Introduction Summaries

Tumbling Blocks by Andrea Boeshaar
Elsa Fritch's dreams tumble from their heights when Shane Gerhard comes to town to collect on the contract between their parents. Could God expect her to endure an arranged marriage with a man who antagonizes her and disregards Him?

Old Maid's Choice by Cathy Marie Hake
Betsy Larkin thinks she must choose between the siblings she is rearing and a man who loves her. Blacksmith Tyson Walker is used to bending iron, but can love and patience bend the will of a woman who is sure she is destined to be an old maid?

Jacob's Ladder by Pamela Kaye Tracy
Samantha Thomasohn dreams of riches and of escaping the mundane life clerking for her father's store. One man holds the riches while another holds her heart. How is true love to be defined, and where will Samantha place her priorities?

Four Hearts by Sally Laity
Diana Montclair covers her loneliness with an arrogant exterior and a drive for perfection that keeps friends at bay. She reluctantly endures the weekly sewing circle. Can Mrs. T.'s words of truth and a newfound friend help her realize she has been seeking the needs of her heart in the wrong places?

Marry for Love by Janet Spaeth
Wild prairie-born Brigit Streeter lacks the domestic and social skills she needs to marry the cultured new minister, Peter Collins, who has come to the Dakota Territory from St. Paul. When Peter's supervising elder brings Brigit a gift of fabric to make her wedding dress, Brigit is lost. She can't sew. Can Brigit become a Psalm 31 wife?

Basket Stitch by Cathy Marie Hake
Bride-who-isn't-to-be Deborah Preston finds herself stranded in No Man's Land without a groom. Rescued and taken to the Stafford ranch, she discovers Micah Stafford is everything she ever prayed for in a mate. Can a sampler-stitchin' city woman soften a rough-and-rugged man's heart?

Double Cross by Tracey V. Bateman
Ignoring Louisa Stafford's vehement objections, Grandma determines to make her granddaughter into a proper lady. The whole venture becomes worth it when circuit preacher Trent Chamberlain starts showing interest in Lou—that is, until a "friend" double crosses her by blabbing all about Lou's tomboyish ways. Will Trent abandon Lou, or will he love her for being true to who God created her to be?

Spiderweb Rose by Vickie McDonough
Josh Stafford's a tease, but he doesn't like it when the joke's on him. The spunky lad he found stranded in No Man's Land has turned out to be a lovely young lady. When Josh and Rachel Donovan are together, tempers flare. When dreams would lead these two in different directions, is God weaving a web of love to keep them together?

The Coat by Tracey V. Bateman
As a jobless widow, Leah Halliday struggles to clothe her son in the aftermath of World War II. When her boy's coat, lined with an heirloom quilt, causes him to be the target of teasing at school, the headmaster's heart goes out to him. But Max Reilly has a scandalous history. Should Leah trust him?

STITCHED
WITH *Love*
ROMANCE
COLLECTION

9 Historical Courtships
Begin in the Sewing Parlor

Tracie V. Bateman, Cathy Marie Hake
Andrea Boeshaar, Sally Laity, Vickie McDonough,
Janet Spaeth, Pamela Kaye Tracy

BARBOUR BOOKS
An Imprint of Barbour Publishing, Inc.

Tumbling Blocks © 2001 by Andrea Boeshaar
Old Maid's Choice © 2001 by Cathy Marie Hake
Jacob's Ladder © 2001 by Pamela Kaye Tracy
Four Hearts © 2001 by Sally Laity
Marry for Love © 2004 by Janet Spaeth
Basket Stitch © 2004 by Cathy Marie Hake
Double Cross © 2004 by Tracey Victoria Bateman
Spiderweb Rose © 2004 by Vickie McDonough
The Coat © 2004 by Tracey Victoria Bateman

Print ISBN 978-1-68322-796-0

eBook Editions:
Adobe Digital Edition (.epub) 978-1-68322-798-4
Kindle and MobiPocket Edition (.prc) 978-1-68322-797-7

Scripture quotations marked KJV are taken from the King James Version of the Bible.

This book is a work of fiction. Names, characters, places, and incidents are either products of the author's imagination or used fictitiously. Any similarity to actual people, organizations, and/or events is purely coincidental.

Cover Photo: Jim Jordan Photography

Published by Barbour Books, an imprint of Barbour Publishing, Inc., 1810 Barbour Drive, Uhrichsville, Ohio 44683, www.barbourbooks.com

Our mission is to inspire the world with the life-changing message of the Bible.

 Member of the
Evangelical Christian
Publishers Association

Printed in the United States of America.

Contents

TUMBLING BLOCKS

by Andrea Boeshaar

Chapter 1

Early March, 1837

Feeling aggravated after his journey, but extremely grateful to have survived it, Shane Gerhard lifted his valise and stepped off the stern-wheeler. What a ride. He'd never experienced one like it in all his twenty-four years. Springtime meant high waters on the Mississippi and Ohio Rivers, high waters and swift currents. But Captain Butch Robertson hadn't seemed to mind either, and the crotchety old man had navigated his mail packet at full throttle in order to beat his competition's time—which wasn't anything to speak of, as far as Shane was concerned. Why, he could have walked to Hickory Corners from St. Louis in the time it had taken the steamboat to arrive.

Well, at least he was finally here. Sort of. He'd been told it was another mile into town. Shane chose to stretch his legs and make the trek on foot. Within ten minutes he passed a rustic-looking sign that read: Welcome to Hickory Corners. He supposed this was it.

Looking around, he took in the modest, if not primitive sights of the small Ohio village. It wasn't anything like the cosmopolitan city of St. Louis, with its paved, tree-lined avenues and majestic mansions, such as the one in which he'd been raised. Walking up a street that ran perpendicular to the river Shane decided his parents' home was bigger than Hickory Corners' boardinghouse, dress shop, and bank put together.

What am I doing? he asked himself for the umpteenth time as he stood across from the boardinghouse. This entire undertaking seemed incredible, if not downright absurd. But, of course, he knew all too well that if he didn't find and marry Elsa Fritch, a resident of this sorry excuse for a town, he'd never get his inheritance.

"And she's probably some homely spinster with a long, pointy nose and buck teeth," he grumbled, crossing the dirt road. But a moment later, he reminded himself that a long, pointy nose and buck teeth were nothing compared to a half a million dollars. For that amount of money, he'd marry his next door neighbor's hound dog. Of course, it wouldn't be a real marriage; he'd have to pay Miss Fritch a tidy sum for her trouble. Then, after the wedding, he didn't care where she resided. Here in Hickory Corners or Paris, France, it mattered little to him. All Shane wanted was the wealth rightfully due him, and he didn't think he would ever forgive his deceased parents for including this most unfair stipulation in their will.

Shane pushed aside his tumultuous thoughts and entered the boardinghouse. One sweeping glance of the place told him this was no palace. To his right, several rough-hewn tables and benches stood in the midst of what was obviously the dining common. Not much in the way of art to admire on the unfinished, plank walls.

"Guten Morgen," greeted an elderly, gray-haired man, perched behind a long counter to Shane's left. His face was wrinkled, etched by time, and his blue eyes resembled dull marbles. "Nice *vetter ve* are having, *ja?*"

"Yes, Sir. Nice weather." Shane immediately recognized the man's dialect, since his own parents had emigrated from Germany years before his birth. While he didn't speak the language fluently, he understood enough to get by. He removed his hat. "Can I get a room?"

"Ja, sure. How long *vill* you stay?"

"Not long. . .hopefully."

The man, dressed in an ivory homespun linen shirt and brown pants supported by suspenders, pulled out a ledger. When he quoted the price for a night's stay, including meals, Shane almost laughed aloud. It was a mere pittance compared to the hotels he'd grown accustomed to in the bigger cities, like New Orleans, Chicago, and New York.

Shane penned his name and paid for a week's lodging.

"Gerhard. . .from St. Louis," the old guy read from the ledger. Next he eyed Shane curiously. "Related to Georg Gerhard, *ja?*"

"Yes." Shane brought his chin back, surprised. "I am his son."

The man's lined face brightened. "I am Arne Fritch!" He shook his head in disbelief. *"Gueter!* Dis is amazing! Do you know me?" He thumped his chest in question. "I know you. I know your *vater*. Ve *ver gute* friends. Elsa! Elsa!" he called up the narrow stairwell. *"Kommen sie her!"*

Shane stood there, feeling stunned by the series of events. So, this was Arne Fritch, Elsa's father. Elsa Fritch, the woman he had to marry in order to receive his inheritance. Shane rubbed a hand over his stubbled jaw. He hadn't meant to present himself to the Fritches looking like some vagabond. And after days on the steamboat without a bath and a close shave, Shane felt even more unkempt than he appeared.

"Elsa! Elsa!"

"I'm coming, Papa."

Shane heard her footfalls on the steps before he ever saw the young woman. When she appeared at the base of the staircase, Shane sucked in a breath, then grinned. *Not bad. Not bad at all. . .*

Elsa Fritch wasn't anything like he'd imagined. She had walnut-colored hair, and he'd bet it felt as soft and smelled as clean as it looked. Her sparkling, indigo eyes were like none he'd ever seen on a woman. They reminded him of untouched pools of deep, deep blue, like the hue of a quiet lake on a cloudless summer day. Her full lips were perfectly shaped and watermelon-pink, just waiting to be kissed, and even her plain brown dress with its starched white apron couldn't hide her buxom figure.

Shane swallowed hard.

"What is it, Papa?" she asked, looking concerned. She glanced at Shane and gave him a perfunctory smile before turning back to her father again.

"Dis is Shane Gerhard," the old man said excitedly. "Gerhard. From St. Louis."

Elsa's expression changed to one of interest. "You mean the same Gerhards who sponsored us?"

"*Ja, ja!* Dey sponsored our journey to America."

"Oh. . ." The young lady stepped forward. "Pleased to meet you, Mr. Gerhard," she stated in a honey-sounding voice that coated his insides. "I've heard much about your family."

"The pleasure is mine, Miss Fritch," he replied with a smile. Moments later, he frowned. "It is Miss, isn't it?" The notion suddenly struck Shane that perhaps she had already married someone else. Of course, that would be in violation of the contract the Fritches had made with his folks some sixteen years ago.

But to his relief, she blushed and nodded her head. "Yes, it's Miss."

Shane grinned.

"But not for long. I'm betrothed."

He felt his smile fade. "Is that right?"

Elsa nodded while Shane glanced at Arne. He wondered why the older man had consented to his daughter's engagement when he'd signed a legal document stating she was to wed Shane as a settlement for his family's passage to this country. Had Arne Fritch forgotten his pact? He'd better not have. Shane's fortune depended on his marrying Elsa.

"Will you be staying with us here at our boardinghouse, Mr. Gerhard?"

He swung his gaze back to hers. "Ah, yes. . .yes, I will."

"We're honored, aren't we, Papa?"

"*Ja.* It vill be gute to visit." Arne grinned broadly.

"Did you arrive by stage?" Elsa further inquired.

"Packet."

"I see. Well, you must be very tired. May I show you to your room?"

"That'd be great."

"Papa, can I have the key to Mr. Gerhard's room?"

"Key?" The old man looked confused. "Vhat is. . .key?"

"*Schluessel,* Papa. Key. . .to unlock the door to Mr. Gerhard's room."

"Oh, *ja, ja.* . .da key."

Elsa gave Shane an embarrassed smile. "Papa is often forgetful these days."

"*Ja,* sometimes my memory fails me," the older man agreed.

Shane nodded his understanding, then followed the comely young woman to the second floor and down a narrow, but carpeted hallway. The walls were white-washed, and after Elsa opened up the bedroom, Shane decided things seemed clean and orderly, from the simple, pearly cotton spread on the bed, to the wooden shutters, opened now to allow the sunshine in.

"Thank you, Miss Fritch. I'm sure I'll be quite comfortable here."

"Please let me know if I can be of further assistance."

Shane set down his valise, pivoted, and grinned. "I will."

She turned to go, then paused just outside the doorway. "Um. . .if you don't mind me asking. . .what brings you to Hickory Corners? We're not really on the way to anywhere."

Shane chuckled. "True enough. The fact is, I have business with you and your parents."

"Oh. . ." Elsa looked troubled. "My mother's in Glory—"

"Excuse me?"

"Heaven."

"Ah, she's dead. I'm sorry to hear that."

"Don't be," Elsa said with a gentle smile. "As I said, she's with the Lord in heaven." Shane rubbed the back of his neck. He never enjoyed discussing religion.

"And Papa, well. . ." Elsa peered to her right, down the hallway. "Papa's mind hasn't been quite right ever since Mama died. Perhaps you could state your business and I could help you."

"That suits me fine. It's really you I'm concerned with."

"Me?" Elsa's dark brows knitted together in consternation.

Shane reached into his overcoat and produced the document he'd been handed by his parents' attorney. "Can you read?"

"Yes, and quite well, thank you."

With a wry grin, he handed her the contract. "This explains my, um, dilemma. You see, Miss Fritch, you are its resolution."

Opening the document, Elsa began to read while Shane watched her expression closely. Though she did her best to conceal her shock at its content, he saw Elsa's chin quiver ever so slightly.

"Mr. Gerhard, I don't know what to say."

"That's easy. Say you agree to the two of us getting hitched."

"But, I'm betrothed."

"Yeah, to me. Ever since you were four years old and I was eight."

Elsa took a step back at his harsh tone, and Shane immediately regretted losing his temper.

"Forgive me," he said. "It's been a long trip, and I'm not exactly thrilled with this setup myself. I never knew a contract between our parents existed until my folks' untimely deaths eight months ago."

"I see."

Shane didn't think she really did. "I cannot acquire my inheritance until the contract is fulfilled, and Miss Fritch, I have every intention of claiming what's mine. . . including you."

She gasped, then paled. "There must be some mistake."

"Yes, I had hoped so, too. But, unfortunately, that contract in your hands is legal and binding and must be executed in order for me to get my money. Lady," he said, inching closer to her, "I want my money. It's all my parents left to me, but it'll see me through life quite nicely. And there's some for you, too."

"I don't want your money. I cannot marry you."

"Yes, you can. And you will."

"I won't."

"You will, or—"

"Or what? You'll shoot me?"

Shane saw her glance at the sleek pistol he habitually wore at his hip. He'd bought the weapon after getting robbed in a gambling den in New Orleans a few years ago.

Elsa shook her head. "I'm not afraid to die, so go ahead and shoot."

Little imp, he thought as aggravation coursed through his veins. "Look, Miss Fritch, the contract," he said, pulling it from her grasp, "is a binding, legal document."

"You said that already."

He ignored the remark. "It means you and I do not have a choice in the matter. We have to get married."

"Then I will go to jail."

Shane rolled his eyes. How could he make her understand? "It's not that simple."

"All right, all right. I will speak to my father about this matter, and if I must, I will ask our sheriff here in Hickory Corners about it...this contract," she all but spat.

Her cheeks were flushed, and Shane thought he could relate to her indignation.

"I understand your anger and upset, Miss Fritch," Shane stated, fighting to keep his voice calm. "I felt angry too. But I hired attorneys in St. Louis to check and recheck this document, and they couldn't find a loophole. I doubt your small-town sheriff will know what to do about it."

Elsa looked like she was about to burst into tears. "But I don't want to marry you."

"I don't want to marry you, either."

"Then let's pretend we never saw this document."

Shane chuckled at her ignorance. "Honey, I'd love to, but there's half a million bucks waiting for me as soon as you and I say, 'I do.' Now, look, I've got a plan. I'll give you ten thousand dollars, and you can go your merry way and forget all about me after the ceremony. How's that?"

Elsa shook her head. "No."

"Well, all right," Shane drawled, "how's twenty thousand?"

"Mr. Gerhard, you could not persuade me to marry you for two million dollars."

"Well, three is out of my price range," he quipped.

Else gave him a look of utter disgust. "You insolent man! No amount of money will do. Don't you know marriage is sacred before God? He created it and designed it to be a beautiful thing between two people who love each other. It's not something you can buy."

Shane shrugged. "Guess I'll die tryin', then."

"Elsa! Elsa!" Arne's voice was filled with concern as he called to her. "Elsa, vhat is happening up dere dat you are shouting like a fishmonger?"

"I'm not shouting, Papa!" she shouted.

Shane laughed at the irony, and Elsa's cheeks flamed when she realized it herself.

"We'll talk later," he said with a wink. *"Schatz."*

She inhaled sharply. "I am not your...sweetheart. How dare you call me that!"

"Elsa. . . ?"

"Coming, Papa," she said, softening her voice. Then, after tossing Shane a scathing look, she made haste down the hallway.

Shane closed the door, leaning against it, grinning. *This might be fun,* he thought.

But one thing was sure—he meant to marry Elsa Fritch, and he would not leave this little hole-in-the-wall town until he succeeded.

Chapter 2

"*N*ein, nein,*" Arne said, shaking his head. "I paid Georg Gerhard."

"Are you sure? You paid him?" Suddenly the hysteria that had been brewing inside Elsa all afternoon began to dissipate. "So there's no outstanding debt, and I don't have to marry Shane Gerhard?"

"*Ja,* das right."

Elsa blew out a breath of relief and continued kneading the bread dough in the kitchen while her father sat at the small table and sipped coffee. He'd just awakened from his afternoon nap and this was the first time Elsa had been able to discuss the matter with him. "Well, it sounds like a misunderstanding," she said. "You and Mama made a contract with the Gerhards after they sponsored us, but later you discovered they made strong drink—beer."

"*Ja,* und I paid Georg und told him no daughter uf mine marries into a family makin' sinful beer."

Elsa worked her lower lip between her teeth, trying to put all the pieces into place. "The Gerhards had been good friends of yours in Germany, is that right, Papa?"

He nodded. "But Vanda und I," he said, referring to his deceased wife, "never knew about da strong drink—und da Gerhards got rich makin' it."

"Despicable." Elsa didn't like Shane Gerhard, and this latest discovery only intensified her negative feelings. Of all the nerve. The man should have made sure of his facts before storming into a person's life and demanding she marry him.

Dividing the dough, Elsa shaped it and put it into two pans, then slipped them on to the iron rack in the hearth. Now to finish supper. Henry Peabody, her fiancé, was coming, and as always, she wanted to display her culinary skills. They would marry next month and live here at the boardinghouse so Elsa could continue to look after her father. Henry disliked the idea, but what else could she do? Her father needed her. With each passing day, he became more and more forgetful.

"I cannot believe da Gerhards are dead," Arne said mournfully, staring into his cup. "Such a shame."

"Yes, I'm sure it is."

"Georg und Lise ver younger dan me. Dey ver your mutter's age. I vas an old man vhen I married Vanda, und yet I outlived her. . .und da Gerhards."

"Don't despair. Mama's in heaven, and I'm glad I have you still around." She glanced over her shoulder at her aging father, who looked so forlorn, she felt tears stinging her own eyes. "Were the Gerhards believers?"

"Oh, *ja*. But dey still made da beer."

"I don't think their son is a Christian."

"Nein?"

"No. He said rude things to me, Papa."

"Vhat did he say?"

Elsa swallowed down the last of her indignation. "He called me. . .*schatz.*"

Her father's guffaw filled the warm, steamy room.

"It's not funny, Papa." Elsa gave him a stern look, and he managed to wipe the smirk off his face. "I think you should speak to him about his manners."

"Nein. Young Shane is, like your brother Herrick, teasing you."

Elsa sighed and gave up the cause. All her life she'd felt like there was no one in the world to protect her. Why should things change now that she was twenty years old? In school, if the boys goaded her, Mama used to cluck her tongue and tell Elsa to ignore the jeering. She said the boys were "sweet" on her, and that's why they harassed her so. Papa always chuckled and told her to be proud of her ample bosom, causing Elsa to feel even more self-conscious about her full figure. Why couldn't God have made her tiny and slender like Betsy Larkin, one of the young ladies at Mrs. Tidewell's Tuesday afternoon sewing circle? Betsy, with her golden-blond hair, brown eyes, and petite frame was everything Elsa wished for in her own physical appearance. Instead, Elsa stood five feet and six inches—as tall as Henry!

"Anybody home?"

Elsa cringed. He'd only been in Hickory Corners four hours, and already she'd grown to recognize and despise the sound of Shane Gerhard's deep voice. To further her animosity, the man walked into her kitchen uninvited, and if there was one thing Elsa couldn't abide, it was a man in her kitchen. She tolerated her papa's presence, but only because the Bible instructed her to "honor thy father. . . ."

"Sure smells good in here."

"Hungry, young Shane?" Arne asked with a wry grin.

"Sure am. I haven't had a decent meal in over a week."

"Vell, Elsa is da best cook in town."

Stirring her pot of stew over the open hearth, she refused to look in Shane's direction.

"From what my nose is telling me," he said, "I'm inclined to believe it."

"Sit. Sit," Arne invited. "Elsa, make our guest something to eat."

"The stew will be done in an hour," she replied curtly.

"Nein, make him something now."

"Aw, that's all right, Mr. Fritch, I can wait."

Without even so much as a glance, Elsa knew her father was frowning at her disobedience. But she couldn't seem to help it.

"I imagine your daughter told you why I came to town," Shane said.

"Ja, und I told her dat I paid your vater da money he put up to bring us to America."

"You paid him?" There was a note of incredulity in Shane's voice.

"*Ja,* dere is no contract. Your vater made strong drink, und I vould not allow my Elsa to be a part of such sin."

Slowly, she turned from the large, bubbling, black kettle to glimpse Shane's reaction.

"My father owned a brewery."

"*Ja,* das right."

"What do you mean to call it sin? I don't understand."

"Da Bible says woe upon dem who is givin' der neighbor strong drink. Breweries make und sell it, und da people get drunk. Drunk is a sin, too. It hurts people, makes dem sick."

Shane shifted, appearing uncomfortable. Then he glanced at Elsa, who nodded.

"Well, before you condemn me," he said on a harsh note, "let me just put things into perspective for you. I wasn't the one who started the business. My father did—and I didn't even inherit it. My oldest brother, Edwin, is now president of Gerhard and Sons Brewery. My second oldest brother, Frederick, was awarded my parents' estate. Being the youngest of three boys, I got a handsome sum of money, except I can't get my hands on it until this contract is satisfied." Shane pulled out the same folded piece of paper Elsa had read earlier. "I don't suppose you'd have receipts, Mr. Fritch, or something showing that you paid my father."

"Receipts? *Ja,* I got 'em."

Shane smiled broadly, revealing strong white, even teeth, and Elsa had to admit he was a handsome man, but in a rugged sort of way. He certainly wasn't her kind of man, and, goodness, but his dark-blond hair could use a good trimming. The tendrils hanging past his collar and over his ears gave Shane a reckless appearance.

Suddenly, he glanced her way, his hazel eyes alight with gladness, and Elsa returned a tiny smile.

"I am as relieved as you are, Mr. Gerhard," she assured him.

"Well, now, I meant no offense," he explained. "I'm just not a marrying man, but if I were, I'm sure—"

"I am already betrothed."

"Oh, right..."

Papa rose from the wooden chair. "I go to find da letters uf payment from Georg."

Elsa watched her father saunter into their family's quarters off the kitchen before she turned and resumed supper preparations.

Shane cleared his throat. "Um, I guess I was a bit brash this afternoon."

"A bit?" Elsa replied, keeping her back to him. "I would say you behaved like a rogue."

Shane laughed. "I've been called worse."

His mocking tone grated on her nerves, and Elsa deliberated on what name she would really like to call him—none being very Christian-like.

"I'll tell you what, Miss Elsa Fritch. How 'bout I apologize for my knavish conduct, and we begin anew?"

Cautiously, she turned around.

"Don't look so suspicious." With a charming smile, Shane stood and bowed. "I am sincerely sorry for offending you this afternoon. I was just having a bit of fun. Of course, I did want my inheritance—still do—but I reckon I wasn't thinking clearly. Now that I've rested up some, I can see the error of my ways. Please forgive me."

"I think you have rehearsed that speech one too many times, Mr. Gerhard."

He replied with a wounded expression. "I'm quite serious, I assure you."

Elsa didn't believe him, and she certainly didn't want to accept his apology. However, she knew it was her Christian duty. "All right, I forgive you."

"Why, thank you."

It was then that Papa appeared at the doorway. "Elsa, vhere is da box uf important papers I keep by my desk?"

"I don't know. It should be there, Papa."

"I don't know. . . ." He shook his head, frowning heavily. "I cannot find it."

"May I help you locate it, Mr. Fritch? Elsa says there's time before supper." Shane swung his gaze around and winked. "I believe she said we have an hour before we eat."

"Yes, that's right," Elsa replied, feeling somewhat flustered all of a sudden.

Ja, come und help me, young Shane."

"My pleasure," he said, crossing the kitchen. Then he paused in mid-stride and glanced at Elsa. "Now, I don't mean that personally."

She stifled a grin. "I will be praying you find those receipts. . .very soon."

Sixty-five minutes later, the table was set, the stew and bread were done, and now Elsa was watching out the window for Henry, her arms folded in front of her. Papa and Shane were still scouring his bedroom for any letter of release that might prove the contract was no longer in effect. But the longer they turned up nothing, the more Elsa began to fret.

"Oh, Papa, what did you do with those papers?" she muttered just as Henry came walking up to the front door. Henry, a clerk at Montclair's Shipping Office just up the street, wore round, wire spectacles, and kept his light-brown hair neatly parted and combed.

Elsa ran to the door to greet him. "I'm so glad to see you," she said, helping her fiancé off with his overcoat.

He cleared his throat. "I'm glad to see you, too. Do you think you could rub the back of my neck? It's been bothering me since I woke up this morning."

"Of course. Come and sit down."

"And my head is throbbing."

"You poor man," Elsa cooed. Once Henry was seated on the wooden benches, she kneaded his neck and shoulders.

"Not so rough, Elsa."

"I'm so sorry," she replied, lightening up her touch.

"Why are there four places set tonight?" Henry asked.

"We have a guest."

At that very moment, Shane and her father ambled through the kitchen.

"Did you find what you were looking for?" she asked hopefully.

"Nein," Papa replied, looking disappointed. "But I know I have dose receipts somevhere."

"What receipts?"

"Oh, nothing, Henry dear," Elsa said quickly. She looked at Shane and silently pleaded with him not to divulge the circumstances. She saw his head dip in subtle acquiescence. "I'll fetch supper. Papa, why don't you introduce the two men."

"Ja, I can do dat."

In the kitchen, Elsa ladled the stew into thick, wooden bowls, then sliced the fresh bread and put in on a platter. Next she filled a pitcher with fresh milk before placing everything on a large tray. Hoisting it above her right shoulder, she carried their meal into the dining room.

Seeing her approach, Shane jumped up from his seat and rushed to her aid, taking the tray from her.

"I can manage," she assured him, even though he had already set it down on the table.

Shane gave her a quizzical glance. "Women should not carry anything heavy."

Elsa laughed softly. "I carry heavy things all the time. Please, Mr. Gerhard, make yourself comfortable, and enjoy your meal."

"I plan to. It looks wonderful."

Feeling oddly pleased by the compliment, Elsa took her place beside Henry. She felt more at ease, probably because her fiancé was here to force Shane Gerhard into behaving himself for a change.

"Papa, will you ask the blessing?"

⁘

Shane listened to the old man pray, thanking God for the food and for Elsa's capable hands that prepared it. Shane remembered as a young boy hearing his parents pray. They were Christians, like Elsa and her father. But over the years, his parents' faith seemed to wane, and Shane figured religion wasn't all that important. They had never talked to him about God. He was Someone who had an omnipresence—similar to the portrait of Shane's grandfather that hung on the wall by the stairwell in his folks' mansion. The painting was there in the background, but no one really paid much attention to it, and that's how Shane viewed God—just sort of there and everywhere, but who needed Him?

"Would you care for some bread, Mr. Gerhard?"

Shane snapped from his reverie. "Don't mind if I do, Miss Fritch. Thank you." He took a slice off the plate she held out to him.

As he ate, enjoying every savory bite, he glanced from her to Henry Peabody and wondered what Elsa saw in the man. He resembled a scrawny little weasel and didn't talk. . . . He whined.

"I think I'm getting another cold. My throat is sore again."

"You poor thing," Elsa murmured in a motherly tone. "Must be your quinsy acting up."

"Quinsy?" Shane sure hoped it wasn't contagious.

"Severe tonsillitis," Henry informed him. "Doc calls it quinsy."

"Oh. . ." Shane chanced a look at Arne, who seemed oblivious to everything around him as he spooned his dinner into his mouth.

Several seconds of uncomfortable silence ticked by.

"So, Mr. Peabody," Shane began, attempting small talk, "did I understand Mr. Fritch to say you're employed at a shipping company?"

"Yes, and I hate my job. My eyes get so tired looking at numbers all day long. From sunup to sundown."

Elsa gave her fiancé a sympathetic smile, while Shane wagged his head at the pitiful scene.

They don't even look good together, he thought, harboring an amused grin. *Elsa has larger biceps.*

The meal proceeded, and Shane couldn't help feeling things were all wrong between the couple. Of course, he was no expert, but he had a good set of eyes. Why didn't Arne see it? Was he really going to allow his daughter to marry a dandy like Henry Peabody? Elsa needed a real man.

Well, it wasn't any of his business. What did he care? All Shane wanted was his inheritance, and as soon as he finished supper, he planned to help old Arne find those letters of receipt. After that, Shane would hop on the next packet leaving Hickory Corners, and he'd never look back.

Chapter 3

S hane didn't enjoy getting up early. Since his college days, he'd grown accustomed to parties until the wee hours of the morning, then sleeping until at least noon. But here he was, up with the sun, no doubt because he'd gone to bed shortly after supper last night. Did all of Hickory Corners close after dark? Why, Arne said there wasn't even a saloon in town!

Walking across the room, Shane grasped the white, porcelain pitcher and poured water into the matching basin on his bureau. He washed quickly, shaved, splashed on some musky-smelling tonic, and ran a comb through his hair. After dressing, he ambled downstairs, where he found the dining common vacant, but delicious aromas wafted to his nostrils from the kitchen. His stomach rumbled at the smell of fried ham, biscuits, and brewing coffee, and Shane began heading in that direction before he could give the matter a second thought.

Entering the kitchen, he found Elsa standing precariously on the service counter and peering into the uppermost part of the ceiling-high cupboard.

He stepped closer. "G'morning."

She gasped, turning. As she did so, she lost her balance and fell backward. Shane rushed forward and caught her easily enough.

"Oh, *mein Schreck!*" she exclaimed with wide, startled blue eyes. "I felt so scared."

"I've got you." He grinned. "Must be my lucky day."

"Lucky day?"

"Sure. It's not every day a lovely lady falls right into my arms."

Elsa gave him a look of reproof. "Put me down at once."

More than a little amused, Shane complied with her wishes and set her feet on the plank floor.

With crimson cheeks, Elsa smoothed down the skirt of her brown dress. She'd worn the same outfit yesterday, causing Shane to wonder if she ever changed clothes. Where he came from, women had morning gowns, afternoon gowns, traveling gowns, evening gowns, and ball gowns. But for the second day in a row, Elsa had worn her simple brown frock with its white apron.

"Thank you for breaking my fall," she muttered.

"My pleasure." Shane leaned against the adjacent service counter and folded his arms. Despite her rudimentary attire, he decided he enjoyed watching Elsa, and he took to wondering what her hair would look like if she freed it from its pinning.

21

"Breakfast will be ready shortly."

"Great. I'm starved." Shane paused while Elsa busied herself with slicing more ham. "So what were you looking for up there? Maybe I can help you."

"I was searching for the receipts from your father," she said over one shoulder. "I thought perhaps Papa had put them up in the cupboard for safekeeping."

"I see. Would you like me to check?"

Elsa shook her head. "The shelf is empty. I was able to see that much before you walked into my kitchen unannounced and scared me half to death."

Shane chuckled. "My humble apologies."

Elsa glared at him, her expression incredulous.

"And don't worry," he continued, "I reckon those receipts will turn up. . .if they really exist."

"Of course they really exist. Papa wouldn't lie."

"I wasn't implying he would. After spending time with your papa yesterday afternoon, I'm confident he speaks the truth. Of course, the question still remains as to why my father never changed his will if the debt had been paid."

"Yes, I thought of that myself."

"I probably won't ever learn the answer to that one," Shane mumbled remorsefully. Now that his parents were dead, there were suddenly so many questions he wanted to ask them, about their faith—and about this contemptible contract!

Returning his gaze to Elsa, Shane thought she appeared fretful herself, and he suddenly longed to change the subject. He preferred to see a little fire in Elsa's eyes, rather than distress.

"Let me ask you something," he began mischievously.

"Yes?"

"Say I was Mr. Quinsy a few minutes ago. . ."

"Who?"

"Your fiancé—the guy with the quinsy."

Elsa huffed with indignation and set her hands on her rounded hips.

"Well, I was just trying to imagine him catching you falling from the service counter."

"And?" she asked with an annoyed expression.

"And I think you'd squish him like a bug." Shane grinned broadly as her gaze sparked, and he thought she looked so pretty, all pink-cheeked and furious.

"Get out of my kitchen before I squish you like a bug!"

Shane chuckled. "Well, now, Honey, you're sure welcome to try—squishing me, that is."

"Get out!"

"I don't suppose I could get a cup of coffee first."

Elsa reached for the closest thing to her, which happened to be an earthenware bowl, and hurled it at Shane. Having anticipated her reaction, he ducked just in time. The bowl hit the doorjamb with a thud before crashing to the floor in pieces.

"Whoo-wee, you've got some temper there, little lady," Shane remarked with a laugh.

"What's going on? Elsa? What's all the racket?"

Her eyes grew wide with horror. "It's Henry," she whispered. "I don't want him to know how angry I got."

Shane quickly scooped up the sections of earthenware from the floor and handed them to Elsa. When Henry arrived at the doorway, Shane donned a well-practiced look of innocence.

"Miss Fritch just, um, dropped her mixing bowl, and I was just about to help myself to a cup of coffee. How 'bout you? Coffee?"

"Yes, but Elsa always pours it," the smaller man whined. He glanced from her to Shane, wearing a curious frown. "Elsa doesn't approve of men in her kitchen."

"Aw, that's just an ugly rumor," Shane quipped, giving her a little wink.

She ignored him. "Why don't you both have a seat in the dining room and I'll take care of the coffee." Walking to the open hearth in the corner of the kitchen, she added, "Papa should return from his morning walk momentarily. When he does, I'll serve breakfast."

Shane figured he'd tried Elsa's patience enough for the time being, and without another word, he followed Henry into the dining common.

·❖·

Elsa's hands trembled as she pulled the pan of biscuits from the iron rack in the hearth. She felt angry, afraid, and humiliated all at once. Angry at Shane Gerhard's insufferable remarks about her and Henry, afraid because he was right about squishing poor Henry like a bug, and humiliated that Shane could antagonize her to the point where she lost her self-control.

Lord, I'm not much of a witness for You this morning, am I? she thought. But in the next moment, she remembered that today was Tuesday and she'd see her friends at Mrs. Tidewell's house for their weekly sewing circle. Elsa decided the meeting would surely put her in a right spirit, and perhaps Mrs. T would offer a piece of advice. Being the pastor's wife, the older woman was good for suggesting godly remedies from the Bible.

Feeling heartened by the idea of escaping the boardinghouse and Shane Gerhard, Elsa gloved one hand with a thick, quilted pad, took hold of the hot coffee pot, grabbed two cups with her other, and strode into the dining room. She found both men reading the newspaper. Without a single glance at Shane, Elsa poured the dark, steaming brew. Afterward, she walked several feet to the box stove, placing the pot on its top to keep warm.

Back in the kitchen, she fried six fresh eggs in the same skillet as the ham, and when she finally heard her father's voice, she served up the meal.

"Won't you be joining us, Miss Fritch?" Shane asked lightly.

Elsa marveled at the man's audacity. "No, I'm not. . .hungry," she stated, looking at the tips of her worn, brown leather shoes. Then she made haste back into the sanctity of the kitchen.

Minutes later, as she sipped a cup of tea at the small, scarred, wooden table, Elsa wondered over the events of the morning. Shane had called her "little." He'd said, "You've got some temper there, little lady." Elsa hadn't been described as "little" since. . .well, she couldn't recall the last time that word and her name had appeared in the same sentence. Always, Elsa had been bigger than her girlfriends and most boys, until later in her teenage years when almost all the young men in her class had grown taller than she. Still, Elsa had never felt "little" around them.

Oddly, however, in Shane's presence she could nearly imagine herself as such. He'd caught her when she'd fallen, and his arms under her knees and around her waist had been strong—strong enough to hold her. Shane hadn't even appeared strained, and Elsa clearly remembered how nice he smelled and how muscular his shoulders felt beneath her palm as she'd clung to him. His hazel-eyed gaze seemed to penetrate her own, and that rakish smile of his. . .

Elsa gave herself a mental shake and reined in her wayward musings. She was engaged and ought not think of any other man but Henry in such an intimate way.

She sighed, steering her thoughts toward today's sewing circle. She was in desperate need of the spiritual uplifting she'd find there. But poor Mrs. Tidewell certainly had her work cut out for her!

Chapter 4

And he says the most outrageous things to me," Elsa lamented as she continued to enlighten her sewing circle of this latest travesty in the form of Shane Gerhard. While she spoke, her needle went in and out of the pieced-together fabric beneath her fingertips. The quilt pattern on which all five young ladies around her worked was called Tumbling Blocks, and Elsa couldn't help but think how the intricate design described her life right now. Tumbling. And all because of one arrogant, highfalutin man from St. Louis who wanted to kick her dreams of marrying Henry right out from under her for his own selfish purposes.

"Elsa, my dear, I don't think you should have thrown the bowl at him," Clara Bucey remarked from her corner of the quilt. She was Charlotte Warner's niece, and everyone in town admired the Widow Warner's commitment to charity. A slim gal with light-brown hair and brown eyes, Clara was following in her aunt's footsteps. "Losing one's temper just isn't ladylike, nor is it Christian."

"I'm sure you're right," Elsa replied, "and I have already asked the Lord's forgiveness."

"I wouldn't have stooped so low as to throw anything," Diana Montclair drawled, sipping her tea and watching the others stitch. The attractive blond rarely attended the sewing circle with the other town girls. Having attended various elite boarding schools, Diana had grown accustomed to more elevated entertainments, and she had been quite vocal about her distaste for such mundane endeavors as needlework. But for some reason, she had graced the group with her presence today. "Of course, I would not have been performing menial kitchen duties," she added with a haughty tilt of her chin, "and, therefore, I wouldn't have had access to an earthenware bowl in the first place."

"You know, Diana," Elsa retorted, "you would make a perfect match for our self-important guest, Shane Gerhard."

Diana glared back, her silver-gray eyes sparkling with resentment.

"Girls, girls," Mrs. Tidewell said, "the wrath of man does not produce the righteousness of God. We must remember that before losing our tempers."

Elsa felt herself blush with conviction. She knew the older woman was right. And she wasn't exactly a Christian role model for Diana Montclair.

Elsa glanced first at Mrs. Tidewell, then Diana. "Please forgive me for my lack of self-restraint."

Diana replied with a bored expression, but Mrs. T readily accepted the apology.

"Of course, Dear," she said, patting her downy-white hair that was pulled back into a prim little bun. "No one is perfect. Now then, let's get on with our prayer requests."

Mrs. T sat down opposite Diana at a small, polished side table in the parlor, while Betsy Larkin cleared her throat.

"I have a request," she said. "I have several requests, actually."

Elsa turned to her immediate left. She had known Betsy most of her life. They'd gone to school together and played at each other's homes. But then Betsy's mother died in childbirth three years ago, leaving her with the responsibility of caring for her four siblings who ranged in age from newborn to five years old. Betsy had been forced to grow up awfully fast in order to fill her mother's shoes.

"Please pray for Karl," Betsy said, her blond hair slightly mussed. "He turned eight on Saturday and suddenly decided he knows everything. And Will is easily influenced by his older brother, so the two of 'em are double trouble."

Everyone laughed softly, except Diana, who appeared infinitely bored with the entire conversation.

"And please pray that I can nurture Marie and Greta," Betsy continued, looking down at the squares on which she stitched, "like Mama would have."

A rueful moment hung in the air.

"Of course, we'll pray for your brothers and sisters," Mrs. T said in a comforting tone. "And we'll pray for you, too, for a nice young man to come into your life and sweep you off your feet."

Betsy brought her chin back while Elsa chuckled softly at her friend's startled expression.

"I'll never get married, Mrs. T," Betsy said. "Who'd have me, what with all my responsibilities at home?"

"A very special man, that's who," the older woman replied with an easy smile. "Now, anyone else have a prayer request? Samantha? What about you?"

"For my mama," she said. Like Betsy, Samantha Thomasohn had been a friend since elementary school. Her father ran the mercantile right across from the boardinghouse.

"Your mother's no better?" Clara asked with a pained expression.

Samantha shook her head, her blond ringlets swinging from side to side. "No, there's been little or no improvement. She's still so sick."

Elsa's heart constricted painfully. She knew what it was like to have an ailing mother. . .and to lose her.

"We'll be sure to pray, Samantha," Mrs. T said with a determined look in her green eyes.

A few other prayer requests were mentioned, and then Mrs. Tidewell asked the girls to stop their sewing and bow their heads. As the older woman prayed, Elsa felt a deep, abiding sense of communing with the Savior, and a verse from the Book of Matthew came to mind: *"For where two or three are gathered together in my name, there am I in the midst of them."*

How awesome, Elsa thought, that a holy God heard their prayers and cared about their welfare!

When Mrs. T ended her petitions with a hearty, "Amen!" Elsa felt renewed, refreshed.

"Now, how about more tea, girls?" Mrs. T asked, looking rejuvenated herself. "Afterward, we'll see if we can finish this quilt."

Midafternoon, Shane ambled down the dusty street of Hickory Corners. He passed a dress shop on his left and the tinsmith to his right, across the road. Both businesses were housed in single-story, rough-hewn buildings, albeit the dress shop had white-washed shutters adorning its two glass windows. Next came the bank, a red-brick building. After that was Montclair's Shipping Office, another wooden structure, and Shane remembered it was Mr. Quinsy's place of employment. He shook his head. What did Elsa see in that guy—and why did Shane even care?

Standing on the corner, he spied a barbershop and decided on a haircut. He crossed the street, nodding politely to a man who was loading supplies into his wagon, and entered the shop. Immediately, Shane saw a feeble-looking, gray-haired man sitting in a chair, reading the morning newspaper.

The old man peered up over the top. "What can I do for you, Son?"

"I'd like a haircut." Shane's gaze roamed over the sparsely decorated shop. He spotted a few shelves of barber bottles that most likely contained scented hair tonic. A few wooden chairs lined the wall near the doorway, and above them were several hooks. Shane hung his black, wide-brimmed hat on one of them.

"Haircut? Why, sure." The old man stood on rickety legs, dusted off the red leather seat on which he'd been perched, and held his hand out, indicating Shane should take his place. "Make yourself comfortable."

Shane strode across the plank floor and sat down.

"You're new in town."

"Not 'new.' Just here on business. . .temporarily."

"I see." The old man fastened a cape around Shane's neck, then took his scissors in one hand a comb in the other. "Folks call me Doc."

"Nice to meet you. I'm Shane Gerhard." Peering through the mirror at the man who stood behind him, Shane saw him tremble with age. "Why are you called 'Doc'? Do people need medical attention when you get done with them?"

Doc laughed until he sputtered and coughed. "Mercy, no! It's against my practice to administer a blood-letting and a haircut at the same time." He cackled again. "I'll have you know, young man, that I have a steady hand once I get going. And, I'm 'Doc' because I'm the physician in these parts."

"You are?" Shane grinned. "No fooling?"

"I wouldn't josh about a thing like that." He began snipping around Shane's ear.

"Well, in that case, I reckon you can sew back on whatever you accidentally cut off."

"Never cut off anything that didn't need cutting off," the old man retorted.

Shane decided he'd best hold real still. . .just in case.

"You staying at the Fritches' place?"

"Yep."

Doc pushed Shane's head forward and snipped around his collar. "Elsa Fritch is one fine cook."

"Found that out already."

"What did you say, Son?"

Shane spoke louder. "I said, yes, she is. . .a fine cook."

"Fine cook," Doc repeated. "And she's grown into a fine-looking young woman, too. Why, I remember when Elsa was just a schoolgirl in braids, playing in the road with her brother, Herrick, and their little sister, Heidi." Doc *snip, snip, snipped* around Shane's other ear. "Heidi got married a year ago, and I think poor Elsa felt badly that it wasn't her having a wedding, since Heidi is younger."

"Mm. . . ," Shane replied, fighting his curiosity.

"Then Henry Peabody came to town. He's from Boston, you know. Works for Mr. Montclair, who's the richest man in southwestern Ohio."

"Is that right?"

"Sure is."

"I haven't met Montclair, but I met Mr. Peabody." Shane closed his eyes as Doc commenced trimming the front of his hair. "He says he's got something called quinsy."

"That he does. Probably should have those tonsils removed."

Shane grinned. "Sharpen up them scissors, Doc."

The old man chuckled. "Oh, no, I don't do surgeries anymore. Henry would have to go to Fort Washington for that. And I suspect he will some time in the future. It's no fun having a sore throat prett' near every day. Perhaps once he and Elsa are married, she'll be able to convince him not to be afraid of having the operation. Although, I wish. . .oh, never mind."

"You wish what?" Shane opened his eyes and glanced at Doc.

"Aw, nothing. I spoke out of turn, Son."

Shane thought it over, told himself it was none of his concern, but still couldn't squelch his curiosity. "Might help if you spoke your mind, Doc, since my business has to do with Miss Fritch. . .and her engagement to Peabody."

Doc paused, his bony hands suspended in midair. "Maybe if you explain your, um, business—"

"Sure." Sensing the elderly man was trustworthy enough, he relayed the predicament and his reason for coming to Hickory Corners—leaving out the sum of his inheritance.

"If that don't beat all," Doc said, wagging his gray head. "What if Arne doesn't find those receipts?"

"Then I plan to marry Miss Fritch as soon as I can find a willing preacher to perform the ceremony."

Doc let out a long, slow whistle. "And does Elsa know this?"

"Yes, Sir, she does."

"I don't imagine she's too pleased about it."

"Let's just say she's as pleased about it as I am."

"I see." Doc sprinkled some tonic water onto Shane's head and proceeded to rub vigorously. "Does Henry know?"

"I don't believe so."

"Hm. . ." Doc combed Shane's hair into place.

"Now, what were you going to say? What is it you wish?"

The old guy produced a wheezing laugh. "I was going to say that I wish Elsa were marrying someone else, not that I don't think Henry is a good man. But he's. . .well. . ."

"Not the man for her."

"That's it," Doc agreed. "Furthermore, my instincts tell me Elsa pities Henry more than she loves him, but she wants to get married and he's the one asking, so. . ."

"So she might as well marry him."

"Uh-huh."

"Look, Doc, just to set things straight, I'm not exactly husband material, got that?" Shane yanked off the striped cape and stood, brushing the loose hair from his clothing. "Elsa would be better off with Mr. Quinsy Peabody than with me."

"You'd know best."

Shane nodded, then paid for the haircut.

"But just the same, I'll keep the matter in my prayers."

"Sure. You do that, Doc."

Donning his hat, Shane left the barbershop, feeling oddly unsettled. He didn't want to get married. He wanted his money. That's it.

He paused, staring across the street. Then why did his gut just tighten upon seeing Elsa heading for the boardinghouse on the arm of Henry Peabody?

Chapter 5

Elsa glimpsed Shane Gerhard from out of the corner of her eye, and chose to ignore him. But she quickly reminded herself that she had to be courteous at all costs. The Lord would not approve of treating Mr. Gerhard with anything less than her Christian best. Even so, Elsa tightened her hold around Henry's elbow.

"Ouch! Why are you squeezing my arm?"

"I didn't squeeze it, Henry."

"Yes, you did."

Elsa clenched her jaw, feeling irked with her fiancé for the first time ever. *Why couldn't he act like more of a man?* Oh, she didn't mean that! Poor, dear Henry didn't feel good again today. He couldn't help being so. . .so sensitive.

Elsa released her hold on his arm, and to her chagrin, Henry rubbed it as if she'd just socked him. At that precise moment, Shane crossed the street, all long legs and broad shoulders, and stood in their way, looking like a bully. Wearing dark trousers, a crisp white shirt under a black, tweed vest and matching jacket, he looked the part.

He removed his hat, nodded politely, and Elsa noticed the haircut. She glanced at the barbershop where Doc stood in the doorway and waved. Forcing a smile, she waved back, then fixed her eyes on Shane again.

"Lovely day for a stroll," he said.

"Yes, I suppose it is," Elsa replied, doing her best to be friendly.

"Will you be joining us for an early supper, Mr. Gerhard?" Henry asked in a hoarse voice. He cleared his throat. "We're on our way to the boardinghouse."

Shane's lips curved into a rather wolfish-looking grin. "I'd be delighted to join you," he said, staring pointedly at Elsa.

"Actually, I do the cooking, not the eating," she stated with an uneasy glance at Henry, who seemed oblivious to Shane's flirtations. "And I really must get back to the kitchen. Excuse me."

Elsa skirted around Shane and made for the boardinghouse. Inside, she removed her bonnet and quickly strode through the dining room. It was then she noticed Zeb and Horace Bunk, sitting patiently at one of the long tables and awaiting their meal.

"Thought you'd never git back," Zeb said with a toothy smile. His wide face was unshaven, as usual, and his brown hair was matted. Even from her distance, Elsa could smell that the brothers were in need of a hot, soapy bath.

The Bunks were what the Hickory Corners called "river rats." They made their living by trading up and down the Ohio River, and Zeb and Horace were quite successful. And, while they were friendly enough fellows, they were a young lady's nightmare for a potential suitor—which was another reason Elsa was glad to finally be betrothed.

"We're starving, Miss Elsa," Horace declared. "Whatcha serving up today?"

"Leftover stew."

"That's my favorite." Zeb's smile broadened. "Yours too, eh, Horace?"

"Yep." He didn't look much different from his brother, same stocky build and short legs, except Horace had rusty-colored hair. Like his brother's, however, it was in need of a good scrubbing. "Say, Miss Elsa, you got some of them biscuits to go with it?"

She nodded. "Coming right up."

Behind her, she heard Shane and Henry enter the boardinghouse. She quickened her step and headed into the kitchen.

"Papa, what are you doing?" she cried, seeing the disarray on the table and service counters.

"I have been searching for Georg's receipts."

Elsa grimaced. "You haven't found them yet?"

"Nein."

Feeling discouragement creeping in, Elsa tried in vain to will it away. She prayed while sliding the biscuits onto the iron rack in the hearth to warm and ladling the stew into four bowls. *Father in Heaven, please allow my Papa to find what he needs to prove the debt was paid so Shane Gerhard can be on his way and out of my life forever!*

Elsa loaded up her round serving tray, waiting a few more minutes on the biscuits before pulling them from the hearth. Setting them onto a platter, she placed that, too, onto the tray. But before she could carry it into the dining room, the object of her troubled thoughts sauntered into the kitchen.

"I thought you might need some help."

"Thank you, but no. And I'll thank you to stay out of my kitchen."

Arne chuckled under his breath.

"Whoa, little lady, I'm just trying to be useful," Shane said, palms up as if in self-defense.

Elsa inhaled deeply, remembering one of the fruits of the Spirit was temperance, although she didn't miss the fact he'd referred to her as "little" again.

She softened her tone. "Thank you for asking, but I can manage."

"Miss Fritch, you are going to hurt yourself if you continue to carry that heavy tray."

"I won't hurt myself, and I only dropped it once, and that was when I was thirteen."

Shane looked at Arne. "Talk some sense into your daughter, Uncle Arne."

Uncle Arne? Elsa swung her gaze to her father, who chuckled.

"You remember, young Shane."

"Yes, I remember. . . ."

"What? What are you two talking about?" Elsa wanted to know.

"Back in Germany, your parents and mine were as close as siblings," Shane explained, "and I called your father 'uncle' and your mother 'aunt.' You did likewise with my folks, although I suspect you were too young to recall."

"I remember, too," Arne said with a faraway gleam in his eyes. "My Elsa followed young Shane around like a puppy."

"I did no such thing!" Elsa exclaimed, feeling her cheeks flame.

"Ah, but you did. Und young Shane put up with it, quite a marvel for an eight-year-old boy."

"If my memory serves me correctly, I believe I gave you, Miss Fritch, horsey-back rides."

Elsa felt so embarrassed, she wished the floor would open up and swallow her. But, no such luck.

With a rakish wink in her direction, Shane picked up the tray and carried it into the dining area.

"Papa," Elsa whispered, "please find those receipts. . .fast!"

"Acht! I am trying, but I cannot think uf vhere to search next." He stood from where he'd been sitting at the table, sifting through various documents and articles of importance. Pausing before Elsa, he patted her cheek affectionately. "Mean-vhile, ve can enjoy young Shane's visit. He reminds me of Georg, und I miss my friend. I vish your mama und I vould not have burned bridges betveen da Gerhards und us. Ve might not have agreed vith der vocation, but dey ver still our friends. Now it is too late to reconcile."

"Papa—"

"But maybe not," he added, the lines on his face deepening with an emotion Elsa could not discern. "Maybe not."

With that, he walked into the dining room.

Flustered, Elsa followed him and finished serving the meal from the tray Shane had carried in for her. When the Bunk brothers grabbed more than their share of biscuits, Elsa smacked both their hands. "Half a dozen each is plenty. There are other mouths to feed here besides yours."

"My apologies, Miss Elsa," Zeb said with a lopsided grin, "It's jest that your biscuits are the best we've ever tasted."

"They're nothing special," she contended. "Why, they're not even fresh. I made them this morning."

"Pardon me, Miss Elsa, but they're a far sight better than the hardtack we've been gnawin' on," Horace said with his mouth full of stew. Gravy dribbled from the corner of his mouth, down his chin, and into his scraggly beard.

Appalled by the Bunks' table manners, Elsa quickly set the platter down in the middle of the table and retreated to the kitchen. She smoothed down her apron and took a deep, calming breath. In that moment, she wasn't sure who disturbed her more, Shane Gerhard or Zeb and Horace.

A knock sounded, and Elsa strode to the back door at the far side of the kitchen and opened it. Mrs. Tidewell's pleasingly plump form stood in the threshold, her beaming face framed by her snowy-white hair. She held out an apple pie.

"I thought perhaps you could make use of this."

"Why, thank you, Mrs. T. I certainly could. I didn't do any baking this morning."

"I figured, what with the sewing circle and all."

The pastor's wife stepped inside, and Elsa closed the door.

"There are five men in my dining room as we speak who will be happy to see this pie."

Mrs. Tidewell chuckled. "Yes, I heard the Bunk brothers were back in town, so I thought they would show up at your dinner table soon enough. You're the closest thing this town has to a public eatery."

"I try my best."

"I know you do, Dear, and I can tell you are feeling overwhelmed."

Unexpected tears filled Elsa's eyes, and she nodded.

"But do you think any of this is a surprise to God? Of course it isn't. No matter what is occurring here on earth, God is still on His throne. He is still in charge."

"Everything would be just fine if Shane Gerhard would go back to St. Louis where he came from," Elsa whispered as she began to slice the pie.

"He's that much of a nuisance, is he?"

"That much and more!"

"Hm. . .well, I have an idea," Mrs. T said as she took plates from the cupboard. "It goes along with what we talked about this afternoon."

"Yes?"

"You need to kill him, Elsa."

"Mrs. Tidewell! How could you even suggest such a thing? You're a pastor's wife."

She laughed. "No, no, I don't mean really kill him. I mean, kill Mr. Gerhard's badgering with kindness. Do what the Bible says in Proverbs 25: 21–22. 'If thine enemy be hungry, give him bread to eat; and if he be thirsty, give him water to drink: For thou shalt heap coals of fire upon his head, and the Lord shall reward thee.'"

"I'm not sure I understand."

"Be courteous to Mr. Gerhard, Elsa. My husband and I have run up against his kind before. He thinks it's fun to tease you because you react, but if you're not rankled and instead you're sweet-spirited, he won't be quite so amused."

"Really?"

"Try it and see."

Elsa liked the idea of heaping coals of fire on Shane Gerhard's conceited head. In her opinion, it was the least he deserved. "I'll do it, Mrs. T."

"Good girl. Now, don't forget about our planning meeting on Thursday, and we'll do our baking the following Friday night at my house. Our Spring Fling is going to be so much fun this year. The unmarrieds in this town need a bit of prodding, I'd say."

Elsa grinned, and for the second time that day, she felt God's peace that passes all understanding fill her being. She wrapped her arms around the older woman, thinking Mrs. Tidewell was as motherly as her own mother might have been, were she still alive. "Thank you, Mrs. T. Thank you for coming over this afternoon."

"You're quite welcome." She returned Elsa's hug with a small squeeze of her own.

Moments later, she was on her way out the door, leaving Elsa to wonder if she'd squish Henry like a bug if she embraced him as heartily as she'd embraced the good pastor's wife.

To her dismay, she presumed she probably would!

❖

The next morning, Shane sat on the outside stoop and watched Elsa hang clothes on the line. The sun's rays felt warm against his face on this March morning, and the breeze felt tepid, comfortable. Arne said it'd been an early spring this year. But Shane didn't give a whit about the weather. He was growing restless in this sleepy little town. He wanted to get back to St. Louis and its nightlife. He wanted his money, just sitting there waiting for him in that trust account. He envisioned the extravagant parties he could throw with that kind of loot lining his pockets.

"You know, I think you're going to have to marry me," he told Elsa. Then he grinned, anticipating a tart reply.

To his disappointment, she sighed. . .and agreed. "If Papa doesn't find those receipts, I'll have no other choice but to fulfill our part of the contract."

"Well, look at it this way, as soon as I get my money you can divorce me and marry your precious Henry."

"I could never divorce you."

Shane frowned. "Why not?"

"Because the Bible says God hates divorce. I could never do something God hates."

"All right, then I'll divorce you."

"Suit yourself."

Shane felt suddenly perturbed. Standing, he walked toward her. "Look, I don't know what you're thinking, but all I want is my inheritance. I have no intentions of getting saddled with a wife."

To his shock and delight, Elsa smiled at him, the prettiest smile he'd ever seen on a woman. A smile that produced dimples in both her cheeks. A smile that caused his heart to flip.

"I completely understand your frustration, Mr. Gerhard."

"Um, sure you do." He swallowed hard but recovered quickly. "I think it's high time you called me by my given name, don't you?"

She looked a bit taken aback. "Well, I don't know. . . ."

"Aw, c'mon," he teased her, "Mr. Quinsy won't mind. He scarcely pays any attention to you unless he wants to whine and complain about his many ailments."

Elsa's cheeks flushed slightly, but not a spark of indignation reached her blue eyes. "If you insist. . .Shane. Then you must call me Elsa."

"It'd be my pleasure."

She bent and picked up one of her father's shirts from the large wicker basket.

"So, what do you do for fun around here, Elsa?"

"There's church tonight."

"Oh, I can hardly wait," Shane quipped.

She gave him an amused glance while pinning the shirt on the line. "There's the

Spring Fling coming up in a week from Saturday."

"What's a Spring Fling?"

"A gathering of all the young people in town and some older ones, too. Mr. Stahl plays his fiddle, and—"

"Don't tell me you all dance."

"Oh, no!"

Elsa looked aghast, and Shane hung his head back and hooted.

"Somehow, I didn't think so," he said.

She reached for several linens and hung them over the line to dry. "This year, we're having a big surprise for all the unattached fellas. We girls are making big, round cookies and baking a slip of paper with our names inside of them. Whoever gets that particular young lady's cookie, has to eat supper with her."

Shane grinned. "You'd best hope and pray Zeb or Horace Bunk don't get your cookie."

Elsa paled visibly.

"Well, now, don't worry," he assured her with practiced charm, "you just tell me what your cookie looks like, and I'll make sure it falls into the right hands."

She gave him a skeptical look. "I appreciate your kind offer, but I'm sure you'll be back in St. Louis by the time the Spring Fling comes around."

"And miss this grand event? Not a chance."

"You can't mean that. I—"

Elsa seemed to catch herself before a sharp retort could pass though her berry-pink lips. They were ripe for kissing, as far as Shane was concerned.

"You're more than welcome to attend, of course," she began again, "although I don't imagine you'll find our simplistic form of entertainment to your liking."

"Guess we'll see about that, won't we?"

After a shrug, she picked up her now-empty basket and headed for the board-inghouse. Shane watched her enter through the back door, thinking he might indeed find the Spring Fling to his liking. . .especially if he chose Miss Elsa Fritch's cookie.

Chapter 6

The man was making her crazy. For a full week, Shane had followed Elsa around like a veritable shadow, albeit a talking, teasing, cajoling shadow! Elsa was at her wits' end.

She sighed as she slipped the blue calico dress over her head in preparation for the midweek prayer meeting. Shane hadn't gone last week, nor had he attended the Sunday service. Then, as now, she looked forward to some reprieve from Shane's company. However, if she were completely honest with herself, she'd have to confess to enjoying the attention somewhat. He paid her compliments, and he offered to help with her chores. They had interesting conversations about their relatives in Germany, and on that account, she and Shane had much in common. They'd grown friendly toward one another, the very thing that disturbed her greatly. Shane Gerhard possessed a charming manner that affected Elsa more than she cared to admit. Furthermore, she found herself wishing Henry would act more like him.

Then, of course, there was the perplexing question as to why Shane behaved as though he were romantically interested in her, and at times, Elsa couldn't discern his intentions. Were they merely friends? Just acquaintances? She did suspect he was trifling with her out of sheer boredom, and she prayed without ceasing that Papa would find those receipts and send Shane back to St. Louis. Her heart couldn't endure much more of that man's flirtations. Unfortunately, Papa liked him and wasn't in any hurry to see him go. Still, her father spent his every waking hour searching for the vouchers from Georg Gerhard, and many times, Shane aided in the hunt.

"Acht!" Elsa muttered in frustration as she brushed out her dark-brown hair. If only her mother were alive and could advise her. . .or if Heidi were home. Oh, what was the use of wishing things were different? Wishing couldn't change her situation. She still had Papa to care for and the boardinghouse to manage. Soon, she could add Henry to the list.

Giving herself a mental shake, Elsa considered her appearance in the oblong, mahogany-framed looking glass. She decided to wear her hair down tonight, save for the combs she wore on either side of her head, above her ears. She wanted to look her best for Henry. . .or was it a reaction from Shane that she secretly coveted?

"You must stop thinking like that," she scolded her reflection. "It's the Lord's opinion you need to care about, and He sees the heart, not physical beauty. And a good thing, too!"

Elsa considered her full figure. Even in Mama's best dress, she didn't feel the least bit pretty. She was tall and big-boned, hardly a delicate, feminine little thing, and surely not the type of woman Shane Gerhard would be drawn to. And even if she were, he'd said he wasn't a marrying man, and if it came down to the contract being fulfilled, he would divorce her once he got his money. Elsa couldn't impress Shane if she tried. In fact, she couldn't impress any man with her physical attributes. . .except for Henry, although she wasn't certain that quality had initially attracted him either.

Elsa often wondered why Henry wanted to marry her. He never said he loved her, not even on the afternoon he proposed. And he never once tried to kiss her, much to Elsa's disappointment. But she sensed he needed her, just like Papa. Poor Henry, chronically ill; however, Elsa had two very capable hands, not to mention a strong back. Perhaps she'd even be the one who would nurse Henry back to health, and maybe God would bless the two of them with children.

She allowed her gaze to wander around the small bedroom she'd once shared with Heidi. Soon she would share it with Henry. On the double bed lay a multi-colored patchwork quilt Elsa and her sister had made two years ago at Mrs. Tidewell's sewing circle. In one corner, there stood a wooden wardrobe Papa had built, and beside it was a small chest of drawers. Elsa had inherited her mother's looking glass, which she'd placed near the tiny dressing area, and she never ceased to marvel at the fact it had survived the trip from Germany.

In a month's time, I'll share this room with my husband, Elsa mused. She prayed that she would be a good wife.

On that thought, Elsa left the bedroom and walked down the narrow hallway toward the kitchen. Dinner had been served at five o'clock sharp this evening to afford her ample time to prepare for the midweek church service. When she'd left the dining room to change clothes over thirty minutes ago, there were several guests still lingering over their coffee, including Papa, Shane, Henry, and Doc. However, it sounded quiet, as though all the men had gone.

Would Papa have left for church without me? Elsa wondered.

Making her way through the kitchen, she peered into the dining room, seeing Shane and Henry. Shane was gazing out the front window, one hand in the pocket of his dark trousers, and Henry was writing on a ledger of some sort at a table.

Elsa took two steps into the room. "Did Papa leave?"

Both men glanced her way, and she watched as Shane's expression brightened with interest. From the sparkle in his hazel eyes to the wry grin curving his mouth, Elsa could tell he appreciated that she'd fussed with her toilette this evening. His next words confirmed it.

"Well, now, don't you look pretty."

"Thank you," Elsa said, feeling herself blush. However, she inwardly acknowledged it was the exact response she had hoped for. Furthermore, she felt amazed she'd accomplished such a feat.

"As for your papa," Shane added, "he went on ahead to church with Doc."

"Oh. . ." She looked at Henry, disappointed that his countenance registered nothing but a pained frown. "Well, we can walk together."

"I'm not feeling well enough to sit through church tonight," he complained. "I think I'll go home." He tossed a glance at Shane. "Mr. Gerhard offered to escort you."

Elsa's heart sank. "But, Henry, it isn't right. . .that is, I'm your fiancé. Shane shouldn't have to escort me."

"He offered. It would be rude to refuse him." Henry cleared his throat and winced, clutching his neck with pale, lanky fingers. "When I get home, I'll make myself some of that tea Doc gave me."

He stood, picked up his ledger, then strode toward the front door of the boardinghouse. No hug or kiss good-bye, no affection whatsoever, not even in his expression. He never once said she looked pretty, or gave her some minuscule promise to hang onto. And he never gave it a second thought that she'd be in another man's company this evening. To sum it up, Henry seemed not to care.

Shane walked slowly toward her, and Elsa blinked back her tears of dejection. She looked his way, and Shane narrowed his gaze.

"You getting the picture here?" he asked, pointing to his temple. "Is it beginning to sink in?"

Elsa swallowed convulsively. "What are you talking about?"

"Mr. Quinsy." Shane shook his head. "He either doesn't love you, Elsa, or he's the biggest fool that ever walked the earth."

"Don't say that. Henry's not a fool. He's just ill."

"More like self-absorbed. Why, I'd have to be dead or dying before I turned my fiancé over to another man's care—especially if he was a man like me."

Elsa had to grin at the irony of his statement.

"There, that's better," he said with a charming smile. "You're far too lovely to be frowning so hard." He held his arm out to her. "Shall we go?"

On a sigh of resignation, Elsa stepped forward and slipped her hand around his elbow. "You're really coming to church?"

Shane shrugged his broad shoulders. "Sure. I reckon it can't hurt."

Arm in arm, they walked down Main Street, heading for Birch Street. As they passed the shipping office, Elsa looked for any signs of Henry, but saw none.

"Who's got the fancy house over yonder?"

At the corner, Elsa glanced to her right. "The one painted dove gray? That's the Montclairs' home."

"Seems out of place, what with all the log buildings around here except for the bank and the church."

"Yes, I suppose it does. But Mr. Montclair is one of Hickory Corners' founders, and perhaps for that reason he maintains a lovely home, even though he and his wife are rarely there to enjoy it."

"So the house is a monument of sorts."

"Something like that."

Despite Shane's attempt at a light conversation, Elsa felt heavy-hearted. She gazed up at him, and in spite of herself, couldn't help admiring his predominant jawline covered with a hint of a shadow. "Do you really think Henry doesn't love me?"

Shane looked at her, and Elsa saw the sympathy in his eyes. "He's a fool."

Elsa shook her head in disagreement. "He doesn't love me."

"Well, look at it this way—at least you found that out before you married him."

"But I thought I could make him love me by taking care of him."

"Darlin', he is supposed to take care of you."

"But—"

"All right, all right," he said as if to forestall any debate, "I imagine marriage is something of a give-and-take arrangement. Wives take care of their husbands by cooking and cleaning and such. Except in your case, life with Mr. Quinsy would be you doing all the giving, and you'd end up one unhappy woman."

Elsa thought of several retorts; however, the truth of Shane's words kept her from verbalizing any of them.

Reaching the church, Elsa and Shane climbed the steps and met a small group of friends chatting in the tiny vestibule. She introduced Shane, and hearing he was from St. Louis, several of the older Stahl boys—no longer "boys" but married men now—engaged him in conversation.

Elsa had to grin. The husky, dark-haired Stahls would keep Shane occupied for awhile. They hailed from a large family whose farm resided on the acreage behind the church.

"Where's Henry?" Betsy Larkin asked.

"He's ill tonight."

"The poor man. Is it his throat again?"

Elsa nodded.

"Are you and Mr. Gerhard getting along better now?" Samantha Thomasohn wanted to know, her brown eyes sparkling with mischief. "It would seem the two of you are quite friendly."

Elsa didn't feel up to the teasing or giving explanations, and merely nodded.

"Does Henry know you and Mr. Gerhard are 'quite friendly'?" Clara Bucey asked, looking alarmed.

"Yes, and it's all his fault, too!"

The girls were wide-eyed with curiosity.

Elsa glanced around the small group. "You're my best friends. You've known me practically my whole life."

They nodded.

"Then you'll understand when I say I'm having serious doubts about marrying Henry. Of course, I haven't breathed a word of this to anyone else yet."

"We'd never repeat a thing," Samantha promised, and Elsa knew it was true. Her friends were not gossips. When they heard of a trial or tragedy, they prayed.

"Mantha and I warned you 'bout Henry," Betsy said earnestly. "We just had a funny feeling concerning the two of you." She suddenly grinned impishly. "Now, you and Mr. Gerhard, on the other hand—"

"Oh, hush," Elsa said, cutting off further reply.

A man cleared his throat, and Elsa turned to see one of the Stahl brothers motioning them into the sanctuary. Bidding her friends a hasty farewell, Elsa walked up the aisle. Shane followed and joined her and Papa in the fourth pew from the front—their usual place.

"I am pleased dat you came tonight," Papa said, leaning toward their guest.

Shane shrugged. "Haven't seen any bolts from out of the blue yet. I reckon that's a good sign."

Elsa smiled at the quip, then sent up a silent prayer that Pastor Tidewell's message tonight would somehow touch Shane in a special way.

Chapter 7

S hane ambled out of the quaint clapboard church and walked alongside Elsa and Arne back to the boardinghouse. He wondered at what he'd heard tonight from Pastor Tidewell's pulpit. Was it true? Was there really a place called heaven and a place called hell? Sure, he knew that's what Christians believed, but was it true? The question continued to play over and over in his mind.

"I'll make some tea," Elsa said once they entered the boardinghouse. She headed for the kitchen, leaving Shane and her father in the dining common.

"So, Uncle Arne, tell me," he began, "do you think the Bible is truly God's Word?"

"Ja." The old man nodded vigorously.

"I always wondered..."

"Your parents did not teach you da Bible?"

Shane shrugged. "I have had some Sunday school lessons. That is, when I didn't get tossed out of class for misbehaving."

Arne chuckled softly just as Elsa reentered the room.

"I set the kettle on to boil."

Shane grinned in reply. He didn't give a whit about tea, but he'd sit and sip it politely just to be in Elsa's company. He watched her take a seat at one of the long tables and marveled that in the course of a little better than one week, he'd begun behaving like some lovesick swain. What in the world was wrong with him, anyway?

"Your vater vas a troublemaker in his younger days, too," Arne said, still grinning broadly. "But after he met your mutter, he settled down. Could be das vhat you need—da love uf a gute voman."

"You think so, eh?" Shane had to keep from glancing at Elsa. He forced himself to walk toward the small window at the front of the dining room. Moving the curtain aside, he gazed out onto the darkened dirt road. Across the way, the mercantile had already closed for the evening. The entire town seemed to close up after sunset. No theaters. No race tracks or gaming tables. No dance halls. "I rather enjoy my life. Carefree, no responsibilities. I don't have to answer to anyone except me. I can stay out all night if I want to. I come and go as I please."

Who am I trying to convince, he wondered, *the Fritches or myself?*

When no reply came from his hosts, he turned to face them. "Getting back to our original topic, I've got another question for you."

Arne nodded as he sat down by the hearth. "Ask, young Shane."

"If what the Bible says is true, and there really is a heaven and a hell, and my folks knew it. . .then why didn't they sit me down, look me in the eyes, and tell me that I was a sinner destined for a godless eternity? My parents loved me, cared about me." He paused, searching his own mind for an answer. "Why didn't they tell me?"

Elsa looked at her father.

"Perhaps, young Shane," Arne began, "your parents did not think you vould listen."

"Maybe. And maybe they would have been right, too, but they still could have said. . .something."

Arne appeared momentarily thoughtful, then said, *Ja*, dey could have said something. But das no longer an excuse, is it? Tonight, you have heard da truth, dat Jesus Christ is God, sent by God da Vater, and salvation is through Him."

Shane nodded out a reply. "Sure, I heard. I just don't know if I believe it."

"That's the decision we all encounter at one time or another," Elsa said.

The warmth in her voice touched Shane's heart in an odd way. He crossed the room and straddled the bench opposite her, the scarred tabletop between them. "So you didn't believe all this Bible stuff at first either, is that what you're telling me?"

"I was twelve years old when I accepted the Lord," Elsa explained. "Papa tried to tell me about Jesus. Mama tried to tell me, too. But I thought I was a good girl, because I always tried to obey at school and at home, and I couldn't understand that I was just as much a sinner in need of salvation as anyone else."

"Hm. . ." Shane thought it over. "Well, I don't have trouble with the sin aspect. Contrary to your childhood disposition, I was always the 'bad' one, the rabble-rouser. In fact, my grandfather often called me a 'ne'er-do-well'."

"It's never too late to change," Elsa stated with a hint of a smile.

Shane folded his arms and grinned back at her. "Are you insinuating that I haven't changed?"

Her cheeks turned a pretty shade of pink. "I think I hear the water boiling for our tea," she said, hastily rising from the wooden bench.

She fled to the kitchen, leaving Shane chuckling in her wake.

-:≡:-

The next morning, Elsa finished dressing two chickens for the noon meal, then impaled them on a spit, which she placed over the fire in the hearth. The Bunk brothers had announced at breakfast that another packet arrived in town. They told Elsa to expect some hungry river men at noontime—themselves included, of course.

Elsa fretted over her lower lip. Perhaps she should roast three chickens. . .no, she'd just double up on the biscuits instead.

"Papa," she called into the back hallway. "Papa, are there more canned beets in the cellar?"

Ja, I think so." He walked slowly out of his room and headed her way. "I vill get you a jar."

"Fetch two please, Papa. We might have several guests today."

He nodded, and Elsa's heart went out to him. Her father had been searching relentlessly for those receipts since awakening this morning. Finding nothing, he looked so defeated. It almost seemed as though he felt his honor was now at stake, although Shane appeared to believe Papa when he said he paid the debt in full.

A disturbance in the dining area suddenly caught Elsa's attention. Wiping her hands on her apron, she strode into the other room, where she found Shane pushing a two-tiered, wooden tea cart on wheels in the front door with Samantha Thomasohn trailing behind.

"What's all this?" Elsa asked.

"Look what Mr. Gerhard purchased for you!" Samantha exclaimed, her cheeks reddening with enthusiasm. "Nathaniel Harmon made it in his carpentry shop."

"For me?"

Shane nodded. "So you won't have to carry that heavy tray anymore."

"First, Mr. Gerhard came to our mercantile," Samantha explained, "but we don't sell what he had in mind, so he ordered it special from Mr. Harmon. I just had to come over and see the look on your face."

"Well, I'm certainly surprised, but I do not need a cart."

"Yes, you do, too, need it," Shane said. "Now, look here..."

Leaving the tea cart in the middle of the dining room, he sauntered into the kitchen, and Samantha gasped.

"He's in your kitchen, Elsa. He just walked right in!"

"He does it all the time," she muttered.

Samantha brought her fingers to her lips in effort to stifle her giggles, while Elsa shook her head as Shane returned with the offensive serving tray.

"See, Elsa? You simply place your tray on top of the cart, load it up, and voila! You push it into the dining room instead of carrying it. Much easier. Underneath the cart, you've got some shelf space for water pitchers and the like." He grinned. "What do you think?"

She opened her mouth to reiterate how unnecessary a tea cart was; however, Shane looked as excited as a little boy on Christmas morning. How could she break his heart?

"I think..." She glanced at Samantha, who gave her an encouraging smile. "I think this is the nicest thing anyone has ever done for me. Thank you, Shane. I'm ever so grateful."

"I knew you'd like it." His grin broadened, and an amused twinkle entered his hazel eyes. "Besides, you can always wheel Henry around on it when you're not serving food. This cart seems sturdy enough."

Elsa narrowed a warning gaze at him, and Shane laughed.

"I think I should be getting back," Samantha said, looking curiously from one to the other. She turned toward the door, and her dark blue skirt swirled at her ankles. "Mama probably needs me. She's still so sick."

"Of course," Elsa replied, walking her friend to the door. "Is there anything we can do to hasten your mother's recovery?"

"Pray." Samantha's blond brows furrowed with concern. "Please keep praying."

"We shall."

Elsa gave her friend a quick embrace, and then Samantha raced back to the mercantile across the road.

Spinning on her heel, Elsa placed her hands on her hips and faced Shane.

"I know what you're going to say," he blurted before she could utter a single word. "You're going to tell me I shouldn't have poked fun at Mr. Quinsy, and I reckon you're right. I apologize."

He gave Elsa a humble-looking bow, and she rolled her eyes. "Always the charmer, aren't you? I'll bet you got yourself out of plenty of whippin's when you were a lad."

"Why, Miss Elsa," he said with a wounded expression, "are you suggesting that I'm being insincere?"

"Yes!" With that, she walked past him into the kitchen. As she suspected, Shane followed.

Papa had returned from the cellar with two jars of beets and a small crate. "Look, Elsa. Look vhat I found." He set his burdens on the kitchen table.

"Do you think the receipts are in the crate?" she asked.

"*Ja*, dey could be."

Shane rubbed his palms together in anticipation. "Want me to help you, Uncle Arne?"

"*Ja*, sure."

The two men pulled out their chairs and began to sit down when Elsa halted them.

"Out of my kitchen," she ordered. "I've got biscuits to bake. You two can do your sorting at a table in the dining room, and Papa, please remember to charge guests who come for lunch today. We forgot yesterday. It's just a good thing our guests were honest."

Standing, her father nodded his head and scooped up the crate with both hands.

"Is she always so bossy, Uncle Arne?" Shane asked with a teasing grin.

"*Ja*. But she keeps me in line."

"Who keeps her in line?" He winked at Elsa.

"Das a gute question, young Shane. Gute question."

The men chuckled together on their way out, and Elsa decided to let them have their fun. She couldn't out-quip Shane Gerhard if she tried. Returning to the service counter, she mixed together the ingredients for her famous baking soda biscuits.

-:::-

It was shortly after the noon hour when the Bunks and six other scraggly looking men clamored into the boardinghouse. Their deep voices and laughter seemed to fill every nook and cranny.

Knowing the men were hungry, Elsa quickly placed the tray onto the tea cart and set several plates of food on it. Next she wheeled it into the dining room, deciding it was much easier to push than to carry.

"Well, well, what do we have here?" a scruffy-bearded man asked.

"Chicken, biscuits and gravy, and canned beets," Elsa replied politely.

"Forget the supper—you're quite a dish yourself, Honey."

Chuckles went up and down the table, and Elsa tried to ignore them as she continued to set a plate in front of each guest.

"What's your name?" the man persisted.

"This is Miss Elsa Fritch," Zeb Bunk answered. "Miss Elsa, that there is Weaver."

"My full name is John Adams Weaver."

Unimpressed, Elsa gave him a perfunctory smile, then glanced over the men's heads to where Shane sat at a nearby table, watching the goings-on with a critical eye. She looked to her far left and saw her papa, sitting behind the greeting counter, busying himself with the funds he'd collected. Elsa quelled her uneasiness by telling herself she was safe with Shane and Papa in the room. Then she wondered why she felt so flustered. She had managed bold men by herself in the past.

The river men began to eat, and Elsa noted only a few bowed their heads and thanked the Lord before digging in. Back in the kitchen, she prepared two plates for Shane and her father.

"Thank you for being patient and waiting," she murmured to Shane as she set the meal before him.

"Aw, Elsa, I'm not that much of a guest."

She replied with a grateful smile, then served her papa.

"Looks gute," he said.

She kissed the balding crown of her father's head before returning to the kitchen.

At the service counter, Elsa sliced the cinnamon spice cake she had baked earlier and lay each piece on a dessert plate. Next she served the river men, taking away their empty dinnerware and stacking it onto her new tea cart.

"You sure are a purty thing," Weaver said. His hair and beard were the color of the brown mud along the banks of the Ohio. His deep-set eyes seemed spaced too far apart on his wide face, and Elsa thought he resembled a reptile. "How 'bout a little kiss for dessert instead of this here cake?"

"I think you'll have your cake," she retorted.

Several guffaws emanated from Weaver's cronies.

"I think I won't." He stood, a determined gleam in his eyes.

Elsa swallowed her sudden fear and tried to back away, but Weaver caught her shoulders. She pushed on his chest, turning her head to escape his eager lips.

In the next moment, Weaver abruptly freed her, and Elsa staggered backward. A strong arm caught her around the waist. Before she even saw him, she knew it was Shane. But then Elsa glimpsed the shiny pistol in his hand, pointed directly at Weaver.

"Don't you ever touch this woman again," Shane said in slow, menacing intervals.

"Das right!" Papa hollered from across the room. "Und you can leave my boardinghouse dis minute!"

Weaver held up his hands as if in surrender. "Now, look, I was just having a bit of fun."

"Get out," Shane demanded.

The river man nodded and grabbed his battered hat from off the bench on which he'd been sitting.

"Me and Zeb'll see to it he leaves for good," Horace Bunk announced.

He took one of Weaver's arms, and Zeb took the other. Ignoring his protests and arguments, they escorted their unruly pal to the front door of the boardinghouse. Then, taking Weaver by the seat of his pants, the Bunk brothers tossed him out onto the road. Elsa winced at the resounding thud of humanity hitting hard dirt.

"Anyone else have a mind to try my patience?" Shane asked, waving his pistol at the other men at the table.

"Nope."

"Uh-uh."

Another man shook his shaggy, blond head and continued to eat his cake.

"Good." Shane tucked away his gun and peered down at Elsa. "You all right?"

"Yes," she stated, feeling embarrassed and grateful all at once. She stared up into his hazel eyes, and in that moment, she determined Shane was something of a hero.

As if divining her thoughts, he suddenly appeared chagrined. Releasing Elsa, he stepped away, nodded politely, and walked off in Arne's direction. When he returned to his place at the table, Arne gave him a congratulatory clap on the shoulder. Shane looked over at Elsa, and she smiled.

My hero, she thought, making her way into the kitchen. *He special orders a tea cart to ease my workload, and he defends my virtue.*

Conversely, she wondered what she'd ever do when he left to go back to St. Louis!

Chapter 8

U ncle Arne, think," Shane beseeched the old man. "Where would you have put those receipts? What about in a safe deposit box at the bank?"

"Nein, nein," Arne despaired. Sitting at one of the long tables, he put his graying head in his hands.

Shane sighed and paced the dining common. He had to get out of Hickory Corners. If he didn't leave soon, he might never get away. There was something strange about this tiny community, and it was drawing him in with its powerful clutches.

This morning, for instance, Doc had come over, and he, Arne, and Shane had chattered on like long-lost friends. Next, he'd met Oskar Bedloe, the wiry-framed tinsmith. Bedloe's place was located between the mercantile and Doc's barbershop. Shane got along well with all three men, as they discussed politics and America's new president, Martin Van Buren. And for the first time ever, Shane felt like he belonged. Doc and Bedloe didn't know about the Gerhards' fortune, so they weren't befriending him thinking they had something to gain. Furthermore, they hadn't an inkling about his past, so they weren't looking down pious noses at him. They accepted him at face value.

Then there was Arne, who behaved like the proud uncle. He introduced Shane to everyone who passed by on the street.

Of course, Elsa didn't help matters. Since noontime yesterday, she had regarded him as if he walked on water. Him! A rake among rakes. Rogue among rogues. Worse, Shane couldn't seem to keep his distance. When she looked up at him and smiled, he felt twelve feet tall. As for marrying Elsa so he could claim his inheritance...well, he wouldn't mind that a bit. Only problem was, he didn't think he could marry her, then leave her behind. He'd want to take her with him, but what kind of life could he possibly provide for a decent woman? And he sure wasn't about to stay here. What sort of vocation could he pursue?

The only viable option was to find those receipts and sail out of this town as quickly as he could!

"All right, all right, Uncle Arne, let's put our heads together. Is there an attic in this place?"

"Ja, but I have searched it."

"Let's search it again."

The old man nodded. "First thing tomorrow vhen da light is better."

Shane expelled an impatient breath and glanced at the windows. Beyond them, he could see the evening dusk rapidly descending.

"Papa, I'm leaving."

Shane swung around, hearing Elsa's voice. She'd removed her apron and had donned a pretty lace collar over her brown linen dress.

She smiled at Shane.

In spite of himself, he smiled back.

"Vhere are you going?" Arne asked.

"To bake cookies with Mrs. Tidewell and a few other ladies. Remember, I told you, Papa?"

"Ja, ja, I remember now."

"Tomorrow is the Spring Fling."

"Oh, that's right," Shane drawled, snapping his fingers. "I plumb forgot. Why, I imagine this is the biggest event of the whole year."

Elsa gave him one of her quelling looks, and he laughed.

She turned to her father. "Henry will be here in a few minutes. He said he had to work late tonight. Papa, are you still going to talk to him for me?"

"Nein, Elsa. Talk to him yourself. I am a tired old man."

"But, Papa—"

"Do not argue," he warned her, rising from the bench. "It is best Henry hears your feelings from you, not me."

With that, Arne shuffled over to his daughter and kissed her cheek. *"Aufwiedersehen, bis Morgen,"* he said, patting her shoulder affectionately.

"Yes, see you in the morning, Papa."

"Young Shane. . .*Gute Nacht."*

"G'night, Uncle Arne."

He watched the aging man head for his bedroom, via the kitchen. Returning his gaze to Elsa, he encountered her perturbed expression.

"May I be so bold as to inquire over what it is you wanted your father to say to Mr. Quinsy?"

Elsa puffed out an exasperated breath but shook her head.

"Aw, c'mon. You can tell me," Shane cajoled. He strode slowly toward her. "Maybe I can help."

"You can't." Elsa folded her arms in front of her and dropped her gaze to the tips of her leather ankle boots.

"Let me guess. You changed your mind about marrying Henry. Someone else came along and. . .and swept you off the service counter."

Elsa let her arms fall to her sides. "You are the most vain man I have ever met."

Shane laughed. "I reckon you're right about that." He took another step forward. "Elsa," he said in all seriousness, "don't fall in love with me. I'll only break your heart."

She sort of rolled her eyes and looked away, so Shane took hold of her chin, urging her gaze to his own.

"Look at me, Elsa."

She did, and Shane's heart splintered seeing fat tears fill her eyes.

"Honey, I'm a no-account gambler. Why do you think my father didn't leave me his company or the family estate? He knew I'd probably lose everything in some high-stakes card game. I've been known for drinking and carousing until dawn. I haven't held a job for more than a few months at a time. That's the kind of man I really am, Elsa. I'm not husband material for a fine, Christian woman like yourself."

"I know what kind of man you are," Elsa said staring back at him with misty eyes that held such tenderness it took Shane's breath away.

He caressed her cheek with the backs of his fingers, fighting the urge to kiss her. He had a hunch she wanted to be kissed, too.

At that precise moment, however, Henry burst through the front door. "Elsa?" he called in his habitual, whiny voice. "Elsa?"

"Over here, Henry."

Shane lowered his hand and stepped backward. "Well, good evening Mr. Qu—I mean, Peabody."

His near blunder earned Shane a rap in the arm. He grinned.

"Come in, Henry," Elsa invited. "Papa has already retired for the night, and I'm on my way to the Tidewells' house, but I'm certain Mr. Gerhard will keep you in plenty of company. He likes to play cards." She made for the door and grabbed her shawl and bonnet. "Good night."

"Whoa, Elsa, just a minute here," Shane called.

But the door slammed shut, signaling her hasty departure.

"Little imp," Shane muttered. He strode to the windows and saw her walking up the street in the company of the blond gal from the mercantile.

Behind him, Shane heard Henry clear his throat. "Imp? Is that what you called Elsa?"

"Ah, yes, it is." Shane pivoted, considering the small man standing several feet away. "You know, if you're not careful, Mr. Peabody, some blackguard is liable to steal your woman."

·:·

With the cookies baked, frosted, and decorated, Elsa and Samantha bid farewell to Mrs. Tidewell and headed for home.

"Won't Betsy be pleased with the cookie we made for her?" Samantha said.

"Yes, it's perfect," Elsa replied, wondering who would choose their friend's treat tomorrow. Betsy's pa deemed it unsafe for her to drive the wagon into town from her family's farm after dark. Besides, she had her siblings to care for and tuck into bed.

"I wonder who'll get my cookie," Samantha mused. "I hope it's Martin Crabtree. He just got home from law school today. He'll be in town through Easter Sunday, so he'll attend the Spring Fling tomorrow."

"Make sure you give him a hint about your cookie before one of the Bunk brothers gobbles it up."

The girls shared a little laugh as they turned onto Main Street.

"What about you? Will you give Henry a hint?"

Elsa shook her head, glad it was too dark for Samantha to see her. "I know I'm betrothed to Henry, but. . .well. . ."

"It's that Mr. Gerhard, isn't it?"

"Yes," Elsa whispered. The admission seemed to float on the breeze and carry through the budding treetops.

"I thought maybe you had developed feelings for him."

"It's worse than that, Samantha. I'm in love with him."

"Oh, dear. . ."

Elsa could faintly see her friend's face peeping out from beneath her bonnet as they paused in front of the boardinghouse.

"Don't worry about me," Elsa said as they prepared to part for the night. "God knows my heart, and He is in control. He knows the situation, and He has already planned for it in His throne room. This turn of events is no surprise to God."

"Very true."

"How's your mother?" Elsa asked, changing the subject.

"She's not faring well. I overheard Doc telling my father that. . .that it's likely she'll. . .die. We should be prepared."

Samantha sniffed audibly, and Elsa pulled her friend into an embrace. "There, there, don't cry." She wished she could say something profound to ease Samantha's sorrow.

"Oh, I'll be all right," she said, giving Elsa a bit of a squeeze before pulling away. "I know God is in charge of my situation, too. But trusting Him is easier said than done. Mama and I are very close."

"Yes, I know. . . ."

A solemn moment hung between them.

"I should get home," Samantha said.

Elsa nodded. "Good night, my dear friend."

"Good night."

With sadness filling her being, Elsa walked the rest of the way to the boarding-house—and nearly tripped over Shane's form perched on the stoop by the front door.

" 'Bout time you got home."

"And who might you be, my guardian?" Elsa asked tartly.

"Guardian angel, maybe."

In spite of herself, she laughed.

"What did I hear about your friend's mother?"

Elsa sobered. "She's sick. . .possibly dying."

"That's a shame."

"Yes, it is. Mrs. Thomasohn is a fine woman, caring in every way. When my mama was ill, Mrs. Thomasohn checked in on Heidi, Herrick, and me, and she made sure things were running smoothly. After Mama died, Mrs. Thomasohn proved such a comfort to us." Elsa paused thoughtfully. "I just wish there was something I could do in return, but it seems Samantha is managing."

"How long since your mother passed away?"

"Almost five years."

"Guess everyone has to go sometime, hm?"

"True. Tomorrow isn't promised to any of us." She tipped her head, straining to see Shane's features in the darkness. Only a small light flickered behind him from inside the boardinghouse. "Do you miss your parents?"

"Some. But if the Bible is true, they're walking the streets of gold in heaven right now. Their enthusiasm for God may have dwindled, but I know they were true believers."

"How did you know about that. . .about the streets of gold in heaven?"

Shane chuckled. "Seems I'm remembering some old Sunday school lessons. I've had a lot of time to think since coming to Hickory Corners. Not much else to do around here after sundown."

Elsa sat beside him. "Did you and Henry get along all right tonight?"

"Did we get along. . . ? I ought to take you over my knee for pulling that prank." Elsa grinned.

"Oh, I suppose Henry and I had a friendly conversation," Shane finally admitted. "I did my best to make him see that he sorely neglects you, but ol' Henry just wanted to complain about his throat. By the way, he feels better today. I thought you'd want to know."

"Yes, thank you. That is good news."

"I told him he should go back to Boston where he wants to have that operation—a tonsillectomy. I believe Henry is seriously considering the idea."

"Really?"

"Uh-huh." There was a smile in his voice when he added, "I hope you'll enjoy living in Boston."

"I'm sure I'll never know. I don't plan to leave my papa and Hickory Corners. Henry knows that. Besides, I've changed my mind about marrying him."

"Is that what you wanted your papa to talk to Henry about?"

"Yes."

"Well, I'm glad you've finally come to your senses, although I hope it's not on account of me."

"Of course it is. You spared me from a loveless marriage. I'm forever grateful."

"Grateful? To me?" He chuckled lightly. "All right, just so long as you're not in love with me."

Elsa chose not to directly reply to the latter. "I have decided something else, too," she announced.

"What's that?"

"I've decided that if Papa cannot find those receipts, I will marry you so you can collect your money, even though I know you'll divorce me soon afterward."

Elsa was fully aware that God's Word warned Christians against marrying unbelievers; however, she rather thought her predicament was similar to Queen Esther's. Surely God would honor Elsa's arranged marriage the way He blessed Esther's marriage to a heathen king. Besides, it wasn't like hers and Shane's would be a "real" marriage.

"You're willing to marry me?" Shane asked incredulously. "You know full well I'm not the husband type."

"I know that, yes," Elsa began. "But in these past two weeks, you have cared more about me than Henry has in all the months we courted. Of course, I understand you didn't mean to show me any special affection," she put in quickly. "You were simply being the brave champion you always are."

"Brave champion?" He chuckled once more.

"You're my hero, Shane," Elsa whispered, leaning closer to him. "You're a regular knight in shining armor in my eyes."

At that, Shane hung his head back and hooted. "Elsa, you've got things all inside out and backward. Didn't you hear anything I told you earlier? I'm no champion, no hero—"

"You are to me." She placed her hand on his arm. "But, I don't expect anything from you. If we're forced to marry, you're free to return to your life in St. Louis while I live mine in Hickory Corners, knowing I spared my father's honor just the way Queen Esther spared the lives of the Jewish people."

"Queen Esther?"

"In the Bible." She suspected her rationale was weak, yet she longed to believe it.

"Ah, yes. . ."

The cool, springtime air caused Elsa to shiver. Standing, she smoothed down the skirt of her brown dress, then pulled her shawl a little tighter around her shoulders. "I guess I'll go in for the night. I think I've caught a chill. See you in the morning."

"G'night, Elsa."

With a parting smile, she walked into the boardinghouse. She had peace about her decisions, but she had to wonder how God would use it all together for His good.

Chapter 9

*S*he thinks I'm a hero, Shane thought, pacing his room the next morning. *A knight in shining armor.* He shook his head. *She sure is mistaken! Why, if Gramps was still alive, he'd laugh till his sides ached. Brave champion, his "ne'er-do-well" grandson? Ha!*

Pausing, he glanced out the window at the sunshine beating down on the building next door. He had to admit, part of him longed to live up to Elsa's expectations, but the other part wondered if it were even possible. A guy like him?

A knock on the door interrupted his musings. Crossing the room, Shane answered it.

"Young Shane, vill you come up to da attic vis me und help me find dose receipts?"

"Um...sure." He gave the older man a quick once-over glance, and decided he looked weary—even more than weary. He looked like he hadn't had a decent night's sleep since Shane arrived. "On second thought, Uncle Arne, why don't we take a little break from our searching?"

"But I thought you ver growing restless und vanted to find da vouchers from your vater."

"I am, but..." Shane smiled easily. "Look, tomorrow is Easter Sunday. Why don't we just wait until Monday to continue our search? We'll give ourselves a couple of days of rest and, who knows, maybe if you're not thinking so hard on this matter, you'll remember where you put those miserable things."

"*Ja, ja*...maybe if I don't think so hard..."

"Give your mind a bit of relaxation."

"*Ja*, I think you are right, young Shane." The old man's lined face split into a grin. "How about some breakfast?"

"Now there's an offer I won't pass up."

Grabbing his hat, Shane followed Arne down the narrow stairwell and into the dining common. Several men, river-faring men, judging from their unkempt appearances, were on their way out. Shane nodded politely, and then a wave of anxiety got the best of him, and he made a beeline straight for the kitchen.

"Elsa, are you all right?" he asked, both hands on either side of the doorjamb. His heart suddenly thundered in his chest.

She turned, a pot in her hands, a dishtowel slung over her shoulder. "I'm fine," she answered, wearing a curious frown. "Why wouldn't I be?"

"I just saw those men leaving. . . ."

"Ah," she replied with a knowing look in her blue eyes. "Not to worry, Shane. I don't think the men from the docks will be getting fresh with me any time soon. I believe word of what took place last Thursday has made the rounds."

"Glad to hear it," Shane said, although he wasn't completely assuaged.

"Vhat is going on?" Arne asked, sauntering to the kitchen doorway.

Shane pivoted to face the elderly man. "Uncle Arne, you just can't leave Elsa unattended when there's a pack of men in the dining common. It isn't safe."

"Oh, Elsa can handle herself," Arne stated confidently. "She vill take her cast-iron frying pan und go. . .bonk! right over der heads."

"Carrying those pots she's going to have arms like a man!" Shane placed one hand on Arne's shoulder and gave it a mild shake. "Look, Uncle Arne, she's a woman, and you need to protect her."

"I do protect her like any gute vater!" Arne said, his voice raised in self-defense. "But you, young Shane, have overstepped your bounds. How I care for my family is none uf your business."

"Papa—"

"No, Elsa, he's right," Shane replied, staring down into Arne's faded blue eyes. "I overstepped my bounds. My apologies, Sir."

With that, he donned his hat and left the boardinghouse. Outside, the sunshine felt warm against his face, and Shane decided if he had even a lick of common sense, he'd set sail on the next packet going anywhere. By staying in Hickory Corners, he was getting involved in all sorts of messes, none of them having to do with his sole purpose for being here—claiming his inheritance.

Strolling up Main Street, Shane had just passed the dress shop when he glimpsed none other than Mr. Quinsy leaving the shipping office. The small-framed, thin man started in his direction, and Shane felt sure Henry was on his way to the boarding-house to see Elsa.

And it's none of my business, he told himself. As Henry neared, Shane inclined his head politely.

"Good morning, Mr. Gerhard. It's a lovely day, isn't it?"

"Sure is."

"My throat is so much better. . .did you notice how clear my voice sounds?"

"Uh. . .yes. Sounds infinitely clearer."

"I no longer croak like a frog." Henry laughed.

Shane forced a perfunctory smile.

"Say, did you recently come from the boardinghouse?"

"Yes, I did."

"Was Elsa there?"

"Sure was."

"Good. I hope she'll be ready to leave on time. I just hate being late for social functions."

"Oh?" Shane arched an inquiring brow. "What social function are you referring to?"

"Why, the Spring Fling, of course. I promised Elsa I'd take her if I felt well enough. Seeing as I do, I thought I might walk up now and break the good news to her ahead of time. The Spring Fling doesn't officially begin until one o'clock."

"Glad you're on the mend," Shane replied, wondering if Elsa would be the one doing the "breaking"—breaking off their betrothal, that is. After all, she had said she'd decided against marrying poor ol' Mr. Quinsy.

"Have a good day," Henry said, continuing on with his trek to the boardinghouse.

"And it's none of my business," Shane muttered, ambling off in the opposite direction. However, the farther away he got, the more uneasy he became. What if Elsa couldn't get herself to relay her decision to Henry? Naw, that wouldn't happen. Elsa possessed a lot of gumption. Of course, she had a soft side to her also—the side that put up with the likes of Shane Gerhard. The side that thought he was a hero.

Against his better judgment, Shane turned around and walked back to the boardinghouse. Entering, he found Arne sitting at the greeting counter.

"Young Shane, I am sorry I lost my temper," he stated, looking sincere.

"Quite all right. Now I know where Elsa gets it!"

"Vhat?" The old man frowned, looking confused.

"Never mind." Shane chuckled. "Apology accepted. But, if you'll excuse me. . ." He glanced around the dining common. "Where did Elsa and Henry go?"

"Out in da back, I think. But, young Shane, dey are having a private talk just da two uf dem."

"Right. I'm aware of that. I just thought maybe Elsa might like some support, you know? Encouragement."

Arne grinned, causing the wrinkles on his face to multiply. "You are fond uf my Elsa, *ja?*"

"*Ja,*" Shane admitted, although he wished it wasn't true. The feelings he'd developed for Elsa only complicated matters.

"She is fond uf you, too," Arne said.

"So I've gathered."

Just then, booted footfalls sounded from the kitchen, through the dining room, and Shane turned in time to see Henry marching for the front door. The man's overall expression registered nothing, although Shane saw the grim slant of his thin lips.

Without a single word, Mr. Quinsy left.

"See," Arne said, "my Elsa alvays knows vhat to say."

⋯⁂⋯

Sitting outside the kitchen door on the back stoop, Elsa felt horrid. She'd crushed poor Henry by stating she had changed her mind—she couldn't marry him. He'd looked so forlorn and disappointed. Nevertheless, he didn't try to talk her out of her decision. In fact, he never even said he loved her. In her heart, Elsa knew she'd done the right thing. . .for the both of them.

Suddenly, she sensed the presence of someone standing behind her. Tipping her head back, she stared up at Shane, who appeared as tall as an elm from her present viewpoint.

He grinned down at her. "Want some company?"

She righted her bearing, nodded, and scooted over to make room for him on the stoop.

"I saw Mr. Quinsy on his way out," he said, taking a seat beside her. "I take it you broke off your engagement."

Elsa nodded.

"Are you sorry?"

"No, only that I'm sorry I hurt Henry."

"He'll get over it."

Elsa had to grin at the piquant reply.

"So, um. . .would you care to attend the Spring Fling with me this afternoon?"

She turned and gazed into his face, expecting to see a sparkle of mischief in his hazel eyes; however, all she saw was the light of sincerity.

"You really want to go?"

"Only if I can take you."

Elsa smiled and lowered her gaze to the skirt of her brown dress. "I would be honored to accompany you, but just make sure you're the one who gets my cookie." Glancing back at him, she added, "You can't miss it, Shane. It has the initials S. A. G. swirled into the frosting."

"S. A. G.? Hm, those sound like my initials."

"They are," Elsa said, leaning a little bit closer and slipping her hand around his elbow. "I peeked at your signature in our guest book."

He stared at her for a good half a minute, searching her face as if her countenance held the answer to some mysterious, universal question.

At last, he grinned and looked out over the yard. "Why do I suddenly feel like I'm sinking in quicksand?"

"What?"

Shane shook his head. "Never mind." He stood, drawing Elsa to her feet. "You just go on and get all pretty for the Spring Fling."

Smiling, she nodded and reentered the boardinghouse.

-:::-

Hickory Corners' annual Spring Fling took place in the one-room schoolhouse across the street from the church on Birch Street. Inside, fabric flowers of all colors decorated the little building, and desserts were lined up on a table, sitting off to one side, enough to satisfy even the Bunk brothers. Shane noticed the Fling drew primarily the unmarried townsfolk. In fact, it seemed to him that this was Mrs. Tidewell's subtle attempt at matchmaking.

"I'm so glad you decided join us," the pleasingly plump, downy-haired woman stated upon meeting him for the second time. The first had been at church last Wednesday evening.

"Yes, well, I'm happy to be here."

It wasn't a fib either. Truth to tell, Shane couldn't think of a place he'd rather be at the moment than here with Elsa. In his eyes, she was the belle of the ball with her walnut-colored hair unpinned and cascading to her waist in silky waves. She wore a fitted, lilac blouse and full black skirt, which she said once belonged to her mother.

Elsa added that she only wore it on special occasions. He figured the Fling was as "special" as it got in this town, but he decided to quit fighting the inevitable and enjoy himself.

The afternoon began with casual socializing. Shane and Elsa chatted first with Samantha Thomasohn. Her mother wasn't any better, so Samantha didn't plan to stay at the Spring Fling for long. Next, they conversed with Betsy Larkin, whose siblings were playing outside in the adjacent school yard, all except the youngest, that is. Three-year-old Greta with her feathery, blond hair and enormous cocoa-brown eyes seemed permanently attached to her older sister's hip. Awhile later, Shane was introduced to Brady Forbes, the Tidewells' nephew, and Lars Douglas, an employee at the grist mill up the road. Shane had to admit, the more folks he met in Hickory Corners, the more he liked the place.

After the mingling, they engaged in an organized game of musical chairs, which the men played a second time blind-folded. The young ladies giggled and watched from the back of the schoolhouse as the gents tripped over each other and missed chairs completely, only to land on their backsides on the hard wooden floor. Shane decided he'd be stiff until Tuesday after that little escapade.

Finally, the event everyone had been waiting for—the cookie caper. Shane managed to acquire Elsa's baked treat, even though he almost had to wrangle it out of Horace Bunk's meaty paw. As the winner, his reward was sharing Elsa's boxed supper out on a grassy knoll in the school yard.

As they strolled back to the boardinghouse that evening, Shane had to admit he'd had a fine time. Good clean fun proved surprisingly enjoyable. Turning onto Birch Street, Elsa's arm looped around his elbow, Shane realized this sleepy little town offered him more than his inheritance could ever buy. Love. Friendship. Respect. Dignity.

They passed the shipping office, and he saw the fretful mar above Elsa's brow which her bonnet failed to shadow.

"I warned Henry a blackguard might steal his woman if he wasn't careful."

"I take it you're referring to yourself," Elsa said with a demure, little smile. "But I hardly think of you as a blackguard. . .and neither does anyone else in Hickory Corners."

"Just shows how little you all know me."

" 'There is none righteous,' Shane, 'no not one.' Every man alive has made his share of mistakes."

Shane wagged his head and chuckled. "Well, Lady, you can't say I didn't warn you."

They paused in front of the boardinghouse, and Elsa peered up at him with questions pooling in her blue eyes. "What does that mean?"

"It means, Miss Elsa Fritch, you're going to marry me whether your father finds those receipts or not. You see, it just so happens that in two weeks' time, I've fallen in love with you."

Chapter 10

As Elsa dressed for church the next morning, Shane's words whirled around in her head. "I've fallen in love with you. . . ."

Hearing them last night was like a dream come true, and Elsa felt tempted to pinch herself to make sure it was truly reality. Shane defended her, protected her. . .everything she'd asked God for in a husband. But she had mistakenly thought she would have to forgo those attributes because of her own capabilities.

The only problem remaining was Shane's unbelief, and if they were to have a real marriage, as opposed to one procreated by their parents' contract, then his lack of faith was an issue. But Elsa felt certain his conversion to Christ would occur in the near future. He had agreed to attend this morning's Resurrection Sunday service, and Elsa claimed the victory beforehand, knowing it was God's will that none should perish but that all should come to repentance.

Wearing her Sunday best, a raspberry-colored, linen frock with white lace adorning the neckline and sleeves, Elsa left her bedroom and walked down the hallway to the kitchen. Breakfast had been a simple fare this morning of porridge and canned peaches, so as to allow Elsa time to prepare for church, and she'd thought all the guests had left. But in the dining room, she heard male voices. They sounded somber. Curious, Elsa slipped into the adjoining area just in time to hear Doc tell Shane and Papa that Mrs. Thomasohn died last night.

"I did everything I could. So did the family."

"Ja, I am sure das true," Papa replied.

"Well, I thought, being neighbors, you would want to know."

Tears filled Elsa's eyes and she bit her bottom lip in effort to thwart them. Poor Samantha. . .

"Was Mrs. Thomasohn a. . .a Christian?" Shane asked hesitantly.

"Oh, *ja,* she loved da Lord," Papa replied.

He nodded. "Guess that's something to be thankful for, huh?"

"Yes, you're right, Son," Doc said, clapping Shane on the back with one arthritic hand. "We don't have to mourn like the heathen do, because as Christians, we know there's life everlasting once we leave this world. In heaven, there'll be no more pain, no more sorrow. . .and God will wipe away all tears from our eyes."

Recognizing the heartfelt promise from the Book of Revelation, Elsa choked on a sob. A moment later, Shane's strong arm was draped around her shoulders, hugging her to him.

"There, there, now, don't cry, Elsa. I know you're sad, but think of it this way—we're all on a journey, and Mrs. Thomasohn's just gone on ahead of us. You'll see her again."

"Amen!" said Doc. "The Good Book says to be absent from the body is to be present with the Lord. I s'pose this is like resurrection day for that dear lady. We call it Easter Sunday when we celebrate our Lord's ascension from the grave, and in many respects, we could celebrate for Mrs. Thomasohn in the same manner."

Doc's analogy lessened Elsa's sorrow, although she knew it would take time for God to heal Samantha's heart, and the hearts of her father, brothers, and sisters-in-law. It had taken a long while before Elsa didn't mourn for her mama, and even now she missed her sometimes.

Shane reached into the inside pocket of his vest and produced a white handkerchief. "Here you go, Darlin'. Dry your eyes. That's right. Now, blow."

Elsa complied, feeling like a little girl. But, finally, her embarrassment overtook her, and she snatched the linen wipe out of Shane's hand. "I can blow my own nose, Shane Gerhard, thank you very much."

Grinning, he allowed her the courtesy, after which time Elsa absently passed back his handkerchief. Shane pocketed it once more.

"See that, Arne?" Doc asked with a chuckle. "Looks to me like true love."

Ja, only true love vill compel a man to return a soiled handkerchief to his pocket."

Elsa winced and looked over at Shane, an apology on her heart. For the first time ever, she saw an expression of chagrin creep across his features.

-:::-

Standing up in front of the church, Elsa sang a solo, and Shane decided she had the most beautiful voice of any woman he'd ever heard. A deep second soprano, she serenaded the congregation with a stirring number. After she returned to the pew and her place between Shane and Arne, Pastor Tidewell delivered his sermon.

On the whole, the Sunday service had a somber feeling to it, Shane thought. Not only were the parishioners grieving for their friend and neighbor, but also Pastor Tidewell chose to speak on a very weighty subject: the Crucifixion. He said in order to rejoice on Easter Sunday, one had to understand what transpired the few days before.

Shane tried not to wince when Pastor Tidewell described how the Roman soldiers nailed the Lord Jesus to a rugged cross, leaving Him there to suffer in bitter agony.

"And do you know who Jesus Christ saw while He hung on that tree? He saw you, and you, and you, and me." Pastor Tidewell pointed at various individuals, and Shane felt sure it was no accident that his gnarly finger included him. "Christ died for all, and if you don't believe me, look here what the Bible says in Romans chapter ten, verse thirteen. 'For whosoever shall call upon the name of the Lord shall be saved.' Whosoever means anyone who has a mind to accept God's free gift of salvation. And how do we know it's a gift? Well, look with me, if you will, at John chapter three, verse sixteen. Let's all read that passage together, shall we?"

Shane looked on with Elsa and read along with her. " 'For God so loved the world, that he gave his only begotten Son, that whosoever believeth in him should not perish, but have everlasting life.' "

"Did you see that word *gave*? That's right, God gave us His Son to suffer in our stead. Now, I want you to read that verse once more, but silently this time," Pastor Tidewell said, "and I want you to substitute your own name where the passage says 'the world'. All right, go ahead. Read it."

Shane did so, swallowing hard. *For God so loved Shane Gerhard, that he gave his only begotten Son. . .*

He sat there and stared at the words now swimming before his eyes. Christ died for him? Shane Gerhard, a no-account, "ne'er-do-well" fellow that didn't deserve anything less than hellfire? Yet, Shane believed it, although he might not have had Elsa not deemed him her "hero." She'd started turning his thinking around. Furthermore, he couldn't explain why, but he suddenly believed the Bible, too. It was like the times when his gut instincts took over during a card game and he called the right deal. This morning, his gut instincts were calling him to choose a different way.

"Did you feel it?" Pastor Tidewell asked, smiling broadly, his gaze roving over his congregation. "Did you feel that little tug on your heartstrings? Why, that's the Holy Spirit. He's trying to get your attention."

All right, Lord, Shane prayed silently, unable to help a small grin. *You got my attention. It's taken You twenty-four years, but I'm listening now.*

-:::-

During the week following, Elsa noted a change in Shane. He seemed more. . . mature, and she wasn't sure what caused it. But instead of pestering her in the kitchen, teasing and talking her ear off, he took to helping Papa around the boardinghouse. He even tilled the plot out back for the vegetable garden and fixed the outer stairwell, which had grown rickety from neglect.

"Uncle Arne," Shane said after supper one evening, "have you ever thought of making this place into a hotel?"

"Nein, too much vork, und I am an old man."

"Well, I'm a young man, and I'd be willing to put forth the funds and some of the labor."

Coffeepot in hand, Elsa slowly turned from the box stove in the dining room and stared at Shane.

"Nein, I do not vant to run a hotel."

"I do. I've given the matter plenty of thought."

Elsa set down the coffee pot and wiped her hands on her apron. "What kind of hotel?" she couldn't keep from asking.

Shane smiled. "A very respectable one. No gaming tables. No strong drink, and I'd like to renovate this boardinghouse and stay in Hickory Corners."

"You would? Why, that's wonderful." Elsa caught Shane's enthusiasm and glanced at her father.

"Vith you und your hotel, den vhat is to become uf Elsa und me?" Arne asked, looking concerned.

"I've got that all figured out. See, as part of the reconstruction, I would erect special quarters for you and I'd build an apartment above the hotel rooms for myself and..." He bestowed Elsa with a meaningful look, and her knees weakened.

Shane cleared his throat and began again. "Uncle Arne, I want to marry Elsa and live here in Hickory Corners."

Arne gave him a suspicious frown. "Marry my Elsa?"

"That's right." He glanced at her again before adding, "If she'll have me."

"Oh, I will!" she declared, stepping forward.

Shane grinned.

"Now, vait a minute, here...." Arne held up a forestalling hand. "Young Shane, I cannot allow my Elsa to marry a man who does not share our faith. Da Bible says so."

"I share your faith, Uncle Arne. I believe."

Arne narrowed his gaze. "I thought you had questions about God und salvation."

"I did, but the Lord answered them."

"Vhen ver you born again?"

"Excuse me?" Shane frowned.

"Born again...da change dat happens vhen you believe."

"Ah, let's see..." He rubbed his shadowed jaw as he contemplated the question. "I would have to say it happened on Easter Sunday."

Watching the exchange, Elsa sensed Shane's earnestness. His reply didn't sound anything like those practiced apologies he had delivered during the first days after his arrival.

"I'm a Christian, Uncle Arne. It's just like that song we sang on Wednesday night—'Amazing Grace.' I once was lost, but now I'm found. That's me. Found."

"Hmpf!" Arne stood. "Ve vill see about dat."

He shuffled passed Elsa and headed into their back rooms. She frowned in his wake, then turned back to Shane. "What do you suppose has gotten into him?"

With a shrug, he rose from the bench and walked toward her. "Will you really marry me?" he asked, taking her hands in his.

"I really will. You're my hero, remember?"

"Sure, I do."

Her father reentered the dining room all too soon as far as Elsa was concerned. In his hands, he carried a leather portfolio. "Look vhat I found just dis afternoon. It vas in my bureau. In da bottom drawer."

Elsa felt the blood drain from her face. "The receipts?"

"Ja."

"Why didn't you say something, Uncle Arne?" Shane asked, releasing Elsa's hands and striding over to the table. He opened the leather packet.

"Elsa called us to supper, und I forgot. But now you don't have to get married. You can go back to St. Louis und collect your inheritance."

Elsa opened her mouth to rebuke her father for trying to dissuade Shane, but suddenly she saw the situation for what it really was—a test of Shane's love for her. She willed herself not to cry while she watched Shane inspect the vouchers. He had a choice to make.

"Looks like everything is in order. The debt's paid." He pivoted and faced Elsa. "Do you see this?"

She nodded weakly and forced a little smile.

Receipts in hand, he stepped toward her. She met his gaze, holding her breath, waiting, wondering. . .hoping. Then in one, two, three smooth moves, Shane tore the documents into shreds. Arne began to chuckle, while Elsa stood by and watched as Shane tossed the pieces into the air. They floated to the ground like fat snowflakes.

Elsa began to half laugh and half cry.

"I no longer care about those receipts," Shane told her. "I don't even care about my inheritance. I've discovered something more valuable than gold right here in this sleepy little town. Now, all I want is to marry you, Elsa. . .because I love you. Because I'm your knight in shining armor, and you need me."

"Oh, Shane. . ." Elsa practically threw herself into his arms. "Papa, say I can marry him. Please."

"Ja, go ahead. You have my blessing."

"Can I kiss her, Uncle Arne?" Shane asked, wearing a desirous expression that caused Elsa to tremble in his arms with anticipation.

"Ja, but only one kiss. You are not married yet, *und* do not forget it."

"Yes, Sir." A rakish gleam entered Shane's eyes. "Reckon I'd better make this one count."

He pulled Elsa close, and then his mouth captured hers in the sweetest of all kisses.

And she immediately knew this man who had first made her life tumble like a child's blocks had just set it aright again.

OLD MAID'S CHOICE

by Cathy Marie Hake

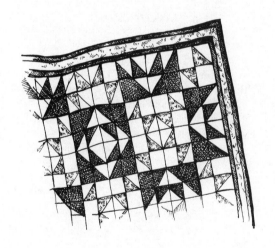

Chapter 1

"Karl, stop your sniveling and hold fast to Will. Will, you'd best quit wiggling, else Marie is going to tumble." Betsy Larkin hoisted little Greta higher onto her hip and held the reins in her other hand. All four of her younger siblings wouldn't fit on their plow horse, so she held the youngest. The other three perched precariously atop the mare and hung on to one another.

"I wanna walk, Sis," Karl whined again. "*You're* walking."

"Only because Jenny came up lame. I'd be riding, otherwise." Betsy hitched Greta again and hoped her petticoat wasn't peeping out from beneath her hem. "If I let you boys get down, you'll be muddy as piglets by the time we get to church."

"Little bitta mud never hurt a body," Karl grumbled.

Betsy ignored his observation. She made it a point to try to enter God's house in a good mood. Scolding her youngers could be the ruination of a glad heart, and she refused to let that happen. Mud sucked at her too-big boots, making each step an effort. She knew the bottom six inches of her dress were spattered beyond redemption, but there was no helping that. Cleanliness might well be next to godliness on most days, but after last night's fierce gully washer, she knew a muddy worshipper would please God more than a vain slacker who didn't make it to church.

They got to the hitching post just outside Hickory Corners Bible Church as the steeple bell pealed. "Here. I'll take Greta," her friend Elsa offered from the steps.

"Oh, thank you!" Betsy handed over her youngest sister and carefully pulled Marie from the nag. Once she did, both brothers flung themselves earthward. "Mind that mud puddle!"

"Aw, Sis!"

She quickly set Marie on the church steps beside Elsa and tied the mare to the hitching post. A bit of grit speckled her chapped hands, so Betsy conscientiously wiped her palms off on her skirt. Satisfied she'd gotten them fairly clean, she took a pair of mended cotton gloves she'd tucked into her sash and pulled them on.

"My, you and Shane are aglow with happiness. Marriage agrees with both of you," Betsy said as she smiled at Elsa and her handsome bridegroom. It was their first Sunday back after their extended honeymoon, and Elsa wore the pale-blue wedding gown the sewing circle had helped her make.

Shane gave Elsa an affectionate squeeze. "Someday, you'll make a man as happy as my Elsa has made me."

Betsy manufactured a smile for him and didn't bother to correct his misconception. She knew better. Because of her family obligations, she was destined for spinsterhood. Men disappeared quickly once they realized her brothers and sisters claimed her time and devotion. One beau actually pretended he'd be happy to farm alongside Pa in the fields, but as soon as he learned the farm was to go to her brothers—not her husband—that one hiked on down the road. Before he left, he listed her liabilities and made her painfully aware there'd be no husband in her future.

Betsy herded her flock on into the chapel and toward the second to the last pew on the left. Once they were seated, she pulled a handkerchief from her sleeve, surreptitiously moistened it a bit with her tongue, and tried to rub a trace of dirt from behind Will's ear. He jerked away. She gave him a stern look, and he made a face as she diligently rid him of the flaw. After gently tucking one of Greta's little blond curls behind her ear, Betsy settled in. She was ready to worship.

❖

Tyson Walker followed the tiny woman into the church. He stood in the back and watched her fuss like a hen over her brood. Her moves were quick, economical, and gentle. A wide-brimmed, flower-bedecked straw hat that had seen better days hid the color of her hair and eyes. Oddly enough, that piqued his curiosity. He waited until everyone took a place in the polished oak pews and looked for an empty spot.

"Howdy!" An old man in a black suit hobbled up. His sparse gray hair looked freshly slicked down. "Josiah Gardner. Folks call me Doc."

Ty accepted his gnarled hand and shook it carefully. His own hands were suited to holding a hammer, and he conscientiously monitored his strength so his grip stayed gentle enough to keep from harming the bony palm, yet firm enough to preserve Doc's dignity. "Tyson Walker. I just bought the smithy."

Doc let out a rusty laugh. "Glad to have you here in God's house and over at the smithy. You'll have plenty of work to keep you out of trouble."

"I was hoping that would be the case." He smiled. "I'd be honored to be your friend, but I hope I don't need your services."

The old gent chuckled. "Just as well that you're healthy. I'm getting too old to make nighttime house calls."

Ty didn't want to make the old man feel self-conscious about his frailty, so he diplomatically changed the subject. "Looks like you have a full house this morning."

"Now that's a fact. We're near to busting out the seams here." Doc looked around and nodded toward the woman Ty had been watching. "Yonder is a seat. You can sit with Miz Betsy and her little brood. Mr. Larkin doesn't come, so you'll have plenty of room."

"Thank you." Ty walked over and slipped into the pew. Miz Betsy turned and tilted her head back a bit to face him. He'd expected a weathered, slightly careworn housewife. Instead, compassionate, big brown eyes glanced back at him. A generous set of freckles sprinkled across her nose. She was young! How young, he couldn't quite say. Her mouth seemed a tad big for a tiny woman, but when a hesitant smile lifted her lips, she radiated kindness. One thing for sure—a pretty face like hers could steal a man's breath away. Even in the dim interior of the clapboard church, she glowed. Ty scarcely remembered his manners enough to nod a silent greeting to her.

Her smile widened. As soon as she'd paid him that polite attention, she scooted a bit to the side and rested her hand on the older boy's leg to stop him from swinging it. "Sit still," she whispered.

As the service went on, Ty watched her manage her brood. The youngest two kids were too short to get back up on the pew after they stood for singing. She lifted them back into place, seated herself, and tucked her skirt a mite closer to her sides without any fuss or nonsense. When the older girl got restless, Miz Betsy deftly folded her handkerchief diagonally, rolled the sides inward, and then flipped back the tip-tops to form a hammock with "babies" for her to use as quiet entertainment. The youngest fell asleep during the sermon, so Miz Betsy cradled her in her lap. No matter what attention her children required, she paid it; but he watched her from the corner of his eye, and Ty felt certain she'd not missed a single word the preacher said.

He thoroughly enjoyed the sermon, but he also fought a strong streak of curiosity that never managed to thin, no matter how hard he tried to tame it. Miz Betsy surely couldn't have borne these children. Simply put, she was far too young to claim them as her own. Had she married their father and taken them as part of the package? She certainly disciplined them with ease. The older of the little girls favored Miz Betsy as far as her wide, brown eyes and delicately rounded chin went. Could they be sisters? Ty wanted to know if Miz Betsy Larkin was already bound in matrimony or if she might be free for a bit of courting.

He wasn't a man to act hastily. The fact that he'd set to wondering about courting her this early on was completely out of character. Mere looks didn't hold his attention—though hers, alone, were sufficient to captivate any man in five counties. She seemed tenderhearted with the wee ones, yet she kept complete control of them. A woman with a level head, soft heart, and hardworking hands was a prize well worth pursuing.

Ty didn't understand how other men said God spoke to them directly and told them to do something. It never happened to him. Still, he'd been praying about his future. The smithy just happened to be listed for sale in a gazette he read, and the price suited his budget. He'd saved up every last little coin he could for years until this opportunity came up and felt maybe the hand of God swept him here. A man couldn't hope to meet a woman at a better place than church—though that wasn't why he'd come to worship. If the Lord had set him in this town, could it be He also set him on this pew, next to this woman, for a reason?

Chapter 2

When everyone else rose for the benediction, Miz Betsy stayed seated. Other folks started to leave, but still, she sat there. Towering over her felt rude. Ty couldn't very well shove his way into the stream of folks ambling down the aisle, though. Big as he was, he worried about bumping into someone. He barely heard Miz Betsy's whisper, "Karl, my boot needs tying."

Karl bobbed his towhead and knelt at her feet. A second later, he held up a bedraggled length of string. "It broke, Sis. I'm sorry."

She sighed softly. "These things happen. We'd best be on our way. Pa will be hungry."

Sis. Pa. That answered that question. Ty felt a surge of delight. She wasn't taken. . .yet.

The church was close to empty. A few folks stayed to visit here and there. Ty left the woman and her kids behind. As he met the preacher at the doorway, he heard an uneven footstep. The slight clump and drag bothered him. Betsy would likely rub a blister on her heel if she didn't knot the ends of the lacing string back together and tie up her shoe.

He and the preacher both turned toward her at the same time. When she'd walked up to the church with the smaller girl perched on her hip, Ty hadn't given it a thought—but now that the little one lay draped across Betsy's arms, he realized she was a fair burden for a petite woman to carry.

When he reached out for her toddler, Betsy gave him a startled look. "I'll tote her for you, Miss."

"Now isn't that nice," Pastor Tidewell said. "Betsy, this is Tyson Walker. He's the blacksmith we've all been waiting for. Mr. Walker, this is Betsy Larkin. You'll be seeing a fair bit of her and her kin. Their farm is the first one on the edge of town, so that makes you neighbors. Being here all on your own, you're fortunate to have friendly folk so close by."

Betsy clung to her sister and dipped her head as she murmured, "Nice to meet you, Mr. Walker."

"Likewise, Miss Larkin. Here. Let me help you." He gently took the child from her arms.

Miss Larkin's smile could light a forest at midnight. "If you could hold her just a moment, I'd dearly appreciate it." She turned her attention back to the parson.

68

"Pastor Tidewell, that message touched me deeply. I surely do appreciate your Bible learnin'."

"Thank you, Betsy."

Ty watched her take off her gloves. She'd bleached them white as could be. Compared to the red, dry skin on her hands, they looked whiter still. Unaware of his scrutiny, she tucked the gloves into her sash, stooped, and modestly lifted her mud-splattered hem just enough to tend to matters. She started to mess with the string she used to lace up what was obviously a man's boot. A boot far too big for someone her size.

His eyes narrowed. Her gown wasn't supposed to be slate blue. Time, sun, and daily wear and tear faded the fabric. . .but they hadn't managed to leech a single dab of this woman's zest for life. He tried to be subtle as he studied the children. They were all clean. Hair combed, slicked, and faces scrubbed pink as could be. They stayed in a huddle beside her, and he reckoned all of them probably felt cowed by his hulking size. To his dismay, kids often feared him.

Miss Larkin didn't quite manage to quell her sigh. She straightened a tad, took off her hat, and pulled a washed-out looking blue ribbon from it. As she used the ribbon to bind the ankle of her boot tight, Ty stared at her. The thick, golden braids she'd looped around her head looked like ripened wheat sheaves.

If a woman have long hair, it is a glory to her." First Corinthians 11:15 sang in his mind. Indeed, the verse applied more to this woman than to any he'd ever seen. He wanted to reach out, touch her plaits, and test their softness. Certainly, a woman who had such a tender heart and gentle voice would have hair soft as spring rain. Instead, he disciplined himself to divert his attention to the tiny girl in his arms. "How old is this little dumpling?"

"She's three," said the other girl. "I'm Marie. I'm five. Karl is eight, and Will is six and a half." Without even blinking, she continued, "Betsy is nineteen. She's the oldest."

Ty winked at her. "Thank you, Marie. It's a pleasure to make your acquaintance. I'm afraid if I bow to you as I ought, I'll drop your baby sister."

Giggles spilled out of the little girl. Her big sister rose and smiled at him. She gently reminded Marie, "Thank the gentleman for his respects."

Marie dipped a surprisingly dainty curtsey. "Thank you, Sir."

"And thank you for holding Greta." Betsy closed the distance between them and made a basket with her arms to receive her youngest sibling.

Ty eased little Greta a bit closer to his heart. He liked holding her. She was soft and sweet-smelling, and the way she nestled close to him in her sleep made him feel glad for his strength instead of clumsy from his size. He tried to keep his voice soft to allow her to slumber on. "You lead the way, Miss Larkin. I'll tote her to your wagon."

"We rode the mare," Karl griped. "Betsy didn't want us to get muddy."

"Washing muddy clothes is hard work," Ty said in a man-to-man whisper out of the side of his mouth. "She and your mama already—"

"We don't got a ma."

"We don't have a mother," Betsy corrected her brother in an even tone. "But we'll see her at the banqueting table in heaven some day."

"Speaking of food," Karl said, "I'm powerful hungry, Betsy. What're you fixin' to have for supper?"

"She put a roast in a pot over the fire before we left," Marie reported, "and there's peach cobbler for dessert."

Ty's mouth watered. He'd not eaten breakfast, so the mention of food caught his attention.

Miss Larkin looked at him, then at the minister. "Pastor, you and your wife and Mr. Walker are welcome to our table. There's gracious plenty."

The pastor chuckled. "Edna ordered me to come home for Sunday supper today. She doesn't want the trout I caught yesterday smelling up the place. Mr. Walker looks like a man who appreciates a good meal." The pastor smiled at the blacksmith. "You're in for a mighty fine treat. Betsy can cook like a dream."

Before Ty could say a word, Karl yanked on his brother's brown, woolen, broadfall pants. "C'mon, Will. If we don't drag Sis outta here, she's going to start jabbering with everyone 'bout quilts and sewing again, and I'm too powerful hungry to last through that."

A fetching blush tinted Miss Larkin's cheeks. She let out a self-conscious laugh. "You don't look like you're languishing, Karl."

Karl tilted his face toward Ty. "Sir, I spent all mornin' smelling something good baking. Matter of fact, that was 'bout all I could set my mind on for most of the service."

"Karl!"

Karl ignored his big sister's chide. "So if you'd take pity on me and head toward our farm, Betsy would race right after you. She keeps an eagle eye on our Greta."

Ty watched as embarrassment and resignation warred over Miss Larkin's pretty face, then shot her a bolstering grin. "Would you rather I ignore him, or shall I threaten to eat his slice of dessert for not attending to the pastor's words?"

Karl let out an outraged yelp as his sisters and brother laughed. Betsy turned to lead her tribe outside. Ty stepped alongside her. Most women shied away when he came close. They'd let their heads drop back and stare way up at him like he was evil old Goliath, come back to life. Miss Larkin didn't. She busied herself hanging onto Will's shirtsleeve and calling to Karl not to step into the mud.

Karl climbed atop a stone and flung himself over the horse's back, then sat up. His independent spirit was fun to behold, but Ty wondered if Betsy sometimes got a bit weary, trying to keep up with him. She cupped her hands around Will's middle and got ready to heft him upward.

"Whoa there." Ty frowned at her. "You're not aiming to hoist a strapping young man like Will, are you?" He temporarily passed little Greta over, lifted Will onto the mare, and then looked down at Marie. "Come here, Smidgen," he said as he peeled off his blue, store-bought suit coat.

"Smidgen?"

"Yes, Smidgen. You're just a little dab of a gal. I think you're just the right size for a piggyback ride." He draped the coat over the hitching post, effortlessly slung Marie onto his back, and settled her hands on his suspenders so she couldn't choke him. He picked up his coat again and reached over to rob Betsy of little Greta.

"Oh, my! They're too much for you to carry!"

He ignored her protest. As he enveloped the toddler in the folds of his coat and smoothly stole her away, he said, "I don't think you have any call to fret, Miss."

"Nope, you don't need to worry none," Karl agreed as he eyed Ty with undisguised interest. "He's pert' near big enough to drag a plow himself, Betsy."

"Karl! Mr. Walker is not a horse!" She looked at Ty with apology shimmering in the brown depths of her eyes. "Please forgive him. He's liable to let any half-baked thought flee from his lips."

Marie shimmied up his back a bit more, peered over his shoulder, and rubbed her soft cheek against his. The action held a catlike affection that warmed his heart. "Karl's wrong. You're not big as a horse; you're big as a mountain! I can see forever and a mile from up here!"

"Oh, mercy," Miss Larkin moaned.

Ty chuckled. "You needn't worry, Miss Larkin. It's no secret I'm a big fellow."

"Which Miss Larkin are you talkin' to?" Marie asked with all of the gravity a self-important child could muster.

"Now that is a knotty problem." Ty craned his head a bit so he could wink at her. "There are three of you."

"Greta's a baby still. Nobody calls her Miss Larkin yet."

"Nobody calls you Miss Larkin, either," Will tattled from horseback.

Betsy unhitched the mare and started to walk. "Nobody's going to eat supper if we listen to your silliness."

Ty paced along slowly, careful to keep his stride short to measure hers. "You might be a smidgen, Marie, but you're still a young lady. What say I call you Miss Marie and call your big sister Miss Larkin?"

"Don't think you ought to do that," Will said. A frown twisted his face. "Makes Sis sound like an old maid."

Ty studied Betsy for a long moment. Until now, she'd been modest enough not to stare at him, but she'd met his eyes. Suddenly, her lashes dropped, and she looked as if she'd rather be dancing barefoot on hot ingots than subjected to his scrutiny. He softened his voice, "No one would ever believe she's an old maid. There must be a dozen bucks coming to your door, wanting to court such a fine-looking, God-fearing young woman."

"Nope." Karl shook his head and had to shove a lock of white-blond hair off his forehead. "Sis feeds 'em and sends 'em packing."

Marie clutched his suspenders tighter. "She's feeding you, but you don't have to go packin'. We like you."

Ty chuckled. "I surely do think I'm going to like being your neighbor. Since I'm the blacksmith, you can bet I'm not going to pack up and leave. The anvil is too heavy to move!"

Though he teased lightheartedly with the children, Ty noticed how Betsy kept silent. Her reserve intrigued him. Why had she sent other men packing? She didn't seem angry or standoffish. Maybe she was a tad on the shy side. With her sister and brothers acting like chatterboxes, she probably didn't get much privacy or peace.

The mare knew her way home. Once they reached the yard, the boys rode her into the barn. Betsy led Ty to the freshly chinked log cabin. He took care to scrape the mud off his boots before he ducked under the lintel and inside.

She watched as he knelt on the blue rag rug between the hearth and trestle table, then coaxed Marie to slide off his back. Not many men were this tolerant of her rambunctious siblings, yet he'd handled them as if they were his favorite little cousins. For such a giant of a man, he managed to keep his bass voice at a quiet rumble. The sound of his deep, soft words made Betsy feel strangely warm inside. So did the way he tenderly looked down at Greta.

"Do you want this little snippet to wake up for supper, or shall I put her to bed?"

"She'll nap awhile longer. I'll take her—"

He shook his head. "No, Miss Larkin. You just tell me where to lay her down."

His dark, wavy hair looked like it needed a trim. Betsy silently scolded herself for thinking anything so personal about a stranger and led him over to the far side of the cabin. She pulled back the thick, green wool blanket that partitioned off the small bedroom she shared with her sisters. For a moment, she wondered what he thought of her home. Though bigger than most log cabins, it wasn't fancy in the least. Farming and frills didn't go together.

A smile broke across his face. "Karl mentioned something about you and quilting. I can see why. That piece you have on the bed is handsome as can be."

"Thank you." She glanced at the Star of Bethlehem she'd pieced out of several shades of blue and green in hopes it would brighten the dim space. "I just finished it last May."

He carefully lowered Greta into the center of the bed the three sisters shared, then smoothed a few curls away from her forehead before he stepped back.

Betsy's heart melted. His gentleness disarmed her. He might be big, but a softness in his hazel eyes and something about the way he took care to leash his strength left Betsy feeling she could rely on him. She silently unhooked Greta's little shoes, gave them each a small twist to help them come off more easily, then took away his coat and covered her with a well-worn, pink-and-white-striped, flannel blanket. Greta wiggled onto her side and popped her thumb into her mouth.

"She's darling," the blacksmith murmured as he slipped the coat back up to cover his brawny shoulders. "All of them are. You take mighty good care of them. Someday, your husband will be glad of all of your experience with children."

Straightening up and ignoring the twinge in her heart, Betsy shook her head. "There won't be a husband, Mr. Walker. My family needs me."

Chapter 3

The next morning, Ty stoked the fire and couldn't get Betsy's words out of his head. *There won't be a husband.* . . . What a terrible thing for her to believe. Shouldn't a young woman with a heart as sweet as hers dream of falling in love? *My family needs me.* She'd said the words so simply, so calmly—as if it were a fact no one ought to question; but there'd been something in her eyes that made him wonder if she'd been hurt by a foolish local buck who told her he didn't need her. A woman deserved to be needed and loved. . .*and Betsy Larkin is some woman.*

Ty turned back to his anvil to examine the horseshoe. He planned to shape the next one just a shade wider. He'd slipped into the Larkin's barn last night and pried the shoe off their mare. He'd noticed she was nodding down—a sure sign something was wrong with one of her hind legs. He suspected the problem lay with the mare's shoe. The least he could do was make a new one—especially after he'd spent all Sunday afternoon at the Larkin table, eating the finest, most flavorful roast he'd ever tasted.

"Excuse me."

Ty set down the shoe as he pivoted around. His pulse sped up. "Miss Larkin! How nice to see you this morning."

Morning sun slanted in through the wide-open double doors and bathed her in a golden glow. The heightened color in her cheeks made her freckles disappear, and the nut-brown color of her homespun dress made her eyes look even more enchanting. She stared at the anvil. "Excuse me, Mr. Walker, but I need to ask if. . .that," she jutted her chin toward the horseshoe, "belongs to me."

"Of course it doesn't." He leaned casually against a rough wood workbench and grinned. "You're a lady. That shoe belongs on a horse."

Her eyes widened, and she gave him a disbelieving laugh. "I see you're a clever man with words. Does that shoe belong to Jenny?"

He lifted a shoulder negligently. "Used to. It was loose and a tad on the small side. I figured since I was just starting up the fire in here today to get a feel for things, we'd do each other a favor—I'd fix up Jenny, and it would allow me a simple task so I could become accustomed to my shop."

"I'll tell Pa so he—"

"No need for that." He waved a hand at the cobwebs and scattered tools left in disarray by the untimely death of the previous blacksmith. "You can see I need to put things in order, and the morning's chilly. I'd have fired up the forge, anyway."

"I'll send Karl over after school to help you clean a bit. He might be on the small side, but he's a good worker. I'll expect you tonight for supper, too."

Ty adjusted his leather apron. "Miss Larkin, am I to figure you and I are starting a habit of swapping howdies and favors?"

"Pa and I have a rule. We won't be beholden to anyone."

"I live by the same standard. Wonderful as Sunday supper tasted yesterday, I'd best put you on notice: I'm going to search for things to do for your farm every now and then since you counter my labors with meals." He waggled his brows playfully. "In fact, lovely Miss Larkin, I have a confession to make."

"Oh?"

"I'm all thumbs when it comes to fixin' vittles, so I just might start making everything from doorknobs to shutter dogs to earn me a place at your supper table."

Her eyes twinkled. "Mr. Walker, you're getting the short end of the deal on that—especially since we also have a policy that there's always an open place at our table."

***

Karl and Mr. Walker arrived about a half hour sooner than Betsy anticipated. She had a length of wool laid across the table and was trying to figure out how to get dresses for both girls and a skirt for herself out of it. No matter which way she worked it, she lacked fabric.

"Hey, Sunshine," her new neighbor said, "why are you wearing clouds?"

Sunshine? No one ever called her anything other than Betsy or Sis. The way he rumbled the sobriquet coaxed a smile from her. "I'm a bit short on the measure." She felt her smile fade when she caught sight of Karl's dirt-and-soot-covered clothes.

"We got his shop all put to rights, Sis," Karl boasted. Like the new blacksmith, his hair was wet, and his face and hands looked freshly scrubbed.

Mr. Walker rested his palm on Karl's head. "Aye, he's a hardworkin' lad." He rumpled Karl's hair and ordered, "Now remember what I said. Go grab something else to wear. Your sister doesn't need you smudging her tidy home. Best if you change outside, then shake these out. When's laundry day?"

"Wednesday," Betsy said. She tried not to show her dismay. She seriously doubted Karl's clothes would ever come clean. She let out a small sigh and resigned herself to cutting britches for him from the wool. She could make do without a skirt for awhile yet.

Pa came through the door. "Tomorrow's Tuesday. You getting ready to go to Miz T's again, Betsy?"

"Yes." She hastily folded the cloth and set it aside. She could cut the dresses out after supper. Hungry men shouldn't have to wait. She put biscuits in the large, shallow kettle and hung it high above the fire so they'd bake without burning. Next, she knelt on the flagstone hearth. The rich aroma of venison stew filled the house as she stirred the pot. "Ruthie Schmidt said she'll mind Greta for me again."

Pa pulled out a bench and sat at the table. He gave her a rueful look. "I ripped the elbow of my shirt."

"It happens," she said. "I'll try to get to it after supper. Will, the wood box is nigh onto empty."

"I'll help you fill it." Mr. Walker walked out the door with her little brother. A minute later, the ring of the ax sounded. There wasn't an immediate need for wood to be chopped. Pa already had seven cords done. Clearly, Mr. Walker wasn't a slacker.

"He's a good man, Betsy," Pa said softly.

"He'll make a fine neighbor."

"A man like that would likely make a good husband, too."

She opened the kettle and pretended to check the biscuits, even though she knew they weren't anywhere near done. She didn't want Pa to see the longing in her eyes. "We'll have to introduce him around, then."

⋙⋘

"So Betsy, tell us about your new blacksmith." Samantha brushed a speck of lint from her black dress the next day as they sat and sewed in Mrs. T's pristine parlor.

Betsy concentrated on mending the rip in Pa's shirt. "He's not mine. His name is Tyson Walker, and I'd be happy to introduce you."

"What is he like?" Samantha pressed.

"I just met him at church two days ago." Betsy wished her cousin wouldn't be so curious or perceptive. She bit the thread and knotted it. "I could scarcely have anything more than a weak first impression of Mr. Walker."

"Weak?" Elsa laughed merrily. "Oh, he's anything but weak. Shane said Mr. Walker shot a five-point buck early this morning and carried it from the woods to his place over his shoulders without a bit of help!"

"Then we can assume he's not going to go hungry this winter," Mrs. T said matter-of-factly. She used her porcelain thimble to push the needle through several layers of wool. "Though with Betsy's good cooking and the Larkins' hospitality, I didn't worry for a moment that he'd starve."

"Speaking of food," Betsy said in an attempt to change the subject, "Samantha, I still want your recipe for that scrumptious squash casserole."

"I'll write it down for you. Mama made that one up. She loved it, too." Samantha blinked back tears.

Betsy set aside her needle and squeezed Mantha's hand. Mantha gave her the "be brave for me" look, so Betsy forced a lighthearted tone. "As much squash as I grew this year, we'll probably eat that casserole for the next month!"

Mrs. T took the cue, laughed, and picked up the Bible from the side table. "The reading I chose for today is about how God abundantly supplies all of our needs."

⋙⋘

Betsy carried the big willow basket full of freshly mended clothes on her hip. Underneath them, a wool dress she'd begun for Greta lay stuffed in a clean sugar sack. Betsy would work on it late at night and use the daytime hours when Marie was at school to stitch on Marie's. Christmas was coming up fast, and she wanted to have something to give each of them. She'd spent much of the summer sitting out on the porch in the evening, spinning while Marie carded the wool.

Pa had planted a full acre of flax. Less than half that would have been gracious plenty to weave the linen they'd need for the year, but Betsy held her silence. Some days, his anger toward God was a fearsome thing. When he grew restless or bitter, she was just as happy for him to be out plowing a field or spending his wrath on the earth. Though he'd come in worn out those nights, he never looked at peace.

He still refused to go to church. He sat in stony silence as Betsy led the children in prayers. Most evenings, when she read to them from the Bible, he'd go out to tend the beasts in the barn. It burdened her terribly to know he'd turned his anger toward God. Still, Pa allowed her to worship under his roof and take her youngers to church. For now, that had to suffice.

Maybe she could squeeze in more time at her loom. With all that extra flax, the extra cloth—no, she shook her head. As it was, she barely seemed to get everything done. Aunt Rachel used to help now and then when the mercantile was slow, but since she'd died, even that little bit of help was gone. With winter coming on, Betsy knew she'd spend more time indoors, but she'd learned to use the cold months to do other things.

Marie and Greta were five steps ahead. Marie had just learned to skip. Greta fancied that she could, too, so she galloped alongside her sister and giggled with glee. Karl and Will dawdled behind her until the smithy came in sight. They both sped up. "Let's go see Mr. Walker!"

"Boys! Don't bother him. He's at work!" Even as she called to them, Betsy knew it was a lost cause. Part of her wanted to hasten, too; but that would be unseemly, and she didn't want to look like she was interested in the handsome, strong, new man in town.

Mr. Walker showing up for church of his own accord spoke volumes. The noon-time conversation on Sunday made it clear he honored the Lord and loved reading the Bible as much as she did. Betsy admired a man who lived his relationship with God so naturally. There was something about having a man say grace or mention the Lord that made a house feel safe and her heart feel warm. Especially with Pa at odds with the Almighty, it would be wonderful to have a Christian brother so close by.

Long before she reached the wide-open doors of the smithy, Betsy could smell the smoke and hear the clang of hammer on metal. The blows carried a rhythm and music the previous smith never attained. It reminded her of the joyful peal of the church bells. Betsy felt her heartbeat change to match the hammer's cadence, and she felt a shiver of delight at stopping by to see Mr. Walker. She stood behind the children, but their chatter had already garnered attention.

"Hello, my new little friends! It's so nice of you to stop to see me when school is over for the day." He looked past them, and his smile widened as he spied Betsy. "I pounded together a small fence there, just inside the door. That way, the children can come watch when they have your permission, but you won't need to worry that sparks or slivers of metal will hit them."

"You're very thoughtful, Mr. Walker. You needn't feel obligated to entertain my little brothers and sisters."

He chuckled. "I have a feeling they'll entertain me far more. You're always welcome, Miss Larkin—you, and the kids. Did you have fun, visiting with your friends as you sewed?"

The tilt of his smile made the welcome personal. She felt her cheeks grow warm and tried to hide her reaction. "Yes, the sewing circle is special. Mrs. T—that is, Mrs.

Tidewell—is a lovely woman. She took to heart the verse in the Book of Titus that exhorts the older women of the church to guide and instruct the younger ones. She invites us over each Tuesday for tea, sewing, and Christian fellowship."

His head tilted to the side a bit. He glanced down at the children, then back at her. A flash of understanding glinted in his eyes. "Must be nice to talk things over with womenfolk and have a chance to sit down for a few minutes."

"I confess, I do look forward to Tuesdays almost as much as I anticipate Sundays. The reverend has a way of making the Bible come alive."

"I noticed." He shoved back an errant lock of hair. "If the ground is wet again this Sunday, I'll stop by with my horse so we can all ride."

"Oh, but you shod Jenny." Though Betsy demurred, something deep inside dared to hope he'd insist.

Concern furrowed his brow. "Even if you and little Greta ride Jenny, these other kids are getting so big, it's precarious for all of them to share a horse."

"I could ride with him, Sis." Marie's awestruck look and tone made it clear she'd be delighted to do so.

"Hey! Me!" Will pounded his chest. "He's a boy. Boys stick together."

"I'll take turns giving all of you rides," Mr. Walker said diplomatically.

"Even Betsy?" Greta asked.

The blacksmith looked at Betsy with twinkling eyes. Her cheeks felt scorched by heat, but he simply chortled and shrugged. "Told you they'd entertain me. Tell you what, kids, I hope to repair the sleigh over on the side of the smithy. When it snows, we'll ride to church in style. That's how your big sister will ride with me."

The children chattered excitedly. "Misser Wakka, can I go, too?" Greta asked.

He leaned over the spanking new fence and hoisted Greta high. Rolled-up shirt-sleeves left his ropy forearms bare, accentuating his strength and making it clear he took pains to be extra gentle as he playfully bounced her up and down. "Hmmm. I suppose you don't weigh too much. We'll tuck you in." He stood her on the fence and kept his huge hands clasped around her. "If we're going to be friends, 'Misser Wakka' sounds like a big mouthful for a half pint like you. Why don't you call me Ty?"

"Sometimes I tie Betsy's apron," Marie said as if the name and the verb were all the same.

To Betsy's amazement, Ty took Marie's childish reasoning in stride and looked down at his sooty leather apron. "Her apron doesn't look anything like mine." He carefully set Greta back down beside Betsy. "Can't say I end up looking very respectable once I set to work."

"Pa gets sweaty and muddy all of the time," Karl declared. "Betsy says that a man who comes home clean didn't mind his work. Course, she makes sure Pa washes up on the porch and scrapes his boots 'fore he comes inside."

"I'll remember that tonight. Your pa invited me to supper. I hope you don't mind, Miss Larkin. He and I were making some neighborly arrangements, and he told me to be there just past sunset."

Glory, what will I fix? I was just going to sliver ham bits in some noodles. . . .

"I brought down a buck this morning," he continued, completely unaware of the panic he'd set her into. "We stuffed a roast in the pan, if that sounds all right to you. Your pa is sowing the winter wheat today, so I figure he's going to have a fair appetite, too."

"Yes. Yes, he will," Betsy stammered. How could one man upset the balance of her day with just a few sentences? "I'd best go slide it on the spit right away. It was very generous of you to share it with us. Come, children."

"Bye-bye, Misser Ty," Greta said. The others echoed her—including Betsy. Once she caught herself being familiar, she felt the telltale tingle of another blush.

"I'll see you later—all of you." He lifted his hammer. "I'm looking forward to your delicious cooking, Miss Betsy."

Chapter 4

They left, and Ty turned back to his forge. He used the bellows to fan the fire and grinned at the collection of implements waiting for repair. Hickory Corners had been without a blacksmith for months, and essential things had fallen into disrepair. Most of the men within a whole day's ride had dropped by with items that needed urgent attention.

They needed him there. Aye, they did—and he'd been a bit of a rascal, inserting himself into the Larkins' life and even daring to address Betsy so familiarly. She had better get used to it. He was here to stay, and he wanted *her* to need him, too.

A steady work pace soon resulted in several sound repairs. Ty set the items on a shelf and carefully kept them with the tags he made to remind him of the owners' names. In a week or so, he'd know them all by name and recall what belonged to whom, but for now, the paper helped him remember names and faces.

The tiny cabin next to the smithy left much to be desired. He'd slept on a pallet of pine needles the past three nights because the iron bedstead needed joint work and the mattress had boasted a nest of field mice. Though he'd gotten rid of the creatures and knocked down the cobwebs, the place clearly hadn't been inhabited for a long while. He'd lived in far worse. Having slept in the woodshed until his stepfather sold him into his apprenticeship, he still shuddered at being in small, dark places.

Thanks to Betsy's fine cooking, he hadn't had to fix a real meal for himself. Just as well, too. He still needed to visit the mercantile to lay in essential supplies. With the bartered goods or money he'd collect from the men who would claim their repaired goods, he'd be able to fill his larder and pick up staples on Friday. In the meantime, the loaf of bread, wheel of cheese, and apples he'd bought would take care of him. . .but he surely did long for sunset so he could go to Betsy's big, happy home and sit at her table.

⋅⋰⋅

"Oh, for goodness' sake!" Betsy stood in the doorway with a quilt wrapped around herself for warmth and modesty. She gaped at Ty. His boyishly handsome, lopsided smile could melt a weaker woman's heart, but she'd just about had enough of him and his early morning wake-up calls. In the past week, he'd arrived with the cock's crow five times. Each time, he brought something he'd managed to hunt. To his credit, he diligently skinned and dressed everything. In addition to the buck, his tally rated as more than impressive: another deer, a full dozen snared rabbits, seven late-migrating ducks, and now, a sizable string of fish.

"You've gotten enough meat to see yourself well through winter," she said as she tried not to let her teeth chatter.

"Not at all, Sunshine. I'm just getting started. Besides, when we butchered your pa's sow so you could make the sausage, we agreed to share."

She gave him a weak smile. Venison sausage tasted too gamy on its own. They'd had a two-day long commitment where Leonard Melvin and his son closed the livery and harness shop and came over to help Pa and Ty slaughter a sow and butcher the second deer.

Betsy called upon Virginia Alexander and Elsa to come help her grind the scraps of pork along with venison to flavor the sausage. They'd spent long, hot hours chopping, grinding, and seasoning meat, washing the tripe, and filling it before they hung the sausages in the smokehouse. Five households—four, if she didn't count Tyson's since Pa invited him to dine with them regularly—all came away with a generous supply. Part of her felt elated they'd have delicious food for the months to come; part of her was too tired to be glad about much of anything. She stared at the fish and compressed her lips.

"Your pa was already going out to milk the cows. He told me to bring these to you. We could have some for supper, and I'll hang the rest in the smokehouse." Ty glanced down and frowned.

She curled her cold, cold toes beneath the hem of her nightgown. It was hard to be gracious when he kept seeing her at her worst. "Go on to the smokehouse, and bring the rest back in a pail of water so they stay fresh for supper. I'll get breakfast started."

"You don't need to feed me breakfast, Betsy. You're already making supper every night."

"You're hunting it!"

"It's the least I can do. My smokehouse is rotted clean through, so your pa is letting me use yours, and he's loaned me wood 'til I can catch up on the repairs everyone needs. You folks take neighboring and hospitality far beyond the commonplace."

Betsy clutched the quilt closer and shook her head. She glanced back at the far side of the cabin toward the boys' bed when Will muttered in his sleep. She found it too hard to look Ty in the eye. "You don't know the difference you're making," she whispered. "Pa's so tired. You sharing your meat takes some of the burden off of him, and the way you shod Jenny and fixed the barn hinges—those things are easing his lot. It's good, too, for Karl and Will to hear a man pray at the table again. Pa stopped praying the day my stepmama died. Bad enough he lost my mother, but losing Frieda when he had a whole passel of children hardened his heart."

She bit her lip. *Why am I babbling? This is so awkward. He didn't need to know that about Pa.*

"Betsy," Ty said softly, "your pa's a good man."

"I know! Yes, I know this!"

He nodded. "Prayer and time. We'll pray and give God time to work. Your pa will let go of the hurt and stop blaming God. In the meantime, I'll come each Sunday so the boys will have a man to accompany them to church."

"Then you must stay for Sunday supper."

He winked. "I was hoping you'd say that."

Something in the way he smiled and winked sent the telltale tingle of a blush straight to her cheeks. *And he thinks* we're *acting more than neighborly?* "I'll. . .um, we'll see you for supper, then." She took the pail from him.

"That thought's enough to make me wish the day away." Ty nodded and left.

As he paced off, Betsy realized the warmth in her heart had made her forget about her cold toes. She hastily shut the door and choked back a sob. She couldn't allow herself these feelings. She needed to mind her obligations instead of day-dreaming about what could never be. Her brothers and sisters needed her. Pa did, too. Ty Walker would have to warm some other woman's heart and feet.

Chapter 5

The first half of autumn blew past so quickly, Ty scarcely could keep track of the days. He cut coal straight out of a four-foot vein in the earth just east of the edge of the township and filled the sledge twice to bring it all back. In the past, he'd done the same chore and thought nothing of it; this time, he'd come back just as filthy as always. He groaned as he caught sight of Betsy taking down her snow-white laundry. Manners demanded he stop.

"Pa said you were going after coal." She unclipped another daintily embroidered pillowslip. "I overheard the sheriff and Mr. Schmidt talking about what a hardworking man you are. It's plain to see they're right." Her smile was honest and sweet as a first spring rain.

"Yeah." He looked down at his black hands and clothes. "I'm well past dirty, going on to squalid."

"It'll wash. After you dump that load, rinse your clothes and bring them over. I left the lye pot for you and banked the fire. If you do them right away and hang them in front of your fireplace tonight, they'll dry just fine."

He cocked his head to the side. She never ceased to astonish him. The wife of the man to whom he'd been apprenticed constantly harped about the black smudges. "You really don't mind the coal dust mess, do you?"

Her brows rose in surprise. "You need coal to earn your living. I'll make a deal with you. I won't notice you're coal black if you ignore how I get covered in wheat chaff, come harvest."

He smiled. "I'm afraid I can't agree, Miss Betsy. It'll just make you look like the golden angel you are." The shocked look on her face made him chuckle. "I'd best get going. Thanks for saving the wash water for me."

In addition to getting the coal, Ty used the next weeks to chop over twenty cords of wood. He repaid the Larkins with four for the one he'd borrowed and knew the satisfaction of being sure he had enough fuel to heat his cabin and fire his forge for the winter. He'd also been careful to buy sufficient lamp oil, wicks, and candles over at Thomasohn's Mercantile to keep from living in the dark. Karl and Will dropped by and helped him chink his cabin.

One day that first week, someone had slipped into his place while he worked and cleaned up the inside. The canning jar with flowers and fresh flour-sack curtains made a difference. Those touches let him think someone cared and reminded him he wasn't a burden to be suffered any longer.

Betsy was too shy to have done the task alone. He suspected she'd pulled along a friend or two from her sewing circle. That sewing circle surely did put a gleam in her smile and gave her a bit of a break. He never once heard her complain about how much work her brothers and sisters created. She set herself to tasks and seemed to keep a glad heart, even though he sometimes wondered if she didn't long to marry and have children and a man of her own instead of tending to her siblings. Anyone who reared kids who weren't their responsibility and treated them well rated high in his estimation. Betsy not only did that—but also went well beyond duty and cherished her little brothers and sisters.

The cabin still felt cramped as could be. It wouldn't take much to heat, but a man could go daft in a cabin he couldn't sneeze in without bumping into the wall or hiccup without hitting his head on the roof. At night, when the fire burned down low, he recited Bible verses from memory to push back the bad memories of childhood. Even now, years later, he loathed dark, small places. When they were cold, that made them even worse. If he didn't want to make a fool of himself by crawling to the Larkins' by midwinter and begging to live in their big house, he'd best do something quick about the situation before bad weather made it impossible to build.

Word was the Thomasohn brothers were hard workers. Ty sought out Zack and asked him for a bit of help felling trees for logs. The next day, six work-hardened men showed up. By that evening, they had it all chopped and ready for a cabin raising. Their neighborliness pleased Ty.

Ty originally planned to simply add on to his existing cabin. To his surprise, Samantha Thomasohn grabbed him by the arm, yanked her biggest brother to the side, and gave them her opinion. She emphatically insisted on leaving the cabin ten feet away. "You can use it to house an apprentice, or your wife can use it as a summer cookhouse. You have plenty of logs. Fix it up right...like the Larkins' or the Schmidts' place."

Though he'd love to have a plank floor, Ty knew he didn't have time to make one. A space not far from the cabin was already fairly even and free of stumps—he presumed it had once been a vegetable patch. He chained a log behind his horses, stood on it, and had them drag back and forth over it to compact and level the ground. As foundations went, it was rugged, but recent rains actually made the ground soft enough to shape but had compacted the earth enough to let him know he'd not have any nasty dips or sinking spots later. He hoped to buy planks and add in a floor come spring.

The next sunrise, even more men appeared and set to work. Soon, women brought baskets of food. It humbled Ty, knowing his neighbors had ceased their own labors without any advance planning and done this to welcome him. The whole church family set to work, and by the day's end, Pastor Tidewell dedicated Ty's home to the Lord's service.

Samantha Thomasohn was among the last to leave. Ty felt a bit awkward. Though a nice gal, she simply didn't strike a spark in him like Betsy did. Nope—he'd already set his heart on the pretty little farm gal across from his smithy. He watched Samantha put a crock of colorful autumn leaves on the table. As she walked past him, she said quietly, "Those were Betsy's idea. She's not just my cousin, Mr. Walker. I count her as my dearest friend, and I do hope you keep in mind a heart as big as hers can be shattered easily."

He smiled. "Miss Thomasohn, Miss Betsy's a woman worthy of a man's highest regard. Her tender heart and her love for the Lord are wondrous qualities. I can promise you, I'll do my utmost to be considerate and mindful of her."

Samantha nodded, drew an inky shawl about her shoulders, and slipped out the door. Ty grabbed a lantern and stretched his legs to fall into pace alongside her. "It wouldn't do for you to find your way home alone after sunset."

⋅⋰⋅

"Do you need any sugar?" Uncle Silas asked Betsy the next afternoon as she dropped off her eggs at the store. "I'm not sure I'll get more in before Christmas."

Betsy thought for a moment and tried to project how much sugar she needed. Most of the time, she used sorghum molasses, honey, or maple syrup for sweetening. The money in her egg account would cover a little real sugar, though. She chewed her lip and thought of how much Ty ate and how partial he was to sweets. "Yes, I'd better get two pounds."

"Fine." As he turned to fetch the sugar, he said over his shoulder, "That new blacksmith seems to be a fine man."

"Handsome as sin, too," Olivia Crabtree interjected. She looked down her nose and waggled her finger at Samantha's father. Her widow's weeds rustled about her thin frame as she stepped closer. "You'd better be sure of him, Silas Thomasohn. He's working fast—mighty fast, if you ask me. I saw him with your daughter last night, strolling down the street, close to her side."

Betsy felt her heart drop into her boots. Her ugly, too-big boots. Her suspicions were true. Ty and Samantha were fond of each other, and they were starting to court.

"You're making a barn out of a berry box, Olivia." Samantha's father shook his head, "I will say, he's a hardworking man. What do you think, Betsy?"

Betsy forced herself to agree, "Hickory Corners is fortunate. We've needed a blacksmith for a long while now." She barely managed to keep a smile on her face until the storekeeper gave her the sugar. She carried it out the door and down the street. The whole time, she wanted to cry. It was silly. She ought to be happy her dearest cousin and a godly man were interested in one another. It wasn't as if she had anything to offer him.

No, she truly was no bargain. She wrapped her braids up in a simple style instead of taking time to curl her hair. Her drab brown homespun gown looked dull as could be, and she never managed to save up quite enough for all of them to have new shoes. What with her youngers growing so fast, she couldn't very well fritter away good coins on a cobbler's services for herself when Karl and Marie could both get good wear out of shoes and still pass them down to Will and Greta. It never bothered her before, but now, she was acutely aware of the fact that she clomped around in ill-fitting boots a hired hand left behind two years ago.

As if her appearance weren't enough to put a man off, Pa's sour attitude and her four rambunctious siblings would make any sane man look for a wife elsewhere. She loved them all—but she knew she couldn't expect a man to share her with her family. No bride saddled her groom with such a heavy burden. She didn't think of them that way, but the men who had come around made no bones about their opinions once they learned she'd never walk off and leave Pa alone with the kids. The apostle Paul talked about how being unmarried allowed him to be a servant of the Lord. He'd been content; she'd have to learn to be content being an old maid.

But deep in her heart, Betsy wept. She wanted to serve God, and she loved her family. Still, seeing how happy Elsa and Shane Gerhard were left her aching with a loneliness she couldn't put into words. Betsy knew in her head Ty Walker would never be hers, but somehow, somewhere, she'd forgotten to keep that fact straight in her heart. He was a wonderful man, and he'd make some woman—probably her very own cousin—a happy bride. Some things in life just happened. This was one of them, and it hurt something fierce. For the first time, Betsy caught a glimpse of the anguish Pa felt in being widowed.

Chapter 6

Ty concentrated on turning the metal strip over the end of the anvil to get the right angle to the twist. He'd messed up on this the first time, and Ed Stahl would be back by sundown to pick up the hoe. If Ty had his way, he'd close his doors and work on fittings for his own place. It needed shutter dogs and a swing arm for the fireplace so he could heat water. Every other house in Hickory Corners needed a fire for cooking, but Betsy fixed his meals as a matter of course.

Betsy. He surely hoped she approved of the house. In fact, he hoped someday he'd carry her over the threshold. The buck's antlers hung over the hearth and held his rifle and powder horn. Each day, he added a shelf or a hook to the cabin to make it feel homey, like hers. He'd built it so it looked much like Betsy's, but he'd planned to do something different. He wanted to put in a real glass window instead of clarified hide. For now, the clarified hide would suffice—especially since he'd taken the cheery yellow, striped curtains Betsy made for his old cabin and hung them there.

From the first time he sat at the Larkins' table, he'd been made to feel welcome. Mr. Larkin spoke to him man-to-man in a way that let Ty know he'd been judged and approved. Mr. Larkin made it clear he didn't want to listen to Ty talking about God, but he'd jaw about anything else, and they'd forged a fair friendship. It saddened Ty to see the pain in Mr. Larkin's eyes and the angry lines around his mouth whenever Betsy and the kids bowed theirs heads for grace—but at least he didn't stop them from praying.

Most evenings after supper, Ty and Betsy traded turns at reading the Scriptures to the kids before she served dessert. Her love for the Lord and the Word were sweeter than anything she baked—and nobody baked like Betsy. To Ty's joy, she made him feel as if she didn't merely set a place at the table for him out of charity— she welcomed him to join them. In fact, she'd even taken to making gingerbread once a week when he'd confessed he had a powerful weakness for the treat.

Mr. Larkin and Betsy wouldn't take money for the meals. They always pointed out that Ty had hunted most of the meat that now filled the smokehouse. He'd chopped cords of wood for them, too. Still, he didn't reckon a man with his hearty appetite was paying his fair way—not for the vittles, and not for Betsy's extra work. Because of that, he made it a game to do chores and make essentials for them.

Nails or pegs used to hold things in the Larkin home. Ty made hooks for the dishcloths and aprons, devised a holder with parallel bars a few inches apart for the towels that held four of them neatly in a small space. Betsy's pretty brown eyes glittered with delight over that invention. He'd made three decorative shelves with porcelain-knobbed hooks for Betsy and her little sisters to use for their clothes. From the joy they showed, Ty might have thought he'd built them a bridge straight into heaven.

Thrice now, he'd taken Karl and Will fishing. When they returned, he told Betsy with absolute sincerity, "I had more fun than the boys!" He'd reinforced a weak spot on the plow for Mr. Larkin, too. A replaced hinge here, a cowbell there. . .all little things Ty hoped would show his appreciation—not just for the food, but for the way the Larkins gave him what he'd not yet had: a place to belong, a family. He knew, too, that Betsy was definitely the heart of that family.

Ty struck one last blow, then plunged the hoe blade into a barrel of water to cool. It took a few minutes to affix it to an elm stick. With that done, Ty picked up the first piece he'd ruined. If he played with it a bit, he could still salvage the metal—Betsy needed a hoe.

Round about a half hour later, Will peeped over the rail. "Whatcha doing, Mr. Ty?"

Ty looked at him and Karl. "Where's Marie?"

Karl jerked his thumb toward the street. "Mary Abner has a new doll. Marie stopped by to see her, and her ma said she can stay for supper."

A smile lit Ty's face. "Shut the door, boys. Christmas is coming, and we have work to do."

⁘

The winter wheat looked like green stubbly grass all over the field. The snows so far hadn't stayed, but they'd moistened the ground. Pa went off with Mr. Melvin and the Bunk brothers to cut lumber. The sawmill paid a bit for logs, and the men made a habit of using a few winter weeks when the fields needed no tending to go saw down trees, take them downriver to the mill, and get some cash money. Since Greta was born and Stepmama died, Betsy dreaded these excursions. She worried about Pa and fretted she'd not be equal to the task if anything went wrong while she carried on alone with her youngers.

She stood on the porch and waved them off to school. Karl carried their McGuffey's primers and readers. A pail dangling from Marie's fingers banged against her knees in a noisy announcement to Ty that his dinner was on the way. Betsy had started packing his dinner pail along with the kids'. It took but a moment more, and it was only fair. Ty did so much for her, she wanted to return his favors and reward his good deeds.

The smoke curling from his forge smelled good. All day long, it served as a reminder to her that she wasn't alone. Greta napped while Betsy went out to bring in the wash. It hadn't dried completely, but most of the water had dripped off, so they'd finish steaming inside without mildewing. She needed to hurry—the sky was getting dark, fast. Betsy cast a look down the road and wished Master Jarrod would let school out a bit early today. It looked like a mighty storm was blowing in.

Indeed, less than an hour later, the wind howled and snow flurries filled the sky. The kids hadn't gotten home from school, and she hoped they weren't lost outside. Betsy cried out, "Protect my youngers, Lord. They're so helpless, and the storm's so bad. . . ."

Loud thumping sounded on the porch. Betsy flew to the door. As soon as she opened it, Ty pushed his way in, swiveled, and shoved his weight against the door to shut out the cold. He opened his coat, and Marie's arms and legs unwound from his neck and waist. She slid to the floor, and Will slowly released his death grip on Ty's left thigh.

Ty gave Betsy a grin. "I knew you'd be worried, so I fetched the kids, and I'll fill your wood box. I had to be sure you'd be all right. Karl is back at my place, warm as can be. Storm's getting worse, so I'll keep him there."

Tears of gratitude filled her eyes. Betsy gathered her sister and brother close and whispered, "Thank you, oh, thank you. God bless you, Tyson."

"He does." Ty shot her a quick smile, then made three swift trips to bring in a generous supply of firewood. He made one last trip, dumped those logs by the front door, and nodded his satisfaction. Before she could say a word, he hiked to the smokehouse and brought back a big bag for her and another for himself. "That's enough to keep you warm and full for a good long while. Do you need anything else?"

Betsy stood on tiptoe and wound a gray-and-blue striped wool muffler around his neck. "This was supposed to be for Christmas, but you're too cold to do without. Thank you, Ty. Thank you for looking out for us."

He smiled and ran icy fingers down her cheek in a tender caress. "I'd do anything for you and yours, Betsy."

They stared at each other, and heat scorched her cheeks. She inched away. Ty tightened the muffler and smiled. "This was a wonderful surprise. I've never had finer. You're quite a woman, Betsy Larkin. There's not a woman on the face of the earth with a bigger heart than yours. Your family is blessed to have you, and God surely must be pleased to call you His daughter. I'd stand here singing your praises all afternoon, but I need to get back to Karl."

She picked up a thick quilt. "Wrap up in this. When you get home, Karl can use it. Hang onto this corner here. I tied a flour sack to it with dry clothes for him."

There wasn't time to waste. The wind howled a warning. As Ty pulled the quilt tight around his shoulders and readjusted his hold on the meat and sugar sacks, he said, "I'm keeping my eye on you. If you have any trouble at all or want my help, tie a red scarf to the west post of the front porch. You can be sure I'll be watching, so don't you hesitate for a single moment. The second you need me, I'll come running. I'll stop by the barn and water and feed the animals, so you won't need to trouble yourself for a few days."

He left, and when he disappeared into the swirling snow, Betsy wasn't sure what to think. Should she be elated that he'd been so good to her and God had answered her prayers to keep her siblings safe, or should she feel bereft that she could never know the joy of marrying such a wonderful man?

It wasn't as if she got to make a choice, anyway. He'd already walked Samantha home. He'd set his heart on a woman who could devote her every waking moment to his happiness. Samantha and Ty were her two favorite people—but Betsy couldn't bring herself to find joy in their romance. She felt guilty for coveting what simply wasn't ever to be in her grasp. . .but that guilt and all of her fervent prayers didn't erase the ache in her heart.

⁘

Four days later, the storm ended. Ty and Karl rode over. Betsy opened the door, and Ty filled his eyes with the sight of her. "You look wonderful," he decided.

"Yeah!" Karl threw his arms around Betsy while Ty gladly hugged the children. He would have happily lifted Betsy up and swung her around, too, but the way she went bashful over his compliment held him back.

After they ate bubble and squeak for lunch, Will and Marie started to squabble. Betsy shrugged apologetically. "The kids are pretty rowdy from being stuck inside."

"That's understandable. It's still bitterly cold outside, but they could probably go to the barn to frolic."

"That's a fair notion. You kids bundle up warmly and tend to the animals while I put Greta down for a nap." The kids obeyed with alacrity. As she came back to the main room, Betsy caught Ty eating the last few bites from Marie's plate. Her delicate brows rose.

"Now don't make fun of me. Smidgen left that for me." A woeful shake of his head accompanied his outrageous claim. "Karl and I were pitiful bachelors. We managed, but nothing we took from the hearth tasted anything like what you make. Truth be told, I could probably knock the center out of my dumplings and sell them as horseshoes."

She stacked the dishes and laughed.

"You have a lovely laugh. I wish you'd do it more often," he said. "It's like a rare gift, seeing you lighthearted." He walked over to her and took her hand in his. "Speaking of gifts, I feel like God gave me the sweetest present in the world the day we met. First time I saw you in church, you nearly stole my breath away. I didn't know at that time, you'd steal my heart, too—but you have."

"No, Ty. Please don't do this." Betsy tugged her hand from his. "Your friendship means so very much. I don't want this to come betwixt us."

He stared at the just-swept plank floor. "It's because I'm so big and clumsy, isn't it? I scare you."

"No!" She didn't hesitate for a single second, and that fact made her response ring with truth. "I always figured a man's strength was a gift God gave him so he could provide for his wife and protect her."

He looked back at her. "Then what's the problem?"

Betsy bowed her head and knotted her hands in her apron pockets. Tension sang in the stiff lines of her stance, yet sadness radiated from her words, "You deserve a bride who pampers you, Ty. A woman who can devote her whole heart to you—someone like Samantha. I can't."

Just then, Marie, Will, and Karl ran in. Will and Marie were both crying. Karl tattled, "They were climbing up to the hayloft and got splinters in their hands."

Ty watched as Betsy gathered them close, soothed, sympathized, and sent Karl to fetch a needle from her sewing box so she could pick out the splinters. As he leaned against the table, the truth finally dawned. Betsy thought he expected her to abandon the children! After years of caring for them, she'd become more of a mother than a sister; and fool that he'd been, he hadn't considered the fact that she didn't know he'd gladly take them all into his home. He'd already opened his heart to them.

Words came cheaply. Actions would have to be his tool. He'd show her over and over again. Yes, that's what he'd do. He'd let her think he'd accepted her refusal and simply be her friend. . .and with time and patience, he'd prove his love.

She could take her silly notions about Samantha Thomasohn and cast them to the wind. In his whole life, no one had ever touched his heart like Betsy Larkin, and she was silly if she thought he was going to give up on her and plug anyone else in just because she'd taken a crazy notion in her head. Her family wasn't a burden; it was an utter joy. Far as he could see, it wouldn't take long for him to prove his feelings. He might not have gotten her pledge of heart and hand today—but Ty felt certain that would come. God wouldn't have brought them together if He didn't intend for this to work out.

Ty left, and Betsy felt like he'd taken her heart along with him. She tried to be cheerful for her siblings, but the fact was, Ty hadn't refuted her assertion at all. He hadn't even offered a token denial that the kids weren't a burden. Just as telling, he'd not contradicted a word she'd said about Samantha. It hurt. It hurt really bad.

She kept busy. That ought to help. She'd been through this four times before. By now, she should be used to it—men simply didn't want a bride who brought a dowry of nothing more than hungry, noisy children. Oh, when the shoe was on the other foot, it was a different matter. Widowers with children regularly remarried and expected their new wife to take on the responsibilities of caring for children. Pa had done that. Frieda married him and had been good about taking Betsy under her maternal wing and shepherded her from being a gawky eight-year-old into early womanhood.

Greta plopped down in the middle of the floor and awkwardly wrapped her dolly in a little baby blanket. She picked it up, cradled it, and crooned. Betsy turned away and tried to blink back her tears. She'd never have a babe of her very own to cuddle. That blanket had been one she'd made to go in her own hope chest, but when Frieda died and the baby things were so worn-out, Betsy had taken it out and used it for Greta.

After she tucked her youngers in for the night and stoked the fire, Betsy sat at the hearth and held her Bible. She had always loved the Word, and she treasured the fact that Ty did too. Because the Good Book was a link they shared, she couldn't bear to even open it tonight. Hands tightly clenched around the battered black leather, she clutched it to her bosom and silently prayed, *God, I'm so thankful for my youngers. Please give me the love and patience I need to rear them. Forgive me for my selfish wishes, and renew my heart. You set me in this family, and Pa and the kids truly need me. Help me to continue to serve them in Your name and with a willing heart. Don't let foolish dreams tempt me, I pray—*

"Sis?"

She hastily wiped away her tears and didn't turn around. "Yes, Karl?"

"Mr. Ty uses tongs so he doesn't get burned, but he's taken to wearing cotton gloves under leather ones now. Funny thing: He said leather lets the heat come straight through, but cotton doesn't. He didn't used to wear 'em, but he started to once he moved here so's his hands don't stay coal black all the time. Old Mr. Willon's gloves were still there, but they're falling apart. I sneaked one and traced 'round it. Since you already gave Mr. Ty the scarf, I thought maybe you and Marie could stitch him some new gloves for Christmas. It wouldn't take long, would it? That way, he'd still have a Christmas surprise."

"That's a fine idea."

"Know what? He's been doin' hunting and not telling folks. Since Mr. Alexander got hurt, he can't bring in food. Ty's been taking meat over to them. After he brought Marie and Will home to you, he went back to the Alexanders' just to be sure they had wood and meat for the blizzard."

"He's a good man," Betsy whispered hoarsely.

Karl padded over and hunkered down. He rested his head on her arm. "I had fun with him. We did some neat stuff, and he taught me some things; but Sis?" his voice dropped to a whisper, "I missed you. Don't tell Will, though."

Betsy pressed a kiss to his rumpled hair. "I missed you, too, and I'll keep it a secret."

"I'm keeping lots of secrets these days."

"Oh?"

The firelight painted her brother's face and made his smile gleam. He nodded. "Can't tell. Christmas is going to be extra fun, though."

"It's only nine days away. I reckon Pa ought to be home in about three more days. I want to finish sewing his shirt for Christmas before he gets back."

"Tomorrow's Tuesday, isn't it? You go to Mrs. T's."

Betsy shrugged. "I might not go. The storm set me behind a bit." She didn't add on the biggest truth: She didn't think she could go and pretend to be happy for Samantha. Best she just stay home and tend to family matters.

-:::-

Late Wednesday morning, Mrs. Tidewell stopped in for a visit. "We missed you yesterday. Karl dropped by on the way to school to say you wouldn't come, but since you're here alone with the kids, I wanted to be sure you were all right."

As Betsy concentrated on pouring steaming tea into their cups, she said, "The storm caught me by surprise."

"It caught us all by surprise. Noah said the Almanac didn't even predict it. Ty was wonderful. It would have warmed your heart to see how he hurried out to the schoolhouse with a rope. The storm came up so fast, he didn't even take time to put on his own coat. He already knows which kids are related to whoever is in town and made them cling to the rope until he reached that building. He dropped them off until he reached his own place."

Honey. Betsy added more honey to her tea. She stirred it around and around and tried to sound casual, "I'm very thankful. I'd been worried and just finished praying, and he appeared at the door with Marie and Will."

"He's become quite devoted to you, my dear." Mrs. T smiled softly. "The girls spoke of little else yesterday at the sewing circle."

Betsy shook her head. "No. It's just a friendship. We're good neighbors."

"Good friends and neighbors are a gift from the Lord." Mrs. T sipped her tea and reached for a small bundle she'd brought. "We decided on a pattern for our next group quilt. I brought you some squares to work on. Since you've begun to teach Marie to sew, I put in a few extras. She could make a little crib quilt."

"Thank you," Betsy said as she opened the bundle and looked at the cream, blue, and rose fabric. "These colors look wonderful together. What pattern are we making?"

"Old Maid's Choice."

The fabric fell from Betsy's hands.

Mrs. T rose and came around the table. She stood behind Betsy and enveloped her in loving arms. "Ah, Betsy. I'm sorry. Please don't feel that was a reflection on you. It wasn't. You've always loved the four and nine patch quilts. Every quilt the group has made went to someone else—you never asked for one, never suggested it was your turn to have us make one for you. We voted that it's well past your turn and started this yesterday because we love you. Samantha chose the colors because she knew they were your favorites, and Elsa suggested quilting it with hearts and lines because your love radiates to everyone."

Tears slipped down Betsy's cheeks. Though her shoulders shuddered with her weeping, Mrs. T held her tightly. That made it even more bittersweet. No one ever held her. Pa didn't, and the kids gave her hurried hugs, but she hadn't had the luxury of being consoled, comforted, and cosseted by anyone for years. The only hugs she'd ever have would be old maid hugs—ones from other women, or from nieces and nephews. . .and that knowledge broke her heart.

Chapter 7

Christmas morning, Ty could hardly wait to get to Betsy's. He'd seen the candle burning in the window at the Larkins' to guide the Christ child to their home. Just as surely, it had beckoned him. He hastily washed with cold water, shaved so he'd look respectable, and quickly hitched the horse to the sleigh. He'd already put the bags of gifts in the sleigh last night, excited to have a family he could celebrate Christmas with. It would be the first time since he was a small boy that Christmas would be filled with love.

The horses pulled the sleigh across the short distance. Bells jingled merrily, proclaiming the joy of Christ's birth. The first rays of sun sparkled on the snow and made the whole world look full of promise.

Karl opened the door and ran out to greet him. "Mr. Ty! It's Christmas! Can we show our secret now?"

Will danced from one foot to the other. "Betsy kept peering out the window, looking for you to come. She even made you gingerbread for *breakfast.*"

"That was 'posed to be a su'prise," Marie chided.

All three kids stared wide-eyed as Ty set both bags down on the porch. He felt a spurt of delight at hearing Betsy had anticipated his arrival. Clearly, she wasn't indifferent to him. Patience. He'd just wait, and she'd finally figure out that they were meant to marry. In the meantime, he chuckled as the kids tried to hide their curiosity and greed. "From that first Christmas, when God gave us His Son, Christmas has been about giving."

Dressed in her faded blue Sunday gown, Betsy came to the doorway. Greta straddled her hip. "The sleigh bells sounded beautiful, Tyson. We've been looking forward to riding with you. Kids, hurry, or we'll be late for church."

"Aww," Karl whined, "I want that gingerbread!"

Ty chortled at Betsy's look of dismay. "I do, too," he admitted. "Nothing on earth compares to your scrumptious gingerbread, hot from the fire. Betsy, would you mind if we all ate a chunk in the sleigh, on the way to church?"

His compliment made her whole face glow. Ty relished the way little things pleased her. He hoped the gift he had for her would bring her joy. Virginia Alexander refused to take any more food unless she could sew for him, so he'd bartered her sewing for his hunting. She'd been good about helping him keep things quiet so Betsy would be surprised.

"Gingerbread and children are a messy combination," Betsy reminded him. "I suppose it's all right, if you don't mind sticky fingers in your sleigh."

"If you pass Greta to me, I'll wrap her in her cape. Boys, no fair peeking—you carry those bags inside."

Betsy passed Greta to him, and he quickly slipped her into her blue woolen cape. She giggled when he gave her a playful squeeze. Marie scrambled in, and he soon had her tucked beneath a big bear fur to keep both girls warm. Once they dragged the heavy, clanging bags into the house, the boys joined their little sisters.

Ty got down and waited for Betsy. He shifted from one foot to the other, eager to have her beside him. She came out and put a fragrant basket into his hands. "Merry Christmas."

"Mmmm." He inhaled deeply. "Merry Christmas to you, too." He passed the gingerbread up to Karl, then turned back to Betsy. "Your pa's not coming?" he murmured softly so the children wouldn't hear.

Betsy shook her head.

He cupped her waist and squeezed gently. "I'm sorry, Sunshine. Maybe soon. We'll keep praying." For just an instant, she dipped her head and rested against his chest. Ty slipped his arms around her and held her tight for a sweet moment. She filled his arms just as perfectly as she filled his heart. All too quickly, she straightened up and pulled away.

She stammered, "We don't want to be late."

He lifted her into the sleigh and climbed up to sit next to her. Once he settled a lap blanket over their legs, he slipped an arm around Betsy and drew her close. It made sense to him that God used Adam's rib to create Eve. With Betsy by his side, he finally felt complete.

Her eyes went wide.

"Huddle close, little lady. It's cold as can be today." He took up the reins and set off. The way she stayed next to him and fed him bites of gingerbread made his heart soar.

—❖—

After church, they went home and had roast duck. Betsy gave Pa and the boys their new shirts and pants, then gave the girls their new dresses and aprons. She shyly put the cotton gloves in Ty's hands. *I hope he likes them. . . .*

"Will you look at these?" Ty beamed. "How did you know I needed these?"

"Karl told me. He traced around your old ones."

"Your stitching is just as clever as his thinking." Ty tried one on. "It's an exact fit!"

Marie proudly gave Betsy and all of the men—including Ty—a handkerchief she'd hemmed. For Greta, she'd sewn a dolly blanket. Pa gave each of the little ones a shiny penny, an orange, and a tin whistle. For Betsy, he'd used a bit of his lumber money and gotten her a paper of sewing pins and a length of green wool, "So you can make yourself a skirt."

It already seemed like the best Christmas ever, and then Ty dragged over the sacks. "Karl and Will have been busy," he said. The boys' scrawny chests puffed out with pride as the set of gardening tools appeared. "They made and painted the handles on these themselves."

"You spent a lot of time with them," Betsy looked into Ty's eyes and marveled softly. "Thank you. Thank you so much!"

"You're welcome!" Will said, oblivious to the fact that his sister had expressed appreciation for the mentor as much as for the tools.

Ty's warm smile let Betsy know he understood her intent. He gave each boy a hammer and a bag of nails. "Young men with your talent need to have tools of their own. This is a start. I'm sure your pa can help you make toolboxes."

"Can you, Pa?"

"Sure enough." Pa smiled. Betsy couldn't remember the last time she'd seen Pa grin. That, alone, made the day.

"I thought we needed something pretty for the little princesses," Ty said as he reached into his other sack. He set rabbit fur muffs in the girls' laps. While they squealed with joy, he stood and carried the still-bulging sack behind Betsy. She sat still and didn't dare turn around to see what he was doing. His deep voice dipped lower and made her shiver. "For the queen of the home."

Something heavy descended on her shoulders and enveloped her—a cape of thick, soft, butternut wool. Betsy gasped as he stepped to her side and gently lifted the hood over her hair. Lined and edged with mink, it was the softest thing she'd ever felt. "Oh, Tyson! It's beautiful."

Ty drew her to her feet, and as he fastened the toggled buttons at the throat, he murmured, "Not half as beautiful as the woman it graces. I chose this," his fingertip brushed the fur, "because it's the same rich color as your eyes."

He didn't ask. He simply nodded to her pa, then escorted Betsy out the door. They went to the barn, and he quickly hitched the horses to the sleigh. "Come on, Sunshine. Let's go for a ride."

Betsy hesitated.

"I have a sled John Altmann had me make for his children that I need to drop off."

Did she want people to see the two of them—just the two of them—together? Betsy didn't know what to do. She wanted to be with Ty, but it was unfair to make him think they were courting. Just as bad, they'd travel straight through the length of town to reach the miller's house. Goodness only knew how many tongues that would set wagging! She averted her gaze. "Tyson, I've told you we can't be more than friends."

He cupped his hands around her waist. "I asked you to ride with me to deliver a sled. I won't try to sneak a kiss or propose again. Come along as my friend. You can help distract the kids so John and I can unload the sled without them seeing it."

His hands stayed at her waist. She could feel their strength all of the way through her new cape and clothes. They could be no more than friends, but she'd learn to accept and enjoy that. So far, she had—and it was good. Betsy nodded.

"There's my girl." His deep, soft tone held approval.

Once Ty lifted her into the sleigh, he put on his jacket and slipped the muffler she'd made for him around his neck. After he climbed up, she turned and carefully pulled it higher, over his ears. "Your ears will get too cold. If you still have some fur, I could sew you a cap."

"I'd be obliged, Betsy." He flicked the reins, and the sleigh pulled out into the snow.

"I'm obliged, Tyson. You were far too generous for Christmas. We're all overwhelmed."

He tilted his head and studied her for a moment. "Betsy, my pa died when I was Marie's age. Ma married up again. The day she had his son, he sent me out to the shed. I thought it was for a whuppin', but I hadn't done anything wrong. Fact is, it wasn't for a whuppin' at all. I lived in the shed. He had no room in his home or heart for me. Ma couldn't do much, else he'd take away her new babe. Almost four years later, they apprenticed me out to a blacksmith."

Tears filled her eyes. "How awful for you!"

"It wasn't good. I'm not telling you this for pity; I'm telling you so you can understand what a gift it is to me that you and yours open your door and welcome me in. The little things I do and bring are tokens of my gratitude. I couldn't ever begin to match what you've given me. The Christian love you share makes every day feel like Christmas to me."

Chapter 8

The weeks after Christmas, Betsy kept busy with sewing on the quilt and doing her winter chores. Ty came over each morning and evening—not just for meals, but for Bible reading. It felt right to have him there—natural. Greta and Marie demanded good night kisses from him, and though the boys didn't ask, they clearly loved it when Ty tucked them in bed. Ty pulled the blanket closed so the boys would drift off, then looked at Betsy. "What're you doing, Sunshine?"

She nudged the table over a bit more. "Making room for the loom. I need to start weaving."

Ty gently set her aside and pulled the table back to its usual spot, then looked at her pa. "If you don't mind, we could go set up the loom in my old cabin. It'll be out of the way, but close by. No use in you being so cramped here."

"That seems like a right fine notion."

"Are you sure you won't mind?" Betsy chewed on her lip. Did he really want her near him all day long? She'd finally admitted to herself that Ty wasn't carrying a torch for her cousin, and Mantha nearly laughed herself silly at the notion that the blacksmith and she might ever be more than friends. Still, Betsy couldn't allow herself to believe. . .

"It'd be a pure pleasure to look out my forge door and see you weaving," Ty said. "There's no reason for you to give up precious room when I've plenty of spare space. Soon as I rise of a morning, I'll start a fire so it'll be cozy for you and little Greta. Having my Sunshine and Sunbeam there will chase away the winter gloom. You just get things ready—I'll tote them over in the sleigh tomorrow afternoon."

Secretly pleased by his words, Betsy murmured, "I'm obliged."

Two days later, Betsy sat in the sewing circle, making another square for the quilt top. Ten to the inch, the stitches marched up her needle before she pushed it through and rocked the needle back and forth again to gather the next inch of fabric.

Diana Montclair was visiting. She didn't work on the quilt with everyone else, but instead embroidered pansies on the yoke of a fine lawn nightgown. "I hear you're at that blacksmith's cabin every day, weaving and cooking for him," she said in a tone as airy as the fine fabric she stitched.

"She's weaving for her family," Samantha said at once.

"The way I see it, her father and the children are there for all of the meals. It's fine for her to cook," Elsa added on. "None of the rest of us would expect Mr. Walker to eat alone—especially since he hunted so much!"

Betsy felt glad of her friends' loyalty. She'd worried about gossip.

Diana arched her brow and stared pointedly at Betsy. "Are you telling me the two of you aren't courting?"

Betsy shook her head. She swallowed hard, and tears filled her eyes and voice, "I've told him we cannot be more than friends. Pa and my youngers need me."

"Well," Diana sniffed, "if you're silly enough to let them use you as a slave so you sacrifice your future, that's your own fault, and I think it's a mistake."

Betsy stuck her finger and quickly pulled back so she wouldn't bleed on the quilt. She looked at Diana and shook her head. "Life isn't always about what you want; it's about others you love and what they need. Most of the time, I'm very happy with my life. Yes, I have days when I start to wallow in self-pity, but then I remember God doesn't glory in a daughter who's being a martyr."

"What verses do you think Betsy can claim for this?" Mrs. T asked quietly.

" 'Seek ye first the kingdom of God, and His righteousness; and all these things shall be added unto you.' " Elsa smiled brightly. "I claimed that one during the days when Shane arrived and turned my world upside down."

"How about Psalm 37:4?" Clara Bucey's beautiful brown eyes sparkled as she quoted, " 'Delight thyself also in the Lord; and he shall give thee the desires of thine heart.' "

"And Psalm 40:8," Samantha added. " 'I delight to do thy will, O my God: yea, thy law is within my heart.' "

"Yes," Mrs. T nodded. "Our covenant with God isn't written on stone anymore; it is written in our hearts by the Grace of Christ. Our focus is to desire to do God's will, to love the things our Father loves. Because He is our Heavenly Father, He wants the very best for us. By trusting in His will, we live in the faith that though we go through trials and are tested, God will bless us in His own way and time."

As she walked home, Betsy paused under a tree and stared ahead at the smoke rising from Ty's forge. *Father, I do want to do Your will, to please and glorify You. Give me discernment and courage to walk the path you put before me. Through Jesus I pray, Amen.*

She continued on toward home with a restored sense of peace.

-:::-

Ty stood in the door and smiled at the sight of Betsy sending the shuttle back and forth with a sweeping rhythm. She'd made several yards of linen from the flax in the past few days. She sang a nonsense song with Greta as she worked, and the small cabin still held the sweet aroma of honeyed corn bread and fried ham steaks she'd made at midday. Her Pa dropped by Ty's new cabin earlier in the day, and all of them ate together before he left to cut more lumber.

As she waved good-bye, Ty noticed how Betsy held little Greta a shade closer than usual. *She's scared.* "He'll be fine, Betsy. If you're worried, I can hurry and join him."

"Don't you dare go off! I couldn't bear having you and Pa both gone at the same time."

Pleased at the depth and speed of her reaction, he still knew better than to play it up. Instead, he pasted on a roguish grin and needled, "Is that your way of saying having me underfoot isn't too big a burden?"

She hitched Greta higher on her hip and got the sassy gleam in her eye he loved so much. "Go back to your forge, Tyson Walker. I have work to do, even if you don't."

He'd tickled Greta's neck, then sauntered off to the forge. Now, he listened to Betsy repeat the tune as she wove. "Sunshine?"

She looked up, startled. A fetching blush stole across her cheeks. "Oh! How long have you been standing there?"

"Long enough to wonder why the pig in your song likes to wear a hat." He chuckled. "I've always thought pigs looked better in shirts."

"No, Misser Ty. The horse wears the shirt," Greta informed him somberly.

He leaned forward and rested his hands on his knees so he'd be closer to eye level with her. "Well, imagine that! What does the turkey wear?"

"Dunno. Sis? What does—"

"A feather duster," Betsy ventured with a playful shrug. "Did you need something?"

"Actually, I do." Ty straightened up and tilted his head toward the smithy. "Reverend Tidewell came to me with a toothache. The molar is rotten and needs to be pulled. I've gotten my tools ready, but I was wondering if you might have a bit of laudanum and cloves."

"Yes. I try to keep a good supply of things on hand. I'll be right back." She took Greta's tiny cape off the hook.

"Greta can stay with me," Ty offered. "She's my littlest sweetheart."

Betsy set the cloak back and started to wrap the one he'd given her for Christmas around her shoulders when Greta tugged on his pant leg. "Who's your biggest sweetheart?"

He carefully lifted the hood and smiled at Betsy. Silly woman still couldn't understand he loved her. "The lady of my heart hasn't figured out the answer to that puzzle. I'll have to wait and let her work on it a bit."

Betsy wouldn't meet his eyes, so he let her go. She brushed past him and murmured, "I'll be back in a jiffy."

Ty didn't like pulling teeth. Somehow, somewhere, someone had determined it was part of a blacksmith's job. He kept a few small pliers and a tiny bullet mold he'd altered a bit to use to accomplish the dreaded task. Betsy set Greta on a workbench out of the way, gave Pastor Tidewell a dose of laudanum, and put three cloves in a little scrap of cheesecloth muslin.

Reverend Tidewell removed his coat. "I expect I'll not feel much like preaching this Sunday. I've asked Brady to fill in for me. You can pass the word we'll still worship."

"Your nephew handled the church hayride just fine," Betsy said softly. "God did a mighty work in Brady's life, and it's a blessing to see him serving his Master."

The pastor nodded, sat on a bench, and Betsy held his head. Greta started to sing about the hat-wearing pig—a strange accompaniment for the event, no doubt. As soon as the task was over, Betsy slipped the cloves in place to help stop the pain and bleeding. By the time Ty got back from walking the pastor home, she'd already washed off his instruments and put them away.

"Betsy, you are like the Proverbs 31 woman—a priceless ruby."

She let out a self-conscious laugh. "Not at all. I'm just a sow with a hat and a feather duster. I'd best better get back to my weaving. Since you've helped Pa with so many of my farm chores, it freed some of my time. I got overambitious and am weaving almost twice my usual amount of linen. I want to have it done by tomorrow."

Ty watched her go back to the cabin. Through the open door, he saw her pick up the shuttle. *She weaves cloth.* . . . Oh, yes, Betsy was a woman who fulfilled all the Scriptures said. One of these days—hopefully soon—the woman he loved would finally realize she was meant to be his wife and pledge her heart in return. She was already his helpmeet in the truest sense of the word.

The next morning, Ty walked out into new drifts of snow and went to the stable. He watered and fed his horse, mucked the stall, and headed for the smithy. To his dismay, the glass pane he'd sent for was broken when it arrived. He'd thought on it all evening and just about the time he'd decided to accept it as a loss, he'd had his devotions and read about how the Stone that was rejected became the Cornerstone. It spurred his thinking. Maybe something beautiful could come from this brokenness.

All morning long, Ty worked on his plan. He kept the door to the smithy almost shut—an unusual thing because of the forge's heat, but he wanted what he was doing to be a surprise for Betsy. By midmorning, he realized he'd lost track of time because he'd gotten so involved with this new project. His stomach growled, making him even more aware of the fact it was almost noon. It seemed odd the children hadn't dropped by on their way to school. Betsy had said she was going to come finish her weaving today, too. Concern furrowed his brow. Ty took off his apron, quickly plunged his hands into the wash barrel, then headed outside. As soon as he looked to the north, his heart leapt to his throat.

Tied to the Larkins' porch post, fluttering in the wind, was a red scarf.

Chapter 9

"B etsy!"

She wearily petted Marie's sweat-dampened hair and raised her voice so she'd be heard over the peculiar coughs that filled their home. "Don't come in here!"

"Wild horses couldn't keep me away." The door swung open. "I came as soon as I saw the scarf—who's sick?"

"Will and Marie. I suspect Greta is, too. She's not herself." Betsy looked up at him and warned, "If you've not had whooping cough, you'd best back straight out the door."

To her relief, he came on in and firmly shut it behind himself. "I'm safe. What about you and Karl?"

"We had it while my stepmama was carrying Will."

Marie started to go into another paroxysm of coughs, so Betsy pulled her upright. The loud, whooping bark had gotten worse since sunrise.

"I've given them pine tar and elderberry cough syrup. It's not helping."

"How much wild cherry bark do you have?"

"Nowhere near enough for this," she confessed.

Ty paced over to Will's bed, gently lifted the boy and cradled him to his chest and shoulder as if he were nothing more than a wee babe. "How much have you gotten them to drink?"

"I made broth. They don't keep it down very well."

"I don't suspect they will." He sat next to her and calmly ironed his big, capable hand up and down Will's shuddering spine as the little boy coughed. He waited until the brace of whoops was over, then said very matter-of-factly, "We'll just have to be diligent to keep them drinking. What say we give them both some apple cider, maybe make a poultice, then I'll go get some more cherry bark. We'll need it. What else do we need?"

She strained to think. "Honey. It'll be impossible to get a lemon. I'm trying to remember what else is good for coughs. Linden, and anise, and—oh!" Frustration had her nearly in tears. "I don't remember!"

"It's going to be all right," he soothed. "After we get the kids settled, I'll go ask Doc what he recommends."

"Doc Gardner's ailing from his rheumatism. He's not been to church for nigh unto a month now. Samantha's father said the cold troubles Doc so badly, he can't go out on calls. I don't think he'll come help."

"I'll get his advice. We can make it through, Betsy. We need to send word to your pa, though."

Her arms tightened around Marie. "You don't think—"

"No, of course not," he cut in quickly. "Everyone's going to get well, but no one's going to get much done or chalk up any sleep around here for almost a month. It'll be good to have his help." He petted Will's head and murmured, "I need you to drink for me, little man. Sips. Loads and loads of sips. No runnin' around. I want you actin' lazy as a 'possum until your cough's all gone."

"Yes, Misser Ty." Even those three words sent Will into spasms of coughs again.

Ty was heartbreakingly gentle with her brother, and that meant the world to her. Betsy wanted to wrap her arms around the two of them.

Ty brushed a subtle kiss on her temple and murmured, "It's going to be fine." Betsy blinked at him in surprise, but he acted as if he'd done nothing out of the ordinary. He calmly reached for Marie and settled her on his other knee. "Come here, Smidgen. Your sis is getting you some cider. It'll make your throat feel better."

A little more than an hour later, Marie and Will stayed side by side in Pa's bed. Karl piled pillows and a rolled quilt up behind them to prop up their shoulders and heads to make them breathe better. Betsy started making cherry bark tea, and Ty brought in firewood and three big buckets of snow to melt on the hearth for water.

"I'll go into town and talk to Doc Gardner." He came close and gently pushed a strand of hair back from her forehead. "I'll be back as soon as I can. Do you need anything from the mercantile?"

"I have plenty of willow bark to bring down their fever. Karl can give you the egg basket. If you trade the eggs for some cherry bark, I'd appreciate it."

He nodded. "Karl, you're going to have to fill in and shoulder a man's place here," Ty said. "You be mindful to slop the hog, milk the cow, and do your stable chores. I want you to fix up the spare stalls in the stable. I'll be bringing over my horses."

"Why?" Karl asked.

Ty cupped Betsy's jaw and tenderly arced his rough thumb across her cheek. "I'm going to stay here until your pa gets home. We're going to see this through together."

Betsy leaned into his gentle caress. Ever since Frieda had died, she'd carried on pretty much alone. For the first time, she couldn't handle matters; but Ty was here, and together, they could manage. This man was a gift from God, and she needed him—not just for the kids, but for herself.

Betsy knew she probably ought to object; it wasn't proper for an unmarried man and woman to stay beneath the same roof. Doubtlessly, Olivia Crabtree would stir up a whole scandal over the arrangement. Then again, with four children as chaperones and three of them sick as could be, necessity seemed more important than propriety. God's mercy counted more than Mrs. Crabtree's pettiness. She covered his hand with hers. "I'm thankful, Ty. Truly, I am."

⊱⋅⊰

He could hear the terrible racket fifty yards from the cabin—loud, barking coughs in long, ugly strings. Ty winced. He'd had whooping cough and still remembered how sore the coughing made him and how sick he'd been. Greta seemed far too small to suffer such a malady, and talkative Marie had been alarmingly silent this morning. Normally a wiggle worm, Will's listlessness seemed all that much more alarming. Ty resolved to make them comfortable...and to make sure Betsy didn't wear herself to a frazzle.

"I'll take your horses to the stable, Sir," Karl said somberly as soon as Ty nudged his horse toward the porch.

Ty dipped his head once in approval. "Son, I'm not sure just who is more proud of you 'bout now: me, Betsy, or Almighty God."

Karl beamed as he took the reins and led the horses off. "I'll take good care of them."

Ty hefted the sacks with essentials he'd brought and went on into the cabin. The place smelled sour. Betsy was holding Greta's head, and the little girl was coughing so hard, she'd ended up emptying her stomach. At night, they'd have to shut the door for warmth, but if he could leave the door open for snatches of time in the day, it'd be wise. Ty used one sack as a doorstop.

"What did Doc say?" she asked without even looking over at him.

"He gave me two recipes for cough syrup. Said to keep their feet and chests warm and their faces cold. Make 'em drink as much as we can. I brought back a dozen of the eggs too, Betsy. Doc said the kids'll do well if you feed them scrambled eggs and custard."

"Oh, but what about getting more cherry bark?"

"Samantha's father has plenty in the mercantile. Mrs. Stahl was there, too. She's already made a cough elixir from cider vinegar and a bunch of other stuff she rattled off that escapes me at the moment. She promised to bring over a pint of it."

"Thank you, Ty. You'll never know how much I appreciate your help." Betsy wiped Greta's mouth, settled her back onto the pillows, and carried the slop jar toward the door.

Ty reached over and took the foul-smelling thing. "I'll get that."

Over the next two days, he and Betsy worked side by side to tend to her little siblings. By the third day, Marie's and Will's fevers broke. Greta's stayed high, though.

"I brought honey," Samantha said from the doorstep. "It'll help soothe their cough. Elsa sent over some bread so you wouldn't have to bake. Is there anything you need?"

Betsy sat on the bench and wearily rested her back against the edge of the table. Greta cuddled close, and her tiny body started to jar with a wracking brace of coughs. Betsy waited until they were over, then said, "Karl gathered the eggs. Can you take them back to the store?"

"Sure." Samantha came on in, calmly straightened up a bit, and started a stew over the fire. "Mary Abner has the cough, too. Her mama is making pancake poultices, of all things. She makes a pancake, puts it on Mary's chest 'til it goes cold, then has her eat it!"

A weary smile tugged at Betsy's lips. "That's better than what Zeb Bunk swears by. He came by with three big, black, ugly beetles and said if I wrap them in a cloth and have the children wear them against their chests, soon as the beetles die, the cough will be gone. Horace came with him. He said the part about the beetle dying was true, but it worked better if I'd keep them in tiny boxes, so he'd carved—"

Samantha went into gales of laughter. "Beetles in boxes! Oh, Betsy! What did you do?"

"Tyson took care of it. He thanked them. You would have thought those beetles were diamonds and pearls to hear him talk. When he took them in his hand, I nearly swooned. Zeb and Horace left, and Ty sat out on the porch like he didn't have a care in the world until they were out of sight—then he hightailed out to the field and got rid of them!"

"Ty's been a godsend, Betsy." Samantha coaxed Marie to have a sip of water. "I think the two of you—"

"Could you please dip this cloth?" Betsy interrupted as she thrust out a soggy rag. It hurt too much to have Samantha play matchmaker. No matter how much she cared for Ty, she couldn't abandon her siblings. "Greta's so hot, Mantha. Her fever still hasn't broken."

Heavy footsteps on the porch warned Ty was back. He'd gone out to see to the animals. Now he filled the doorway and held her big washtub.

"I thought maybe our little Greta would like to cool down in her very own bath," he rumbled gently. He crossed the floor and set the washtub down by the hearth. Betsy couldn't imagine how he'd carried it so easily—it was half full of water! Unaware of her astonishment, he dunked several cloths into the fresh water, wrung them out, then handed two to Samantha. As she tended Marie and Will, Ty came toward Betsy. "Here, Betsy."

Betsy gratefully accepted the cloth, but before she could start to gently wipe Greta, Ty sat down and pulled the toddler into his own lap. He bowed his head and tenderly kissed her sweat-dampened curls. "God bless you, Dumplin'."

Betsy folded the wet rag around her hand and started to cool Greta's sizzling brow. To Betsy's astonishment, Ty lifted his hand and gently ran the last moist cloth over her cheek! She gave him a startled look.

"It's all right," he soothed. "I'll sit with her awhile until the water warms up. Why don't you go nap a bit?"

Betsy moistened her lips. "No, I'm fine." She fought the urge to lean against him. The way he trailed the cloth over her cheeks and forehead felt heavenly. Her eyes fluttered shut with bliss, then flew open as Greta began to cough again. Over on the bed, Marie started hacking, too.

Betsy automatically started to rise, but Samantha called over, "I have her." Indeed, she did, so Betsy slumped back down.

Ty slipped his arm around her and tucked her close to his side. She sagged against his strength and rested her cheek on his suspender. Greta stopped coughing and didn't even have enough strength to lift her thumb to her mouth. That fact nearly tore Betsy's heart in two.

"O worship the King," Ty started to sing softly.

Betsy barely managed to keep her composure until he hit the last verse. "Frail children of dust, and feeble as frail. . ." Tears ran down her face and wet his shirt. He still cradled Greta to himself, but his other hand cupped Betsy's head and slowly stroked through her mussed hair.

·⁙·

"Here. I'll take her."

Samantha's quiet bidding let Ty know he'd lost track of time while praying over Greta and trying to comfort Betsy. Was it sheer exhaustion that finally dragged Betsy to sleep, or had she found some comfort in his arms? He loosened his hold, and Samantha claimed the limp toddler.

"The water's tepid. I'll bathe her—it'll cool down her fever. I folded back the covers on Betsy's bed."

Ty nodded and turned his attention toward Betsy again. In all his years, he'd never once seen a woman this bone weary. She nestled into his side as if that was where she belonged, and her words echoed in his mind. *I always figured a man's strength was a gift God gave him so he could provide for his wife and protect her.* Ty would gladly have her as his wife, provide for and protect her—but regardless of their wishes, only God ruled over life and death, and Ty felt every bit as helpless as Betsy did in the face of the children's illness.

Silently, he found the strings to her apron and untied them. As he eased the apron straps over her head, a loose hairpin caught and halted the progress. Soon, he had half a dozen hairpins in his hands, and Betsy's breathtakingly soft plaits tumbled down. He'd known her hair to be long—but the sight of her thick, golden plaits reaching her waist made him wish he could see it hanging loose and free. Even with the kids as sick as they were, she'd been careful to slip behind the blanket partition to tend her hair each day.

The soft plop of water and Samantha's sweet singsong reassured him Greta was in good hands. Ty carefully scooped his arm beneath Betsy's knees and twisted so his other arm cradled her shoulders. As he stood, she slipped neatly into his possession. Her head lolled over his heart as he carried her to the bed Samantha had prepared. Ty stood at the bedside, whispered a prayer as he snuggled Betsy close, then brushed a kiss on her brow.

Once he slipped her onto the thick feather bed, he winced at the high neck on her dress. Certain she'd never sleep well with it constricting her throat, he carefully slipped the uppermost button free, then trailed his fingers down her soft, sweet cheek. She might be a slightly built woman, but her backbone was forged steel, and her soul was pure gold. "Betsy Larkin," he whispered, "you're worth waiting for. I reckon if that fellow in the Bible waited for fourteen years for Rachel, I can be patient for you."

Ty quietly unlaced her boots and took them off. He loathed them. Pretty little Betsy wearing dreadful, heavy, men's boots—it was a shame. He'd given serious consideration to getting her dainty kid boots for Christmas, but decided not to because he feared he'd embarrass her by doing so. Her feelings were far more important than her looks. Satisfied she looked comfortable, Ty drew up the beautiful quilts he knew she'd made and left her to slumber.

Chapter 10

Betsy pushed back the blanket divider and stopped. Still a bit disoriented from her nap, she couldn't quite believe her eyes. Karl sat at the table, slurping soup. Marie sat on the edge of the boys' bed, absently swinging her stockinged feet as she drew on her slate. She set it aside to cough, then, calm as you please, picked it up and continued to draw afterward.

Ty sat in a chair across from the fire. Will sat on one of his thighs and leaned against his chest; Greta slumped on his other leg. Ty's massive arms wrapped securely round both—and all three were fast asleep. Will's body started to quake with his heavy coughs, and Ty's huge hand automatically ironed up and down on his back to brace and comfort him. When Greta started in, Ty simply drew her a tad closer so his forearm would support her.

"Mr. Ty said you're 'posed to eat when you woke up." Marie's voice was croaky from all of the coughing. She probably needed another dose of elixir.

Betsy tiptoed over to the dish shelf. They didn't own a timepiece and simply depended on the church and school bells. The Montclair's housekeeper, Millie Sanderson, had graciously lent her a mantle clock to determine when to give the children their medicines. Afraid the rising heat from the hearth might damage the beautiful timepiece, Betsy had placed it on the dish shelf. She looked at the clock and gaped in astonishment. Eight thirty! She'd slept the whole afternoon away!

"Mr. Ty gave them their cherry cough stuff at sunset. Greta got willow bark then, too," Karl reported dutifully. "Mr. Ty made me promise you'd eat straightaway. He already ate two bowls of Miz Samantha's stew."

Betsy debated whether to eat or take her siblings from Ty's arms so he could sleep better. He didn't seem troubled in the least to be holding them. Then again, he never acted as if they were a bother at all. She'd just eat quickly and have a little bowl. . . .

As she ladled the aromatic stew into her earthenware bowl, Betsy marveled at Samantha's strength. It hadn't been easy for Mantha to come help. She'd spent the spring caring for her own mother. Even with Mantha's fine nursing, Aunt Rachel slipped to the hereafter. Being here, seeing the children sick, had to stir up Samantha's grief—yet she'd come. Betsy whispered a prayer of thanks.

All three kids started coughing again. At the same time, a cold blast shot through the cabin. Betsy wheeled around. "Pa! We didn't hear you over the racket!"

"I came right away." He shut the door and peeled off his coat. Deep lines etched his pale face. "How are they?"

"Noisy," Ty rumbled with a tinge of humor. He gave Betsy a sleepy wink.

Marie sidled up to Pa and clamped hold of his leg. He immediately picked her up and crossed over to see Will and Greta. "Has Doc been by? What does he say?"

"Doc's not up to traveling out here," Betsy said. "Will and Marie are weary from barking all of the time, but they're doing well enough—"

"And my Greta?" Anguish filled Pa's voice as he knelt. His hand shook a bit as he reached over to touch her cheek.

"She's still feverish," Ty said softly. "It's harder on her."

"Here, Pa." Betsy shoved her bowl into his hand. "Eat and warm up a bit. Elsa sent bread. I'll slice you some."

Though he probably should have gone home, Ty spent the night. He didn't offer to leave, and no one suggested it. Just past midnight, Greta's fever climbed higher still. Betsy put her in the washtub again. The door slammed shut, and she could hear Pa out in the yard, yelling, "Why, God? Why? You took Hilda. Then You took Frieda. Two wives. Two! Wasn't that enough? Not my Greta, too!"

Betsy bowed her head and started to cry. Ty dipped down, kissed her temple, and walked outside.

⋆⋆⋆

Ty whispered a prayer for wisdom and stepped off the porch. Matthew Larkin stood out by the pump, his hands fisted and his head thrown back as he continued to rail at heaven. A man with that much anger and pain deserved comfort.

Betsy's pa spun around and growled, "So you came out here to give me all the answers, did you?"

Ty shook his head. "No, I came to be with you—to share your grief and be with you so you didn't have to stand alone."

"Stand close, and God might well strike you dead by mistake," Matthew sneered.

"God makes no mistakes." Ty closed the distance between them. "Things happen. I can't understand them. I don't know His reasons why, but still, I trust. He sent His Son and watched Him die. He understands your anguish. He's big enough to listen to you bellow."

"He sent His Son. He got Him back again."

"True," Ty agreed promptly.

"I didn't get Hilda back. I didn't get Frieda back. If He takes my little Greta—" Matthew's voice cracked.

Ty stood next to him and simply reached around and cupped his shoulder. He didn't have the right words. He didn't have a perfect answer, so he stayed silent.

A horse whinnied, and the cow lowed. They could hear the kids coughing inside the house. An icy wind clawed at them.

"Why did you come out here?" Matthew finally asked in a defeated tone.

"I came to stand alongside you so you wouldn't be alone. There've been times in my own life when I needed such a person. Sometimes, it's been a friend. Other times, there was no one—but in those times, I learned to lean on Christ. He was with me. If

107

you feel you don't have the comfort of the Lord, you at least deserve to have someone to help you shoulder this pain so you aren't crushed by it."

"Why would I want anything to do with a God who might take my baby daughter, my Greta, away?"

Ty thought for a moment. "Because He made her and lent her to you. She brought love and laughter to you. I pray she stays to fill our days with joy. Still, if God calls Greta home, He would hold her on His lap until the day you go to join her and Him in heaven."

"God would hold my child? Mine? I'm the man who hates Him!"

"God is bigger than your hatred, Matthew. He already conquered it on the cross."

"I wouldn't know what to say to Him."

Ty slowly exhaled, then ventured, "Maybe it's time you stopped shouting at Him and started listening. Wait a moment. Tell me what you hear."

"My sick children."

"And Betsy's sweet voice, soothing them."

"The wind."

"Sweeping away the snow clouds so tomorrow will be warmer."

Matthew shot him a grim smile. "You're trying to show me how I look at the wrong things. I'm a contrary man."

"You're a man who hurts. Maybe it's time you're a man who healed. Just be sure you seek God because you want to be right with Him—not to make a bargain for Greta. Even if He spares Greta, life will demand other sacrifices later. Faith doesn't mean we walk a smooth path—it means we don't walk the path alone."

"I'm so tired of being alone," Matthew confessed in a hushed tone.

"You don't have to be alone any longer. Can I pray with you?"

Chapter 11

Betsy carried her mending into Mrs. T's house. "Hello!"

"After being cooped up for over two weeks, I imagine it feels good to get out," Mrs. T said as she hugged her.

"Yes, it does." Betsy turned and gave Clara and Elsa quick hugs. "Pa's staying home today. Marie and Will are springing back nicely. Doc said since they're strong, the cough will run its course in about three weeks."

"How's Greta?" Samantha asked as she joined them.

"Still puny, but she kept broth and cider down for the past three days." Betsy smiled. "She'll just take a mite longer, but God was merciful."

Everyone sat down and started to sew. Betsy popped her thimble on her finger and deftly let down the hem in Marie's dress. Her needle stopped midair when Samantha blithely announced, "Betsy, we were talking about you last week when you weren't here. We all agree—you and Ty ought to get married."

She felt the tingle of a blush start at her bosom and climb straight up to her forehead. Bad enough Mrs. Crabtree scurried all over town, whispering tales. Now her own friends were imagining things! "Mr. Walker and I are good friends—nothing more."

"There's a pity," Elsa muttered.

Mrs. T patted her hand. "Things have changed since you refused his suit. Your father went to church this past week. He's finally shedding his anger at the Lord. He'll be sure to tend to the children's spiritual lives."

"I know, but—"

"Your other concern was that the children needed daily care," Mrs. Tidewell continued.

"Oh, for goodness' sake!" Samantha impatiently shoved her sewing aside. "You live right next door. The kids already practically live at the smithy. You did all of your weaving there this past winter. They can spend the daytime with you and the nighttime with your father."

"We have it all planned out." Clara grinned at her.

"And don't you dare try to convince any of us that Tyson won't welcome your little brothers and sisters. He's crazy about them." Samantha paused. "When Greta's fever was so high, he called her 'our Greta,' and his love for all of them is plain as can be."

Mrs. Tidewell picked up her Bible and started to read 1 Corinthians 13. " 'Charity suffereth long, and is kind; charity envieth not; charity vaunteth not itself, is not puffed up. . .Beareth all things, believeth all things, hopeth all things, endureth all things.'"

She looked up at Betsy. "Charity is love—love freely given. You've been so busy loving others, you've been blind to how much someone loves you. Ty Walker's a fine man. He's been patient and gentle, trying to earn your heart. Think on how he hasn't envied your time with the children, how he's prayed and believed alongside you 'til your father returned to the Lord, how he's still hoped to capture your heart without asking you to sacrifice anything that was dear to you. For years, you put everyone's needs ahead of your own. Ty's come to town and done that for you."

She let out a small laugh. "Betsy, you're two peas in a pod. Surely God fashioned you to be together. Don't you think it's time both of you were free to receive love, too? The man adores you. You love him, don't you?"

"I do love him," Betsy confessed quietly. "He's everything I ever dreamed of as a young girl. I lost my heart to him weeks ago, but I couldn't ask him to take on my family." She smiled. "I guess I've been pretty silly—he's already done that from the day we met, but I lived by fret instead of by faith."

"That settles that! I'll bake the wedding cake," Elsa planned.

"We'll all finish that quilt for you," Clara agreed.

Samantha rubbed her hands gleefully. "I just got new fabric in. You can choose something pretty, and we'll make a dress for you, too!"

"I don't think I can go to him. It's so—so. . .bold!"

"Nonsense," Mrs. T said. "Ruth went to Boaz. That was way back in the Bible days when women were far more reserved. She did it; you can, too!"

"Oh, what will I say to him?" Betsy fretted.

Mrs. Tidewell drew her out of her chair and nudged her to the door. "Love will find a way."

Betsy started down the street. Her heart beat twice as fast as normal, and her boots scuffled the clumps of snow. Did she dare go speak her heart? The air was redolent with smoke from chimneys. As she drew closer to the smithy, she could hear Ty's mighty hammer at work. Her nerves jangled with every strike. *What do I say?* Moments later, it wasn't the metallic clang of hammer and anvil, but the solid sound of a mallet on wood.

The moment he spied her, Ty set down his mallet and hastened to her. "Betsy! What is it? Is our Greta all right?"

Our Greta. Samantha was right—at some point, Ty had already wormed his way right into the family. "She's fine."

He wrapped his hands around her arms. "What is it, then? Where is your cape? You're cold!" He pulled her close to the forge and briskly rubbed her arms. "Do you need something?"

I need you. The words sounded too stark, too forward. Betsy hitched a shoulder and shivered as he took her chilly hands in his, gently blew on them and rubbed them until they warmed. *How could I have doubted that this man loves me?*

"I was working on something special. Want to see it?"

She nodded.

Ty turned and lifted a big, wooden frame. As he swiveled, her jaw dropped open. A beaming smile lit his face. "The glass was broken in several places. I asked Mrs. Tidewell for a few patterns. This is the one she said would work best. What do you think?"

He'd taken the broken pane of glass and cut it into more pieces, then added in a few pieces of colored glass. He'd connected them with leaded cames into his own version of a stained glass window. "I got the pieces of blue and green glass from the peddler who came through last week. Elsa and Shane were by the other day. She said her grandma called this quilt pattern Old Maid's Puzzle."

She choked out, "Mrs. T calls it Old Maid's Choice."

"Don't you think it'll look wonderful in the cabin?"

Betsy reached out and tentatively ran her fingers over the edge of the frame. She whispered a quick prayer for courage, then asked, "Would you be willing to let me share this window with my youngers during the daytime if they still slept at Pa's each night?"

Ty stared at her, set down the window, and gathered her in his arms. "Sunshine, I'd share that window with them day and night if it meant you were mine."

"So this old maid doesn't have to make a choice between her family and the man she loves?"

"You're a beautiful young woman, not an old maid. Love, my sweet Betsy, isn't something that draws lines and shoves others out. Love is a bond that draws others in. You already took my heart. Are you ready to take my name?"

"Yes," she whispered before his lips met hers.

⁎

Two weeks later, as soon as the kids' coughs settled, everyone in Hickory Corners met at the church. Betsy wore the pretty yellow dress her friends helped her make. She wiggled her toes in the soft kid boots Ty had given her and brushed one last kiss on Pa's cheek before he walked her down the aisle.

The wedding ceremony was sacred and beautiful until Pastor Tidewell asked, "Do you, Tyson, take Elizabeth to be your wife—"

"No!" Greta cried. "No!" She stood up on the pew and burst into tears.

Betsy's heart flipped for a moment, but she squeezed Ty's hands and promised, "Give me a minute. I'll be right back."

Greta wasn't about to wait. She planted her little hands on her hips and piped out, "You marry our Betsy. Not 'Lizbeth. You're ours!"

Folks in the church muffled their laughter.

Ty kept hold of Betsy's hand. He led her over to Greta, and said very evenly, "Betsy is a little name. Your sister's whole, big name is Elizabeth—just like my name is Tyson, but you call me Ty."

Greta wound her arms around his neck and gave him a weak hug. "I didn't want nobody else to get you. You b'long to us!"

"Yes, I do," he agreed. "Now if you let go and sit back down with Smidgen, Betsy and I will finish here so you can have some yummy cake."

Later that afternoon, Ty carried Betsy over the threshold of their cabin. He kicked the door shut, and afternoon light flooded through his beautiful window and spilled across the quilt the sewing circle had finished just days before.

He kissed his bride long and deep, then set her down and held her close. "Welcome home, Sunshine."

Betsy beamed up at him. She knew she'd made the right choice.

JACOB'S LADDER

by Pamela Kaye Tracy

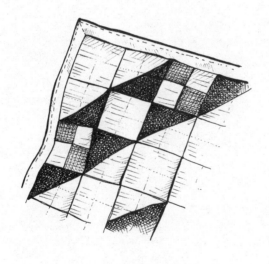

Chapter 1

S amantha Thomasohn loved weddings. . .until this one.

A footprint of melted snow glimmered on the wooden floor of the crowded church. Samantha snuck a look up and down the family pew, lifted her blue skirt, and placed her black leather boot over the wet spot. With the tip, she wrote, "No." Then, carefully, she enlarged the word. She'd been eighteen for a week, and so far nothing good had happened. She wanted seventeen back, and her mother. What if this melancholy feeling never went away? An itch developed under her white stocking, near her ankle. One more annoyance to add to her memories of 1838.

"Samantha, stop fidgeting." Zack's blond eyebrows pinched together in a frown. Only two years older, this brother —who looked so much like her, right down to the light-blond hair and slight build—always managed to make her feel amiss.

Samantha sighed. It was more than Zack making her feel out of sorts. This morning, at her father's insistence, she'd shed the black mourning dress she'd worn for *only* five months.

Zack elbowed her. Oh, it was fine for him to sit there all pious. He did not have to share quarters with the soon-to-be new Mrs. Thomasohn, a woman unknown to the family a mere two months prior. No, Zack would leave the wedding celebration, take his bride home to their farm, and the burden of dealing with a new stepmother would fall to Samantha. Thank goodness her papa hadn't indulged in a three-day wedding celebration like Zack. Of course, marrying in blustery, late February took some of the punch out of the fifty-year-old man.

The population of Hickory Corners stood. Zack took her elbow. Did he worry she wouldn't stand? Dare he think she might faint! Samantha clenched her teeth tightly and tried to breathe. Today couldn't be happening. It was all a dream, except there really was a woman walking up the aisle and a silly grin on a groom's face.

Across the aisle Betsy Larkin—er, Betsy Walker—leaned against her new husband. The sweet voice of Elsa Gerhard sounded from behind. Any other service, Samantha would listen and enjoy, but now the perfect harmony didn't belong. Today wasn't perfect, didn't deserve perfection, and Samantha wanted to scream. Elsa chirped on. Looking behind her, Samantha tried to send a warning glance to her friend. Instead, she caught the gaze of Jacob Stahl, and *he* winked.

How dare he! Fresh! Quickly Samantha turned to face the front, hoping he'd not noticed her face redden. This day couldn't get any worse. What if somebody had seen?

The bride stepped to the altar wearing the white silk that had arrived at the store months ago and been deemed too fancy by most of the female clientele. Cecilia hadn't batted an eye at the price tag or color. Samantha had refused the offer of a new dress. There'd be whispers as to why she wore her old blue linen. There'd be more whispers speculating why she'd shed the black.

Love? Could it happen in two months as her father claimed?

Looking over at Betsy and Ty, Samantha knew it could. And, if anything, Elsa sang even better since becoming Mrs. Gerhard.

The congregation sat, and Samantha stared at Cecilia's back. Brown hair coiled under a white veil. She looked so different from the woman who had been ushered into town a few months ago by river men. Then, grieving her husband, Cecilia's long hair hung in a tangled mess over garments too thin for the Ohio cold. Two hundred miles to the east and Cecilia might have called Fort Harmar home. One hundred miles to the west and Fort Washington would have been the lucky spot. Cecilia James settled in Hickory Corners, took a room at Elsa's boardinghouse, and started helping out Virginia Alexander, the dress shop owner.

Samantha's father, Silas Thomasohn, took a shirt over. At the time, Samantha puzzled over the fact. Her mother, Rachel, had patched his sleeves until last year. After her death, Samantha took over the job. The basket, the needles, the worn thimble all belonged to her mother. Touching them inspired beloved memories.

It took her father five shirts to woo the widow. The day after the wedding announcement, Samantha tucked the last of her mother's personal belongings into the old cedar chest and tried to hide the fact that with every fiber of her being she didn't want a stepmother.

The ceremony began. "No" dried into nothingness on the church floor. A silent cry unheeded by all. Samantha's brothers stared forward, unperturbed. Even Raymond, who'd hurried home from Ohio's Willoughby Medical University, seemed calm about the nuptials.

If only Mama had lived.

Up front, Noah Tidewell, the minister, looked to be enjoying himself. A tuft of white hair nodded in agreement to every word he said. He acted like it was every day a local businessman married a woman twenty-two years his junior. *Only nine years older than me,* Samantha thought, closing her eyes. Cecilia James—*oh, and with the minister's words it became Thomasohn*—claimed the same birth year as Samantha's oldest brother, Trevor.

Samantha tried to sneak a glance back at Jacob. He stared at her instead of straight ahead. The nerve of the man. Her stomach tightened. He'd traveled home with Raymond, intent on helping Doc. It had been a year since she'd last seen Jacob. Her memory had him patting the top of her head, *as if she were a child,* and going off with her brother. Just one scant year later, his chestnut hair was a bit longer, his shoulders a shade wider, and his manner a whole lot brasher.

Raymond intended to finish school and switch places with Jacob. Both men agreed that Doc's eyesight impaired him more than the crippling arthritis. Samantha suspicioned that Jacob was out of money, and thus his college days were over. The Stahls thought little of education. They were of the land. Samantha often heard Gunther Stahl question Jacob's choice of professions. When the Stahl men came into the store, they seemed to think that she heard nothing as they jawed about prices, crops, and Jacob.

Doc certainly never winked at women during church. Jacob must have learned a few things at college besides how to mend bones. His mother would be none too pleased. The Stahl family always set the perfect example of how one should behave during church services. Samantha shifted uncomfortably. Why was Jacob behind her instead of in front of her? Had the Stahls finally overflowed their favorite bench? Zack said if many more Stahls were born, they'd need to change the name of the town to Stahls' Corners.

"I do."

It was over. Done. Samantha had a stepmother.

"And you're seventeen, Dear?" Cecilia asked the first time they'd met. *"Why aren't you married?"*

Because I won't marry the first person who asks, Samantha had thought, *and because I'm happy where I am.*

Never mind that no one had asked. It hadn't mattered until today, when suddenly Samantha wasn't happy.

The minister called for a prayer. Samantha bowed her head. She'd been continually praying Cecilia would disappear. Instead, today, the woman would be moving into the upstairs of the mercantile. Obviously God wasn't listening to Samantha Ann Thomasohn.

Zack cleared his throat. A sound designed to inspire reverence. If she ignored that first hint, she'd get nudged again.

I will not cry.

Silas Thomasohn beamed as the congregation stood. Well-wishers surged forward. Zack touched Samantha's elbow, meaning to usher her up front. Always the brother to make sure appearances were met, Zack usually had the shovel ready before the snow flurried. Shrugging off his hand, Samantha tried to turn down the middle aisle.

Zack's fingers gripped her elbow. "Papa is expecting you."

She'd sensed Jacob's presence before she saw him. Was it a scent? A feeling?

He easily removed her from Zack's grip. "Samantha, Mrs. Crabtree was hoping you'd open up the store so she can get a few staples before heading out to your brother's."

The slight beard and mustache were new. Samantha didn't like facial hair, much. And, she certainly hadn't liked the wink. Still, Jacob was offering her an opportunity to escape.

"That can wait—" Zack began.

With a jerk, Samantha freed her elbow and clutched at Jacob's sleeve, noticing for the first time how he towered over her. At five feet, three inches, everyone towered over her—just not with Jacob's bearing. Oh, pshaw, the wedding had befuddled her. "I'll go right away. Thanks for fetching me."

The sting of winter greeted her at the church's door. Samantha breathed deeply till it almost hurt.

"I'll help you." Jacob's voice came right at her ear.

117

He took her cape from the peg and handed it to her. How he knew the correct one, Samantha had no idea. His fingers brushed hers, and she shivered. The cape dropped to the floor. Samantha bent to pick it up and finally scratched at the spot just above her ankle. So what if Jacob Stahl thought her unladylike. Truly this day could get no worse. Her father remarried, and she acting clumsy in front of Jacob Stahl. As if he mattered. He shouldn't have winked. He was her brother's friend, not hers.

She felt so removed from everything. As if her world tilted and suddenly she no longer stood on firm ground. Taking a deep breath, and holding her chin steady, she marched toward the mercantile.

⁘

Jacob watched Samantha. He'd never seen her so tense. Looked like the little princess really disliked having Cecilia James as a stepmother. That Samantha had managed to stay single nigh until age eighteen was an answered prayer. He'd wait a bit longer, to let her get over the misgivings she had with her stepmother. When he took her hand in marriage, he'd know that she was leaving home *to be* with him and not leaving home to *get away* from Cecilia Thomasohn.

God would show him when the time was right.

Jacob believed in prayer.

So did Olivia Crabtree, who marched with Samantha toward the mercantile. She had Samantha all picked out for her son. Martin Crabtree had graduated from college last semester and was apprenticing with a lawyer in Capital City. To Jacob's notice, Martin had no designs on Samantha.

Only God knew Jacob's feelings. Samantha was sunshine and elegance, and Jacob was nothing more than an oversized bear. He admired her high-spiritedness and the way she so easily shone during the town's spelling bees. He liked to see a woman add a sum in her head and challenge the town miser.

Jacob had fallen in love with Samantha the day she'd tricked Oskar Bedloe into paying his mercantile bill. She'd been fifteen, with blond hair pulled back in a knot that showed the graceful curve of her neck. Her cheeks had been flushed.

Jacob liked the thought that he could bring a blush to her cheeks. He'd make the wedding celebration at Trevor's an opportunity. The cocoon of Samantha's family was hatching open, exposing her to the world, and maybe he'd be the one to help her spread her wings.

But, first, he needed to get there. Jacob walked to the barbershop. The red-and-white-striped pole symbolized haircuts and surgery. The curtains were drawn. Doc's hands could no more manage the scissors than they could the knife. So far, no one seemed interested in trusting their hair to Jacob. Pushing open the door, he took the stairs two at a time until he got to Doc's rooms. For years, Doc had lived in one room while using the other for patients. Now both rooms were for patients, Doc being one.

"How was the wedding?" Doc's deep voice belied his condition. A person might expect the man to jump out of bed and do a jig, so strong was the sound. Only when the listener saw his glassy eyes and gnarled fingers did the truth dawn.

Covering Doc's feet with a blanket, Jacob answered, "Seemed like most weddings. It was too long."

"I stood up with Silas when he married Rachel."

"Really? I wasn't aware of that." Jacob adjusted Doc's pillow and grasped the frail man by the arms. He pulled him to a sitting position and placed a water glass on the bedside table.

"Silas wasn't a rich man then. No, his family came from New York. They were craftsmen. The money was Rachel's."

"The Gustefans are good people."

"They are, and Silas was the peddler."

Jacob blinked. "He was?"

"Yes, he'd come through twice a year. He always had a treat for Rachel. Got so she looked forward to his comings. Then, she looked forward to him."

"I didn't know that."

"It caused a stir for awhile, then they built the store and started nesting."

"He has such bearing."

"Sometimes confidence comes from inside, not from your surroundings."

"And is that my piece of advice for today?" Jacob smiled as he held the water glass up to Doc's mouth. Doc often dispensed medical wisdom; today the topic had turned to something a bit more personal.

"Go after what you want."

"Oh, I intend to."

"She's worth it."

Jacob blinked. "And you'd be talking about?"

"Miss Samantha."

"And how—"

"You talk in your sleep, Boy. Don't think you're ever going to be able to keep many secrets from a wife."

Chapter 2

If March intended to go out like a lamb, it had better hurry, Samantha decided. She propped herself up on one elbow and peeped out the window while still cocooned in the warmth of her bed. She let the curtain go and lay back down. It was time to get up, but she didn't want to.

The comfort of the green and yellow quilt wrapped her in a momentary peace. She'd been seven years old when Mama put the quilting needle in her hand. Her feet hadn't even touched the floor as she sat beside Rachel Thomasohn. Hunched over the quilting frame, Samantha learned about the family and how the girls were always slight of build. She'd learned how to behave around boys, and about her mother falling in love with her father. It seemed like the past was sewn right into the threads of the Shoo Fly, their first quilt. Samantha stroked a ragged corner. Some of the stitches, probably hers, were breaking loose.

Outside, a plop of snow fell from the roof and hit the ground. The sound reminded Samantha of other March mornings and snowball fights with her brothers. She wished Raymond still lived at home. The three rooms above the mercantile echoed with the footsteps of three people tiptoeing around each other. Raymond would joke the rooms back into being a home. No matter how Samantha tried, she couldn't muster the effort, and it had been over four weeks.

She shivered as her bare feet touched the cold, wooden floor. Hurrying, she found her slippers. She rid her hair of the rags she'd slept in. Since Mama died, she'd rarely managed a decent curl. She took her day dress from the peg, slipped it on, and picked up her brush. Instead of brushing twenty-five strokes, as Mama had suggested, she did ten before heading downstairs. She wanted to help Cecilia open the store, and then be off to the sewing circle. Lately, it had been her only source of comfort. Not that she dared share her unhappiness with her friends. Mrs. Tidewell would quote a scripture about selfishness and remind Samantha that her father was lonely.

No, Father wasn't lonely, but Samantha was, and she didn't know how to rid herself of the feeling. For the first time in eighteen years, Samantha's prayers were full of muttering what-ifs instead of heartfelt thanks. She never felt better after "amen."

Hurrying through the main room, Samantha stopped to bury her face in Mouse's fur. The cat slept—without complaint—in the box Cecilia made for it, right next to the Franklin stove. He meowed now, annoyed at his nap's interruption. The sound perked Samantha up, taking away a bit of the silence. Father must be at the docks supervising a load. Cecilia would either be downstairs in the store or over at Virginia's dress shop. Checking the weather out the back door, Samantha saw it was cold enough for snow but not cold enough to beg off fetching the water. She changed from her slippers to her boots. Grabbing her cloak and the water bucket, Samantha headed outside to the community well. In the summer, the green grass and the daffodils encouraged her steps. In the winter, the wind pushed against her, warning her away. Fetching water was her least favorite chore, Cecilia's, too, which was why the job now daily fell to Samantha. When Mama was alive, they'd taken turns.

Old snow, streaked with gray and footprints, crunched underfoot. Samantha shivered and hurried. The well waited behind Oskar Bedloe's shop. Perhaps because of her mood, it seemed to regress into the distance as she hurried closer.

Only one other person fought the winter wind. Samantha knew better than to offer help to Charlotte Warner, who drew on the rope to the well. The gray-haired widow pooh-poohed the assistance of others. She claimed the day she couldn't take care of herself was the day she wanted to go meet her maker.

"Surprised to see you here," Mrs. Warner said.

"Why?" Samantha sat down on a stone bench to wait her turn.

"You been by to see Betsy?"

Samantha fidgeted with a hole forming in the mitten of her right hand. She needed to mend it, but had forgotten. Like she'd completely forgotten that Betsy's little sister, Greta, was sick. And that Betsy was torn between caring for her new husband and taking care of a little sister who grew weaker every day.

Like Mama had.

Sickness Samantha could deal with; death had her running scared.

"Has something new happened?" Samantha asked slowly. Betsy was an elbow cousin and almost like a sister at times.

"I saw Doc Stahl's sleigh go by last night. Didn't see it return, couldn't stay awake that long. I hoped you had news."

"No." Samantha clutched her bucket tighter, almost wishing the cold would seep through her mittens so she'd have something to jar her into action. So, Jacob was at Betsy's again. Since returning to town last month, he'd been away just as often as when he'd been at school. Only once had she seen him at church. The townspeople buzzed about all the good he was doing. It bothered Samantha that she felt the urge to know his whereabouts. It also bothered her how little she'd done to help out Betsy. She'd change that today. "Thanks for letting me know what's going on. I'll let you know when I find out."

"You do that, Girl." The look Charlotte Warner gave Samantha sent chills down her spine. Samantha had seen that look before. Master Jarrod had used it when he'd caught her letting one of the younger students copy sums from her slate. Mrs. Tidewell had used it when Samantha was nine years old and threw a doll in the baptismal to see if it would float or sink. Father used it last night, when Samantha had sassed Cecilia.

The bucket seemed weighed down by more than water as Samantha trudged back to the store. Little Greta had been bedridden for weeks, ever since Silas and

Cecilia's wedding. Both the Walkers and Jacob Stahl had been called away from the wedding reception almost as they walked in the door. Betsy had missed three sewing circles because of Greta. Clara and Elsa, missed too, when they were helping Betsy. Samantha tried to quell the shame that spread through her. In a town the size of Hickory Corners, Samantha was one of the few too busy drowning in her own sorrows to lend a helping hand with Greta.

Twenty-seven steps it took to get to the upstairs dwelling of the Thomasohns'. In summer weather, Samantha could make it without spilling a drop. In winter, it took more effort. Today she didn't lose any. And the bucket just got heavier.

"Good morning." Cecilia's words were cordial. The hem of her new pink linen dress barely missed brushing the floor. The smell of frying bacon lingered in the air.

"Good morning." It sounded like a croak to Samantha's ears. The kitchen table, which had for so long dominated the middle of the room, now resided against one wall. Cecilia's doing. It looked so small. When the three of them sat there, Samantha felt cramped. Her feet curled in fear of contacting Cecilia's. Samantha often thought she'd not manage to swallow.

"Your father is still at the dock. I thought we'd eat breakfast then clean up the store a little." Cecilia dumped the water into the pitcher. She poured two glasses and motioned toward the table.

Mouse curled on Samantha's chair. Picking him up, Samantha cleared her throat. "If you don't mind, I'd like to go over to the Larkins' and help. Charlotte said that Greta took a turn for the worse. I'll imagine Betsy is beside herself."

Cecilia nodded. "I can start in the store."

Thirty minutes later, as Samantha marched up the front walk to Betsy's old house, the thought occurred, *The store isn't dirty and just what is Cecilia starting?*

-:⁑:-

Jacob closed his hands around Greta's fingers. They were cold and limp. He'd been there for over four hours and couldn't think of a thing he'd done to improve Greta's health. *Father, this is one of Your precious ones. She is much beloved. I fear that I am too unskilled to help her. Guide me, Lord. She is in Your hands.*

"Well," Betsy encouraged, "what are you going to try now?"

He'd been doctoring Hickory Corners and the neighboring towns for all of a month and already knew that worriers came in all shapes and sizes. There were the weepers: they weren't much good, as they huddled in the corner and gasped out answers to his questions. There were the gripers: they thought he took too long to get to them. Why they could have died! They spent their time scolding him as he tried to help them and their families. There were also the misers. How dare he act like they owed him something for his visit. Indeed, they'd begun to feel better minutes before he arrived, but since he was there, it would do for him to give an opinion. And there were the helpers: Betsy Walker rated as queen of that list. He figured if he asked her to climb on the roof and sing a ditty, she'd do it if she thought it would help Greta.

"I think you ought to let me take her to Doc's."

Betsy's eyebrows raised. "I can put on another quilt, if you think that will help. You trying to bring on a sweat?"

"No, I just think she'd be more comfortable."

"Kids, go outside." Betsy ordered.

The other Larkin children bundled into their winter clothes and were out the door in minutes, too subdued to argue.

"Tell me the truth," Betsy ordered.

"She's not getting any better. I want to keep a closer eye on her."

"What do you think is wrong?"

"I'm thinking it is pneumonia, but it could be typhoid fever."

Betsy collapsed against the wall, her face as pale as Greta's. Jacob knew why. He'd already lost a little girl up toward Wabash Springs, the same symptoms, just last week.

Jacob didn't intend to lose Greta, but unless he got her temperature down, inflammation of the kidneys or an ear infection would follow.

Betsy didn't look convinced, and Jacob wished he had more of a way with words. He needed a wife to advise him on how to speak to the women. Doc always said that the ladies often wouldn't tell doctors what was ailing them due to embarrassment. Now was not the time to be thinking about wives—and that meant Samantha— Greta needed his attention.

Betsy took a drawer from the dresser and started packing. "She can come home with me. I should of thought of it earlier. It will be much easier?"

Jacob started to move toward Betsy. Poor woman had enough on her plate. Just as he let go of Greta's hand, he heard a thump upon the door and then a hesitant knocking.

"It's Pa," Betsy said. "He's not going to like this."

But it was Samantha Thomasohn, opening the door against the cold and looking like she'd faint dead away. Still, Jacob had to admire her. She stood shivering from the cold, with her chin in the air, clutching her reticule like it was her only hold on sanity. Behind her stood the other Larkin children. The look on their faces said it all. Sickness was no stranger to this clan.

"What can I do to help?" Samantha herded the children to the kitchen table. Everyone looked at Betsy. She held onto a nightgown of Greta's and frowned. Jacob started to stand, but stayed crouched. The little girl, if possible, had grown even hotter to the touch.

As if realizing she was the center of attention, Greta woke up and whined.

"I'm so glad you're here," Betsy said.

Jacob wasn't sure if the words were directed to her siblings or to Samantha. Giving Greta a quick pat on the shoulder, he moved over to Samantha. "Take the drawer and put it in the sleigh. Betsy, you need to talk to the little ones. It will frighten them that Greta is gone."

Betsy lay the last nightgown in the drawer and nodded.

"I'll get Greta settled over at your place," Samantha said. "I want to."

A few minutes later, Jacob stopped the sleigh in front of Betsy and Ty's place. He tethered the horses before reaching for Greta. He wanted to help Samantha down, but she followed too quickly. He heard her behind him. Even taking careful steps, her shoes were slippery. Silly female whim. Her feet might look small and dainty in the pretty, black leather boots, but the hard, flat sole acted much like an ice skate. If he weren't already carrying Greta, he'd sweep Samantha off her feet to keep her from falling.

"Jacob, you feeling all right?" Samantha stared at him.

He'd gone right to their door and stopped. Greta stared at him, awake, not coughing, and curious.

"Come on, then." Jacob pushed open the front door and carried Greta the few steps to Betsy's bed. Soon the little girl snuggled into the sheets. She probably smelled Betsy and felt secure. Jacob checked her pulse and tongue. No change since he'd done that the first time an hour earlier. "Greta, does it hurt when you breathe?"

"Um dra hgum now." Greta closed her eyes and went to sleep.

Jacob pulled the blanket up to the child's shoulders. "What did she say?"

Samantha settled on the edge of the bed. "She said it doesn't hurt now."

Chapter 3

At six foot, Jacob was the runt of the Stahl litter and had an easygoing manner that his family lacked. He'd helped Raymond with pranks, mimicked Zack's seriousness at times, and always listened closely when Trevor read aloud to the family. When he'd played at Samantha's house, he'd bossed her as bad as her brothers had.

At the schoolhouse, and even the few times she'd seen him at her home, she'd considered Jacob clumsy, inept. But now his fingers worked magic as he bathed Greta's forehead. The little girl went to sleep, soothed by the gentle touch of a man who couldn't roll a decent snowball. Only the child's labored breathing broke the silence in the room.

Samantha was suddenly very aware that she was practically alone with Jacob. Stepping back, she tried to focus on something—anything—else. Betsy's home smelled of gingerbread and peppermint. No, Betsy's home smelled of gingerbread. Jacob Stahl smelled of peppermint.

Pushing herself off the bed, Samantha stepped closer to him. "What can I do to help?"

"Boil some water. Steam will help her breathing."

Glad for something to do, Samantha hauled the black cast-iron pot from the fireplace and went outside. The slim piles of snow still holding their own at the Walker place were a tad cleaner than in town. Samantha scooped handfuls into the pot and hustled back toward the house. Since March hadn't turned, the wicked wind sent tendrils of frost inside Samantha's cape.

Betsy came running up the road, caught up with Samantha, and hurried to the front door. Samantha struggled to follow. Her bonnet blew back, and blond hair streamed behind her, caught in the wind that strained to keep her outside.

Samantha shivered then, not from the cold, but from the realization that Betsy was hurting and no matter how much help was offered, hers was a pain to be borne alone. They'd tried steam on Mama, too. And Samantha had made countless trips to the well to keep the water supplied.

The door closed behind them. Samantha took the pot to the fire and hung it on the spit. Jacob left Greta's side, opened his doctor's bag, and withdrew a bag. Samantha recognized pulverized Peruvian bark. Her father carried it at the store.

"What do we do now?" Betsy asked her favorite question.

Jacob's lips formed a thin line as he gave a slight shrug and pulled the blanket tighter about the child's shoulders.

The seconds ticked by, and the room grew smaller. Jacob's attention focused on Greta. Betsy put away Greta's belongings and all but collapsed on the kitchen table.

Ten minutes later, with a bundle of laundry—the least she could do—Samantha headed home. Her boots clamored on the slick, frozen ground. Struggling to keep her balance, she passed the sheriff's office, and the cold wrapped around her. She told herself the sharp, prickling sensations were penance for being selfish—for leaving Betsy alone; but in the pit of her stomach and even in the back of her mind, she knew herself a coward.

Once home, she climbed the stairs and dumped the clothes in the hamper. Usually, home was the place Samantha Thomasohn most wanted to be. She hadn't appreciated the security of her family enough. She wanted to be involved in a family Bible reading, with Raymond tickling the back of her feet, trying to make her laugh so she'd get in trouble. She wanted to watch the face of Zack as he nodded in agreement to everything Father said. She missed the homey feeling that settled in her stomach when Trevor took his turn reading the Scriptures.

Thumps, from downstairs, echoed through the room and jarred Samantha from her melancholy. Father never unloaded during business hours. He insisted that stocking should take place either early morning or late at night. And Father hadn't returned yet with the wagon.

The door leading down to the store stood open. Samantha took a few hesitant steps and stopped. Even from there she could see the changes. Bolts of material now took up space on the top shelf of the east wall. Coffee grinders were arranged artistically on the high shelf behind the counter.

"What do you think?" Cecilia grinned. A streak of dirt across her nose made her look even younger.

"I think you've put much of our stock out of my reach."

"What do you mean?"

"I mean that if someone comes in wanting to buy a sausage gun or meat chopper, I won't be able to sell it to them, unless of course the customer happens to be six-foot tall and can reach it themselves."

"Why—"

"Who told you you could do this?" Samantha's stomach hurt. She put one hand on the wall to help her stand straight. No way did she want to hunch over and show weakness.

It didn't look like Cecilia felt any stress. The woman's eyes blazed. "Nobody told me. I thought—"

"You're changing everything!"

"I'm just trying to help."

"You call this help? I can't reach anything. I wish you'd just go—"

"Samantha, that's enough." Father stood at the top of the stairs. His hair, once dark brown and thick, now mimicked the picture of a monk Samantha had seen in one of Master Jarrod's many books. At the moment, what was left of Father's hair stuck out in jagged lines, half frozen from the Ohio winter and anger.

"But—"

"You will apologize to Cecilia."

Samantha's lips went dry. Her tongue snaked out, back in, and her mouth went as dry as her lips.

"Now."

"I'm not sorry." Her voice betrayed her, becoming an embarrassing squeak.

Father moved closer. Even the echo from his boots sounded fierce. The back of Samantha's throat tightened. Those stupid tears; they were trying to surface.

"I'm sorry."

Before her father could say another word, before Cecilia could open her mouth and really bring tears to Samantha's eyes, she sailed out of Thomasohn's Mercantile. She only managed the boardwalk and a few steps toward Oskar's before bumping into a solid form. Anybody sensible would have moved.

"Whoa, whoa. And what sends a comely gal fleeing without a coat?"

The funny thing was. . .anger had a warmth to it, and Samantha didn't feel a single chill, although she noted the difference when a black frock went around her shoulders.

"When did you get back in town, Martin?" If possible, Samantha noted, he had grown handsomer. Yet the observance didn't pool in the pit of Samantha's stomach like it usually did.

"This morning. Now what vexation has you knocking me over in the street?"

"If I was knocking you over in the street, Martin Crabtree, I'd certainly have waited until a cart was going by!" The words came easily, slipping from her tongue like the hot butter on Elsa Gerhard's sourdough rolls.

"You wound my heart, Samantha. Now, who wounded yours?"

Tossing back her head, and glad that she could blame her tearing eyes on the weather, Samantha forced a grin. "Ah, but you have to have a heart in order for it to be wounded. I've probably given mine away while you've been gone."

Martin laughed. He plucked off his Cumberland top hat and set it on her head. It was too big and quickly blinded her. The buoyancy of her curls made the hat lopsided. He tucked her hand in his elbow. "Walk with me over to Elsa's."

Samantha pushed the hat up. Martin didn't deserve her wrath. He was an innocent bystander in the path of her anger.

"Come on, Mantha, you know you can't stay vexed long."

He tickled her under the chin and forced a smile from her. Martin was considered a prize by all of the eligible young ladies in Hickory Corners. Her *oma*, Rosie Gustefan, said he could charm the starch out of fresh laundry. Samantha began to calm down and even forgave him for calling her Mantha.

"Come with me while I call on Elsa." Without any further encouragement, Martin tugged Samantha across the street. Each step took her farther away from the mercantile and the ugly memory of what had just happened inside.

The Hickory Corners Boardinghouse offered warmth, not just from the roaring fireplace. Elsa and Shane had created a real showplace. The dining room, once outfitted with hand-hewn benches and uneven tables, now sported a set of furniture unequaled in Hickory Corners. It was the rocker in the corner of the room that caught Samantha's eye. Working in the store had given her an eye for craftsmanship, and this piece didn't come from the hands of Nate Harmon, the cabinet maker. Harmon was good, but this was exquisite.

"Where did you get this?"

"Jacob Stahl."

Samantha rubbed the fine-grained hickory wood with the tips of her fingers and remembered the sounds of Raymond and Jacob whistling as they sat on the side stairs whittling. It had been over a month since he'd had the audacity to wink at her. Oh, what was Jacob Stahl doing on her mind! And especially when Martin, in his double-breasted tailcoat and tight-fitting trousers, still had his hand on her arm long past the time he should have let go.

⋯

Jacob rubbed the sleep from his eyes as he exited Betsy's home. Little Greta had finally fallen into a healing sleep, at least he hoped it was a healing sleep. At college, many of the professors held fast to the ideas of Benjamin Rush. Steaming was one of the great man's favorite cures. So far, Jacob could not add any names under the list of those cured by steam. If Greta didn't show some improvement soon, Jacob intended to try a treatment of calomel.

The horses stamped their impatience. They wanted the livery and food. Normally, Jacob would have walked to the Larkins', but he'd started his morning with two distant house calls before settling down with Greta. Jacob clucked and drove them the mile into town. After turning the reins over to the livery owner, Leonard Melvin, Jacob headed for Doc's place. In the irony of fate, Doc was improving while Greta sagged. Doc's aged body daily grew stronger, not from steam or purging, but from sheer will to survive.

The ancient clock above Doc's mantel showed ten o'clock. Jacob picked up the key and wound it. Doc was sleeping, not an unreasonable pastime for a man of his age and health. His forehead was cool and his breathing even. Without waking Doc, Jacob rubbed Professor Low's liniment on the old man's hands, paying special attention to the joints. No matter how many times Jacob reminded Doc to lubricate his hands, he didn't do it.

When there wasn't a patient in the other room, Jacob used it. Since he hadn't made the bed, he took the time to do it, then glanced at the cradle on the floor near the window. Elsa Gerhard was turning into a regular customer. The cradle was a prize. He was tempted to keep it and make Elsa another. A Stahl child would look fine in the contraption.

The thought of a babe turned into a vision of Samantha seated in a rocking chair like the one he'd made Elsa and Shane. He could see her Madonna-like features soften as she looked at a babe in her arms, their babe.

All thoughts of sleep vanished. Jacob went to the basin and splashed cold water on his face. Samantha had surprised him this morning. First, she'd shown up to help. Second, she'd looked at him as a man, rather than as her brother's annoying friend.

Well, maybe she'd given him a similar expression when he'd winked at her during church.

Since her mother's death, Samantha had avoided illness with a determination unequaled. Was a bit of healing finally coming along? Jacob figured if that was true, then maybe the time had come to act. So far the only hint he'd given Samantha that he was interested was that wink at church. Winking might have gotten her attention but was not all that fulfilling.

He changed his shirt, stuck a peppermint in his mouth, and picked up the cradle. Might as well deliver it before Elsa headed to the sewing group she so loved on Tuesdays. Besides, Samantha and Elsa always walked together. If he timed delivery just right, he might get to wink—or something more—with the girl he intended sparking.

Chapter 4

Jacob adjusted the cradle under his arm and took a deep breath of the March crispness. Most of the people who scurried along Main Street were bundled up against the cold. They held the neck of their cloaks together and wrapped their chins with brightly colored scarves. Not him! He relished the brisk breeze that reminded him how good it was to be alive.

His jubilation waned as his thoughts returned to Greta. Somehow it didn't seem right for him to be in high spirits when at Miss Betsy's a small child struggled to breathe. He'd pore over Doc's medical books again when he got back to the barbershop. Surely there was something he'd missed, some remedy yet to try.

Just as he turned the corner, Olivia Crabtree came out of the dress shop. Her black mourning dress, worn since he was knee high to a grasshopper, knew better than to brush the ground. She didn't clutch her coat or wear a scarf. Weather didn't seem to affect her. She tipped her head to the side, an inquisitive gesture by anyone else but from her more a demand, eyed the cradle, and asked, "Is that for Elsa?"

Jacob didn't know how she did it, but Mrs. Crabtree was the only woman in town who had her dark and graying hair drawn so tightly into its bun, it didn't dare move. He'd soon make some extra money from prescribing headache powders. Forcing a pleasant smile, he responded, "Yes, what do you think?"

She pressed her thin lips together and stepped closer, clearly hoping to find a flaw. Begrudgingly she admitted, "I'm thinking someday you'll be making one for my boy and his wife."

Jacob's fingers grasped the cradle harder. To his knowledge, Martin had yet to act on his mother's advice, but then, being a dandy took up a lot of his time. With the ink on his law degree still drying, Martin just might be thinking it was time to settle down. Mrs. Crabtree would be talking up Samantha.

Jacob studied the cradle. Yes, he should have kept this one, but if he knew Samantha, she'd be pleased he chose to give it to her friend.

Samantha was free, done mourning, and much too gentle to deserve a mother-in-law like Mrs. Crabtree. The woman didn't know how to smile. It was unnatural.

He hoisted the cradle onto his shoulder, uttered a terse excuse, and hurried to the boardinghouse. It was well past noon, yet as he opened the door and stepped inside he heard voices coming from the dining room. Jacob followed the sound. Samantha sat in his rocking chair. Next to her, with his hand on her arm, stood Martin.

She was wearing his coat and hat.

They looked good together.

Samantha's gaze met Jacob's. She reached up and took Martin's hat off. Handing it back, she shrugged his hand off her arm and started to slip out of his coat. Martin silently helped her.

Once, years ago, Jacob watched as a fox grabbed his mother's prize chicken. An uncanny grin graced the carnivore's face as it made off with its booty. Smug was too polite a word.

Martin Crabtree looked a bit like a fox.

Jacob Stahl had often been compared to a bear.

No way was the fox getting the prize this time.

"Jacob." Elsa rushed toward him. "Are you finished with my cradle already? I figured it would be at least another week."

He carefully set it on the floor. "I've had some sleepless nights."

Samantha's eyes turned misty. Were the tears still from this morning? From watching little Greta suffer? Jacob wished he were standing next to Samantha. He'd do more than touch her shoulder. He'd sweep her into his arms and promise her the moon. Well, he'd promise her undying love anyway, which was all he, a struggling doctor, had to offer.

Shane helped his wife to her feet and picked up the cradle. "Where do you want it, Wife?" His jovial tone and dancing hazel eyes were aimed at Elsa.

Envy took hold of Jacob, not a comfortable or familiar feeling. Martin was standing too close to the woman Jacob wanted. Jacob didn't like it one bit. "I saw your mother, Martin. She said she'd someday order one for you."

"Did she now? I say a cradle's a fine place for storing fire kindling. Don't you agree, Samantha?"

"Hush," Elsa said. "Such nonsense. Come on, Samantha, let's go to my room, and you can help me decide where to put it."

Before Jacob had time to catch his breath, the Gerhards and Samantha were gone. Martin remained behind the rocking chair, fingering his hat and grinning.

A good general always prepared for battle. Jacob hadn't realized how close to camp the enemy had maneuvered. With fierce determination, he forced himself to study Martin Crabtree as a possible adversary.

Martin eyed him with a gleam. "It would bother you to make a cradle for me, wouldn't it?"

"No, not a bit."

"Good, then maybe you should see about assembling the piece. I mean, no sense waiting for the last minute. You never know what might happen."

"I'll wait a bit."

"Really, you think there might be surprises in store?"

"No, I don't think. I know."

⁘

Elsa barely gave Shane time to place the cradle on the floor of their bedroom. Nudging him past the oak vanity and out the door, she whirled to face her friend.

Samantha protested, "Really, Elsa, Shane probably wants to help decide—"

"Oh, pooh, he'll rearrange it the way he wants later. Now he's talking about ordering me one of those fancy bathtubs. He read that half of Pittsburgh owns one. Imagine," Elsa patted her swollen abdomen, "as if I could even fit into one." Perching on the edge of the bed, Elsa pulled Samantha down with her, folded her hands in her lap, and with an amused expression asked, "So, do tell."

"Do tell what?"

"I mean, when you walked in with Martin, I wasn't a bit surprised. You've swooned over him since first primer, but then in walks Jacob Stahl, of all people, and suddenly I saw two men sizing up the territory."

"They didn't," Samantha insisted. Her stomach lurched. Maybe they had.

"You've taken off the black. You're beautiful and of marrying age. It makes sense the men will come courting."

"It's too soon," Samantha whispered.

"That's not the problem." Elsa's foot tapped on the floor, a steady *trip, trap, trip,* of reproach.

"Things keep changing." Samantha knew her friend only meant to give comfort, but the walls were closing in. Elsa was married, with a babe on the way. Betsy had a ring on her finger. Not only did Samantha feel alone within her family, but also her friends were growing up and away faster than she could count to ten.

"Jacob's a good man," Elsa said.

"So is Martin."

"Martin has his moments, I'll agree. But think, you know Martin will never stay here. We've no need of a lawyer, and he'll chafe under the dictatorship of that mother of his."

Samantha stood up and offered Elsa a hand, changing the subject as she did. "That reminds me. Martin brought news from your sister."

It worked. Elsa put a hand to her heart and scurried from the room amazingly fast for a woman in her condition.

Samantha followed slowly. Elsa was right, Martin would never stay in Hickory Corners. Moving would be good, Samantha decided. She wouldn't have to watch Cecilia contrive to change the look of Mama's home. Moving would be bad—Samantha changed her mind. Everything that had ever spelled comfort was right here in Hickory Corners.

"Samantha, we're late! Mrs. T will wonder what's keeping us." Elsa's voice dragged Samantha from her musings. Looking at the grandfather clock Shane had shipped in as a wedding present for Elsa, Samantha quickened her step.

"Keep the coat," Martin suggested, handing it to her. "I'll fetch it tonight when I come calling."

Before she knew what she was doing, Samantha looked at Jacob. His chin jerked to one side and back, a minute indication of *no*.

Samantha blinked. What was she thinking? Looking to Jacob Stahl for permission! "That would be fine, Mr. Crabtree. I'll tell Papa to expect you at seven." Grabbing Elsa's hand, she barely gave her friend time to grab a cloak before pushing her out the front door.

"Don't say it," Samantha warned as they hustled up the street toward Mrs. T's.

"Don't say it? You've got to be joshing. I can hardly wait to tell Betsy. Do you think she'll be there?"

"No, Greta's taken a turn for the worse. Jacob and I—"

"Jacob and you?"

"No, not us together. He was already at Betsy's house when I went to help this morning."

Elsa gave Samantha a hug as they turned onto Birch Street. "And to think I was worrying this winter would be dull. I do believe Hickory Corners is due for a high time."

Mrs. T opened the door and hustled the girls in. The minister's wife always kept the stove hot and the sweets ready on quilting day. "Samantha, I'm sending Brady to your father's store. He stopped by earlier. Seemed right concerned about your whereabouts." Squinting, Mrs. T stepped closer. "Did you get a new coat?"

Clara jumped in. "Is that a man's frock?"

"I'm wearing it for a bit," Samantha defended. "It means nothing."

"Martin Crabtree's," Elsa piped in.

"He happened along, and I was cold."

"Where were you? When did Martin get back in town? Why—"

"Girls." Mrs. T expertly stalled Clara's questions. "Let's settle down, and perhaps Samantha will fill us in. . . ."

Samantha shook her head.

"And perhaps not." Mrs. T left the room, and soon the girls heard her calling Brady's name.

Samantha slipped from the room and caught hold of Brady's shoulder before he headed for the store. The Tidewells' nephew was pretty easygoing. He wouldn't mind traipsing through town with a flowered basket.

"Brady, will you ask for my sewing basket, please?"

Deep blue eyes twinkled. "Why, Miz Samantha, if you can walk through town in a man's frock, I'll surely get by with your sewing basket." He laughed all the way out the front door.

The girls busied themselves at the quilting frame. Elsa saved Samantha from more questions by chattering about the upcoming baby. Although, from the looks Elsa cast Samantha, the subject was not dropped.

Mrs. T delved into her Bible, not bothering to join the girls at the frame. She left the Scriptures to accept Samantha's basket, then delved back in, a troubled look on her face. Samantha knew the minister's wife looked forward to the sewing circle as much as the girls did. Betsy's absence left a void. Mrs. T probably hunted for Scriptures of comfort.

Glancing over at Clara Bucey, Samantha noted that she'd already turned the point of the Pieced Star. Not one stitch had Samantha managed. Running her finger along the silver dimples of her mother's thimble, she remembered the first time she'd tried it on. She'd been five, and it had slipped right off her finger.

Mama's thimble. Samantha blinked back tears and tried to shake the sadness. Instead, she shivered.

"I'm going to read today from the Book of Ephesians," Mrs. T said softly. "Chapter six, the first few verses: 'Children, obey your parents in the Lord: for this is right. Honour thy father and mother; which is the first commandment with promise; That it may be well with thee, and thou mayest live long on the earth.'"

Strange, Samantha considered, the verse had nothing to lessen the pall of Betsy's absence.

The thimble slipped from Samantha's finger and fell to the floor.

"Oh." Clara immediately pushed back her chair and went to her knees. "I don't see it."

Samantha gently rubbed her left middle finger. It felt warm and tender, much like her heart.

Elsa peered under the quilt's edge. Mrs. T started to stand up. The frame trembled as Clara crawled through to the other side.

"It's lost," Clara announced.

So am I, Samantha thought.

Chapter 5

S amantha couldn't remember the schoolroom being more crowded for a Friday Night Social. Enterprising men had moved some of the benches from the church so families would have a place to sit. Older children stood against the wall. Master Jarrod sat at his desk. Usually the schoolhouse was as tidy as Mrs. T's house, *except for Master Jarrod's desk.* Slates, primers, a giant hourglass, and all kinds of homemade gifts called the top of his desk home. Today only the bell occupied space. In contrast, the mud from the townsfolks' boots marred the floor. Reticules, baby blankets, and even a few dried beef droppings decorated the floor. The Bunks occupied the dried beef corner. They tended to leave a trail wherever they ate. More than once, Samantha had swept the mercantile floor after the Bunk brothers vacated. She figured Master Jarrod would rather not cross the river-rat brothers, otherwise the two men would have already seen the ruler rap their knuckles, and the dried beef would be long gone.

Master Jarrod reminded Samantha of a stork. She felt a bit guilty about the comparison, especially since the only reason she knew what a stork looked like was from a quick peek at one of the teacher's personal books.

Mrs. T darted from one end of the schoolhouse to the other. She whispered in Charlotte Warner's ear, glanced out the window, and nervously fingered the teacher's bell. She had put together tonight's April gathering. During the winter months, the church tried to organize a few social events to break up the monotony.

A fire roared in the stove. Samantha was warm, but not from the fire. Wedged between Millie Sanderson and Martin, Samantha felt firmly buffeted from the faint chill sent by the early April wind. For a moment, as Millie scooted closer to make room for another latecomer, Samantha wondered where Clara was. Surely not at home sewing? Clara would leave for New York in two weeks, and for the last few days all she talked about were relatives and the excitement of visiting.

The cuff of Martin's sleeve brushed Samantha's wrist. Startled, she looked up. Martin smiled and took her hand. This wasn't the first time she'd attended a social with Martin. Before Mama's illness, and when he was in town, he'd often squired her around town. This wasn't the first time he'd taken her hand either.

It was the first time the gesture made her start. It used to make her tingle.

Looking around the schoolroom, she noticed that only Roy Schmidt, the banker, wore clothes of the same quality as Martin. Pride? Is that what she felt when regarding

Martin's ruffled shirts? He'd taken off his frock. He sported the only silk damask vest in the room.

Samantha straightened the skirt of her blue cotton dress. It had fit perfectly when Mama tailored it, but after putting on the mourning black, Samantha lost weight. She wondered if Martin noticed that her sleeves had the fullness a bit too high. Fashion changed quickly, or so Cecilia had reminded her as they dressed for the evening's event.

Leaning forward, Samantha searched for her father. There he was, sitting near the front, with his arm protectively around his new wife. Clothes didn't matter to Silas Thomasohn; family did; Cecilia did.

"Stop letting her bother you," Martin whispered.

Samantha took her hand out from under his. Was she that obvious? "I'm not."

"I've listened to you recite that 'obey your parents' Scripture at least ten times during the last week."

"It's helping."

"You know what comes after verse one, don't you?"

Samantha's brow wrinkled. She should know it.

Martin didn't give her a chance to think. "Fathers, provoke not your children."

It did give her pause, but she shook her head. "Oh, Martin, that has nothing to do with what's bothering me."

"Used to be, you stared at me during our evenings. I don't think you've looked at me even once this evening."

"That's not true."

Master Jarrod chose that moment to ring the bell.

Once everyone had quieted down, Reverend Tidewell started the evening with a prayer. Mrs. T nodded from her perch by the window. The school door burst open, and an outrageously tall man ducked in. He was padded with what looked like, Samantha squinted, quilt stuffing. As he scuffled up the aisle, she noticed the coffee cans tied to his shoes. They must be made of rock, she thought, to hold Tyson Walker up. The blacksmith easily outweighed and outstood every man in town, including the Stahl brothers, who'd towered over everyone until Ty moved to town. Briefly, she wondered why he wasn't home with Betsy helping take care of Greta.

He turned once he reached the front of the room and boomed, "I hear tell this town is tired of winter. Is that true? I said, IS THAT TRUE? Well, the same thing happened over in Michigan in '26. So I let out a hot breath, melted that snow quicker than you could say Jehoshaphat. The townspeople were mighty obliged, especially when they realized that the melting water formed one of the Great Lakes."

The school door opened again. After being surprised by such a "tall" entrance, Samantha expected to see something big enter. Big was correct, but blue was a better description. Unless she missed her guess, the blanket the mystery guest wore came straight from Mrs. T's bed. The horns were made from two of Doc's hearing aides. Children laughed and scrambled out of the way. Samantha noticed the Larkin children, minus Greta, in the corner. That explained why Ty was there. Betsy probably told him it was important for the young ones to have some fun.

As the unconvincing ox clumsily moved up the aisle, its head swung right and left. Samantha's eyes caught sight of Ole Babe, and she felt tingles go down her arm.

Jacob Stahl.

He'd taken to dropping by the store regularly and not just to purchase dry goods. Yet he didn't ask her father for permission to court as Martin had. No, instead he told her what nursing he wanted her to do over at Betsy's. And because Samantha loved Betsy, she obeyed. And she pretended she didn't want him to wink again.

Martin leaned over and whispered in Samantha's ear. "An improvement in the sawbones' wardrobe, wouldn't you say?"

"Ah," cried Paul Bunyan, saving Samantha from having to answer. "My trusted friend, Babe."

Jacob snorted and pawed at the ground. His ragged boots, a Stahl brothers' hand-me-down, did not make oxenlike noises. Children giggled, and parents smiled indulgently. Checking the schoolroom for Jacob's parents, Samantha located them in the back row. They didn't usually come to town for socials, thinking them frivolous. Jacob's mother had a smile on her face. The first Samantha had seen.

"He looks a bit ridiculous," Martin whispered in her ear.

"Hush," she whispered back. She wasn't about to tell Martin that betwixt the two men, Jacob came out the winner in more ways than one.

⁘

The blanket added more heat than Jacob needed. Sweat pooled at the back of his neck and ran down his spine. Perhaps he should dress Greta up in the getup and see if it helped. Before coming to the social, they'd practiced their act in front of Betsy, Mr. Larkin, and Greta.

Not even a smile came from the child.

It was easier dealing with Mrs. Cullen over in Taylorville. During his first visit, she'd been in denial over her illness. Now she was angry. Anger sometimes cured people, to Jacob's way of thinking. They decided to get better by sheer will power, and it worked. Jacob knew prayer had a lot to do with it. Greta had prayer, but it surely looked like God was calling her home.

Jacob had no speaking lines, unless snorting counted. From beneath Mrs. T's blanket, he could watch as the audience *oohed* and *aahed* at Ty's monolog. As Ole Babe, Jacob pretended to move a mountain—Brady Forbes in disguise; danced with a hurricane—Shane Gerhard in disguise; and gave the sheriff's young son a ride. Just as Tyson ordered a tornado—Benjamin Melvin's role—the schoolhouse door burst open, and Mr. Larkin rushed in. One look said it all. Without missing a beat, Brady ducked under the blanket and took over Jacob's role. Jacob moved down the crowded aisle, grabbed his doctor bag and coat, and followed Greta's father to the wagon.

"Are you sure you want to come?" Mr. Larkin's face had a gray cast to it. His eyes were bloodshot, and his hands shook.

Jacob started to answer what he considered a silly question, but then a soft voice came from behind him.

"I might be able to help."

Samantha clutched her coat to her neck. Jacob helped her into the wagon and

137

scooted in beside her. Reaching behind the bench, he grabbed the blanket to tuck around them, although he didn't feel the cold.

"Tell me what's changed," Jacob ordered.

"Her lips turned blue, as blue as that blanket you were wearing."

"Go faster," Jacob urged.

Chapter 6

The sun shone broadly in Samantha's eyes as it reflected off one of the few remaining patches of snow at the cemetery behind the church. She shivered, but not from the cold. Father slipped his arm in hers and hugged her. Cecilia stood a few feet away looking decidedly forlorn.

Reverend Tidewell cleared his throat as he paused beside the newly erected headstone. "Greta Larkin wasn't but four. She was a special child, full of God's love. She often sought comfort in my wife's lap."

Samantha looked over at Mrs. T. Her cheeks were moist, and not even the constant dabbing of the handkerchief hid the sorrow. Mama's words came back: *They have no children of their own, so you girls and Brady are their family.*

There were not many dry eyes that Samantha could tell. Neither Crabtree showed emotion, nor did Oskar Bedloe, although he did seem to have a never-before-seen bothersome twitch.

Blinking, Samantha tried to make the tears come. Greta, who had often called Samantha "Tha" because she couldn't manage the whole word, had left this world. Then, Samantha noticed Greta's father. Matthew Larkin stood as close to the coffin as possible, as if determined to retain contact with his youngest child. He wasn't crying. Not a drop. His head was bowed, but there was a peace to the expression. He'd fallen apart at Greta's mother's funeral. Reverend Tidewell had tried to offer comfort back then, but Mr. Larkin cursed at the preacher and at God.

Samantha moved closer to her father and wished she was anywhere save there. Unable to stop herself, she peered over at her mother's grave. Jacob stepped in front of it.

Did Jacob think she didn't know what her mother's grave looked like? Even with him standing in the way, she could see it clear as—but she couldn't see it, nor could she see the head-stones for Mama's two babies who'd gone to Heaven before her. All Samantha could see was Jacob.

He rolled his hat in his hands. Samantha noted the pain in his eyes and felt it. He'd tried everything! The onion poultice drove Samantha, eyes and nose running, from the room. Betsy heated stones in the fire to put at Greta's feet. For three hours the girl lingered, caught somewhere between life and death. Yet despite Jacob's best effort, death won. And why did Matthew Larkin have a peaceful look on his face when Jacob looked so torn?

The Reverend droned on, his face red from the cold. A few tufts of white hair escaped from under his hat. Samantha shifted from one foot to the other. Greta's wake was on its second day and would be ending soon. They'd moved to the cemetery less than an hour ago, and the mourners were all stamping their feet trying to ward off the cold that paid no attention to the bright, shining April sun. Bright and shining like Greta's smile.

Samantha turned her attention back to the coffin, closed now and looking hauntingly insignificant among so many mourners. People came from as far away as Wabash Springs. Funerals always garnished a crowd. They brought food, comfort, and other things as well. This morning, Samantha had brushed away the salt and earth that the Bunk brothers had placed on Greta's stomach. They were superstitious men claiming that salt was a symbol of the spirit and earth represented the flesh. All Betsy wanted was for Greta's dress to stay clean. The coffin was lined with the Pieced Star quilt the sewing circle had been working on. Mrs. T left it incomplete, saying that like Greta, more time was needed.

Everyone bowed in final prayer. Samantha mimicked the others and tried to concentrate. From the corner of her eye, she could see Martin inching closer. He'd stayed away the last three days, partly in respect, partly in anger. He hadn't liked it a bit when she left with Jacob Stahl, no matter the reason.

With a start, Samantha realized that Martin wasn't sad, because Martin didn't *know* Greta, indeed didn't *know* most of the townspeople. Oh, he knew their names, what they did, where they lived, and possibly a family background, but he didn't *know* them. He'd always been with the crowd but never in it. Why hadn't she noticed that before? He'd be the perfect lawyer—detached.

Betsy leaned against Tyson. He'd come to the store yesterday for crape. Samantha had refused to charge him for the material and visually dared Cecilia to interfere. To her surprise, Cecilia had added some black muslin after Samantha hurried upstairs to fetch the mourning attire she no longer wore.

Today, Betsy wore the black Samantha had so unwillingly shed only a few months ago. *Did I look that forlorn?* Samantha wondered. Looking at her father, she noted his eyes on Mama's grave. Rachel was gone but not forgotten. For the first time, Samantha felt an inkling of relief that she'd taken off the mourning. *Yes, God,* Samantha thought, *You knew that Betsy would need it more than I do.*

Reverend Tidewell ended his eulogy. Samantha took a step toward her father and Cecilia, but before she could catch up with them, Martin stopped beside her. "Sap's rising. Mother wants to know if you'd like to go with us tomorrow for a gathering."

"This is hardly the time to be talking about having fun."

"This is exactly the time. Greta is gone, and you were barely an elbow cousin. Don't start grieving again, Samantha. This time I might not wait."

Samantha felt her mouth fall open, very unladylike, and she hurriedly closed it. Looking around, she noticed that everyone had moved in the direction of the Larkin farm. Most women would be stopping by home to gather up more food to take. Her father and Cecilia tarried by the schoolhouse, keeping Samantha in sight.

"Wait for me, indeed, Martin Crabtree. You were not even here while I was mourning. Besides, you're waiting in vain."

He blinked, and unreasonably, Samantha felt a bit smug. Then, she caught sight of Jacob beside the Stahl clan. He looked back at her, and Samantha knew that at the slightest provocation, he'd leave his family and stand beside her.

That's what it was about: God, family—

Family? When had she started thinking about Jacob and the word *family* as a combination. The dreaded blush rose to her cheeks. Jacob Stahl made her uncomfortable. No, not uncomfortable. Jacob made her feel like she'd never felt before. No, she couldn't deal with it now. She hurried to catch up with her father and Cecilia.

Everyone knew the Stahls had the best maple trees. Jacob jumped off his wagon and started unloading the sap buckets and yokes. He'd spent six days without a crisis. Greta's death weighed heavy on his mind. What could he have done differently?

Master Jarrod drove up in a hay wagon. He'd wedged in almost fifteen school-children. Laughing and singing songs, they served as a good reminder that life went on. Behind them came at least four more wagons from town.

Jacob's heart lightened when he saw Samantha scramble down from the Gerhards' wagon. Not wanting to appear too eager, Jacob slowly walked over as Elsa handed down the troughs and paddles. "Let me take that for you." Jacob reached over Samantha's head. Her bonnet had slipped, and blond curls beckoned his fingers. He wanted to touch her. He wanted to bury his face in the fine strands of her hair and tell her he loved her.

She'd made some huge steps in recovering from her mother's death and accepting Cecilia. Jacob knew Greta's death set things back some. It only made him want to grasp life and love with both hands before it was too late.

"Thought things would have been started by now," Shane remarked.

"It's still early." Jacob put a hand to Samantha's back and liked the way she moved in the direction he guided. It was the first time he'd touched her without it being a tease as a boy, or a doctor giving comfort. It felt better than he'd dreamed.

Then she sent him a smile meant just for him, and he experienced a taste of heaven.

Not counting the schoolchildren, over ten adults came to the Stahls' land to gather sap. Jacob set the men to boring holes in each maple. Jacob had whittled out the insides of ash branches to form the tubes, which the older schoolboys now bored into the holes. When that was done, the men drove nails under the tube. The women came behind and hung buckets on the nails.

As children screamed with delight to watch the sap drip, Jacob watched Samantha. He noted the way her hair swayed in the wind and how it blew against her cheeks. He fought the urge to brush her hair back. She'd not like it if he touched her so intimately in public. Not when he hadn't bothered to ask her father permission to call. He needed to get his affairs in order, garnish a nest egg, and prepare for family life. Right now his pay had more in common with the barter system than the monetary one.

The noise from the children putting their tongues at the end of the spouts to taste thin, icy-cold sap drew him from his meanderings. The afternoon, spent with Samantha, proved what he already knew. He was in love.

❖

"I saw you at the sap running," Clara said, settling into a chair at Mrs. T's house, and pulling out her piecework. "You certainly looked all cozy with Jacob Stahl."

The blush started at Samantha's cheeks and spread clear to her ears.

"Oh." Clara clasped a hand over her mouth. "I was just teasing, but there is something to tell, isn't there?"

Samantha started to say no. The word wouldn't surface.

"Are you throwing over Martin?" Clara's piecework dropped in her lap. "Did something happen? What?"

"Clara, leave Samantha alone. You're making her uncomfortable." Mrs. T's scissors cut a perfect square for her new pattern.

"Jacob's a good man." Betsy spoke her first words. She'd arrived late to the sewing circle, somberly nodded a greeting to her friends, and sat down to sew without talking. They'd left her to her thoughts. Two weeks had passed since Greta's funeral. Betsy's needle shook as it wove in and out of the fabric with such determination that, left up to her, the quilt pieces would soon be finished.

"Of course he is," Elsa agreed.

Surely there was a comment to be made, Samantha thought. *And by me.* The words stuck in her throat. It felt so strange to be thinking these thoughts about Jacob. He was nothing like Martin. Martin was excitement, adventure, and mystery. Jacob was more like an old shoe. One that fit comfortably but had been in the family forever.

"Jacob is a good man," Samantha finally said.

Betsy's head stayed bowed. Elsa nodded with a knowing gleam in her eye. Clara frowned, clearly aware that somehow she'd missed a major upheaval in the midst.

Mrs. T changed the subject. "Girls, I have today's Scriptures. I think Ecclesiastes, the third chapter, will do: 'To every thing there is a season, and a time to every purpose under heaven: a time to be born, and a time to die.'" Mrs. T paused, as did every thimble.

Betsy's piecework lay in her lap, the needle carefully threaded into the edge. For a moment, Samantha thought Betsy would make a move, but she didn't.

Elsa rubbed her stomach, almost an unconscious movement. Looking at her friends, Samantha was struck by her love for them.

Mrs. T continued, "'A time to plant, and a time to pluck up that which is planted.'"

Clara gave a little gasp. Her needle flashed in and out of the handkerchief she hemmed. At least six times this afternoon, she'd mentioned her trip and the importance of having enough toiletries. She would leave tomorrow morning. Samantha tried to drive the thought from her mind, but Mrs. T, with her infinite wisdom, reminded the girls to cherish the remaining time.

"'A time to love, and a time to hate.'"

This time Samantha's flush had nothing to do with Jacob Stahl. Hate? Did she hate Cecilia? No, not possible. Samantha had been taught better than to hate. Dislike maybe. Resent probably. But hate?

142

" 'God shall judge the righteous and the wicked: for there is a time there for every purpose and for every work.'" Mrs. T closed her Bible and bowed her head in silent prayer. The other three girls did the same.

Yes, thought Samantha, changes were coming. Not only in the lives of her friends, but in her own life as well.

And there was nowhere to hide.

Chapter 7

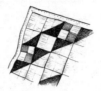

T he docks were busy and cold. Everything was brown. April swept a warm hand over Hickory Corners but never touched the ground. Through her black boots, Samantha felt a chill stealing steadily upward. Her toes almost curled from the force of it.

Clara couldn't manage to stand still. Her light-brown curls bobbed with excitement. Her Aunt Charlotte didn't even reprimand her. For over ten years, Charlotte Warner had been more mother than aunt to Clara. Watching her ward leave couldn't be easy. Noticing how eager she was to go surely made it harder.

Eager to go, that described Raymond as well, and Samantha worried that once he finished medical school, he'd not return. The worry had intensified after Jacob took over Doc's practice.

He was with his brothers today, she figured. She'd seen him load up his wagon and head in that direction. And she was at the docks saying good-bye to Clara.

The Ohio River moved like a herd of schoolchildren late for school. The river men seemed filled with the same anticipation.

"I'll take these, Ma'am." Horace Bunk pretended not to recognize Clara as he reached for her valise.

"It's me," Clara exclaimed. "Clara Bucey."

Horace winked at the girls. "Ah, all growed up and off to play in the big city. You know, folks often get a taste of the *wanderjahr* and never return to the place of their birth."

Clara's eyes brightened.

What was this? *Never return?* Samantha hadn't realized Clara's dreams were so vastly different. Had she? Truth? She had realized, just pretended not. Clara always had her nose in a geography book. She and Master Jarrod had played Spin the Globe many a school day morning. Clara had willingly written essays on the places her finger landed.

A time to pluck up that which is planted.

Too soon, Clara's luggage was taken aboard. A too-quick good-bye, then Clara's steps faltered a bit as she walked up the loading plank of the *A. M. Phillips*. Yet she didn't look back.

No, wait! Samantha wanted to cry.

Horace must have noted Samantha's distress. He stepped off the loading plank.

"Don't worry, Miss Samantha, we ain't got no preachers or white horses aboard. It will be smooth sailing."

"Thank you, Horace," Samantha managed, resisting the urge to push him into the water. White horses, indeed!

A violin started playing from somewhere on deck. Ropes left their moorings, river men scurried to their posts, and the mighty steamship pulled away from the dock.

Samantha expected to cry—wanted to—but Elsa wept instead.

"I cry all the time," she excused. "Last night, Shane remarked that his potatoes were cold, and I broke down right there. Poor man, when I fed him potato cakes this morning, he looked at them in fear."

The bugle blew as the *A. M. Phillips* sailed out of sight.

"I'll miss her," Betsy said, bringing a black handkerchief to her nose.

"Me too," Elsa echoed.

Samantha was the first to leave the group as they returned to town. As she entered the store to see Cecilia waiting on a customer, she had to admit her stepmother had been good lately about allowing her time away from the store and chores.

A few people lingered inside. Victoria Alexander fondled a French silk that had arrived just yesterday. Sheriff Abner had Pa off to one corner questioning him about the recent purchases of two Ottawa Indians who now resided in the town jail. Jacob Stahl leaned against the counter chatting with Cecilia.

Samantha took a breath. She hadn't sassed, snapped, or even scoffed at her father's wife for weeks. The Thomasohn home was a bit quieter since the effort sorely limited the words that popped out of Samantha's mouth.

"'A time to love, and a time to hate.'"

Samantha bit down until a coppery taste filled her mouth.

"Here she is, Jacob. I told you she'd be right back." Cecilia positively glowed.

What had they been speaking about? Samantha felt it again! The flush that betrayed her emotions. Never had anyone looked at her so appreciatively, so admiringly. It nigh took her breath away.

"Go ahead. Show her," Cecilia urged.

She hadn't noticed his smile before, not really. It started at the corners of his mouth and spread until his whole face was a mass of approval.

He approved of her. She didn't deserve it, not lately.

"I knew you'd be feeling down some," he said, "what with Clara leaving. Elsa told me how much you liked her rocking chair, so I made you this."

He'd made her a rocking chair? Oh, dear. Rocking chairs made her think of Elsa and babies. It was much too forward a gift, just like that wink in chur—

She'd seen ladders before, only not quite so short and squat. Cecilia pushed while Jacob tugged, and soon his creation sat in the center of the store.

"It's so you can reach the top shelf. I'm going to lean it against the wall here. It's really rather light. Just push it where you want, and you'll be able to reach anything."

"And in a ladylike stance, too," Cecilia added.

"That's quite a ladder, Jacob." Victoria bent down and fingered the smooth sanding. "I'd like to order one for my shop."

Samantha stared down at Jacob's ladder. There were no elegant lines; this was made to be sturdy. He'd painted it brown, and, like Olivia Crabtree, the ladder didn't cotton to elegance. Three steps up, a platform, and three steps down, the ladder looked a little like the giant wooden blocks her brothers had played with as a child.

Elsa got a rocking chair and a cradle. Samantha got chunks of wood stuck together.

For a moment, she felt disgruntled. Then, she remembered Martin whispering to her the verse, *"Fathers, provoke not your children."* She looked around the mercantile, at the shelves of dry goods, at the barrels of beans on the floor. She thought back to helping Mama arrange the window display. Samantha knew that as much as upstairs was her home, this store held just as many cherished memories.

Jacob had made something that felt all wrong—the store not looking the way her mother arranged it—into something that felt almost right. How wise he was. What a wonderful father, husband, he would make.

"Thank you, Jacob. It's the nicest gift anyone's ever given me."

And she kissed him on the cheek.

"Come on, you can do it." Sheriff Abner sat in the old barber chair Doc had inherited from his father.

Jacob much preferred getting a haircut to giving one. Just what was up with the sheriff's hair anyway? A man his age should be thinning some.

"You been using Professor Low's hair tonic?" Jacob asked.

Abner laughed. "No, I figure chasing bad men must stimulate growth or something. Fact is, my wife gets plumb annoyed at this mop of mine."

Jacob used the strop attached to the barber chair to sharpen the scissors.

"You sharpen those scissors much more, Son, and you won't have nothing but a file." Abner chuckled. "Don't know as I want a young pup in love messing with my hair."

"Keep talking, Sheriff, and I'll tell your wife what Low puts in that medicinal elixir you prescribe to."

Abner kept chuckling, and Jacob slowly circled the man. The sheriff wore his blond hair a bit longer than most of the Hickory Corners men. Dime novels, combined with pride, no doubt.

Trying to remember what Doc had done, Jacob gently gathered a hank of hair between his fingers. The scissors sliced through the strands as easily as his mother's paring knife cut through husks of corn. But corn husks neither yelped if they didn't like their shape nor carried handcuffs.

A beetle scurried across the floor and Jacob wished it needed a haircut so he could get the practice.

The door opened, and Silas Thomasohn entered. He headed for one of the three-legged chairs by the front door. Paying no attention to the dust lining its seat, Silas sat down.

The sheriff and Jacob both stared. The man didn't have enough hair to cut. Surely he didn't want a shave, Jacob hoped.

Pulling out a piece of ash wood, Silas took to whittling.

"Are you here for a haircut?" Abner asked, saving Jacob the words.

"Nope."

Jacob finished Abner's trim and grabbed the bar of soap still on the shelf. It took some doing, but finally he managed a lather and soaped the back of Abner's neck. Doc kept three straight-edge razors. Jacob chose what looked like the sturdiest. He flicked it open and grabbed the strop again. After sharpening it, he scraped an inch of soap off the sheriff's neck.

Now that Abner had shown faith in testing the new barber's abilities, others would follow suit. At one time, the barbershop had garnished quite a gathering of men wanting to jaw the time away. It was good for Mr. Thomasohn to see a reliable business. Jacob guessed he'd have to check behind the back curtain where two tubs waited for filthy customers to bathe.

It was a part of Doc's profession that Jacob hadn't considered taking over. Yet, it would be an income. Doc had already hinted that he'd move out of the upstairs room if Jacob wanted to move Samantha in.

Eyeing Mr. Thomasohn, Jacob wondered why the man was here. This morning, Jacob had intended to pull Samantha's father aside, ask permission to court, and lay out his intentions. Instead, Silas had been huddled in the corner with Abner, and Cecilia had beckoned to Jacob. Once she'd seen the little ladder he'd made for Samantha, any hope of talking with Silas disappeared.

A bit headstrong was the new Mrs. Thomasohn. Jacob could see why Samantha, who was fully capable of caring for a home, might feel stifled.

"Doc never took this long," Abner complained.

Jacob stared at the back of the man's neck. As smooth as a baby's behind, there wasn't a single nick. Jacob dropped the razor into the mug.

What next? A hot towel? Doc always cleaned the back of the customer's neck with a clean, hot towel. Jacob looked down at the stove. Since the weather had warmed, he'd not even thought to fire it up. If he intended to make a side living at barbering, he'd need to keep the thing going during trade hours.

Even the towel was a bit dusty. Jacob whacked it against his knee a few times before applying it to the sheriff's neck. "Sorry, Sheriff, you're my first haircut, and you're going to have to make due with a dry towel. I'll do better next time."

Abner stood and stared into the broken mirror. He ran a hand across the back of his neck, as if to assure himself that it was still there. "You did fine."

A nickel richer, Jacob set the shaving mug on the table beside the barber chair. "A shave?" he questioned Silas.

"No, I can get that at home. I came by to ask about your intentions toward my Samantha." Silas carefully put away his whittling. He brushed his hands as he stood.

Jacob was a tall man, but looking down at Samantha's father, Jacob realized that height offered no advantage when dealing with a doting father.

"I intend to marry her, Sir. I came to your mercantile this morning to ask permission to court."

Silas nodded, "I figured as much. I'm sorry, Jacob. You're a good man, but I cannot give you my blessing. The answer is no."

Chapter 8

Jacob couldn't remember the last time he'd sat at his parents' kitchen without a whole herd of siblings traipsing through. Arlene Stahl expertly pinched the ends off a handful of beans and broke them in two while his father sat looking guilty for leaving the fields during daylight hours. His eyes were on the window, and the flax outside waiting to be harvested.

"What I want to do," explained Jacob, "is take the plot of land you've allotted me and sell it back to you."

"Why," Gunther said, "that land—"

"Let him finish," Arlene interrupted.

"I've asked for permission to court Samantha."

"I knew it." The beans in his mother's hands became a blur as she doubled her speed. "When's the wedding?"

"Her father didn't give me permission to court."

Gunther sat straighter. "Why? Is he thinking there's something wrong with her marrying a Stahl?"

"No, Pa, that's not it. He says a doctor is married to his profession, and that I'll be gone more than I'll stay put. He doesn't think the two rooms above the barbershop constitute a home."

"Marrying a Gustefan certainly gave the man airs." Gunther slammed a fist down on the table.

The bowl of beans shuddered. Arlene put out one hand to steady it. "So, what are you thinking, Son?"

He'd prepared for the question, knowing his practical mother. Opening his doctor's bag, he drew out a plan he'd worked on for three weeks. Three agonizing weeks. He'd spent part of the time over in Wabash Springs amputating the arm of a farmer who'd gotten too close to an ax. He'd delivered a baby out at the docks. Mother, father, and child were staying at the inn for a few days.

Jacob had spent some of the time conferring with Reverend Tidewell, praying, and figuring his next course of action. He lay that action in front of his parents now. "Doc says he'll sell me the building, barbershop and all. I'm going to tear it down and build a combination doctor's office, barbershop, and home. I want to order bricks from the kiln over in Wabash Springs. Once Silas sees that Samantha will live in town, instead of out here, I think he'll reconsider. Then, there's also the fact that

Raymond still intends to practice here. With two doctors, we can share the out-of-county calls. What do you think, Pa?"

"I think you're going to a lot of trouble for a man too blind to see how much you love his daughter."

"In all honesty, Silas only voiced concerns I already had. I owe him thanks. He made me take action."

"Does Samantha know how you feel?"

For three weeks, Samantha had watched him with curious eyes. During week one, he'd imagined those eyes longing for him to say something. During the second week, she withdrew, a slight frown on her face as if something puzzled her. This week, her chin jutted in the air as she carefully avoided him.

"She does, and she returns the feeling. But," Jacob carefully folded the plan, "I don't think she knows her father refused me permission to call."

Fifteen minutes later, Jacob Stahl headed for the bank.

⁘

Samantha cut through a yard of muslin.

"Martin left for New York this morning. Oh, what a job offer he has." Olivia Crabtree narrowed her eyes into slits. "He'll be back in a month. He'll be wanting to pack up the last of his things. Why, he might ask me along. He'll need someone to take care of the big house he'll be able to afford. Some people don't know what's good."

It had been three weeks since Jacob stopped by with the sole intent of seeing Samantha. Oh, he'd been by to purchase goods. He'd also attended church and sat with his family. From her pew, sitting next to Father, she'd longed for a wink.

"New York's far away," Silas said. "You think he'll stay there forever? Hickory Corners is growing. Two new families this last month. Soon we'll be needing a lawyer."

To Samantha's chagrin, Father looked at her. Lately, he'd been bringing up Martin just as often as Olivia.

"'Tis possible," Olivia agreed. "Let's hope the future works itself out." The look she sent Samantha said it all: Samantha was upsetting Olivia Crabtree's carefully constructed plans.

Folding the material into a neat square, Samantha gathered matching thread and a few buttons. Olivia moved over next to Father.

One thing Samantha knew, Martin Crabtree wasn't husband material. She'd recognized that at Greta's funeral. Oh, to be honest, she'd figured it out at the Friday Social.

After Olivia left the store, peace returned. Samantha returned the sewing paraphernalia to its shelf. Cecilia was upstairs, and Samantha enjoyed the time spent with Father alone. For a moment, she pretended that nothing had changed. In all honesty, the Thomasohn home seemed a bit more tolerable. Less and less, Samantha felt resentment taking hold. Lately, Cecilia spent more time piecing together a quilt than she did interfering.

The afternoon toiled on. Samantha sold a seventeen-cent broom and a handful of lamp wickings. Father whistled over his ledger as he tallied profits and losses.

A feeling of happiness overtook Samantha and lasted until five o'clock when Father closed the door and Samantha finished pricing the beeswax she'd taken in exchange for a yard of bleached sheeting.

Cecilia had supper on the table, but instead of hustling to serve Father, she struggled in the corner of the living room next to where Samantha used to sleep.

She'd lowered Rachel's quilting frame from the ceiling. It swayed gently under the pressure of Cecilia valiantly trying to fasten the quilt to the tacks stuck in the edges for just that purpose. Samantha couldn't remember Mama ever trying to set up the quilting frame on her own.

Father quickly tugged on the opposite end and pulled it taut. "Samantha, get the other end."

Cecilia chuckled as they set the frame together. "My mama always said when you finish a quilt what you need to do is put a cat in the center. Then, everyone tugs on the sides. When the cat runs off, whichever girl he passes by, that will be the girl to get married next. Perhaps when I finish this quilt, Samantha, we can try that."

The quilting frame swayed under Samantha's hands. Weeks ago Samantha would have figured the words were Cecilia's way of hinting that Samantha should leave, but now she didn't know. She didn't know anything except that feeling the soft fabric under her hands made her remember crawling underneath this very frame with Raymond and watching Mama's needle dipping in and out, a silver blur. They'd felt so safe with the quilt over their heads and Mama's feet tapping to thoughts they couldn't hear.

Samantha climbed the ladder to the loft, dropped to her knees, and leaned against the bed to pray. The resentment hadn't left, but what she'd learned from the scene below told her the problems lay with her and her alone.

❖

"I want to go visit Opa and Oma for awhile." Samantha tried to eat a piece of toast. Her stomach rolled, and she set the bread back on her plate. She'd thought long and hard about it. Visiting her grandparents would give her time to work through all the turmoil.

"Are you feeling okay? Shall I call Doc Stahl?" Father felt her forehead, as he'd done hundreds of times before.

"Let her go, Silas." Cecilia looked pale today.

For the first time Samantha wondered how acutely her stepmother felt the animosity. Cecilia probably thought Samantha's leaving a good idea.

"Why? I don't understand. I thought things were better." Father looked confused. He stared at Cecilia for a long time, then turned a stern gaze at Samantha. "Are you sure that's what you want?"

She thought of the quilting frame in the corner. She saw Cecilia hunched over it every night. Cecilia's foot tapped in the same way Mama's used to. "Very sure."

"Well, then, Zack is heading out there with some supplies later today. Pack your things. You may go."

For a moment, Samantha had it in mind to give her father a hug. But she didn't feel happy. She'd expected him to put up a bit more fuss.

It didn't take long to pack a valise. It had been years since she'd spent time at Opa and Oma's. The Gustefans lived a good eight hours from town. Zack would be spending the night before returning to his farm. It would be different staying there now that she was older. Maybe Opa would let her help milk the cows. She'd loved that as a child. Then, there were the banty hens. One summer, because Oma wanted fryers, Samantha and Oma stuck Barred Rock chicken eggs under the banty hens to set. Samantha always wondered if the banty hens marveled at the size of their much-larger offspring, or if the hens had any clue about the switch. Samantha closed her eyes. The last time she'd stayed with Oma, she'd been so small she had to stand on a chair to see out the window.

Zack didn't waste any words when he pulled in front of the store at noon and found Samantha waiting. "Pa needs you."

"Cecilia's here to help him."

"You're running away. It's time you faced whatever it is that has your lips looking like you sucked on a lemon."

"Leave me alone, Zackery Gus Thomasohn, you only come to see Father once a month when you deliver these supplies. You have no right to tell me what to do."

"You're a spoilt brat, that's what you are."

Eight hours she'd have to spend with him in the wagon. Of all her brothers, she understood him the least. Trevor was the silent one, only offering words when he deemed it important. Raymond would have scolded her, too, no doubt. But first he'd have mussed up her hair and given her a peck on the cheek. Zack must have been dropped as a baby, that's the only thing Samantha could figure. "I'm going to walk over and say good-bye to Mrs. T. I need you to do me one favor."

He shot her a look of disbelief.

"I want to take Mama's old cedar chest."

"You need to get over this, Mantha." He surprised her by using the nickname that no longer echoed through the upstairs of Thomasohn's Mercantile.

"I know. I'm trying." Her feet grew heavier each step she took. The town looked brighter, and Samantha wondered if that was because she didn't know how long it would be before she saw it again. She crossed to the other side so she wouldn't have to walk in front of Doc's place. Her feet dragged as she slowed a bit. All the Stahl brothers were busy loading Doc's belongings into farm wagons. To the side, Samantha could see at least a thousand bricks stacked taller than Jacob. The man didn't deserve a good-bye. He'd winked at church, prayed with her at Greta's side, made her a ladder, flirted with her over maple sap, then backed away so fast that if Samantha didn't know better, she'd think maybe a giant wart had appeared on the tip of her nose. What was he up to now?

She forced herself not to walk backward. She didn't care what Jacob did.

"Everybody is talking," Mrs. T said from her front step, "except Jacob."

Samantha stared back at the sight of chaos on the corner of the street. "You'll have to write and tell me what's going on."

"Write? Oh, Darling, not you, too?"

"Just to Opa and Oma's and just for awhile."

Mrs. T insisted on packing up a hefty lunch. Samantha hadn't given thought to that, although Zack's wife probably had.

"I'll tell the girls," Mrs. T promised. She hugged Samantha close. "Oh, now you don't stay away too long. Our little sewing circle is dwindling down. We need you."

Zack knocked at the door. A moment later, he took the box of food from Mrs. T. "Not too late to change your mind," he said out of the corner of his mouth.

"I need to go."

Zack looked down the street. "Doc's staying at the inn, and I think Jacob's lost his mind. I wonder where he got the money?"

As the town of Hickory Corners disappeared from sight, Samantha wondered if she'd been wrong about Jacob's reasons for leaving medical school.

⁛

Rosie Gustefan didn't bat an eye at Samantha's arrival. She opened up the extra bedroom and set about enjoying her granddaughter.

Living on the farm was vastly different than visiting. Milking the cows lost its appeal after four days. At the mercantile, they'd never needed livestock. They took everything in trade. The third time Old Bess slapped Samantha in the face with her tail, leaving a residue Samantha would rather not think about, she wished she had a tail to slap back with.

The chickens were another matter. There existed something called a pecking order. The dominant chickens actually cornered a cowering Rhode Island Red and pecked it half bald. Samantha removed it from the brood and stuck it in a pen all by itself. Instead of saying thanks, the chicken pecked her! Of course, the daring rescue of the Rhode Island Red gave the rooster an opportunity to escape. The silly thing frantically stayed near the pen wanting back in but was too stupid to take advantage as Samantha held open the door. Five hours Samantha spent chasing Wilber the rooster. Oma didn't name the farm animals, but Samantha named the ones she scolded. She also named what she fell in love with, like the collie puppies in the barn. Opa grumbled that her favorite, Ike, would not learn how to walk if she didn't put him down.

While there was more work at Oma and Opa's, there was more time for solitude, too. Samantha sat in the living room in the evening and read the Bible aloud to Opa.

On Sunday, they met in the home of a cousin. The men took turns preaching. It was very different than the church in town. Not the words or the feeling of reverence, but the absence of friends who were more family than anything else. Samantha wondered if Elsa had delivered the baby. She wondered if Betsy still visited Greta's grave every day. She wondered if Father missed her. And she wondered what in the world Jacob Stahl was doing with all those bricks.

They rested on the Sabbath but made up for it on Monday. Samantha knelt in the dirt beside Oma and patiently listened to the lecture on how to tell a weed from a tomato plant.

Oma said, "The leaves on the tomato plant have tiny little hairs. Oh, there he is."

Samantha leaned closer to stare at the leaves. Just which "he" was Oma referring to?

Oma's knees popped as she stood. Samantha looked down the road. It wasn't Zack's wagon, although he was due any day now. This was a buggy.

"Who is it?" Samantha asked.

"Why, he's finally come for you. I knew he would."

Jacob pulled up in front of the house. Samantha looked down at her blue cotton dress. Sweat stained under her arms. Dirt smeared near her knees. She was pretty sure dirt streaked her face, too.

"Jacob Stahl," Oma greeted. "About time you got here. The cobbler said you were building a house for your bride. Can't figure why you let her stay here a month. You don't have second thoughts, do you?"

"Oma," Samantha whispered frantically. "He's not building a house for me."

"Sure he is. Cobbler said so."

Jacob never looked more handsome. He wore a brown vest over a white shirt. Brown homespun pants hugged his thighs. His chestnut hair danced in the wind; it was longer than she would have liked. . .on anyone else.

Oma brushed the dirt from her hands. "Close your mouth, Samantha, and let's pack you up."

"I'm not going."

Jacob somehow had grown taller. His voice held that same commanding tone he so often tried to use with her. "Yes, you are. Morning, Mrs. Gustefan."

Samantha gazed up, intending to argue, and instead felt her breath quicken.

"You can call me Oma. Might as well start getting used to it. She never completely unpacked, so it shouldn't take long. Sure you don't want to spend the night? You look spent."

"Can't," Jacob said. "Cecilia is sick. I need to get Samantha back there as soon as possible. Silas needs help."

Numbness washed over Samantha. He hadn't come for *her*, after all. He'd come because of Cecilia.

⁘

Jacob took it easy on the way back. The horse looked as weary as Jacob felt. Samantha sat silently by his side, her posture as straight as the ironing board his mother propped against the kitchen wall. It made him tongue-tied to watch her grip the side of the seat to keep from bumping into him.

She'd changed out of the blue dress and now wore a simple yellow cotton. A white petticoat peeked out near the same silly boots that often had her accidentally ice-skating in winter. They made her feet look dainty and small. He liked having her beside him in the buggy. He'd have gone another seven hours to retrieve her. "You might as well tell me what's bothering you. We can't fix it until I know what's broken."

"Nothing's broken. I just didn't want to come back to town, that's all."

No, that wasn't all. He knew that much. Her eyes had lit up at the sight of him, but they'd dimmed just as easily. He replayed his words, but couldn't think of anything he'd said amiss. Surely, Samantha didn't feel such ire at Cecilia as to consider not pitching in.

"I missed you," Jacob said softly.

"I didn't miss you." She stared straight ahead.

Jacob smiled. For someone who didn't miss him, she sure seemed bent on pointedly ignoring him. He grinned. "I think your pa missed you, too."

"Why didn't he send for me sooner?"

"He didn't send for you at all. I took it upon myself to come get you."

She forgot to hold herself erect. She let out her breath and slumped against the back of the seat. "That doesn't make sense. I always help out."

"I think he was worried about how you would take it."

"Take what?"

"Cecilia's in the family way."

Chapter 9

The sound of Hickory Corners carried over the trees. People's voices raised in conversation. She'd gotten used to the silence of the farm. The *rat-a-tat* of Ty Walker's hammer welcomed her home.

They passed the Larkin farm. Matthew waved from atop a pile of hay. His oldest boy, Karl, immediately took off in the direction of Betsy's house.

The corner where Doc lived looked completely different. The clapboard building no longer stood. In its place, bricks formed what would someday be a grand building.

"There is a lot to say for having ten brothers." Jacob grinned.

Samantha smiled weakly. It indeed looked like it could be a home for a bride. Glass windows, leaning against a wagon, glittered in the sun. A porch, that only needed a swing, waited for a family to move in. The cobbler claimed the bride was her. If that was true, why hadn't Jacob come calling?

Oh, she had more to worry about than Jacob's wishy-washiness. Too soon, Jacob pulled up in front of the mercantile. Samantha hopped down, again forgetting to let Jacob help her, and scurried up the steps.

Trevor stood behind the counter. Shane Gerhard counted out money for a pound of sugar. Taking the steps two at a time, Samantha hurried up the stairs. Father set in a chair by the bed, spooning what looked like broth into Cecilia's mouth.

"She's a bit older than most first-time mothers." Jacob's voice was so near Samantha's ear that she could feel his breath. There came that tingle, and at such an inopportune time, too.

"Father, I'm here to help."

Silas turned so fast that some of the broth spilled out of the bowl. Jacob took over. He patted Cecilia's arm and cleaned up Silas's mess with a towel.

It was only for a moment, but the look in Father's eyes said it all. He touched her on the chin, nodded, and took off down the stairs.

"He's a little choked up," Cecilia said. "He's prayed every night, even before I took sick, that you'd come back."

Jacob set down Samantha's valise and felt Cecilia's forehead. "Keep her still. She keeps asking to get up, and the answer's no. Read to her, she can do some piecework if you prop her up, and she stays in bed."

"Thank you, Jacob."

"I'll talk to you later." His eyes made promises his words didn't encourage.

155

She nodded and took his place next to Cecilia. "First, let's change you out of this damp nightgown. It can't be comfortable to lie with broth seeping down your neck."

"I can manage on my own." Cecilia sat up, grimaced, and tried to swing her legs over the edge of the bed.

"Don't be silly. I'm here to help."

"Did it ever occur to you, Samantha, that I'm as uncomfortable around you as you are around me?"

Mouse chose that moment to skid to a stop at Samantha's feet. Glad for something to do with her hands, she picked the cat up.

Cecilia's brown hair was flat on the side. She'd always kept it so carefully coiled, Samantha knew her stepmother must feel truly terrible.

"It's my little brother or sister you're carrying. Seems we can make a truce until you feel better." Samantha set Mouse down and took a clean gown from the armoire. Cecilia didn't look pregnant, but she did look vulnerable. Samantha took the woman's hand. "Maybe truce is the wrong word. You make my father happy, and that should make me happy. I really want to help. Will you let me?"

Cecilia gripped the edge of the mattress in much the same way that Samantha had earlier gripped the buggy's edge. It took a bit of bullying, but Samantha managed to slip off Cecilia's gown, give the woman a sponge bath, and tuck her into bed. Sleeping, Cecilia looked young enough to be part of the sewing circle. Well, once Cecilia got better, Samantha would go again. It would be fine to see Elsa's shining eyes and hear Betsy's dour humor.

Samantha looked around the room. The place needed cleaning. First, Samantha tidied up the kitchen, and then she started on the main room. It felt good to be needed. The quilting frame acted as a magnet, drawing her attention, until she gave in and went to look at Cecilia's work.

Jacob's Ladder.

"She's making it for you, you know." Silas silently crossed the room and sat in the chair meant for the quilter.

"Really?"

"She's a smart woman, and strong. I knew that when she went to work for Virginia. Cecilia still hurt as bad as I did from the loss of a spouse, yet she dug in her heels and kept living."

"I understand, Father."

"Do you?" Silas looked over at his sleeping wife. "I wish you'd give her as much of a chance as she keeps giving you."

Samantha's teeth hurt and she unclenched them. Of its own volition, her head shook. "I am trying."

"You call running away trying?"

"I call coming back trying."

Father ran his fingers over a section of stitching. "I didn't even know the name of this quilt until she told me. Jacob's Ladder. Then she had to tell me why she chose the pattern. Seems she recognized something I missed. I always knew Jacob had feelings for you, but I didn't realize you returned them."

"He doesn't—"

"He asked permission to call, you know."

"Jacob did? When?" Her cheeks flamed, and this time her stomach didn't hurt because of Cecilia.

"A few weeks before you left for your grandparents'."

"He didn't call."

"I told him no."

"Father!"

"Don't go scolding me. Cecilia's done nothing but. Then, that crazy doctor starting building nothing less than a brick house."

"For me," Samantha whispered.

"That's what the cobbler says." Silas reached down into the sewing basket by his chair. "Is Jacob Stahl what you want?"

"Yes."

"Then, I'll give him my blessing."

Samantha flew across the room. It had been months since she'd felt his arms around her in love.

"You did good, Husband," Cecilia said from the bed.

"One more thing," Silas said. He pushed something in Samantha's hand. "The reverend's wife thinks you'll be happy to see this. Seems it had somehow landed in the hem of her skirt."

Mama's thimble.

No longer lost.

❖

Dust drifted with the wind as the town settled down for the evening. Samantha adjusted the bodice of her favorite dress and took a deep breath. Down the way she could see Jacob sitting on the front step of his building. The boardwalk echoed under the soles of her boots. She and her brothers had often gotten in trouble for making too much noise when they played in the shade under the awning.

Jacob looked tired, but then the trip to her grandparents' farm had cost him fifteen hours.

All her life Samantha had striven to be the perfect lady, but always she'd failed. Walking toward the man she loved felt like the scariest and bravest step she'd ever taken. To know Jacob had asked her father for her hand weeks ago made her the happiest girl in Hickory Corners. To know that her own stubbornness put that precious love in jeopardy made her a fool.

"Hello, Jacob."

He stood so fast, whatever he'd been whittling fell.

Samantha picked it up. The wood felt smooth and strong in her hand. "What are you making? Something for the business?"

A lantern sat on one of the porch rails. Its light flickered across Jacob's face. "Do you really want to know?" He wrapped his fingers around the piece of wood and her hand.

Feeling bold, Samantha stepped closer. "Yes."

"I'm making another cradle. I've decided not to wait for the last minute. In many ways, I've let too much time pass by."

"I agree."

"Do you?"

"Yes. Did my father come by to see you tonight?" Samantha stepped back as Jacob moved closer.

His hand traveled up to cup her chin. "He did."

"And?"

"And what?"

"Did you ask him any questions?"

"No."

She would have stumbled and fallen had not his hands gripped her shoulders. Was she mistaken about—

He tugged her even closer, the grip on her shoulders turning into a caress. "I do have a question to ask you, though."

"Yes," she whispered.

"You need to hear the question before you say yes."

"Yes."

He kissed her then, right on Main Street. Samantha quickly glanced right and left. Why, anyone could have seen!

Fresh!

And just in case somebody was looking, Samantha kissed him back.

FOUR HEARTS

by Sally Laity

Chapter 1

The *Blue Hummingbird*'s engines shut down, and the wakes behind her paddle wheel smoothed out as the ornate white steamship coasted over the swift indigo current of the Ohio River to the broad, wooden wharf. Dock workers seized the stout ropes tossed from the vessel and secured them to the stationary landing posts, while at the wheel, silver-haired Captain John Sebastian hollered orders to his bustling crew.

Diana Montclair, her lace-gloved hands grasping the iron railing, blew wisps of honey-blond hair from her eyes while she watched the familiar activity, a mixture of resignation and anticipation flowing through her. Home again. . .at this place that had never truly been home.

Filling her lungs, she glanced around at the tiny hamlet nestled against a rolling scape of forest just donning the variegated greens of late spring. Changes were slight in Hickory Corners. A new doctor's office of the same red brick as the bank now complemented the quaint white clapboard church, but the rest of the town was made of plain or rough-hewn log dwellings. The dirt streets often blew with dust, or worse yet, lay ankle deep in mud from frequent rains. Yet she had to admit the town had a certain warmth and charm. A surprising array of shops and enterprises provided just about any service needed. Even the smallest home appeared tidy and inviting, and the local inhabitants seemed cheerful and content. What a pity she had so little in common with any of them.

She would never understand why her father insisted upon maintaining a house in this rural outpost in southwestern Ohio, with Cincinnati but a few hours west. Surely prestigious Montclair Shipping Line would fare much better with the larger city as its headquarters. Not that her mother and father ever deigned to spend any more time than necessary in this provincial settlement they had helped found. "And I shan't, either," she declared under her breath. "There is nothing for me here. Nothing at all."

"Diana! Over here!" a voice called from ashore.

Diana shifted her attention to the older woman waving so enthusiastically from the quay, and she smiled. Mildred Sanderson, the family's faithful housekeeper for what seemed like forever, had been the single mainstay in Diana's nineteen years. At least Millie always seemed happy to have her around. Drawing comfort from that, she lifted her arm and returned the welcoming gesture.

"Looks like somebody's glad to see ya, Miss Montclair," Ozzie Mallory teased from a few yards away.

Diana hiked her chin at the curly-haired "rooster," as the roustabouts were commonly called. He stacked cartons of supplies brought up from the hold to be delivered to the various business establishments in town. Barely older than herself, the sandy-haired sailor had known better than to make unwelcome advances to the boss's daughter. He had kept his distance, making only polite conversation in her presence. Nevertheless, she hadn't missed the admiring glances the ruddy-cheeked young man and other crew members cast her way from time to time.

"Mrs. Sanderson always meets me when I come home," Diana answered, subtly correcting her posture to that of a proper young lady.

"Guess we won't be havin' ya aboard much, now your schoolin's over. I wish ya the best, Miss. Good day." With that, the sturdily built seaman hefted a bulky crate to his muscled shoulder and headed for the gangway being lowered.

Watching after him from the shade of her bonnet's brim, Diana drew her woolen shawl snugly about herself and tried not to think about how her travels to Hickory Corners for Christmases and summers had come to an end. There might be some things about growing up in Boston's best boarding schools and finishing schools that she hadn't particularly liked, but free trips on her father's numerous ships and other sailing lines had pleasured her. Thanks to his reputation and influence, she always enjoyed the best accommodations and service. She knew the captains so well, they were almost like uncles, and every one of them took exceptional care of her.

Gathering the skirts of her stylish plum linen ensemble, Diana went to see if Mrs. Woodwright, the assistant teacher-chaperon provided by Prentiss Finishing Academy for Young Ladies, had finished repacking the trunks Diana would take ashore.

The broomstick-thin widow stood within the close confines of the tiny cabin they'd shared during this leg of the journey. The somber navy traveling suit on her slight figure only accented the darkness of the bunk-lined room as her nimble fingers fastened the buckles on the second piece of Diana's luggage. "All set," she announced a little too brightly. "It's been a singular pleasure accompanying you, Diana. I trust you'll enjoy being home with your family now."

"Thank you." Diana saw no point in elaborating on how little she really knew her parents. "Will you be taking tea at the boardinghouse before returning to Boston?"

The chaperon raised a pale hand to knead temples framed by tight brunette curls. "No, I think not. I'm fighting a bit of a headache just now. At times prolonged sailing does not agree with my constitution."

"I'm sorry. Shall I request a tray for you, then, before the ship weighs anchor?"

"Thank you, no. I'll just lie down for awhile and have something brought in later. Remember all the things you learned at the academy, Dear. You were one of our finest students, and I have every confidence you will find success in all your domestic ventures."

For a split second, Diana expected the dark-haired woman to hug her, but the awkward moment passed without an embrace. Diana moistened her lips and smiled.

"Thank you. . .for everything."

The bun atop Mrs. Woodwright's head bobbed with her nod. "God be with you, Dear."

"And with you," Diana whispered. Plucking her mulberry satin reticule from the built-in cabinet separating the two narrow bunks, she cast one more smile over her shoulder, then took her leave.

In moments she descended the gangway, one of a scant few arrivals. But then, who would come to Hickory Corners on purpose, she wondered caustically.

Diana's black kid traveling boots scarcely touched the dock's wooden planks before Millie Sanderson hastened over and enveloped her in loving arms. The housekeeper's plump frame and braided gray coronet emitted the spicy smell of apples and cinnamon, evidence that today was baking day. How strange to see her without her ever-present bib apron.

"Oh, my little darling," the older woman gushed, leaning back, her creased face absolutely beaming, her smile adding even more squinty lines at the corners of her small blue eyes. "So lovely to have you home. Did you have a good trip?"

"Oh, yes. Very. Except for two rainy days, the weather was ever so mild and lovely."

"Well, even so, I expect you're tired. We'll let the menfolk deal with your trunks. I'll draw you a hot bath, and you can have a nice soak while I whip up some supper." Sliding an arm around Diana, she waved to the brawny Bunk brothers working at the wharf as usual. "Tote her belongings up to the house, when you've a minute, and I thank you kindly."

"Will do, Ma'am," the stringy-haired pair chorused, then jabbed one another in the ribs and grinned before resuming their duties.

"I've been counting the days, little one, till you got here," Millie confessed, her button nose as rosy as her cheeks. She escorted Diana along the nearly straight route up Main Street toward the big two-story Montclair house occupying a sizable chunk of Birch Street.

"Will Mother and Daddy be coming to visit soon?" Diana hadn't meant to ask, but the words popped out seemingly of their own accord.

"Well, now, they know you were expected to arrive today, so mayhap they'll arrange their travels in a way that'll bring them our way one of these days."

I won't hold my breath waiting, Diana affirmed inwardly. Her unwelcome birth late in life to parents still grieving the loss of the son who'd been the light of their world had never quite been forgiven.

Catching a glimpse of Elsa Gerhard sweeping down the front steps of her father's newly renovated hotel, Diana ventured a small smile at the buxom brunette she knew from the stitchery group that gathered weekly at Edna Tidewell's home.

"Good afternoon, Diana," the blue-eyed girl said, resting a hand on the top of the broom handle. "Home to stay now?"

"So it would seem," she answered casually.

"Well, perhaps we'll be seeing you at the sewing circle, then. Oh, I think I hear little Georg waking up. I'd better run." And with that, she turned in a swirl of tan calico and dashed inside.

"Such a sweet new mama Elsa makes," Millie said.

Diana nodded politely, keeping pace with the older woman's slower stride.

"And doesn't the old boardinghouse look grand, now that all the improvements are completed?" Millie went on. "Elsa's husband worked night and day to turn the place into a real hotel, with Brady Forbes lending a hand whenever needed." She paused. "You remember Brady, don't you? The Tidewells' nephew."

"Quite," Diana muttered. Recollections of the bold young man who possessed an uncanny ability to rankle her on every visit home filled her with chagrin. Whenever she left to return to school, it would take weeks to dismiss him from her thoughts. . . which also vexed her to no end.

"Good day, ladies." As if hearing his name being mentioned, the person in question hailed them cheerily on his way out of the mercantile across the street.

Diana gave the lanky, square-jawed carpenter a casual nod as they went by. With that glossy brown-black hair and deep blue eyes, he was far too handsome for his own good. She sensed his gaze following them as they continued walking, but resisted the impulse to glance back and find out for certain. No sense in giving him the idea she was interested. Besides, this was the last place on earth she'd look for a mate, handsome or not. He probably had his cap set for some local girl himself.

Her gaze flitted over the simple but stylish dress displayed in the single window of the dress shop as they strolled by. Suitable for the town's special occasions, it was considerably less elegant than even the simplest frock Diana owned. Most of her wardrobe arrived at school in parcels shipped from New York, Philadelphia, or Paris, compliments of her mother. In truth, however, though always lovely and the latest fashion, not one of them had been Diana's personal choice.

By the time they passed the bank and her father's shipping office and crossed Birch Street, the peacefulness contrasted pleasantly with the noise and bustle so prevalent at the docks. Diana felt a measure of pride at the sight of the neatly kept grounds surrounding her parents' stately residence. She loved the fresh dove-gray paint and black shutters, the broad front door in gleaming federal blue, the wrought iron eagle weather vane atop the cupola. This was one of the few buildings in town sporting anything other than a weathered log or whitewashed exterior.

Millie had even made new cushions for the settees on the front porch, Diana noticed. Mounting the steps, she easily imagined herself curled up in the pillowy softness on sunny afternoons, reading James Fenimore Cooper or Keats or Shelley. Thank heaven, her father had a decent library of books here.

When the door latched behind them, Diana inhaled deeply, smiling with pleasure. The interior of the house bore sweet scents of baking. When had she last eaten? Before she finished calculating, her stomach growled audibly.

"Oh, you poor dear," the housekeeper crooned, taking their shawls and bonnets and draping them over a hook on the hall tree in the wide entry. "Let me fix you a bite to eat while the water heats for your bath."

"You're too kind," Diana said, a touch embarrassed. "I know you've been busy this whole day, then that long walk down to the wharf. . ."

"Nonsense. What's a body to do, if not keep busy? You go have a seat in the parlor, and I'll holler when the food's ready."

The offer was far too tempting to resist. Still smiling, Diana crossed the gleaming wood floor and entered the arched doorway to her right, where matching settees in striped silver damask caught the light pouring through white lace undercurtains and satiny burgundy drapes. Choosing an upholstered wing chair near the fireplace, she set her reticule on a marble-topped side table and kicked off her boots to rest her feet on the padded footstool. Home. She leaned her head back and closed her eyelids.

In what seemed the briefest of moments, Millie's light touch on her shoulder awakened Diana. Much to her surprise, she'd dozed off.

Upon entering the cheery kitchen with its shiny walls and yellow curtains, she took the proffered seat at the pine trestle table where a dainty feast of coddled eggs, raisin scones, cinnamon applesauce, and hot tea awaited her. "It looks delicious."

The housekeeper glowed. "Well, you just take your time and eat, little one. I'll start filling the tub. And after your bath, you just go on up to your room and have a snooze. There's church tonight, if you've a mind to go anyplace after you've rested up a bit. If not, there's always Sunday."

"I'll think about it," Diana promised as the older woman carried the first kettle to the round wooden tub kept in a small side room off the kitchen.

Later, however, bathed and changed and snuggled in the comfort of the feather bed in her rose-and-white room, Diana didn't know if she could bring herself to appear in public just yet. She'd only been in Hickory Corners in snatches and bits since she was old enough to be sent off to live with her Aunt Eunice, then to school. Everybody in town knew everybody else, and all of them lifelong friends.

And at nineteen, she didn't have the slightest notion how to make friends...with anybody. Never had. None of the girls at school had cared a whit about her. Only the teachers. And Millie. The dear, sweet housekeeper whom Diana wished for the thousandth time had been her mother.

At least in Boston there were theaters and museums, social soirees and activities to keep herself occupied, to say nothing of her studies. She hadn't counted on her school years coming to end just yet, before she'd decided what she wanted to do with the rest of her life. A sigh of depression came from deep inside at the bleak future now looming ahead. Her teachers expected the domestic skills they'd taught her at school would be put to use in a fine marriage, but Diana saw no hope of finding a suitable mate in this tiny place. How in the world was she supposed to endure being stuck here...perhaps for good?

❖

That does it, Brady Forbes thought, pounding the last nail into the steps he'd replaced on the porch of his aunt and uncle's parsonage. He picked up the tools scattered about him and placed them inside the toolbox he'd borrowed from his employer, Nathaniel Harmon, the cabinetmaker. The man had taught him more than he'd imagined there was to know about working with wood. Thanks to the skills he'd picked up through Nate's tutelage, these new steps would probably outlast the rest of the house, no matter how many feet traipsed up and down them in their comings and goings.

For a hamlet small as Hickory Corners, the parsonage saw much more than its share of visitors, Brady conceded, heading back to the shop. Aunt Edna's gracious spirit seemed to blossom when surrounded by ladies. Older ones attended a new prayer circle every Thursday, and the younger ones made up a sewing circle on Tuesdays. But far be it from him to find fault with those weekly gatherings. Truth be told, he held parsonage repairs in reserve for those very occasions. That way he could get in on all the delicious goodies served to the guests.

Brady's mouth watered as he recalled the peach tarts the banker's wife provided for today's prayer circle. Fit for a king, they were, and the ladies had persuaded him to have more than one. . .not that he'd put up much of a fight.

The sewing circle, though, was where the really good stuff was. Sometimes one of the gals would whip up some fudge or bake gingersnap cookies, two of his favorites. Those and the melt-in-the-mouth currant scones of Mildred Sanderson's.

Now that his thoughts had meandered in that direction, he wondered if little Miss Montclair ever deigned to soil her soft pink hands with floury dough. The golden-haired beauty dressed like a plate in a fashion catalog at Thomasohn's Mercantile. He chuckled, envisioning her in the voluminous apron she'd have to don to protect those fancy gowns of hers.

Then Brady's smile flattened. Of course, a guy would have to be blind not to recognize true beauty when he saw it. Glorious curls the color of warm honey—and likely as silky. Eyes of misty gray. The first time he'd lost himself in those silvery depths, his ability to speak coherently vanished. Took considerable joking around before he regained strength in his knees. To this day he didn't even remember all the asinine remarks he made to that ever-so-proper girl. But a few too many must have hit their mark, because she scarcely gave him the time of day now.

Funny thing, but he didn't see her as snobbish or haughty, the way some of the other young women in town did. He never had. Yet he did view Diana Montclair on an entirely different plane from the rest. . .and not merely because of her money and grand house. Not even because of her outward beauty. Something else about her called to his spirit, made him want to find out who she truly was inside. That intense loneliness in her eyes, maybe. Or the droop of those fragile shoulders when she neglected that rigid posture. The sad wilt to the corners of her rosy, upturned lips.

Whatever the elusive quality, he would try harder to be her friend, now that she'd come home to stay. Perhaps this time he'd get it right.

Chapter 2

A tantalizing blend of cooking smells from downstairs prompted a smile as Diana exited her bedroom late the next morning. More of her favorites, no doubt. Millie, bless her heart, always made sure that whenever her charge came home, there'd be a steady supply of dishes and baked goods Diana especially liked. But since this was no mere visit, a bit of discretion might be prudent. Too much indulgence, and soon enough, none of her gowns would fit.

Passing the older woman's bedroom, next door to hers, Diana couldn't help but note the homey quality. So different from the cloudlike rose-and-white frills that made up her own domain, the bright, warm colors in Millie's room invited a person to come in, sit down, linger. She admired the reds, yellows, and blues of a Log Cabin quilt draped over the walnut sleigh bed, the complementing hues in the shirred curtain. The coziest cushioned rocker occupied the corner. A last wistful glance, and she continued toward the staircase a few yards away.

But instead of going down, an impulse took Diana beyond them, to her parents' quarters at the end of the hallway. She stopped respectfully in the open doorway, as if visiting a museum or the bed chamber of one of America's founding fathers, feeling like an intruder.

Immaculate, as always, the room appeared ready for occupancy at a moment's notice, with hand-crafted furniture proof of Nathaniel Harmon's incredible talents. Sunshine glinted across the emerald and ivory satin coverlet on the four-poster bed, lighting upon the cut glass trinket dish on the carved wooden bureau and scattering miniature rainbows about the pristine walls. A plush Oriental carpet's intricate pattern graced the floor. Such splendor, Diana thought sadly, and no one here to see or enjoy the beauty. She would never understand why. Hiking her chin, she turned and retreated to the stairs, clutching her lavender-striped dimity skirts in both hands as she descended.

"Mmm. Something smells delicious," she said, upon reaching the kitchen, where fat cinnamon rolls cooled on the sideboard, creamy icing trailing down their puffy edges.

Stirring a pot of porridge at the hearth, Millie turned. "Good morning, Dear. Sleep well?"

"Like a dream." She took the spot awaiting her at the table.

"Good. Perhaps you'd like to run a few errands with me, then." Ladling out some oatmeal, she carried the bowl to Diana, then brought over a pitcher of milk.

"Thank you, Millie. I doubt I'll ever be the cook you are."

"Stuff and nonsense, Child. All a body needs is practice." She replaced the lid over the pot.

Spreading the linen napkin across her lap, Diana bowed her head for grace, knowing the housekeeper would expect that much. Even the school kept up that ritual, though it didn't carry much significance for Diana. She had difficulty with the concept of a *loving* Father. "What sort of errands?" she finally asked, pouring milk over the hot cereal.

"Oh, I wanted to take some baked goods to Charlotte Warner."

"The widow down the street?"

Millie's gray head nodded. "The old dear sprained her ankle a few days ago. Of course, she's much too self-reliant to allow anybody to do things for her, whether she's hobbling around or not. But she's so good about fixing meals for others, even making sure if there's a prisoner at the sheriff's place the fellow has a decent supper. About time somebody does her a kind turn. She shouldn't find fault with a couple cinnamon buns."

Chewing thoughtfully, Diana had to agree. "I'd be more than happy to tag along."

"Splendid. And since I made so many, I'll take a few to the Tidewells while I'm at it. That nephew of theirs about eats them out of house and home when he comes in from working at Nate Harmon's."

The oatmeal suddenly tasted like straw. Brady Forbes, with that quick wit and smart mouth of his, had embarrassed her to no end on her last visit. Just as she arrived at the sewing circle, she caught the cad doing an exaggerated impression of her. She could still hear the stifled giggles and snickers from the other girls at Mrs. Tidewell's gathering, and she didn't relish being the butt of his jokes again any time soon.

Not picking up on Diana's discomfort, Millie whipped off her big apron without missing a beat. "Edna promised to let me borrow a new crochet pattern that came all the way from Philadelphia, too. While you finish eating, I'll just run upstairs for my bonnet, make sure I don't have flour on my nose. Shouldn't be more than a minute."

"Take your time," Diana mumbled in the housekeeper's talkative wake.

But Millie turned out to be amazingly spry for someone of her age and returned to the kitchen before a single minute had gone by. She removed two baskets from the cupboard and filled them with baked goodies, spreading a checked cloth over top of each. "There. All ready. We'd best hurry. My old bones feel a storm coming."

"Yes, Ma'am." No longer hungry since Millie mentioned visiting the home of Brady Forbes, Diana left the remains of her breakfast and rose. She washed her hands on a damp rag and hastened after the housekeeper.

"The shawl you wore yesterday should do nicely," Millie suggested, plucking it and Diana's straw bonnet from a hook in the entry and handing them over. With no further ceremony, the two of them stepped out into the crisp morning, baskets looped over their forearms.

The Widow Warner's small dwelling, a few houses down Birch Street, sported an uncustomary light coat of dust on the porch, evidence that the woman's mishap had slowed her down. But greenery in the flowerbeds on either side promised a bounty of geraniums to come, now that winter was but a memory and summer just around the corner. Millie rapped softly.

"Come in," came the labored reply.

"It's Mildred," the housekeeper announced as they entered the dimly lit cabin, "and our Diana, come to visit. How are you getting along, Charlotte?"

"Oh, fair to middlin'," the slight widow responded from the padded rocking chair where she sat tatting lace, her brownish hair askew, the heavily splinted ankle propped on a pillowed footstool. A thin fire crackled in the hearth, casting a golden glow over plain, but serviceable furnishings. "Set a spell." She gestured to the faded settee and smiled as they sat down. "Don't mind sayin', it's been kinda lonesome around here lately. Seems odd not to be up and about the way I'm used to. My backside is purely tired of stayin' in one spot."

"I'd imagine. You are a person who keeps hopping." Millie paused. "I thought you might enjoy some sweets. You know me, always making too much."

"Yes, and I do appreciate your kindness, Millie." She switched her attention to Diana. "Home for the summer again, Child?"

"No, to stay this time," she answered. "I've finished my schooling, and my aunt back East has passed on."

"Well, the town can always do with another young face," Mrs. Warner said kindly. " 'Specially one pretty as your'n."

"My sentiments exactly," Millie affirmed, precluding Diana's response.

Diana averted her attention to some samplers and embroidered proverbs on the walls while the two older women chatted for a time about local happenings.

"Can I fix you some tea while I'm here?" the housekeeper eventually asked.

"Thank you, no. Just finished a pot. Thought it might help keep me awake, since settin' around makes a body sleepy."

"Well, then, we shan't keep you from your rest." Standing, Millie moved to put the basket within the widow's reach. "We've a few more errands to run before the sky completely clouds over. We'll come by again real soon."

"God bless you, Mildred, little Diana. Many thanks."

Neither spoke for several moments after taking their leave. Then Diana broke the silence. "I wonder if Mrs. Warner would like one of us to drop in and read to her now and then, while she's laid up, I mean. Since she can't get out at all, her days must seem overlong."

Millie beamed at her. "Why that's a splendid idea. Wouldn't seem so much like we were keeping a close eye on her that way. I do worry about the old gal, seeing as how she's by herself so much."

"Then let's look through Daddy's library when we get home and see what we can find." Though she had never done anything of that nature before, Diana actually found herself anticipating the possibility of reading to a shut-in. She'd always gotten along with older people. Somehow they didn't seem so critical and judgmental as people nearer her own age.

But as she and Millie neared the parsonage, the elation faded. Would *he* be around?

STITCHED WITH LOVE ROMANCE COLLECTION

"New steps," the housekeeper remarked with an appreciative eye when they started up to the porch. "No one can accuse young Mr. Forbes of not being handy. Those old ones were starting to sag in the middle."

The front door opened before they knocked. "Saw you two comin', I did," short Mrs. Tidewell informed them. "Come in. Come in." The woman's little round face had a glow about it that Diana always found endearing.

"We can't stay long," Millie said. "Just brought over some cinnamon buns from this morning's baking. Thought perhaps that nephew of yours might appreciate them when he comes home at noon."

Brady's dark-haired head peeked around the kitchen door at the opposite end of the room. "Is that what I'm smelling? Let me at 'em."

Diana's pulse thudded to a stop when, grinning broadly and rubbing his hands together in anticipation, he crossed the expanse between him and his aunt in a few long strides. His presence somehow made the air around them seem charged, as if a thunderstorm were directly overhead, though why he had that effect on was a mystery. After all, it wasn't as if she was interested. Anything but.

Mrs. Tidewell bestowed a proud smile on him and slipped an arm about his trim waist. "Brady came home a little early today, since he's in the middle of some project or other that needs long, involved work this afternoon." A light dawned over her sweet features. "In fact, the two of us were just about to sit down to dinner. Noah's visiting some of our sick folk in the outlying areas. We'd love to have you join us."

No! Diana pleaded silently, her gaze studiously avoiding his. She'd only just had breakfast a short while ago, even if she hadn't consumed all of it.

"Well," Millie hedged, "I did have a few more things to do before we head home, but the sky doesn't look too threatening just yet. We'd be glad to stay." With that, she shrugged out of her shawl, then waited for Diana to do the same.

Moments later, they gathered around the long, linen-covered table in the dining room, Mrs. Tidewell and Millie occupying the end chairs. Diana and Brady sat opposite one another on the sides. A hearty beef vegetable soup and crusty hot buns with butter lay before them. Diana tried to focus on that and the tidy familiarity of the parsonage in general, while she picked at the food.

"We're so happy you've come back to us, Diana," the minister's wife gushed. "All finished with school now?"

Diana swallowed the bite of roll she'd been chewing. "Yes, Ma'am. I won't be returning to Boston."

"Splendid. The girls will love having you at the sewing circle again."

"Should make for a livelier group," Brady said.

Having caught the teasing glint in his eyes, Diana lowered her lashes and concentrated on her meal.

"Well, it certainly is much livelier at home," Millie admitted. "Not so many echoes, and I don't feel I'm rattling around in all that empty space anymore."

"You know? Noah and I felt the same when our Brady came to us," Mrs. Tidewell said wistfully. "Just having him here made us feel young again. I can barely remember what our life was like before that. And he's so good about repairs. This old house has never been in better shape. All one has to do is mention something needing attention, and he does it."

Detecting a slight puffing out of the manly chest across from her, Diana gave intent consideration to repositioning the napkin on her lap.

"I'd imagine Nate Harmon keeps you pretty busy, then, Brady," Millie said, offering the plate of rolls to her friend's nephew.

"Thanks." He helped himself. "Yes, he keeps me hopping."

Relief flickered through Diana. Perhaps his job would keep him too occupied to pop in during sewing sessions. Even diminish the chance of running into him elsewhere. If so, living at Hickory Corners probably wouldn't be so tiresome after all.

"I still have a little time for other projects, though," he said. "Something in particular you need done?"

"Now that you mention it, yes. But there's no real hurry. Perhaps sometime when you have a spare minute or two you might stop by and check the roof. I noticed a damp spot on the ceiling after the last rainstorm."

Diana's gaze shot to him just in time to see a broad grin spread across his face.

"Sure thing. Be glad to."

"Oh, good. When you come by, I'll take you right to it. In the upstairs bedroom. The one on the left."

But that's my *room!* Diana's heart gave a lurch. Even if she wasn't likely to endure his presence at the sewing circle, or chance meeting him in public, the clod was coming to her own private domain. She felt warmth rise over her cheekbones.

"I'll try to come over one day this week, Miz Sanderson," he promised. "Of course, I don't have much experience with roofing, but I should be able to figure out the problem."

"I'd appreciate that. And so will Diana, since the problem concerns her room."

"Ah. In that case, I'll make it a top priority." The man had the audacity to flash a wink at Diana.

Suddenly devoid of even the hint of an appetite, she sank back against the chair's spindles, no longer caring whether her spine had the proper arch.

"Might I offer everyone some apple tarts?" Mrs. Tidewell asked, rising to clear the dishes. "Made fresh just this morning."

"They do sound tempting," Millie confessed. "You know the weakness I've always had for those little pies of yours."

"Good. I'll be just a second." With that, she toted away the soiled things.

"I'll help, Aunt Edna." Brady carted to the kitchen what she couldn't carry. He returned with a stack of plates, which he set out with a flourish one by one, his unrelenting gaze lingering a touch overlong when he placed Diana's.

His aunt brought in a platter of folded, golden-brown pastries and passed them around before pouring tea into everyone's cups.

"Excellent, as always," the housekeeper commented shortly, smacking her lips. "Just excellent. I must try this recipe sometime."

"There's none easier," the minister's wife told her. "Oh, and don't forget, I promised to let you borrow the new pattern I received the other day. You can adjust the stitch count to make either doilies or scarves." She tilted her head at Diana. "You crochet as well, I believe?"

"Yes, but it's not my favorite pastime."

"What is, Miss Montclair?" Brady challenged, obviously endeavoring to maintain a straight face. "If you don't mind my asking."

She met those taunting indigo eyes evenly. "I particularly enjoy going to the symphony or visiting museums. . .neither of which is available at Hickory Corners, of course."

"Of course. Well, we'll have to come up with something to provide you with a few *pleasant diversions* then."

Diana opened her mouth to issue a crisp retort, but Millie rose at that instant. "I do thank you, Edna, for your hospitality. We had a delightful visit."

The minister's wife smiled. "Always a pleasure to be in your company. And Diana. So nice to have you back home again. Please don't be a stranger. We hope to see much more of you at church. And don't forget the sewing circle."

Blotting her lips on the napkin, Diana stood to her feet and smiled sweetly as she and Millie went to put on their wraps and take their leave. "Thank you, Mrs. Tidewell. I'll definitely make time to visit with the other girls."

"My little group is changing so quickly," the older woman mused. "Three of the dear girls married already, one with a baby, another in the family way. But we still relish our sewing sessions. Of course, we don't always labor over quilts or items for hope chests these days. Nowadays it can be a wedding dress, a baby blanket, what have you."

"Well, I'll look forward to being part of the circle again."

"And I'll look forward to more of that fudge you used to bring," Brady called from the dining room.

With a disbelieving roll of her eyes, Diana followed the housekeeper outside. The man was worse than the mosquitoes of summer. There was just no getting rid of him.

Chapter 3

"O ff to a brilliant start, Dunderhead," Brady muttered, striding purposefully back to Nathaniel Harmon's place of business. All those gallant plans, and what's the first thing he does in Diana Montclair's presence, but act the village idiot? Maybe he should borrow one of Nate's wood clamps...that ought to keep a big, overgrown mouth shut.

What quality about the gently bred gal made him act like a clod or blurt out the first thing that popped into his mind? Shaking his head in a futile attempt to slough off his frustration, Brady glanced toward the well-kept mansion positioned halfway between the parsonage and Nate's place. So the front bedroom belonged to her. . . .

A barely discernable movement behind the ruffled pink curtains stirred the gauzy panels. He didn't immediately avert his gaze, but merely adjusted it slightly, as if trying to spot a missing shingle above the chamber. Nothing seemed amiss, at least from this vantage point.

At the *clop* of approaching horse hooves, Brady redirected his attention to the wagon turning from Main Street onto Birch. He waved when he recognized Betsy Walker at the reins.

The brown-eyed blond tipped her bonneted head and smiled a greeting while the rig clattered past him, its bed laden with supplies to be divided between her own home and her father's farm. Though married, she still did the marketing for both households. Aunt Edna had mentioned that Betsy's father and siblings managed breakfast on their own, but they ate dinner and supper with Betsy and Ty each day.

Once the dust cloud settled, Brady angled across the street to the carpentry shop, where spring's sweet freshness gave way to the more pungent smells of cut wood, resin, and glues emanating from the squat building. He'd grown to appreciate those distinctive odors.

The front door stood open, amplifying the high-pitched whine of the lathe as he went inside.

"Oh. You're back." The master carpenter looked up from the foot-powered machine now slowing to a stop. The warmth of Nate's smile and a merry twinkle in his eyes kept him from being downright homely. The twitch of a grin widened his graying handlebar mustache, curled on either end to the size of a two-bit piece. Somehow, the waxed perfection detracted from the man's underbite, lessening the prominence it might otherwise have. "Edna feed ya good, did she?"

173

"Yep," Brady replied, patting his stomach. "To the gills." He navigated the clutter of partially completed projects scattered about the remaining floor space. Even in a town the size of Hickory Corners, Nate found a ready market for the excellent cornices, cabinets, and finely crafted furniture produced in his shop. What didn't sell locally he transported to settlements in the outlying areas, so the livelihood generated a steady income.

Brady went to check the joinings on the mahogany desk he'd been working on before noon.

"Lookin' good, don't ya think?" Nate prodded, his faded blue eyes making a slow perusal from where he sat. "Right fine job on the carvin' and joints. You'll soon be puttin' me outta business, Lad."

"That'll be the day. You've taught me everything I know. If not for you, I wouldn't be able to tell a chisel from a keyhole saw."

The older man gave a nod. "Well, holler if ya need any help. I'm almost finished with these table legs."

"Will do." Brady returned to measuring lengths of the woods he'd use to construct drawers. Then he began sawing, taking care to keep the angle of the cuts straight, the way he'd been taught. He smiled to himself, picturing the piece finished and in Uncle Noah's office at the church. The unassuming minister had made do with a dilapidated relic long enough. His upcoming birthday would provide the perfect excuse for a well-deserved surprise. Little enough thanks, Brady mused, after he and Aunt Edna took him in, showed him what love is. The two of them turned him around. Saved his wayward life from ruin.

Now, if only he could learn to corral his mouth. A golden-haired vision stole into his thoughts, adorned in translucent colors as delicate as the hues of a rainbow. Would she ever forgive him for embarrassing her last summer?

"Whatcha stewin' over?" His employer set down the table leg he'd finished shaping. "Considerin' the season, must be gal trouble."

Brady shot him a droll grin. "What makes you say that?"

"A man don't get to be nigh onto two-score years without learnin' a thing or two."

"Reckon not."

They both resumed working, the whirring of the lathe and the sharp grating of the saw's teeth echoing off the hard planes of cabinets and shelves. Then Brady stopped mid-stroke, waiting until Nate did the same. "I don't suppose—" he began, feeling uncomfortably warm in the vicinity of his neck. "Aw, shucks. Ever get yourself on some young lady's wrong side?"

"Whoo-ee." The man's guffaw accompanied a smart whack on his sturdy knee. "Ain't nobody on this earth done that more'n me. In case ya never noticed, I don't have myself a little wife t'home, greetin' me of an evenin'."

Brady shrugged. "I figured you just weren't interested."

Running stubby fingers through his graying hair, the carpenter grew thoughtful. "I was interested enough, all right, in my younger days. Just seemed to have this talent for puttin' my foot in my mouth. All the way up to my belt buckle."

"Somehow, I know what you mean." Brady wagged his head.

"Well, time helps more often than not. Eventually a gal forgets what the problem was." With a decisive nod, Nate fingered a section of smooth, turned wood on the machine and began pumping the treadle with his booted feet once more.

Brady tried to draw comfort from his employer's words, but couldn't quite believe things could work so smoothly in this case. A goodly number of months had gone by since he'd humiliated her in front of the other girls, unintentional or not. And before he had a chance to apologize she'd been on her way back East. He had his work laid out, all right, trying to redeem himself in Diana Montclair's eyes.

※

Sunday dawned surprisingly clear after a day and a half of steady rains. Glancing up at the damp circle on the ceiling above the maple chest-on-chest that contained her frilly "sit-upons," as the teachers from the academy so delicately termed "underthings," Diana wondered how long it would be before a chunk of wet plaster would come crashing down on her head, shingles and all.

Much as she cringed at the thought of Brady Forbes stepping foot in her private boudoir, she knew Millie had been right in seeking help. Expelling a breath of resignation, she looped a fresh chemise and some drawers over one arm and moved to the matching wardrobe to choose a gown for church. The russet silk, perhaps, so as not to show the inevitable mud she and the rest of the congregation would track in.

An hour later, after a delay caused by a loose button on the housekeeper's dress, Diana and Millie arrived at Hickory Corners Church mere moments before the start of the service. They took seats in their customary pew. Although the rustic meetinghouse could not compare to some of the loftier houses of worship Diana had attended in Philadelphia and Boston, she found the atmosphere here noticeably friendlier and more welcoming.

Even with most of the churchgoers facing forward in anticipation of the opening prayer, Diana realized how many of the townsfolk had become familiar to her during her many visits. She tried not to be obvious in picking out the ones easiest to recognize.

In their Sunday finery and seated with their respective husbands now, rather than being clustered shoulder to shoulder the way they used to, Elsa Gerhard, Samantha Stahl, and Betsy Walker offered tentative smiles of greeting. So did the Widow Warner, whose makeshift crutches lay propped against the wall alongside the pew she occupied. Diana returned their smiles with a polite one of her own, wondering if any of the girls would approach her afterward to visit.

Her meandering gaze idly drifted across the aisle. . .and met Brady's lopsided grin. Even before she could lower her lashes, she noticed how tall and splendid he looked in a chocolate frock coat and matching trousers, every strand of his nearly ebony hair in place. She couldn't suppress a tiny smile, but assured herself it was only proper to return his, after all.

Interrupting her musings, Reverend Tidewell, in his best black suit, his tuft of white hair slicked back, stepped to the lectern. He raised a bony white hand to signify silence, then bowed his head. "Our most gracious Father and Lord, we ask Thy blessing on this Sabbath service. May all that is said and done in Thy name be honoring and glorifying to Thy precious Son, in whose name we pray.

"Now," he continued, "let us begin by standing and singing 'A Mighty Fortress Is Our God,' page twenty-seven in the hymnal."

The pump organ wheezed out a few chords in introduction, and Millie edged closer to share the open book in her hands. The older woman's contralto blended pleasantly with Diana's clear soprano through every verse, yet the lovely lilt of Elsa's sweet voice stood out ever so slightly above the rest. Brady, she noted, only held a hymnal and followed the words in silence.

But directly behind Diana a rich tenor belted out the lyrics. Recognizing the particular range, she surmised that successful attorney Martin Crabtree must also be visiting from Capital City. The handsome bachelor possessed considerable charms, and with his fine education seemed somehow out of his element in rustic Hickory Corners whenever he came to visit his gossipy mother.

"Please be seated," the minister said, his expression gentle as ever as he assessed his flock. "I must say, it's gratifying to see such a goodly number of folk present this morning, after yesterday's rain."

Nods and smiles made the rounds.

After a slight pause, he cleared his throat, removed reading glasses from a breast pocket, and put them on. His kindly eyes scanned the congregation over the gold wire frames. "The title of my sermon this morning is, 'Ye Are the Salt of the Earth.' Turn with me if you will to the Gospel of Matthew, chapter five."

In the ensuing shuffle of pages, Diana stifled a yawn and sought a more comfortable position on the hard pew, bolstering herself for a long half hour's tedious dronings. She didn't exactly see any connection between living people and the common substance, salt. Besides, she had other things to occupy her mind, such as ignoring the surreptitious glances from a certain bachelor across the aisle. And the occasional brushings of a man's booted foot against her heel—which occurred a touch too often for it to be merely accidental. No one ever accused Martin Crabtree of being subtle. Straightening in her seat, Diana moved her feet safely out of his reach. She stared unseeing toward the minister, while her fingers toyed with the lace-edged handkerchief from her reticule, folding it a dozen ways, then rolling impossibly narrow rolls.

Eventually she heard the good reverend announce the closing prayer. Revitalized at having endured the Sunday service, she smiled with satisfaction and stood for the benediction.

A noticeable rustle of skirts and scuffle of feet immediately followed the minister's final "amen," and Millie moved a few steps away to chat with her lady friends.

"My, my." Fair-haired Martin stepped in front of Diana, his most dazzling smile focused on her as he gave a somewhat-formal bow. His expertly tailored suit enhanced his manly form to perfection. "If it isn't the lovely Miss Montclair, gracing our little hamlet with her glorious presence. Home for another summer?"

The rust-colored plume on Diana's bonnet fluttered as she tilted her head with cool reserve, first at him, then at his sharp-nosed mother. Obviously the young man had inherited his marvelous features from his late father's side. "Mr. Crabtree. Mrs. Crabtree. How nice to see you both."

"You've not answered my question," Martin prompted. "How long will we mere mortals be treated with the benefit of your angelic face?"

From across the aisle, Brady snickered, then shook his head and blended into the departing crowd waiting to shake his uncle's hand.

"Actually, I've come home to stay this time," she admitted, a little miffed at the departing carpenter's attitude.

Martin's golden eyebrows rose high. "Do tell. That is splendid news, is it not, Mother? Just splendid." A smugly serene look passed between the pair.

At that moment Elsa stepped nearer, her sleeping cherub in her arms. She looked every inch the doting mother. "So glad to see you at service, Diana. I do hope you'll be coming to Mrs. T's on Tuesday."

"I'm considering it, yes," Diana said.

"See?" Martin Crabtree said, adding a knowing smile. "You're in great demand with the locals."

In the distance, Diana caught Samantha's and Betsy's decidedly frosty glares in the attorney's direction and furtive glances in her own as the two took their leave. Her confusion gave way to doubt. Even if she attended the sewing circle every week from now until doomsday, would she ever truly be part of their close-knit group?

Chapter 4

Tuesday. The dreaded day had come.

Even as she dressed for breakfast, Diana still debated whether to go to the sewing circle. Conflicting thoughts warred in her mind. The other town girls shared the memories and experiences of a lifetime in Hickory Corners. She did not know how to relate to them. Surely they would believe she was trying to elbow her way into that close-knit group.

"All ready for your special day?" Millie asked with a cheery smile when Diana entered the kitchen. The housekeeper dished up a generous serving of scrambled eggs and feather-light biscuits and brought them to the table.

Diana forced a smile. "I. . .thought perhaps you might need me here at home. To. . .help with. . . ," she fluttered a hand, trying to think of a word, "something."

Millie tucked her chin, a baffled expression scrunching her features. "Nonsense. I haven't a thing pressing, and even if I did, what couldn't wait a few hours? Now that you're home to stay, you need to spend time with the other girls again. Rekindle those friendships."

Diana heaved a sigh. Millie had no idea, no idea at all. Only one thing would make her understand. Honesty. "But that's just it, Millie," she confessed at last. "They're not my friends. They've never been." Maddening tears came dangerously near the surface, their presence stinging the back of Diana's eyes, causing moisture she couldn't quite suppress. She swallowed hard. "If my own mother and father don't consider me worth being around, why should anyone else?"

The older woman's mouth fell open with a gasp. She dropped the dish towel she'd been using and flew to Diana's side, wrapping comforting arms around her. "Don't think such things. I have a hard time myself, understanding your parents' actions, but I know they love you. They truly do. Your brother's sudden death hit them real hard, and the only way they could get through that sorrow was to throw themselves into that shipping business. Things were just coming together for them when you came along. It just wasn't the best time for them to let up."

"What about now?" Diana asked miserably. "Everyone knows Montclair Shipping Line is one of the biggest enterprises on the Ohio and Mississippi Rivers. When will there be enough success and enough money for them to make room for me?"

"I don't know that," the housekeeper crooned. "Only the Good Lord can see into the future. But I pray every day that He'll open their eyes to see the treasure they have right here." She hugged harder.

Diana didn't know if she should set any hopes on that or not. Even if her parents did decide to come here and make a life with her, the house would be filled with inhabitants who barely knew one another.

"In the meantime," Millie went on, straightening and returning to her chore, "there are people in town who'll accept you, if you'll only let them. You have to remember, though, in order to make friends, you must *be* a friend."

Be a friend.

A simple concept, yet profound. Diana pondered it throughout the remainder of the morning and during dinner.

Afterward, with the housekeeper's admonishment still ringing in her ears, Diana couldn't help but take her time walking the short distance to the minister's home. What sort of reception would she have? Did the others truly want her to come, or had the invitation at church merely been a pretense, a polite gesture one might make to any regular visitor in town?

Happy chatter wafted out of the parsonage's open window, along with the hem of a lacy curtain fluttering on the breeze. Her reservations intensified. Gazing idly at her feet, she did notice the new steps sported a coat of paint since her and Millie's visit, a gray reminiscent of the decks on her father's steamships. Grasping the skirt of her pale-green lawn gown in her hands, she drew a strengthening breath, approached the door, and rapped.

"Oh, Diana," Mrs. Tidewell said, her gracious smile more than welcoming. "Come in, my dear." Disposing of Diana's shawl and bonnet, she ushered her inside to the comfortable sitting room, where the other girls from town were positioned around a quilt frame. The older woman raised her voice slightly. "Everyone, our little group is complete once again."

Elsa, Betsy, and Samantha, looking fresh in crisp muslin and calico dresses, paused in their stitching and glanced up, their smiles pleasant, their demeanors expectant.

"What did you bring to work on?" Mrs. T asked, guiding Diana to the padded rocker in the corner which she'd always preferred.

"Nothing, really." Venturing a step into the unknown, Diana cast caution to the wind. "I. . .was wondering if I might learn to stitch on the quilt, if it isn't too much trouble to teach me. I must confess, sewing has always been my weakness. I've only ever done well with embroidery." She held her breath, expecting a rebuff.

"Sure, we'd love to have you." Elsa scooted her chair to one side, making room between her and Betsy.

Diana, greatly relieved, pulled up a seat for herself, while across from her, Betsy's cousin Samantha offered a tentative smile. Perhaps this wouldn't be so bad after all, Diana decided.

The pastor's wife brought a quilting needle, a thimble, and a spool of thread to her from the sideboard. "Let me show you how to get started."

She threaded the eye expertly and sat down, one hand above the quilt, the other below while she rocked the needle, collecting a series of ten stitches on that minuscule length. Watching her, Diana immediately lost heart. Her best efforts at sewing had been miserable failures. How could this one be any different?

Mrs. Tidewell's conspiratorial smile put her at ease. "That's how you'll quilt once you've had some practice. But for now, merely poking the needle straight down, like this, then up again from below, will do nicely. Down, up. Down, up. Here, you try." Mrs. Tidewell relinquished the chair and handed her the needle and thimble.

Diana drew an uneasy breath, took the seat, and set to work, not even daring to imagine attempting two stitches in a row on the needle, even with these lightweight layers of fabric. She gave all her concentration to laboring over the simpler method.

"You should have seen me trying to master this process," Elsa said kindly, an understanding sparkle in her blue eyes as she worked on her section. "Poor Mrs. T must have sat for hours after we'd all gone home, ripping out every pathetic stitch I'd done and redoing them."

An astonished gasp issued from the little woman. "I did no such thing." Coming to peek over Diana's shoulder, she perused the crooked stitches and nodded her encouragement. "On the contrary, I shall always treasure those first sweet projects completed by my fledgling seamstresses. One of my greatest joys has been witnessing your progress over the years. None of us is born with any ready-made skills. We learn things by practice. Including quilting."

Somewhat more optimistic, but still feeling all thumbs, Diana jabbed the needle into the bright material. She stopped now and then to give a critical eye to her work while the other girls chattered in the easy way she'd always envied, sharing special memories of events unknown to her. Perhaps it was her own fault she had virtually no pleasant memories of classmates from her school years.

Diana contemplated the unique design of the quilt, each block of which held four hearts in different patterns, but complementing colors, with the points meeting at the center. To her, the theme seemed symbolic of the sewing circle. . .at least how it might have been, had she not lived away from town. Four girls, growing up together, forever friends.

Yet, part of her still felt like an intruder. Perhaps always would.

Just then, the grandfather clock across the room chimed the hour, and then Elsa yawned and stretched, a sheepish grin widening her rosy cheeks.

"Sounds like somebody had another long night with baby Georg," Betsy said. "I'm learning what to expect when my own little one makes his entrance into the world." She patted her blossoming tummy and blushed becomingly.

Elsa ceased stitching momentarily. "After being wakeful much of the night, I expect he'll sleep the afternoon away. Of course, that should make it easier for Shane to look after him. Now that our little angel is toddling around, he finds some rather interesting things to get into when our backs are turned."

Diana's curiosity got the best of her. "He wakes you up in the night?"

Elsa nodded. "He must be cutting new teeth again."

"I should think that's why people hire nannies," Diana blurted without thinking. "How can one function during the daytime if deprived of sleep?"

A peculiar look passed between the others.

"I really don't mind tending to Georg," Elsa said, her tone gentle. "I consider the responsibility a joy and a blessing. He's growing so quickly, he'll soon be out of this stage. Then I'll get more sleep."

Mrs. Tidewell took advantage of the awkward moment to cross the room for her Bible. "I believe we'll read the Twenty-third Psalm today, pertaining to the way our Lord looks after His own."

Listening to her soothing voice while continuing to sew, Diana paid close attention to the words being read. On Sunday, the Reverend suggested that God's children were salt. Now it seemed they were also considered sheep. How very strange, those two mental images.

After the Scripture reading, the girls took a break for refreshments, serving themselves from the sideboard, where the minister's wife had just poured cups of tea.

"These gingersnaps," Samantha said dreamily, munching a cookie, "are truly delicious, Betsy."

"Thank you. Ty especially likes them, so I bake them pretty often. Of course, with little brothers and a sister popping over to gobble every batch warm from the oven, I have to hide some, or he'd never get any."

"It's much the same at the hotel," Elsa confessed, "trying to keep up with boarders and guests."

Diana almost injected something about the benefits of having Millie around, but caught herself just in time. It seemed difficult to relate to people who did things for themselves, when she'd been waited on practically her whole life. In reality, however, the very fact the other girls were so self-reliant only made her envy them all the more.

"Would you care for more tea, Dear?" Mrs. Tidewell asked, making the rounds with the china pot.

Diana peered into her cup, amazed to see the bottom. She'd been so absorbed in her thoughts, she couldn't recall drinking a drop. "Yes, please."

"Are you glad to be home for good now?" Elsa asked, coming to sit beside her on the settee.

In all Diana's years, she could remember no one ever asking her opinion on anything, only an endless string of *go here, do this, do that,* to which she'd submitted with no other recourse. Now, however, she dared another step into this strange new life. "I'm. . .trying to adjust. Everything's so different."

"I would imagine. I've often wondered how it must have been for you, going far away to the big city, living in boarding schools, taking excursions to see wonderful sights, traveling all that way home again. You must miss those benefits."

"I did enjoy sailing on the steamships," Diana confessed, some favorite memories surfacing. "Watching the lovely countryside passing by."

"Mind if we listen in?" Betsy asked. "I haven't traveled anywhere." She and Samantha, obviously having overheard at least part of the conversation, drew up chairs and perched on them.

Having an audience who actually appeared interested in what she might say gave Diana a heady feeling she'd never before experienced. She felt some of her guard melting away as a yearning for the other girls to like her came to the fore. Was this what it was like to make friends? She looked from one face to the next, their sincere interest enabling her to relax and smile. "The schools I attended were quite lovely, with sprawling grounds one could stroll across between class hours. I most enjoyed visiting museums and going to the symphony."

"I'll probably never see anything beyond Hickory Corners," Elsa mused, "though my family did travel some when I was a youngster. Shane has been all over, of course. He tells me lots of stories."

Mrs. Tidewell, restoring order to the sideboard, smiled their way. "Perhaps we could continue sharing our recollections as we get back to work."

"Yes, Mrs. T," they singsonged.

Scarcely had they settled back into their places, when lively footsteps sounded from outside. The door opened, admitting Brady, unrolling the sleeves of his blue homespun shirt while he craned his neck in the direction of the baked treats. "Any good stuff left?" His unabashed grin made the rounds.

At least, Diana surmised, it included more than just her. She'd looked down so quickly, she could only guess. She had quite enough to focus on, remembering how the stitches were supposed to go.

"Oh, pshaw," his aunt said. "As if we'd let a grown man starve. I've a plate already fixed for you out in the kitchen. Then if you're still hankering for sweets, you can help yourself to the cookies."

His not-so-quiet steps clumped across the plank floorboards, diminishing only a little as he disappeared into the other room.

"So what's it like, going to an actual symphony?" Samantha asked Diana, her eyes aglow as she held her needle poised to sew. "To be in some huge hall, with music filling all the nooks and crannies. I should think that would be heaven."

"Much better than having only a string quartet providing the entertainment," Diana said with a smile. "Although, they, too, can be quite. . .entrancing."

"I hope to go to a grand music hall one day," Samantha said. "We don't have much entertainment here in town."

"What's this about entertainment?" Brady echoed, carrying his dinner in one hand on his return. He plopped down onto a side chair next to the wall. One with a direct line of vision to Diana as he ate. "You saying you don't like Nate's fiddlin' at socials?"

"We like it fine," Betsy said. "But I'm sure we'd also enjoy some more refined music now and then."

"*Refined.* Ah, yes. You're hearing about the advantages of city life, as opposed to the more lowly lifestyle of country bumpkins." A smirk took up residence on his face as his gaze slid to Diana.

Diana felt her cheeks burning. "I merely answered their questions," she said in her own defense, miffed that he'd butted in.

"I reckon. But quiet towns have some benefits of their own. I wouldn't discount country life altogether."

"I wasn't doing that." Aware of her mounting emotions, Diana clamped her lips together, lest she really speak her mind. Here she'd been, on the verge of relating to the young women who'd been practically strangers to her over the years, and *he* had to come in and ruin everything. "Oh, would you look at the time," she said in a rush. "I really must be going." Knotting her thread, she clipped it off and rose. "Splendid visiting with you all," she told the others, then smiled at her hostess. "Thank you for the refreshments and the sewing lesson. I had a lovely time." She marched right past Brady Forbes without so much as a glance, her clipped steps beating a staccato tempo on her way to the door.

"Actually," Elsa remarked, "I need to get back to the hotel myself. We're expecting a ship around the supper hour." Dropping her sewing supplies in Mrs. T's basket, she snatched up her belongings and followed after Diana.

Outside, Elsa placed a hand on Diana's forearm. "Thank you for coming to the circle this week. Don't mind Brady, though. He's far from being the town rake. He's really quite the wit and takes singular pleasure in teasing us all, as you'll discover week by week. Please don't let him get to you."

"What makes you think he gets to me?" Diana asked through gritted teeth.

The dark-haired girl merely smiled. "Oh, I don't know. Intuition, perhaps."

Despite herself, Diana calmed a little. But reliving the humiliation she'd suffered last summer thanks to the Tidewells' nephew, it was pointless to correct the new mom. "Thank you, Elsa."

"For what?"

"For helping me to feel less a stranger today. I appreciate it."

"You're most welcome. The other girls and I, well, we've always wondered what you were really like. Now you're home to stay, we'll finally have a chance to get to know you. So you'll keep coming every week then?"

"I'll try. I really will."

"Good. I'm glad. See you at church on Sunday." Swiveling on her heel, she crossed Birch Street, heading for the hotel.

Diana watched after her, amazed at how truly *friendly* Elsa Gerhard seemed now that she was married. Samantha and Betsy had made an effort to make her feel at ease today, too. If those girls were willing to accept her presence in Hickory Corners, perhaps it was time she accepted her fate and did the same.

At least *some* of her new life would be easier to endure. With a scathing glance over her shoulder at the parsonage, Diana headed for the nearby sanctity of her parents' big house.

Where *that man* would appear soon enough, to fix the roof.

Chapter 5

onsiderably lighter at heart after the gathering at the parsonage, Diana would have skipped home, except for the conviction that such childish behavior hardly befit a proper young lady. Nevertheless, she hurried, eager to tell Millie about how the town girls had welcomed her into their group and made her feel a part of the sewing circle.

The only dark cloud had been Brady's appearance. The very sight of him dredged up the memory of the incident when he'd embarrassed her in front of those same girls. Did they remember, too? Hoping not, Diana ignored thoughts of him and focused on her new friends as she traipsed up the porch steps and went inside.

"That you, Honey?" Millie called from the kitchen.

"It is, indeed." Not even attempting to control her smile, Diana followed the housekeeper's voice to the room that seemed the woman's personal haven.

"Well, well. Look at that face." Millie paused in rolling a batch of biscuits and propped floury knuckles on one hip. "Methinks you had a pleasant time at Edna's this afternoon."

"I did. And you were right. The other girls, they—"

A knock rattled the front door.

"I'll run my bonnet upstairs while you see who's come," Diana said. "I'll tell you all about the sewing circle later." Upon reaching her room, she flung the straw hat gleefully toward her wardrobe and flopped across her bed to relive every minute of her experience at the parsonage. Or rather, almost every minute of it. Part of her couldn't help wondering if Elsa's parting comments about Brady Forbes were true. If so. . .

Those musings hung in suspension when footsteps approached her door and stopped.

"Diana?" Millie rapped lightly.

"Come in." She eased to an upright position as the housekeeper entered.

He strolled in behind her.

Diana blanched and sprang to her feet, her pulse beating in her throat.

"Miss Montclair," Brady said, with a polite nod, the brim of his everyday hat clutched in those long fingers, while midnight blue eyes made a sweeping circuit of her private boudoir.

"There's the problem," Millie told him, pointing to the discoloration bordering the crown molding on the ceiling. "And it's getting worse every time it rains. Or even sprinkles, as it did last night."

"Hmm." He tipped his dark-haired head back and assessed the spot from where he stood. "Don't suppose you have a ladder."

"Matter of fact, I do, out back. Not the sturdiest one around, but it's handy. I'll take you to the shed."

"Great. Much obliged, Ma'am."

As the two took their leave, Diana exhaled a nervous breath. She gave fleeting thought to making herself scarce, but before she figured how to do so without being obvious, Brady came clomping up the stairs again. Alone this time. Cutting off any hope of an exit. . .but was she really certain she wanted one?

He seemed so much. . .taller. . .up close. How could his presence fill up so much of the room's space?

A knowing grin softened those angular features. "Miz Sanderson had to tend to some biscuits, then said something about reading to Miz Warner later."

Diana gave a mute nod and fidgeted with a fold of her skirt, watching him survey the feminine trappings surrounding them both. Realizing she was gawking at his strong, noble profile, she quickly averted her gaze.

"Nice place you've got here. Real pretty." He carried the ladder over below the water stain and propped it against the wall, adjusting the footing a time or two. Then he swung her a sidelong glance. "Suppose you could hold onto this while I climb up? Looks like the thing's seen better days."

"I. . .of course." Even with the little experience she'd had around workmen, and the tools of their trade, Diana knew a rickety contraption when she saw one. She put aside her reservations and went to help. So far he didn't seem threatening in the least. "What should I do?"

He shrugged. "Hold the sides. If the thing collapses, cushion my fall, okay?"

Eyes widening, she took a step backward. "You can't be serious!"

His grin broadened as he chuckled and shook his head. "I'm sorry. Really. I don't know what there is about you, Diana Montclair, that makes me act the fool. But I really would appreciate your help here. Just take a firm grip on the sides. I'll only be a second. Promise."

Be a friend. With Millie's encouragement ringing in her ears, Diana chose to give him the benefit of the doubt and moved to do his bidding. As Brady ascended the few rungs required to reach the ceiling, she tried not to be brazen enough to stare at that masculine form while her fingers absorbed the vibrations of his movements. But when he stopped, she couldn't help checking to see what he was doing.

Brady pressed his fingertips against the darkened spot. "Soft, all right." He climbed down again, more confidently, then brushed his hands on his trousers. "This place have an attic?"

She nodded. "The door leads off the hall."

"Let's go see what we can find up there, shall we?"

Inside, Diana knew he spoke in generalities. He might need to be guided to the attic door, but he didn't need her tagging along up into those dark recesses after him.

Still, she went anyway. . .the *friendly* thing to do.

Reaching the dusty top landing, Brady stood aside so she could join him. Then he glanced around. "Let's see. If my calculations are correct, over there's about where your room is." He strode toward where he'd pointed, and knelt down. "Sure 'nuf. It's damp here, too."

Diana swung her gaze upward the same instant he did, and saw the tiny gap where some skylight shone through.

"Well, would you look at that," Brady said with a quirk of his mouth. He cut her a glance. "How are you at climbing roofs?"

Despite herself, Diana had to laugh. "I'm afraid that wasn't one of the subjects covered at the Prentiss Academy."

"Pity," he quipped. "Well, looks like I'll have to get me a real ladder over at Nate's and see what needs done up top. Thanks for the help, Miss Montclair."

"You're quite welcome. . .and Diana will do." She hadn't meant to add that last part, but the words popped out all by themselves. More than that, she was glad they had.

His slow smile did amazing things to her insides. Perhaps Elsa was right in assuming he wasn't really so horrid. Maybe the time had come to forget the hurtful past. After all, both of them were older now. Perhaps they, too, could become true friends. The delightful possibility tickled her heart.

Somehow she refrained from watching out the window while Brady strode over to the carpentry shop. But after he left, Diana headed back downstairs where the aroma of Millie's biscuits permeated the air. Turning at the bottom to go to the kitchen, she noticed that the small rag rug the housekeeper kept on the porch had caught in the door. She stepped outside to straighten it.

"Associating with the riffraff, are we?" a woman's nasal voice called from the next house.

Diana moved farther out on the porch, where she could see acid-tongued Olivia Crabtree's insinuating sneer. The widow knew everyone's business and didn't hesitate to express her opinion about it. "I beg your pardon?"

Making a pretense of sweeping the always immaculate stoop, the gaunt woman stood rigid, gnarly fingers still grasping the broom handle as her close-set eyes peered over her hook nose. "There's not a soul in town who doesn't know that one's sorry background. I'm sure your parents would prefer you to keep company with someone more. . .suitable. My Martin, for example. Any young woman would be fortunate to have his attentions."

"I'm sure they would."

Her jaw gaped, but she recovered quickly. "Splendid. He'll be happy to hear of your high opinion of him." With that, she turned and strutted back inside.

The woman's movements reminded Diana of a black crow she'd once been fascinated by as a child. Moistening her lips, she frowned and shook her head, wondering what in the world that was about. This truly had been the most surprising day. She had a lot to relate to Millie. . .and something to ask about Brady Forbes, as well.

※

Brady whistled all the way to the shop.

Practically a castle, that Montclair house, he conceded. Little wonder the shipping magnate's daughter dressed like royalty. She didn't act regal, though, at least while he'd been there. On the contrary, she'd been rather ordinary. Not ordinary enough to give a guy like him a second look, but then he wasn't exactly in the market for a significant relationship. What did he have to offer a gal—especially one like her? What started him thinking along those ridiculous lines anyway?

"Hey, Nate," he hollered, entering the shop. "Where's that big ladder of yours?"

The cabinetmaker peered around the door he'd been attaching to a large walnut wardrobe. "Leaning against the outside of the shop, like always. Find that leak at the Montclair place?"

"Yep. Must be some roofing blew off when we had that windstorm last month. Thought I'd climb up and see for sure."

"Give a yell if you need help, Lad. I've patched a roof or two in my day."

"Thanks, I'll do that."

Nothing to offer a gal. The grim reality bounced around in Brady's head while he toted his ungainly burden back to the Montclair mansion. He'd never given much thought to fortunes or worldly goods before. He had his hands plenty full enough working at Nate's and keeping the parsonage and church in good repair. The only thing he'd ever considered important was repaying his aunt and uncle for their faith in him. Along with all his free labor, he turned over every cent he earned. Figured they'd put it to better use than he ever would.

Funny, though. There'd been a lot of changes in town the last couple years. The guys he used to joke around with had moved on with their lives. Married. Started families of their own. First Shane Gerhard, then Tyler Walker, and not long ago, Jacob Stahl. Maybe it was time to give some thought to his own future. Or did he want to spend the rest of his days going to work and coming home to pore over his uncle's theology books till he was as old and snowy-haired as Uncle Noah?

That unsettling possibility fit like a square peg in a round hole. Perhaps the time had come to start looking for some nice gal to settle down with. He wasn't dense enough to daydream that one as classy as Diana would give him a tumble, of course. Still, it beat everything the way she stuck in a guy's mind. Maybe the reason he didn't already have a girl of his own was because he'd been comparing them all to her in the first place. Drawing an unsteady breath at that realization, Brady crossed the street to the Montclair house.

There on the front porch, Diana chatted with that foppish Martin Crabtree.

The sight of that dandy, spruced up as always in his fine, city-bought suit knotted Brady's stomach. Diana's musical laugh over some ever so clever remark hardened his jaw. What more proof did he need that his earlier convictions were right? Compressing his lips, he tromped right on by to the side of the house. He had a job to do. Best he get on with it.

·:·

Even with the unexpected guest seated between her and the opposite end of the porch, Diana caught the blur of Brady's movements as the handyman went around the far side of the house, a long ladder tucked under his arm. Surely that sour expression on his normally jovial face was a product of her own imagination.

". . .So, with this being a particularly fine day," Martin was saying, "I thought to myself, perhaps Diana might enjoy going for a stroll along the river." He arched his brows suggestively. "The birds are singing, the flowers are coming into bloom. . .certainly too nice an afternoon to go to waste. What do you say?"

This did seem to be her day for making friends, but she'd had virtually no experience with young men her age and had no idea how to conduct herself. "Well, I. . ." She hesitated a fraction too long.

"See?" He stood in his shiny shoes and gave an exaggerated bow. "I knew you'd have no reason to refuse." He held out a soft, pale hand, waiting.

Gratified at being the recipient of her good-looking neighbor's attention, Diana politely acquiesced. "I'll just get my bonnet," she said, returning in moments.

She managed not to glance in Brady's direction as she hooked her fingertips in the crook of Martin Crabtree's arm and accompanied him across the street. Nevertheless, she sensed the carpenter's gaze on their backs. Perhaps even his displeasure, though she could find no reasonable explanation for that. After all, this making friends was getting more enjoyable by the hour.

"Millie tells me you've earned your law degree from Capital City and apprenticed with a barrister there," Diana began, her tone casual.

"Quite true." Beneath his crisp bowler, her sandy-haired companion's chin rose a notch.

"Then what brings you back to Hickory Corners? I should think you'd prefer living someplace where your education might be put to better use."

Martin nodded and gazed down at her. "You speak my own mind. Mother, however, had some legal matters that required my assistance, so I'm here to take care of them. But I also have a few personal decisions to make. Regarding my future." His intense gaze lingered a touch overlong.

"I see." Purposely diverting her attention to the dress shop as they went by, Diana observed the new ensemble displayed in the window. She also noticed the lady who owned the business eyeing them. . .along with a few other individuals on Main Street. No doubt by tomorrow news of this innocent stroll would be broadcast from one end of town to the other, yet she could see no cause for worry.

The spring breeze gathered a little more strength in the open expanse near the Ohio, stirring the trees and ruffling the long grasses. As she and Martin slowly walked along the bank overlooking the fast-moving river, a playful draft tugged at her bonnet's brim, and she reached up to hold her hat in place until the gust passed.

A large side-wheeler from her father's line sat at anchor, the flawless white paint stark against the blues of sky and water. The vessel Elsa had mentioned, no doubt. It appeared deserted, and Diana imagined the crew partaking of the delicious supper at the hotel. She couldn't help feeling a twinge of disappointment that she wouldn't be setting sail with them as she had so many times before.

"Do you ever give thought to leaving this hamlet?" Martin asked. "Making a life in some big city?"

"Yes, I do, actually," she confessed in all honesty. "After spending most of my life in Philadelphia and Boston, there are many things I miss, being here."

A satisfied smile spread across his patrician face. "Doesn't that strike you as for-tuitous? Both of us preferring the advantages of civilization to the rustic style of life in this tiny town?"

"It is rather funny, isn't it?" Diana mulled over the amazing coincidence that in this rural hamlet, of all places, was a handsome bachelor who shared some of the same deep longings as she did. To think she expected never to meet a young man with whom she had anything in common as long as she lived here.

"Well, perhaps we can do something about that. . .you and I."

Meeting Martin's speculative gaze, a niggle of uncertainty crept up Diana's spine, bringing a shiver. "I–I'm a little cold just now. Perhaps we should go back."

"As you wish." He turned and guided her toward the homeward route.

Chancing an oblique glance at her companion, Diana detected a hint of smug-ness in his expression. The same one she'd seen at church. It had made her a little nervous then, and still did, even though she had no idea why.

For some reason, she had misgivings about rushing into a relationship with Widow Crabtree's pride and joy. Friendship was one thing, but perhaps her son's expectations exceeded those bounds.

Diana couldn't help feeling it was simply too soon to encourage him—or anyone else—along that line. Not that there *was* anyone else to encourage.

Yet a certain lopsided smile drifted across her memory, one as playful as the spring breeze itself, and the recollection of the twinkling dark-blue eyes that went with it warmed her like summer sunshine.

Chapter 6

When Diana returned home from her stroll with Martin Crabtree, a sweeping glance alongside the house revealed no sign of Brady. An unexpected wave of disappointment coursed through her. Could he have discerned and repaired the roof problem in just the short time she'd been gone? Even as she chided herself for feeling let down, her companion's voice derailed her train of thought.

"I'm so pleased you accompanied me, Diana." Coming to a halt at her porch steps, Martin removed his bowler, took her hand, and gave a slight bow. "No doubt I was the envy of all the locals, keeping company with the most beautiful belle in town." The slanting rays of late afternoon sunshine glistened over golden highlights in his hair, lending added richness to his clear complexion.

Martin certainly knew how to charm a lady. A flush rose over Diana's cheeks. She'd always wondered how it would feel when a young man sought her company. The fact that the individual was as learned and sophisticated as he, made it even more enjoyable than she imagined. "Why, thank you, Martin. I had a lovely time. Thank you for inviting me."

"I'll be staying at Mother's awhile longer before I leave Hickory Corners again. Perhaps we might go for a stroll another time." His fair brows acquired a hopeful arch.

Diana saw no reason to discourage him. "I would like that."

His eyes probed hers, and he gave a satisfied nod. "Then I shall call again. Perhaps we might discuss a decision I'm facing. For now, I bid you good day."

"And to you, Martin. Thank you for the pleasant time." She watched him straighten to his full height and turn on his heel. A tip of the head, and he replaced his hat and strode away, his bearing cheerful and confident. Any woman's dream.

Smiling after him, Diana gathered her skirts and started up the steps, but her wayward gaze darted alongside the house once more. When Brady didn't materialize after all, her smile wilted.

⁖

Diana dawdled over supper, savoring Millie's succulent roast chicken and light, flaky biscuits. She'd already related the day's happenings to the older woman, including the sewing session and the walk with her neighbor. Odd, how the housekeeper made so few comments about Martin during the discourse. Diana tried not to make too much of that. She had other things on her mind, like mustering nerve to bring up a different subject.

Millie stood and took her own plate to the sideboard before returning with the teapot to refill their cups. "Me thinks the sewing group will be the high point of your week now. That's a real answer to prayer." She set the pot on a trivet on the table and reclaimed her chair.

"You pray about such trivial matters?" Astonished, Diana forked a slice of chicken breast to her mouth.

The housekeeper smiled gently. "Believe me, my dear, nothing that affects His children's dear ones is a trivial matter to the Lord. He's concerned about every part of our lives."

To Diana, the notion sounded far-fetched, yet it struck a tender note in her heart. Did God truly care so much about her? Did He even remember her? Years ago, she'd heard the accounts of various Bible heroes and martyrs of the faith. Once as a child she'd even prayed and asked Jesus to come into her heart and be her Savior. But on her own at boarding schools, those sweet childhood memories faded, gradually losing importance. Most of her teachers had more modern ideals, the sophisticated sort that fit well with city life.

Here in the country, however, surrounded by His handiwork, a person perceived the Creator in a whole different way. Perhaps the time had come to revive some of her former beliefs. Surely her father had a Bible amid all those leather-covered books in his library. She had plenty of time now to read and get reacquainted with the once familiar contents.

Millie's voice cut across her musings. "Edna and I prayed often for you, especially when we knew you'd be coming back for good. We wanted you to fit in and feel at home."

"I'm hoping not to miss a single sewing session," Diana assured her. "There's so much to learn—about stitching and my new friends." Pausing in thought, she drew her lips inward momentarily, then released them. "Millie?"

"Hm?" Squinty blue eyes blinked, then focused on her.

"What has Mrs. Crabtree got against Brady Forbes?"

The housekeeper gave a wry huff. "That old biddy? There's hardly a person in town she doesn't have something against, except for that *faultless* son of hers, of course. Seems her lot in life to aggravate decent folks. She's like a toothache. Some of us hope Martin will yank her off to Capital City for good, to live with him."

Hoping the attractive young man wouldn't be too hasty along those lines, Diana squelched a smile. His sudden interest in her was quite intriguing. "But why would she consider Brady riffraff?"

"She said that?" Stray hairs from the older woman's coronet of braids stirred as she slowly shook her head. "There's not a finer young man in town, in my opinion— and that includes her beloved Martin."

Recalling how polite and attentive Widow Crabtree's son had been on their walk earlier, the end of Millie's statement baffled Diana. He'd been the perfect gentleman. How could one ask for more? She took another sip of tea.

"Young Brady did have a bit of a questionable past, and that's the truth," the housekeeper went on. "After his folks died, he got mixed up with some bad company in Cincinnati. Older ruffian troublemakers who were headed for jail and finally ended up there."

Diana raised her eyebrows, and her lips parted in surprise.

With an understanding nod, Millie continued. "Seems the judge at the trial took Brady's youth into consideration and decided discipline and guidance could still salvage him. That's how he came to live with his aunt and uncle. Been here a good four or five years already, and is turning out fine as can be, if you ask an old lady like me. Edna and Noah just love him to death. He'll do anything for them—and for anybody else who needs help. He's more than proved himself."

"I'm. . .astounded," Diana said, though the word scarcely expressed her shock. "I have to admit, he does strike me as having a few rough edges." *He's not half as polished as Martin,* she nearly added. At twenty-four, three years older than Brady, her neighbor's attributes made her opinion of him take a decided turn in his favor.

"Well, once you get to know him better, you'll see those as the facets that reflect God's love and grace the brightest." Millie's cheeks plumped into a smile. "He's quite the wit, too, in case you haven't noticed. He has a unique gift. He can imitate anybody around town. Plays each one to the hilt, too. You should see him portray old Olivia herself!" The housekeeper laughed until she had to dab at tears with her apron.

"He imitates everyone?"

"Oh, yes. He makes merciless sport of all the girls in the sewing group. But they're all so used to it, they pay him no mind."

Diana frowned. Elsa had alluded to the same thing. Could it be that Brady hadn't set out purposely to embarrass her at all last summer? She'd arrived at the gathering awhile after it was under way, only to walk in on his portrayal of her. In retrospect, it had been rather comical, too. She shouldn't have stomped off in a dither.

Still, she couldn't ignore how much more at ease she felt in Martin's presence. He seemed so worldly wise and treated her like a real lady.

Brady, on the other hand, had a teasing way about him that made her feel self-conscious and tongue-tied. Much less sure of herself. Thoughts of him were as hard to shake as a summer cold.

Diana stifled a smile. Scarcely a week ago she'd expected she'd languish away in this little hamlet with no hope of attention from any respectable bachelors, and already she found herself comparing two completely opposite men. . .both of whom fascinated her in entirely different ways. The summer was turning out far more interesting than she ever imagined. Who knew what lay ahead?

<hr/>

"That's it, Dear Heart. I can't eat another bite." Uncle Noah leaned back in his chair and patted the vest straining over his slight frame.

Aunt Edna feigned indignation as she rose to clear the table. "Not even a slice of your birthday cake?"

"It's your favorite," Brady added, enjoying the interplay between the two. He truly admired their loving relationship—as constant in the privacy of the house as it was at church. One day he hoped to emulate the godly example they'd set for him. . . assuming he ever found a woman with whom he'd consider a lifetime commitment.

Presently that hope seemed quite slim. Or had, until recently.

"Well," the white-haired minister drawled, "mayhap a smidgen wouldn't hurt. Never could resist that chocolate cake of yours."

"I figured that's what you'd say." With a conspiratorial wink at Brady, she carted the remaining food to the kitchen.

He sprang to his feet, stacking soiled plates and gathering utensils. From the day he finally rid himself of the chip on his shoulder, he'd made a habit of helping out in as many ways as possible. Another of their examples he liked to follow.

"I hear you've taken on another sideline of late," Uncle Noah said, blue eyes twinkling when Brady and his aunt returned with the dessert. "Roofing, is it?"

"Just another of my many talents," he quipped, accepting the slice of cake passed his way. "Miz Sanderson's roof had a leak she needed fixed."

"I'm surprised you found the time." The older man sampled his own chunk of the rich sweet. "Seems Nate's been working you night and day for awhile now."

Brady swapped furtive glances with his aunt, but maintained a relaxed expression as he contemplated the newly finished desk now gracing the minister's study. "The project's done now, Uncle Noah. I'll take you to see it as soon as you are through."

"Can't say as I'm up to hoofing down the street just now," he returned with a pained look. "Not after tramping about the countryside calling on sick folks all day. My rheumatism's kicking up again. Must be a storm on the way."

"It's not at the shop," Brady assured him. "Just next door."

"Next door? At the church?"

"Yes, so hurry and finish," Aunt Edna coaxed, her own pride on the verge of popping her apron strings. "You've really got to see this."

He looked from one to the other and back. "With both of you set on getting me over there, I'm getting a mite curious. Remember, though, it takes a lot to surprise a man my age." Taking a last gulp of coffee, he brushed crumbs from his hands and stood. "Lead the way."

Shortly thereafter, standing before the gleaming example of Brady's finest workmanship, the normally eloquent man stood speechless for the first time in his life. "I. . .don't know what to say." He blinked wetness from his eyes, then grabbed Brady in a back-thumping hug, while his wife stood on the sidelines, mopping tears with her apron.

It took Brady a few seconds to speak past the lump in his own throat. "Happy birthday, Uncle Noah. This is only a fraction of what you deserve. I owe you and Aunt Edna my life. Likely it'll take that long to repay you both."

The older man held him at arm's length and shook his head. "Love doesn't charge for its services, Lad. Your aunt and I couldn't be more proud of what you've become since allowing God to direct your life. And as sure as this magnificent desk will outlast the three of us put together, I know He has some wonderful plans for you ahead. You're going to make some fortunate young woman a good husband one day soon."

"A good husband, indeed," Aunt Edna echoed. Moving closer, a secret smile on her guileless face, she hugged the two of them.

The older woman emitted faint scents of lavender and roses, and Brady inhaled deeply. His aunt kept sachets of dried flowers in her armoire. . .lacy, frippery things made by Diana Montclair. Now that he thought about it, those enticingly feminine fragrances seemed to fill up a room, whenever Diana was present.

He liked them. A whole lot. In fact, a guy could get used to such fripperies, if he set his mind to it.

Even as he smiled inwardly, Brady felt his spirit plummet like a broken kite. The problem was what a gal like her would have to give up, if she chose a guy with so little to his name. He ought to back off and let that foppish Martin have her.

⁙

Diana set the Bible on the bedside table and lay back on her pillow. The Psalms were pleasant enough reading, but her active mind kept drifting to the events of the day. Had it been only this afternoon Brady Forbes had been right here in her bedroom? His presence had so filled the air around them, it left very little air for breathing. She could still see the mischievous sparkle in those blue eyes, still envision his playful grin.

Considering the poor start he'd had in life, did any of the rough character of his youth remain hidden to surface again? Was that the mysterious quality about him that she found so disconcerting? So. . .utterly fascinating?

Diana shifted to a more comfortable position, propping an arm beneath her head. Better to direct her thoughts toward a safer, more predictable route. Martin Crabtree. Now there was a fine example of manhood, a person of means and culture, who would make something of himself. Diana had seen him only a few times in her life, yet she could never imagine Martin doing anything one might find scandalous. She chuckled. More than likely, he'd be so predictable and practical he'd be an absolute bore.

What had gotten into her anyway, with so much of her time suddenly claimed by thoughts of those two bachelors? Her teachers affirmed that the domestic skills she'd learned at school would enable her to make someone a worthy bride, but Diana didn't really know if that was what she wanted for her life. There had to be more to one's existence than courtship and marriage and raising babies. Many intellectuals alleged that women would eventually enter fields once forbidden, fields other than domestic ventures and teaching. Soon there would be women doctors, women lawyers, and who knew what else? With all her father's resources behind her, Diana knew she could get the required training for whatever she wanted. All she had to do was figure out what that was.

But in the meantime. . .

A smile tickled the edges of her lips.

Chapter 7

T here. Good as new, almost." Avoiding Diana's eyes, Brady climbed down the ladder in her bedroom, a white-tipped paintbrush still in his hand.

Diana watched him from the padded rocking chair where she'd sat embroidering, a few feet away, aware that her presence made him uncomfortable. Tiny dots of white speckled the strands of his dark brown hair and the bridge of his nose, adding even more appeal to his square-jawed face. He made quite a sight in that faded cambric shirt and trim-fitting trousers. Despite herself, she couldn't help gawking at him or enjoying it. The very thought warmed her cheeks. "You do excellent work, Brady. Thank you."

With nothing but a lackluster grin, he bent over and began rolling up the oilcloth protecting the floor beneath the work area. "I'd keep the windows open the rest of the day so the fumes don't give you a headache."

Diana already had a headache, and it had nothing to do with the smell of new paint. Aside from a few wordless glances in her direction while he worked, Brady had studiously ignored her since her first stroll with Martin Crabtree last week. He hadn't even dropped in on the sewing circle for baked treats. The uncharacteristic silence bewildered her. She missed his easy smile, his funny remarks. More than that, she missed the new friend she thought she'd found in him. Had someone told him to mind his place around her? Had it been Martin?

While Brady had been occupied covering the water stain on her ceiling, she'd tried to picture Martin doing something enterprising like repairing a leaky roof or repainting a ceiling. But the widow's son had hands even whiter and softer than Diana's. Most likely if the young attorney were to be faced with such needs around the home, he'd have to hire the work done for him, as her father did.

That had been her own mind set, until coming home to stay. How different things were here. Everyone appeared self-reliant and competent enough to handle most tasks. Not only would folks in town not pay someone to do common repairs, but they would also help each other out, when possible, with no charge for the service. *Being neighborly,* they called it, a term Diana appreciated more each day.

The roll of oilcloth under his arm, paint supplies in hand, Brady gave a tight-lipped smile on his way to the hall. "Stay dry, Diana."

"You too. Don't fall off any ladders." But her attempt at levity drew no response whatever. "Thank you," she repeated lamely as he clomped downstairs.

Diana gave a resigned sigh and put down the bookmark she was embroidering for Elsa, the last of three she'd made to surprise her sewing circle partners. She couldn't let it pass, this—whatever it was—between her and Brady. She had to learn what was amiss.

She found the kitchen deserted on her way through, but the scent of Millie's scones lingered. No doubt the housekeeper had taken some over to Charlotte Warner. Though the widow's sprained ankle had healed well enough, she'd caught a chill a few nights past and was abed once again.

Exiting the house through the kitchen, Diana spied Brady in the backyard, putting away the paint things. His none-too-quiet movements and the closing of the squeaky shed door masked the sound of her footsteps as she approached. Just what she'd hoped, since she hadn't an inkling what to say.

Brady secured the latch and turned. Indigo eyes focused on her, and his dark brows flared high. "Did I forget something upstairs?"

Why did he seem so much taller up close? Diana swallowed. She shook her head.

A frown etched a pair of grooves above his nose. "Then what is it?"

"That's what I've been wondering." Feigning bravado to conceal her quivering insides, she schooled her expression to remain calm.

With a grimace, Brady ran spattered fingers through his hair. "Look, Diana, I'm kinda busy right now. If there's something you need me to do, spit it out. Otherwise, I gotta get back to work." He shot a sidelong glance toward the Crabtrees' house. "Besides, you wouldn't want to keep His Loftiness waiting. It's probably time for your little stroll."

Her jaw gaped. "You've been keeping tabs on me?" she asked incredulously.

The tips of Brady's ears reddened. With an offhanded shrug, he shifted his stance. "Well, it's not exactly a secret, you know. The whole town watches the two of you strolling the riverbanks together every day."

"We are not together every day." But even as she defended herself, Diana fought to temper the offense caused by his remark. She placed her hands on her hips. "And I've only gone walking with Martin twice. . .not that it's any of your concern."

He raised a hand in concession. "Forgive me. You're right. It's none of my business who you spend time with. Now, if you'll excuse me, Miss Montclair, I have to get back to the shop. Some of us common folk must work for our living."

Diana elevated her chin and arched an eyebrow. "Well, far be it from me to detain you," she flung back in her haughtiest tone. "I've neglected my needlework too long as it is. I. . .I just—" Her shoulders sagged, and she softened her voice. "I just missed the friendship I thought we shared. Excuse me." Snatching her skirts in both hands, she bolted for the house before completely humiliating herself by bursting into tears in front of him.

Inside, she sagged against the door. What made her think she needed Brady Forbes anyway? Widow Crabtree was probably right. If Diana ever wanted to be accepted in her parents' world, she'd be wiser to cultivate a relationship with a man they'd approve of.

⁘

"My, but you're quiet today, Diana," Mrs. Tidewell remarked the next afternoon. Reading silently in the rocking chair, she closed the Bible, but kept a finger in place.

"Most likely has her head in the clouds," Elsa said on a teasing note. "Strolls along the river, drinking in the beauties of approaching summer. . .I remember when I first fell in love." A dreamy smile curved her lips.

Diana stopped stitching. The whole town *did* know of her walks with Martin. But just what was everyone saying about the two of them? "I assure you, I am not in love," she insisted.

Directly across from her, Samantha regarded her but did not speak as she exchanged significant glances with her cousin Betsy. It never ceased to puzzle Diana the way those two always had their heads together. . .especially whenever Martin Crabtree's name cropped up in conversation. Frowning inwardly, she worked harder at her stitches.

She'd spoken the truth about not being in love. Nevertheless, Martin gave the distinct impression he was concocting some sort of scheme. He'd dropped hints on their last walk, regarding the possibility of a future for the two of them. As tempting as the idea appeared on the surface, Diana wasn't completely convinced she wanted to deepen their relationship. She certainly didn't know the man well enough to consider marriage, if that's what he had in mind. She hadn't even written to her parents to let them know she was interested in anyone. Likely they'd be relieved if she were no longer their responsibility.

On the other hand, if she did marry Martin, it would effectively get her out of Hickory Corners, back to civilization. Away from disturbing thoughts of Brady Forbes. Wasn't that what she'd been hoping for?

Gradually, from the background, Mrs. Tidewell's voice overpowered Diana's contemplations. ". . .So I thought I'd pass on some verses I've been reading about wisdom," she said, opening her old Bible once again. "In the fourth chapter of Proverbs, Solomon refers to wisdom as the 'principal thing.' I'll begin at the first verse."

Listening to the Biblical admonishment to seek after wisdom, Diana became even more perplexed. How could one be sure if a particular choice would be considered wise? She remembered that Millie often prayed about things. Perhaps therein lay the secret. Tonight at bedtime, Diana would ask God for wisdom. Somehow even the thought itself comforted her, and her spirit breathed a wordless petition on the spot.

After the gathering, Elsa hurried away to tend her son, and Betsy drove off in her wagon. Diana and Samantha took a turn helping Mrs. Tidewell restore order to the parsonage. Exiting when they'd finished, Samantha started toward the mercantile, but halted abruptly and turned back. "Diana? Wait."

Diana stopped until the fair-haired girl came to join her. "What is it?"

Samantha released a troubled breath. "I wasn't going to say anything. Betsy says you'll think I'm prying into your personal affairs. But I wouldn't be your friend if I didn't tell you."

"Tell me what?"

"About Martin."

Diana stiffened. Samantha had once kept company with the young attorney herself. But she was married now. Was she actually *jealous* that Martin was lavishing attention on someone else?

"I got a letter from Clara a few days ago," Samantha said, her words tumbling out of her like water over a fall. "You remember her, don't you? Clara Bucey? She used to be part of the sewing circle, only she left Hickory Corners to visit some out-of-state relatives. Now she's decided to stay and live in New York."

"Yes," Diana said, trying to make some sense out of the one-sided conversation.

Samantha caught her lower lip in her teeth as if struggling over how to go on. "Well, it seems Martin's going to relocate in New York City; did you know that?"

"I thought his practice was in Capital City."

"Yes, it is. Or was. He's gotten a new position, in a rather prestigious law firm back East. That's why he's here. To settle his affairs, sell his mother's house, and pack up. He'll be taking her along, of course."

Diana shook her head. "I don't understand. He's mentioned nothing of that to me. Nothing at all. Well, he did hint of some change coming up, and how I might be a part of it. . . ."

"Don't trust him, Diana. He's a real bounder. He gives all the girls in town the eye when you're not around. He's always been like that. Take it from someone who knows."

"But. . .but he seems the perfect gentleman when he's with me," Diana insisted. "So sincere."

Samantha grimaced. "Martin Crabtree hasn't a sincere bone in his body. I might as well tell you the rest. Clara says he'll be working for her uncle. . .and that one of the stipulations for securing that lofty position is marriage to her spinster cousin."

"So, I'm what one might call a 'last fling,'" Diana said in a flat tone.

"More like a way out, I'd venture to say. He's told Clara's uncle he's practically engaged to someone 'back home.'"

"Me."

Samantha nodded. "But believe me, the only person Martin loves is himself. He's positive all women find him irresistible, so he uses that. He always has. I just thought you needed to be told, in case. . ." She bit her lip again, letting the unfinished thought dangle.

Searching her friend's eyes, Diana sensed she'd spoken from her heart. There was no reason not to trust her. Stepping nearer, she gave Samantha a hug. "Thank you. I appreciate your telling me that. I know it couldn't have been easy."

"I just couldn't bear having him hurt one more of my friends," she returned, blinking against gathering tears.

Diana couldn't speak. She smiled instead, and with a nod, turned and walked home.

To her dismay, her handsome neighbor waited on the porch. Diana's stomach lurched.

"Ah," he said smoothly. "The fair mistress of the house returns at last. Would you care to come strolling? I've something of import to ask you."

Forcing a smile, Diana effected her most refined posture. "Thank you, no, Martin. I'm afraid I've promised not to see you again."

His features fell flat. "Promised whom?"

"Why, Brady Forbes, of course," she blurted, then decided a fabrication ought to be elaborate enough to be believed. "Just last evening he asked me to marry him, and I accepted."

"Forbes!" Martin spat. "You can't be serious."

"Oh, but I am." Smiling gaily, she pranced up the steps and took hold of the door handle, opening it as she spoke. "Good day, Martin. All the best in your new life. . .in New York." With that she sailed inside.

Right into a grinning Brady Forbes.

Chapter 8

"Well, now. That was interesting. Very interesting, indeed." His tongue in his cheek, Brady rocked back on his heels, arms crossed over his chest.

Diana wished the floor would open up and swallow her, scarlet face and all. She'd never been more mortified in her life. Surely she could provide a reasonable explanation for her *faux pas.* Gathering her dignity as best she could, she squared her shoulders and raised her chin. "I. . .needed a way to put Martin off for good," she said breathlessly, hating the unnatural high pitch of her voice. "I figured that if I told him you and I. . . ," she fluttered a hand in exaggerated nonchalance, "were *involved. . .*"

"I believe the term was *engaged,*" he corrected, his face maddeningly straight.

Diana swallowed the huge lump in her throat and dipped into the fragile remains of her fortitude to continue. "And I surmised that, *friend that you are,* you wouldn't mind if I. . ." Wincing, she shrugged.

"Bandied my good name about?" he finished. "So freely?"

The last of Diana's composure evaporated, and her knees gave out. She sank to the floor in a puddle of skirts and covered her still burning face in her hands. "I must ask you to leave now," she moaned, her fingers muffling her words. "Just let me die in peace."

"No need for you to go to that extreme," Brady said gently. He dropped down beside her. "Anyway, he's gone now. That's what you wanted, right?"

She nodded.

"That makes two of us."

Diana uncovered her face and ventured a look at him. "You're not mad, then?"

"Naw. I've been wanting to punch the stiff out. You saved me the trouble. Nothing worse than sore knuckles when you're trying to build things."

The beginnings of a smile trembled on her lips.

The kitchen door banged shut, and Millie came into the entry hall, her arms full of folded linens. "What's happened? Someone get hurt?"

Diana swapped a conspiratorial grin with Brady. "No one who matters."

The housekeeper eyed him. "You checked that repair in the ceiling?"

"Yes, Ma'am. Seems to be holding fine."

"Well, then, I'll just go put these away." With a curious look encompassing both of them, Millie carted the clean sheets upstairs.

The carpenter stood and offered Diana a hand.

She placed her fingers in his, and he assisted her effortlessly to her feet, sending delicious shivers through her being.

"Guess I'll be off. I need to see Uncle Noah," he said with a wink. "Takes awhile to plan a wedding."

"Oh, you. . ." Diana had the strange feeling she'd never be able to stay mad at Brady for long.

Partway out the door, he stopped in his tracks and looked over his shoulder, his expression incredibly vulnerable, for once. The sight stopped her heart. "So, does this mean you would consider keeping company with a poor working man, if he asked?"

"Why doesn't he ask and find out?" she murmured.

"He might. Soon. Very soon." With a lopsided grin, he left.

Suddenly aware of the hall's emptiness, Diana hugged herself and smiled. "I'll be waiting, Brady Forbes."

-:::-

A gentle autumn breeze rippled across water as blue as Brady's eyes. Diana watched the fascinating movement of his muscles as he rowed the boat to the picturesque grove they'd found some months ago. It had become their favorite picnic spot, a place where they could talk and pray and watch the steamships chugging to and from town. A place where they could share their dreams and their hearts.

She'd found him to be thoughtful and considerate, and she reveled in the respectful way he treated her. He allowed her the freedom to be herself. For that, she loved him more than she'd dreamed possible.

Reaching their haven, Brady veered toward the shallows and beached the rowboat, then, as always, got out and carried Diana to dry ground. "What would you do if I never put you down?" he challenged.

Arms looped about him, she rested her head on his shoulder. "I guess I would just die happy."

Diana felt a chuckle rumble through his chest as he swung her around, then set her on her feet without releasing his hold. "You'd leave me all alone, huh?"

Her gaze rose to meet his. "No. Never. I couldn't bear being without you."

"Funny, I feel the same way," he said huskily, all levity vanishing from his expression. "I want to be with you all the time. To come home to you at night, take care of you through good times and bad, raise a family with you. Diana. . .would you honor me by becoming my wife?"

"Oh, my sweet Brady." She snuggled closer, trying to quiet her throbbing pulse enough to speak around it.

"I'm willing to wait until your parents can come and check me out," he added.

She gave a small huff and eased away slightly. "By that time, we'd both be old and toothless and doddering about on canes. They've never cared about anything else in my life, why should this be different?"

Disbelief clouded his eyes as Brady stroked gentle fingers through her hair. "They don't know the treasure they've wasted. If God blesses us with a daughter someday, she'll never doubt that her parents love her every bit as much as they love each other."

Drawing her close again, he kissed her tenderly.

When the kiss ended, a hopeful light shone in Brady's eyes, and his expression held the vulnerable quality Diana always found endearing. She hesitated only a heartbeat. "My answer is yes, Brady," she whispered. "I was only waiting for you to ask."

His arms tightened around her as he crushed her to himself. . .and even the birds sang out with joy.

Epilogue

O
ctober is such a perfect time for a wedding," Elsa said on a sigh. She handed Diana the final gift from the stack of presents surrounding her. "Yours and Brady's was the loveliest Hickory Corners has ever seen."

Samantha and Betsy nodded in agreement

"I'm so glad you were all part of our special day." Diana grinned at the trio of attendants who over the past several months had become her best friends in the world. How lovely they'd looked during the ceremony, in gowns of crushed gold satin, and carrying bouquets of yellow and white roses. Mother and Father sent funds enough to cover the best, plus deeded the house to Diana. . .an excess they assumed would make up for never sparing time in their lives for their only daughter, she surmised. Sadly, they were still off on a tour of Europe.

Diana had long ago accepted their disregard. She sat straighter and looked around at her new family, the one God had given her. . .Millie, the Tidewells, and the threesome from the sewing circle. People who truly cared about her and Brady.

Her fingers toying with the ribbon on the gift Elsa had placed in her lap, she glanced across the room to her new husband. Tall and respectable in his new suit, he chatted with some well-wishers who'd waylaid him at the refreshment table. She dragged her gaze away to finish unwrapping the big present.

Raising a fold of the paper, Diana looked closer at the contents, and her eyes grew misty. "Why, it's the quilt we worked on together!"

"Four Hearts," Samantha supplied. "We each signed our name in a corner. Mrs. T embroidered yours, so you'd always remember this past summer."

"How sweet. This will make the memory even more special. My forever friends. Thank you all so much."

Diana's heart felt full to bursting. The Tidewells had presented the newlyweds with a bank account containing every cent Brady had earned over the years. That, along with the big Montclair house and a housekeeper who doted on them, would give them a much better start in their married life than most people had. But Diana had grown enough to appreciate the value of things more precious than money. She knew now that happiness lay in friends and neighbors all striving to help each other, and in honoring the Lord. That true contentment was found in giving, in sharing.

She and Brady had a lot of love to share. He'd make a good life for her and, hopefully, for the little ones to come. In time, the big house would boast four hearts of its own, possibly more. Its walls would ring with joyful laughter. What more could she ask?

Brady crossed to her side once more and held out his hand. Tugging her gently to her feet, he wrapped his arms around her. "I'm the luckiest guy in the world," he murmured, his warm breath feathering tiny hairs on her neck. "I plan to spend the rest of my life making you glad you chose a poor working man for your husband."

Diana looked up at the features that had grown so dear, at the dark-blue eyes that could see into her soul. "Poor, my dearest Brady, is being surrounded by wealth, without love. Having you and knowing how you feel about me has given me more riches than I've ever had."

He smiled that heart-stopping smile and lowered his lips to hers with a kiss that fulfilled all her dreams. "Then let's go home, my love."

To Diana, there seemed to be no one else in the room as she placed her hand in her husband's and strolled with him toward the door.

MARRY FOR LOVE

by Janet Spaeth

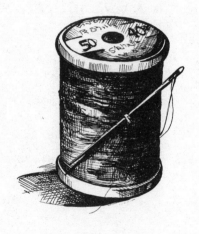

Dedication

To my parents, Margaret and Bill,
who gave me the patchwork of my own history.
Daily the hand of God draws thread through
that cloth and binds us all closer.

A woman that feareth the LORD, she shall be praised.
PROVERBS 31:30

Chapter 1

Dakota Territory—1879

Brigit Streeter ran into the small house, hooting with laughter. "Fulton and I just raced a rabbit," she said to her father, "and we won."

Mr. Streeter sighed, and Brigit knew she was in for the usual litany of *Why can't you act like a girl instead of a wild animal? Do you think this is a barn instead of a house? When will you grow up?*

"It's good exercise," she protested as he opened his mouth. "It keeps Fulton healthy so he can pull the plow. Horses need to stretch out their muscles, you know. Plus, running and riding keep my arms and back strong. What would you do with a weak daughter?"

Her father seemed to shrink, and Brigit wished she could bite back the words she'd just spoken. She didn't have the life he'd wanted for her, presiding over a grand house with lace curtains and plush carpets. Instead, she was a farmer, working just as hard as any son would. She knew it pained him.

She stepped behind his chair and threw her arms around his shoulders.

"Oh, Papa, you know I didn't mean anything by that except that I love being here with you and I will never, ever leave you."

He smiled, and she relaxed. The crisis had been averted—for the moment.

They'd been on this farm, just the two of them, since she was born. She'd never known her mother, who had died giving birth to her. All of Brigit's life, there had been her and Papa, and it was enough.

It always would be.

But now Papa had a crazy thought rolling around in his head—that she should be thinking about getting married.

What a foolish idea that was. First of all, she had no interest in getting married. Second of all, there was no one in the entire Dakota Territory who was even faintly husband material.

That pretty well summed up her situation. It didn't bother her one whit that her prospects were at best slim. She didn't care. She was perfectly happy staying on the small farm with Papa, watching the sun set on the Dakota fields.

Days like these were precious, the first true moments of spring with their fragile beauty, so full of promise. She could feel life bursting from the land right into her veins.

"What did you do this afternoon, Papa?" she asked, flopping into the only other chair in the tiny room. This one was hers, and the thin cushion on it now fit her body perfectly.

"I went into town to see about some new boots. These are getting to the point where they're like vanity: from the eyes they look good, but from the *sole* they're sorely lacking."

Brigit laughed at father's pun. He was a God-fearing man, always had been, always would be. Even her mother's death hadn't swayed him from his abiding belief in the Lord.

"Papa, why didn't you become a minister? You would have been a wonderful preacher." It was a question she'd pondered for many years, and although she'd asked it before, she'd never gotten an answer that totally satisfied her.

"I'm a farmer. It's in my bones and in my blood. A minister is a farmer, too, I suppose. He plants the seeds of hope and love and awe in the hearts of his congregation. And that's lofty work. But me, I need to feel the dirt in my fingers, and in my hair, and yes, in the cracks of my feet."

He lifted up his foot and smiled ruefully as the sole flapped away from the upper. "If I don't get these boots fixed soon, I might as well go barefoot."

"You said you went into town to get some boots. Why didn't you?"

"I guess I got waylaid by some news. And mighty big news, too."

Brigit wriggled to the edge of her chair. "Tell me! What happened?"

"A new minister is headed our way."

"Really?"

"Really. Our very own minister! Just for us."

Archer Falls was so small that it didn't have a minister. Marriages and baptisms had to take place in Fargo, a two-hour wagon ride away. For Sunday morning worship services, the townspeople relied on each other, with the sermon duty handed from man to man.

Brigit didn't mind it at all when her father brought the message, but she dreaded the days that Milo Farnsworth, the owner of the feed store, stood in front of the congregation. Mr. Farnsworth apparently felt that the significance of his sermon could be absorbed only if he hollered it so loud that Brigit's ears rang for the rest of the day.

Mr. Streeter smiled at his daughter. "And this new man, according to the rumor, has two very interesting attributes."

Brigit knew he was teasing her. "Attributes, huh? Let me guess what they are. He's breathing, and oh, let's see, what else would be important? Wait, don't tell me. Could it be—he has a heartbeat, too?"

"Very good. But I was thinking of two more. One is that he is young, fresh out of the seminary, and the other is that he's a bachelor."

The joy evaporated from the day. "Then let me guess two more things, Papa. He will be as horrid looking as a dusty toad, and he'll be equally as boring."

"Brigit, don't do this. All I mean is, he's going to be our new spiritual leader, and we're certainly in need of that."

Immediately she regretted her outburst. She knew that her father had longed for the presence of a permanent minister, not just for Sunday services, but to expand his own understanding of the Lord and the world. She'd seen his subtle grimace—although he must have thought it hidden—when Milo Farnsworth bellowed forth dire predictions of a fiery afterlife for those who didn't follow in his oversized bootsteps.

She kissed her father's sun-dried cheek and smiled. "We are indeed. And he can start working on my heart right away after words like that! I'm sorry, Papa."

"Not to worry." He smiled at her reassuringly. "Reverend Collins will be conducting services next Sunday morning. They're expecting an overflow crowd."

He touched her tangled strawberry-blond hair, and she laughed. "Yes, my dear father. I will clean myself up and wrap this messy mop into a respectable bun. I'll look so splendid, even you won't recognize me."

"You're a beautiful young woman." His voice was so quiet that she knew he was talking more to himself than to her. "When did that happen? When did you stop being that little girl who ran beside me, catching grasshoppers as I put in the wheat?"

She dropped a kiss onto his head and noticed how his hair was starting to thin. As she was getting older, so was he.

She ignored the catch in her heart and answered lightly, "It just wasn't fun anymore when you made me stop putting them down the back of your shirt. But if you're getting nostalgic about that, well, dearest Papa, we still have a quarter to plant. Better guard your back!"

⁜

The train shuddered to a stop. The newly ordained Reverend Peter Collins leaned over to retrieve his hat, which had slid to the floor with the last jerk of the brakes.

He glanced out the window at the station. The presiding elder had told him that someone would be waiting for him, but which one was it? The man wearing overalls? The presiding elderly woman, balanced on her cane? The family of three, finely dressed in what must be their Sunday best?

Excitement fluttered in his stomach. This was his first real assignment as a minister. He'd been given it so easily, he suspected no one else had wanted it.

How could they not, though? Who wouldn't want to live in a town like Archer Falls? It had the best of two worlds: it was small and rural enough to be a true community yet large enough to have the world of possibility open to it.

And the Dakota Territory! The very words evoked the images of a land rich in soil and belief. The closest he'd ever come to being one with the earth was putting a petunia on his windowsill at the seminary.

As he stepped out of the car, he blinked at the vast panorama that greeted his eyes. He'd underestimated the expanse of sky and the stretch of land sprinkled with the bright green of new grass that seemed to go all the way to the ends of the earth.

And it was now officially where he lived.

"Reverend Collins?" The fellow in the overalls spoke, and when Peter nodded, the entire group moved forward. He took a moment to realize that they'd come to greet him—and that they were all beaming as happily as he was.

Introductions were made—names Peter knew he would know better soon—and he was taken to a waiting wagon.

He had never been happier. Never.

God had truly brought him home.

·⁘·

Brigit struggled with the bag of rice, succeeding at last in spilling half of it across the table. *Waste not, want not,* she reminded herself, but her attempts to sweep the grains back into the bag only sent them skittering onto the floor.

A call at the front door diverted her attention. It was Mary Rose Groves, her best friend, motioning madly to her.

"Brigit, did you hear? Did you? A new minister, and he's single!" Mary Rose's slightly nearsighted brown eyes glowed with excitement, and she pushed up her wire-rimmed glasses with a finger.

The two of them plopped on the edge of the shallow porch boards.

"Papa told me. I just hope he isn't going to scream the Word at us the way Mr. Farnsworth does. My ears can't tolerate that anymore." Brigit shuddered at the thought.

"I think the damage has been done." Mary Rose frowned. "There's something already wrong with your ears."

"What?" Brigit watched an ant industriously carrying a minuscule bit of something under the boards.

"Didn't you hear a word I said?" Mary Rose demanded. "I said he's single. Not married. A bachelor."

"If there were any hope that he's handsome as well, I might let myself get excited, but the fact is, Mary Rose, there isn't a man in this territory that I would have for a husband. Not a one."

"You shouldn't be so negative, Brigit." Her friend stared at her earnestly. "This could be the fellow, the man you'll share your life with. You never know."

"Oh, I know perfectly well. I know all about the so-called eligible men in Archer Falls. I'd have to be a desperate woman to marry one of them. Look who I have to choose from: Lars Nilsen, who doesn't speak a word of English, at least as far as I can figure." Brigit rolled her eyes.

"Jerrod Stiles would make a terrific husband, wouldn't he, assuming I could wave my way through that constant plume of pipe smoke to see what he looks like," she continued. "Or maybe I'd be happiest with Arthur Smith, who's a hundred ten if he's a day but thinks he's fourteen."

Mary Rose kicked her friend's leg lightly. "You are exaggerating, but not by much. There aren't good pickings here; that's the truth."

Brigit grinned. "Between you and Papa, you'll have me married by the time I'm twenty-one or die in the trying."

Mary Rose's slightly myopic gaze got dreamy. "I only want you to be as happy as I am. Just think, by autumn I'll be Mrs. Gregory Lester."

"You had to go and get greedy and take the last good man in the territory," Brigit teased, "and look what you left me with. My choice of a fellow I can't understand, one

I can't see, or one I can't abide."

"Maybe so," her friend argued back lightly, "but you've got to admit that this new minister might be just the one."

"If he is even palatable, Mary Rose Groves, I will eat my hat. I promise that to you. I will sit in front of the school and eat my hat, ribbon and all."

-:::-

"I hope that hat is as tasty as it looks," Mary Rose whispered as she slid into the pew next to Brigit. "I've heard that straw is quite flavorful."

"Mmmm-hmmm."

"Don't you think Reverend Collins is handsome?" Mary Rose insisted.

"Mmmm-hmmm."

"Brigit, why don't you say—oh, I see." Mary Rose leaned back and smiled in satisfaction. "You agree with me. And for some reason, I think you're happy to lose this wager."

"Mmmm-hmmm."

The Reverend Peter Collins was the kind of man who had inhabited Brigit's dreams—when she'd dared to let her thoughts drift to that vague fancy that somehow, someday, she would find true love.

Standing to the side, silhouetted against the newly painted wall, was her hope personified. Tall, with dark hair that would silver elegantly when he aged, he stepped easily to the front of the small sanctuary. With every move, he stepped closer to her heart.

Then he turned and faced them. His gaze settled on each member of the congregation, as if recognizing every individual, and Brigit held her breath.

Finally, her turn came, and during that moment when their gazes met, she saw a true faith glowing in his deep brown eyes.

He began to speak, and his glance flitted away to the rest of the people packed together. But Brigit knew what she had seen, and she liked it.

Mary Rose jabbed an elbow into Brigit's side and motioned expressively toward the new minister. Brigit understood what the motion meant. Yes, he was handsome beyond belief. But more important, he radiated faith. That, as far as Brigit was concerned, was more important than his appearance.

She peeped at her father. His weathered face was not going to grace any advertisements for genteel menswear, that was certain, but she saw beneath the wrinkles and the leathered skin what was more valuable: a trustworthiness, a security, a steadfastness that far outweighed his physical appearance.

A pang stabbed her heart. She hadn't known her mother more than a few moments, just long enough, her father had told her, for the woman to hold her newborn daughter and whisper some words in her ears.

She'd often asked what those words were, but he'd turned away, sudden tears in his eyes even after all these years, and shaken his head. She no longer pursued the issue. She did not want to hurt him any more than he had already been hurt.

As if aware that she was thinking about him, he turned to her and smiled. From the relaxed expression on his face, she could tell that his heart was filled with gratitude as the new minister's words filled the room.

Piecing together their faith in this small town had been like making a quilt of scraps. Bit by bit, the ragged edges had become smooth, the small unmatched bits turned into a beautiful unity, with each color, each shape enhancing the others. *It has been,* she thought, her heart filling with gratefulness for her father, *an extraordinary work of love.*

Now Reverend Collins's strong, young voice filled the hall. ". . .Seminary in St. Paul, when the call came for this church. I was eager to come here. I have lived in the city my entire life. Admittedly, twenty-four years isn't an eternity, but I was ready to commit to another twenty-four years spent under God's sky, watching the country grow before my eyes."

His smile swept the crowd. "I was delighted to accept the assignment."

Then he paused. Only the sparrows chirping in the lilac bush outside the open window made any sound. The listeners stopped all motion and stared at their new pastor.

"I'm not being entirely honest with you," he said at last, his voice dropping to a near-whisper. "I have a confession to make."

The assemblage leaned in to hear his barely audible words.

"I begged to come here." He grinned at the surprised faces. "I wanted to come to the Dakota Territory—I have since I was just a lad and saw all those wonderful notices about life out here. More than anything, I wanted to see the sun overhead, the clouds floating like white puffs of God's breath against the blue vault of the firmament. I wanted to be able to look at the horizon and see the curve of the earth without any buildings crowding it from my sight. I wanted to be able to dig my hands into rich, black Dakota valley soil, to feel with my fingers where the seed finds its root and, I pray, where I might find mine."

If it were at all seemly, Brigit thought, the church would have stood and applauded. She realized she'd been holding her breath and exhaled.

Around her, the people of Archer Falls were smiling happily. This was the moment they had waited for, for a long time, ever since their community had been nothing more than a cluster of sod houses. It had grown board by board, building by building, until it lacked everything except a man of the cloth to lead them.

And now they had their minister.

Brigit looked at the new young minister, and he looked at her. . .and her heart stirred.

At that moment, Brigit Streeter fell in love.

Chapter 2

"Reverend Collins, I'd like you to meet Alfred Streeter and his daughter, Brigit," Milo Farnsworth shouted at them.

Brigit's heart, which had been busily fluttering in her throat, seemed to rise even farther and take over her speech. She nodded mutely, unable to take her eyes off the minister's face, yet at the same time completely incapable of looking directly into his coffee-colored eyes for fear of what her own eyes would reveal.

This is ridiculous, she scolded herself. *You've just met the man.* She took a deep breath and tried to calm her shaking fingers as she reached to clasp his hand.

"I'm very delighted to meet you," he said, and she found herself returning his easy smile.

She'd always loved Archer Falls, always felt that she was so much a part of the prairie that its rich soil was part of her blood and bone. But she had never been as glad to be standing where she was as at that moment in the newly painted church with late-spring sunlight streaming through the windows—and holding Peter Collins's hand.

She was suddenly aware of how she'd flown into her clothes this morning, having overslept by at least an hour, ripped a brush through her knotted locks, and quickly bound her hair into a braided bun.

Her shoes were probably irretrievably scuffed. Brigit looked down at the leather-shod toes that peeked from under her blue and white calico skirt and grimaced. Not only were her shoes dusty, but also one of them was untied and the lacing hopelessly frayed. She tucked the offending shoe behind the heel of her other foot and attempted a smile.

This man had the speaking skills that Lars Nilsen lacked. He wasn't wreathed in odorous pipe smoke like Jerrod Stiles. And he most certainly was nowhere near as old as Arthur Smith.

No, the Reverend Peter Collins was about as perfect a piece of work as God could have made. She could only pray that his heart was as good.

"I'm very delighted to meet you." She felt stupid and quite dense. He'd certainly think she was not very bright if all she could do was parrot back his line.

His smile was a candle in a dark room. "I'm looking forward to being here."

His fingers moved in her grip, and she realized that she was still holding his hand. She dropped it as if it were on fire. Quickly she mumbled a few incoherent words and turned, nearly tripping on her shoelace as it caught on her heel.

No wonder he was smiling. She was a foolish, foolish young woman. He was so elegant, so cultured, so perfect, and she was nothing more than a prairie chicken scratching in the dust.

-:::-

Her father filled the uneasy silence on the ride home with a running commentary on the reactions to the new minister.

"That was quite the picture, let me tell you," he said to Brigit as Fulton pulled them along the lane. "Milo Farnsworth was puffed up, proud as a pigeon; and you know, I think I heard him claim responsibility for the Reverend Collins's presence here."

He slowed the wagon to look at a deer that wandered out of the shelterbelt. "Of course, Milo was part of the committee that requested a minister, so I do suppose he has some credit due him on that."

She didn't respond. She couldn't. Her mind was too occupied to manage speech at the moment.

He glanced at his daughter. "Remember, he's a bachelor."

"Mr. Farnsworth?" Brigit looked at him in confusion. "No, he's not."

"I didn't mean Milo," her father said. "The new minister isn't married."

Suddenly the day didn't seem as bright as it had. Couldn't she simply meet Reverend Collins without her father and who knew who else pushing them together? Didn't he think she was capable of finding her own sweetheart without his interference?

"He's not married," she snapped, "and interestingly enough, neither am I."

Her father didn't respond to her outburst. He merely reached across the wagon and patted her hand. "We farmers can only trust in our Lord for our daily bread, but He trusts us with the seed."

She loved her father dearly, but right now figuring out what he was talking about required more thinking than she was willing to do. Somehow, though, she knew this had to do with Reverend Collins.

She should guard her heart closely with the new minister, because there was no way he'd want a farming woman like her with calluses on her hands and no social graces at all. The gap between them was as wide as the Mississippi River.

Brigit sighed. At last someone who was handsome and charming and educated had come to Archer Falls, and she had no choice but to look the other way.

Her father had quit talking and was now singing softly. It was a hymn that she'd grown up with, "Rock of Ages." He'd hummed her to sleep with the melody many nights when she was a child, and it never failed to calm her.

Even now, she felt the tightness in her throat relax and her heart ease. God was good. He had given them a minister.

He would give her love, too—in time.

All He asked of her was patience.

-:::-

Peter placed his new Bible on his bureau. It was the one that the presiding elder had given him as a first-assignment gift. The rich burgundy leather cover had his name stamped in gold letters on the front. He'd never had anything as fine, he had assured the Reverend Armstrong at the time, but that wasn't quite true.

His fingers ran across the words HOLY BIBLE on an older copy that was also on his bureau. The black leather was cracked, the pages were dog-eared and bent, but it meant more to him than the new volume.

This Bible had belonged to his father, and before that, his father's father. He opened the cover and let his fingertips trail across the notes that three generations had added.

The last page was the Our Family page. There were his grandparents' names, and his parents', and their children's. His brothers and sisters and their spouses were on the family tree, along with the "twigs," as he liked to call his six nephews and nieces.

But his branch was empty save for his name. No spouse. No twigs.

The only corner of his heart that wasn't filled with joy moved sadly—yet with hope.

Maybe here he'd find his love, and his tree would grow and bloom on this prairie.

God, he prayed silently, *dearest Lord, might I find love here? Is the woman Thou meanest for me—is she here?*

The image of a young woman, her hair the color of orange marmalade, floated into his mind.

Brigit Streeter. Brigit Collins?

The tiny empty corner of his heart seemed to sigh with a sense of hope.

·⁂·

If only Brigit hadn't decided to take a late afternoon run through the cottonwoods on Fulton's back. But the house had been too closed in for her. Spring was already nearly over. Summer was lurking behind every leafing tree, ready to leap out and embrace her.

The new minister had been there for five weeks already, and his sermon that morning had been about enjoying the beauty of God's creation. She had gone out of the house, not planning on doing anything beyond sitting on the log seats and doing exactly what Reverend Collins had suggested, when she discovered that one of the harbingers of summer had already arrived—the voracious mosquito.

She quickly slapped that insect into history and ran into the barn to saddle up Fulton. Mosquitoes were already in his stable area, and his tail switched furiously in a mostly futile attempt to keep the pests away.

Within minutes they were one being, woman and horse, and the memory of the nasty mosquitoes was left behind them.

These were the times she loved the most, when she could shake herself free of the responsibility of house and farm. Fulton seemed to enjoy it, too, and Brigit allowed herself the fancy that he was imagining himself running free across the prairie with no saddle on his back, no plow fastened to him, and only the wild grasses to feed upon.

At last they both tired, and at the end of the farthest tree line, they turned back, moving in a companionable canter as the ever-present wind cooled the sweat.

The mosquitoes found them immediately. Brigit brushed and swatted, swatted and brushed until they arrived home and she could lead Fulton into the barn and clean him up.

Voices were coming from the house, and Brigit glanced at the wagon that was parked in front of their house. It was probably one of her father's friends come to chew over the events of the day.

Fulton was, without a doubt, the best horse in the world, and Brigit told him so as she curried and fed him. "I wish I could do something about the mosquitoes, old friend. Someday someone will invent something that really works to make them go away."

She gave him one final pat and left the barn.

The voices still floated from inside the house in a quiet, murmuring stream. Automatically she began separating them. Her father. Mary Rose's father, Calvin Groves. But who did the third voice belong to?

She pulled the straggling bun out of her hair as she walked toward the house. There was no point in trying to keep it in place. The ride had effectively torn the hairpins from their moorings so that the chignon trailed down one side.

Men surely had it nice, she thought as she tried to untangle her hair from the pins. Just snip-snip and they were done. It certainly would be wonderful if she could have short hair, too. Her life would be much easier: no snarls to try to comb through, no trying to braid and wrap her hair behind her back.

"Hello, Papa," she sang as she stumbled into the house, her eyes not used to the darkness of the inside after the glare of the afternoon sunshine. A pin fell, and she dropped to her knees to find it. Her fingers searched blindly; against the floral background of the rug, it was nearly impossible to see the pin. "Fulton—"

Her words stopped mid-throat as she realized who the third voice belonged to.

The Reverend Peter Collins was in her house, and she was crawling on the floor, her hair a matted mess, her dress stained and wrinkled. Plus she smelled like a sweating horse.

Lovely, she thought. *Just lovely.*

There was no hope for her. None. At least, she consoled herself as she stood and worked up a smile for him, there was one good thing to be said for all this.

It couldn't get any worse.

Chapter 3

If Peter was horrified by Brigit's appearance—and her aroma—he didn't show it as he stood and bowed slightly to her. *He's probably too genteel,* Brigit thought. There was no way that he couldn't notice how disheveled she was.

She stole a look at her father. From the expression on his face, she knew that she looked as terrible as she feared. His left eyebrow was arched almost up to his hairline, a sure sign that he was dismayed at what he was seeing. She'd seen that often enough growing up to know it as a danger signal.

"Brigit," he began in his warning voice, but Peter interrupted him.

"You look as if you've been enjoying this wonderful spring afternoon that the Lord has provided us," the young minister said, his eyes alight with laughter. "We should take advantage of all of them without worrying about the winter that is always lurking around the corner."

Milo Farnsworth stepped from the shadowed corner of the room. "Brigit Streeter, sometimes I think you are more horse than woman." He smiled, a frosty action that touched only his lips, not his eyes. "How fortunate your father is that he has you as a daughter. Why, you are as strong and capable as any son. Didn't I see you last week plowing the field north of here?"

A quick retort sprang to her lips, but her father gripped her arm tightly. She didn't dare look at the minister for fear of what she might read in his expression.

These were not simple, innocent words. Mr. Farnsworth's sentences hurt. Like a vengeful hornet, he had found the most painful—the most effective—target for his sting.

Her father's fingers dug in a bit more, and this time she knew it wasn't done to keep her from lashing out at Mr. Farnsworth. No, the words had struck a spot in his heart that still ached with loss. Plus there was something else, something that even Mr. Farnsworth couldn't know.

Albert Streeter couldn't farm without his daughter.

They had never spoken about it, but she knew from the way he sank into his chair at the end of the day. He wasn't sick—she could tell that. He was simply tired. The farm he had was too big for him to run by himself.

So the two of them had done it together, father and daughter; and it had been a good partnership. Now it was, in her father's eyes, time for her to move into a marriage home.

He could sell off part of the farm, but she knew he'd never stop farming. He'd. . .

Her thoughts were abruptly ended when Reverend Collins turned to her and said, "She looks wonderfully capable to me. Any man would be fortunate indeed to have her grace his home."

The look on Mr. Farnsworth's face made up for any hurt that she was feeling. His cheeks were flushed, and for the first time in her life, Brigit saw him at a loss for words.

He started to speak, stopped, started again, stopped again.

Her father's fingers relaxed their hold, and he spoke behind her. "I am always proud of Brigit. Always."

Mr. Farnsworth harrumphed. "Of course, of course. She is an—"

Brigit had to suppress the smile that twitched around her lips as he struggled for the proper way to describe her. She could tell that he wanted to say more, but social correctness kept him from doing so.

She turned to look again at Reverend Collins and was surprised to see him watching her, almost as if he were studying her. He smiled. "No, there'd be no mistaking you for someone's son."

If she'd thought the day couldn't get worse, she hadn't figured on him saying *that*. The blood rose right from the tips of her dusty toes to her cheeks.

Oh, she hated blushing. Just hated it. She didn't turn pink or blush gently. No, her whole face flooded into a bright red. Why on earth had God ever thought it would be a good idea to make her face turn crimson whenever she was embarrassed? Couldn't He just have given her a brightly colored flag to wave or a sign to hold—"I am mortified"—or perhaps a trumpet to blare?

Reverend Collins smiled at her, and the world collapsed into a space that was just big enough for the two of them.

This was not real, a little portion of her brain told her. It wasn't possible to fall in love this quickly.

There were other people in the room. She could hear their voices indistinctly. Mr. Groves said something vague and left.

Mr. Farnsworth stood off to the side uneasily, as if not being at all accustomed to being in that position. He said a few words, something about a piano, and Reverend Collins turned to him and nodded.

"Friday evening? Why, thank you. I do enjoy good music, and from what you've told me, your wife is quite an accomplished pianist. I'm looking forward to getting to know you and your family better."

If he had thrown a knife right into her heart, it couldn't have caused more pain. The Farnsworth house was the grandest one in Archer Falls. The windows that overlooked the fertile valley were draped in snowy white organza. The dishes—she had seen the dishes—were blue and white patterned china. She'd never seen cups as delicate as these. Her father once described the Farnsworth china as "thin as a hurried promise."

She looked down at her stained dress and sighed, which reminded her that the Farnsworths undoubtedly smelled better.

But then, she thought, they'd never had the joy of riding Fulton full-bore along a young shelterbelt, nor known the satisfaction of seeing wheat that they'd planted themselves from tiny seeds sprout up in sun-warmed earth.

She summoned a smile from the depths of her soul and tried to stand tall and proud. What was done was done, and she couldn't do much to change that, now could she?

"It's been wonderful seeing you both," she said, imagining herself in front of a grandly sweeping staircase, "and I do hope you both drop in again to visit."

She put her hand on her father's shoulder, and as she did, she noticed a piece of straw dangling from her cuff. Of course it wasn't a small bit. It was at least four inches long and caught the late afternoon sunlight so that it glowed golden.

The men noticed at the same time. There was no way to ignore it, so she did the next best thing.

She held her arm up and admired the straw as it reflected the rays. "Look at this. God gives some of us gold in coins. For the rest of us, He grows it in our fields."

Her father's lips clamped shut, but she knew it wasn't because he was offended by her audacity. Quite the contrary, he was probably trying to control his amusement.

Mr. Farnsworth gaped at her, obviously astonished at her words.

Reverend Collins, however, smiled broadly and chortled. "Amen, Miss Streeter! Amen!"

Mr. Farnsworth glanced uncertainly at the minister and joined in the laughter. "Ha ha. Good one, Brigit. Gold in the fields. Ha ha." He harrumphed loudly. "On that cheerful note, I will take my leave. Reverend Collins, it is indeed a joy to have you with us in Archer Falls. Streeter, we'll talk more this week about putting some paint on the schoolroom walls."

Some people could simply leave a room, Brigit thought, but not Mr. Farnsworth. He took a good five minutes to finally get across the room and out the door.

"Farnsworth is a good man," her father told the minister. "A good man."

"I can tell he is," Reverend Collins agreed. "He certainly has the heart of a stalwart citizen. If I hadn't already been inclined to come to Archer Falls, he would have swayed me in this direction."

"We are glad you chose us." Her father winced a bit as he leaned back into his chair, and he rubbed his leg. "Brigit, would you walk the reverend to his wagon? I'd do it, but this charley horse has got the better of me."

"I'm sorry to hear about your leg, but I'd certainly enjoy Brigit's company," Reverend Collins said, touching her hand.

People had touched Brigit's hand before, many times. But the action had never had this effect. She had to remind herself to breathe as they walked out of the house and toward his wagon.

She was very aware of how the sun sat just so on the cottonwood trees. How Fulton whinnied softly to her from his stall. How the mourning doves cooed a forthcoming rain that the sky didn't yet show.

And how very tall and handsome Peter Collins was.

"It's quite lovely out here," he said. "This has a beauty of its own. The sky is incredibly blue. You know, in St. Paul I didn't get to see but patches of the sky. The buildings got in the way."

She looked at him, startled. Most of the city people who came to Archer Falls saw only empty prairie, barren and in need of more buildings, more trees, more things.

"In Dakota," he continued, apparently unaware of how much his words had surprised her, "the sky goes on forever. I am awed by what our God has done."

"He's done a good job." Her voice sounded small and tiny.

Reverend Collins glanced at her, and his lips curled into a grin. "Yes, He has. He has made many wondrous creations, I'm finding."

That furious blush started its crawl up her neck, and she quickly changed the subject. "I hope life in Archer Falls is to your liking."

"Oh, it is. As I said in church on Sunday, Archer Falls is exactly what I've been looking for."

"It isn't too. . .backward?"

He reached down and picked a just-blossomed daisy. "Backward?" He studied the flower thoughtfully. "Not at all. Oh, the buildings aren't as grand as those in St. Paul, and the stores don't have the variety of wares, and there's no opera house, but none of those matter. What's important is the people. And the land."

"I'm glad to have you with us," Brigit said. Then she added hastily, "We've been in need of a minister for a long time. As it is, the men of the community have been trading off the sermon duties, and while my father's sermons are intelligent and thought-provoking, I can't say that's true of the other men's sermons."

"Does Mr. Farnsworth preach?" he asked.

"Oh, yes. He does." She thought she should stop with that short answer.

He continued, "And how are Mr. Farnsworth's sermons?"

"Loud."

The word popped out before she could stop it, and they both laughed.

"You know, Brigit," he said, "there's a lot of work ahead of us, building a church."

"Yes, there is."

"Can I ask you something? I don't want to rush you but. . ."

Oh, this is great, she thought wryly. *He's going to ask me to sew altar cloths or polish candlesticks or something, when my talent would be more in laying the floorboards.*

"I don't know if I can help you much," she admitted. It was better to get it out in the open, in case he hadn't figured out that she was sadly lacking in the finer feminine skills. "It's not my forte."

Reverend Collins seemed surprised. "Not your forte? What do you mean?"

"You want me to do something with the church, right? Embroidering pew cushions or hanging drapes?"

He didn't answer. Instead, he studied first her face and then the daisy. "Well, that would be helpful, but that's not what I had in mind."

She groaned silently. This wasn't sounding at all good. "Reverend Collins, I—"

He shook his head. "Let me finish. First of all, I like you—quite a bit. Would you be willing to let me visit you?"

"Of course," she said. "Our door is always open. Or almost always open. Except when it's closed."

Oh, stop babbling like that, she scolded herself. *Not only have you made a splendid impression on him with your first meeting, but you've also undoubtedly cemented his opinion of you with today.*

"I want to visit you," he began, and then he paused and took a deep breath. "I want to visit-you-because-I'd-like-to-get-to-know-you-better." The last words came out in one long whoosh of breath.

He handed her the flower, and to her amazement, he flushed a deep crimson.

If there had been any doubt at all, it vanished with that simple act.

"I'd be honored to have you visit," she said, aware that she'd never smiled as broadly and as joyfully before.

⁙

Peter got into his wagon, and as he drove away, he realized he was singing. This wasn't something he often did, for although God had given him many talents, singing wasn't one of them.

He warbled—shakily—the last line of the morning's hymn, and a flock of quail flew out of a cluster of brush by the road.

At least he thought they were quail.

She's the one, isn't she, God?

Life was good. God was good. The future stretched ahead like this road that seemed to head toward the horizon, a golden thread in the afternoon sunlight, a golden thread with no knots, no snarls, no—

Oh no!

He sat upright so suddenly that the horse whinnied a question.

He clicked in encouragement, and the horse continued down the road, but his afternoon had taken on a less glorious glow.

He'd forgotten about the evening of piano music at the Farnsworth house on the coming Friday. It wasn't that he didn't think he'd enjoy the recital—quite the opposite—but for some reason he didn't relish the evening.

Maybe it would be all right, he tried to console himself. Maybe it would be just a simple evening of good music in a lovely house.

In the interim, he had something wonderful to look forward to. Odd that Brigit hadn't mentioned it to him.

⁙

Brigit watched as Reverend Collins's wagon got smaller and smaller until it was part of the horizon. She hugged herself with delight, thinking of what he'd said.

She tried not to think about the upcoming evening at the Farnsworth house, though. The fact of the matter was that comparing Farnsworths to Streeters was like comparing silk to homespun.

"You must have found a lot to talk about," her father said when she came inside. He was grinning. "Even Milo Farnsworth doesn't take that long to leave."

The dear was trying so hard not to ask her what the minister had said to her.

"We visited about the community and the church."

221

"Yes?" His curiosity was ill reined, and Brigit didn't keep him in suspense.

"Yes. He also asked if he could come to visit."

Her father frowned. "Well, of course he can visit. Maybe he wants some information from me about the materials of worship that we have, or—"

She smiled broadly as the realization struck him.

"He isn't coming to see me, is he?"

"He could be."

"Or not."

Brigit stood in the fading summer light, watching hope play across her father's face.

She tried to refuse to let the nasty little voice in, the one that reminded her how unsuitable she was for the minister. *He really should be married to someone like Mary Rose,* the voice nagged, *someone who is well versed in the social graces.*

Someone not like you.

"I'm glad," he said at last. "Very glad."

He was smiling a bit more than she was comfortable with. She didn't try to figure it out. Her father was having some very strange moments lately.

She patted his hand. "He's a nice fellow, Papa."

He nodded and stood up. "I'd better check to make sure that chicken wire is still good. Groves brought over some of his newest hatchlings."

She grinned happily. Baby chicks! She loved them. Maybe Mary Rose could come over later and they could play with them. She loved the sensation of their little chick feet on her hands when she held them.

"You don't mind, do you?" he asked as he ambled toward the front door. "I meant to ask you, but just like old Groves's rooster, it flew out of my mind."

He stepped outside and almost immediately popped his head back in. "I did tell you that I invited Reverend Collins for supper, didn't I?"

Chapter 4

Y ou did *what?*

Brigit's father turned and faced her, a faint frown creasing his forehead. "Didn't I tell you?"

She studied his face. Was that slightly confused expression also slightly faked? "No, you didn't tell me."

"I'm sorry. I certainly meant to." He sounded sincere, but a mischievous glint in his eyes gave him away.

She shook her head. What was she going to do with him? "When is he coming over?"

Mr. Streeter stepped out of the doorway before answering. "Tonight."

Tonight?

Brigit took a mental survey of what was on hand. It was a very quick survey: they didn't have much at all.

She slumped into the chair. There were some women in town who were quite adept at taking a chicken, a carrot, and a sprinkle of seasonings and coming up with something delicious. She wasn't one of those women. If she couldn't boil it, it didn't get cooked.

Why had her father done this? He knew how limited her culinary skills were. If he were really trying to marry her off, he had chosen an odd way of advertising her assets.

There was no ignoring her predicament, though. Her father had really done it this time. With a sigh, she pulled herself out of her chair and checked to see what was possible for a dinner.

She grumbled to herself as she gathered together a pile of vegetables. It certainly wasn't much, and it definitely wasn't going to be fancy.

The Farnsworths weren't going to be eating thick stew with carrots and potatoes cut into large chunks because Brigit didn't have the patience to dice them into tiny cubes. No, they'd be served food with French names that she couldn't pronounce on dishes that she didn't dare touch for fear she'd break them.

Here she'd be serving stew on heavy mismatched plates with chips in the sides. The delicate china that had been her mother's had long ago been discarded, the victim of her father's inept washings.

Why hadn't he asked her before he invited the minister to dinner?

She muttered as she chopped potatoes and sliced carrots. Griped as she cut up the chicken. Complained as she shoved wood into the cookstove and heated the small kitchen area to an unbearable temperature.

But even as she did so, part of her was rejoicing.

He was coming back!

She smiled at the unpeeled carrot she was holding. Had ever a vegetable looked so beautiful? How could its brilliant orange coloring develop like that underground? Had there ever been such a miracle as a carrot? She almost hated to scrape the skin off it, but into the pot it must go.

If only she had some of those seasonings she'd heard the women at church talk about. She'd never paid any attention to those discussions. Salt and pepper were all she and her father ever used.

The liquids began to burble in the pot. It would be awhile before it would be ready. She had time to turn Fulton out to graze one last time before evening. She didn't like to have him out after sunset. The mosquitoes were getting fierce at dark, even this early in the season.

Her horse whinnied softly as she went toward his stall in the barn. He'd been with her so long that she'd almost forgotten a time when he hadn't been there. Even so, his canter was still good and strong. She loved to watch him playfully fling his head or nibble the grass.

She couldn't resist. Within minutes, she was up on his back, racing down the road toward the river and then back again. There was nothing like the wind on her face to clear her mind of her foolishness, she told herself.

After they'd come back to the farm and she'd brushed him down, she turned Fulton into the fenced area of the yard.

Brigit watched Fulton soak up the afternoon sun for a while, and then she realized with a start that it was almost time for Reverend Collins to arrive, and she was still as smelly and messy as she had been—even more so since she'd added peeling an onion to her day's activities.

She tore inside and washed and combed and patted and brushed until she looked as good as she could, given the circumstances. She had just finished when her father lumbered through the door, calling to her.

"Brigit, are you—Oh no! What is that smell?"

She poked her head around the corner, a ready retort on her lips. "I smell just fine, thank you very much, thanks to—oh, that's awful!"

She covered her nose and ran to the kitchen.

The pot with the stew in it had boiled dry, and the carrots and potatoes were now a hardened mass at the bottom. She gave them a tentative poke with the fork, but it was as bad as it appeared—and smelled.

"What are we going to do?" she wailed. "What are we going to do?"

※

Peter stood in front of the mirror and straightened his tie for the seventh time. It simply would not stay put. No, it insisted upon sliding over to the side, and that wouldn't do at all.

Not when he was going to visit Brigit Streeter. He was smitten. There was no other word for how he felt. She lived life with a vigor he envied. Customs and conventions didn't seem to hold her back.

He sighed. Customs and conventions were part of a minister's life. He had known that from the very beginning. And they fit him very well.

Brigit Streeter, though, touched that part of his soul that longed for a closer relationship with the Lord, one that saw His face in every flower, His hand in every bird.

She had also touched his heart.

"So what are we going to do?" Brigit asked her father again.

He shook his head in disbelief. "I don't know. I just don't know."

She opened the cupboard door and stared in at the nearly empty whitewashed shelves.

The stew was beyond salvaging, and there wasn't enough of anything left to make dinner from on such short notice.

She sank to the spindle-legged chair in the small kitchen and buried her face in her hands. This was not good. She wanted to make a good impression on Reverend Collins, not continue to reinforce what he must surely think of her—that she was a tomboyish mess.

There was something inordinately unfair here. Here she was, stuck on the prairie with the saddest assortment of "suitable" men imaginable, and what happened when the most eligible bachelor this side of the Mississippi showed up—and was interested in her, to boot?

The pain in her soul was almost palpable. *I want him to like me,* she cried silently, moving as naturally to prayer as if it were breath. *Dearest Lord, Thou art probably trying to teach me something here, but apparently I am a horribly slow student. What am I supposed to do? Please help me!*

A knock sounded at the door, and she raised her head, startled. She hadn't expected God to answer quite this quickly, and she dreaded His answer.

"Mary Rose, what a surprise!" Her father's voice rang through the small house. "I wasn't expecting to see you this evening."

Brigit stuck her head around the corner and stopped mid-step when she saw what her best friend was holding out toward her father.

It was round and wrapped in a blue and white checked cloth, and it smelled heavenly.

Could it be that God had answered her prayer in the rotund form of Mary Rose Groves?

"Brigit, Mother sent this over. She said that you—"

Mr. Streeter took the dish out of her hands and gave it to his daughter. "Please tell your mother that we send our thanks. Now, Mary Rose, you must hurry home, isn't that right?"

Mary Rose started to say something but stopped. "Oh, absolutely."

When Mr. Streeter left the room with the dish in his hands, Mary Rose leaned over and whispered conspiratorially, "I think your father is playing matchmaker."

Brigit groaned. "I am really in for it, then. He is relentless when he gets an idea in that balding head of his."

Mary Rose winked behind her glasses. "Sometimes, Brigit, you have got to admit that he is right. Some matches *are* made in heaven."

⁘

Birds twittered and a slight breeze rustled the leaves of the cottonwoods as Peter's horse walked the road to the Streeter home. There couldn't be a nicer afternoon, he thought. This was the Dakota Territory in its sunlit glory.

He spoke softly to the horse and slowed its pace until it stopped. He jumped from the horse and turned around in a complete circle, taking in his surroundings.

God had truly excelled in this land. The sky was an azure arch over his head, reminding him of the vision that far exceeded his own. A faint puff of white, a lone cloud on an astonishingly blue canvas, drifted across the sky. Peter's heart immediately sought prayer.

Lord God of all beings, I thank Thee with all my soul for bringing me to this place of extraordinary beauty. I beg of Thee to let my ears be open to Thy way and my mouth speak only those words assigned by Thee.

He paused and listened to a meadowlark warble its prairie opera, watched a jackrabbit bound across an open field.

The only thing missing was someone to love. . .someone to love him.

He sighed. There was no use in getting philosophical about that in the middle of a country road. Then he smiled and finished that thought. . .especially when love might possibly be waiting at the end of this very road.

He put his foot back into the stirrup and swung himself easily onto the saddle. He clicked to the horse and urged it into a trot. Time was wasting away.

As Peter drew closer to the Streeter home, a wagon passed him. Its driver waved, and he thought he recognized her as someone from the church, although he couldn't remember her name. What a friendly place Archer Falls was!

He was looking forward to this. He really was. His stomach growled in anticipation of the wonderful dinner that was awaiting him.

He'd had enough of his burned stew to last a lifetime.

⁘

"He's here."

Brigit's heart leaped up to flutter somewhere in her throat as, from the doorway, she watched Reverend Collins dismount from the horse. He spoke quietly to the animal and then greeted her father, who'd gone out to meet him.

They tended to the animal and returned to the house, and as they did so, she tried to calm herself. She probably had the wrong idea about his feelings for her. To him, perhaps she was simply another parishioner, someone to love only in a godly sense.

He smiled at her as he took off his hat before entering the house. His hair gleamed like coal in the late-afternoon sunlight, and his eyes were as dark as warmed chocolate.

"Miss Streeter, it's very kind of you and your father to invite me to your house."

She took his hand, trying very hard to remember to breathe. "The pleasure is ours, and please call me Brigit. Let me take your hat, and you go ahead and have a seat, and my father can show you around."

His face lit in a smile. "I'm not sure I caught all that, but I'm delighted to be here with you."

She knew she should let go of his hand, but she couldn't release her grip. The message that flashed from his eyes told her that she hadn't misread anything. How could her heart leap around like this? Why didn't it stay in place in her chest where it belonged rather than jumping from place to place inside her?

At last she came back to her senses and dropped his hand. "I'm really glad you're here, Reverend Collins."

Somehow she managed to bumble her way through the next few minutes as they got themselves seated and ready to eat.

"Reverend Collins, would you do us the honor of praying over our food?" her father asked.

"It would be my pleasure." He bowed his head and began to pray. "Blessed Lord, Father of all we have been, all we are, and all we will be, have grace upon us this day as we gather to eat the gifts of this fruitful land. Shower our time together this afternoon with joy and caring. We ask this in Thy holy name. Amen."

"Tremendous words," Mr. Streeter commented as he shook his napkin out into his lap.

Brigit beamed at her father and at Peter and at the casserole. Life had rarely been this good.

What they talked about was as simple as how pleasant the weather had been, how the wheat was coming up good and strong this year, how Archer Falls was growing into a real community.

And all the time, Brigit heard only bits and pieces of the conversation. She felt as if she were dreaming the entire event.

The men's voices brought her back to reality.

"And that's why I've decided to stay in Archer Falls," he was saying. "I know I've only been here five weeks, but they've been a persuasive five weeks, enough to convince me to stay. I suspect the presiding elder will let me do so, that is, if the congregation will ask me to stay."

He turned his winning smile on her and added, "I received a letter from him this week, saying he was satisfied with my work, so I am ever hopeful that he will agree to let me remain."

"You have determined to stay?" her father asked, and there was an edge to his voice that surprised Brigit. It was almost an anxiety that she heard.

"Yes." Reverend Collins looked at her, and his eyes spoke secrets that she'd only dreamed of.

Something was going to happen. The air almost sizzled with it, like the way the air was charged before a lightning storm, when the earth waits for the celestial fireworks yet to come.

"I've grown quite fond of the area," he continued, "and the people."

A nervous smile that she was unable to control twitched around her face. What was she supposed to do? Her romantic contacts had been limited—actually, there hadn't been any—and she was in the dark about what she should do next.

This was the kind of thing that she and Mary Rose had talked about long into the night, and she was sure that Mary Rose had told her what she should do, but as usual, Brigit hadn't paid any attention.

It hadn't mattered then. The idea that she might some day want to attract and keep the attention of a young man had seemed so unlikely. Certainly none of the men in the community had caught her eye. How Mary Rose had ferreted out Gregory Lester was a miracle. The fellow lived across the river, and they'd met through the help of some far-flung distant relatives who were determined to see them married, preferably to each other.

Speaking of miracles, here was one sitting across from her, and he was clearly waiting for a response to something he'd just asked.

She tried to recover and not look flustered and undoubtedly failed at both.

Chapter 5

Summer moved along at a clip. Brigit loved the busyness of the season, when the earth seemed to explode with life. It was also the best time to fall in love, with long walks along tree-lined roads and picnics on violet-strewn grass. Brigit and Reverend Collins had just returned from such a walk on a Sunday afternoon.

"Isn't this a glorious day?" she asked, twirling around and sending her bun plummeting down. "What more could you ask for, Reverend Collins, than a day like this?"

His reply was soft. "What I would ask for, Brigit, is for you to stop calling me Reverend Collins. We can't have you calling me Reverend Collins all the time."

"What else would you have me call my minister?" She knew that color was rising in her cheeks, but she was incapable of stopping it.

His voice dropped a level. "You would call him Peter. Or maybe even Dear."

That did it. Her heart flip-flopped its way up her throat and back down again. *Peter.* Had there ever been such a beautiful name? *Peter.*

❖

"Nice sermon."

"Excellent."

"Next week."

Peter stood at the church door, staring at his parishioners as one by one they delivered terse compliments and sped out of the small building. They'd never been in that much of a hurry before, he thought. What had it been today? Had the building been too hot and close? Had there been a terrible smell that he hadn't, literally, gotten wind of? Or—horrors!—had his sermon been so awful that they felt compelled to flee from his presence the moment the service ended?

He watched them leap into wagons or onto horseback and hurry away. This was very odd. He leaned against the door frame and absently swatted away a persistent horsefly.

Maybe he shouldn't have come across so strongly about the gifts of heaven. Had the congregation interpreted his message as looking for increased donations?

"Going over your sermon again?" Brigit asked from behind him. "Trying to figure out what you could have said about the loaves and fishes that would be offensive?"

"Can you read my mind that easily?" he asked, only partially teasing.

"I can when your thoughts are written across your forehead." She laughed. "Actually, I can explain this odd behavior in one word: harvest."

"Really?" Peter was fascinated. This was another angle of farming he knew nothing about.

"Oh, don't get me wrong. They're not going home to work in the fields. No, they'll sit in their living rooms and think about their crops and the future. For them, each tiny seed that goes into the ground is a life, and they'll bring it through with prayer.

"They'll become preoccupied and worried and jubilant all at the same time. Remember, they've been looking forward to this day ever since that May morning when the first shoots curled up through the slumbering soil, changing winter to spring overnight."

She made it sound like a poem, he thought, and when she spoke, it was easy to forget how hard the process was, how capricious the weather could be, how much of a struggle the farming life was.

"We live for this," she continued, and he noticed how the sunlight behind her lit her hair into golden strands. "We even dream about the harvest."

"I hadn't realized it was so all-consuming."

"It is," she replied adamantly. "But don't expect much of a drop-off in attendance. We know who gave us these crops. We know who made the miracle of the plant inside the seed. We know, and we must praise Him."

At that moment, he knew what his next sermon would be on. Genesis 8:22 had long been one of his favorite verses. How could he forget it? "While the earth remaineth, seedtime and harvest, and cold and heat, and summer and winter, and day and night shall not cease."

The loving continuity of the Lord—it had been a theme that had sustained him throughout his life, and it continued to support him now. But he'd never seen it through the eyes of farmers, how their very work echoed the promise of the Lord.

How could he, who had been carefully schooled in the seminary, have missed that? He'd needed Brigit with her honest faith and her instinctive understanding of God's love to bring it to him. And now he needed to bring this message to his congregation.

They already know it.

He heard God's voice as surely as if He'd spoken in his ear.

It was a lesson that he, the preacher, was learning from his flock. God was real to them in ways Peter had never thought of and even now only vaguely understood. They saw God's face in the sunflower and heard His voice on the wind.

The yearning in his soul was almost an ache as he thought of what they had—and he didn't. What Brigit felt—and he didn't.

It wasn't that God wasn't very much a part of his life. He was. But Peter longed for the deeply personal relationship these farmers had with God, a deep-seated, internal knowledge that flowed through their veins like blood itself.

Bit by bit, though, Brigit was bringing him closer to his God, and it made him love her even more. Standing there, backlit by the glorious summer sun, her greenish eyes glowed with laughter, and something in his heart sang for the joy of her. She was truly beautiful.

"You're thinking," she said.

"I wish it weren't that obvious," he replied ruefully, dragging his thoughts back to the daily world. "Although I would hope that I'm thinking all the time, not just when it shows."

"Good point. But can I ask what occupied your thoughts so greatly today?" She tilted her head, and some golden-red strands slipped out of the bun and curled into tendrils around her face.

He leaned over and touched her cheek. "Nothing more than a glorious August day and an equally glorious woman. Would you like to go for a walk with me this afternoon?"

"I'd love to."

When Brigit smiled like that, Peter was sure he could hear the angels sing.

-:::-

The cottonwoods whispered among themselves, and once in a while a crow cawed a noisy protest about the antics of a lively rabbit.

Inside her small house, Brigit hurried through her meal, barely even tasting the slab of ham her father laid across her plate and gulping down the boiled potatoes mindlessly.

Mr. Streeter watched her silently until at last he said, "Is there a train coming through here that I should know about?"

"A train?"

"I was just commenting that from the way you're wolfing down your meal, there must be a train headed our way."

"Oh, I'm sorry, Papa. No train, just a minister."

He didn't say anything, but from the way his face softened, Brigit knew that her father was fond of Peter, too.

She jumped out of her chair, ran over to him, and threw her arms around his shoulders, trying to ignore for the moment how thin they were. "Papa, dearest Papa, what should I do? About Peter, I mean. We are from two very different worlds."

"Does it matter, Brigit?"

"I believe it does, Papa. You see, I think, I hope, I worry that he is starting to love me. What should I do?"

He held her tightly, and his voice was muffled as he answered, "Love him back."

-:::-

The afternoon sun was warm on Brigit's shoulders as she and Peter walked down the road leading away from the small farmstead.

"If it weren't for the insects, I think this would be heaven on earth," he said to her, as he smacked a relentless mosquito. "I know our Creator had His reasons for everything on this earth, but I fail to see how the mosquito quite fits into His greater plan."

"They're food for other animals." Brigit sent up an unspoken prayer of thanks for a long-ago schoolteacher who had explained it to her. "Dragonflies, for example, eat them. I remind myself of that whenever the mosquitoes are especially fierce, since I think dragonflies are amazing insects."

"I think the dragonflies had better get busy." He swatted another mosquito. "There's plenty to eat at their table."

"I think it's an uneven battle between them and grossly stacked in the mosquito's favor," she replied. "At least the dragonflies don't go hungry."

A large dragonfly buzzed toward them, its body and wings a kaleidoscope of emerald greens and cobalt blues.

"Isn't it beautiful?" she asked, leaning down to observe it as it paused on a road-side daisy. "God put extraordinary effort into this creature. Look at how it shines! And the wings are so transparent and thin, you'd think they'd tear in the wind, not keep this beauty aloft."

She stood up and smiled at him. "I'm sure I'm not telling you anything you don't already know. I don't know how anyone could not believe in God from simply look-ing around the everyday world. The perfect symmetry of a snowflake. The perfume of freshly laid straw. The delicacy of a newborn kitten's nose."

"That's right," he said almost to himself. "This is truly God's world."

"Sometimes I have to tear myself away from it or I'd be spending all my time looking at the miracle of a daisy." She touched the flower as the dragonfly flew away. "Here I am, a farmer myself, trying to make plants grow where I want them to, and at the moment, I can't think of a better place than right here for this daisy to grow. God decided that, and His mind was perfect, as always."

"I've never heard it put quite that way." His voice was barely above a whisper.

She felt herself redden. Of course he hadn't. Her views of God must seem mighty simple compared to the theology he had learned in the seminary.

"Do you know what surprises me the most about the Dakota Territory?" he asked, and before she could answer, he said, "The colors. Everything is so intense. The sky is so blue, the wheat is so golden, the trees are so green."

"Listen to this." Brigit pulled a shiny leaf off a poplar and bent the green heart in half. She blew into the bottom edge of it, and the shrill whistle from the folded leaf pierced the air. She grinned as a squirrel overhead scolded her for breaking the peace of the afternoon.

Peter laughed. "Let me try it."

He plucked a leaf and folded it in half. After a futile attempt at producing any sound at all, he relinquished it to Brigit.

"You are a silly goose. I thought a minister was educated and knew everything."

"Is making a poplar leaf into a whistle part of the curriculum of a seminary now? If so, I must have skipped class that day," he teased her.

"Let me show you. You fold it like this, and then you kind of purse your lips a bit, and then you—"

"Kiss."

"What?" Brigit stopped, the leaf still in her fingers. "I said, you. . .I mean, you. . .that is, why. . .oh, dear."

"It certainly sounds to me like you were describing perfectly how to kiss. But I'd rather kiss you than a poplar leaf. May I?"

For once in her life, Brigit was speechless. She could only nod.

He leaned over, and she raised her lips. A memory of how she and Mary Rose had practiced kissing their pillows shot into her mind, and she almost laughed, but then his lips touched hers. There was nothing pillow-like about Peter Collins's lips.

At last he drew back, but he held her lightly around her waist. "I've been wanting to do that for a long time. Brigit, I—"

"Is that Reverend Collins?" Mr. Farnsworth's voice boomed across the landscape. "It is! Good! I want to talk to you about the men's meeting next Tuesday."

Peter leaned over and whispered in her ear, "Apparently the only way I'll get to kiss you in private is to marry you."

She stood in the shade of the poplars and stared at him as he grinned at her. He squeezed her hand quickly and went to talk to Mr. Farnsworth. She couldn't have heard him right. He must have said he would *tarry* her. *Carry* her. Or even *bury* her.

Peter lounged against the Farnsworth wagon. He didn't seem to look like a fellow who had just proposed. Or not.

She ran the words through her mind again. He hadn't said, "Brigit, will you marry me?" Actually, he hadn't asked her a question at all. It was probably a joke—not a good one, but a joke nonetheless.

The hope in her heart evaporated except for one stubborn bit: *He wouldn't have said it if he didn't mean it.*

The two men talked at the wagon, oblivious to the turmoil in her soul.

What did she want? Did she want Peter to love her? The answer shot back, clear and pure: *Yes.*

Did she want to be his wife? Again the answer was: *Yes.*

Could she be a minister's wife and mingle with church dignitaries and hold teas and serve fancy dinners? The answer this time was no.

She was the kind of woman who knew how to make poplar leaf whistles and could bring in a field of wheat by herself. These were not the talents asked of a minister's wife.

Peter motioned her over to the wagon. "I hate to cut our afternoon short, but I need to get back into town. There's a telegram from the presiding elder that's marked *Urgent.* Mr. Farnsworth has volunteered to drive me in. Can we drop you off on the way?"

His eyes pleaded with her to understand, and she did. She shook her head. "No, but thank you just the same. I believe I'll walk on home."

"Are you sure? Then I'll pick you up tonight around six thirty for the pie supper at church?"

She nodded. "I'll be ready. But don't worry about my walking. It's such a nice day, and as we all know, such warmth is fleeting in Dakota. All too soon it will be cold, and I'll be pining for this heat."

Besides, she added mentally, *I need some time to work out my feelings about you.*

But it wasn't, she acknowledged as she walked slowly back to her home, that she had to sort out how she felt about him. She knew that. She loved him with every bit of her being.

She just had to determine what to do about it.

⁙

Peter straightened his tie yet again in the mirror. He wasn't a vain man, but he lamented his inability to center his tie. No matter what he tried, it simply wouldn't stay in line.

He was really looking forward to the evening. Pie suppers were apparently great fun. But that wasn't why his tie had to be straight. No, it was because of a young woman with wild strawberry-blond hair who would be there, too.

His heart warmed at the thought.

Clearly, Lord, she is the one Thou hast intended for me. I had no idea that my soul was capable of such love. It seems to grow, to expand inside me. I must thank Thee, O Lord, for bringing her to me.

Tenderly, he touched the daisy that she had picked for him earlier that day. How could he have never noticed the delicate white petals, the velvety yellow center, the texture of the slender green stem?

He grimaced one last time at his reflection and gave the recalcitrant tie one last tug, which sent it completely askew. Peter resisted the temptation to rip the offending item off entirely and jerked the tie back toward the center. By the time he got to the Streeter house, the ride would knock it farther out of line.

The clock in the hallway bonged six times, and he ceased his struggle with his tie. If he was going to get to the Streeter house, collect Brigit and her father, and bring them back into town without being late, he had better get going.

He bolted down the stairs and out the door singing. It was going to be a good night whether his tie was lined up or not.

Some of his joyous mood was, he had to admit, due to the contents of the telegram. He touched his coat pocket where the paper crinkled reassuringly. Yes, it was real. He couldn't wait to share the news with Brigit.

Peter sang all the way to the Streeter farm despite the loud objections of the squirrels and crows along the way. He was no musical prodigy, that was sure. It was a good thing tonight's show did not require audience participation, he thought wryly.

Brigit was in the barn. He could see her outline against the open door. He couldn't wait to see her reaction to his news. That was the best part of love: being able to share joy like this.

Chapter 6

"B rigit!" Peter tore into the barn, startling Fulton, who reared up slightly in protest. "Oh, sorry there, Fulton. Brigit, guess what! You'll never guess! Just guess!"

She leaned against the stable door and studied the man she loved. "Why don't we spare us all the pain of my trying to guess something I'll never guess, and you just tell me?"

"Oh, right. Let me take a deep breath. Is he going to be all right?" Peter shot a concerned glance at Fulton, who was watching the minister warily.

"He's fine. What's the news?"

"Reverend Armstrong, the regional presiding elder of the church, is coming right here to Archer Falls!" He reached into his pocket and withdrew a crumpled piece of paper, which he waved in front of her. "That's what the telegram was about!"

Why this was such exciting news was beyond Brigit, and she said so, with polite modifications.

"He's coming here for a visit, Brigit, to see us!"

"To see you and me? Why?"

"No, to see all of us. To see the church and how it's doing. How I'm doing. He was my mentor when I was in seminary."

"You're not worried, are you?" she asked him.

"I suppose I am a bit," he confessed, "but mainly I'm excited to have him meet the congregation and to see how blessed I am."

He grew serious. "I've learned so much from all of you, and I'm eager to share you with him."

She studied his eyes for signs of tension and saw none. If she were in the same spot, she'd be a nervous wreck. Maybe he was simply hiding his feelings well.

"Is there anything I can do to help?" she offered.

His face lit up. "Interesting that you should ask that. There is. Reverend Armstrong's wife would like to meet the ladies of Archer Falls."

Her smile froze. She couldn't meet someone as important to Peter's career as the presiding elder or his wife. She was only a farm woman.

"I'm thinking a tea would be good." He ducked his head and cleared his throat. "I don't know how much trouble something like this would be—I'm not exactly sure of what one would even have to do to have a reception of this sort. So tell me if I'm asking too much. Could you put together a tea for her?"

Could she put together a tea for the presiding elder's wife? Could she flap her arms and fly to Minneapolis? Of course she couldn't.

Her brain knew that, but her heart knew something else, and her mouth apparently had a mind of its own. "Of course I can."

Was she out of her mind? Frantically she sought a way to take back the words. "I mean, I can't. . .I don't. . .I. . ."

But the expression on his face stopped her. What she saw there wasn't just gratitude; it was also relief. And then it struck her: he wanted her to do it.

That alone was enough to stem her objections.

She, Brigit Streeter, was putting on a tea.

⁘

"Mary Rose, what do you know about teas?"

Brigit's friend turned her nearsighted gaze at her as they sat in the yard of Brigit's house. "I like strong black tea the best. One and a half spoonfuls of sugar or a quick slurp of honey to sweeten it. No cream. Why?"

"No, not that kind of tea." Brigit shook her head. "I'm supposed to put on a tea for Mrs. Armstrong, the presiding elder's wife, and I have no idea how to start."

"A tea? You, hosting a tea?" Mary Rose laughed uproariously. "How did that happen?"

Brigit picked a clover blossom and shredded it. "I'm not really sure. I certainly meant to say no, but somehow I said yes."

Mary Rose nodded knowingly. "Ah. I understand. When is this tea?"

"In two weeks."

Her friend frowned. "I can't help you then. I'm going to St. Paul with my mother to pick out the material for my wedding gown. Did you see the pattern we found? It looks a bit like Queen Victoria's. . ."

Brigit paid only minor attention as Mary Rose launched into the details of her wedding preparations. It wasn't that she didn't care. On the contrary, Mary Rose was her best friend ever. But things like patterns and dresses ranked quite low with her.

Right down there with hosting teas.

"And Reverend Collins said he would," Mary Rose finished with a triumphant beam.

Brigit had no idea what Mary Rose was talking about, but her mention of Peter brought her back to the conversation. "Peter said he would do what? I'm sorry, but I got lost in my own world there for a minute."

Mary Rose laughed. "I do tend to go on and on when I get to talking about my wedding. I was just saying that Reverend Collins agreed to officiate at the wedding in September, depending on how the harvest is going. I want my honeymoon to be far away in Minneapolis, in a big fancy hotel, not in a wheat field here in Archer Falls."

Suddenly the import of what Mary Rose had been saying these past three months since her engagement to Gregory struck Brigit. Mary Rose would be going away to live with her new husband.

What a day this had been!

⁘

Some days crept by, thought Brigit, and others simply tore past. It had been fourteen days since Peter had spoken to her about the tea, but she had managed to put off even thinking about it.

That was, until Peter mentioned it from the pulpit in church. "Reverend Armstrong will be visiting us this week. He and his wife are, in fact, arriving around noon today, and I'm looking forward to introducing all of you to them through some very special occasions. I'd like to remind you again that there will be a ladies' tea this afternoon to honor Mrs. Armstrong."

He smiled at her, apparently oblivious to the turmoil that churned in her stomach.

They were arriving today? She hadn't done anything about the tea. What on earth should she do? Why hadn't she given this any thought? Why did she always put things off until the last minute?

These were excellent questions, she realized, but they didn't help her at all. She was still stuck, completely and totally stuck, in a dire predicament.

"Where shall they meet, Brigit?" Peter had spoken from the front of the church and was looking at her expectantly.

She had no idea where they could have this thing called a tea. She ran through the options. The church? Not with the pews. Her house? There were only two chairs. Peter's house? If he'd wanted that, he would have offered.

She wanted to put her head down and cry. Peter would think—rightly so—that she was terribly inept. Again, the differences between them were brought vividly to light. In the same situation, he would have known what to do and, furthermore, done it right away.

Brigit did the only thing she could. She smiled brightly and said, "Let's meet at the front of the church, and we can walk."

Peter's sermon was undoubtedly superb, but her thoughts flew around in her head like unsettled sparrows. She had to find a solution.

The worst part of it all was that it wasn't only about her. This was about Peter and his career in the ministry. If she in any way made his situation perilous with the presiding elder, it could change his life's work—and the countless souls he might yet touch with the Lord's Word.

There was only one thing to do. Pray.

God, I am really in a pickle here. I don't know what I can do, but I know I have to do something. Please help me out, God. Please!

Somehow she got through the service and was trying to slide out the side door when Peter caught her. "The plans for the tea must be going extremely well," he said. "I haven't heard of any problems at all with it. I suppose you decided on having it at the school. There really isn't any other place. . ."

He chattered on happily while Brigit breathed a quick prayer of thanksgiving. How a tea held in a school could be elegant was beyond her, but she'd have to make it do.

She began to relax. Perhaps this tea was not going to be all that difficult.

As soon as she could gracefully slip away, she darted outside and ran across the square to the schoolhouse. She pulled on the handle. It was locked.

"Well," she said to herself, "when a door is locked, you must find a key." It was one of her father's sayings, and she'd heard it often enough when growing up to have it ingrained in her brain.

A key. She needed a key. Who had the key? Her thoughts tumbled around each other like baby puppies, impossible to settle down.

"Brigit!" Her father called to her from the wagon. "Are you coming?"

She ran to him. "Papa, I need to get into the school. I have to set up the tea in there."

"You're having the tea in the school?" From the expression on his face, she knew it wasn't her best choice. Sadly, it was her only choice.

"Yes, I am, and I haven't got a lot of time to set it up."

He studied her face solemnly for a moment and then asked, "Have you prepared at all for this, Brigit?"

She shook her head. "No, Papa, I haven't." Quick tears sprang to her eyes. "And to make it worse, I can't even get into the schoolhouse. Peter will think I'm dreadfully disorganized because. . .because. . .because I *am*!"

Wordlessly, he leaped from the wagon and walked to the school and unlocked the door and returned to her. "You're a fortunate young lady, Brigit. The only reason I could let you in is that I mended the window sashes in there yesterday and neglected to return the key."

She dropped a kiss on his weathered cheek. "Thanks, Papa. You are a dear." She dashed to the schoolhouse and in the front door.

The room itself was quite tidy but horribly inappropriate for a tea—at least what she knew of such functions. The first order of business was to move the desks out of their orderly rows.

She pushed. She shoved. She pulled. She tugged. The desks would not move. They were nailed to the floor.

She sank to the nearest chair and put her face in her hands. This was terrible. Just terrible. What was she going to do?

A sound outside reminded her that the guests would be soon arriving, and her chaotic thoughts scattered even more. What could she do to make the room more presentable?

The teacher's desk was clear. Maybe a centerpiece would make it seem less. . . desk-like? Was there any way to salvage this?

The presiding elder and his wife wouldn't see the beauty of the prairie, she thought sadly as she looked around the room. If only she could show them—

That was it! She knew what she could use as a centerpiece. She leaped out of the chair and ran outside, nearly running into a cluster of women who were standing by the steps of the school. "Oh, I'm sorry. Last-minute details, you know. Be ready in a minute!" she caroled to them as she tore past.

She knew exactly where to go. Behind the church, there was a stretch of even land where she and her father had often picnicked. Right now that area was flush with wildflowers. She scooped up as many daisies as her hands could hold, and she raced back to the school. This would have to do.

Well, she still had at least an hour. Even as she formed the thought, she knew it wasn't good. Having a tea wasn't the same as having tea. Why hadn't she asked for help earlier?

An hour, an hour. It had to be enough time.

She came around the corner of the church and found herself facing Peter and an older couple.

"Brigit, this is Reverend Armstrong and his wife, Mrs. Armstrong," he announced proudly.

"I'm pleased to meet you," she said, not knowing if she should curtsy or bow or shake their hands. *They were early!*

Mrs. Armstrong smiled graciously at her and said, "Oh, my, those are lovely flowers. Are they for me?"

Brigit stared, horrified, at her erstwhile centerpiece, and said the only thing she could. "Of course."

Mrs. Armstrong took the flowers and smiled. "Daisies are my favorite. I have no idea how you knew this, but thank you so much. Dear, we have a few minutes before the tea. Would you mind showing me around the town a bit? I'd like to stretch my legs after that long train ride."

There went any shred of a chance Brigit had to remedy the tea. *I'm sorry, Peter,* she said silently to him. *I'm really very sorry.*

Mrs. Armstrong was very kind as she and Brigit strolled through the small town, so much so that Brigit felt comfortable confiding as they returned to the school, "This tea isn't going to be nearly as grand as what you're used to. I do hope you won't think badly of us when you—"

Her words froze in her throat as they entered the school. The ladies of the church were all gathered there. The desks were still in their utilitarian rows, but they were all graced by spring-hued napkins. Marie Farnsworth was setting out a bowl of grated sugar. Sarah Bigelow was arranging the last teaspoon. Mary Rose Groves winked at her from behind the tea urn, and Brigit realized what she had totally forgotten—tea! Yet somehow the tea was brewed, and there were even assorted cookies on a tray.

"Why, this is lovely," Mrs. Armstrong said. "Absolutely lovely!"

Brigit introduced Mrs. Armstrong to the church women and pulled Mary Rose aside. "How did. . . ? Who did. . . ? I mean, what. . . ?"

Mary Rose smiled. "You can thank your father and the very organized ladies of the church. He just sent out the word, and they showed up, ready to help. All they were waiting for was someone to ask them."

Brigit nodded, too overcome to speak. But when the time came to introduce Mrs. Armstrong, she thanked the members of the church for all their work. What would she ever do without them?

And so she—and Peter—had been saved again.

·:·

That evening, Peter and Brigit walked through the dusty streets of Archer Falls. "This town feels like home," he said to her. "I'm very comfortable here, and I really do want to stay."

He turned to her and asked suddenly, "Have you ever wanted to live somewhere else?"

"Do you mean like Chicago or Rome or London?" She looked at the line of houses all built so close together that they almost seemed to be standing shoulder to shoulder against the prairie wind. "Maybe only for a moment. In my heart of hearts, I think I always want to live in Archer Falls. Why?"

He turned to her and took her hand. "This isn't exactly the way I'd intended to do this, Brigit. Well, the truth is that I didn't have anything planned. I couldn't decide how to—"

"How to what?" She'd never seen him at such a loss for words.

"Do you remember when we were out walking, and you were talking to me about daisies and kittens' noses, and I kissed you?"

Her breath stopped in her throat. How could she ever forget that? She nodded, and he continued.

"And Mr. Farnsworth interrupted us? And do you remember what I said to you then?"

"That if you wanted to kiss me. . ." Her voice trembled.

"I'd have to marry you."

"Yes." It was just a whisper.

"Will you, Brigit? Will you marry me? I can't offer you much, just all of my love, which, to be honest, is quite a lot."

"Peter—"

"I know what I want. I want to live here in Archer Falls with you and raise a family." He took her hands and said earnestly, "I think God brought me to this place to meet you. Until I met you, I was incomplete. You are the other half of my soul. Of my heart. Of my mind. Will you marry me and be a minister's wife?"

She swallowed. "Yes. Yes. Yes."

There was never, she thought, a more inappropriate match. And yet there was never a more perfect match.

"Yes."

⁕

Brigit's father smiled happily at her as she waltzed into the small house. "You look as if someone has crowned you queen of the summer!"

She plopped down beside him. "I think someone has. Papa, Peter asked me to marry him."

"And you said yes, I hope."

"My darling father, of course I did." She ran her hand over his work-worn fingers. "But there is something I must ask you. What will you do about the farm? Can you do it without me?"

"You worry too much." He leaned back and frowned slightly. "Has this been worrying you?"

She nodded, unexpected tears gathering in her eyes. "I love Peter, but I want to farm here with you, too."

"The land is in your blood, isn't it?" he asked.

"It is."

"Ah." He leaned back and shut his eyes. The conversation was abruptly over, but he was smiling.

Chapter 7

P eter awoke the next morning surprised that the sky was overcast. How could it be this dreary when his heart was so happy?

The Armstrongs met him at the church after breakfast.

"You seem especially happy this morning," the presiding elder said to him.

Peter tried to keep the grin off his face, but it kept popping back into place. "Yes, I am."

Mrs. Armstrong smiled. "Could it have anything to do with the charming woman we met yesterday?"

"Yes, it could." Peter straightened the already-neat altar banner.

"If you'd like to share something with us...," she began.

"She said yes!" he interrupted happily. "She said she'd marry me!"

"Lovely choice," Mrs. Armstrong said, and her husband agreed.

A thought came to him—a wild, crazy thought—but maybe, just maybe... "Would you do us the honor, Reverend Armstrong, of performing the wedding? My parents, you might remember, have gone on to be with the Lord. Having you perform the ceremony would mean so much to me."

The presiding elder's face broke into a wide smile. "Why, I'd be honored." His brow wrinkled. "But I'll be out of the country for the next year. We're leaving right after we return from this visit."

"Could you marry us before you leave?"

"Well, I could. But bear in mind that I'm only in this region for two weeks, so this wedding would have to take place soon."

Peter briefly considered that. Certainly he and Brigit hadn't known each other long, and he hadn't given any thought to a quite abbreviated engagement, but an early wedding shouldn't present any problem.

"We can do that," he said.

Mrs. Armstrong tugged on her husband's sleeve. "Might I suggest something?" she asked softly.

"Of course," Peter answered.

"Could we discuss this with Brigit? She might have something to say about it. A woman does only have one wedding in her lifetime, you know." Her eyes lit with a soft love for her husband as she looked at him.

"Did I hear my name?" Brigit spoke from the doorway of the church.

Peter's heart skipped a beat at the sight of her unruly hair, which was, even at this early hour, escaping the pins that vainly tried to hold some kind of a bun arrangement in place. He crossed to the door and took her hands in his and led her to where the Armstrongs stood.

"Brigit, I've told the Armstrongs that you accepted my proposal last night," he began, "and—"

Mrs. Armstrong gave Brigit a quick hug. "I'm delighted for you," she said. Then with a meaningful glance at her husband, she added, "I think that Charles and I would like to take a walk in the fresh air before we return to the dusty world of church records. We'll leave you two alone for a bit."

"But I thought—"

"Didn't you want to—"

Both men spoke at once and were promptly hushed by Mrs. Armstrong, who looped her arm through her husband's. "Come along, now."

Brigit looked befuddled as the Armstrongs left the church, a slightly confused look on the presiding elder's face. "What was that about?"

Peter drew her close and kissed her gently. "I hope you don't mind, but I asked Reverend Armstrong to perform our wedding ceremony."

The thought that he was going to spend the rest of his life with her was almost too much to bear. She was so beautiful, so free-spirited. What a delightful experience life was going to be with her.

"That's fine with me," she said, her voice muffled against his shoulder. "I hadn't thought about it, but I suppose you can't perform your own wedding."

"So it's all right with you to have him officiate?"

"Of course. It would be an honor." She leaned her head back and ran her finger down the side of his face. "Shouldn't we set a date then? I don't know anything about weddings, but I can ask Mary Rose. She's an expert."

Finally his brain clicked into place. Weddings. They took time. "How long has Mary Rose been engaged?" he asked, trying to sound casual, but he dreaded the answer.

"She's been working on it since Christmas, but she's marrying Gregory Lester, and there are Lesters all throughout this part of the territory. Their wedding is going to be the event of the year."

"So our engagement doesn't have to be that long, right?"

"Oh, not at all."

He took a deep breath. "So, how does two weeks sound?"

She jerked out of his arms. "Two weeks? Two weeks?"

"Too long?" His bad attempt at humor warranted golden sparks in her light green eyes.

"Two weeks?" she repeated. "Two weeks?"

⁘

Brigit rode down the row of poplars. Fulton looked over his shoulder as if to ask, *Why aren't we running?* But she needed the time to sort through her thoughts.

This was going much faster than it should. She still had to come to grips with being a pastor's wife. Could she do that and get married—in two weeks?

God, I'm turning to Thee again, she prayed silently. *Once again haste is my enemy. I've never paid attention to much in life, just rushed pell-mell forward, and somehow Thou hast always caught me when I might have fallen. What should I do?*

There was no answer except the soft sound of the wind in the poplars and the soft neigh from Fulton as he again questioned why they weren't running.

When she was a pastor's wife, would she have to forgo these cleansing rides on Fulton's back? Or making poplar leaf whistles?

"Come on, boy. Let's go!" She urged him forward, and together they raced against the day.

By the time she had Fulton stabled for the night, she had her answer. She loved Peter, and she was going to marry him whether it was in a year or a day.

Later that evening, she lay in bed wide awake. Too much was happening for sleep to come. In less than two weeks, she'd be married to Peter. She'd be Mrs. Collins, Mrs. Peter Collins! Brigit Collins. She tried the name on for size and found it fit very nicely.

She sat up in bed, startled, as a sudden thought came into her mind with the force of a prairie whirlwind. Getting married in two weeks wasn't going to be a problem. She couldn't be expected to put on a fancy wedding with that little time. She and Peter would quietly get married with no folderol.

Life was good, very good.

⁖

The Armstrongs handed their baggage to the boy loading it onto the train. "We'll be back in two weeks for the wedding then," Reverend Armstrong said.

"I've enjoyed this visit," Mrs. Armstrong confided to Brigit, "but the wedding is going to be joyous indeed."

She handed Brigit a small, tissue-wrapped package. "I hope this can make the day a bit brighter for you."

"What is it?"

"Open it, dear, and find out."

Brigit unwrapped the packet, and a neatly folded length of material spilled across her hands, as soft and delicate as a baby's breath.

"It's lovely." The words didn't begin to express how much the gift touched her.

Mrs. Armstrong smiled and held the material against Brigit's face. "As I thought. The green matches your eyes."

Impulsively Brigit threw her arms around the older woman's shoulders. "Thank you so much!"

"I never had a daughter of my own," Mrs. Armstrong said, "only one boy, and he's not big on spring green dresses. It would be an honor if you would wear a dress made out of this fabric on your wedding day."

"I will, I will," Brigit promised, nearly beyond words as she held the incredible material. "I will."

Mrs. Armstrong dropped a kiss on Brigit's cheek. "I'll look forward to seeing what you do with this. I just know that any woman Peter has selected will be a true Proverbs 31 wife."

Proverbs 31 wife? What did that mean?

She watched the Armstrongs board the train and numbly waved good-bye as the train pulled away, its wheels chugging out the message: *Two weeks, two weeks.*

Peter hooked his arm around hers, and together they walked back to Fulton and the wagon. She couldn't linger today, for the harvest was in full swing, and her father needed her help.

"What did Mrs. Armstrong give you?" he asked.

She showed him the swath of fabric. "She thinks it would make a lovely dress to be married in, and I agree. What do you think?"

He squeezed her hand and helped her into the wagon. "I think you'd be the most beautiful bride in the Dakota Territory if you were dressed in Fulton's feedbag."

Brigit laughed. "Now that's something the people of Archer Falls would be talking about for years!"

⋅⊰⋅

Mr. Streeter was hard at work in the field, and he motioned to Brigit. "Mary Rose came by to see you. She'll stop by tonight after supper. Meanwhile, can you take over here? I have to run into town to get a part for the baler."

She loved the harvest. The smell of the wheat as it fell to the blade, the warmth of the sun upon her shoulders, the glorious azure sky overhead—all of these made this time exciting.

Plus it gave her time with her thoughts. This year she had plenty to consider. She was about to marry the man she loved. What was she supposed to be doing? There had to be something besides making her wedding dress.

The thought nearly stopped her mid-step. Making her wedding dress? It was insane. She couldn't sew. She couldn't!

She was the only young woman her age who couldn't sew. Whenever something needed mending, her father actually took up needle and thread.

As far as her dresses went, her friends' mothers had always taken pity upon the poor motherless child and tried to help her with making her dresses. But despite their best efforts, Brigit had never learned. Was there ever a duller subject? While the enterprising mothers had talked of needles and seams and selvages, she'd daydreamed of racing Fulton through the fields.

Oh, why hadn't she paid attention—not just to sewing, but to the whole realm of the household arts? She was getting married in two weeks and had only the vaguest idea of how to cook a dinner and certainly no concept of how to entertain or make a dress or even mend a ripped seam.

What a foolish choice she was for Peter. There was no way for her to learn what she didn't know in two weeks.

That evening she unfolded the delicate material and spread it out. How long she sat there, the material around her like a pool of pastel green, she had no idea. At last a sound at the door made her look up.

"Daughter, what are you doing?"

"I'm making a dress." She didn't sound at all convinced of the fact, but she bravely smiled for her father.

He came and knelt beside her. "Where's your pattern?"

"Pattern?"

"You're going to need a pattern to tell you where to cut. What is this material for, anyway? Why don't you wait for one of the women in town to make it for you?"

She buried her face in her hands. She was not a crying woman, and she wasn't about to start now, but this project had vexed her beyond her capabilities.

"Why are you doing this?" he repeated.

"It's my wedding dress. Or it's supposed to be."

Mr. Streeter smoothed her tangled hair, as if by doing so he could smooth her tangled thoughts. "I think you should wait for someone to help you."

"How can I?" She looked up at him with worried eyes. "They're all busy with the harvest. I barely have time as it is to work on it myself. Mary Rose is in Chicago this week, looking at shoes of all things. That's what she wanted to see me about today, to tell me that. So she can't help me."

"I can help."

"Papa, I need to make the dress myself. Mrs. Armstrong expects, and Peter expects, and I—"

"And you expect," he finished for her. "I understand. Might you take some advice from an old farmer? The wheat grows straighter if you line up the seeds."

Brigit gaped at him. He had clearly spent too much time in the sun.

"Plan before you cut, dearest daughter. Plan before you cut."

She studied the cloth a bit more. She could see the imagery. The fabric as the land. The scissors as the plow. The needle and thread were like planting.

Her soul began to rise, ready to take on this next challenge. She could do it.

After all, how hard could it be to make a dress?

Chapter 8

The next day, Brigit stared at the material and pondered what to do. This, like farming, would take some planning. It wouldn't be right to just cut into the cloth, willy-nilly. She had to be in the right frame of mind, ready to focus.

The fields called to her, a ready excuse. The harvest needed to come in. That couldn't wait, whereas a dress—oh, how long would it take to sew some seams together?

The next day, she wasn't prepared to cut into the material, nor the next day, nor the next.

"How are the preparations for the wedding going?" Peter asked her as they strolled down past the poplars once again.

She couldn't meet his eyes. "Fine," she lied, and then, because she couldn't bear such dishonesty, changed from an outright lie to a little fib. "There isn't much that can be done, not with such short notice. The ladies of the church are putting together a reception, and they're decorating the church with some flowers. That will be about it."

"I've asked Reverend Armstrong to read Proverbs 31 as one of the scriptures. It reminds me of you."

Proverbs 31 reminded him of her? Was she misremembering it?

"You have such talents," he continued, "like cooking—that was a wonderful dinner you made when I first came to town. You're superb at entertaining as I saw with the tea. Plus, you're making your wedding dress, and I'm sure it'll be breathtaking."

Yes, she thought, *it easily could be.*

She needed to stop him, to tell him the truth, but she couldn't. She loved him so much that she couldn't imagine not spending her life with him.

He hugged her waist. "I'm counting the hours until we become man and wife. When you walk down the aisle toward me in your green dress."

Her mind guiltily fled to the pile of green fabric on her bed. Every day she had duly spread it out, and every day she had packed it back up.

Tonight she would begin.

⚜

"At some point, you will have to cut the cloth," her father said gently that evening.

"I'm afraid," she said, her voice barely audible. "I'm afraid I will make a mess of it, just as I made a mess of the dinner, and the tea, and everything else. And now I've waited so long that I can guarantee you it will not work out at all well, and the

Armstrongs will think I'm not good for Peter, and what's worse, Peter will know that I won't be a good wife."

"What have you done about it?" he asked.

She shook her head, and half of her bun came unpinned. "I don't know what you mean."

"Who have you talked to about it?"

"Mary Rose, of course. And, well, you."

"Ah." He leaned back in his chair. "Have you talked to God about it?"

"God isn't going to sew my dress, Papa!"

"No, but He has certainly helped you out before, hasn't He? It seems to me that the dinner went fine. The tea was a success. Why don't you trust Him now? Ask for His help. At least do that."

She picked up the well-worn Bible. "For a woman who's marrying a minister, I certainly have been wrapped up in my own worldly issues, haven't I?"

"Brigit." He stopped.

"Papa?"

"I never told you what your mother said to you with her last breath, did I?" His words were thick and his eyes moist.

She could only shake her head no.

"She kissed you and. . ." His voice broke. "She told you why she chose Brigit as your name. It means strong. She wanted you to be strong. Brigit, she would have been so proud of you. You're strong and capable, and I know that you've made your mother very proud in heaven."

She stood up, and as she dropped a kiss on the top of his head, a few tears mingled in. "Thanks, Papa."

-:::-

By the next afternoon, it was quite clear to Brigit that God was not going to step in and save her. She had already taken apart her favorite dress to use as a pattern. The first lesson she'd learned about sewing was that she had to lay the pieces out carefully or she'd run out of room.

One arm of the dress was going to be spliced from two end pieces, thanks to her carelessness in not laying the pieces out neatly.

The second lesson was that she should cut slowly. The collar looked like it might end up lopsided, because there were some scraps of the pattern dress laying on the floor, and she knew that wasn't right.

The third was that fabric was very slippery and should be pinned or held down while being cut. Pieces that were supposed to be the same certainly didn't look the same.

The fourth lesson had to do with seam allowances, and the fifth and final one was that it was always a good idea to know what piece went where. She had long thin bits that could be sleeves, or they could be—well, she didn't know. But she couldn't be sure they weren't sleeves.

The needles pricked her fingers mercilessly, and she was forever swabbing blood droplets from the pale fabric.

People do this for a living, she thought with amazement. She'd rather muck out pigpens than do this.

Someone knocked at the door, and she smiled. This was the help that God was going to send her, at last. Mary Rose wasn't due back until the evening train, but perhaps she had gotten home early.

"Come in," she sang out.

"Brigit, Rever—" Peter's voice stopped midword as he surveyed the scene in front of him. Behind him, the Armstrongs stepped into the room, and she could see the shock in their eyes. The room was chaotic, and she was not better.

She leaped up from the floor where the pieces of the dresses were strewn about, and as she did so, the pins holding the bun on the back of her head sprayed out, and her hair, tangled and curling wildly like a madwoman's, showered around her shoulders.

"It's good to. . .please excuse the. . .I'm a bit. . ." She couldn't pull the words together.

"It looks like we've caught you at a bad time," Mrs. Armstrong said. "Is there, uh, anything I can do?" She looked at the disarray doubtfully.

Brigit summoned a smile. "Oh no. Just last-minute things. I'll be fine. See you tomorrow!"

She didn't dare look at Peter for fear of what she might see in his eyes.

She probably pushed them out the door rudely, she thought, but other things were more important, like making the pieces turn into a dress.

Proverbs 31 ran through her mind endlessly. Everything God expected of a wife was right there. She got the Bible from the table and read through it again with a sinking heart. Peter was wrong: this was everything she was *not*.

Brigit looked at the destruction around her. "She maketh fine linen," but Brigit cut it up. "She maketh herself coverings of tapestry," but Brigit couldn't get the needle threaded. "Strength and honor are her clothing," but Brigit had been living a lie to Peter.

She shouldn't marry him. He needed a wife who wouldn't be an embarrassment to him.

She heard his voice outside. Her father had come home, and Peter and the Armstrongs were still there.

Brigit gathered up the bits of the soft-green cotton and called to him from the door. "Peter, please come here. I—I have something I must say."

The sunlight glinted across his hair as he turned to her, and from the way his smile flashed at her, she knew that whatever else might be wrong in her life, he was the one thing that was right. She loved him. He loved her. They needed to be together.

Nothing else mattered.

"Brigit, did you want to say something?" Peter asked as he came back to the house from the wagon.

She smiled at him. "I love you. Just that, I love you."

Reverend Armstrong called from the wagon, "We'd better go, Peter. The poor girl has enough to do without our interference. Remember, she's getting married tomorrow!"

Brigit stood in front of the altar of the small church, and it all seemed like a reverie. Reverend Armstrong read the marriage ceremony, and from somewhere in a dream, she heard herself saying, "I do," and saw Peter's warm gaze.

And then it was over.

The congregation surrounded them with good wishes and congratulations. Even Milo Farnsworth, although he seemed puzzled by the whole matter, shook Peter's hand heartily and nodded awkwardly at Brigit, clearly not sure what to say and finally settling for a vague, "Yes, yes, excellent."

Mary Rose, though, knew exactly what to do. She hugged her good friend. "Mrs. Collins! Who knew you'd be able to marry for love!"

"The dress is lovely on you," Mrs. Armstrong said when the crowd had thinned.

"Don't look too closely at it. If I take a deep breath, the seams are likely to spring apart," Brigit said confidingly.

"We do what we need to do," the presiding elder's wife said wisely, "and we learn. My dear, I have one more gift for you—a sewing basket. Life is going to give your heart more rips and rends than a simple silver needle pulling thread can fix, but it's a start. God bless you, dear."

Brigit hugged Mrs. Armstrong, wondering if the woman had any idea how inapt the gift was. Already the seams of the green dress were loosening, but it didn't matter.

The dress, Brigit realized as her handsome new husband joined them, was just outerwear. It was the love that she and Peter shared that was important.

Her father's eyes were suspiciously red as he approached them. "Peter, she's my girl. She's always been my girl, and she always will be. I have just one request of her."

"Yes, sir?"

"She's part of this land, you know. She was born in Dakota and raised here, too. Farming's in her blood."

Peter smiled as Mr. Streeter continued. "So I think we should tell her what the surprise is."

Brigit's new husband turned to her. "I've been living in a rented house. It's small and cramped and no place to raise twigs."

"Twigs?" she asked blankly.

"Twigs, on our family tree," he explained. "Children."

The thought of their children warmed her heart.

"Your father is building us a house on the farm," he went on. "We can live there and farm together, all of us, your father, you, me, our children—"

"Our twigs," she added laughingly.

Chapter 9

Peter, can you come here, please?"

He put down his book and joined Brigit by the back door where she was washing clothes. Life with her was sweeter than he'd ever imagined. "Yes, my dear?"

Brigit dipped her hands into the washtub again and again, pulling out piece after piece of sodden green cotton. "Look at this, Peter. Do you know what this is?"

He shook his head. "Stockings? Gloves? Towels?"

"No," she said sadly, retrieving yet another bit of cloth from the water. "This is my wedding dress. It came apart when I washed it."

He bit his lip, trying to stop the inevitable quivering.

Brigit went on. "I'm a terrible cook, and I can't organize a tea, and I have never sewn a dress before in my life, and when I did sew it, look what happened."

He bit harder on his lip.

"I'm not a Proverbs 31 wife," she continued, "not at all, but I love you, and I want to be with you always."

Peter gave in to his laughter. "Darling Brigit, I don't care about cooking or teas or sewing. All I care about is that you love me."

She studied the damp pieces of what had been her wedding dress. "Peter, do you know what I'm going to do with these? I'm going to use these to teach myself to sew. I'm going to put that sewing box Mrs. Armstrong gave me to good use, and I'm going to make a quilt. I will teach myself to be a Proverbs 31 woman."

He held her closely. "Don't you remember what else is there? 'A woman that feareth the Lord, she shall be praised.' You, Brigit, my dear, are already truly a Proverbs 31 wife."

He kissed her roundly and soundly while the green scraps dripped, unheeded, onto the floor.

Epilogue

My dearest son,

This quilt is the story of your family and the love that binds us together as truly as the threads that hold together these pieces of cloth.

I began this quilt as a new bride. I didn't know any more about sewing than I did about being a wife, but I knew about love. The pieces of my wedding dress are in here and form the center block. They are the delicate spring-green swatches. It's the same green, by the way, you'll see when the first wildflowers poke their brave stems through the winter-worn earth.

There are a few patches of white in this quilt. They are cut from the shirt your father wore when we got married. Ah, John, what a fine figure he presented that day! I can still see him in my mind, so elegant, so handsome, so sure. . .and so very much in possession of my heart.

The little patches were once your blanket. This was the first earthly fabric that touched your newborn skin. Yellow-spotted flannel looked so warm against your infant skin, like God had poured sun around your tiny body. It was cold the night you were born—so cold the doctor's breath froze midair—but you quickly warmed our hearts.

As our family grew, so did our love—and the quilt. Notice how the stitches get more even and practiced on the outer patches. I was just learning in the center section, but the patches, straggly though they may be, are still holding together after many years of hard use.

Love is like that, John. At first, it's all very new and awkward, but if you're willing to put your heart into it, it'll hold steadfast. There aren't any silk or satin or velvet pieces in this quilt, but to me, its beauty far exceeds the grandest coverlet. Even the littlest, most mundane pieces of life make an extraordinary tapestry when united by love. . .these scraps of love.

Your loving mother,
Brigit Streeter Collins

BASKET STITCH

by Cathy Marie Hake

Chapter 1

*No Man's Land—the strip of land between Kansas and Texas
not claimed as a territory by the U.S. government
Summer 1886*

"Dustin Travis? Sorry, ma'am, but he up and died 'bout a week or so ago. Got trampled flatter'n a griddlecake in a stampede."

Deborah Preston braced herself against a barrel. Her fiancé was known for pulling pranks, and his horse was hitched outside. She scanned all she could see of Foster's Food and Feed for him. "Dustin? Please don't tease me just now."

The gangly young clerk shoved away from a teetering stack of multicolored calico sacks. "Miss, I wasn't funnin' you." He smoothed back his stringy hair. "Don't you fret yourself none. I'll be happy to marry up with ya."

"I–I'm afraid. . . ." Words failed her.

"No need to be afeered, ma'am." He reached for her arm. "I'm Bently Foster. I'll take good keer of ya."

Deborah evaded his touch and shook her head.

"Well, well. My eyes weren't playin' tricks on me after all," a man's voice said from the doorway. "That's a woman—and a purdy one, too."

"She's mine," Bently said as he stepped in front of her. "Go find your own woman, Testament."

"I'm not your woman." Deborah frowned at him, then glanced over at the man approaching them. "I came to marry Dustin Travis."

Three other men tromped in behind him, all big, blond, and homely. Two whistled. The other spat out a wad of tobacco and smiled at her. The first one shrugged. "No use wasting the trip. I'm claiming you."

"Now wait a minute here!"

"Hush up, Foster. She already said she don't want you." The men started arguing over her.

Normally, Deborah could appreciate a fine joke, but after days of travel, weariness swamped her. Dustin must have taken appreciable time to cook up this elaborate charade, but she was too tired to be a good sport. Backed against a post and hot and dusty as the road she'd been on, Deborah hit her limit.

"Stop this. Stop it at once!" She shoved the basket she'd been carrying onto the

255

nearest barrel, then thought better of that move and grabbed it back. "I'm not a juicy bone to be fought over by a pack of wild wolves."

"All wolves are wild," a woman said from somewhere to Deborah's left. Her voice carried an entertained lilt.

Relieved that she wasn't the only female around, Deborah craned her neck to locate the woman. Once she spied her, Deborah's hopes for any assistance or sisterly support wavered. The woman wasn't quite twenty, and she was handsome in the way only a young, raven-haired woman could be—however, she wore a holster instead of a sash, and her hair wasn't up in a lady's fashion but braided in a long tail that fell over her shoulder.

"I need Dustin, please. Dustin Travis." Head pounding, mouth dry, Deborah silently prayed this woman would take pity on her and put an end to the tasteless joke.

"Hardheaded little thang, ain't she?" One of the men moved closer.

"King Testament," the strange young woman said in an exasperated tone, "you're not going to claim this girl."

"Mind yer own business, Lou."

Having decided Dustin wasn't planning to rescue her anytime soon, Deborah pushed back an errant tendril of hair. "Gentlemen, I'm going to need to appeal to—"

"Oh, you appeal to me just fine."

She pretended she hadn't been interrupted. "—Your chivalry. Perhaps you could direct me to the nearest boardinghouse."

"Lady, these men don't even know what chivalry is," Lou muttered. "Now you men just go on home."

The men didn't seem the least bit interested in the women's opinions. King chuckled. "Petunia ain't got no boardinghouse, and you won't need one. You're coming home with me."

Deborah realized these uncivilized men must not be part of Dustin's joke and couldn't be reasoned with. Even if Lou had a gun, Deborah knew they were outnumbered. She figured the time had come for her to rely on what she had on hand and good old-fashioned common sense. She could use the derringer in the basket. Her amethyst-topped hatpin would make for a wicked weapon, and she still had Papa's favorite pocketknife, an arsenal of knitting needles, and her sewing scissors. Yes, the time had come to defend herself and her virtue. These men weren't being honorable, so she was going to fight as dirty as she could. Deborah took a deep breath, let it out, and burst into tears.

"Now look what you went and done to that poor gal, King One." The tobacco spitter yanked off his hat and whacked the foremost man with it.

Deborah sucked in a choppy breath, took a better look at him, and decided she'd been out in the sun too long. He looked just like the man beside him. That wouldn't have been quite so alarming, but the other two men looked exactly the same as one another. *Seeing double. I'm just seeing double. It's not as bad as I thought. No, wait. It's worse. I'm sunstruck and—*

"Sugar, don't pay them Testaments no mind." Bently patted her arm. "I'm not gonna let 'em have you. Yore mine."

Deborah flinched. She stuck her hand into the basket and blindly searched for the derringer. The least Dustin could have done was show up to meet her instead of leaving her to fend for herself. Tears blurred her vision and thickened her voice. "Leave me alone."

"You done went and ruint it for all of us," another complained as he elbowed past and stepped closer to Deborah. "Calming a sobbin' gal is harder than puttin' socks on a goat."

"You boys back up," the woman said as she hopped up and stood on a nearby crate. The action managed to reveal the scandalous fact that she wore men's boots. "You don't know what she has in that basket, but you sure enough know I have my pistol."

One of the men snorted, and two of the others snickered.

King went ruddy. "You just keep that Colt in your holster, Lou. My brothers would hate to have to wing you. As for me worryin' 'bout this gal posin' a threat— she's bawling like a baby and just as helpless."

Bently muttered, "Lou, she's a regular girly girl—not a scrappy she-coyote like you."

The soft angora yarn brushed the back of Deborah's hand as it toppled out of the basket. She refused to look down and watch where it went. If she couldn't find the gun, at least she could grab something.

The closest man stuck out his hand and caught the ball of pink yarn. He lifted and inhaled deeply. "How d'ya like that? Smells like them flowers of Ma's."

"Gimme that and git outta here." The clerk grabbed the yarn.

Looking quite earnest, the man with the hat pressed it against his chest and shuffled so close she caught a whiff of the beer he'd been drinking.

"C'mon, sweetheart," King crooned to Deborah as he shoved aside the man with the hat. "You ain't got no call to cry or—ouch!"

The minute he touched her wrist, Deborah yanked a knitting needle from her basket and poked him. He jerked back, but she lost hold of the needle. It pinged as it hit the floor. She hastily sought a replacement from her basket.

"That's the way!" Lou stayed on the crate and cocked her pistol. "Now you boys just mosey on back home."

"Lou's got her hackles up," one of the brothers groused.

"And my gun drawn. You Testaments already know I'm not shy about pulling a trigger when it's necessary."

"Louisa Stafford, what stunt are—" The unseen man's impatient voice changed to a bellow. "Put that gun back in your holster, girl!"

"Not 'til the Testaments leave this lady alone, Wally."

Boots grated on the floor as an older man walked up. Wrinkles and impatience creased his face. "You boys kick up more trouble than a cyclone. I can't have you hassling my customers."

"Your customers are bothering us. Lou's drawn her gun, and this other—" He scowled at Deborah as he rubbed his wrist. "She pert near poked a hole clean through me with a pig sticker."

"Watch what you say about pigs." Wally pulled Lou from the barrel and set her on the floor. Deborah noted he hadn't repeated his order to holster her weapon. With that in mind, she took out another knitting needle.

"Now you went and done it." Another whap with the hat punctuated that exclamation of disgust. The speaker lowered his voice more. "We're all gonna have to listen to another Petunia story."

"Miss Eleanor, she thought highly of my Petunia. Didn't she, Lou?"

"Yes, Grandma sure did." Lou bobbed her head. "She named the town after your pig. It's not every day you see a pet like yours."

He has a pet pig? Oh, the sun really did bake my brain. Deborah bit her lip to keep from letting out a cry of despair. She tried to wipe away some of her tears, but the knitting needle kept prodding the brim of her bonnet.

"Gonna put out her eye, First Chronicles. Lookie there at how she's poking that stick around. Somebody oughtta help her out."

"Not me. Already drew blood on my wrist with the other one."

"Women wouldn't have to defend themselves if you'd behave and leave them alone." Lou holstered her gun.

"You boys are already in enough trouble." The old man shook his head. "Your ma's gonna skin you alive when she finds out you've let Chronicles drink again."

"Aw, you ain't gonna tell her, are you?"

Lou hurriedly said, "Not if you promise to leave us alone."

Wally folded his arms and glowered at the Testament men. "You *are* your brothers' keepers."

The wobbly feeling in Deborah's legs should have gone away when the muttering men tromped out of the feed store, but it didn't. She leaned into the post. "Thank you. Thank you both so much."

"You'll be safe enough now. Come on over here and sit a spell. Pay no mind to those louts, and rest your bones a bit. I'll tell you all about my pet."

The odd man had a kindly face, and Deborah decided she might stand a chance of reasoning with him. As he tucked her hand into his crooked arm and led her toward a disreputable-looking stool, she promised, "You can tell me all about Petunia after we find Dustin Travis."

"Why, I suppose that's easy enough." The old gent's face drooped mournfully. "They're buried right next to each other just out back."

Chapter 2

Micah took one look at the contents of the buckboard and couldn't believe his eyes. A blond woman in widow's weeds lay amidst a collection of trunks and baggage. The shallow rise and fall of her bosom reassured him she was alive. Little comfort, that. It still meant a heap of trouble.

He halted his sister before she could get down from the seat. "Louisa Abigail Stafford," he ground out in a hiss of a whisper so the strange woman wouldn't awaken, "you drive right back to town and don't come home until you take care of that problem."

"She's a girl not a problem."

"Same thing." Micah glowered at his kid sister.

Dust flew from his chaps as he smacked his work gloves against them. "She's not a stray, Lou. She's a person." He dared to take another glance and winced. Bad enough, Lou's latest stray was a woman, but this one was downright comely. "Take her back where she belongs."

Lou ignored his order, set the hand brake, and jumped from the opposite side. "She doesn't have anywhere to go."

"She has to." He glowered at his sister and rumbled accusingly, "She's a *lady.*"

"Worse than that. She's a fancy, big-city lady."

"Have you taken leave of your senses? She doesn't belong—"

"She swooned."

His sister's words lit his temper worse. As he strode around the wagon so he could scoop up the woman and tote her into the house, he hissed, "Didn't Grandma teach you what to do for that?"

"I know better than to loosen someone's stays in the middle of a feed store." Lou grabbed a pair of flower tapestry valises and headed up the porch. "No fair being mad. I still got the chicken feed."

The buckboard squeaked and rocked as Micah leaned over the side and started to reach for the young widow. Lou hadn't made it easy on him—she'd wedged the woman dead center between bags of feed and the trunks. She stirred as he made contact, so he decided to be civil.

Micah drew back, shoved his Stetson more firmly on his head, and folded his arms across the top board. "Ma'am." He nodded. "If you lean this way, I'll help you out of the wagon."

She jolted, and the movement tilted her face toward the sunlight. Micah's irritation disappeared in a heartbeat when he saw the dried tear tracks on her dusty cheeks. "What did Lou do that made you cry?"

She continued to stare at him with those much-too-innocent blue eyes as if he were going to sprout horns and a tail at any moment, and she struggled to scoot farther away. Her tongue peeped out to moisten her lower lip, but the nervous action didn't seem to bring her any comfort. Micah's eyes narrowed. At first, he'd thought her pallor was from fright, but now he thought differently. Her awkward moves and agitation took on new significance.

"You're thirsty, aren't you?" He kept his voice pitched low and gentle as he rounded the wagon with long, deceptively lazy strides. She'd moved enough that all it would take was a simple tug to catch decent hold of her. "Let me take you inside, out of the sun."

Micah saw the rapid pulse at the base of her throat and the fast little panting breaths she took and suspected that while part of it was fright, the rest came from heat exhaustion.

"There aren't two of you." Her words came out in a dazed tone.

"You're right." Not that the observation made sense, but he figured if he agreed with her, she might feel safer. Indeed, it barely took any effort at all to hoist her into his arms.

A tiny, frightened sound shivered out of her.

"Shhh. I've got you." Her black wool skirt and the flurry of several petticoats explained why she'd overheated. Too listless to struggle, she lay draped over his arms.

"Oh, dear." Grandma came out onto the porch and wiped her hands off on her apron. "Bring her in right away."

"Told you she needed help." Lou clomped back down the porch steps.

Josh sauntered up and took a look at the woman swagged across Micah's arms, then at Lou and the buckboard. "Don't tell me you ran over her!"

"Of course I didn't." Lou gave him a disgruntled look.

"If you had, your aim would be getting better. That skunk you hit the last time—"

Micah left his siblings to argue and headed into the house. "She's weak as a kitten. Where do you want her?"

"I was making up my bed. Put her there."

Grandma's bedroom was the only one downstairs. The quilts rested over the quilt stand, and she'd been interrupted after putting a sun-bleached sheet on the mattress. As Micah slid his burden onto the bed, Grandma popped a pillow into a fancy, crochet-trimmed pillow slip and tucked it under the girl's head. He hastily untied her fancy, city-gal balmorals and yanked them off her feet as Grandma deftly unfastened the jet buttons at the woman's cuffs.

"Looks like heat exhaustion," he murmured as he poured water from the washbowl pitcher into a cup.

"And no wonder. Forget that water. Have Lou bring in some sweet tea and towels." Grandma winced. "Her buttons are in the back. Help me turn her onto her side before you step out."

Micah stepped to the far side of the bed, rested one knee on the mattress, and decided he'd best say something before touching the woman. "Ma'am, I'm aiming to twist you my way. No need to get riled."

She turned to look at him and blinked. "Who are you?"

"Micah Stafford." He pushed a strand of her honey-colored hair off her forehead. "That's Grandma on your other side. Who are you, sugar?"

"Deborah Preston."

"Deborah, you're in good hands." Grandma patted her shoulder. "We're going to take care of you."

Figuring they'd spent more than enough time with the niceties, Micah cupped his hands around their guest's far shoulder and hip and pulled. It took no effort at all to make her roll onto her side. He cranked his head toward the wall and stared at the blue-and-white floral material Grandma had tacked up to insulate and prettify the room. Grandma grew up in a fine home with servants. Judging from the quality of Deborah Preston's clothes and manners, she had, too.

He'd send her right back there as soon as she recovered.

-:::-

Deborah limped across the bare, hardwood floor and donned the flowered flannel robe someone had left draped on the back of the rocking chair. It felt odd to help herself to someone else's clothing, but she couldn't see her own garments anywhere in the room. Since someone had dressed her in a white lawn nightdress, she assumed they'd not be offended if she made use of the robe. After securing the sash, she left the room.

Odd, but she stepped from the bedchamber straight into a parlor. Gingerly, she walked past an ornate family tree sampler, by an upright piano, and toward folks all seated at a supper table. To her relief, Lou perked up and waved.

"Well, don't just stand there! Come on over and meet my family."

Everyone at the table stopped talking, and the men rose at once. *At least they're gentlemen—not like those horrible men at the feed store.* Deborah wasn't sure what time of the day it was, but at least if this was Lou's family, she was probably safe. She flickered a smile and ventured, "Hello."

"It's so nice to see you've improved, dear." The old, white-haired woman's velvety Virginia drawl poured over Deborah like a balm. "Come sit here by me. Samuel, get Miss Preston a chair. Louisa, fetch a place setting."

"Thank you for your hospitality, but—"

"Micah, go help her. What with the terrible way her limbs cramped, the girl probably can't take another step."

The tall, black-haired man at the head of the table started toward her, and his piercing silver-gray gaze made her aware of just how weak in the knees she'd become. Surely, it was from the heat, not from him. "I'm not. . ." Hopelessly embarrassed, she glanced down at her borrowed attire.

"You've been sick. You're decent." He reached for her.

She took a step backward and stammered, "I—I can walk."

"You're going the wrong way." His quiet words made her shiver.

Memories of the men at the feed store closing in on her flooded her mind.

Deborah took another backward step and bumped into something big and heavy. She tried to recover from the clumsy move and managed to plink several treble keys of the piano.

"If you're still of a mind to, you can play a tune for us after you've had supper." He stood beside her, took her right hand in his right hand, then cupped his large, warm hand on the left side of her waist.

The last time she'd been escorted in such familiar fashion was at her engagement party when Dustin had led her to the center of the room to make the grand announcement. Deborah couldn't decide whether to bolt or to lean gratefully into this man's strength. He seated her, scooted in her chair, and rested a proprietary hand on her shoulder.

"You've already met Lou. Grandma—Mrs. Stafford—is beside you. I'm Micah, and these are my brothers, Samuel and Joshua."

"I'm Deborah Preston. Thank you for taking me in."

Micah continued to stand behind her. "Lou, soon as supper's done, I want you to loan the lady a suitable day gown. She'll swelter in that black wool she was wearing."

"Thank you, but I have summer weight in my trunks." Deborah suddenly halted, the unfolded napkin halfway to her lap. "My trunks!"

Mr. Stafford pointed behind the oak and burgundy brocade folding screens that divided the dining room from the parlor she'd just edged past. "Four trunks, two valises, a barrel of what sounds suspiciously like broken china, and a basket."

She smiled at him. "Thank you for seeing to my things. I'm sure Dustin will be by shortly to help me with them."

Silence descended over the table again. Micah rested his heavy hands on her shoulders. Grandma reached over and squeezed her arm. Dread snaked through Deborah. She looked at the old woman's compassionate face, then up into the man's concern-lined features.

"It wasn't just my fevered mind?" She stared at him in horror. "I wasn't dreaming?"

He shook his head. "Dustin's not with us any longer."

"I hope it comforts you to know the town gave him a fine Christian burial," Grandma said.

Deborah couldn't help herself. "Right next to a pig?"

"Well, it was Petunia," one of the other men drawled.

"Hush, Josh," Micah ordered. "Miss Preston, you just calm yourself with some warm tea. After supper, we'll discuss what to do, but for now, everyone needs to eat."

Deborah stared at the platter in the center of the table and felt her stomach lurch.

"She went white like that in the feed store, too." Louisa's words sounded distant and muffled.

"Don't you go fainting again," Micah ordered. He turned her chair around, cupped her chin in his callused hand, and tilted her face to his. "You don't have some special reason for being swoony, do you?"

"Micah Reed Stafford, apologize to Miss Preston this very minute."

"Not until she answers my question." His eyes went the same shade as gunmetal, and he didn't turn loose of Deborah.

It wasn't until his grandmother's shocked response that Deborah understood what he'd implied.

"She was wearing widow's weeds," he said in a calm tone. "There was nothing sordid about the question. I'm not trying to be indelicate, but someone ought to ride to Wichita and see if there's something special we should do to help Mrs. Preston recover from her heat exhaustion if she's in the family way."

Tingling from hairline to heels with the heat of embarrassment, Deborah quietly said, "I assure you, there's no need. It's *Miss* Preston. I'm in mourning for my father."

"My condolences," Micah said in a remarkably even tone. He scooted her back toward the table, stepped over the bench, and sat next to her. He moved with assurance and masculine grace.

"So," Joshua said, leaning forward and grinning, "Dustin was your brother?"

Lou snorted. "Her name is Preston. Dustin's last name was Travis."

"Could've had different fathers, just like Micah had a different mother," Josh shot back. "Travis and Miss Preston are both blonds. A man would be proud to have a picture-pretty sister like Miss Preston."

"Pay them no mind, Miss Preston." Micah stabbed his fork into a piece of meat. "I'll arrange for you to travel back to your family as soon as possible."

Clutching the napkin, she said, "I have no family."

The fork halted in midair. Micah glared at her. While his grandmother murmured empathetic sounds, he acted as if being an orphan was akin to committing a terrible crime. "Surely you have friends back home. You don't belong here."

"Micah! Where's your hospitality?" His grandmother patted Deborah's arm. "Don't worry, dear. We—"

Deborah stood. "I'm not worried, Mrs. Stafford. I'll manage."

"How?" Lou wondered aloud.

Grasping at straws, Deborah blurted out, "Dustin's house. We were to be married. He built it for me. I'll take over his claim."

Joshua and Samuel looked at her as if she had lost her mind, then broke out in guffaws.

"The lady wasn't trying to be funny." Micah's much-too-quiet voice silenced them immediately. He turned to Lou. "Finish eating. We're going to show Travis's place to Miss Preston."

Thirty minutes later, Deborah sat in a wagon, clutching her parasol against the summer evening sun. Wedged between Micah and Lou, Deborah didn't say a word as they bumped over ruts and small stones. She'd agreed to this ridiculous trip with the understanding that Micah would deliver her possessions tomorrow. Now that they'd been on the so-called, seemingly nonexistent "road" for a while, Deborah had to admit to herself that she'd have gotten lost out here on her own.

"Give Miss Preston another drink," Micah ordered his sister.

"Thank you, but I'm not thirsty."

"Best you go on ahead and have a few swigs anyway." Lou shoved a canteen into her hands. "Can't have Grandma nursing you back again. She's weary from staying up with you the last two nights."

"Oh, my." Guilt speared through Deborah. She quickly twisted off the stopper and tried to time her sips between the worst jostles so she wouldn't spill. "I didn't mean to discommode anyone."

"You being out here is more than an inconvenience; it's a disaster waiting to happen." Micah shot her a wry look. "A hornet in a birthday cake would be more welcome."

Stung by his comment, Deborah clutched the handle of her parasol tighter and remained quiet. The wagon continued on until they approached a small hill. Micah stopped the rig and set the brake. "Here's Dustin's place."

"It's lovely land." She looked at the area and wondered aloud, "Does it begin or end at that little creek?"

Lou jumped down from the wagon, and Micah hopped down from his side. He shook his head and reached up to help her down. Deborah had reasoned it all out. Dustin didn't have any family, so surely his land should belong to her now. She'd stay at his home and pay his cowboys to do whatever it was ranchers did.

Once her feet touched down, Micah threaded her arm through his and began to walk. She saw a cow standing quite close on a small hillock. "Is that one of Dustin's?"

Micah squinted, then shook his head. "Crossed S brand. Mine." He led her on a small path diagonally down the hillock, toward the cow. "Here you are."

Lou galloped ahead and opened a door built into the earth. "Not much, but it's home." She grinned.

Deborah stood rooted to the ground in shock.

"Didn't Dustin tell you he'd built a soddy?" Micah asked softly.

She turned and looked at him in shock. "Your cow is standing on top of Dustin's house?"

Chapter 3

S he'll move when she's good and ready." Micah swept his hand in a gallant gesture toward the door.

Deborah gulped and headed toward the opening.

Lou stayed by the door. Micah left Deborah and went inside. He bumped into something, then she heard the scratch of a lucifer. A circle of light radiated from a lantern. "Okay. You can come on in."

A cave? Dustin had been living here like a mole? Thoughts tumbled in Deborah's mind as she stepped inside. She had hardly any money and no place left to go. Faced with that awful truth, she squared her shoulders and decided to make the best of this situation. The place smelled of dirt and moisture. With Lou right behind her, blocking out the light, she had only the meager glow of the lamp to light the interior.

An iron bedstead took up a third of the tiny dwelling. The blankets on it were a rumpled mess and spattered with dirt and mud. A pair of crates with a board atop them served as a table, and the backless portion of a cast-off chair was the only seat in the place. On the far wall, a shelf crammed into the wall held a few odds and ends beside a small, pot-bellied stove, and a shirt hung from a peg.

"Well," she said, trying to sound confident, "as soon as my things arrive, I'll be able to fix this place up."

"You can't stay here."

She acted as if she hadn't heard Micah's pronouncement and walked to the stove. "If you give me a moment, I'll see what I have on hand."

"We just had supper." Lou gave her an odd look.

"Yes, well, perhaps a cup of coffee or tea before you take your leave." Deborah stuffed tinder into the stove and tossed in a dried disk she hated to touch. She'd read about buffalo chips, but she hadn't thought she'd actually have to cook with them.

"Now that you mention it, coffee sounds mighty good." Lou sat on the chair and watched her.

"Come to your senses." Micah glowered at his sister, then turned to Deborah. "You're not staying out here alone. It's not safe. Pack up anything you want to keep."

Just standing inside this place, Deborah felt like she was being buried alive. She swallowed hard and knotted her hands together.

Lou pulled a small, pasteboard box from beneath the bed. "Found your letters to your intended. A few got sorta mouse-bit."

Deborah cleared her throat. "Just leave them there." She swiped a handful of weeds from the wall and headed toward the stove.

Micah stopped her. "What are you doing?"

She glanced down at her fist. "Making use of what's available. This will serve as fair kindling."

"You already put kindling in the stove," Lou reminded her.

"You're not," he growled, "starting a fire."

"Of course I am."

Lou said, "Chances are, birds are nesting inside the pipes."

Micah glared at Deborah and repeated himself in a tone she supposed was meant to be well modulated, but the muscle in his jaw twitched. "No fire, Deborah."

Deborah didn't argue. Once they were gone, she'd do as she pleased. Lou must be crazy to think birds would nest in this place. Even if they had flown into the pipe in hopes of establishing a home, they would have rushed right back out. *They have more sense than I do. I have to start a fire for light and heat once they leave, or I'll panic.* Deborah scooted past Micah and stubbornly shoved the weeds into the stove.

"Those are too damp," Lou informed her. "Even if they catch fire, they'll just cause a bunch of smoke."

Why doesn't that surprise me? The rest of my life has gone up in smoke, too.

-:::-

Micah watched Deborah with mounting dread. The crazy woman grabbed some beans and put them to soak for her supper the next day. Dirt sifted from the ceiling and fell into the pot. Though Deborah didn't quite manage to suppress her shudder, she turned away and whisked the quilt off the bed. "Lou, could you please help me shake this out?"

Micah figured the minute prissy little Deborah saw the soddy, she would dissolve into a puddle of tears. He'd been wrong. Deborah was trying to nest here just like the birds in the stovepipe!

Micah rasped, "Enough of this. Time we left."

"Yes," Lou agreed hastily. "It's going on dusk soon. We can't risk the horses and wagon in the dark."

This situation was impossible, and they'd played it long enough. He'd brought Deborah to prove she couldn't survive here, and the silly woman was actually planning to stay! She'd likely die of fright the first night she spent alone. Oh, but there she stood, a smile on her delicate face, her slender-fingered hands holding that filthy quilt.

Behind her, a sudden fall of dirt warned she was about to entertain another guest. Micah wondered if she'd ever seen a gopher, but he wasn't about to introduce her to this one. He grabbed Deborah's wrist and hauled her out the door.

She dug in her heels. "This is all—"

Her sentence ended in a surprised shriek as Micah tilted her over his shoulder, carried her to the wagon, and unceremoniously dumped her in the bed.

"Lady, somebody's got to save you from yourself."

·:·

"Took you long enough." Lou slammed the door shut and climbed into the wagon. The whole thing squeaked in protest as Micah got in at the same time. "Did you see that—"

"Yes." He cut off whatever his sister was about to say, and his tone made it clear she wasn't supposed to pursue the subject.

Deborah got up on her knees and clutched the back of the seat. "I saw it. What *was* that thing?"

"A gopher. Sure as toads hop, he'd land on your bed." Micah swiveled around and gave her a heated look. "You were supposed to get out here and show enough common sense to go back to where you came from."

She lifted her chin. "That's not possible."

"Nothing is more impossible than you living out here."

"He's right." Lou's inky braid danced up and down as she vigorously bobbed her head. "I wouldn't even try it, and I know how to shoot and ride."

"Thank you for your opinions," Deborah said as she reached out and brushed a spider off Micah's sleeve. "But Daddy always said God would put me where He wanted. I'm not going to argue with the Almighty." Having made that statement, she gathered her skirts and awkwardly swung out of the wagon.

"That spider was the size of an apple!" Lou squawked.

Micah clicked, and the horse pulled the buckboard past Deborah until the rear wheel was right in front of the soddy's door. Micah looked down at Deborah. "I can be every bit as stubborn."

"I have no doubt of that."

He cracked a grin. "So are you going to take pity on the horses if you don't feel much of it for Lou and me? Climb on up here."

She let out a sigh. "I need to do something first."

He nodded and pulled the wagon forward a bit more.

Deborah opened the door to the awful habitation, bit her lip to keep from crying, and went inside. She nervously scanned the habitation and saw no sign of the gopher. Nothing in this filthy place mattered to her—other than the letters she and Dustin exchanged. She lifted the gritty box and turned to leave.

Micah stood in the doorway and wordlessly extended his hand. She trudged over, slipped her hand in his, and let him take her back to the wagon. He didn't sneer or gloat with any "I told you so's." Instead, he cupped his big hands about her waist, gave her a little squeeze, then lifted her up. When they got back to his ranch, he helped her down and gave her that same reassuring squeeze.

Lou scampered up the porch steps, opened the door wide, and called, "Micah brought her back, Grandma."

Micah's voice was low and steady as he said, "You're welcome to stay awhile 'til we decide what to do with you."

She might be stranded, but she wasn't stupid. Staying here was far better than being in the soddy or near any of those men in town. Deborah looked up at his craggy face in the dimming light. "Thank you. I'll try not to be too big of a bother."

"Sugar, you're a lady." The left side of his mouth pulled, but she couldn't decide whether it was a wince or an arrested grin. "Ladies are bound to be bothers out here."

Chapter 4

O h, she was a bother, all right. Micah saddled Gray and rode off the next morning with the sweet scent of Deborah's tea-rose perfume haunting him. She'd been in the kitchen at the crack of dawn, baking bread and helping Grandma make breakfast. The two of them got along like kindred spirits. Micah knew he'd need to find a place for Deborah to go—and soon—before Grandma decided to adopt her.

"Grandma's getting older," Sam said as he rode Buck alongside Gray. "Seems to me having someone around to help her isn't such a bad notion."

"Louisa can do whatever Grandma needs."

"If Grandma can nail her down long enough. Lou's barely eighteen and still half wild. It occurs to me that having a young lady around might help tame her." Micah glowered at him, but Sam pretended not to notice. "Sis will grow up fast enough, Micah. Once she does, she'll marry and move away."

Micah shot his brother a withering look. "Are you starting to have designs on Deborah?"

"She's pretty and makes fine-tasting bread, but I'm still too itchy to settle down. Figure I have a few years left before I put my neck in the parson's noose."

Josh rode up, cramming something in his mouth. After he swallowed it, he grinned. "That gal sure can fry up a fine bacon sandwich. We ought to keep her." He took the last bite. Mouth still full, he nodded at Micah. "I say you ought to marry her. That'd work just fine."

Sam snickered.

Micah shook his head and forced a grin. "I thought Deborah was the only sun-struck one. Looks like you're suffering from the sun, too."

"Not at all." Josh eased back in his saddle.

"Good. Then you can go over to Masterson's and see if he's done with the plow."

"Aw, Micah—" Josh gave him a pained look. "Masterson's? All I said was that it's 'bout time for you to take a bride."

Micah stared at him. "Once you get the plow, go ahead and do that patch for Grandma."

Sam chuckled after Josh rode off. "I'm no fool. I'm not going to mention any-thing matrimonial to you, else I'll get stuck with something I hate doing, too."

Throughout the day, Micah kept banishing thoughts of Deborah. She'd said nothing more about Dustin's fate or how her dreams had been broken. She was wearing black—but it was for her father. He couldn't help wondering what had become of her that she'd be in such straits. Whatever the cause, as soon as he could spare a few hours and a few bucks, he'd send her back to civilization. It would keep her safe and keep him sane.

⠸⠬⠇

"You're sure you don't mind?"

"Don't be silly." Lou bounced on her bed. "All three of my brothers share a room. This one's big enough for the two of us."

Since her arrival, Deborah had shared Grandma's room, but because she'd be staying awhile longer, it had been decided that she'd move upstairs with Louisa. Pale-blue walls and white furniture made the room an airy haven. The flowers painted on the headboard and washstand made her wonder if Lou had once been feminine and lost her sense of womanhood after living in the wilds for so long.

Deborah smoothed her hand over Lou's lavender and blue grandmother's-flower-garden quilt. "I admire how you've used what you have on hand to make your home so charming. I have to admit, now that I'm here, I'm starting to think this isn't No Man's Land. It feels more like No Woman's Land!"

Lou smiled at her, then dipped her head as she tugged up a stocking and frowned at a small hole in it. "Paint only comes in two colors over at Foster's: white and barn red. After we were done painting the house and barn, Daddy said Grandma could have the leftover paint. Micah and Sam were hauling the stove here, and they brought back a little tube of blue tint."

That explained why the downstairs walls were dark blue below the wainscoting and pale blue above. Deborah could imagine Grandma mixing the three colors she had on hand in cups and bowls to create the pink, violet, and lavender. She'd probably spent days to brush the flowers on the kitchen wall and create the handsome burgundy design that bordered the parlor walls.

Lou fell back on the pillows and rolled to her side. She got a sheepish look as she confessed, "According to Grandma, I sleep like a bobcat. I don't want to seem selfish about the bed."

"Oh, no. The cot will be fine. Believe me, after staying at some of those stage stations, the floor of a brickyard would be soft." Deborah decided her basket-of-tulips quilt would match best and planned to get it out of the trunk on her next trip downstairs.

Lou dug her elbows into the bed and propped her chin in her hands. "I've been thinking about something ever since you hopped back out of the wagon yesterday."

"What is that?" Deborah started unpacking her valise. She'd been given the bottom drawer of the dresser and half a dozen pegs off to the side of her cot.

"You said God would put you where He wanted you. What if He wants you here with us?"

"I want to live in the center of the Lord's will, Louisa. I just don't know where that is." Deborah slowly set Daddy's Bible on her side of the dresser.

"I've got three brothers, all of them handsome and smart. Every last one of them is of marriageable age and able to support and provide for you."

Deborah stayed silent. She couldn't very well confess that she'd thought the same thing, then promptly decided Micah was the only one who made her heart skip a beat. What kind of woman was she, to be chasing a man?

"Grandma says you're in mourning for your papa and for Dustin, too. She figures you need time to grieve. I suppose she's right, but it would be far more comfort to lean on a strong man rather than to go it alone, if you ask me."

⁙

Now if that didn't beat all. Someone had put a basket of wildflowers in the bathroom. Micah stood in the doorway from the mudroom that led into the washroom and stared at the ridiculous thing. It sat on the little table between the big, galvanized steel bathtub and the smaller, copper hip bath. He let out an impatient huff, then turned to the washstand, only to discover the mirror over the basin reflected the basket of flowers.

Resolved to ignore the flowers, Micah rolled up his sleeves and poured water into the basin. When he reached for the soap, he came up with a cake of something pink. He dropped it back on the china holder and snatched the amber, oval bar of Pears.

Washed up and hungry for supper, Micah exited the washroom, through the mudroom, and into the kitchen. Instead of being at her usual station by the stove, Grandma was "In the Starlight" on the piano. Lou was setting the table, and Deborah leaned over the hot oven, humming along with the hymn in a sultry alto. She bent down to check on something that smelled good enough to be on the menu at heaven's wedding feast. Only nobody wore black to a wedding, and he had yet to see her in anything other than crow-black mourning.

Her wearing black was a great notion. Dustin hadn't been her husband, so she needn't wear widow's weeds on account of him. As for her father—back East, they might observe all of those rules, but here, she *could* be in something more colorful. Grandma hadn't made Lou wear black on account of Mama's or Father's passing.

The dreary shade put a man off, and that fact pleased Micah to no end. The fellows in No Man's Land weren't going to get near enough to catch a whiff of her perfume or hear her sing. They'd spy her crow-black dresses and keep their distance—all except for the Testaments, but he'd take care of them. Satisfied, Micah nodded to himself. Nothing would stand in the way of his plan to send her back to the city, where she could hitch up with some fellow who'd treat her like a queen.

"This is about ready," Deborah said as she shut the oven door. "When will the men be here?"

"I'm home." He smiled at how she'd jumped. Surprising her made him glad he'd oiled all the door hinges just last week. He sniffed appreciatively. "Judging from the smell, I think I ought to send Josh and Sam off to do late chores so I can eat their share."

Deborah laughed. It was the first time he'd seen her happy, and her eyes sparkled like a handful of stars. "You might reconsider that. Josh seems quite put out with you over the plow."

"Weather's nice and the water level's good. Grandma said she had plenty of time yet to plant more garden and put up more yield. No reason Josh shouldn't pitch in."

"I love to garden." Deborah perked up. "I brought some seeds along in my trunk."

"Which one?" Sam lounged in the doorway and gave her a playful wink. "I helped carry in those trunks, and I'd swear in a court of law all but the smallest is chock-full of sad irons."

"You poor man." Deborah pressed a hand to her bosom in a gesture of horrified concern. "You'd better hasten to the table to replenish your waning strength."

"Not 'til he uses the washroom," Grandma called out. "Be sure to comb your hair tonight, too, Samuel. You still had specks of sawdust in it last evening. I only serve the civilized at my supper table."

"No need to put in more of a garden, then. Nobody but you is going to be sitting there," Josh grumbled as he came down the stairs.

"We'll see about that." Micah caught the look in Grandma's eyes as she said those words. She'd glanced over at Deborah and gave her I've-got-a-secret-plan smile.

The hair stood up on the back of his neck.

The floor creaked. Deborah froze, held her breath, then slowly relaxed as she realized it was just the wooden structure settling for the night. She quietly slipped into her robe and whispered a prayer of thanks for the fact that though Lou flipped over in bed like storm-tossed waves, it would take cannon fire to wake her.

One arm clutching the pasteboard box to her side, Deborah cautiously opened the door a crack and peered out into the dark hall. The door to the large room the men slept in was closed. No light shone up through the staircase, so the downstairs would be vacant.

Relieved, she tiptoed down the hall, past the men's door, and descended the stairs. She'd banked the fire in the stove at bedtime, so it would be easy to accomplish what she needed to do now.

Deftly using the hook, she lifted a stove lid and set it aside. One by one, she slid the letters she'd sent to Dustin into the flames. Each caught fire and turned into curling ashes. All of her girlish dreams of romance, of finding excitement in the West, of wedding a dashing rancher burned away with those pages.

When the last one turned to ash, she bent the lid of the box and stuffed it into the stove, too. It took longer to burn, and as it flared, Deborah gasped.

Micah stood less than a yard away, arms folded across his chest, silently watching her.

Wishing she'd been able to do this in complete privacy, she said, "I didn't know you were up."

"I heard someone on the stairs."

"I'm sorry I disturbed you." She stared at the bottom of the box and wished Micah would have waited just a few more minutes so she could have gotten rid of all of the evidence of her actions.

"Need help with that?" He nodded at the box.

"I just. . .it's. . .mice."

He drew closer. "Here." He took it from her hands and methodically found the paper seam, tore along it, and disassembled the container. Acting as if he did this all the time, he casually said, "With the fire going, I wouldn't mind a cup of coffee."

"I'll make a pot."

Deborah started the coffee, then headed for the stairs, only to have him hold her back.

"Share a cup."

They sat across from each other at the table. Heat radiated from the stove, and Deborah curled her toes beneath the hem of her robe as she sipped from her mug.

"Why did you burn them?" Micah studied her with an intensity that made her want to squirm. "Didn't you want them as a keepsake?"

Deborah sighed. "Not particularly."

"I considered stopping you. I thought you might want them when your grief wanes."

Deborah pensively traced the handle of her mug. It felt dishonest to accept his sympathy. Quietly she admitted, "It's not like that."

"But you came clear out here to marry him."

"I was brought up to honor my mother and father. Daddy approved of Dustin. He felt Dustin showed a lot of potential and it would be a sound match. The week after we became engaged, Dustin took a mind to come claim some land and promised to send for me." She paused. "That was three years ago."

Micah didn't say a word. He stared at her and took a slow sip of coffee.

"Papa counseled me to wait on God's timing, but when he died, I didn't have anywhere to stay. I wrote Dustin, and he sent a telegram telling me to come." She didn't mention that one word comprised the entire message on the cheap telegram. Some things were too humiliating to reveal.

"Did you love him?"

Deborah kept her gaze trained on the table. "I wasn't given a choice. Dustin and Daddy thought it would be clever to place an announcement in the *Gazette* and use it as a surprise proposal."

"Why did you allow him to court you if you didn't hold any tender feelings?"

Stung by that question, Deborah dumped more sugar into her coffee and stirred it until the whirlpool threatened to spill over the edge. "We didn't court. Daddy invited Dustin to the house about once a week for supper, and then they'd play chess. Daddy appreciated his intellect and humor; Dustin liked my cooking. To them, it added up to a suitable match."

She dared to look up at Micah. "I came here because I didn't have any other choice."

"You're a beautiful woman, Deborah. Surely, there are men back home who would be happy to marry you."

His words made her heart flip-flop. He'd complimented her, yet he'd made it clear he held no interest in her. She shrugged. "I'm not marketable. I'm nearly penniless and well past my prime."

"A gentleman isn't supposed to ask. . ." His brows rose, making it clear he still expected an answer.

"I'm twenty-two." She took a sip of her coffee and almost gagged on how sweet it tasted. "If you'll excuse me. . ." She rose.

Micah's bench scraped the hardwood floor as he stood. He shadowed her to the sink and said nothing about the granular sludge she poured from her cup down the drain. His voice stirred the tendrils that escaped her braid and curled around her face and nape. "Deb, matrimony shouldn't just be a union of practicality. I'm sorry Travis passed on, but I'm not sorry you escaped marrying a man whose fondness for you revolved around your stove instead of yourself."

"You're most kind."

"No, I'm not. Don't ever fool yourself into believing that."

"How did you end up out here?"

He lounged his large frame against the counter and shrugged. "Dad was mourning Mom, and he wanted to get away from the memories. Grandma insisted on coming along to help with Lou, so here we are."

"Is your father away on business?"

A shadow passed across his face. "No. He died after the first winter here. By then, we'd set down roots and decided to stay."

"I'm sorry for your loss." Her heart ached with empathy.

He trailed his rough fingers down her cheek. "Folks just say those words out of convention, but I know you understand and mean them."

He withdrew his touch, and she felt lost.

·⁙·

The earth smelled rich, and the air carried a tang of cut grass. The men were scything and storing the tall, wild grasses to use as winter fodder for the cattle. Deborah gathered her slate skirts and scooted down the row as she planted more beans. A shadow fell over her.

"You're in the sun. I don't want you getting sun sick again."

Deborah tilted her head back and peered from under the wide-brimmed straw hat she'd borrowed. "Your grandmother's bonnet casts enough shade for the whole family to hold a picnic beneath it!"

Micah took off one of his leather gloves, cupped her chin, and rubbed her cheek with his thumb. He nodded approvingly. "Not too hot. Make sure you stop and rest awhile in the shade, and drink a dipper of water every hour."

"Thank you for your concern."

He nodded and walked away with that long-legged, loose-hipped stride of his. He stopped and turned around, and Deborah felt her cheeks grow warm because he'd caught her watching him. "Sugar, that hat isn't anywhere big enough for a picnic. Stafford men all have big feet."

"Bigger hearts," she tacked on.

He let out a derisive snort and turned to walk off, but Deborah caught the flash of his smile.

Later that afternoon, Micah wasn't smiling one bit. He stomped up the porch steps and grabbed her sewing basket. "Inside. Now."

She hopped up. "Why?"

Chapter 5

Testaments on the way." Heedless of the grass stains on his hands or the blades that clung to his clothes, Micah curled his hand around Deborah's arm and towed her toward the front doors. They stood wide open to allow the breeze to cool off the house, but once Micah had her inside, he slammed both doors shut. "You sit on the settee. What're you stitching?"

She held one of his shirts that had frayed cuffs.

He nodded approvingly. "Keep working on that." Micah pushed her around the screens, into the parlor. "Grandma! We're about to have callers."

Grandma came out of the pantry. "Oh?"

"Testaments—the whole clan." Micah gave her a steely glare. "Don't let them near Deborah or Lou. Where is Lou, anyway?"

"Fishing at the creek." Grandma pursed her lips. "Send Josh to join her. I can send Nehemiah Esther down to visit with them. They'll bring back supper, and we'll make this a friendly get-together whilst setting out the way things are."

Micah turned around and waggled his forefinger at Deborah. "Don't cook anything good. Burn it. Salt it too much." Before she could formulate a response, he left.

Grandma was wreathed in smiles as she seated Deborah on the burgundy-and-blue striped settee. "Just play along, dear. It's all for the best."

About ten minutes later, someone halted a team of plodding horses out front. The folding screen kept Deborah from seeing Grandma open the door, but she heard the old woman greet the neighbors with gentility. When they rounded the screen, Grandma waved a hand at Deborah. "You just stay seated, dear. We wouldn't want you to waste your strength. These are Exodus and Ruth Testament."

"A pleasure to meet you," Deborah murmured. Social convention forced that response, but she felt like bolting when she spied the rest of the family.

Grandma glided over to her as graceful as a swan, but Deborah was sure the tiny woman hadn't walked that fast in ages. Grandma sat down beside her and patted the spot on her other side. "Ruth, I do believe there's enough room for you here. Exodus, do make yourself at home in one of my grandson's chairs. Deborah, these are the Testaments' sons, First and Second Kings and First and Second Chronicles, and their daughter, Nehemiah Esther."

"No Ezra?" she asked weakly.

"Pages in my Bible stuck." Exodus's cheeks went ruddy. "Family never skips a name.

Ruth felt sorta bad for a girl getting saddled with Nehemiah, so we tacked on Esther."

"And the good Lord above blessed us with twins on both the Kings and Chronicles," Ruth gushed.

As if on cue, one of the big blond men shuffled forward. He yanked the sorriest-looking rose that ever bloomed from behind his back and stuck it out. "This is for you, Miss Deborah. So's you won't have no bad feelin's about us funnin' you when you first got here."

The folding screen slammed multiple times as Sam pushed it back and made the dining room and the parlor into a single, huge room. Micah plowed across the floor. "What's this about you funnin' Miss Preston?"

"We didn't do nothing wrong. Peas and gravy, Micah, she drew my blood with her knittin' needle!"

"The Miss Preston I've come to know would never behave in such a manner unless she felt it necessary to protect herself." Micah yanked over the dainty chair that matched the settee, planted it on the floor right beside Deborah, and sat in it. The delicate cherry wood piece wasn't constructed with a strapping man in mind, and Deborah expected it to shatter into bits of kindling any second.

Micah glared at the flower, and Deborah watched as it seemed to wilt in First Kings's—or was he Second Kings's—hands. "I suppose Miss Deborah would allow you to put that on Dustin Travis's final resting place."

First Kings exchanged a bewildered glance with his twin, then shot a questioning look at his mother. "The rose is yourn, Ma. I reckon Travis won't appreciate it much. You wanna keep it, or is it gonna go to waste, just like all the bacon and pork chops did when we all let Wally Foster plant that pig of his in the ground?"

Grandma pulled an ivory and silk fan from her sleeve, opened it with a whispered swish, and started to fan Deborah. "Dear, I'm afraid this is all too much for you."

It was too much—in more ways than one. Deborah blinked and nodded.

Micah slapped his knees, shot to his feet, and swept her right off the settee. "I'll take her on upstairs and let her rest."

"But we was just starting up a nice, neighborly visit," one of the Testament men said.

Micah charged past them, across the parlor, and headed straight up the stairs. He put her down just inside Lou's room and bent so his breath whispered across her cheek. "Naming children after books of the Bible isn't the only quirk of the Testaments. They come from a backwoods mountain clan that practices bride claiming—which is just a fancy term for kidnapping. Stay up here."

Deborah grabbed the front of his shirt and whispered back, "Don't worry. I have a derringer in my knitting basket up here."

"Do you know which end the bullet comes out of?"

Deborah smiled sweetly and batted her eyes. "Well, I suppose while I'm waiting up here, I could take a look at the pictures when I take it out of the presentation box."

‐∷‐

"Go on upstairs and get that derringer," Micah ordered the next morning at the breakfast table.

"After you convinced the Testaments I'm sickly and probably wouldn't survive long enough to—as you so delicately phrased it—'whelp a single man-pup,' I doubt I'm in any danger from them."

"Sugar, that little pop gun's going in the kitchen drawer. Grandma can use it the next time she needs to butcher a chicken, because that's about all it's good for. I'll teach you how to fire a pistol today."

"I'm coming along!" Lou thumped her glass on the table and jumped up. "I'll get some cans—"

"You're not coming." Micah stared his sister down. "The last thing I need is you getting winged because you distract Deborah or wander off."

"You can go into town with me, Sis," Sam offered. "I need more nails. Gotta reinforce the fence."

Micah gave Sam a questioning look. This was open range; they had only one fence other than the two surrounding the gardens out back. That fence corralled their two prized bulls, Hercules and Mercury. The pair were far too foul-tempered and dangerous not to keep penned up.

"Herc's been charging the fence, and Merc's leaning on his sector. I need to reinforce it."

"Fine. While you're in town, find out when Goodman's passing through again."

Deborah's jaw jutted forward. "If that inquiry is regarding me, you can spare yourself the trouble. I'm not about to travel with that man. He hated me."

"Wally and Bently already got an earful from Happy." Lou shook her head. "None of it was good."

"I can't imagine the man can do more than grunt or growl. He barely spoke five words the whole three days I rode here with him, and he has the uncouth habit of pointing out a stone or plant and expectorating his tobacco to hit it."

"Happy does have genuine talent in that direction," Josh agreed.

Sam snorted at the pun while Lou gave her a you-poor-dense-thing smile. "You didn't praise his skill. It hurt his feelings."

Josh shoved away from the table. "Happy said he won't haul fancy folks and vows if they tried to hire a seat for you, he'd never haul anything to Petunia again. I can promise you, no one's letting you get near a Goodman Freight wagon."

"I didn't do anything wrong!"

Micah figured he'd better not remind her that coming here was wrong. He'd be putting a gun in her hands in a few minutes. The last thing he wanted was to rile her. He stood and pulled out her chair. "Do you know how to ride?"

"Of course I do. I can also drive a buggy."

"Fine. I'm heading out to clear a few things with the hands. Josh can bring you out to Cherokee Creek. We'll do some practice shooting there."

Grandma gave them a sweet smile. "That's a good choice. I can see that sector of the sky from the kitchen window. If I notice buzzards wheeling in the sky, I'll send the hands to rescue what's left of you."

⁘

Deborah decided it would be acceptable for her to stop wearing mourning attire. When she wasn't in mourning, Father directed her to be "a lady of solemnity," which meant he expected her in stylish attire of somber browns and grays. White shirt-waists with stylish lacework received his grudging approval, much to her relief. She didn't have a riding skirt, so she needed to wear the gray day gown with the fullest skirt. By foregoing the bustle, she had a little extra room.

Doug and Pete were mucking out stalls when she entered the stable. Josh and Slim stood in a corner, chuckling. Slim walked past her and tipped his hat in that mannerly, wordless way cowboys seemed to have ingrained.

"Here's your mount." Josh walked up.

Deborah bit her lip and shook her head.

"Tulip's gentle as they come. Grandma even rides this mare."

"I need a lady's saddle."

Josh tilted his head to the side and smiled patiently. "This is a special saddle—a western woman's saddle. See the fancy stitchwork on it?" He lifted her into the saddle and turned his head a moment so she could smooth down her skirts. "You tell me when you're ready for me to adjust the stirrups."

"They're about right."

A quick peek, and he nodded as he handed her the reins. He led her out into the sunlight and swung up onto Sultan. "Slim needs some help from me. If you feel safe enough, I'll get you most of the way there, and then you can follow Cherokee Creek the last little bit."

Deborah had a difficult time riding. The saddle chafed and felt awkward. For being gentle, the mare seemed rather skittish, too. Josh kindly set a slow pace and gave her an occasional word of encouragement. Finally, he pointed ahead. "See that red speck? It's Micah."

Micah whistled, and Deborah thought he waved, so she waved back. Her mare continued to walk sedately toward him. Unwilling to look like a child who had to be minded every moment, she said to Josh, "Since I can see him, you're welcome to go back and help Slim. I've already taken up enough of your time."

"You sure, Miss Deborah? It's no trouble." He almost looked disappointed.

"Positive." She sat a bit straighter in the strange saddle. "I'll be off Tulip and shooting that pistol in no time at all."

"If you say so. Follow right along the creek. The ground's softer—easier on the horse," he quickly tacked on.

Deborah laughed and continued alone. Once he couldn't see her face, she grimaced. Riding the rest of the way was going to challenge her, but she refused to give up or show any weakness. The Staffords made her sound downright feeble yesterday, and she wondered if it was all an exaggeration to keep her safe from the Testament twins or if they truly counted her as delicate-unto-death. Well, she'd show Micah Stafford she could do anything his sister could do.

Micah had his hands propped on his lean hips as she came to a swaying stop. His scowl would make midnight look light by comparison. "I thought you said you can ride."

"I'm accustomed to a different style saddle."

He snorted. "Do you need help, or can you dismount?"

She'd secretly hoped he'd help her, but this was an opportunity to prove her abilities. "I'll manage, thank you."

"Oh, for cryin' in a bucket!" Micah reached up and grabbed her arm. "Swing your. . .ahem. . .limb over the back of the horse not over her neck!"

Deborah could feel heat fill her face as she looked down at him. "You forget, I'm in a lady's saddle."

He grumbled something under his breath, gained purchase on her waist, and swept her out of the saddle. Her boot caught the back of the saddle, causing the mare to move. Only Micah's strength and quick reflexes kept them from falling.

Feeling clumsy as could be, she brushed her skirts and gave him a perky smile. "Well, now. I'm ready for that pistol."

"Not a chance, princess."

"What? I rode all of the way out here for a lesson."

"There's no way I'm going to put a gun in the hands of a woman who can't tell she's saddled her horse backward!"

Chapter 6

"Backward!"

As soon as he saw her reaction, Micah got a terrible feeling. "Who saddled Tulip?"

"I don't know. She was ready when I got to the stable."

He tilted her face up to his and softened his voice. "Sugar, didn't it occur to you that all of the other horses are saddled with the pommel forward?"

"Yes. Josh said this was a special western woman's saddle. He even pointed out it has special stitching."

He'd deal with Josh later. For now, he shook his head.

Deborah cleared her throat. "The pommel is a completely different shape, size, and tilt than yours or Josh's."

He had to admit, she had a point. Micah crooked a brow. "If I put a pistol in your hand, do you promise not to shoot Josh?"

"Vengeance is mine, saith the Lord." She patted his arm. "I would never aim a firearm at your brother."

"I hear you have several knitting needles."

Giggles spilled out of her. "Want a few to melt down for bullets?"

"It's not funny, woman." He followed her over to the spot where he had the pistols waiting and swiped the gun she'd lifted. "You could have fallen and broken your neck."

"Grandma would see the buzzards and send someone to help you drag my dead body back home." She grabbed the other pistol and gave him an impish smile. "Why don't you calm down and tell me which end the bullet comes out of this thing?"

About an hour later, Micah slipped the reloaded pistols into his holster and shook his head. "If it comes to protecting yourself, you'd better have a whole basket of knitting needles with you, because you couldn't hit the broad side of a barn."

"I'm getting better."

He gave the bale of hay a dubious look. She'd hit the edge of it once—in thirty shots. "Sugar, the only chance you'd have of someone not hurting you is that they'd run for cover because a *loco* is pulling the trigger."

He switched her saddle around, lifted her up, and got the shock of his life when she managed to ride with considerable grace. Her eyes sparkled as she cantered alongside him. "Oh, this is marvelous! And your land is beautiful."

"I'd like to think it's mine, but legally, it's not. Kansas stops at the thirty-seventh parallel, and Texas starts at the thirty-sixth. That leaves thirty-four miles here that the government thinks is too small for a territory. We're all planning to claim squatters' rights because the land will have to be annexed sooner or later."

"It's hard to imagine you as squatters. You have a lovely home."

He saw her shudder. "We freighted in the lumber. It was expensive as all get out, but there aren't many trees hereabouts. Even then, we ran out of wood, so the other half of the upstairs turned into a balcony."

"I see."

She hadn't said much at all about Dustin after she'd spoken so frankly the night she burned the letters. Micah decided maybe he ought to stand up for the man. "I'm sure your intended would have built you a nice little place once he got established. Most of the folks out here live in soddies, you know."

She shrugged and refused to say more. Micah decided to let the subject drop and started thinking about what he'd do to Josh when he got home.

"Micah?"

"Yeah?"

"Since Josh played that stunt on me, would you be upset if I found a way to surprise him back?"

"I thought you didn't believe in vengeance."

"I don't, but I do believe in justice. What would you think if I. . ."

⁂

"Micah says I couldn't hit the broad side of a barn if I tried," Deborah announced merrily as she popped the buttermilk biscuits she'd made into a basket.

"She's a terrible shot."

"Probably had the wrong target." Lou licked her finger after scooping mashed potatoes into another bowl. "Shoulda used a basket. Deborah's the basket-est woman in the world. Her quilt is even a basket pattern."

"Just how many baskets do you have?" Micah asked as he took the basket of rolls from Deborah and set it on the table beside the basket of flowers she'd gathered by Cherokee Creek.

"I never bothered to count." She shrugged. "Whenever the need strikes, I just whip out another one."

"You mean to tell me that trunk that was real light is just stuffed with baskets?" Josh hooted with laughter.

"Reeds, rods, splints," she corrected.

Micah slanted a look at her. "You wove the baskets we've been seeing?"

"Why, yes."

"Now there's a fine skill to have," Grandma said. "My aunt tried to teach me, but I couldn't get the knack of it. Now, my fingers are too stiff to even try such a craft. Sewing is about the best I can do."

"I'd be happy to help you with anything that needs to be done." Deborah took the coffeepot off the range and started walking around the table to fill the mugs.

They all sat down for the meal and bowed their heads, and since it was his turn,

Samuel prayed. A split second after they all chimed in to say amen, Lou snatched the basket of rolls and popped one onto her plate. It went all the way around the table, and Josh got the last one. Beneath the table, Micah nudged Deborah's heel with the toe of his boot. He made a show of slathering butter on his roll. "Mmm-Mmm. Deborah, you do bake a fine biscuit."

"Better than mine," Lou agreed.

Josh laughed until he snorted. "Anyone's is better than yours!" He grabbed the biscuit from his plate, dunked it into the gravy on his mashed potatoes, then took a bite—or more accurately, tried to take a bite. His eyes grew huge.

Everyone else at the table pretended to be busy cutting meat or sugaring coffee.

Josh gave his sister an outraged look. "You little sneak! You baked this. I can tell. It's hard enough to use as a sinker the next time I go fishing."

"Now wait a minute!" Lou glowered at him.

"Fish is about all I'll be able to eat," Josh continued as he pounded the rock-hard biscuit on the edge of his plate, which resulted in an astonishing, bell-like chime. "This thing'll chip every last tooth in my head."

"There's nothing wrong with my biscuit." Micah made a show of pulling his apart and sinking his teeth into a flaky half.

"Mine, neither." Sam did the same.

Deborah looked across the table and tried to look innocent as could be. "Josh, I'm so sorry. I wanted to do something extraordinary for you. You helped me with that special western woman's saddle this morning, so. . ."

Josh's ears went red, and he looked down at the biscuit and groaned. "What did you put in this thing?"

"Flour, salt, and milk," she began. Finally she couldn't tamp down her smile as she added, "Of course it was Epsom salts; talcum powder, not baking powder; and, um, milk of magnesia."

Josh glared at Micah. "You put her up to this."

"Nope." Micah gave her a slow, heart-melting wink. "The little lady cooked this one up all on her own."

"See? I knew she belonged with us," Lou declared. "She fits right in."

Deborah continued to look into Micah's fathomless gray eyes. *Oh, if only I truly belonged here, with you. . . .*

·:·:·

"I don't suppose you ever smile," Deborah said as she set her sites on the target.

"Only when there's reason." Micah judged the angle of her pistol and estimated, "You're going to overshoot. Lower your aim a smidgen."

Her hands stayed steady, and she looked over at him with merriment dancing in her eyes. "A smidgen?"

The minute he'd used the word, he'd regretted it. He knew she'd nab him on it, but it was too late. "You here to gab, or to—"

"Gun?" she cut in. Her sassy grin made him break into a grin. "Well, well, do my eyes deceive me? Micah Stafford actually can smile. This is a red letter day, indeed!"

"It'll be a red letter day if you ever fire that weapon and hit a target. I'm starting to think I should have left you with that peashooter instead of trying to teach you how to use a real weapon. With that thing, even if you wing yourself, you'd live. The way you handle that Colt, I'm half afraid you're going to blow your head off."

"Only half afraid?"

"The other half of the time I fear for my own skin."

"My, my." Deborah let out a cheerful laugh. "And to think I expected you to tell me it was because you've decided I have only half a brain!"

"You said it, lady. I didn't." He nodded toward the target. "Now stop lollygagging and get busy."

"Yes, sir." She closed one eye, squeezed the trigger, and *bang!*

To Micah's astonishment, the bottle shattered. "You hit it! Now do it again. Hit the next one."

Deborah bit her lip, closed one eye, and fired again. And again. And again. She emptied the chambers.

"Look! I got two!"

"Yeah, cupcake. Two out of six shots. If you have enough time to empty your gun, you should have run away."

"Oh, don't be so sour. We made progress."

"Yeah. You'll pull your gun and talk 'em to death."

Suddenly, the brightness of her smile dimmed. Deborah turned the Colt around and carefully handed it back to him. As he stuffed new bullets in the cartridge, she wiped her hands on the sides of her dark-brown skirt.

"I'm sorry. I didn't realize I was talking so much."

"No more than usual." He glanced up at her and saw the momentary flash of hurt in her eyes before she looked away. He shoved the pistol in his holster and took hold of her arm. As he led her toward the horses, he tried to lighten her mood. "At least you hit something this time. That's a definite improvement. It'll take more practice before you develop any accuracy or confidence. I'll bring you back here in a few days."

"There's no need."

He stopped at Tulip's side, checked the cinch out of habit, then curled his hands around Deborah's slender waist. "I'll be the judge of that."

"You've taught me gun safety. Lou could—"

"You're plumb loco if you think I'd let you and my sis come shooting." He tightened his hold and lifted her into the saddle. She smelled just like that pink soap in the washroom—flowery, fresh, and far too delicate for this rough land. Micah turned immediately, both to allow her a moment of privacy to adjust her skirts to modestly cover her layers of ruffled petticoats and trim ankles, and to mount up himself. He'd escort her home, then get back to work. He squinted at the shadows and estimated they'd spent a solid hour out here—not all that much, but more than he could afford. He also noted a dust cloud coming toward them at appreciable speed. As he swung up into his saddle, he clipped, "Let me do the talking."

Chapter 7

D eborah moistened her lips and nodded solemnly.

"We'll head toward the house, but we'll have company before we get there." He kneed his horse and they started off.

"Hey!" One of the Testament men shouted as they drew abreast to Deborah ten minutes later. Micah rode so close to her other side, their legs bumped. "We come runnin'. What's awrong?"

"Nothing's wrong." Micah glowered at King—whether he was the elder or younger King Testament, only his family could tell.

"Shots came from over this way—a bunch, all in a row."

"Three, evenly spaced, is the come running signal. Those shots weren't evenly spaced, and there were more than three." Micah kept heading toward the homestead. "As you can see, everything's fine."

"You are lookin' mighty fine, Miss Preston." Micah figured that greeting might have come across as a bit more charming if Chronicles didn't precede it by spitting out a wad of tobacco.

"She's been out in the sun long enough. I need to get her home."

Deborah took her cue wonderfully. She pulled a handkerchief from her sleeve and dabbed at her forehead.

"Hot as the hinges of Hades out here today," King said in a conversational tone.

Micah heard Deborah's gasp. "That's no way to talk around a lady. You men best go on back home."

The Testaments grumbled but did turn their horses and head back toward their own spread. Micah felt a spurt of relief, but it didn't last long.

The ride back to the house was quiet—but not in a good way. Deborah listened to whatever he said, nodded, or gave abbreviated answers in a muted voice. By the time they reached the stable, Micah was irked at her attitude. He dismounted, closed the distance to her mount, and swept her out of the saddle without so much as a word of warning. He didn't put her down, either. Instead, he pivoted and plunked her down onto an upended bale of hay.

She looked at him in open-mouthed surprise.

He knocked his hat against his thigh. "Suppose you tell me why your back's up?"

"I'm not angry; you are."

"Oh, don't try twisting this around. All of a sudden, you've clammed up and have your lips shut tighter than a widow's purse."

"You said I talk too much."

His brow furrowed. "When did I say that?"

"You said I could talk someone to death and that I'm not talking any more than usual. Clearly, I owe you an apology. I didn't mean to make you uncomfortable in your own home."

"Aw, come on now, Deb. You're blowing this out of proportion—"

"Please excuse me." The hay rustled as she wiggled and scooted to get down. The minute her feet hit the floor, she dashed toward the stable door.

He effortlessly caught and held her. "Just where do you think you're off to?"

"I promised your grandmother a new basket to use for gardening."

"Do you ever just sit still? You're busy as a bee."

Her laughter didn't ring true. "That's what my name means. Deborah, the bee."

"Seems like a mighty nice name to me. Honeybees are industrious. It's a Bible name, too."

Hurt flashed across her pretty face. "That's what my mother said. My father named me, though. He said it was because it stung that I wasn't a son."

"Pardon me if I insult him, but your father was a nitwit."

Deborah shook her head. "No, he wasn't. He said God put me where He wanted me. Father just made sure I earned my keep and reminded me I was to be seen, not heard."

"Your mother—"

"Became an invalid when I was thirteen. She passed on when I was sixteen. She loved me in her own way, but I know she regretted that she hadn't given Father the son he craved."

"So they pined for what they didn't have instead of cherishing the blessing they did have?"

She gave him a winsome smile. "I've never been called a blessing before."

Their sheepdog streaked by, something in his mouth. Lou dashed in after him. "Why didn't you stop him? Grandma's going to have a conniption when she finds out Shane just swiped one of the chickens she planned to roast." Lou tried to corner the dog in a pen. "He could have at least taken the one I hadn't plucked yet!"

Micah looked back to see Deborah's reaction, but she was gone.

⁛

His boots were caked, so he used the bootjack and shucked them. Micah had rolled his sleeves up earlier in the afternoon heat, so his muscular, tanned forearms looked strong and masculine. Deborah turned back toward the bowl of peas she was shelling at the table. She noticed everything about him—his leonine walk, the perceptive gleam in his eyes, the way he listened. . . .

Oh, the way he listened. She felt a heated wave of embarrassment wash over her as she recalled the dreadfully personal things she'd revealed to him yesterday. Dodging him last night took every scrap of her imagination. To keep from sitting by him at breakfast this morning, she stood at the stove and kept making flapjacks. Now, though, with supper started, she needed to stay put—and from the look in Micah's eyes, he knew it.

His loose-hipped, long stride carried him across the floor. He poured two cups of coffee, set them on the table, and took the place directly opposite her. Without asking, he added sugar to one cup, then nudged it along the smooth surface of the table toward her.

Unnerved, Deborah fumbled and sent a pea arcing through the air.

Micah's arm shot out, and he caught it. He held the pea up between his thumb and forefinger. "Sweet little thing."

Deborah drew in a sharp breath. *He wasn't looking at the pea when he said that—he was looking at me!*

"Micah's partial to peas—especially if I drizzle a scant bit of honey on them once they're drained," Grandma said. "Micah, weather's plenty hot enough. Can you get out the screens so we can dry some peas?"

"I'll do it on Monday." He popped the raw pea into his mouth and chased it with a gulp of coffee. "Seems to me that new parson's due to be here for tomorrow's service. I suppose you've got something in mind for Sunday supper. What're you going to want me to get out of the smokehouse?"

"I'll think on it."

Deborah concentrated on the peas as she said, "I didn't see a church in town."

"Petunia has nothing more than a saloon and Foster's Food and Feed. We hold church here."

"Oh, my." Deborah looked about herself.

"We fold up the screen that partitions off the parlor and move the dining table into the kitchen," Grandma explained. "By pulling in a bunch of benches Sam built, we turn the dining room and parlor into a regular church."

Micah rapped his knuckles on the table. "We'll keep you away from the Testaments. Don't you dare cook anything. They get a taste of anything you make, and it's all over."

"What's over?" Lou asked from the doorway. She absently scratched the back of her hand.

Micah's eyes narrowed. "Louisa Abigail, turn around and get right back outside."

"Now what did I do?" She gave him a disgruntled look.

"Unless I miss my guess, that's poison ivy clinging to your skirt."

Micah was right; Lou ended up covered in a miserable rash.

With Lou hiding out upstairs, speckled and itching to beat the band, and Grandma complaining her fingers were too stiff, Deborah ended up playing the piano for church the next morning. Josh accompanied her on his guitar, and the parson started them off on the last of the morning's hymns. Once the music ended, Deborah turned around on the piano bench, and Micah sat beside her. For once, he didn't mind that the bench seemed on the dinky side. It meant he could catch a whiff of Deborah's perfume.

She wore a black dress today—at his request. He didn't want her in one of those frilly white blouses she wore with her fashion-plate skirts. They looked delicate and fancy as a wedding gown, and the last thing Micah wanted was for some local yokel to crave her as his very own bride. At Micah's urging, she'd also scraped her sunshiny hair back into a tight knot at her nape, but instead of it making her look pinched and sour, the style only served to make the fineness of her features more apparent. It was too late for him to order her to change it, so Micah stuck by her side to keep all of the ranch hands and bachelor boys away from her. Most of all, he made a point of herding the Testaments to the far side of the dining room so they sat as far away from her as possible.

The new parson preached a fine sermon. Young, tall, earnest, he'd started the circuit almost two months ago. This was his second service, and folks all flocked in to listen to the Word of the Lord.

"Withersoever you go, I will go...."

Micah listened to the Bible reading and looked about the congregation. Exodus elbowed Ruth, and they both sat up straighter, clearly happy the new parson was preaching about her biblical namesake. Deborah subtly slipped off the piano bench, took a wiggly toddler from Opal Piven, and brought him back to sit on her lap. Opal gave her a shy, thankful smile. Opal did just what Ruth—the Ruth in the Bible—had done: left kith and kin, came to a strange place, and was working hard at her husband's side.

Grandma had come for the sake of family. Now that he thought on it, Micah recalled her quoting that verse the day they set out to come here.

Deborah shifted the little tyke on her lap, and he snuggled close. Micah winced. She'd been obedient, too. She came but not because love would sustain her. She'd come because she'd been boxed in and didn't have a choice. It was wrong. No woman ought to be dragged to the outer reaches of civilization unless she stood a fair chance of being content there.

She looks pretty happy at the moment. No. No, she's not. She's learned to settle for what life throws at her. For once, she deserves to choose for herself. A fine woman like her—a lady—ought to be cared for, cosseted, cherished. She's suited to live in a city where a gentleman can squire her to a symphony or she can take tea or visit a library.

Micah scanned the room and realized every last unmarried man managed to either sneak a peek or openly gawk at her. Not one of them would provide for her. If pink-and-pretty Deborah stayed here long, she'd end up like poor Opal—living hardscrabble in a soddy with a passel of hungry young'uns.

"Boaz. Now there's an interesting man," the parson mused. "He made sure Ruth and Naomi had plenty to eat. Oversaw their safety. Was a good, decent man. But when it came to the possibility of marrying Ruth, he balked. He was sure someone else ought to be the happy groom. Figured he'd step aside. But you see, God had a plan. When God's got a plan, you can be sure He's going to work it out...."

-:⁑:-

Seeing the Pivens' children barefooted at church made Deborah's heart ache. That evening, while Grandma was upstairs dabbing witch hazel on Lou's rash, Deborah decided to find Micah and talk with him about the Pivens. She found him hunched over a calf in the stable. The acrid smell of singed hide told her what was going on. He was tampering with the brand.

"Need some help?" she asked from a few feet away.

"Get back into the house, Deborah." He didn't even look over his shoulder at her, but she could tell he issued the order through gritted teeth.

The calf let out one last bawl as Micah rose and expertly released the rope he'd used to bind him. Sam came in through the opposite door of the stable and called softly, "Josh found another one. You—"

The minute he spied Deborah, he came to a grinding halt. "Uh. . ."

The calf scrambled past Deborah and headed out toward his mama. Micah heaved a deep sigh as he took a stance beside her. He rested a heavy hand on her shoulder. "It's not what you think."

Chapter 8

I know exactly what's going on here." She turned to him. "That calf came in here Crossed S and left Box P."

"At least she knows we're not rustling." Sam came closer and relief rang in his voice.

Deborah didn't bother to turn toward him. She continued to look into Micah's beautiful, steady gray eyes. "You're honorable. You'd never do such a thing."

"You can't breathe a word of this," Sam told her.

Micah lifted his hand and trailed his callused forefinger across her lips. "She won't. Deborah knows when to keep quiet."

Warmth coursed through her.

"Here you are. I—" Josh bumped into Sam, took one look at Deborah, and groaned, "Oh, no."

"You two go ahead. Deborah and I are going to have a little talk." Micah wrapped his arm about her and walked her past his brothers and out into the yard.

Deborah relished the feeling of being sheltered in his strength and kindness. She fought the powerful urge to cuddle closer. As she passed by the unbranded calf Josh had in tow, Deborah understood: They'd searched high and low to find calves that got skipped during spring roundup and branding. The cow nuzzling the just-branded calf bore the Crossed S mark.

Micah stopped by the clothesline, reached up, and casually curled his long fingers around the pole. "In January, we had a real bad cold snap. Folks are calling it the Big Die-up because so many cattle froze. Everyone did the best they could, and cattle from north of here came south to try to survive. Piven lost more than most."

"I see. Is that why Lou said the spring roundup was such a mess this year?"

"Yes. Plenty of ranchers were hoping to find livestock, but no one rode away very happy. Next month, we'll be driving the cattle to Tyrone."

Deborah remembered overhearing one of the ranch hands talking about the upcoming drive. *Taking a four-dollar cow to a forty-dollar market.* "But Mr. Piven won't sell those calves, will he?"

"He's forced into selling more of his cows than he ought to, and it'll end up cutting his stock in future years. This isn't much, but it's a way of helping him out without hurting his pride. Why did you come out here, anyway?"

"I wanted to ask if someone could take me to town to get fabric. I could make the baby some clothes."

"Grandma already has material. She sent back to Maryland for it. Happy Goodman hauled it in when he brought you."

"She sent to Maryland?"

"The Mastersons sent their daughter back there to husband hunt." His voice softened. "Hope she has better luck than you."

Later, as Lou slept soundly, Deborah sat on her cot. Micah's words echoed in her mind. *Hope she has better luck.*

By the light of a single candle, Deborah took the wedding sampler she'd made with Dustin's name beside hers. Carefully, she snipped the threads and pulled Dustin's name off. *I don't need luck. God put me where He wanted me to be. I'm not in No Man's Land; I'm in my man's land.* She looked at the empty spot on the sampler. Micah's name would fit there far better.

·:÷·

Micah shoved the book across the table and wearily scrubbed his face with his hands. He'd promised himself he'd find a good place in a decent town for Deborah, but time just got away from him. He'd be leaving on the cattle drive to Tyrone tomorrow, and Deborah still lived under his roof.

If prices held and the cows didn't lose too much weight on the trail, he'd have enough to buy lumber to finally finish the upstairs. Happy Goodman could freight it in. *Deborah is happy here. I could just add on a room for her.*

The thought made him slam the book shut and bolt to his feet. He should have followed his first instincts and sent her away the day she arrived. Everywhere he turned, he saw evidence of her nesting in this house. Her baskets, her soap, the scent of her perfume, cookies, rolls. . .

Grandma even ordered material from back East so Deborah could have new clothes—ones that were dainty prints and girly colors. He'd burned his tongue, gulping scalding coffee so he wouldn't put in his two cents' worth on what she ought to get. His plan to keep her in black hadn't made any difference. Every single man in the area ignored the mourning color and admired the woman—and for good cause.

After I sell the cattle, I'll search Tyrone and see if there aren't some possibilities for Deborah. She can't stay there—it's too rough for her. The newspaper or telegraph office might have a posting for a finishing school back East. She'd be a shoe-in for a position like that. It's respectable, safe.

He put the book on a shelf and went into the little washroom to brush his teeth. Until Deborah came, they'd used baking soda, but she brought tooth powder that she shared with them. She'd embroidered a horse and three cows across the bottom of the hand towel, and her rose glycerin soap seemed to fit next to the cake of Pears quite naturally now.

The sight of her soap bothered him. So did the taste of her toothpowder. He lay in bed and tried to go to sleep, but he struggled with his plan to send her back East. *It's so far away, and I won't be able to keep an eye on her. She's alone in the world. It's not right for a woman—especially Deborah—to be on her own.* He wrestled with the quilt and grunted. *Ever since she came here, I haven't had a decent night's rest.*

"Oh, my. It looks just like the picture of baby Moses in my Bible picture book." Opal Piven timidly touched the basket Deborah had woven.

Grandma laughed. "I said the selfsame thing." She nudged her way into the soddy, and Deborah followed in her footsteps. In the past two weeks, they'd stayed busy while the men were gone on the cattle drive. She and Grandma stitched baby clothes, blankets, even a nightgown and dress for Opal in preparation for today. Lou managed to tangle threads, prick her finger, and beg off most of the sewing, so she'd volunteered to do the cooking for the three of them.

Opal had sent her ten-year-old over to get help for the birthing since Seth wasn't back from Tyrone yet, and after dashing off a hasty note to tell the men where they'd gone, the ladies came to the Pivens' soddy.

The basket nearly overflowed—and a quick look about the soddy told Deborah this family desperately needed everything they'd brought. She wished she had enough money to buy shoes for Opal and the children—they were all barefoot.

Lou followed with a crate full of food. "Grandma got too enthusiastic planting her garden again."

Opal caught sight of the brimming crate and pressed her fingers to her mouth. Unsure whether she was having a labor pain or was simply stunned by the gift, Deborah reached out to brace Opal.

"Those are tomatoes from the seeds you gave me, Opal," Grandma said. "In all my life, I've never seen more or bigger ones. It's been too hard for you to garden much, and it would be a sin for us to let those vegetables go to waste."

Looking around, Deborah gulped. Squirreling away the jars, cans, and bags took Lou barely any time at all. In those few minutes, Deborah got an eyeful. *If Dustin hadn't been killed, this is how I'd be living, too.*

-:::-

Maddening, crazy woman! Two days later, Micah lifted Deborah out of the buckboard. All dewy-eyed and glowing, she acted as if helping Grandma attend Opal's labor was a miracle instead of a frightful opportunity for any number of disasters to strike.

"Thank the Lord, everything went just fine," Grandma said as she walked up the porch steps. "Lou did a fine job keeping all of the little children busy. One of these days, she's going to make a fine mama, herself."

Micah gave Deborah a searching look. "What did you think?"

"Opal's a strong woman. She loves her children and is doing the best she can."

"The best isn't good enough," he rasped as he curled his hand around her elbow and escorted her up the steps. "Seth had no business bringing her and the kids out here. He's a hard-working man, I grant you that. But his dreams eclipsed good sense."

She diligently wiped the dust off her fancy town-girl balmorals on the mat, then stepped into the house. Micah barely scooted the soles of his boots on the mat and followed directly on her heels. He didn't like the direction her thoughts were taking. "At least Dustin didn't haul you out here when he couldn't provide."

"The Pivens don't have much, but they have each other and are content. I'd rather live in a hovel with a husband I love than in a fine house with someone who didn't care."

"Your problem, Deborah, is that you're willing to settle instead of hoping for the best." Micah shook his head. "Stop selling yourself short."

She looked at him and lifted her chin. "Seth was happy Opal had another daughter. *Happy,* Micah." Tears glossed her eyes. "That little girl might live in a crumbling soddy and go barefoot, but she's rich in love. Opal and her children have what counts most of all. If God sees fit to match me with a man who cares for me and will cherish all of our children—daughters as much as sons—I'll count myself blessed beyond my wildest dreams."

Sam stood by the mantel, winding the walnut, camel-backed clock he prized. "Glad to have you back." He grinned. "I had my fill of bad food on the cattle drive."

"I'm tuckered out." Grandma rubbed the small of her back. "I hate to admit it, but it's the truth."

"Go take a nap," Deborah urged. "I'll see to supper."

"Great!" Sam grinned at her. "Make plenty. We're going to make pigs of ourselves."

"Same as usual," Lou teased.

"Aren't you tired, too?" Micah studied Deborah carefully. The whole time he'd been on the trail, he'd thought of her. She looked a hundred times prettier than he remembered, and though she looked delicate, she didn't seem like the fragile flower he'd thought of.

"Trust in the Lord with all thy heart and lean not on thine own understanding. In all thy ways acknowledge him, and he shall direct your path." The verse flashed though his mind. *I haven't sought God's will about her.* The thought stunned him. All along, he'd tried to make a sound, safe decision instead of a godly one.

"Tired?" She laughed. "I'm hearty as can be." She went to the kitchen and pulled her apron off the hook. As she reached around to tie it behind her, the movement accentuated her willowy, womanly form. "If you're desperately hungry, I can fry up eggs, ham, and potatoes. If you want to wait a bit, I can have sausage cabbage rolls ready in about an hour."

"I'll take both."

"Samuel Stafford," Micah rumbled in heated displeasure, "this isn't a cheap diner in Tyrone. Deborah doesn't have to cook up a bunch of meals to suit your gluttony."

"Well, she offered," Sam muttered.

Josh stomped the mud off his boots and tromped in the front door. "Grandma, where do you want all these parcels? Wally Foster said they came in a few days ago."

Grandma scurried back out of her bedroom and waved at the table. "Put them there. It'll be the fabric we asked Hope Masterson to send!"

As Lou and Grandma started stripping the brown paper wrapping from the parcels, Deborah quietly set to work in the kitchen. Micah watched her and frowned. "You got material. Don't you want to see it?"

"It'll wait. You men are hungry."

He made an impatient sound. "We can hold tight for a few minutes. You've waited for weeks."

"He's right, dear. Look—this is for you." Grandma unfolded a length of material the color of summer sky.

Deborah gasped. Reverently, she touched the material with the tips of her fingers. "I've never had anything this beautiful."

"It's just plain blue, Deborah." Lou laughed.

"It's *blue*," Deborah said in a wonder-filled voice. "Father wouldn't let me wear anything this impractical or showy."

Micah's jaw dropped. He thought for a moment and realized her skirts were black, brown, or gray. He'd assumed perhaps she'd been sensible because of the ever-present dirt. It never occurred to him that a woman would be denied the simple pleasure of a pretty color.

"What else did you get her?" He started to dig through the dress lengths and pulled out a rosy-colored one with little maroon threads here and there.

Sam hooted. "Try putting Lou in that!"

Lou glowered at him. "Me, in pink?"

Deborah shook her head and drew out a buttery yellow piece. "I love Lou for being who she is. She doesn't have to change herself. She's all sunshine and warmth. This is suited to her."

Micah watched his kid sister's reaction to those wise words, then turned to Deborah. She knew what it meant for someone to shove her into a mold that didn't fit, and she'd just made sure Lou didn't get bullied into the same trap.

Come to think of it, Deborah showed plenty of gumption. After staying overnight in a soddy and helping birth a baby, she was downright chipper. Like a sapling, she had the ability to bend and yield in the winds of life and still stay grounded. *Maybe she could make it out here. Maybe God's showing me that I've underestimated her.*

⁘

Life had never been sweeter. Deborah smoothed the skirt of her rose dress, spiraled a few tendrils around her fingertip, and dabbed on a touch of tea-rose fragrance as she looked at her reflection in the washroom mirror. *In the week since he's come back from the cattle drive, Micah hasn't once mentioned sending me away.*

Lou was off fishing with Josh and Nehemiah Esther, and Grandma was having her devotional time. Deborah wanted to go pick a few tomatoes and check the shirts on the line to see if they were dry yet. *Of course, it wouldn't hurt if Micah caught a glimpse of me in my new gown.*

She walked across the yard and opened the garden gate. The cottonwood picket fence kept the free-grazing cattle out of the food, but as usual, the gate stuck. A quick, unladylike kick did the trick. The action scuffed the toe of her balmorals—something Father would have disapproved of. Here, it didn't matter. Deborah laughed aloud with sheer joy. She had sunshine on her face, a new dress, and a heart full of hope and love.

She picked a few tomatoes, popped them into a basket, then hung the basket on the tip of a picket. On her way back from the clothesline, she'd grab it. Shirts flapped in the wind, and the sleeves of Micah's blue chambray lifted—almost as if they were beckoning her. A quick check showed the shirts were still too damp to take down, but Deborah lingered for a few extra seconds as her fingers tested Micah's worn work shirt.

When she turned back around, her heart stopped.

Chapter 9

The bulls had gotten loose. Josh and Sam had Hercules cornered, but Shane's crazed barking made Micah glance back toward the house. Drawn by the laundry flapping in the breeze, Mercury was jogging toward the line—a nuisance, to be sure, but when Deborah stepped around a sheet and the wind whipped her reddish dress, the bull picked up speed.

I can't get to her in time! Micah bellowed in anguish as he turned Gray toward the yard and rode for all he was worth.

Deborah ran behind the laundry, out of sight. Merc plowed through the clothes, scattering them and revealing how Deborah twisted and changed direction.

Lord, protect her. Keep her safe. Let me reach her in time.

Mercury snorted and ran toward her billowing skirts. Deborah let out a scream as she changed directions again and ran. Shane headed off the bull, nipped at him, and bought her a few seconds. *It won't be enough. . . . God, please. . .*

She was heading for the garden. Micah knew she wouldn't make it in time. He spurred Gray on and drew his pistol. He couldn't shoot—Deborah zigged. He would have shot her. Seconds later, she flew over the garden fence.

Mercury plowed into it, and pickets scattered like toothpicks. Micah could see the horror on Deborah's face as she whirled around. He strained forward, Gray streaked ahead, and Micah swept her out of what was left of the garden just before Merc reached her.

The commotion had ranch hands scrambling. Micah let them take care of the bull. He clasped Deborah to his chest and strove to calm himself so he could handle her.

Only she wasn't hysterical. She clung to him and let out a breathless gasp as the bull charged the clothesline again and shredded a shirt. Burrowing in close, Deborah laughed. "I was just thinking that shirt didn't have much life left in it."

"The shirt!" Micah fought the urge to shake her; he fought the urge to kiss her silly.

"Is she all right?" someone yelled.

"I'm perfectly fine!"

Micah rode up to the house, slid her onto the porch, and grated, "Go pack."

⁂

"I saw Deborah today," Lou said as she pulled burned rolls from the oven. "Basket Stitch is a hit."

Micah gritted his teeth. He'd determined to take Deborah to Abilene or Tyrone and put her on a train, but she'd taken a mind to dig in her heels. Stubborn woman decided she liked Petunia and promptly wheedled her way into the Fosters' hearts and home. She took over a small corner of the feed store, where she wove baskets and did sewing. With all of the bachelors working on the ranches, she didn't lack for work.

"Three days, and she already has enough work to keep her busy for a month." Lou dumped the rolls into a basket—one Deborah made.

It's been four days not three. Micah scowled at the table. It looked naked without Deborah's place setting next to his. The whole house felt empty. All of the little touches were missing: wildflowers on the table, the scent of tea rose. . . .

"She makes the best of things." Grandma set a bowl on the table. "I never once heard her complain. If my daddy matched me with a man the way hers did, I would have pitched a fit."

"You mean the newspaper announcement?" Micah winced after he spoke. If Deborah hadn't shared that with anyone, he'd just broken her confidence.

"That, too." Grandma slipped into her seat. "He and Dustin agreed to the marriage like they were hiring a brood mare or a maid."

"What?" Micah leaned forward.

"Instead of providing a home, Dustin was to move into her father's house. He'd have a wife, and she'd still do her daddy's cooking, cleaning, and laundry. Dustin just up and left town a week later—left a note about coming out here. She didn't know why."

Sam whistled. "And she still came out here to marry him?"

Restless, Micah paced into the parlor. Of all places, he stopped in front of the family tree sampler. His was the fourth generation to be on it, and for the first time, the blank place by his name intended for his mate seemed wrong.

"Everyone needs someone," Grandma said.

"She should have stayed back in civilization and woven her baskets there."

"It's none of your business what she does, Micah Stafford." Grandma gave him a look of regal disdain. "Now sit down and ask the blessing. The food's going cold."

The food wasn't just cold; it tasted awful. Each bite stuck in his throat like the sawdust from the work they were doing, finishing the second story of the house. But what good was a bigger house when it already felt so empty?

-:::-

"There you are, Hank. Nearly good as new." Deborah handed the shirt she'd mended to the cowboy. He tipped his hat and hobbled off on bowed legs. She turned and smiled. "Ready, Cynthia?"

Though Lou's age, Cynthia Connelly was nothing like Lou. She was polished, prissy, and spoiled. She'd also come with a length of lavender taffeta. That came as no surprise. Fosters carried a single bolt each of white cotton and brown denim. They had red, white, and brownish-black thread and a single card of shirt buttons. Three shelves held the sum total of the items suited for people. Those sewing items, cans of coffee, ready-made shirts, spices, lamp oil, beans, and a box of borax made for unlikely partners in that meager space. Beautiful fabric such as this had to be brought in.

"I want this to be special." Cynthia leaned closer. "It'll be my new Sunday best."

"It's a lovely color."

"She hopes the new parson thinks so, too," Jake Connelly teased. He lounged against Deborah's worktable and gave her an assessing look. "Gals of a certain age have to start thinking of marrying up."

Deborah forced a laugh. Almost every single man who'd come in to have her write a letter, mend a garment, or conduct business with the Fosters managed to wrangle marriage into the conversation with her. There was only one man she wanted, but he didn't want her.

I'm not giving up. Grandma said he'd come to his senses, and Lou said he's miserable.

"Boys have to be dry behind the ears before they start considering matrimony."

The sound of Micah's deep voice slid over her and made her shiver. "Cold, honeybee?" He stepped from behind her to beside her and slipped his arm about her waist. If he hadn't been holding her, Deborah was sure she would have melted into a puddle on the floor.

"You had your chance, Stafford. She didn't want you." Jake squared his shoulders.

Micah chuckled. "It wasn't proper for me to court a woman under my own roof."

She didn't know how he managed it, but Micah steered her out of the corner of the store where she'd set up shop and took her out to a grassy little spot that had a sprinkling of wildflowers. He turned her toward him and tilted her face to his. "Remember the night when I took you to Dustin's soddy? You said God would put you where He wanted you."

"I remember."

"He did. You belong back home. With me."

It wasn't what she'd hoped and prayed for—he hadn't proposed. Deborah had spent her whole life settling, but she refused to settle this time. She lifted her chin. "I'm not boasting when I say I can cook and clean and sew a fine seam. I'm earning enough here at Basket Stitch to make my way."

His eyes darkened to the color of thunderclouds. "You don't have to earn your keep. You earned my heart—that's all it takes."

Deborah gave him a wary look.

"Honeybee, I've fought this every last step of the way. From the moment you told me you weren't a widow, I wanted you for my very own. This is no place for a lady. Life here is rugged, and you're such a delicate woman. I've tried every way I can to let go, but I can't. You've filled my heart and my home. No matter what I'm doing, you're always on my mind. Now I know why Dad left Virginia and moved here—he couldn't bear the memories of Mom in every room in the house. Come home, Deborah. Come home to me. Be my wife."

Slowly, she nodded. He let out a whoop, scooped her up, and spun her around, then kissed the very breath from her.

Micah wanted to take her home at once, but Deborah needed to pack. As if he was afraid she'd climb out the window and run away, he stood in the doorway and watched her stuff her robe and brush into her valise. Mrs. Foster slipped past him. "Don't forget your sewing basket."

"I'll take that." Micah caught one handle but missed the other. To Deborah's mortification, the contents of the sewing basket spilled all over the floor. Micah bent over, picked up the wedding sampler, and ran his fingers over where she'd neatly stitched his name next to hers.

A slow grin tugged at his mouth. "Well, it's nice to know you care for me. I wondered."

She knelt by him and straightened the sampler. "Read further."

"Love unite us, and God keep us together forever." He looked back at her.

"I've hoped, Micah. When I met you, for the first time, I dared hope and pray for love. God answered my prayers."

-:¦:-

"You may greet your bride."

The words were barely out of the parson's mouth when Micah gently pulled Deborah into his arms. He put his heart and soul into their wedding kiss.

Sam chuckled, and Lou, dressed in her new yellow gown, let out an embarrassed moan.

As they cut the cake, the parson turned to the Testaments and gave them a stern look. "This is a sacred union. No shivaree."

"No shivaree!" they protested.

"They're so uncouth," Cynthia Connelly simpered as she rested her hand on the parson's arm.

"She's just sour 'cuz none of us'll have her," King One shot back. "We all thought Miss Deborah was a fine prospective wife. It's a matter that we're of discriminating taste."

Folks stayed and celebrated, and Grandma happily pointed out how Deborah's name had been stitched into the family tree sampler. Micah finally tugged Deborah through the kitchen door and out to the little cottage in the back. Sam, Josh, and the hands had all done their best to make it as a wedding gift. Micah and Deborah would spend their honeymoon in it, but they'd have to move back into the big new suite upstairs in the house until the rest of the work was done.

They reached the threshold, and Micah swept her into his arms. She wrapped her arms around his neck and smiled up at him. "Whithersoever thou goest, I will go."

"Honeybee, coming here was your last flight." He kicked the door shut behind them. "You're home now."

DOUBLE CROSS

by Tracey V. Bateman

Dedication

To my brothers and sisters:
Steve, Jack, Sandy, Linda, Rod, and Bill.
I couldn't have convincingly written about these wonderful,
crazy siblings if I didn't have my own wonderful,
crazy brothers and sisters.
Thank you for encouraging me and loving me.

Chapter 1

No Man's Land
April 1886

Trust me, Lou. Baby skunks don't spray. They're not strong enough."

Lou Stafford eyed her brother Josh suspiciously, knowing full well that he wasn't above stretching the truth in order to make her appear foolish. She looked once more at the litter of baby skunks huddled together in their den. The early spring breeze coming off the creek was awfully cool, and Lou's heart went out to the shivering babies.

In a rush of spring fever, she and Josh had grabbed a couple of poles and hiked down to Cherokee Creek, hoping to catch a mess of catfish for dinner. As usual, Shane, their sheepdog, had accompanied them. He'd found the rock den, and Lou had barely grabbed him in time to keep him from harming the babies.

Now, Josh held the cur by its scruffy neck, fighting hard to keep the animal from going after the helpless kittens.

"Come on, Lou. Are you yella?" Josh asked, an obvious attempt to cinch the deal.

Somewhere in the back of her mind, Lou recognized his baiting and even realized she should probably beware, but being called *yella* was almost more than her fragile ego could take.

"What are you waiting for?" Josh pressed. "You know as well as I do that those kittens were abandoned by their mama. If we don't take them back to the house, they'll die."

Lou took another look at the four baby skunks. How could such adorable creatures possibly bring about the same smelly consequences as their larger counterpart? Perhaps in this instance she should believe her brother. She scrutinized the expression on his face. He appeared to be genuinely concerned. Innocent, in fact. Still. . .

"You take one first," she bargained. "Then I will."

"Are you daft? If I turn loose of Shane, he's going to snatch one of those babies before either of us can grab him. Is that what you want?"

Of course she didn't want the canine to make a meal of the little creatures, but neither did she want to smell like a skunk for a week or have her skin rubbed off with Grandma's lye soap and firm hand. Things had smelled bad enough the time she'd accidentally run the wagon wheel over a skunk in the road. The brothers had barely stopped teasing her about that every time they had a chance. All she needed was another skunk incident to make her life unbearable.

A low growl rumbled in Shane's throat as one of the kittens shifted.

"I'm having me a hard time keeping this animal still." Josh's voice sounded strained. "You best decide if we're saving those skunks or if they're a snack for Shane, here."

As though he understood what Josh said, Shane wiggled with anticipation, looking from Lou to the kittens and back to Lou.

Lou scowled. "Forget it, you mangy critter. You're not touching these babies."

Did she detect a note of triumph in Josh's eyes? She shot a glance back to him, but the expression of utter innocence remained fixed.

Lifting the hem of her skirt, she moved forward, her gaze focused on the animals she was about to rescue. As far as Lou was concerned, the only thing a skirt was good for was carting orphaned animals and apples. Otherwise, she preferred the trousers she'd worn to help around the ranch before Grandma had put her tiny foot down about the whole situation a few months ago.

What riled Lou more than anything was that her three older brothers had agreed with the family matriarch. Imagine! Those double-crossing varmints agreeing with Grandma that she, Lou, the best ranch hand on the Crossed S, needed to concentrate her efforts on learning to run a household, cook, clean, sew, and try to hogtie a husband before she got too old. Hrummmph! Eighteen years old wasn't exactly ancient.

Anyway, that was neither here nor there, as Grandma would say. Right now, being forced to wear this ornery skirt was a blessing in disguise. She could carry all four kittens to the ranch while Josh kept Shane at bay.

"Uh, Lou."

"What?" She reached for the first kitten.

"Don't make any sudden moves. The mama skunk is behind you."

"Stop fooling around, Josh. I'm not falling for that." Lou sniffed and gently scooped up the remaining kittens one at a time. That Josh would love to have her panic and turn around. Everyone knew a mama skunk didn't leave her babies in a den unless she was abandoning them. Unless. . .well, she might have gone to look for food and might not have gone far. In which case. . .

"I'm not fooling, Lou."

The sound of Josh's low tone filled her with a sense of dread. She started to rise. Slowly.

"Watch out!"

With great care, she turned and came face to face with the skunk. The full-grown, angry mama skunk.

A shriek escaped Lou's throat, and the world slowed its spinning as the black and white animal turned. Startled by Lou's sudden movement, the kittens wiggled and without exception did the unthinkable.

Josh stood a safe distance away, howling with laughter. As the full force of the grown skunk's spray doused her, and the kittens sprayed her from their nest inside her skirt, Lou knew she'd been double-crossed in the worst way.

She moved slowly, depositing the babies on the ground, then ran toward the creek, dropping her holster from her hips and jumping in before the mama skunk decided to spray her again.

"Josh, stop that laughing. You sound just like a sick coyote! Go home and get me some different clothes."

"Okay," he choked out. "I'll be back."

She stripped underwater and tossed everything but her undergarments up on the shore where she could burn them later.

On the western horizon, the sun, now a ball of orange, sank low. Already its warmth had fled. Soon it would disappear altogether, leaving in its stead a cold moon. "Hurry, Josh," she whispered.

A solid hour later, Lou realized Josh wasn't coming back. Her lips quivered with the cold, and her eyes filled with angry tears. How could he do this to her? A prank was one thing. But to leave her in the cold water was another matter. She debated whether or not to put the skunk-sprayed clothes back on but dismissed the thought. She'd be sick before she made it home.

Gathering a deep breath, she opened her mouth wide and did the only thing that came to mind.

"HEELLP."

❖

Trent Chamberlain's ears perked up at the mournful sound.

"What do you reckon that is?" Timmy asked, his freckled brow wrinkled with worry.

"Could be a wolf," his brother, Davy, suggested.

There it was again. Trent wasn't sure what the sound was, either, but he knew the dangers of this country. Not too many years ago, Indians had roamed freely, wreaking havoc on settlers. And rightfully so, some might say. In local feed stores 'round the pickle barrel, speculation often gave voice to the fear that bands of renegades still hid in caves, waiting for the right time to attack and reclaim their land. Trent was skeptical. Regardless of the source of the mournful sound, he had no intention of taking the boys along to investigate.

"Run up to the house over there. I'm going to check out that wailing." At best it was nothing more than a calf bawling for its mother. At worst it might be a wild animal caught in a trap. That could be dangerous for the boys, and he didn't want to take any chances.

As the protesting boys rode double toward the two-story house, Trent turned Melchizedek, his horse, toward the sound. He paused a moment and waited until he heard it again. Then he nudged the roan forward.

"Heelllp!"

His heart beat a rapid rhythm as he recognized the cry of a child.

"Hang on," he called. "I'm coming."

Spurring the horse to a gallop, he stopped short at the edge of a creek that was full from the spring rains. The child was splashing about in the water but seemed to be swimming away.

"Try not to panic," Trent called, trying to ignore the noxious odor of a recent skunk spray. "I'll get you."

"Y–you stay away."

The child sank so far into the water that Trent could barely see eyes, nose, and mouth.

He took another step toward the water.

"I–I mean it, mister. You best stay where you are or I'm going to—to—"

The thundering of horse's hooves interrupted, cutting off the threat.

"Lou, what's going on?" In a cloud of dust, the rider pulled his horse up short and dismounted in one fluid movement.

"Oh, Micah," the child cried. "I'm so glad to see you. Tell this. . .this. . .man to leave me alone."

Guilt or the fear of appearing guilty slithered through Trent. "The boy was crying for help," he explained to the rider, "but he won't let me come get him."

"Who says I was crying?" came the belligerent voice from the water.

The man grabbed a bundle from his saddlebag and chuckled. "She happens to be a girl."

"A girl named Lou?"

He grinned and jerked his head in a nod. "Short for Louisa."

"Well, she's freezing in there. You should probably try to talk her into coming out."

"Lou, get out of the water." His tone was impatient, exasperated, as though he'd traveled this road before and was in no mood to revisit the trail.

"Not with you two out there. I don't. . .I'm not. . .decent." The girl smacked hard at the water. "Josh was supposed to bring me something to wear, but that lousy varmint ran off and forgot about me."

"Relax. Seth Piven brought his new quarter horse around. You know Josh. Mention a new horse and he forgets his own head."

"He forgot about me because of a dumb ole horse?"

"You should see this animal, Lou. It's a dandy. Anyway, he remembered when a couple of youngsters rode up to the house and told us they heard bawling from a sick or hurt animal. Guess that must have been you." Chuckling, he tossed a ball of clothing onto the bank of the creek. "Grandma sent these old clothes for you to put on."

"Well, get out of here so I can get dressed."

"Fine. We're going. Grandma said to go straight to the barn so she can scrub you down."

The man turned his gaze upon Trent and offered his hand. "Name's Micah Stafford. My family owns the Crossed S. Grandma says you best come on up to the house for supper, and we'll find a place for you and your boys to bed down for the night. Your boys told us you're the circuit rider. Grandma's so excited she can barely contain herself."

"Thank you." Trent's mouth watered at the thought of a home-cooked meal, and his muscles warmed to the image of a bed to sleep in.

"Will you two get out of here? I'm freezing half to death in this water."

The girl's testy, quivering voice rallied the men to action.

"We're going!" Micah mounted his horse and headed back through the brush. Trent followed. "Will the little girl be okay by herself? It's getting dark."

"Little girl?"

"Louisa. In the water." Trent's defenses rose a bit. Was this family neglectful of the child?

Micah Stafford chuckled. "Believe me: Lou can take care of herself."

Trent only had the man's word and seeming affection for the child to go by, but he'd be watching closely, and if the girl wasn't being treated right, he'd do whatever it took to see her to safety.

When they reached the welcoming, white, two-story ranch house, Trent said a prayer of thanks for the opportunity to give Timmy and Davy at least one night of normalcy before they headed back on the trail.

Riding the circuit, preaching in a different town every week or two, was a hard life. And even more so since the boys had joined him. He'd found them huddled together, freezing and half-starved before Christmas last winter. Both parents had died within weeks of each other—their mother from childbirth, their father from sickness—leaving the boys to fend for themselves. Timmy, ten, and Davy, eight. Such a heavy load for children to bear. Life on the trail wasn't easy. But it beat the alternative: an orphanage.

Trent was taken aback when he stepped inside the Stafford home. The cozy atmosphere drew him, and the sight of Timmy and Davy sitting at the table, which was laden with food, caused a needle of guilt to prick him. These boys needed a home. But he needed to be faithful to the call of God on his life. Ministering on the circuit fulfilled his sense of destiny as much as finding the boys had filled up the loneliness.

A white-haired, elderly woman set a platter of fluffy biscuits on the table and glanced up, a smile lifting her weathered, heat-flushed cheeks.

"Welcome, Parson!" Her soft, southern drawl charmed him, and he smiled, sweeping his black hat from his head.

"Thank you, ma'am."

She grabbed his hand and shook with such vigor, he was afraid the tiny creature might come off the floor. "It's an honor to have a man of God in our humble home. Please, take a seat at the head of the table."

Trent felt his ears warm. By now he should be accustomed to the place of honor he occupied whenever God provided a home in which he could rest for a night. But Trent didn't think he'd ever become accustomed to well-meaning women ousting their hard-working men from the place of honor at the table just to accommodate him.

He felt a hand clap him on the shoulder. Turning, he faced Micah's grin. "It's a privilege to have you sit in my spot, Parson. A real privilege."

Another young man rose from across the table and stuck out his hand in welcome. "I'm Sam Stafford."

"Nice to meet you, Sam," Trent replied, accepting the proffered hand. He sat at the head of the table, feeling a little more at ease.

"Did you see to Lou?" the old woman asked Micah, lowering her voice at the last moment.

305

"Sure did. And Josh was right. Those skunks got her good. The smell is so strong it made my eyes water. I reckon Lou had better bed down in the barn for a few nights to air out."

Trent tried not to eavesdrop, but forcing a child to sleep in the barn just because she was sprayed by a skunk? That seemed a little harsh. What if she had a nightmare?

"I sent Josh out to fill the tub. I have a plate set back for her. She can eat as soon as she's had a good bath."

Micah rolled up his sleeves and took a seat at the table. His amused gaze met Trent's. "Lou gets herself into more scrapes by bringing in stray animals. She can't resist an orphan."

"Sounds like a lovely child."

Micah laughed and exchanged glances with Samuel.

"Yeah, real lovely," Sam said, a grin widening his lips.

"Josh, you double-crossing varmint. Get out here!"

The bellow coming from outside the door made Trent jump. He knocked his knee against the bottom side of the table, upsetting the glass of milk that Mrs. Stafford had poured. "I beg your pardon," he said, humiliated by the white liquid stream headed toward the edge of the table at an alarming rate of speed.

"Josh, you get out here this minute, or I'm coming in after you!"

Mrs. Stafford grabbed a towel and began soaking up the spill. She gave Micah a pleading glance. "Take care of her, will you?"

"Be glad to."

As Micah went to take care of the belligerent child, Mrs. Stafford finished sopping up the spill. She sat and smiled at Trent and the boys as though nothing were amiss. "How about we go ahead and say the blessing? These boys look hungry enough to eat a bear."

"Yes, ma'am!" Timmy replied, nodding his agreement.

Trent folded his hands and bowed his head. As he did, he caught a whiff of something that smelled suspiciously skunklike. With his head still down, he cut his gaze around to the open window next to the table. Wide blue eyes stared back at him from a face surrounded by long, black, wet curls.

Trent caught his breath. The child was no child, but a lovely young woman. And for the life of him, he couldn't pull his gaze from hers. Her lips parted ever so slightly, and she took in a gasp of air. Vaguely, Trent was aware that he was supposed to be doing something other than staring at this woman, but what that task was, he couldn't remember.

A loud clearing of throat distracted him from the window. He cast a guilty glance about.

Oh, yes. He was to say the prayer. "Pardon me," he mumbled and bowed his head once more. Shamefully, he was hard-pressed to concentrate on thanking the Lord for the bounty before them, as springy curls and blue eyes invaded his mind.

Chapter 2

Six months later

"Grandma, I'm just not cut out for sewing these little stitches." *Or any kind of stitches for that matter.* Lou tried once again to reason with her grandmother, but the lines on the dear woman's face scrunched together in a scowl that told Lou to stop whining and get to work.

Heaving a sigh, Lou jabbed the needle into the fabric.

"You'd do fine if you would stop staring out that window. I gave you the easiest stitch in the world. Double cross. Two lines one way, two lines the other. You just need to concentrate on what you're doing. Now turn your chair around so that you're not tempted by that window."

Lou obeyed, knowing her grandmother was more than likely right. The outdoors drew her to the point of distraction. She hated the confines of being indoors. Especially on a day like this, when the gentle autumn breeze whispered through the crisp leaves. The honking of the migrating geese called to her, beckoning her to run after them through the pasture, to loosen her long braid and let her hair flow free in the prairie wind.

She longed for the feel of a horse beneath her, the exhilaration of roping a steer. She hated to disappoint Grandma, but she wasn't cut out to sit demurely indoors attending to domestic things while the outside teemed with the excitement of life and adventure. Cooking and cleaning held no appeal for her, nor did keeping her stitches dainty. And if that meant she never landed a man, then maybe God hadn't intended for her to get married in the first place.

A stab of pain caused her to wince as a crimson stain dotted the fabric. She popped her finger into her mouth to ease the throbbing.

Grandma scowled, and Lou felt the weight of her disappointment.

Lou jerked her finger from her lips. "I'm sorry, Grandma, but this is all so worthless. I mean, really. I feel as though I'm not accomplishing anything."

Grandma harrumphed. "That's because you're *not* accomplishing anything. Take out those stitches and get another piece of cloth. You'll have to start over. We can wash that one with the others. But try to be more careful. That's the third square you've bloodied."

With jerky movements, Lou huffed her displeasure and yanked out every bit of thread she'd labored to stitch into the fabric over the past hour.

"I just don't see the point in trying to stitch flowers into a pillowcase just to put it away in a trunk on the remote chance some man might marry me." Lou's foul mood darkened further as she tried to thread the needle.

"When the right man comes along who doesn't mind your peculiar ways, you'll be glad to have a pillowcase for him to lay his head on after a hard day's work. Then you'll thank me."

"If a man wants to marry me, he'll have to take me as I am, or he can forget it."

Setting her lips into a firm line, Grandma gave her a dubious look but remained silent.

Once more Lou tried her hand at reason. "I'm just not the sort who enjoys this frilly work, Grandma. Some women enjoy it, and some don't. Take Deborah, for instance. Micah found himself a wife who takes to this nonsense like a duck to water."

Pushing her bony finger toward Lou, Grandma scowled. "Don't you go slandering your brother's new bride, or I'll have to take you over my knee."

"Slandering?" Lou blinked her surprise. "I think Deborah's the best thing that's ever happened to Micah."

Apparently mollified, Grandma's expression softened. "Well, I have to agree that she came along at just the right time." Grandma looked past Lou to the window. "Looks like we have company."

Lou followed her gaze to the horizon, where three riders approached. "I suppose I should put away the sewing basket." She kept her gaze innocently staring out the window and forced a regretful tone.

Grandma let out a cackle. "You're not fooling anyone, Louisa Abigail. But go ahead and put it away. We'll take it back up tomorrow."

Relief washed over Lou like a warm summer breeze. Freedom at last. Her heart sang a lilting tune as she snatched up the shears, thread, and needles. With relish, she put away the sewing supplies, anxious to escape the confines of four walls and a roof.

But Grandma's next words dashed her hopes to the ground. "As soon as you put away the sewing basket, set the table for the midday meal. Set three extra places. Looks like the preacher and those sweet boys of his are back."

Lou gathered in a sharp breath and flew to the window. "It *is* him!" she said, then wished she could rein the words back in. She spun away from the window with as much nonchalance as she could muster. "Should I put out the china or everyday dishes, Grandma?"

"Don't you think the good dishes are a bit too much for lunch?" Grandma searched Lou's scorching face.

Lou shrugged. "I don't know. I thought since we're having special guests, we might not want to put out the everyday. Two of the plates are chipped."

"I suppose the parson is special. But I believe we'll save the china for Sunday dinner." She peered closer. Lou stared at her boots to avoid eye contact. But that did nothing to defer Grandma. "You taking an interest in the parson, Louisa? You could do a lot worse."

Lou felt her heart pick up a beat at the thought. She'd never been smitten with a fellow before. And there would be no living it down if she admitted to the new condition of her heart. Especially when it was so obvious that Cynthia Connelly had set her cap for the parson. The girl had practically draped herself across him like a shawl the last two times the parson came through. Cynthia might be a sour apple, but she looked sweet enough on the outside, and the parson had seemed to enjoy the attention.

Lou refused to make a fool of herself by trying to compete with the likes of Cynthia. She squared her shoulders and gave her very best attempt at appearing as though she didn't know what Grandma was referring to. "An interest? Really, Grandma. I've never heard anything so ridiculous."

"You telling me you haven't taken a shine to him?" Grandma's hawklike gaze followed her across the room.

"A shine?" Lou reached for the stack of everyday plates. "I mean, he's a man of God, so naturally I think highly of him. But. . ."

"I see." Lou watched Grandma walk toward the door, her all-knowing tone of voice sending a wave of apprehension through Lou. When Grandma made up her mind about something, there was no talking her out of it. Not that she was wrong in this case—Lou *had* taken a shine to the Reverend Chamberlain. And even if she couldn't compete with Cynthia, this time she was determined, at the very least, to make a better impression. No skunk smell, no stringy wet hair. No bellowing at any of the brothers, despite how riled they made her. She would be the perfect lady even if it killed her.

⁓⁂⁓

Trent smiled at the sight of Grandma Stafford waving from the porch of the white, two-story frame home. Her face shone with a welcome that warmed him from the top of his head all the way down to his booted toes.

Six weeks ago, he'd had the honor of presiding over the wedding of Grandma Stafford's oldest grandson, Micah, and his lovely bride, Deborah. He'd promised Grandma Stafford that he'd plan to stay over a Sunday next time he rode through so that they might have a real service on the Lord's Day. Her pleasant smile was all the welcome he needed to know she looked forward to his visit as much as he did.

"Afternoon, Grandma Stafford!" he called. He and the boys dismounted.

"This is the best surprise I've had all day, Parson. Louisa's setting the table. You three are just in time for lunch."

A jolt hit Trent full in the gut at the sound of Lou's name and the sudden memory of her lovely black tresses swept up into a loose chignon, the sides of her slender neck visible and inviting. He could scarcely believe the lovely creature he'd met at the wedding, that vision of decorum, was the same girl who had run into the creek. But one look at those startlingly blue eyes framed with long, bristly lashes had convinced him. No one else in the world could possibly be graced with eyes as blue as the sky and wide as an innocent child's.

Leaving the boys to care for the horses, Trent climbed the steps to the porch. An indignant bellow blasted through the open door.

"Shane, you ornery varmint! Drop that!"

Trent jumped out of the way just in time to avoid being barreled over by a hairy dog clutching something that looked suspiciously like a hunk of meat in his jaws. The animal flew across the porch and sailed off the top step. A flash of blue wielding a broom blurred past in pursuit.

Grandma Stafford's face went red, and she planted her hands on slim hips. "Louisa Abigail Stafford. Come back here this instant."

As though she hadn't heard, Lou continued to run after the animal. Timmy and Davy appeared at the barn door and immediately joined the chase.

"Corner him, boys!" Lou called. "Grab that roast."

"Mercy, Louisa. Let the dog have it." Apparently, realizing the girl was too focused on her mission to hear a word she said, Grandma shook her head and looked at Trent. "It's not like I'm going to serve a slobbery roast anyway. I hope you've no objection to having bacon sandwiches for lunch. They're quite tasty, and no one makes them finer than our Deborah."

Feeling a little bewildered by this return of the rowdy Miss Stafford, Trent merely nodded his agreement. He watched as the dog, now backed against the barn door, kept the meat locked firmly in his jaws and eyed the three intruders closing in on him.

Alarm seized Trent—the new worry that had appeared at the same time he became an adopted father. "Be careful, boys."

"Oh, you don't have to worry about Shane. He wouldn't hurt a flea, let alone a couple of sweet boys like those two." Grandma gave an exasperated huff. "Even if he is the biggest thief that ever lived."

Trent chuckled, trying to come to grips with the disappointing loss of a roast beef meal after two weeks of nothing but rabbit roasted over a spit, whatever fish they'd managed to catch along the way, and if all else failed, jerky.

"Lou, leave the dog alone," Grandma called. "There's no sense upsetting him."

The young woman turned, her jaw slack. "Me, upsetting him? That varmint stole the parson's lunch. We going to just let him have it?"

Warmth slid through Trent like fresh honey. Her outrage at the dog was due to his lack of a proper meal? That might just be the sweetest thing he'd ever heard.

He only had a moment to revel in the charming revelation, however, because, as though knowing this was his only chance to make a break for it, Shane took advantage of Lou's lack of attention and darted between her and Timmy.

"Oh, no you don't, you mangy critter!" In a flash, she dove after the dog, landing on her stomach while simultaneously grabbing him around the middle. The animal yelped and struggled to wiggle away, half dragging Lou after him.

Trent swallowed hard watching the tussle. His heart raced as though he were the one tangling with the beast. "He won't bite her, will he?"

Grandma waved aside his concern. "The dog would sooner bite off his own tail than hurt Lou."

The boys whooped excitedly over the wrestling duo in the dirt. "Hang onto him, Lou!"

Keeping her grip and showing surprising strength, Lou somehow maneuvered until she was sitting up, holding Shane firmly with her legs and arms. She reached around with one hand and grabbed the mangled roast. "Turn loose," she ordered.

Obviously knowing he'd been bested, Shane obeyed, allowing the meat to fall into Lou's grip.

Relaxing her hold, she ruffled his longhaired head. "Now get out of here!"

He bounded away, then stopped to be petted by the laughing boys. Lou climbed slowly to her feet, staring at the mess in her hands. "I guess you probably don't want it now, do you, Grandma?"

"Probably not," the elderly southern belle replied with a droll smile. "The dog fought hard for that roast. Why not just give it back to him?"

"After he snatched it right off the table? You might as well cook him a big meal every day for all the manners that'll teach him."

Grandma let out an unbellelike snort. "That dog isn't the only one around here that needs to learn some manners. Give it to him, and go get yourself cleaned up."

As if understanding that the meal was his for the taking, Shane sprang into action and sped toward Lou. Before she knew what hit her, the dog snatched the meat from her hand. The action spun her and knocked her to the earth once more. Trent heard the thud as she landed with an *oomph*.

He shot from the porch without touching a step and reached Lou in a split-second. She groaned and sat up, rubbing her forearm. Stooping to his haunches, he allowed his gaze to sweep over her. A trickle of blood making a slow trail down her arm through a ripped sleeve nearly stopped his heart. "Are you okay, Miss Louisa?"

She nodded, lifting her wide blue eyes to meet his gaze. Even with dirt smudging her face, her raven curls springing from the braid down her back, and the men's boots peeking from the bottom of her dusty calico skirt, she was quite appealing.

"That was the funniest thing I ever saw!" Timmy said, beating Lou on the back as though she were a buddy.

"Yeah, you sure ain't like no girl I ever knew." Davy's echo sent a bolt of reality through Trent. Louisa wasn't like other women.

"I'm sorry, Parson," she said. "I guess that wasn't such a good example to your boys, was it?" Her eyes clouded with remorse, and Trent felt his heart turn to mush.

"Come on. Let's get you inside. You need to see to that cut."

"Cut?"

"Right there." Trent pointed to her arm.

She looked down, then gave him a sheepish smile. "I guess that explains the stinging. I'm such a mess."

Feeling himself responding to her good-natured self-deprecation, he smiled back. "Here, let me help you up."

Her brow shot up. "Thank you." Her voice was like velvet, soft and smooth, as she leaned on him and allowed him to lift her to her feet.

Enjoying her closeness, Trent held her a little longer than necessary before releasing her arms.

"Th–thank you," she said again, her face now a beguiling pink.

"Lou, come on up to the house, honey." Grandma Stafford's voice filtered through the air, firm but mildly amused in tone. "We need to start lunch over."

"Yes, Grandma." Clearing her throat, she smoothed her hands over her unkempt hair. She swept her gaze to the porch, then back to Trent. "I. . .um. . .it was kind of you to help me up off the ground, Parson." Giving him a shy smile, she darted toward the house, then slowed her pace and walked calmly away. Trent's gaze trailed after her.

"Yessir."

Trent startled at Timmy's voice. He glanced down to find his son staring pensively after Lou.

" 'Yessir' what?"

"She sure ain't like other ladies, is she?"

"What do you mean?"

Timmy shrugged his slender shoulders. "All afraid of a little dirt and sweat. A ma like that wouldn't always be yelling at us for being rowdy or dirty or loud."

"Did you see that blood on her arm?" Davy joined in. "She didn't cry or nothing. I like her. I think you ought to marry her, Parson."

Trent's jaw dropped as he stared after the boys. Words, along with the ability to speak, fled his mind. How could they have casually flung the shocking and absurd statements in his face, then walked off toward the house as though they hadn't just upended Trent's world?

Chapter 3

L ou studied herself in the mirror and gave an exasperated huff. Tears formed
in her eyes, and she tried once more to twist her hair into the fashionable
chignon she'd worn at the wedding last month. Her arms ached from the
repeated attempts. She was just about to start all over again when a tap on her door
made her snarl.

"What?"

"May I come in?" Deborah's soft voice filtered from the other side of the door,
and Lou nearly fainted in relief. She jumped from her vanity chair, opened the door,
and practically dragged her sister-in-law inside, shutting and locking the door after
them.

"Deborah, I'm so glad to see you."

"You look lovely, Lou. I don't think I've seen you wear that dress since the wedding."

"That's because I haven't," Lou said flatly, in no mood to explain her reasoning
even to the one person she could count on not to tease her.

"Grandma said you should hurry. The Testaments are pulling up, and I'm sure
everyone else will be arriving for services soon." She peered closer, and Lou felt her
cheeks warm under the scrutiny.

Deborah gave her a kind and understanding smile and, to Lou's relief, didn't pursue a conversation about the parson. She merely reached for the hairbrush clutched
in Lou's hand. "May I?" At Lou's nod, she gently untangled the curly mop, then
went to work weaving and pinning until Lou barely recognized herself. Gentle curls
sprang attractively from her temples, and a few trailed down the back of her neck.

"You're a lovely young lady, Lou," Deborah said, giving her a quick squeeze
around the shoulders from behind.

Embarrassed, Lou ducked her head and mumbled her thanks.

Through the mirror, Lou noticed her sister-in-law's brow crease into a frown.
"What's wrong?"

"I'm not sure you should go out there looking like that."

Heart sinking, Lou gave herself a harsh perusal. She looked ridiculous. Who was
she trying to fool? The brothers would never let her live this down.

Jerking to her feet, she reached around and began to unfasten the buttons at the
back of her neck. "You're right."

Deborah's laughter filled the room. "Oh, Lou. I'm only teasing. What I meant was that you look so beautiful, the parson won't be able to keep his eyes off of you."

A flush of pleasure burned Lou's cheeks. "You really think so?"

"I can almost guarantee it." She gave her a wry smile. "Of course, there's another problem."

"What's that?"

"The Testaments might decide to run off with you after all. King One seems smitten still."

Lou snorted and reached for her holster hanging on a peg by the door. "If one of those mangy Testament boys comes after me, I'll give them what I gave King One last year."

The Testament men's method of acquiring a wife was nothing short of kidnapping, and Lou was determined not to be a victim to their version of wooing.

The whole lot of them had pretty much left her alone after King One tried to snatch her up when she'd been fishing alone at Cherokee Creek. She'd warned him not to come any closer. But a man like that only knew one kind of discouragement. And a bullet to the shoulder convinced him he'd best leave her be if he knew what was good for him.

With a laugh, Deborah grabbed her hand. "You are not wearing that holster belt. Your brothers will see to your safety today."

Hesitating for a moment, Lou nodded and released her grip on the belt. "All right, but those Testaments better not come anywhere near me."

⁙

Trent swallowed hard and fought to remember the point he was trying to drive home to his bewildered congregation. This had to have been the most difficult sermon he'd ever preached. From the moment Lou stepped into the room wearing her yellow gown, he'd been tripping over his tongue.

Watching her slender fingers move across the piano keys had effectively robbed him of the long-familiar words to "Blessed Assurance." If Grandma Stafford hadn't rescued him by singing extra loud in her slightly off-key voice, he'd have been a laughingstock.

As it was, he detected amusement amid loud clearing of throats. With a disappointed sigh, he glanced about the room and gave up. He hurriedly finished his woefully lacking sermon, then said a quick closing prayer, adding his silent apology to the Lord.

"Just the way I like my preaching, Parson." Wally Foster pumped his hand, his face lit with a wide, toothless grin. "Quick and not too much to ponder."

But Trent quickly discovered not everyone was pleased with the lack of spiritual relevance.

Exodus Testament scowled. "I think maybe you ought to pay more attention to your preachin' duties and less attention to the gals. Ya plumb confused me."

Humiliation burned Trent's neck as the man moved on. His wife, Ruth, slipped a work-roughened hand into his. "Don't you worry none about Exodus. It don't take much to confuse him. I thought you done a fine job, Parson."

"Thank you, ma'am." Trent dreaded the line of parishioners behind the lady. Was everyone going to critique his performance today?

He squeezed Ruth Testament's hand, then released it, expecting her to move on. Rather, she dropped her tone and pressed in closer. "You be careful casting sheep eyes at that Lou Stafford, Parson. That one's got a mighty harsh temper. Took a shot at one of my boys just a year ago. Winged him in the shoulder, though I imagine she could've sent him to glory if she'd had a mind to. So I'm grateful he didn't rile her more than he did."

Trent didn't have to guess which one she winged, as three of the Testament boys guffawed while another scowled, red-faced.

"King One still has a hankerin' for Lou. 'Specially after getting a look at her to-day." The identical Chronicles, One and Two, nudged each other and snorted their laughter at their brother's expense.

"You boys stop teasing," Ruth admonished. "He ain't running off with Lou Stafford."

Alarm seized Trent. He knew exactly what Mrs. Testament meant when she said, "running off with." From what he'd heard, the Testaments came from a long line of men notorious for kidnapping their wives. No wonder Lou shot King One. Animosity burned his chest. He'd shoot the man himself if he laid one finger on her.

He scanned the room. He swallowed hard when he saw Lou standing against the far wall. Timmy and Davy stood with her, each vying for her attention. She smiled at one, then the other. Seeing her like this made yesterday's tussle with Shane, the sheepdog, seem like a distant memory. Now this Lou he could definitely picture settling down with, raising Timmy and Davy and, if the Lord willed, children of their own.

A loud clearing of the throat drew him from his musings, and he looked back to see that the Testaments had moved on. Next he shook hands with Seth Piven.

"Nice message, Parson." Seth pushed his wife forward. "You remember my missus. Say hello, Opal." Babe in arms, Mrs. Piven glanced shyly at him. Twin spots of pink appeared on her cheeks. "Howdy, Parson," she said barely above a whisper. "I'm afraid I can't shake your hand, what with holding the baby and all."

Trent's heart softened to the woman. He knew her husband wasn't intentionally a poor provider. The man just didn't seem to realize that shoes and clothing for his family needed to come before buying a new horse or gun or whatever else took his fancy.

He glanced at the line of Piven children, ranging in age from ten years old down to the new baby. They dressed neatly in threadbare clothing that was either too big or too small depending on where the child fit in the family line-up.

They were all clean—other than their feet, which he suspected were dirty from running barefoot in their soddy. He had to hand it to Mrs. Piven; she did her best and seemed to remain cheerful despite a thoughtless husband and the poorest of living conditions.

Reaching forward, he patted her forearm and smiled. "Of course I remember. The baby's growing fast." He trailed a finger over the baby's chubby cheeks. "And she's even prettier than last time I was through."

Her face brightened. "Thank you, Parson. They grow so fast."

"She likes babies, don't you, honey?" Seth nudged her and, to Trent's dismay, sent him a wink, jerking his thumb toward the other children. "There's always more where those came from."

At a loss for words, Trent gave Mrs. Piven a sympathetic smile and swallowed a sigh of relief as the family moved on to the yard, where tables were set up for a picnic.

The next time Trent came through this area, the weather wouldn't be mild enough to accommodate an outside get-together. He had a suspicion these good people would find some way to enjoy a common meal. Despite their peculiarities, they knew each other. Cared for one another. He longed to be a part of their close-knit community. He'd had an offer for a permanent position from a small congregation a day's ride from here. But so far he hadn't committed. He supposed deep inside, he kept hoping this group would make the same offer. Only a small twinge made him question his desire. If he took one position, would God have him abandon the rest of his flock?

"Fine preaching, Parson." A soft voice arrested his attention, and Trent turned, coming face to face with a pretty blond he knew as Cynthia Connelly. As he returned her pleasant smile, he had to wonder why the Testaments hadn't run off with her yet.

He took her proffered, white-gloved hand. "Thank you, Miss Cynthia."

"Lou's a mighty lucky girl to have caught your eye." She glanced at him through pea green eyes.

"Well, now. . .I didn't exactly say."

"Oh, then she hasn't caught your eye?" Her look of innocence belied the all-knowing tone.

"I'm interested in all my sheep, Miss Cynthia."

"Well, tell me then." She leaned in slightly. "Are you interested in me?"

Without waiting for an answer, she released his hand and moved away.

Feeling as though he'd been caught doing something wrong, Trent cast a hurried glance toward Lou. Inwardly, he cringed as he met her scowl. He felt the urge to hurry to her side and assure her he hadn't encouraged the other girl. Then he chided himself. After all, he hadn't courted Miss Lou. And he hadn't done anything wrong.

So why did he want so badly to go to her and explain?

Finally, after everyone had taken their turn shaking his hand, Trent made his way across the room to where Louisa and the boys still chatted.

Timmy grinned a welcome. "Hey, guess what, Parson?"

"What?"

Lou gave him a half-smile, then averted her gaze.

"Lou says she'll loan me her copy of *Tom Sawyer.*"

"But he had to promise not to let it fall into a creek like he did his own copy." Lou smiled fondly at the boy.

"That's kind of you, Miss Stafford." Trent searched her face and noted with relief that she wasn't holding a grudge over the other young woman.

"It's my pleasure. We can't leave the boy hanging halfway through the book. That would be torture."

"I'll be careful. I promise!"

Lou reached out and ruffled his hair. "I trust you."

Something about the maternal gesture tugged at Trent's heart. He wished for a few minutes alone with her—as alone as possible in a room crowded with women preparing food.

"Boys, I noticed there's a baseball game started outside. I thought you might like to join the fun."

"Yes, sir! Bye, Lou." Davy took off toward the door without hesitation.

Timmy hung back. "You want to play with us, Miss Lou?"

Lou's face brightened, and for a second Trent thought she might say yes, but she slumped back against the wall and shook her head. "I'd better not. Grandma would skin me alive if I got this dress dirty."

"Aw." The boy scowled and headed off after Davy.

Trent smiled. "I happen to agree with your grandma. That dress is much too lovely to risk."

A short gasp escaped her throat. "You think so?"

Taken aback by the unexpected question, Trent raised his brow and studied her expression. Wide eyes indicated she wasn't fishing for compliments. Still, it was obvious the young woman wasn't accustomed to receiving them. "As a matter of fact, I do think so. It's a lovely dress, and you look fetching in it."

"Th–thank you, Parson. I. . ." Her face turned scarlet, and her gaze darted from one side of the room to the other. Finally, she glanced at him. "Excuse me, but I think I hear Grandma calling."

She bolted across the room toward Grandma, who clearly hadn't been calling but seemed grateful for the help anyway.

With tunnel vision, he watched Lou grab a towel, remove a pie from the oven, and set it on the counter. Then she turned as though summoned by his attention. She caught his gaze, and Trent felt a jolt pass between them.

"Do I need to be asking your intentions toward my sister, Parson?"

Trent's scope broadened to include Micah. He cleared his throat. "I. . .well, I didn't mean any disrespect toward Louisa."

Micah clapped him on the shoulder. "Relax, Parson. I'm just teasing. No one expects a man like you to take a shine to a girl like Lou."

Defenses raised, Trent frowned. "What do you mean, 'a girl like Lou'?"

Micah followed his gaze to the other side of the room where Lou stood with Deborah, Micah's new bride. "Well, come to think of it, she cleaned up pretty good, didn't she? And you did seem a little distracted during the service."

"Louisa is a lovely girl." He hesitated, embarrassed by Micah's raised-brow scrutiny. "And quite. . .nice."

"You think so? She's got a temper like a polecat. Just ask King One Testament."

In no mood to hear the story again, Trent nodded. "True, she's a little high-spirited."

"She certainly is that."

The eldest male Stafford's amusement was beginning to grate on Trent. So the girl wasn't exactly prissy. That didn't mean she wasn't feminine when it mattered. And from her appearance today, there was no doubt she was a beautiful young woman, able to hold her own in a kitchen.

"Parson, you can rub a piece of glass 'til it shines, but that won't make it a diamond."

"And you can rub a diamond with mud, and it's still a diamond underneath. It just needs to be cleaned up and given a chance to shine."

Micah gave a conceding nod. "If you want to think Lou's a diamond, I won't be the one to discourage you. I'd be pleased to welcome a man of God into the family. Just don't say I didn't warn you. You can't give her back once she's yours."

"Now, just a minute. I didn't say. . ." But Micah had already moved away.

Trent watched him put his arm around his wife and whisper in her ear. Deborah's eyes widened, and she stared straight at Trent, an approving smile curving her lips. Feeling the heat rush to his face, Trent made a beeline for the door before Deborah went to Lou and repeated whatever Micah had just said.

Had he just effectively made an offer of marriage? Maybe Micah considered his interest and defense of Lou as equal to the Testaments' peculiar—and somewhat criminal—method of acquiring a wife.

It wouldn't be so bad if he could be sure which Lou was the real one. It wasn't that he minded a spirited woman who could hold her own against a thieving dog or a teasing brother or even a would-be suitor bent on kidnapping, but he had to be certain she could be proper when the need arose. Did she have the necessary skills to be a wife and mother?

The type of woman he married wouldn't matter so much if he had chosen to be a rancher or a farmer. But God had chosen his path for him. What if he settled into one congregation soon? He had to marry a woman who could keep a proper home, or he'd lose all credibility in the community. Towns had been scandalized by a lot less than the things he'd already witnessed from Louisa Stafford.

As much as he'd love to ignore petty propriety, he knew it existed in society, and right or wrong, folks tended to lump propriety with godliness. His first priority was to see that he was able to minister to his sheep.

He leaned against the porch railing and watched Timmy and Davy playing their ball game with the local children. The boys had lost so much; they deserved to have a home.

Father, show me what's right for me and the boys. And if Louisa Stafford is the wife You've chosen for me, give me peace. If not, help me to forget the color of her eyes, and help me to push away my tendency to want to reach out and test the tendrils of hair brushing against her neck. And about her neck, Lord, help me not to wonder what it would be like to run my finger down the length of it and see if it's really as soft as it seems.

"Look out, Parson!" Trent looked up in time to see the ball flying toward him. The last thing he remembered was the bruising pain on his forehead right before he landed hard on the porch. Then everything went black.

Chapter 4

"He's coming around."

Lou chewed the inside of her lip as Grandma waved smelling salts under Trent's nose. He'd been out cold for a full five minutes, and a goose egg had formed on his forehead.

His eyes opened slowly. A collective sigh of relief *whooshed* through the neighbors clamoring around the poor man.

"You okay, Parson?" Grandma asked as Sam lifted Trent's shoulders to help the dazed man sit up.

"We told you to duck." King One scowled and shook his head. "How come you just stood there gathering wool like a woman?"

"I guess I was a mite sidetracked." Trent appeared to be trying to focus. "I was thinking about Lou's eyes," he mumbled.

Shouts of laugher rocked the porch. Lou's face flamed.

"You *did* get knocked in the head, Parson, if you're thinking of courting that Lou Stafford," Ruth Testament piped in. "I told you what she did to my boy."

Lou averted her gaze as the woman glared at her.

"I beg your pardon, Louisa." Trent glanced at her as though suddenly aware of his slip of tongue. "I'm a bit rattled."

"It's all right," she whispered. Guilty glee shifted through her at the thought of him pondering her eyes. Although, he hadn't actually said he liked them. Only that he'd been thinking about them.

Grandma stood and nodded to Sam. "Help the parson inside."

"I'm fine," Trent protested. "I don't want to be any trouble."

"A little late for that, ain't it?" groused King One.

Lou threw the full force of her glare at the Testament. "Leave him alone."

He glared right back. "Lou Stafford, I officially withdraw my offer of marriage."

More chuckles sounded from the group.

"Good!" she flung at King One as she followed Sam and Trent. "It's about time. I wouldn't marry you if you were named after King David!"

The crowd roared. The Testaments sputtered. "I think we've worn out our welcome," Exodus shouted, his face red with anger. "Ruth, pack up the vittles we brought and get to the wagon."

"Oh, Exodus, simmer down," Grandma said. "Now, you know good and well these folks are only having a little fun. Dinner's just about ready, so how about everyone gather 'round? Since the parson's a bit addled at the moment, may I suggest Exodus Testament ask the blessing?"

Visibly mollified, Mr. Testament removed his hat. "I'd be honored to stand in for the parson."

Lou shook her head and inwardly cheered Grandma. The genteel graces with which the southern lady had been raised came in handy at each gathering. At least one person—usually a Testament—got ruffled feathers that had to be smoothed.

Bowing her head, Lou waited as a hush fell over the group of neighbors. They stood on the porch and in the yard—the men with hats in hands, women with their hands clasped in front of them.

A chill slithered down Lou's spine as Mr. Testament began his prayer. This sort of gathering was what building a community was all about: families joining together to honor the Lord's Day, to fellowship, knowing that even if there were disagreements, anything could be settled with a handshake and a prayer.

As Mr. Testament droned on past a simple blessing, Lou found her mind wandering despite her best attempts to stay focused. The little community was quickly becoming a town. All they needed was a school and a church, and then more and more people would start settling around Petunia. And if they did, it wouldn't be long before Petunia needed a teacher and a permanent minister.

Lou drew in a breath, and her eyes popped open despite the fact that Mr. Testament was still voicing his long-winded prayer. She glanced at Trent leaning against the door pane for support, and then her gaze roamed until she located Timmy and Davy. They belonged here. It was time the parson settled down and took a wife—her, for instance—and raised those boys up right. They shouldn't be on the trail. Who was seeing to their schooling? Timmy loved to read. But how long would that last if he was denied books and the opportunity to continue his education?

Noting that Mr. Testament was winding down, Lou hurriedly shut her eyes. But she had every intention of speaking with Grandma and the brothers about offering the parson a place to settle.

⁘

"I think Lou's got a point."

Lou's brow rose at the agreement coming from Josh.

"I agree, too," Deborah said quietly. "We need a permanent church and a preacher. The parson has those boys now and needs to be in one place. It sounds like a good solution to me."

Grandma's eyes sparkled with pleasure. "I'm all for the parson settling down here among us. And I think donating an acre of land to build the church is a wonderful idea."

Micah nodded and smacked his thigh. "It's settled then. As soon as the parson heads back out, we'll call a town meeting and get a vote." His lips twitched as he glanced at Lou. "I'm not altogether sure what your motives were, Lou, but you came up with a sound idea."

Feeling the perusal of her family, Lou's cheeks warmed. "I just think we need to snatch him up before one of his other congregations offers him a place to settle."

Josh snickered. "I reckon what you really mean is that *you* want to snatch him up before some other girl does. Never thought I'd see the day Lou would be setting her cap for a fellow. And a parson at that."

"Stop it," Grandma admonished before Lou could form a crushing retort. "Lou has another point about Timmy and Davy. Someone needs to see to their education. What do you think about offering to let them stay on here while the parson finishes up his obligations on the circuit? Between Lou and Deborah and me, we can get some book learning and manners drummed into them. And I noticed they're both in need of some new trousers. We should get started making those pretty soon."

Deborah stood, cradling her stomach, her face suddenly void of color. "Excuse me, I need to. I'm. . ." She ran out of the house.

Lou frowned at Micah. "Deborah ailing?"

His worried gaze settled on the door Deborah had left wide open. "I don't know. Maybe I should go after her."

Grandma stood. "I'll go. You fix your wife a nice hot water bottle and take it upstairs."

"Yes, ma'am."

Lou scowled. All they needed was to have a bout of sickness sweep through the whole house. She had planned to ask Deborah for some advice about Trent. But she supposed she'd have to wait now. She couldn't chance getting sick when she was about to start teaching the boys, who could quite possibly be her future sons.

⁜

When it rained it poured. So far, every congregation Trent had attended this time out on the circuit had offered him a permanent position. All but Petunia. He figured he'd blown his chances there, what with his poor excuse for a sermon, followed by getting himself knocked out and admitting he'd been daydreaming about a girl—just like a love-struck boy.

Trent had to admit this particular offer was everything he'd hoped for. A moderate but livable salary, a place for the boys and him to live. It was everything he wanted except for the location. As fine as these good people were, they weren't the Staffords or the Pivens or even the Testaments. Trent's heart was in the town of Petunia.

He glanced around at the group of men waiting expectantly for his answer.

"Gentleman, I'm honored by your offer." The men exhibited grins all around.

"Do we have a deal then?" The town's founder, Edward Kline, stepped forward, extending his hand.

"Well, I'll certainly pray about it. I've recently had a couple of similar offers, and I want to make sure I walk through the right door."

"You mean you might take another church?"

"Does that mean you'd stop coming around here?"

"Gentlemen, please." Trent held up his hands for silence. "I haven't made any decisions. But I will have a definite answer for you when I come back through in six weeks."

"You didn't answer the question, Parson. If you take a position somewhere else, does that mean you won't be preaching here anymore?"

"Well, if I accepted your offer, wouldn't you expect me to be here each Lord's Day?"

"I reckon." Mr. Kline glanced around. "Maybe we ought to take back the offer. Seems to me a once-in-a-while preacher is better than no preacher at all."

"Whether you take the offer back or not is certainly your decision," Trent said, keeping his voice even. "But I have my boys to think of. They need a real home. So I will be finding somewhere to hang my hat before long. As a matter of fact, I'm hoping to settle in some place by Christmas."

"Christmas! That's only a few weeks away."

"Yes, sir. I know. But that's what I feel is the right thing to do for my boys." Trent rubbed his hand over his face, wishing he didn't feel so many conflicting emotions. "Timmy and Davy have been staying with friends for the past weeks, and I have to admit I miss them more than I thought possible."

Mr. Kline gathered a slow breath and nodded. "Then I suppose we'd like you to keep our offer in mind. We'll surely be praying that God will give you the right answer."

Trent's heart warmed. "Thank you."

"Oh, Parson. Betsy says stop by before you leave town. The children have plumb outgrown every pair of boots they own, and she wants to donate them to your basket."

"Thank you, Mr. Kline. That's kind of you both."

By evening, Trent had his second horse loaded with one more bag of serviceable hand-me-downs for the Piven children. He'd been so moved by Mrs. Piven's attempt to keep the children neat and proper with the little she had that he'd decided to put the word out and see what he could turn up. He grinned. The Pivens would more than likely be the best-dressed family in Petunia after this Christmas.

His thoughts turned to the boys, and he wondered how Timmy and Davy were getting along. He pictured the two of them running around with Shane, doing their chores and lessons. Were they happy? Or did they resent him for leaving them behind?

In three days, he'd be home. Home. Was Petunia home? Releasing a sigh, he looked heavenward to the blue, blue sky and thought of Lou.

Chapter 5

T hat's right, Timmy. Hold the rifle firmly against your shoulder. Just like that so that it doesn't knock you down."

Lou smiled at the look of concentration on the boy's face. His tongue slipped between his lips and pushed to the side of his mouth as he closed one eye and aimed.

"Okay, take it easy. Squeeze the trigger. Don't jerk it."

Gunfire cracked through the air. A loud whoop followed as Timmy hit his mark, and the tin can flew up and back before landing on the ground a few feet beyond its original location.

Lou grinned and pounded his back. "You're a natural!"

His face glowed, and in a moment of adulation, he threw his arms about her. A lump formed in Lou's throat as she gave him a quick responding squeeze. "Set it up again. We have time for a few more rounds."

Watching him swagger forward to reset the targets, Lou couldn't keep back a proud smile. True, at nineteen years old, she wasn't old enough to actually be his mother, but that knowledge didn't stop the maternal feelings that had sprouted in her breast during the past few weeks.

She had discovered that, contrary to her belief, boys had more than a rough-and-tumble side to them. Timmy, for instance, had shown an interest in playing the piano. And despite frowns from the brothers and teasing from Davy, the two of them had spent hours in front of the ivories. Much to Grandma's delight, he was already playing hymns. The boy had a gift and shouldn't be discouraged for fear of looking like a sissy.

"Wish Davy could have seen that shot!" Timmy exulted as he stomped back to Lou's side.

"Well, your brother should attend to his lessons a little more instead of staring out the window so much."

Lou inwardly cringed at the words she'd actually spoken aloud. How many times in her life had Grandma said those very words to her? She understood Davy's plight, but the fact remained that Trent was counting on her to see to the boys' education. Well, he was counting on all of them really, but she had taken over instruction of reading, literature, and history. Sam, with his love for woodworking, had volunteered to teach the boys carving and building. Deborah had quite a head for numbers, it seemed, so she had volunteered to teach arithmetic and penmanship.

Josh was teaching the boys all about horses and tracking game, while Micah had agreed to teach them the ins and outs of ranching and had even allowed the boys to take part in day-to-day activities when their lessons allowed for it.

As for Grandma. . .she loved them to distraction and fed them endlessly. And everyone agreed that was the best contribution she could make.

The wind whipped up from the north, sending a blast through Lou's collar straight to her neck. She shivered. Too bad she hadn't listened to Grandma and brought a scarf.

"Fire off one more, and then let's get back, Timmy. It's about time for me to help Grandma and Deborah with supper."

Lou mounted her golden mare, Summer, and waited while Timmy climbed onto his saddle. Another gust of chill wind blew across the field. Lou shivered. "I think the weather's starting to turn. I wouldn't be surprised if we end up with a little snow on the ground for Christmas."

"Think the parson's going to make it back by then?"

"He said he would, didn't he? Christmas is a full two weeks away. I'm sure he'll make it."

The boy's face lit. "You really think so?"

"Sure, I do." Lou knew the boys missed Trent. They'd spent their Thanksgiving without him. But both had agreed that even though they missed their adopted father, the day had been a hundred times better than last year when they were on their own.

Lou's words could have been prophecy. "Timmy, look!" Two horses were tethered in front of the house. And Trent, Grandma, and Davy stood on the porch.

"Pa–Parson!" Timmy nudged his horse into a gallop.

Lou had to restrain her own urge to do the same. Inwardly, she felt like shouting for the joy of seeing Trent again.

He bent down and hugged Timmy, then glanced up at her as Timmy pointed. Suddenly self-conscious about her appearance, Lou wished she could hide until she made herself more presentable. For the shooting lesson, she'd donned one of Josh's cast-off plaid shirts and his old coat from last year. For the first time ever, she wished her skirt was long enough to cover the pair of men's boots she preferred for the toe room. But at the moment, she would rather suffer the pinched toes and be a little more ladylike.

She dismounted and tethered Summer to the hitching post in front of the house. "Glad to see you made it safely, Parson."

Her skin felt hot despite the chill in the air as his gaze perused her attire.

"Timmy tells me you're teaching him to shoot a rifle."

"Yeah. I just figure a ten-year-old boy ought to know how." She knew she sounded defensive and cringed. Grandma always said, "You can catch more flies with honey than vinegar." Until now, Lou hadn't cared much about the adage. But the look on Trent's face revealed his offense at her words.

"You don't think I'm doing right by the boys?"

Lou shrugged. Better to keep her trap shut than risk making the situation worse.

"Now, Parson. Don't go getting your feathers ruffled." Ever the peacemaker, Grandma patted his arm. "Lou didn't mean a thing by it. Did you, honey?"

"No, ma'am."

"There, you see? How about letting the boys attend to the horses? Lou, go put on some fitting clothes and help me with supper. Deborah's feeling a bit under the weather again."

Alarm pressed Lou's chest. "Think I ought to ride for the doc? She's been sick an awful lot lately."

A gentle smile tugged at Grandma's lips. "I think Deborah will be fine. This will pass in time."

Not quite convinced, Lou climbed the porch steps. Grandma didn't seem concerned, so she was sure Deborah would be fine. Still, when a person got sick day after day. . .

Her mind wandered back to the present where the parson hung back, allowing her to enter ahead of him. Her knees went weak at his nearness. He smelled like the trail. Woods and wind. The subtle hint of soap revealed he'd stopped off at the creek and washed up—and probably changed his shirt—before riding to the house. A girl had to appreciate that sort of thoughtfulness, especially given as many cattle drives as she'd been on when the men smelled of cows and sweat and didn't care.

Ducking around him, Lou entered the warmth of the cozy room. The house overflowed with the smells of fresh bread and the sweet, spicy smell of apple tarts.

Lou headed for the stairs. For the first time she saw the wisdom in taking up room space for the washroom the boys had recently added for Deborah and Micah's comfort and privacy. She occupied the other side of the upstairs and had every intention of making the most of that washroom. When she came back downstairs, she planned to make the parson forget all about her minor suggestions that maybe Timmy should have known how to shoot a rifle before now.

She tiptoed past Deborah's open door and couldn't resist the urge to peek inside. "Deborah?" she whispered.

"Lou." The weak response prompted Lou to step inside.

"Grandma says you're ailing again. Can I get you anything?"

"No. I'm starting to feel a little better. Did I hear company downstairs?"

Lou's cheeks warmed. "The parson's back."

Deborah's pale face brightened. She squeezed Lou's hand. "What are you going to wear?"

Releasing a frustrated breath, Lou shook her head. "I don't know. I guess I'll just have to get my other skirt. Grandma will skin me alive if I wear my Sunday dress for a plain old Tuesday night supper."

"Didn't you burn a hole in that skirt building a fire last week?"

"Oh, yeah," Lou said dully. "Well, I guess I'll just have to wear this one."

"No, you're not." Deborah rose slowly and with determination. She knelt before the trunk at the foot of the bed and opened the lid. "Honestly, if you'd have just let us start sewing those new dresses a month ago like we wanted to, you'd have a couple to choose from."

"I know, but the boys needed new clothing. Then we got busy with lessons. There's an awful lot to raising children."

"Yes, I know," Deborah said softly. "But it's worth it."

Lou had to agree. She smiled broadly. "That Timmy is a crack shot. And Davy has a real love for animals. I think that's why he gets along so well with Josh. They both love horses."

"All right. Here it is." Deborah pulled a white lacy blouse from the trunk and a simple light-brown skirt.

"I haven't worn this since I made the new gowns. I know it's not exactly pretty. . . ."

"It's perfect." Lou gave her a quick squeeze. "Thank you, Deborah."

"Come back after you get washed and dressed, and I'll help with your hair if you'd like me to."

"I will." Lou headed toward the door, then hesitated. "If you're sure you feel up to it."

"I do. I promise."

Lou felt her heart skip a beat as she walked toward the washroom. This time she was determined to show the parson she could be a lady.

∗∷∗

Trent sat where Grandma had motioned him, bewilderment forming a lump in his throat. He just never knew what to expect from that Louisa Stafford. She'd slipped out of her worn, sheepskin coat, revealing a man's plaid shirt. The boots peeking from beneath the patched gingham skirt were obviously men's. Her single holster hung from her hips, and he had the feeling she could probably outshoot most of the men he knew.

His mind wandered to the churches he presided over on a regular basis. They were brimming with proper women. Yet no one had come close to capturing his attention despite the attempts of more than one mother to make her daughter appealing. Just why Lou Stafford had invaded his thoughts, he wasn't sure. Perhaps it was her unique personality and dress. But were those necessarily traits he could afford to condone in a wife?

"Have a cup of coffee, Parson." He turned to find Grandma studying him.

Clearing his throat, he took a seat at the table and accepted a mug of steaming liquid. "Yes, Ma'am. This'll hit the spot, for sure."

Grandma joined him a minute later with a mug of her own and a plate of pastries.

"Help yourself to an apple tart. Supper won't be on for a while. I thought you might be hungry."

"That's kind of you." Trent's mouth watered at the cinnamony, apple aroma, and he reached for a tart without hesitation. He took a bite and sighed at the burst of flavor exploding over his tongue.

"Now I want to talk about you and my granddaughter."

Trent nearly choked. He covered his mouth with his fist and tried to keep from spitting apple tart all over the table. "Excuse me?"

"Don't try to deny it. You've been casting sheep eyes at each other since Deborah and Micah got married."

"Sheep eyes? I'm sure you've misunderstood."

"Maybe. But there's no mistaking getting yourself knocked senseless because you were daydreaming about Lou's eyes."

She had him there. He gave her a wry grin.

"They are quite remarkable."

Grandma harrumphed. "They're eyes."

How could she even suggest they were anything less than sensational? "I don't want to seem disagreeable. . . ."

"The girl's eyes are identical to Sam's. But I didn't hear you mumbling about him when you were coming to that day on the porch. I would like for you to make your intentions known."

He studied the determined expression on the woman's face and knew he needed to be honest. "There's no denying that Louisa has some attractive qualities, but. . ."

Grandma's eyes narrowed, and he could tell she was about to let him have it. So he hurried on, speaking the truth from his heart. "But there are some quirks that make me stop and wonder if she would be a proper minister's wife."

There. He'd said it. Now the Stafford matriarch knew he had honorable intentions toward Lou, if a few misgivings.

"Our Louisa lost her ma when she was barely past girlhood. It. . .changed her somehow. Turned her from a girl just like any other to the tomboy she is. We've done our best with her, but I admit she'd rather rope a steer than stitch a pillowcase."

Grandma stood and patted his shoulder as she walked past him to the oven. She pulled out a pan of bread and straightened up, her face pink from the heat. She set the pan on top of the stove to cool, then turned to him, the expression on her face pensive. "Love has a way of softening a woman. Lou's growing. She's learning. She'll always love the outdoors, but when she's finished blooming, she'll be the best of both types of woman. The one that captured your interest is the rowdy Lou. So don't try to understand why you like her, and don't talk yourself out of liking her just because she's not like other women. Trust the Lord and me that we'll get her into shape to be the woman you need by your side if that's His will."

Trent's reply was cut off by a blast of cold air shooting through the room as the door opened, allowing Timmy and Davy entrance. "Can we go out and shoot the rifle, Parson?" Timmy asked. "Miss Lou says I'm a natural."

Trent smiled and ruffled the boy's brown hair. "How about we wait until tomorrow? Grandma Stafford's getting supper. Grandma Stafford, you think I can hole up in the bunkhouse?"

The old lady fixed him with a fierce frown. "No, sirree. You're not staying in the bunkhouse. The boys got the cottage finished. But Deborah's not up to moving, so she and Micah will stay put upstairs for a bit longer. They discussed it and gave me leave to tell you that you're welcome to the cottage for as long as you'd like to stay." She turned her gaze upon the boys. "Did you take your pa's things to the cottage?"

"Yes, ma'am," Davy replied without hesitation. Trent's heart leapt. These boys were his sons. They would be forever. But hearing Grandma call him "Pa" made it seem even more real, and he longed to hear it come from their mouths.

"How long do you get to stay this time, Parson?" Timmy asked, his hazel eyes filled with query.

"As a matter of fact, I'm not going back out until after Christmas."

The boys whooped, and Grandma gave him an approving smile. "A lot can happen in two weeks," she said pointedly.

Lou breezed into the room. "I'm sorry I took so long, Grandma."

"That's all right. You can set the table."

Trent swallowed hard as, once again, Lou took his breath away. Grandma was right. A lot *could* happen in two weeks, and he had the feeling that his time off would prove to accomplish one of two things. He would either know for sure Lou wasn't the right choice of a wife for him, or he would be completely in love.

Chapter 6

Lou felt like crying and probably would have if not for the fact that she refused to look like a fool in front of the late-afternoon stragglers at the Sunday get-together.

Resentfully, she watched Cynthia fawn all over Trent. That Cynthia Connelly had obviously sunk her claws in the poor, unsuspecting parson.

She'd give anything for some advice from another woman who would understand how it felt to be in love, but Deborah was ailing again, and Micah had sent her up to bed for the rest of the day. All the other women were old, unmarried, or had been married too long to remember what it felt like to be in new love.

"Why don't you call her out?"

Nehemiah Esther Testament's gruff voice made Lou jump. "You scared me to death, Neh."

"You going to tell that bobcat to get her claws out of your man?"

"Don't be ridiculous."

"Well, it'd be better than standing on the porch watching them walk off toward the creek like a courtin' couple."

"If Trent prefers Cynthia, there's nothing I can do about it. Besides, what do I care anyway?"

"You care. That's plain to see. And if a man I cared about was about to get hisself caught like a worm on a hook by that sneak, Cynthia Connelly, I wouldn't stand for it."

"Well, you aren't me." Lou turned and sat on the railing. She couldn't watch anymore. Trent wasn't exactly pushing Cynthia away, so who knew if he really wanted to be rescued?

"Fine. Personally, I think you ought to just carry him off and find another preacher to do the marrying."

Lou grinned. "Is that how you're going to get your man?"

"Sure. That's the way we always do it. How else?"

"You could let a man take a shine to you," Lou said dreamily. "Then he'll ask you if he can come calling, and in a few months you'll be betrothed. And not long after that, you'll be married. And no one had to be forced or tricked into it."

"You got it bad for the parson, Lou."

Lou jerked her chin and stared at the girl. "We weren't talking about me. We were talking about you."

"Maybe so. But if you don't do something, your parson is going to get tricked into marrying Cynthia, and by then it'll be too late for you to carry him off to a preacher. You're worth ten of Cynthia; everyone around here knows that. But you have to make sure the parson knows it, or you're gonna lose him."

Lou would have replied, but the sound of Mr. Testament's voice interrupted. "Nehemiah Esther, get yourself to the wagon, girl."

"Comin', Pa!" She glanced back at Lou. "Remember what I said, Lou. Don't let another girl have the man you want for your own. That Cynthia don't deserve a decent man. Even my brothers don't want nothin' to do with her, and you know they'll pretty much spark to any girl that's old enough to get married." She hopped off the railing and headed toward the stairs. "And don't forget the parson's boys. Do you want Cynthia to be their ma?"

A jolt of reality shot through Lou at those words, and she stared silently after her friend. The girl might be uncouth and a little warped in the head about the way things should be, but that wasn't her fault. In this case, she had a point. Cynthia wasn't going to get free and unfettered access to Timmy and Davy if Lou could help it. It was one thing to let Trent fall for the annoying girl. But it was another thing altogether to stick the boys with Cynthia for a mother.

Armed with a sense of purpose, she strode to the barn and saddled Summer.

Timmy entered just as she was walking the horse to the door. "Where you going, Lou?"

Lou smiled. "Just for a ride. It's been a few days. I can't have Summer getting fat and lazy."

"Can I come with you?"

"Not this time."

The disappointment on his face almost caused Lou to relent, but she knew if he came along, she wouldn't have the gumption to tell Trent how she felt about him. With Cynthia hanging onto his arm, it was going to be difficult enough. But Lou had always believed in the direct approach, and Trent needed to make a choice.

She rode down the trail toward the creek, her heart pounding, unsure of what she was going to say. As much as she'd like to tell Trent all the reasons Cynthia wasn't right for him, she knew that speaking ill of someone—even someone who deserved it— wouldn't be right. Slowing Summer to a walk, Lou felt the heat sift from her. Trent was a good man with a heart after God. If he chose Cynthia to be his wife, then it would be for a good reason. She had no right to tell him whom to love. Tears pricked her eyes at the thought of Trent marrying someone else, but she turned Summer back to the house. If she turned him away from Cynthia through underhanded means and vicious slander, she'd be no better than the Testaments in her methods.

A scream sliced through the air just as Lou was about to kick the horse into a trot. She reined the mare hard and whipped around.

⁘

Trent eyed the snarling dog warily. Cynthia had a stranglehold grip on his arm, and he knew there was no way he could fend off the animal if it sprang on either one of them.

He could kick himself for not paying closer attention to their surroundings. Cynthia's constant chatter and his pounding headache had worked together to disorient him until they were facing the large dog, which was obviously a mixture of some kind of pet and a wolf. It stood in their path, matted gray head down, teeth bared. The poor animal looked half-starved, but as sympathetic as Trent was, he didn't want to offer any part of his anatomy for a meal.

"Shoot it, Parson," Cynthia screeched.

"Shhh."

The foolish young woman was making the dog more nervous with her screaming and obvious terror.

"Do not try to shush me when I'm staring at a rabid dog. Hurry and shoot it before it kills us both."

"I don't wear my gun on the Lord's Day."

A gasp escaped her throat. "What kind of man doesn't wear his gun?"

Irritation clamped hard within Trent's chest at her berating. "Apparently the kind of man I am. But rather than argue, how about slowly backing up before the dog pounces?"

The dog advanced, its yellow teeth bared.

Cynthia buried her face in Trent's shoulder and screamed. The dog crouched menacingly. Trent tensed, aware that they were in immediate danger.

In a bold move, he disentangled himself from Cynthia's grip and shoved hard, sending her sailing to the frozen ground just as the dog lunged.

Knowing there was no time to evade the attack, Trent raised his arms to defend himself and said a quick prayer for mercy. *Crack!* A gunshot rang through the air, and the dog yelped, landing inches in front of Trent. *Thank You, Lord.*

"Are you all right, Trent?" Louisa reined in her horse and dismounted.

Now that the fear of the moment was over, Trent's chest filled with shame. What sort of man needed to be rescued by a woman?

She looked him over. Relief washed across her face, and Trent couldn't help but smile. "Thank you for coming along at the right time."

"Glad I was nearby."

"Doesn't anybody care whether or not I'm all right?" Cynthia's voice broke.

Giving her a quick glance, Louisa nodded. "You look fine to me."

She knelt before the wounded dog. A low, warning growl came from its throat.

Even wounded, the animal had the power to do harm if a person got too close. "Be careful, Louisa."

"If you had shot straighter in the first place, that creature would be dead!" Cynthia's tearful voice rang shrilly into the dewy air.

Rallying, Trent collected his thoughts and his manners. He walked to where the poor girl still lay on the ground and crouched down beside her. "Are you hurt, Miss Cynthia?"

To Trent's dismay, the girl jerked her chin and turned away. "Not that you care, but I'm fine. A gentleman would never manhandle a lady and shove her to the ground when she's just trying to get him to protect her."

Just as he was about to apologize, Louisa spoke up. "He saved your ungrateful hide, Cynthia Connelly. You should be kissing his boots instead of trying to make him feel bad."

Trent blinked as Louisa stood and shrugged out of her coat. She regarded Trent evenly. "Can I bother you for your belt, Parson?"

"Louisa Stafford." Cynthia rose to her feet, jerking away from Trent's offered assistance. "That is absolutely indecent."

A scowl twisted Louisa's face. "I want to muzzle the dog so I don't lose a finger carrying her home on Summer."

Alarm seized Trent. "Wait a minute. What do you mean you're taking the dog home? Don't you think you should go ahead and. . .finish it off?"

Louisa's eyes flashed as she turned on him. "If I had wanted to kill the dog, I wouldn't have shot it in the shoulder."

Cynthia gasped. "You mean you missed on purpose?"

"Of course." Louisa frowned, turning her gaze on Trent. "I could never kill an innocent animal just for trying to protect itself."

"Protect itself?" Cynthia's shriek was beginning to grate on Trent's nerves like a squeaky wagon wheel, and he'd had just about enough. She pressed her hands to her hips in an unladylike manner and huffed. "Louisa Stafford, you need your head examined."

"Do you need help?" Trent asked Lou, handing over the belt she'd asked for.

A smile curved her generous mouth, and he swallowed hard. Oh, how he'd love to kiss those lips.

"What's goin' on here?"

"We heard a gunshot up at the house."

Trent jumped as though caught stealing from the candy jar.

To his relief, it was only Kings One and Two.

Cynthia burst into tears. "It was just awful, King One. That horrid animal attacked me."

"It did?"

He pulled out his Colt, determination carved on his face.

"Don't you go anywhere near this dog, King One, or I'll wing you again," Lou warned.

"You see?" Cynthia said, through her tears. "Louisa and the parson care more about that horrible, vicious creature than they do me. Will you please take me back to the ranch?"

"Of course I will, Miss Cynthia. Don't fret none. Lou's just one crazy gal. You know that." He dismounted and lifted the trembling young woman into his arms. In true Testament-like fashion, he carried her to his horse and deposited her in the saddle.

Trent watched in bewildered fascination as King One was transformed from uncouth simpleton to knight in shining armor. He swung up behind her, and they left without so much as a good-bye.

"The dog's lost a lot of blood, Trent." Lou's eyes glistened. "We need to hurry if

I'm going to be able to save her."

Moving slowly, Trent and Lou worked together to get the belt around the growling animal's nose and jaw, effectively robbing the dog of her ability to bite.

The animal whined when Trent lifted her, wrapped in Lou's coat, and carried her to the horse.

He turned to Lou. "Climb up, and I'll set her in front of you."

"Thank you, Trent. I couldn't have done this alone."

Though he reveled in the appreciation, he knew Lou Stafford could do anything she put her mind to. After she was sitting in the saddle with the dog lying in front of her, they headed back up the trail toward the house.

"What were you doing out riding alone?" he asked, more for something to say than because he needed an answer. Lou loved to ride and often did so on the spur of the moment.

"To be honest, I was looking for you and Cynthia."

"Oh? Was something wrong? Are the boys all right?"

"They're fine. But they won't be if you marry Cynthia Connelly. They'd be miserable, Trent."

"Marry Cynthia? Why would you think such a thing?"

Louisa sniffed and gave him a wry grin. "Let's just say she looked mighty comfortable on your arm."

He couldn't resist a sly glance upward. "Jealous?"

"Never in a million years, Trent Chamberlain, and don't you forget it." She sat ramrod straight and stared ahead.

The dog growled as if in agreement.

Trent shook his head. He'd effectively offended two women and a dog today. One he wasn't so worried about. The dog had a muzzle around her mouth and couldn't hurt him. The other woman intrigued him beyond belief.

As they walked in silence, curiosity began to burn a hole inside of him. When he could stand it no longer, he voiced his question. "What did you plan to do if you'd caught up to Cynthia and me under other circumstances?"

Lou's face flushed. "I was going to try to make you see the error of your ways."

"I see. And how were you planning to do that?"

She gave an exasperated sigh. "If you must know, I was going to tell you that you can't marry Cynthia because..."

Trent drew in a sharp breath. "Because?"

"Because I love you."

Taken aback, Trent felt his head swim with the news. "Lou..."

A gasp escaped her throat. "Don't say it, Parson! I don't expect you to feel the same way about the likes of me. Go on and marry Cynthia Connelly if you've a mind to, although after today, I doubt she'd have you."

She nudged Summer into a trot, leaving Trent to stare after her. His mouth hung open, and he knew his world would never be the same again.

Chapter 7

L ou sat next to the wounded dog, which they had named "Belle," and watched the animal sleep. At Micah's insistence, Lou had tied Belle to a stall just in case she rallied faster than any of them thought she would. No sense taking a chance the animal might hurt one of the horses or anyone else.

The bullet had come out easily enough, but the dog would need care for several days before she could be turned loose. Grateful for an excuse to hide out, Lou stayed with the animal. And she'd been staying with her for the better part of a week. The family assumed it was because of her love for any living creature, large or small. Only she and Trent were aware that she'd opened her heart for the first time in her life, only to be thwarted in the worst possible way. He'd opened his mouth and tried to let her down easily.

What a foolish girl she was! She'd let the emotions of the moment carry her away and force her to admit something she should never have admitted. Poor Trent.

A moan escaped her even as the barn door creaked open. Timmy entered. "How's the dog?"

Pushing aside the unsettling emotions, she forced a smile for the boy. The boy who would never belong to her. She swallowed back tears. "I think she'll be just fine. Just need to keep an eye on her for a few days."

"Miss Lou?" Timmy kept his attention focused on the dog.

"What's wrong?"

"I was just wondering if you're mad at the parson."

"Of course not. Where would you get such an idea?"

He shrugged. "I overheard him talking to Grandma Stafford. He said he offended you and didn't quite know how to make things right."

"He did, huh?"

Timmy nodded.

"Well, don't worry, kiddo. It takes an awful lot to offend me. Besides, if the parson wants to make things right, he knows where I am."

"I reckon he does." Timmy turned. "You coming in for supper?"

"I'll eat a bite later."

He nodded and turned to go.

⁘

A sharp northern wind assaulted the plains and whipped around Trent like Indian arrows, shooting through his clothing straight to the skin underneath. Fat, gray clouds promised a white Christmas. He thought of the two hand-carved sleds Sam had crafted for the boys and smiled. He hoped it snowed a foot.

He gave a relieved sigh when the familiar white, two-story house came into view. He could use a hot cup of coffee to warm himself up. The morning had been long as he'd conferred with the newly elected, four-member council of Petunia. His heart had soared when Micah presented him with the offer he'd been waiting for: to be the permanent pastor of this flock. But just as quickly as his joy had risen, it fled, and in its place had come that now familiar sense of struggle associated with each offer over the past couple of months.

How could he leave all the other congregations and settle into one? What would the others do? They were all members of the flock God had appointed him to reside over. On the other hand, God had also called him to nurture two young boys who needed stability. During the ten-mile ride from town, his mind had traveled different possible trails. Now, drained and confused, all he could do was pray.

His heart warmed and a smiled tugged at his lips as he drew closer and spied Timmy and Davy running toward him, waving frantically.

Trent waved back, then frowned, nudging Mel into a trot.

"Parson! Come quick. Lou's in trouble!"

"What's happened?"

"That new dog. She's in the barn. Hurry!"

Trent slid off his horse and ran toward the barn, his heart pounding in his ears.

"Lou!" he called as he opened the door.

He stopped short at the sight of her. She sat, her back against the barn wall. Trying to assess the situation, he stepped forward.

"You okay?"

"Of course. Why wouldn't I be?"

"The dog didn't hurt you?"

She gave him a look that clearly indicated she thought him crazy. Belle's head rested on Lou's lap, and Lou's long, slim fingers caressed the animal's head. Clearly the boys had lied. He was about to turn around and demand an explanation when the door shut tight. With a sense of dread, he heard the slat fall into place. They were locked in.

"What's going on, Trent?"

"I'm not sure." He scratched his head, trying to make sense of it all.

Lou gently moved Belle and stood. She glared at him as though he'd planned the whole thing.

"For some reason, Timmy and Davy told me you'd been hurt and then locked us in."

Lou gasped. "Those little double-crossers! Why would they do such a thing?"

Trent let out a chuckle. "I have a pretty good idea."

"What's that?"

"They want you to be their mother. They figure there are only a few more days before I leave again, and since you won't come into the house, they had to bring me to you."

Lou's mouth made an O.

"I'm sorry they forced this on you." He'd been trying to respect her desire to stay away from him over the last week, but in a way, he was glad the boys had contrived this forced meeting. He'd gotten her a Christmas gift that he prayed she would accept.

"What do you mean you're leaving in a few days?" She frowned, obviously pushing aside the situation in which they found themselves. "Didn't Micah and the rest of the men talk to you about staying on as the regular preacher?"

"Yes." He took a step closer. "But I haven't found a peace about doing it."

"What about the boys, Trent?" Lou moved closer to him, further shrinking the distance between them. "They need a stable home."

"They have one with you, don't they?"

"Well, of course. They're more than welcome to stay here for as long as necessary. But that's not the same as spending time with their pa."

"What about their ma?"

"O–oh." Lou stopped and stared at the barn floor.

Trent took another step until he was close enough to reach out and snag her around the waist. But he held back.

"I know God gave me those boys to raise. But I also know that He called me to preach."

"You'd be preaching if you stayed here full time."

"Yes, but I wouldn't be feeding the souls of all the sheep God has placed me over."

"Have you considered that maybe God is settling you down? Changing your ministry?"

"The thought has crossed my mind several times over the past weeks." Reaching out, he fingered a loose curl. She shuddered.

She cleared her throat. "Well, then?"

"I can't leave four congregations without a minister just because I'd rather be here with you."

"W–with me?"

His heart nearly burst with love for her. But he knew what he was asking wasn't necessarily fair. Dread gripped him at the thought that she might say no.

Taking her hands in his, he looked into her sweet, heart-shaped face. "I'm sorry I was such an idiot when you told me how you feel. To be honest, I've been struggling with that same emotion toward you."

Her wide eyes glistened. "I don't understand what you mean. Why struggle? Am I that repulsive?"

"Repulsive?" In a flash, he released her hands and slipped his arm around her waist. She didn't resist as he pulled her close and kissed her trembling lips. She melted against him and returned his fervor. When he pulled away slightly, he whispered, "Do you still think I find you repulsive?"

Smiling, she shook her head. "Then why the struggle?"

"Because if you marry me, you'll have to understand that I'm not going to be around all the time. We can pray that God will provide ministers for the rest of the congregations in my circuit, but until that time, I am the one responsible for ministering to them."

"Marry?"

Trent chuckled. "Is that the only word you heard?"

She slipped her arms around his neck, shaking her head. "I heard every word you spoke. And I admire you more than you know."

"You wouldn't mind marrying me and raising the boys even while I'm away?"

"I'm not saying it won't be a challenge and that I won't miss you while you're gone, but I have my family to help me."

Trent nodded. Lou was a smart, capable woman, able to be tough when she needed to be, yet also soften into a beautiful woman when the occasion called for it. He could trust the safety of his boys to her until God saw fit to allow him to stay in one place. For the first time in weeks, peace settled over his heart.

He pushed her slightly away from him and reached into his pocket. He felt the cold metal and smiled as he pulled it out. "This was my mother's. I'd like to give it to you as a token of our engagement."

Lou drew in a cold breath and lifted the diamond-studded lady's watch. "Oh, Trent, are you sure you want me to have this? It's so. . .elegant."

"I'm sure. My mother wore it as a brooch, but if you prefer, we can get a ribbon and you can wear it on your wrist like those society ladies in the cities."

"I love it as a brooch." She threw her arms around the man she adored and hugged him tight.

"Is that a 'yes, Trent, I'll marry you'?"

"You know it is. Of course I'll marry you and raise those wonderful boys." Her eyes filled with tears, blurring her vision. "Thank you, Trent."

"For what?" The tenderness shining in his eyes filled her with warmth and contentment.

"For loving me and wanting to marry me."

He dipped his head and kissed her. "Thank you, back. For loving me and wanting to marry me even though it means you won't have a normal life."

Lou laughed. "Normal? I've never had normal in my life."

"Then I suppose God brought us together for a reason."

"Shall we go and tell the family?"

"The door's locked, remember?"

A sheepish grin curved her lips, and she took his hand. "There's a side door. Come on."

An inch of snow had fallen in the amount of time they'd been locked in the barn.

Lou squealed. "We're going to have a white Christmas!" She grabbed his arm in her excitement. "The boys can sled."

Trent threw back his head and laughed. "Do you really think those two double-crossers deserve those sleds after the stunt they pulled?"

A grin tipped her lips. "If you hadn't asked me to marry you, I'd be the first one in line to throttle them. But considering how it all worked out, maybe we could just tell them not to pull anything like that again and let it go?"

He dropped a kiss to her nose and smiled. "If that's what their new ma thinks is best, then I guess I'll go along with it. . .this time."

They laughed as they opened the door. The heavenly smells of pies baking and corn popping greeted them, and Lou realized she was famished for the sight of her family all together at once.

"Oh, Lou!" Deborah hurried to greet her. "It's so good to see you. I thought you'd never leave that barn again."

"Hey, how'd you get out?"

Davy's outraged face grew red as all eyes turned to him.

"What do you mean, David?" Grandma asked, a stern frown creasing her brow.

"N—nothing." He gulped and cast a guilty look at Lou. She winked and lifted the watch slightly, for his eyes only. His countenance changed from worry to surprise to joy as obvious understanding dawned.

Micah stood. "Now that everyone is here, Deborah and I have an announcement to make."

Lou glanced at Deborah. Her sister-in-law glowed. A smile lit her eyes as she clung to Micah's arm.

No one moved.

"It appears that God is about to bless us with a new addition to the family."

As understanding sank in, Lou couldn't hold back her delight. She went to her brother and Deborah and hugged them both tightly.

She moved out of the way so the rest of the family could congratulate the parents-to-be.

Trent took her hand. "Shall we share our news as well?" he whispered against her ear. Lou smiled but shook her head. "Not yet. Let's give this moment to Deborah and Micah. We'll tell them tomorrow on Christmas morning. Okay?"

"Sounds wonderful. Mind if I tell the boys tonight after we go to the cottage?"

"I think you should."

Trent squeezed her hand, his heart of love shining from his eyes. Lou felt more content than she had in years. And Grandma was right. As she thought ahead to her wedding day, Lou was glad for the pair of stitched pillowcases folded neatly in her trunk. The irony of the double-cross stitch struck her, and she laughed aloud, thinking of Davy and Timmy's ploy to lock them together in the barn.

At the sound of her laughter, everyone stared, but she shook her head and waved them back to the joy of Micah and Deborah's news. It was enough for her to know that Trent loved her and that the years ahead would be filled with love and family. Closing her eyes, she breathed a silent prayer of thanks.

SPIDERWEB ROSE

by Vickie McDonough

Dedication

I'm so grateful to my husband, Robert,
who didn't laugh when I first told him I was writing a book.
His gracious and generous support and encouragement has
made it possible for me to write the stories of my heart.

Chapter 1

No Man's Land
Spring 1887

I sure made a fine mess of things this time." Rachel Donovan blinked away the tears stinging her eyes. She picked up a rock and hurled it halfway across the stream that lapped at the toes of her oversized boots. If not for her need to get out of Dodge so fast, they wouldn't be stranded in the wilds of No Man's Land, and her grandpa wouldn't be injured. She wiped her face with the back of her hand then squatted by the smooth-running stream.

Her papa's denim trousers felt stiff and unnatural against her legs. She longed for the familiar petticoats and the feel of soft cotton twisting about her legs. But she'd made a promise to Grandpa, and while traveling across No Man's Land, where they might encounter outlaws or other unsavory types, she had no choice but to keep her word and pretend to be a boy.

Rachel glanced around, thankful none of the brigands had stumbled onto their campsite. She bowed her head. "Please, God, heal Grandpa's injuries, and don't let us run into any of those dangerous men. And help me find our horses today. Amen."

It seemed her dream to live on a ranch would never come true, but here they were almost halfway between Dodge City and her uncle's ranch in Amarillo. If only. . .

A sigh escaped. She dipped a battered tin cup into the creek. The cool liquid ministered to her dry lips and parched throat but did nothing for her sagging spirits.

Cupping a palm over her eyebrows, Rachel studied the serene landscape. A bright-red cardinal and its mate flittered in the fragrant honeysuckle bushes across the creek. Locusts and crickets dueled each other in song. After the revelry from the myriad saloons and gunfire in the Dodge City streets, the gentle voice of nature comforted her wounded spirit. If only she hadn't created such a horrible mess.

The soothing creek rippled its way across the dry countryside, but peace and tranquility forked off to the left, while Rachel and her troubles turned right. With their horses gone and Grandpa injured, she wondered how they'd ever make it out of this dangerous territory.

Rachel drew in a deep breath. Self-pity wouldn't put food in their bellies or find help for Grandpa. The good Lord helped those who helped themselves, so she'd best get busy. She dipped her cup for a final drink.

Snap!

Rachel's heart jumped at the unnatural crack of a twig. She froze.

"Hold it right there, mister," a deep voice boomed behind her. "This is Stafford land, and we don't cotton much to squatters. Get your hands in the air where I can see them. And turn around. Slowly!"

Rachel leaped to her feet. The cup slipped from her grip and tumbled to the ground, clinking against the rocky creek bank. Turning, she tried futilely to stop her arms from trembling.

Her gaze took in the lone man, and then she scanned the nearby trees and brush. Hope soared a fraction before plummeting back to Earth. Did she have a chance, even against one man? She eyed the gun aimed at her chest and struggled to swallow the lump in her throat. *How could I have let down my guard?*

With his free hand, the cowboy pushed back his black Stetson. Strands of raven-colored hair slipped down, fanning a forehead tanned lighter than the rest of his bronze face. Dark-blue eyes, previously hidden under his hat's broad brim, widened in surprise. "Why, you aren't much more than a kid! I've been watching you for some time." He waved toward the steep bluff behind him. "I know you're alone. Care to explain what you're doing way out here by yourself, boy?"

He watched me? For how long? Rachel's pulse raced faster than the mustangs she'd seen a few days ago on the open prairie. *Good thing I decided not to bathe this morning.*

Ever so slowly, she exhaled. *Lord, thank You that he didn't see through my disguise.* She peeked toward the bluff overlooking her campsite where the cowboy had pointed. Obviously, he hadn't spied her grandpa resting in the shadows.

The unwelcomed masquerade worked again. This wasn't the first time since they'd left Dodge City she'd been mistaken for a teenage boy. Her papa's old clothes swallowed her, even though he'd been a small man, and she tried to ignore the tight fabric around her chest, binding her feminine attributes. The hardest part of the facade had been cutting her long, wavy tresses. A thin piece of leather held back her shoulder-length hair, and an old floppy felt hat added to the illusion.

Rachel studied the stranger, praying desperately. The man didn't have the look of a hardened outlaw, but she well knew looks could be deceiving. "Can I p–put my hands down?"

"I reckon it wouldn't hurt. I'd be the laughingstock of my family if I couldn't whip a kid your size." Amusement flickered in the eyes that met hers, and his lips curled into a broad grin.

The man took a good look around. Seeming satisfied she posed no danger, he holstered the gun and casually crossed his long arms over his wide chest. The confidence oozing from him did nothing to calm Rachel's pounding heart. She thought again about him watching her, and the hard, dried biscuit she'd had for breakfast churned in her stomach.

"Well?" he prompted.

"Well, what?" She lifted her chin to meet his gaze. He must have been more than six feet tall by the way he towered over her.

"The name's Joshua Stafford, and all the land you can see for miles around belongs to my family. Why are you camped here?"

Rachel straightened to her full height, which barely brought her to the bottom of the cowboy's slightly cleft chin. The man's tanned chin was darkened by several days' worth of stubble. She boldly met his gaze. Bluffing her way out of this mess would require showing the absence of fear.

"Do you have any proof of ownership? If so, I'd be obliged to see it."

Instant surprise registered on the man's handsome face.

Her gaze darted to the large boulder, ten feet away, where her Sharp's carbine rifle had fallen when she'd set it down to wash up. A clump of tall weeds hid it from the man's view. Looking straight at the cowboy again, she eased toward the weapon. "Maybe you're just a squatter, and you want this nice camping spot for yourself."

One dark eyebrow rose, and his cocky grin broadened at her challenge. A dimple creased his left cheek, giving him a charming, boyish look. When he smiled like that, his eyes all but disappeared in a squint under his thick, dark lashes. In spite of her nervousness, she couldn't help admiring the man standing in front of her.

"You've got spunk. That's good, kid. Might just keep you alive." With hands resting on his holster, he stepped closer. "But I still don't know your name or why you're out here alone. C'mon, you can trust me. Let me help you."

Rachel slowly moved to her right. Joshua Stafford seemed decent enough, but so had many of the men in Dodge City until she'd gotten to know them. *Trust him?* Only about as far as she would trust the hind end of a spooked skunk. She needed to draw him away from where her grandpa slept in the shadow of the cliff—and she needed her rifle.

"Tell me your name at least."

"Lee. Lee Donovan." He didn't need to know Lee was her middle name, and she wanted to avoid lying. To protect her, Grandpa had stretched the truth a mite to some of the people they'd encountered, but she'd promised God and herself that she wouldn't.

Joshua Stafford moved another step closer, touched the brim of his hat, and nodded. "Well, Lee Donovan, it's a pleasure to make your acquaintance." The warmth of his voice echoed in his wide smile. For a moment, Rachel wanted to trust him more than she'd ever put faith in anyone. But that could be dangerous. He stared intently at her for a few seconds, then his eyebrows slanted and his smile faltered.

"What're you doing way out here on foot?" He waved his hand through the air. "You can't be more than fourteen or so."

Fourteen. Rachel schooled her features to keep from smiling. Wouldn't he be surprised to find out she was a twenty-year-old woman?

"This is dangerous territory. Where's your horse? And where are your folks? A boy your age has no business out in this wild country alone." He yanked off his sweat-stained hat and smacked it against his thigh.

Rachel took advantage of his chatter to edge closer to her goal. A few more steps and she'd be within reach of her Sharp's. A blur of movement snagged her attention. She'd taken her eyes off the handsome cowboy a moment too long.

Quick strides of his long-legged gait brought him dangerously close. Rachel lunged to her right. The cowboy slammed his hat to the ground and reached for her arm, snagging her sleeve. Rachel jerked and twisted loose from his grasp and dove toward her weapon. She landed on the hard ground with a thud. Pain radiated through her head and chest. She secured her tilting hat with one hand while the other stretched toward the rifle. *Please, God, I almost have it.* She dug her toes in the dirt and inched her body forward. Her fingertips brushed the cool metal of the gun barrel just as the cowboy grabbed her ankles.

"Oh, no you don't."

Rachel desperately clawed the ground for a fingerhold as the man pulled her by the ankles through the dirt.

"Let me go!" Like a fish out of water, she flopped and twisted, fighting against his firm hold. She felt her feet slipping loose from Papa's oversized boots. *Please help me, God*, her mind screamed. One more hard jerk and her feet slid free. With empty boots suddenly in hand, the stranger stumbled backward. Rachel jumped up, pressing her hat back down, and grabbed her rifle.

She heard her boots hit the ground behind her. "Stop it," the man roared. "You fool kid. I'm not going to hurt you."

Ignoring him, Rachel cocked the carbine and pivoted to face Joshua Stafford— if that was his real name. Once again she stared down the barrel of his revolver. Without taking her eyes off him, she spat out the dirt that coated her tongue and teeth. Her wrist and side ached; her pulse throbbed in her ears. She wondered if Joshua Stafford had any idea how deep her fear ran. If only she *could* trust him. But how could she trust a stranger holding a gun on her?

"Well, kid, look's like we've got us a Mexican standoff."

His cocky grin returned.

Chapter 2

Josh might have kicked himself if his leg hadn't still been throbbing from where Lee had walloped him during their scuffle. If his brothers could see him now, standing here squared off against this puny kid, he'd be the laughingstock of the Stafford family. It was one thing to be the one making the jokes, but he didn't like being on the receiving end.

He refocused his thoughts on the boy in front of him. The kid couldn't be more than five foot four. Lee's faded blue shirt hung loose, shoulders sagging. The cuffs had been torn off, probably because they would have hung clear past his fingertips otherwise. Ragged dingy blue pants held up with a frayed rope belt dragged on the ground.

The kid had guts all right, but deep in those big brown eyes, Josh recognized fear and vulnerability. He could never shoot this boy.

"Lee, put the rifle down. I told you, I mean you no harm." With one hand held up in surrender, Josh took a chance and lowered his pistol. "See, I'm gonna put my gun away."

Just like the mantel clock in the parlor at home, Josh's heart pounded out the seconds as they ticked by. The creek's peaceful rippling and the birds singing their cheerful serenade seemed out of place in light of the tense standoff. As Josh lowered his gun into the holster, from somewhere behind him he heard a noise. A human cough.

With a skill earned by years of practice, Josh whipped out the pistol again. He spun around and scanned the area, listening for human sounds. For a full hour, he'd watched the kid from the cliff above and seen no other signs of life, not even a horse. He still didn't see anything except for a pitiful old mule munching grass in the shadow of a huge oak tree.

"Is everything okay, Ray?"

Josh stiffened at the gravelly voice. There *was* another person here, maybe two. The man had called for Ray. Squinting, Josh stared into the shaded area next to the cliff. He saw a small lean-to with a man lying inside. He took a step toward the man but stopped suddenly when something jabbed his side.

"You can stop right there," Lee hissed.

Closing his eyes tightly, Josh berated himself for his carelessness. In all his twenty-one years, he'd never been on the wrong end of a rifle. He could probably wrestle it away from the boy, but he didn't want to get shot in the process.

"All right, kid, I'm putting my gun down. Just don't get trigger-happy."

Josh squatted and laid his revolver on the ground. He stood and slowly turned to face Lee. "Now what?"

"Back up." Lee jerked the end of the rifle through the air, motioning him back.

When Josh had moved halfway to where the man lay, Lee stepped forward. Never taking his eyes off him, the boy squatted and picked up the gun. Josh narrowed his eyes. This might be his best chance to take the kid since he couldn't shoot the heavy rifle one-handed and Josh's revolver was most likely too heavy for him also.

"What's going on out there? Ray, you okay?" the man's raspy voice called again.

"Nothing, Grandpa. Everything's fine."

Grandpa. So the kid had an old man with him, hurt or sick from the sound of him. What happened? And where were their horses? Josh glanced around but still didn't see signs of them. Surely they had more sense than to travel cross-country with just that old mule.

"There's no one else here, if that's what you're looking for," Lee volunteered.

"So, who's Ray?"

"I am," the kid said.

Josh narrowed his eyes. "But you said your name was Lee."

For a fraction of a second, something akin to panic flashed across Lee's face. His pursed lips and furrowed brow betrayed the inner struggle taking place. Josh wondered what he was hiding.

"Don't you have two names? Grandpa calls me Ray, but Lee is my middle name. You can call me whatever you want. It doesn't really matter."

"Okay, kid. How 'bout I call you Peewee?"

Lee's eyes flashed with outrage. "Stop grinning like a possum."

With effort, Josh forced the smile from his face. "So, where are your horses?"

Josh stared at the boy. If he wasn't mistaken, the kid blushed. . .or maybe he was flushed from their tussle and all those clothes he wore.

"Gone," Lee whispered. His lips pursed into a thin line.

"Did you say gone?" To lose your horse in this part of the country could be deadly. Josh bit back his retort when he looked at Lee. The kid seemed to be on the verge of tears. Josh didn't handle tears well.

"Umm. . ." Lee sucked in a ragged breath and straightened. "Grandpa's horse had a run-in with a rattlesnake. Scared her so bad, she reared and threw him, then ran off. I jumped off my horse to check on Grandpa, and mine followed his. The only one I managed to hang on to was our pack mule. I know it's stupid." With Josh's gun in his hand, Lee tapped his hat back down and looked off in the distance. He murmured, "I think Grandpa's leg is broken."

The weight of both the gun and rifle was taking its toll on Lee's thin arms. His head hung down, and he stirred a circle in the dirt with the toe of his holey sock. Every few seconds, Lee would glance up at Josh and raise the rifle as if to hold him back. Then, slowly, the rifle would drift toward the ground again.

Josh's heart ached for the boy. Coming from a large family, he couldn't imagine what it must feel like to be stranded out there with only an injured old man for companionship. He wanted to help them, but first he had to gain the kid's confidence.

"At least you hung on to the most important thing. You managed to save your supplies and your rifle. I'd say that's rather smart." Keeping his eye on the rifle, Josh took a deep breath and slowly closed the space between the two of them. He laid his hand on Lee's shoulder. The kid shrugged it away but not before Josh caught a hint of a smile on his lips.

"Lee," Josh spoke in a calm, soothing voice, like he'd use on a spooked horse. "I can help you and your grandpa if you let me. You can't stay out here alone. My family has a big ranch, and we can put you two up 'til your grandpa mends. My grandma's done a fair share of doctoring in her time. I'm sure she can help your grandpa."

Lee shook his head, but his expression softened. He was wavering.

"I have a big family, and we're God-fearing folk. You'll be safe with us." The kid's eyebrows quirked up at his comment. Obviously something he'd said hit home. "Think of your grandpa. If he does have a broken leg, we have medicine for the pain. He's probably hurtin' real bad. C'mon, let me help you."

Biting his bottom lip, the kid looked toward his grandpa for a long moment then back to Josh. His coffee-colored eyes penetrated clear into Josh's soul, as if searching for some truth to cling to. With a long sigh, he glanced away. When Lee looked back, his face was steeled with resolve. He nodded his head. Once. Barely discernible. Lee lowered his rifle and Josh's gun.

Josh realized he'd been holding his breath and released a loud sigh. For a moment, he thought he'd have to fight to get the weapons. He plastered his ever-present grin back in place, and Lee's expression darkened. With a sizzling glare, the kid slammed Josh's gun back into his hand.

I like your spunk, kid. Josh chuckled to himself and shook his head as he watched Lee snatch up his boots and march toward his grandpa.

Chapter 3

Sitting on a sun-warmed boulder, Rachel twisted the worn sock around so her big toe didn't stick out the hole, then slid her boot back on. She stared at the contraption attached behind Emma, her mule. "What did you call that thing, Mr. Stafford? A trapeze?"

He secured the rope to Emma's pack and turned around, grinning at her. The lunch she'd just eaten, courtesy of his fine hunting skills, did a flip-flop in her stomach.

"A travois. I learned how to make it from some Indians who passed through with an injured brave when I was a kid. And call me Josh—everybody does."

"You're sure it's safe, uh, Josh?" Rachel stared at the apparatus, feeling almost as uncomfortable about Grandpa using it as she did calling Josh by his first name.

Josh had taken two long, straight tree limbs and stripped them of their smaller branches. With his lariat, he'd woven a weblike section between the two branches. Rachel folded Grandpa's blanket and placed it over the ropes. Josh attached the long poles to either side of Emma and lashed them to the pack carrying their supplies.

Chuckling, Josh checked the rope. "Don't look so worried. My brothers and I made a travois once, and we gave each other rides. May be a little bumpy, but it'll serve its purpose. Your grandpa will be more comfortable riding on it than he would with his leg hanging down and being jostled around on my horse." He jerked the knot tight. "That ought to hold the pack. Let's see if your grandpa's awake." Josh glanced up at the sky. "We need to head out soon."

A short while later, Rachel watched Josh's plaid shirt tighten across his broad shoulders as he lowered her grandpa onto the contraption. She took a steadying breath, squelching further thoughts about Josh's physique. She looked at the trav. . .thing again, still not too confident in the flimsy device, but surely if she walked beside him, Grandpa would be fine.

"How's that feel, Mr. Donovan?"

Josh squatted beside Grandpa. The tall cowboy had been nothing but kind and respectful to him. Though she'd never admit it to his face, Rachel was grateful for his take-charge attitude. The pressure of worrying over her grandpa and the lost horses had taken its toll on her frayed nerves. She wondered if a home in Texas was worth all the risks. In her excitement to get to their new home, she never dreamed crossing No Man's Land would include facing outlaws, snakes, bugs, and runaway horses;

sleeping on the ground on the open range; and wrestling for a rifle with a ruggedly handsome cowboy.

"This thing feels fine and dandy, young man. Call me Ian. Nobody calls me Mr. Donovan, 'specially someone who might jes' have saved my life."

"Yes, sir, Ian. We'll go slow and take our time so it won't be too rough on you. Normally, my ranch is about a half day's ride from here, but at our pace, it will take us until tomorrow evening, most likely, to get home."

Rachel threw her blanket over her grandpa and smashed her hat down again. Grandpa had told her to never take it off in anybody's presence, or they'd probably be able to guess she was a woman.

"You ready, Lee?"

"Doesn't Grandpa need a hat to cover his eyes? Somehow his got lost when the horses ran off."

"So, can't you give him yours?" Josh suggested.

"No! Uh, it's too small." Rachel smashed the old felt hat tighter on her head. She held it down just in case Josh had any funny ideas about taking it away.

He squinted at her like he wanted to say something, but he didn't. He looked past her to Grandpa, and his face exploded into that crazy grin. "Let it never be said that a Stafford refused to help an old man or a kid." He doffed his hat, bowed stiffly, then walked over and handed it to Grandpa.

"Thanks," Ian mumbled.

"Let's mount up." Josh picked up his horse's reins.

"I'm walking next to Grandpa," Rachel said.

Josh folded his arms across his chest. After a moment, he brushed a hand through his straight dark hair and sighed. "No, you're not. We've got many miles to cover, and I don't need you getting hurt, too."

"Well, I can't exactly ride on Emma with her carrying the pack and pulling Grandpa."

Josh sighed. "You can ride with me."

Rachel sucked in a breath and felt her eyes widen. She hadn't even thought of that. Josh walked toward her as she shook her head.

"You're not still scared of me, are you?"

She took a step back. Scared wasn't the word she had in mind.

"The way you're acting, you'd think I were Jesse James. Come on, we need to get going. We don't have time for this nonsense." Josh smashed his fists to his waist.

How could she sit all day, riding behind this stranger? Every man she'd ever spent time with in Dodge City had either asked her to marry him or tried to force himself on her. Even though she'd wanted so badly to be married and have a family, she'd never been able to get close to a man she liked. Now she was supposed to sit behind Joshua Stafford for two whole days.

She shook her head. "No. I'm walking next to Grandpa."

Rachel turned and strode over to the travois. Grandpa lay there with Josh's hat covering the top part of his face. She stiffened when she heard Josh's footsteps behind her.

Quick as a flash of lightning, her feet left the ground. She clawed the air, grabbing hold of the back of Josh's shirt as he flung her over his shoulder. Her stomach smashed hard against his solid shoulder, jarring her insides. One-handed, she grabbed for her hat as it flew off her head and flopped to the ground.

"Are you always so stubborn?" Josh's breath, warm against her leg, sent frustrating tingles down her spine.

She could hear Grandpa's muffled laugh from underneath Josh's hat. The last thing she wanted was for Grandpa to side with this rugged hooligan. Rachel pummeled his back. "Put me down."

"As you wish, your majesty."

Rachel felt Josh suck in a deep breath. The next moment, she flew through the air, arms flailing, and landed on the back of his horse. She clawed the saddle horn to keep from falling, and both boots slipped off her feet from the jarring landing. Her chest heaved with anger and humiliation.

"Here, your majesty."

Josh smacked her hat against her thigh. Rachel dared to glare down at him. Their gazes locked, and his self-confident smile evaporated into a confused frown. She quickly snatched her hat and slapped it back on her head. Disconcerted, she crossed her arms and pointedly looked away.

·:⁝:·

Josh tucked Lee's boots in a corner of the supply pack. This way, he rationalized, he wouldn't have to worry about them sliding off Lee's feet all the time. He glanced at the pitiful excuse for boots. Never could he remember having to wear any that scruffy. What was the story behind them?

For the third time, Josh checked Emma's lead rope. Firmly tied to his saddle, and with Lee's leg anchoring it down, he felt certain it was secure. Josh glanced at Lee's stiff back and the shoulder-length hair pulled back patriot style and tied with a leather strip. He could see why the kid wore that scruffy hat all the time. He knew some women in town who'd kill for curly golden hair like Lee's. First thing after getting the boy cleaned up and fed would be a haircut.

Josh shook his head in an effort to rid it of the strange thoughts he'd been entertaining. With those long eyelashes and big brown eyes, the poor kid looked almost pretty enough to be a girl. All that would change, though, soon as he filled out and started growing whiskers.

No wonder he'd fought so well—probably had to in school. Josh could imagine the teasing the boy must have endured. He knew. Being the youngest of three boys, he always fell prey to his brothers' pranks and schemes.

With Ian injured like he was, the pair would probably be around the ranch for several weeks. Maybe he could use the time to toughen up the kid.

Josh led Sultan over to a large boulder and climbed onto it so he could mount without knocking Lee off. He glanced up at the golden curls that had escaped the confines of Lee's hat. *Poor kid.* He sighed, shaking his head. The saddle squeaked as he sat down in front of Lee. Sultan snorted and pawed the hard ground, anxious to be on the way.

Josh shook his head. *Too bad the kid doesn't have an older sister. If she had his wavy wheat-colored hair and big brown doelike eyes, I'd be a goner.*

Chapter 4

Rachel felt herself falling and awoke with a jerk. She yawned then smiled when she realized she wasn't dreaming. Her arms were wrapped around her father's waist, and his warm hand held tight to her forearm. He wouldn't let her fall. Her head rested against the rock-hard muscles of his back. The steady rocking of the horse's gait and the soft squeaking of the saddle threatened to lull her back to sleep. Gentle vibrations tickled her cheek as she listened to the mellow song her pa sang. What was that tune? It sounded vaguely familiar. "Carry Me Back to Ole Virginny."

Rachel bolted upright! Though the War Between the States had ended nearly a quarter of a century ago, her papa had remained a Yankee all his days. He'd never sing such a song. Her nostrils flared, and her jaw tightened as she clenched her teeth. She'd been lying against Josh's back, and he still maintained a tight grip on her wrist. The once warm sensation now burned her forearm like a branding iron. She tried to jerk it away, but he held it firmly.

"Let go of me," she hissed with the venom of a diamondback rattler.

"So, you're finally awake," he drawled in a smooth accent that held just a hint of the South. "Thought you might sleep the whole day."

"Why are you holding on to me?"

"Me? You started to fall and grabbed me around the waist, hanging on for dear life."

"Did not!" she said, jerking her hands free with such fierceness that she lost her balance. Her arms flapped in the air like a chicken with clipped wings until she managed to grab hold of Josh's waist again. His low, rumbling chuckle made her want to punch him. Instead, she released him and crossed her arms.

Josh went back to his singing. His voice, though not as deep as many men's, had a clear, crisp tone. Rachel could envision him crooning with his ranch hands around an evening campfire.

After a while, he quieted, and they rode in comfortable silence. "So, you gonna tell me what you two are doing out here?"

His words jarred her out of her musing. "I don't see how that's any of your business."

"I reckon it is since I came to your rescue."

That seemed fair. He probably saved their lives. She bit down on her bottom lip and contemplated how much to tell him. "Grandpa and I are traveling to my uncle's

351

ranch near Amarillo. We're going to live with him."

"Where do you hail from?"

"Dodge City."

Josh rubbed the back of his neck. His tanned hand ruffled the long, dark hair that fringed his collar, and Rachel had a fleeting desire to smooth it back down. She shook her head to rid it of the errant thought. There was no sense allowing herself to be attracted to Joshua Stafford. She wouldn't be staying long at their ranch—and besides, she still hadn't decided whether she could trust him or not.

"Well, looks like you made it about halfway. Why didn't you just take the stage? Would have been a lot faster and safer."

Rachel stiffened and took a quick breath. She couldn't tell him they were running away from the man who killed her papa. Cyrus Lawton. A snake who used his appealing good looks to charm women. She'd fallen under his spell, but when she realized her mistake and tried to cut off their relationship, Cy had tried to force himself on her.

Rachel straightened, determined not to cry, though remembering that tragic day always made her weep. She sniffed and wiped her moist eyes. If she didn't get control of her emotions, Josh would surely figure she was a woman.

Rachel remembered the scene as if it just happened. She'd been alone, cleaning Pa's barbershop, when Cy confronted her. He'd made the mistake of pulling down the shades to hide his deed. When her pa came back from the bank and saw the shades down, he must have become suspicious because he came into the shop instead of going on home. Cy had already wrestled her to the ground. Her pa grabbed the broom as he raced toward them. But Cy deftly pulled a small pistol from his jacket and shot her father. *Oh, Papa.*

"Hey? You fall asleep again, or did you just fall off?" She heard the smile in Josh's voice. When she didn't respond, Josh lithely lifted his right leg over the saddle horn and twisted around, sitting sideways in the saddle.

Rachel felt her eyes widen, and her breath slowed at the closeness of his face. Her heart raced as her gaze locked with his. Sapphires—his eyes reminded her of dark-blue sapphires, just like the ones in Melba Phillips's wedding ring.

Rachel lowered her gaze. A dark shadow of whiskers shaded his tanned face, and his strong chin was etched with a shallow cleft. Why couldn't she have met him before . . .before her life had broken into fragments like the tiny shards of a shattered mirror?

She clenched her fists and squeezed her eyes tightly shut. *Stop it! Stop it!* She had to stop thinking this way. Anger filled her being. Anger that she'd lost their horses. Anger over her papa's senseless death. Anger that Cyrus Lawton had nearly had his way with her. Anger that Josh Stafford could affect her so.

She opened her eyes and glared up at him.

He leaned back a fraction, and his eyebrows shot up. "Whoa! What'd I do now?"

"Nothing," she blurted out. "Just turn around."

Josh's lips tightened into a mock smile, and he gave her a brief salute. "Yes, sir, whatever you say, boss."

Rachel breathed a sigh of relief when he turned. She was tired, weary, and would like nothing more than to close her eyes and go to sleep in a big, soft bed.

Why, God? Why did You have to let Papa get killed? You already have Mama. Wasn't she enough? Don't You know how much I needed Pa? Are You going to take Grandpa from me, too?

⁘

Near the end of her second day of riding behind Josh, a soft mooing drew Rachel's attention away from counting the squares in Josh's blue plaid shirt to a herd of cattle peacefully grazing on a nearby hill. As they rode through the herd, the cows raised their heads almost in unison and stared at them with bovine incredulity. She'd never seen so many cattle. She glanced back at Grandpa then inched closer to Josh.

"Are all these yours?"

Josh nodded. "Yep! But this is only a small herd. We have a lot more out on the south range. We brought this batch up a couple weeks ago so we could brand the new calves."

"Do you like raising cattle?"

He didn't answer her immediately, and she'd begun to think he didn't hear her.

"Well, since you asked, I don't dislike it." He paused again. "But my secret dream is to raise horses. I love working with horses. They're so much smarter than cows. Besides, I think there's a real opportunity to sell good stock horses to the army and to other ranches in these parts."

He reached back and massaged his neck. After a deep sigh, he continued. "My brothers won't give me a chance to try; they keep me busy working the cattle all the time. It's just that they'll always think of me as the younger brother. Lou, my sister, is younger than me, but she gets more respect than I do."

Josh looped his leg around the saddle horn and turned sideways again. Rachel leaned back a fraction and grasped hold of the saddle's cantle to keep from falling off. She thought about asking him to turn around, but his serious tone held her silent.

"When I was little, I had a hard time concentrating on one thing for very long. I tended to start a job and not finish it. My dad was always quoting the verse in the Bible to me about finishing the race. 'Be a finisher, Joshua,' he kept telling me." He looked down and fiddled with the reins. "School was hardest for me, but Grandma and Lou never gave up, and I finally learned. I even read more than my brothers now. But Micah and Sam still look at me as that flighty kid. No matter what I do, I can't seem to prove myself to them."

Rachel noticed the rise and fall of Josh's chest as he released a huge breath. She wondered how hard it had been for him to share his feelings. This was the first time he had shared anything personal, and she realized that this strong, confident cowboy might be vulnerable, too. Her heart softened toward him in that moment.

⁘

Why did I tell that scrawny kid all my secrets? Josh smacked his forehead with his palm. It was too late to take it all back. He sighed and wondered what Lee would do with the information. *Probably nothing. Maybe I'm just making a mountain out of a molehill.*

The truth was, he'd felt an instant connection with the stranded boy, at least he did once Lee had quit trying to shoot him. He smiled at the memory. Grandma would call Lee a kindred spirit. Josh wondered if this was the way a man felt toward a younger brother. He scowled. Well, he wouldn't make the same mistakes his brothers had made. He would trust Lee and try to teach him and guide him while he was at the ranch. This could actually be fun—if only he could get Lee to fully trust him.

Josh thought back to the time Lou had been sprayed by a skunk. He sighed. It had been funny at the time, but now he saw how immature he'd acted. And he had failed to bring Lou's clothes back—all because of a horse. When would he quit failing people? Taking Lee under his wing and toughening up the sissified boy might just go a long way in showing his family that he'd matured and could be trusted.

He heard Lee's loud gasp and reined Sultan to a stop atop the hill.

"Is that your ranch?" Lee asked, the astonishment evident in his voice.

"Yep! That's the Crossed S—actually we've been on it ever since I found you."

This location was one of Josh's favorites. Whenever he'd been gone for a time, he liked to stop on top of this hill and survey his home. Warmth and peace flooded him. Spring was the best time of year to enjoy the view, before the killing heat of summer dried everything out. Thanks to recent rains, fresh sprigs of newborn grass created a lush green carpet across the countryside. White and yellow wildflowers lifted their tiny faces toward the sky as if in praise to God. Normally, he would breathe in their fresh, floral fragrance, but with a couple hundred head of cattle nearby, Josh reconsidered taking a deep whiff.

Eager to be home, he spurred his horse forward. As they rode down the hill toward the ranch, he realized something for the first time. Someday, when he met the woman he wanted to spend his life with, this very hill was the spot where he'd propose. He smiled to himself, surprised at the direction his thoughts had taken him. *I wonder just how many years will pass before that happens.*

He shook his head and directed his thoughts back to his brothers. Though they didn't totally put their confidence in him, he knew without a doubt they loved him. And then there were Lou and Grandma. Josh thanked God again for his close-knit family. They weren't perfect, but he loved them all.

"I didn't realize it would be so big."

"It has to be big; lots of people live there. Micah, my oldest brother, and my sister, Lou, are both married. Deborah, Micah's wife, is with child. Then there's Grandma. She's a wildcat and needs lots of room. And there's Sam and me."

"You're lucky to have such a nice home and a big family." Lee's sigh tickled the hairs on the back of Josh's neck. "I always wanted to be part of a big family."

Josh barely heard the whispered words. The yearning in Lee's voice tugged at his heart.

"What about your parents?" Lee asked.

"They're dead. Have been for a while."

"Guess we have something in common."

Josh nodded and pointed out a smaller building near the large barn. "That's the bunkhouse. I'll drop you off and get you settled before I take care of the animals."

Lee inhaled a sharp breath, making Josh wonder what he'd said wrong this time.

Chapter 5

The bunkhouse. *I never even considered that. I can't stay in a bunkhouse full of men. Oh, Lord, what am I going to do?* Rachel's stomach churned, and she looked down at her trembling hands.

Josh reined his horse to a stop in front of a long wooden building. Several rocking chairs and discolored spittoons decorated the simple porch. The windows were raised, and blue gingham curtains could be seen flapping in the light breeze. *Probably Grandma Stafford's handiwork*, Rachel thought.

Josh hopped down and tied his horse to the hitch in front of the bunkhouse. "Hang on a second, and I'll get your boots."

Rachel chewed on her bottom lip, contemplating what to do. She couldn't stay in that bunkhouse with a bunch of men. Maybe she should tell Josh she was a woman and just get it over with. She shook her head, knowing the truth. *I'm chicken. I'm scared of his reaction.*

"Here, give me your foot." Josh slipped on one boot. "You sure got little feet," he said as he walked around to the other side. After sliding the other boot on, he looked up at Rachel. "Need help getting down, city boy?" He grinned from ear to ear as if it was the best joke he'd heard all day.

He has no idea that I really am the joke of the day. Rachel shook her head and gave him a tight-lipped smile. "I think I can manage. Maybe you could get Grandpa some fresh water."

"Good idea. Wouldn't mind some myself," he drawled. Rachel liked the smooth, easy timbre of his voice. Josh had mentioned that his family came west from Virginia when he was young. He still maintained a hint of a southern accent. It was a good thing her papa wasn't here, because that would have been enough for him to dislike the man. Rachel breathed a sigh of relief that Grandpa wasn't so prejudiced.

Now, what to do? She looked around and saw several men gathered at the corral watching another cowboy working with a spirited horse. They hee-hawed and nudged each other in the side when the rider got bucked off and landed on his back in the dirt.

"Lee, come here. I need you to hold the mule steady while I pick Ian up."

"Sure." Rachel grabbed hold of the saddle horn and half slid, half fell to the ground. Dusting her hands on her filthy pants, she walked toward Josh on shaky legs and grabbed hold of Emma's halter. "How you doing, Grandpa? You feeling okay?"

355

"I'm okay. Just a bit tired from all the jostling around. I'll be right as rain soon as I get me a good night's sleep and somethin' to eat."

"Come on, sir. Let's get you in bed, and then I'll get Grandma or Lou to take a look at your leg. They're both mighty good at fixin' things."

Rachel stood there holding the mule and watched Josh carry Grandpa into the bunkhouse. She contemplated whether she could stay in the bunkhouse with him until the men came in then make a quick exit. Maybe she could find a place in the barn to sleep tonight—but that would mean deserting Grandpa.

Just then, a tall, skinny man with a beard came around the corner of the barn and walked directly toward her. He gave a brief nod of his thin head and walked past her and into the bunkhouse. *So much for that idea.*

Josh came back out, walking with purpose. He had retrieved his hat from Grandpa, and it was back on, covering up his sunburned forehead. "I'm gonna run up to the house and get Grandma or Lou. Can you get your grandpa that drink and water the animals? The pump's over there." He waved a hand toward the barn and took off, not waiting for a response.

Rachel was grateful for the reprieve. It took her awhile working at Josh's tight knots before she was able to get the mule untied. She gathered the horse's reins and led the two animals to the trough near the barn. While they drank, she wrestled with the pack until she managed to pull out her beat-up tin cup. One day, she'd have some pretty dishes and glasses and maybe even a fine house like Josh's.

Rachel studied her hands. Never before had they looked so awful. Every fingernail had dirt under it, and each was chipped from the hard, physical labor of the past weeks. Her mother's hands had been beautiful, soft, and gentle. Rachel had loved to sit next to her mother and watch her sew. Rose Donovan was famous in Dodge City for her expert embroidery. Before she died, she had taught Rachel her signature stitch—a spiderweb rose. She longed to get back to her sewing. It was one of the few times she still felt close to her mother.

She heard scuffling and looked up to see Josh and a young woman about her own age coming toward her. "Lee, this is my sister, Louisa Chamberlain. She'll take good care of your grandpa. I'll take the animals to the barn and feed them and give them a rubdown." He flashed his trademark grin then took the reins and her tin cup from her hands. "I think we can supply you with a decent cup. You won't need this old thing anymore."

Rachel scowled as he walked away. That "old thing" was her only cup.

"Call me Lou."

Rachel turned toward the young woman.

"Josh told me all about finding you two. Must have been pretty scary being stranded like you were. Come on, let's have a look at your grandpa. You think his leg is broke?"

Rachel liked Lou. She seemed to have the same easygoing gift of gab as Josh. The resemblance between the two amazed her. They both had the same big smile and dark hair. Lou's eyes were a lighter shade of blue than Josh's stunning sapphire eyes. Lou stood a few inches taller than Rachel, probably making her about five foot six.

"Hello, in the bunkhouse. Everyone decent?" Lou called.

"Yep." A single deep acknowledgment rang forth.

Lou marched in as if she owned the place. Come to think of it, she did. Rachel followed, stopping at the doorway. If Lou could go in, why couldn't she? After a moment, she stepped across the threshold and allowed her eyes to adjust to the dim interior.

"Hi, Slim," Lou said.

"Hey, Miss Lou. I'll just head back out 'til you've finished up in here."

"No need for that. I shouldn't be too long."

"Ain't no problem, ma'am. I'll come back later." Slim rose from his bunk and slipped quietly out the door.

Lou knelt beside Grandpa's bunk and began unwrapping his leg. Gently, she probed it and tried to bend it at the knee. Rachel bit the inside of her lip when Grandpa winced and cried out. Lou shook her head.

"There, there, I'm done for now. You just lay back and rest, Sir." Lou patted Grandpa's shoulder.

"Thanks, Ma'am," Grandpa's hoarse voice whispered.

Lou nodded her head toward the door. Rachel followed her outside, apprehension swirling in her belly.

"It looks like it might be broken, but it's so swollen that I'm not sure. We need to have Grandma take a look at it. I'll go see if she can come down before dinner and check your grandpa. She was up to her elbows in biscuit dough when I left." Lou smiled. "I think he'll be fine, Lee. I'll be back in a little bit. Can I bring you anything?"

Rachel wanted so badly to confess her secret to this friendly young woman, but she was unsure. She shook her head. Lou smiled and walked toward the house.

Suddenly, Rachel knew she couldn't let her leave without knowing the truth. "Lou, wait."

Lou stopped in her tracks and spun around. Her dark braid swirled, smacking her in the chest. She rubbed at the spot and stared back, dark eyebrows raised.

"I need to talk to you for a minute before you go. If that's okay?"

Lou smiled. "Of course."

Rachel walked over to her and saw Josh exiting the barn. *It's now or never.* She leaned toward Lou, taking her gently by the arm, and quickly whispered the situation in her ear. As Rachel stepped back, she heard the quick intake of Lou's breath. Her eyes were wide with astonishment, but she recovered quickly and nodded. Her mouth tilted in a one-sided, tight-lipped grin as she watched Josh coming toward them. Lou leaned toward Rachel and whispered, "Don't tell Josh yet. This will be *so* much fun."

⁙

Josh slowed as he closed the gap between himself, and Lou and Lee. He narrowed his eyes as he watched his sister. Lee whispered something in her ear, and Lou looked shocked half to death. What could the boy have told her? Surely Lee wasn't already sharing Josh's dream with everybody.

Lou crossed her arms and glared at him. Uh-oh. This didn't look good.

"Joshua Stafford, you should be ashamed of yourself. Why in the world would you bring a man injured as badly as Mr. Donovan to the bunkhouse? You just march in there and get him and take him up to the house."

Josh stood there with his mouth open. What had gotten into her? Lou sure had gotten bossy in the few weeks she'd been married. She didn't say anything earlier about bringing Ian to the house.

He glanced at Lee. The boy's cheeks actually looked pink with embarrassment. Josh felt a small measure of relief that Lee looked almost as surprised as Josh felt. Lou grabbed Lee's arm as if they were best friends and pulled him toward the house.

Dumbfounded, Josh watched them go. Lee looked back over his shoulder, and Josh read his lips. *Sorry.* He was beginning to think he was sorry he ever ran into Lee Donovan. It seemed as if he'd been in trouble ever since.

Chapter 6

L ou burst through the door of a small cottage, dragging Rachel with her. Her laughter echoed through the tiny house. "Did you see his face? That was so much fun."

Rachel didn't think it was much fun. Josh had been so kind to her and Grandpa. She didn't think he deserved being the brunt of a mean joke.

"Rachel, you probably think I'm crazy, but you have to understand. Josh is always teasing us, and we rarely have a good chance to get back at him. Remind me to tell you the skunk story. He's so meticulous in everything he does that we rarely ever catch him off balance."

Rachel considered that for a moment. Obviously, Josh wasn't aware that his family considered his work nearly flawless.

A tall, good-looking man entered from the other room.

"What's all the ruckus, Lou?" He looked at Rachel and smiled.

Lou danced over and hugged him. "You won't believe this, Trent."

Rachel watched the transformation of Trent's face as Lou relayed her story. When she finished, he shook his head. "You're asking for trouble. I don't think this is a good idea."

"Oh, pooh." Lou swatted his arm. "It'll be fun. You'll see. Could you please fetch some water so Rachel can have a bath and get changed before dinner? We have to hurry."

"All right, but let it be known I said this was a bad idea." He turned to face Rachel. She liked his kind face. "By the way, I'm Trent Chamberlain, Louisa's husband. It's a pleasure to make your acquaintance."

Lou put a hand to her mouth. "Oops, sorry. In my excitement, I forgot the introductions. We have two boys running around here somewhere, too. I'll introduce them later."

She tugged Rachel's sleeve. "Come on, Rachel. We need to see if I have anything that will fit you." Lou looped arms with her and dragged her to a small bedroom. Rachel loved the hominess of Lou's cottage. *Someday I'll have a nice place like this.*

Lou tugged open a wardrobe and thumbed through the clothes inside. "Do you mind taking a cold-water bath? We don't have time to heat water before dinner."

Rachel shook her head. "Any kind of bath will feel heavenly. Thank you for what you're doing for Grandpa and me."

There was a loud bang against the wall and a scuffling sound then a knock on the bedroom door frame. Trent stood there with a large round tub. "Is it safe to come in?"

"Sure thing," Lou said as she pulled the door open.

He set the tub in the corner and quickly exited.

Lou rummaged through a trunk, holding up several undergarments. "My yellow dress should fit you, but I don't know if these will work. I'm a bit taller than you." She tossed the pile of off-white bloomers and chemises back into the trunk and slammed the lid. "Oh, I know. While you get your bath, I'll run over and borrow some under things from Deborah. She can't wear her regular ones anyway since she's in a family way."

A short time later, Rachel stepped out of the small tub and reached for the towel on the bed. She felt so invigorated. Her damp hair dripped rivulets of cold water down her back as she dried off. Rachel stiffened at the soft knock on the door. She'd always had privacy when dressing. Papa and Grandpa had been very gracious about disappearing when it was her time to bathe in the small house.

"Yes?"

"It's me. . .Lou. Can I come in?"

Rachel took a deep breath. "I—I guess so."

Lou tumbled into the room, her arms laden with undergarments and clothing, which she dumped on the bed. "Oh, your hair. It's so curly—and blond! Josh will love it."

Josh will love it? Rachel had to stop and think for a moment. *Do I care if Josh loves it?*

Lou's chatter intruded on her thoughts. "You should have seen Grandma's eyes twinkling when I told her about you. She's anxious to meet you. She said another woman would help even the odds with all the men around here. Do you like this one? It's mine. I think it will look good with your blond hair and brown eyes."

Rachel stared at the beautiful yellow dress. It looked like a Sunday-go-to-meeting dress and store bought, too.

"Look!" From behind her back, Lou produced a pair of balmorals.

Rachel gasped. How many times had she stood in front of Jennings Footwear and dreamed of owning a pair of the front-lacing shoes?

"They're real nice, aren't they? Deborah had an extra pair. She said you could keep these if they fit." Lou folded up a brown skirt and soft-blue blouse then laid them on the bed. "You can wear these tomorrow."

Rachel looked at Lou, blinking back the unshed tears stinging her eyes. Never since her mother died had she owned such nice things. Papa and Grandpa had been virtually ignorant in things that were important to a growing young woman. "I don't know how to thank you. Your family has been so kind."

Lou enveloped her in a warm hug. "Now don't you worry about that. I'll have my reward tonight at dinner when I see Josh's face."

A short while later, after Rachel had dressed, the two women sneaked over to the big house. Lou peeked around the mudroom doorway for a moment, and then she ducked back into the small room with an ornery grin lighting her face. Her eyes twinkled, and she bounced with excitement. "Are you ready for your big entrance?"

Rachel shrugged and breathed in the enticing aroma of home-cooked food. Her stomach grumbled, urging her forward. It had been weeks since she'd eaten a real meal.

Though she wondered what Josh would think of her as a woman, she had a very bad feeling about Lou's scheme. But after all the Staffords had done for her and Grandpa, how could she refuse? "Will Grandpa be there?" she whispered.

Lou shook her head. "No, he's on the couch in the office. Grandma took him a plate already, and he's sleeping."

Rachel heaved a sigh. Somehow, she didn't think Grandpa would approve of Lou's little game, either. But what else could she do? Lou had been so nice to her and rescued her from the bunkhouse dilemma. Rachel thought of Josh's cocky smile and his bossiness out on the trail. Maybe it wouldn't hurt to take him down a notch.

"Grandma's seated. Let's go."

"Where's Lou?" Rachel heard a deep voice ask, right before they entered.

"I'm right here, and I've brought a friend." Lou grabbed Rachel's hand and pulled her through the kitchen and into a huge dining room. She felt all eyes turn toward her. Chairs squeaked against the floor when the four men rose to their feet. Two young boys slowly followed their example. Rachel tried to swallow the lump that had suddenly risen to her throat. The tantalizing odor of home-cooked food that moments before had teased her senses now made her stomach roil.

She looked at Josh, and her heart did a little dance. His whiskery face was freshly shaven. A pink, sunburned forehead stood out against his tanned face. The cost of being gallant. She smiled at him. He looked handsome in his dark-blue shirt and black pants. She read the question in his gaze, *Have we met before?*

Rachel felt as if her heart had lodged itself in her esophagus.

Lou cleared her throat and pulled Rachel forward. "Everybody, I'd like to introduce my newest friend, Rachel."

Rachel looked at Lou, who grinned mischievously, winked, then turned toward Josh. "Josh, I believe you already know her."

Every head pivoted toward Josh. His forehead crinkled, and he seemed to be thinking deeply. He shook his head and grinned charmingly, his dimple winking. "Nope. I seriously doubt I'd ever forget meeting someone as lovely as her."

Lou snickered. "Maybe you know her better by her full name. Rachel *Lee* Donovan."

Josh shook his head again, and then it jerked to a stop. Rachel felt impaled by his intense scrutiny. His expression grew still. Serious. His smile held no humor but rather a hint of sadness.

Rachel knew she'd made a terrible mistake.

⁛

Josh couldn't believe his eyes. Lee was a woman, a very pretty woman—and she'd played him for a fool. *Ray stood for Rachel. How could I have been so stupid and blind? I should have listened to my gut.* He knew deep in his gut there was something unusual about that kid. Only she wasn't a kid—not by a long shot.

Suddenly, the whole room exploded in a gale of laughter. Josh looked at Micah and Sam. Both hooted, slapping their palms on the table.

"She really pulled the wool over your eyes, didn't she?" Micah roared.

Sam slapped his thigh and dropped to his chair. "This is the boy you planned on toughening up? Whoowee! This is the best joke to come along in years."

Lou leaned forward in mirth, swiping at the tears running down her cheeks. Deborah turned away but not before he saw her smile. Even Grandma sat there with hand over mouth, trying to hide her chuckling. Timmy and Davy stared at each other as if wondering what was so funny. Josh looked at Trent. He was the only somber one of the group. Josh could tell he didn't approve of Lou's joke.

He glanced at Rachel. Her pretty face looked pale. What had he done to her that she would make him the laughingstock of his family? He'd done his best to make her grandpa comfortable. He'd cared for them and brought them into his own home. And she still didn't trust him enough to be honest with him.

He gritted his teeth and pressed his lips together, seething with anger, humiliation, and hurt. "Well, you all have had your joke; now have your dinner," he uttered in a contemptible voice he barely recognized as his own.

With one last steaming glare at Rachel, he could see that her expression was bleak and she looked on the verge of tears. *Good. She deserves to cry.*

Josh looked to his grandma. "Excuse me, Grandma. Suddenly, I'm not hungry."

He pivoted quickly, knocking his chair back. It crashed loudly behind him as it landed on the hardwood floor. With both hands, Josh shoved open the screen door. Its loud bang reverberating against the wall followed him outside.

It wasn't bad enough that Lee—no, Rachel—had humiliated him in front of his whole family, but even his own heart defied him. In spite of everything, he couldn't deny his instant attraction to the real Lee—Rachel Lee.

Chapter 7

That's about all you can see of the Crossed S on foot." Sam waved his hand in an arc in the direction they'd just come.

"It's very impressive." Leaning on the rails, Rachel lifted her foot onto the lowest rung of the corral fence. "I wonder if my uncle's ranch will look anything like this."

Sam leaned his arms over the railing. "Maybe. Might even be bigger. Some Texans have huge spreads. Where did you say it was?"

"Near Amarillo." Rachel rested her hands on the top rung of the corral and leaned her chin against them, watching two men saddle a horse whose eyes were covered with a red bandana. "What are they doing?"

"That mare is fresh off the prairie." Sam flicked his finger toward the dark-brown horse. "Not broke yet."

"Why do they cover his eyes? Seems like it would scare him."

"Her. That's a female." Sam grinned. Her stomach lurched. He looked so much like Josh. "Actually, covering her eyes calms her down so the men can get her saddled easier."

Josh walked out from behind the back of the barn. Rachel's heart picked up its pace. She hadn't seen him since the previous night's dinner, and he'd been conspicuously absent at breakfast.

Her foot slid off the corral rung, and she straightened. Josh slipped through the rails on the opposite side of the corral and walked toward the horse, yanking on a pair of worn leather gloves. He looked up, and his gaze locked with hers. He stopped so fast the cowboy following right behind him stumbled to a halt, nearly slamming into his back.

"Hey, Josh, don't haul back on the reins so fast," the tall cowboy teased as he hurried by.

Josh's dark brows narrowed into a straight line, and his lips pursed together. One hand reaching toward his well-worn Stetson, he gave her a curt nod then turned toward the saddled horse.

Rachel's pulse kicked up another notch. Josh was still mad. Well, why shouldn't he be? He'd done nothing but help her, and she all but betrayed him. If only she could go back and change things. In her evening prayers last night, she had felt God's prompting to apologize, even though what happened hadn't really been her fault. Still, she could have stopped it if she'd pressed Lou.

Josh hopped onto the back of the horse with the skill of one who had ridden all his life. The jittery animal froze when he landed in the saddle. With a quick flick of his wrist, one of the cowboys yanked the bandana off the horse's eyes. The mare jerked her head, the whites of her eyes showing, nostrils flaring. She held all four legs stiff. Her skin quivered. She snorted twice then exploded.

The next instant, all four hooves were off the ground. Josh held a thick rope rein wrapped tight in each hand. Rachel wanted to scream, "Hold on to the saddle," but couldn't since her heart was lodged in her throat. The horse hit the ground with a loud thud, sending dust flying. Josh's backside landed so hard against the mare's back that his hat went sailing through the air.

Rachel raised a fist to her mouth. He was going to get killed before she had a chance to apologize. The mare arched her back and twisted, looking something like a pretzel Rachel had eaten at a Dodge City carnival. Josh flew through the air, just like his hat had done. Rachel gasped, clutching the corral railing with a white-knuckled grip. He landed hard, stirring up so much dust that it looked like a cloud of smoke. For a moment, he didn't move.

The cowboys' hee-haws and loud guffaws filled the air.

"C'mon, Josh, you gonna let that little filly best you?" a cowboy in a brown plaid shirt hollered. Two others chuckled, nudging each other with their elbows.

"Go on, Josh," Sam yelled. "Show her what you're made of."

Rachel gasped and turned to him. "Don't say that. He's going to get himself killed."

Sam blinked. "Josh lives for this. He loves working with horses."

"I don't care. He's going to hurt himself. If you won't stop him, I will." Rachel bent down and stuck one foot in the corral. The bucking mare flashed by, almost tromping on Rachel's toe. She lunged back, landing on her backside in the dirt.

Sam squatted beside her. "You can't stop him. He'd die of embarrassment if you made a fuss in front of the men. Best you don't cause him any more humiliation after last night. He's still upset." Sam gave her a tight-lipped smile and patted her arm. "He'll come around soon. Josh likes to tease everyone, but he's always had trouble being on the receiving end. Still, he can't hold a grudge for long. It's not in his nature."

Rachel peeked up in time to see Josh knock the dirt off his denim pants and hop back onto the trembling horse. She shook her head at his foolishness. At least she didn't have to sit there and watch him kill himself.

Sam offered her his hand and pulled her up. She left him at the rail, already engrossed in Josh's next ride, and entered the barn. Stalls lined one side of the huge red building. The pungent aroma of wood, hay, and horses blended together, reminding Rachel of the livery stable back in Dodge. Several horses hung their heads over the door of their stall and nickered for handouts. With the double doors at both ends of the barn open, the warm sun shone in. Rachel moseyed along the stalls, stopping to pat each horse that stuck its head out looking for treats.

The last stall was empty, gate wide open. Rachel started to pass by but heard a tiny squeak. Curious, she peered inside. In the corner of the stall, nestled in the sweet-smelling hay, five small puppies growled and frolicked with one another. "Oh, how cute!" She knelt in the hay and picked up the runt, a fluffy golden ball of fur.

"Aren't you a sweetie? Where's your mama?" Rachel rubbed the puppy's soft ear between her finger and thumb. "I bet Shane's your daddy, huh?" She thought of the Staffords' ornery sheepdog.

Leaning her head back against the rough barn wall, Rachel listened to the sweet puppy noises. Their yips and squeals reminded her of a family at play. She'd always wanted a big family, but her mother hadn't been able to carry any of her other four children to term. The last baby had taken Rose Donovan's life when Rachel was just twelve. Did Josh know how lucky he was to have a big, loving family? And this ranch—Rachel had only dreamed of ever living on a ranch. Did Josh appreciate his fine home?

She thought again of her uncle's ranch. What would it be like to live there? Would her cousins be kind and accept her and Grandpa, or would they resent their presence? Anxiety twisted her stomach. As much as she wanted to live on a ranch, she had major reservations about going to her uncle's, but·it had been the only option available after her father was murdered. She closed her eyes. Prayer with her heavenly Father was the only thing that could soothe the anxiety twisting her insides.

"You never listen to me." Rachel recognized Josh's raised voice as he entered the barn.

"I do listen. I'm just not convinced it's a good idea—or that it's the right time."

Rising to her knees, Rachel peeked through the slats of the stall. Josh was talking with Micah, who rested his hand on Josh's shoulder. She wondered what to do. She didn't want to eavesdrop but didn't feel right intruding on their heated discussion.

"You know I'm the best wrangler on the ranch. Between the rustlers and Mother Nature, we never have enough good horses. We gotta have more and better stock." She heard a smack and knew Josh had just whacked his hat against his leg. " 'Sides, last time I was in town, I heard the army's needing good horses, and they're willing to pay top dollar."

Rachel couldn't see Josh's face, but she felt sure he wasn't smiling. Did his brother realize this was Josh's dream—to raise horses?

"Yeah, I've heard that, too. But with things as dry as they are here most of the year, I'm not sure we have enough grass to support the stock we have now plus more horses. I'll think on it and talk to Sam. Right now, though, we need to concentrate on checking out the new calves, and I need your help."

"Micah." One of the cowboys from the corral stood in the barn entrance. "Pete needs you to look at the cows in the south pasture. Seems there's a problem."

"Be right there, Doug. We'll talk later about this idea of yours, Josh." Micah turned and followed the cowboy outside.

"Yeah, sure," Josh mumbled, "always later."

Rachel ducked her head to peer below the stall rail and see what Josh was doing. He yanked on his gloves as he walked over to a large burlap bag filled with something. The overstuffed bag hung from the rafters by a thick rope. He balled his fists and threw a punch that sent the solid bag flying several feet. It drifted back toward him, and Josh hammered both fists into the defenseless object.

Any thoughts Rachel had of making her presence known quickly flew away, just like the dust particles scattering out of the bag with each punch of Josh's fist. She eased back against the wall. The pup, cradled against her arm, slept upside down in blissful puppy-dog ignorance, pink belly showing between four sprawled stubby legs. *Wouldn't it be nice to have so few worries?*

A shadow crossed Rachel's feet just as she heard a hideous snarl. She looked into a mouthful of dingy, pointed yellow teeth. A huge, multicolored dog—or was it a wolf?—stood three feet away. Its black ears lay back against its thick mottled-gray head.

It growled, low and menacing. Rachel set the puppy on the ground and pulled her legs up to her chest. The dog closed its mouth for a second, sniffed at her pups, then snarled again.

At that moment, she didn't care if Josh knew she'd been eavesdropping. She just wanted out of there. "Josh," she whispered. Her voice squeaked. She licked her lips and cleared her throat. "Josh," she called, louder this time.

The pounding on the bag instantly ceased.

"Josh." She would have screamed if she weren't afraid of upsetting the dog even more. She heard the thud of his boots as he walked toward her. His head appeared over the top of the stall, and his brows narrowed into a single line.

"What are *you* doing here?" he snarled almost as viciously as the dog.

Rachel squeezed her eyes together and swallowed the bile burning her throat. "Just hoping to live another hour." She opened her eyes, and for a fleeting moment, she'd have sworn she saw a hint of amusement grace Josh's nice lips.

"This is how we handle liars and deceivers. Feed them to the dogs."

Rachel studied his face, hoping to see that cocky grin. He looked dead serious. "I never lied to you, Josh," she whispered.

"Yeah, right. For two days you paraded in front of me dressed as a boy. You said your name was Lee."

Rachel wrapped her arms around her knees and pressed her back against the barn. A splinter from the rough wall pierced her blouse, but she tried not to wince. She glanced at the dog. It stood there, eyeballing her, as if waiting for Josh's orders to have her for dinner. The puppies whined and fidgeted, wanting to nurse.

"My middle name is Lee. It was my mother's maiden name." She gazed up at Josh, who peeled off his gloves and stepped through the stall gate.

"Settle down, Belle," he said.

The ugly dog wagged her tail and edged over, leaning against his leg.

"Grandpa made me dress like a boy. He said it was for protection. He told me never to tell anyone the truth until we got to Texas."

Josh winced, and she wondered what was going through his mind.

"He even made me cut my hair. It went all the way to my waist. Used to be so pretty." She raised her hand and twisted a curl around her finger, wishing Josh could've seen her hair when it was long.

He reached out his hand. It smelled of sweat, leather, and horse. Eyeing the dog, she pressed her hand into his, and he pulled her up. Her palm tingled from his warm touch, and his nearness threatened her composure more than the snarling dog had.

He reached up, fingering the hair that hung just past her shoulders. Rachel couldn't breathe. "It's still pretty, even if it's shorter than it used to be." A smile tilted one side of his mouth, and his dimple winked at her. "I thought it looked too pretty for a boy, and I'd planned on having Grandma cut it when we got back."

His winsome smile faded as his eyes darkened. "Why didn't you trust me with the truth? I told you that you could."

Rachel looked down at their feet. A thick layer of dust covered Josh's boots and pants. How could she tell him of her run-ins with the ruthless men of Dodge? She'd never encouraged their advances, but because she had been one of the few unmarried women in town, they readily sought her out. It got so bad that she never left home after dark.

"Rachel?"

She closed her eyes. Josh had called her by her true name for the first time.

"Is it so hard to trust me? I know I'm just an ornery ol' cowboy, but I tried to treat you kindly." The pain in his voice stabbed like a knife twisting in Rachel's stomach.

"I do trust you," she whispered.

"You have a funny way of showing it."

Tears burned her eyes, and she willed them to go away. They didn't. Instead, they escaped and streamed down her cheeks. She didn't want to hurt Josh. He'd been only kind to her. He'd even shared his hopes and dreams, though he thought her to be a boy at the time.

She felt Josh's hand on her chin, lifting her head. She looked up and stared into his dark blue eyes. "I'm sorry," she said. "Things got out of hand. I never meant to embarrass you in front of your family. I'm so grateful that you rescued Grandpa and me. We might be dead right now if you hadn't come along."

Josh winced, and his lips tightened into a pale line. She wondered if he would accept her apology.

"Josh, I know you thought I was a boy when you shared your dreams with me." He stiffened and looked off in the distance through the barn doors. Rachel laid her hand on his forearm. He glanced down at it then captured her gaze again. "I'll never tell a soul. I promise. It meant a lot that you shared with me. And I do trust you— more than you'll ever know."

He studied her face as if searching for the truth. After a moment of intense scrutinizing, he exhaled heavily then lifted his hands and cupped her cheeks. With his thumb, he wiped away her tears. His mouth slowly tilted in that cocky grin she was quickly coming to love. "I'd be a liar if I didn't tell you I much prefer this version of Lee to the scruffy one I found on the prairie."

Josh leaned forward; his warm breath tickled her face. He studied her gaze as if waiting for her objection, and then he brushed a feather-soft kiss across her lips. Rachel heard wedding bells clanging.

"I forgive you, Rachel." He grinned as he straightened. "I'm starved. Let's go eat. That's the lunch bell ringing."

Chapter 8

Rachel glanced up from her stitching just as Grandma Stafford peeked in her bedroom door. She pulled her thread taut and held it secure with her thumb.

"Aren't you coming to the shindig?" Grandma asked.

Rachel shook her head. She couldn't explain that being around the Staffords' big, loving family had rekindled the hurt of losing hers. "I thought I might stay here and work on my tea towels." She held up the flour-sack towel she'd been stitching.

"How pretty! You do lovely work." Grandma eased down beside her on the bed. "That looks just like a red rose. How'd you do that?"

"It's called a spiderweb rose stitch." Rachel smiled. Thoughts of her mother drifted across her mind. "It was my ma's favorite stitch. Her name was Rose, and the stitch reminds me of her."

"That's so sweet. What happened to your mother?" Grandma Stafford fingered the rose then handed the towel back to Rachel.

"She died in childbirth when I was twelve."

"I'm so sorry. The kids lost their mother at a young age, too. Poor Micah lost two mothers." She smiled and smoothed a wrinkle from her dark-blue skirt. "It's difficult to lose someone you love whether it's a child or your parent. So, is that stitch hard to make?"

"No, not at all." Rachel shook her head. "I can show you how if you'd like. See, here's one I just started." Rachel smoothed the towel on her lap. "You start with five lines about one-half inch long, stitched to look like wagon spokes. Then, you take a thick thread or thin ribbon, and starting in the center, you weave over and under the spokes to make a rose design, like this." She wove her red thread over a spoke and then under the next one, pulling the thread taut. "Here, you try it."

Grandma held up her palms. "I'm afraid these old hands are no longer nimble enough for such an effort."

Rachel bit back a smile. She knew Grandma Stafford's hands were just fine.

"Grandma, where are you?" came a muffled call from somewhere in the house.

"In here, Lou." Grandma stood and smoothed her dress. "Have you seen the sampler in the parlor?"

Rachel shook her head.

"Have a look at it some time. I've stitched the children's names in it, and as each one marries, I add their spouse's name."

Lou stepped in the doorway. "You two comin' to the party?"

Rachel shook her head. "I don't think so. It's a family gathering. I'd just be intruding."

Trent came to the door. "Come on, Lou. I can already hear Josh singing."

Josh was singing? Rachel thought back to their time on the trail. She loved to hear his strong, clear voice. Maybe she would go and stand in the shadows.

"Oh, come on. It's not just family," Lou said.

"That's right, the ranch hands all come," Grandma offered. "They'd love to dance with you. A few of the neighbors might even show up." A wry grin curved her lips.

"Course, if the Testaments show up, Josh will have to hide you somewhere." Mirth danced in Lou's blue eyes.

Rachel smiled, not sure what Lou meant by the Testaments. "Maybe I will go for a little bit. You go ahead, and I'll just put this away."

She finished the spiderweb rose, folded the flour-sack tea towel, and set it on the little table next to the bed. She hoped to eventually have towels that represented each of the nine Fruits of the Spirit. As she stitched each towel, she asked God to fill her with that particular spiritual fruit. She'd already completed the love, joy, and peace towels, though God had yet to perfect those characteristics within her. Now she was working on patience.

Patience seemed the slowest in coming.

The longer she stayed at the Staffords' ranch, the more she missed her parents and the brothers and sister who died before she could even hold them in her arms. It would be weeks before Grandpa's leg was healed enough so they could travel. Somehow, she had to get hold of her emotions. At least she and Josh were talking again. He'd even done more than talking. Remembering their kiss sent butterflies dancing in her stomach in time with the lively music outside.

Rachel walked downstairs and peeked in the room where Grandpa was staying. His chest rose and fell in peaceful slumber. Lips that had kissed her cheeks many times puffed out with each breath. Love for him flooded her heart, but concern gnawed at her gut. His strength hadn't returned since his accident. What would she do if he didn't get well? If he died, she'd be alone.

Have faith—and patience. Don't think on those things.

She pushed away from the door frame and walked through the dining room; the music outside beckoned louder with each step. Rachel started out the front door then turned back to the parlor. She scanned the homey room, and her eyes came to rest on the Stafford family sampler. Bright colors accented the usual alphabet, numbers, and flowers. Along the bottom, she read the names of the Stafford children. Two were already married, but Josh and Sam remained single.

Rachel ran her finger along Josh's name. Joshua James Stafford. Well, not quite Jesse James. She grinned. Josh seemed a fitting name for a teasing cowboy with a heartwarming smile. His cocky grin certainly warmed her heart.

"Hey."

Rachel jumped at the sound of Josh's voice. Had he seen her tracing his name? Cheeks burning, she turned to face him, realizing that she no longer heard singing, just peppy guitar music and an occasional *yee-haw*. Why did her heart take off like a racehorse from a starting line whenever Josh came near?

He nodded his head toward the sampler. "Kind of nice having a family record like that."

Rachel smiled and tucked her trembling hands behind her back. "Yeah, it is." She tried not to stare, but Josh looked handsome cleaned up and in fancy clothes. His black pants and freshly shined boots accented his dark hair, which was free of his hat for a change. As if conscious of her gaze, his hand lifted and smoothed back the straight black hair that insisted on falling rebelliously across his forehead. The indigo shirt brought out the deep blue of his eyes.

"So. . .uh. . .you coming to the shindig?"

Rachel nodded, and a charming grin brightened Josh's face.

"I was hoping to get a dance with the prettiest gal in the territory." He crossed his arms, then dropped them to his side, then shoved his hands in his back pockets.

Rachel bit back a grin at his nervousness. The tough, bronc-busting cowboy seemed more like a shy schoolboy. Josh looked down at his boots, and she noticed his long, dark lashes.

When he glanced back at her, she couldn't hold back her grin. Josh thought she was pretty—and he wanted to dance with her. He raised his head and straightened when he saw her smile. Rachel slid her hand around his offered arm.

"Did I tell you how pretty you look?" he said.

"It's Deborah's dress. She let me borrow it." Josh held the screen door open, allowing her to pass in front of him.

"Well, you look good in green. Must get tiring borrowing clothes all the time." Josh stepped beside her. He picked up her hand and looped her arm back around his. "You know, Lou and Deborah are planning a trip to town later this week. Why don't you go and get something to wear? You probably lost 'bout everything when your horses ran off. I. . .uh. . .have some money saved. I'll give you some to spend."

Rachel stumbled, and Josh tightened his grip. She couldn't let him spend his savings on her. "Thanks all the same, but I don't think it would be proper for you to buy my clothes."

"Why not?"

She shrugged. "It just wouldn't. That's all."

Josh turned her to face him. "Maybe you could work it off somehow."

"How?" Rachel narrowed her eyes at him, wondering what she could possibly do for him.

"Oh, I don't know." Then he flashed her an ornery grin, and her stomach did a jig. "Dance with me, Rachel Lee."

⁘

Josh spun her through three dances before he agreed to allow Sam to claim her, and even then, he didn't want to let her go. She was quite a fair square dancer. It worked well having another woman around so that there were four pairs of dancers instead of the usual three. Grandma, who opted to sit this round out, rested on the porch, fanning herself.

Feeling empty without Rachel to fill his hands, Josh picked up his guitar and started strumming along with Hank, one of the ranch hands. They played and sang "Oh! Susanna" and "Buffalo Gals," but when Hank started into the slow-moving "Aura Lee," Josh set his guitar aside. Slipping up behind Doug, he tapped his shoulder. The ranch hand scowled but relinquished Rachel to him.

"Aura Lee, Aura Lee, maid of golden hair; Sunshine came along with thee. . . ." Hank's haunting words left Josh breathless. Rachel Lee, his own Aura Lee, hair of gold. . . So her eyes weren't azure but a beautiful brown. He tugged Rachel closer and tightened his grip on her waist. As he stared into Rachel's lovely face, he saw the question in her eyes.

He pulled her hand to his chest as Hank began the last verse. What was he feeling? Could it be love? He'd never felt so strongly about a woman before. Never considered spending the rest of his life with one before now. Sure, his affection had grown quickly, but he had bonded with Rachel, even when he thought she was a boy. There'd been a connection between them from the start. The soft guitar strumming and the quiet voices of talking cowhands faded into the background as Josh listened to the words of the song.

"Sunshine in thy face was seen, kissing lips of rose. Aura Lee, Aura Lee, take my golden ring. . . ." Josh captured Rachel's gaze. When Hank sang about kissing and wedding rings, Rachel's cheeks turned so crimson that he could see them well in the fading daylight.

All too soon, the song ended. Rachel stepped away, barely giving him a fleeting glance. "I—I need some air." She fanned her face with her hand. "Too much dancing." She turned and hurried toward the barn.

Chapter 9

Rachel rushed past the barn, the noise of the gathering fading the farther she went. Deborah's dress swished around her legs. Though she didn't care much for them, pants were definitely better for running.

What had she read in Josh's gaze? Could he possibly feel something for her, or was he just being nice? Rachel stumbled and caught herself then slowed to a walk. Her breath came in quick gasps. What was the point in even thinking about Josh or her feelings for him when she'd be leaving in a few weeks?

With everything enveloped in the inky darkness of a moonless night and her vision blurred with tears, Rachel couldn't see anything. She slowed to a stop.

Why, God? Why did You bring me here? Isn't it enough that You took my family? Do You have to show me what I'm missing by not having a big, wonderful family like Josh's?

"Rachel?"

"Oh!" she squealed, grabbing her chest. "Stop sneaking up on me, Josh." She resented his intrusion but felt thankful he couldn't see her tears because of the darkness.

"Don't you know it's not safe to wander around in the dark this far from the house? Even with the dogs out, varmints sneak around at night looking for grub."

Rachel shivered. What would Grandpa do if something happened to her? She wiped her cheeks then crossed her arms over her chest and moved closer to Josh. He was the last person she wanted to be with just now, but maybe a critter wouldn't get her if she stayed near him. Now that her tears had stopped and her eyes had adjusted to the dark, she could see the shape of his body silhouetted against the distant glow of the shindig campfire.

"What's wrong?" He reached out in the darkness and grabbed hold of her shoulders. "Did I do something to upset you? I know I didn't step on your toes." He choked out a halfhearted laugh.

What could she say? That she didn't want to leave him when Grandpa was well? That she was already growing to care for him? That she loved his family and wanted to be a part of the Stafford clan forever, but she'd never let Grandpa leave without her?

"Rachel, talk to me." Josh pulled her toward him. She stiffened, not wanting to give in to her feelings, but then melted against his chest and wrapped her arms around him. Just this once she'd enjoy being alone with him, because it couldn't continue. Tears burned her eyes again.

"What's wrong?" Josh leaned back, loosening his hold. His hands burned a path up her arms, warming her cheeks as they rested there. "You're crying. Why?"

"Y—you have no idea how wonderful your family is, do you?"

"My family? That's what you're crying about?" He wiped her tears with his thumbs. "Come on now. Don't cry, honey."

Rachel's heart momentarily swelled at his endearment then plummeted, knowing she wouldn't be the one he'd be speaking them to after tonight. She sniffed. "You have everything I've ever wanted, and you don't appreciate it."

"Hang on. What does that mean?"

"You have a great family, and you live on this fabulous ranch. Even though you smile most of the time, you're not happy. You want to raise horses, but you can't get your nerve up to face your brothers and make them see how important your dream is to you."

Josh dropped his hands to her shoulders. "When did this become about me?"

"All my life, I've wanted what you have, but God took my family." Rachel swatted the tears from her cheeks, instantly remorseful for blaming her troubles on God. And why did she always cry when she was upset? "I wanted to get away from the craziness of Dodge City and live on a ranch, but in my effort to realize my dream, I may have killed my only living relative."

"Oh, honey, your grandpa's not gonna die. And what happened to him wasn't your fault."

"Yes, it is."

Josh cupped her cheeks again. "No. It's not. Accidents happen out here. You should have taken the stage instead of trying to cross No Man's Land on your own, but don't blame yourself. Besides, I'd never have met you if you hadn't."

"Maybe that would have been for the best. I've only caused you trouble."

"No," he whispered, "meeting *you* was the best thing that ever happened to me."

Rachel caught her breath.

"Don't you know how I feel, Rachel? I felt a bond with you even when I thought you were a boy, and now it's even stronger. I don't want you to leave." Josh's hand slid down to her chin and tilted her face upward. She felt his breath warm her cheek as he leaned forward. "Stay here with me. Make my family yours. Please."

She blinked in the darkness. Had he just asked her to marry him? He didn't actually say the words. Josh's boots scuffled against the ground as he eased closer. One hand slid around behind her head, entwining in her hair as the other grasped her waist. Faint guitar and harmonica music blended with the nearby cricket chorus serenading them. Josh lowered his face to hers; his warm lips pressed gently against hers. The odor of campfire smoke from the shindig and hay from the nearby barn mixed with Josh's own distinct scent.

This was the kiss she'd dreamed of. Sweet, warm, with a promise of more to come. Rachel looped her arms around Josh's neck and kissed him back. He tasted of coffee. Josh pulled her tighter, deepening his kiss. Butterflies danced in her stomach. *This* was the man she loved—the man she wanted to be with forever. But Grandpa would never stay here. How many times had he said how much he wanted to spend his remaining years with his brother in Amarillo? And she couldn't let Grandpa leave without her. Rachel's dream skidded to a halt like a galloping horse being jerked to a sudden stop.

Josh must have sensed the change in her. He loosened his grip.

She had to push him away. If she didn't, she'd never be able to leave him. Rachel squeezed her eyes against the hurt she was preparing to inflict. Josh or Grandpa? Why did she have to choose one over the other? Grandpa was her only living relative except for the uncle and cousins she'd never met. Grandpa needed her. Josh had his whole family to support him. *God, where are You when I need You?*

"Rachel?" Josh held her by her upper arms.

She clutched her arms to her chest. "Is this what you meant when you said you'd figure out a way to pay you for the clothes you offered to buy me?"

Josh's loud gasp sliced her gut. "That's a low blow. I can't believe you'd think that." The pain in his voice brought tears to her eyes. He dropped his hands and moved back.

"I–I'm sorry, Josh, that wasn't fair." Her misery weighed her down like an anvil around her neck, pulling her deeper into the dark depths. "I know you wouldn't barter kisses for clothes, but don't you see, I'm leaving in a few weeks." Rachel sniffed back her tears. "Grandpa and I are heading to Amarillo. There's no point in us pursuing a relationship. It'd only make leaving all that much harder."

"How do you know God didn't cause your horses to run off just so I'd find you and we could meet? Maybe that was His plan. Did you ever consider that?"

Rachel cringed at the tone of his voice. That thought hadn't occurred to her. Was this God's answer to her prayer? Would He really make her dream come true? A dream of living on a ranch and having a big family and a wonderful husband like Josh. But such a dream would require her to be separated from Grandpa. Did she want the dream more than Grandpa?

"I–it doesn't matter," she whispered.

"What do you mean? Have I just imagined that you feel something for me?" Josh's voice sounded flat. The festive music in the background now seemed out of place in light of Rachel's emotional turmoil.

"You don't understand." She wanted to shout how much she loved him, but she didn't have the right. "Grandpa's all the family I've got. I can't let him go to Uncle Lloyd's without me."

Josh stepped closer. "Maybe God wants to give you a new family."

"Not if it means being separated from Grandpa. I—I can't."

"Rachel," he said, his voice full of entreaty. Josh's hand cupped her cheek, and she wanted desperately to lean into his caress. "Why can't you have both?"

Rachel blinked. She could barely think with Josh's thumb gently stroking her face. Could she have a life with Josh *and* Grandpa? If she did, it would mean Grandpa would have to give up his dream—and she couldn't ask that of him. Years ago, he'd given up his own dreams to stay in Dodge and help raise her after her mother died. At his age, he'd earned the chance for a little happiness, even if it meant sacrificing hers.

"No, Josh. Grandpa won't stay here once he's well. He wants so badly to spend his remaining days with his brother. I won't ask him to give up his dream for me."

"That doesn't make any sense." Rachel knew if Josh had his hat right now, he'd be smacking it against his thigh in frustration. "You'd sacrifice your dream for Ian?"

"Isn't that what you're doing?"

"What do you mean?" Josh dropped his hand from her face and stepped back.

"You want to raise horses, but you won't stand your ground with your brothers."

"It's not the same thing. I've tried to talk to Micah, but he just thinks he's the biggest toad in the puddle. He doesn't listen to me."

"Have you even prayed about your dream? Have you asked God if that's His will for you?"

"Uh, sure I've prayed. Probably not enough. But it's still not the same thing."

Rachel crossed her arms over her chest, thankful to have the conversation directed at Josh instead of her. "Yes, it is. You're smart, capable—everyone sees that except you."

"Rachel, this isn't about me."

"Well, it isn't about me, either. I'm leaving in a couple of weeks."

"Fine. If that's the way you want it, I'll stay out of your way until you and Ian leave." His voice sounded resigned, and Rachel wanted to throw herself back in his arms. But it had to be this way. She couldn't leave Grandpa for a man she'd known only a few days—no matter what his cocky smile did to her heart.

Chapter 10

Grandpa patted the side of his bed. "Come sit fer a spell, Ray."

Rachel gently eased down on the bed, hoping to not hurt his splinted leg. She thanked God his color had improved and his appetite had returned. Micah and Sam had even helped him out to the porch last night so he could get some fresh air. A smile tilted her lips as she remembered how Grandma Stafford had insisted on bringing him some hot tea and cookies then sat with him until the sun set.

"Sure feels good to be feelin' good again. Thought I wudn't gonna make it there fer a while."

Rachel studied him as he rubbed his thigh. "Does your leg hurt much?"

He shrugged. "A tad bit. Eleanor's been making me swallow this nasty-tastin' tea stuff. Just ain't right fer a man to be drinkin' tea, though it does seem to ease the pain."

She bit back a smile. "How long do you think it'll be 'fore you can travel?"

"Why? You anxious to be movin' on? Thought maybe you'd decided to stay."

Rachel blinked. "Why would you think that?" With Grandpa laid up, he had no way of knowing about her attraction to Josh.

"Just seems to me a certain young cowboy's mighty interested in you. I figured you might return his affections."

"You have been laid up in this room all week. How do you know if Josh is interested in me?" Rachel eyed him with curiosity. He always had this uncanny way of knowing what she was going through.

He struggled to scoot up on the bed. She hopped up and fluffed his pillow then helped him ease back against it. "I've had me some visitors. Josh's been by a few times and played checkers with me while you was helping in the kitchen. He's pretty good fer a young whippersnapper. Ain't seen him around for several days, though."

"He's gone. Out checking one of the herds somewhere." Rachel broke his gaze and plucked a piece of lint off her skirt and dropped it on the floor, wishing she could discard her troubles as easily. "He left the day after the shindig." She tried not to wince, knowing she was the reason he was gone.

"I've talked with Eleanor, too. She seems to think the boy's a goner for you."

"That doesn't matter." Rachel couldn't look at him and stared at her hands, hating that she told him a falsehood.

"Why not? You have feelings fer him—or am I mistaken?"

Rachel heard a sound at the door and looked up to see Lou entering. "There you are. I've been looking all over for you. Ready to go?"

Rachel nodded. "I'm going to town with Lou and Deborah, Grandpa. We'll be gone most of the day." She leaned forward and kissed his whiskery cheek.

"I'll meet you at the wagon," Lou said as she slipped out of the room.

"Give me my boots." Grandpa flicked his hand toward the corner.

Rachel eased off the bed, grabbed his boots, and handed them to him. He reached inside one and pulled out a wad of dollars. "Here. Been saving this in case we had us an emergency." He unrolled several bills and stuffed them in her hand. "Get us some clothes and whatever else you think we gotta have."

"You've been holding out on me, Grandpa." Rachel smiled, relieved that she wouldn't have to take any money from the Staffords for the things they needed to finish their trip.

"We'll talk later, sweetheart."

"There's nothing to talk about, Grandpa."

His knowing smile told her that this wasn't the end of the conversation.

⁘

Lou slapped the reins of the two horses pulling the buckboard to speed them up the hill as they left the small town of Petunia behind them.

"I love getting away from the ranch. It's probably the last time I'll get to go before the baby comes." Deborah patted her swelling stomach.

"You got some darling baby clothes. I love that snow-white christening gown with the soft lace." Rachel smiled.

"Soon as we get home, we'll have to get busy sewing some more clothes and diapers out of that soft flannel you bought. We've only got a couple of months 'til the baby comes." Lou glanced at Deborah, who sat in the middle of the wagon seat. "Oh! Deborah, have you seen the beautiful roses that Rachel sews? Wouldn't some small ones be precious on the yoke of an infant gown?"

Deborah nodded. "Oh, yes!" She turned to Rachel. "Would you mind sewing a few on some gowns—or at least showing me how?"

Rachel tightened her grip on the side of the wagon and pressed her foot to the floor to brace herself as they rolled down the gentle hill. "I'd love to sew some for you or teach you how, either one. I've never made tiny roses, but Lou's right. They'd look precious on an infant's gown—as long as you have a girl."

"Oh, Micah insists it's a boy. I don't know what he'll do if I have a girl," Deborah said.

Lou giggled. "Can't you just see his face if you have a boy and we dress him in a gown with roses on the bib?"

The three women laughed aloud. "Maybe we'd better make some gowns without flowers, just in case." Deborah smiled.

"Yeah, we could sew tiny little bows made out of pink ribbon on the chest instead." Lou snickered, her eyes gleaming.

The women laughed again. Rachel loved their easy camaraderie. They had become good friends in a mere week. She wanted so badly to stay and make a home with the Staffords. With Josh. If only Grandpa would, too. But what was there for him to do at their ranch? Would the Staffords let him stay if she and Josh were to get married? She knew they would.

Rachel thought of Josh's grin—the one that had so irritated her when she first met him. Now she loved that rogue's smile. If only. . .

"What are you grinning at, Rachel?"

She looked at Lou, who had a twinkle in her eye. Her face warmed, and she knew she was blushing. Turning away from Lou's smug I-know-your-secret expression, she studied the abundant yucca and sage plants off to her right. Two tumbleweeds rolled past as if in a race.

"You know, Deborah," Lou said, "we just might have to make a wedding dress before we sew those baby clothes. That Irish lace we bought would sure spiffy up a wedding gown."

"Can you imagine how beautiful a soft-blue or pale-lavender dress would look with Rachel's roses and seed pearls sewn across the bodice?" Rachel could hear the smile in Deborah's voice and feel her stare.

"So, we gonna have a wedding, Rachel?"

She desperately wished she could enjoy their good-natured teasing, but the pain of her decision weighed heavily. The sound of galloping horse hooves intruded into her troubled thoughts, and she glanced over her shoulder. "Three riders are coming up behind us, Lou." She breathed a sigh of relief to be able to change the subject.

Lou turned her head and looked back. "I don't recognize them. And they're coming fast."

"How far to the ranch?" Rachel asked.

"Too far to outrun them. Besides, we can't take a chance jostlin' Deborah around with her being in the family way." Lou pulled back on the reins and slowed the horses. "We'll just have to take our chances." She reached for the rifle on the floorboard as the men on horseback pulled up beside them.

"Drop the rifle, little missy." A man with shoulder-length, dingy brown hair looked past Lou once she set down her rifle and stared at Rachel. Warning spasms of alarm erupted within her. Take the scraggly beard away and she was certain the man was Cyrus Lawton. Pain like a stab from a Bowie knife sliced through her whole being. Rachel gasped. An eerie grin crept across the man's face.

"That her, Cy?" the slender man on Rachel's right side asked.

"Yep. Her hair's shorter though." He scratched his whiskery chin and grinned. "Couldn't believe my eyes when I saw you in town. Thought for sure you'd given us the slip, princess."

Lou and Deborah both turned to face her. "You know them?" Deborah asked.

Rachel nodded, glaring at Cyrus Lawton. "He's the man who murdered my father."

"Well now, murder's a harsh word, 'specially when the man attacked me first."

A burning fury almost choked Rachel. She jumped to her feet. "How dare you. You know you murdered him. Papa was just trying to defend me, and you shot him."

"I don't recall that you needed rescuing. We were just having ourselves a good time."

"Liar!"

Cyrus Lawton raised the pistol that had been resting on his saddle horn and waved it in the air.

"Now don't go doing something that will get your friends hurt."

She glanced down to meet Lou's and Deborah's wide-eyed stares. For the first time since she had met her, Lou seemed speechless. Rachel lifted her chin and met Lawton's chilly glare. "Your fight's with me. Let them go."

"Oh, I don't know. You got a wagon full of supplies and me a-hankerin' for a home-cooked meal."

"I'll fix you something to eat," Rachel offered. "Just let them go. Deborah's with child." She laid her hand on Deborah's shoulder. "She needs to get back home."

"No." Cy stroked his beard. "I'm thinkin' you'll be more agreeable if'n I take them along with us. Y'all turn that wagon off the road ahead and follow me." He leaned over, retrieved Lou's rifle, and holstered his gun. "Carter, you follow along behind and make sure they don't try nuthin'."

Lou guided the wagon off the road, following Cy Lawton as he headed toward the mesas in the distance.

"What are we going to do?" Deborah whispered.

Lou shrugged. "You just hold on tight for now, and I'll try not to jostle you too much, but being off the road will make the going rougher."

"I'm so sorry about this." Rachel shuddered inwardly at the thought of what might happen to them. This was her fault. Somehow she had to get her friends out of this mess. *Dear Lord, You see our situation. Please help us find a way to escape.*

"Though I walk through the valley of the shadow of death, I will fear no evil." Deborah's quote of the Psalms touched Rachel's heart, bringing encouragement.

"Amen," she whispered.

Lou gripped the reins so tightly her knuckles grew white. Her eyes flashed daggers at the kidnappers. "Micah and Trent will find us. Don't you worry."

"Josh and Sam will help, too," Deborah whispered.

Cyrus Lawton turned an angry glare toward them. "Be quiet. No talkin', ya hear?"

What would Josh do when he realized she was missing? Would he even know since he was out working the herd somewhere? Tears burned Rachel's eyes, and a tightness in her throat threatened to choke off her breathing. What if she never saw Josh again? He'd never know how much she really loved him.

Oh, Josh, I'm so sorry for pushing you away.

Chapter 11

J osh reloaded his pistol and aimed at his hostage. The once multiarmed sage-brush now raised only three measly branches skyward. He aimed, firing off a trio of rapid shots. Each branch exploded into tiny shards. Staring with satisfaction at the stub of a shrub, he reloaded his pistol again and shoved it into his holster.

Women. His brothers had warned him about their fickle ways. Sam evidently believed the warning more than Micah, since he'd remained unmarried.

Josh glanced over at the pretty gray mare he'd lassoed out of a herd of mustangs. The moment he saw her, he knew she was the horse for Rachel. After four days of intense workouts, she now let him handle and lead her without a fight. She had spunk and spirit, but she had the wisdom to know when to give in and accept her fate. If only Rachel had the same good sense.

After the initial sting of her rejection had worn off, Josh realized in his heart that she didn't mean what she'd said about trading kisses for clothes, but he couldn't for the life of him figure out why she'd say something like that.

Talking with Ian had helped. He'd reinforced the fact that Rachel had always wished for a big family, but instead, it had only been the three of them until her father had been killed. Ian was the only family Rachel had left. How could he expect her to choose between her grandpa and him? There had to be a way to work things out. Josh knew in his heart that Rachel was the woman he wanted to marry; he just had to make her see it, too.

For the third time since noon, Josh sank to his knees. *Come on, Lord, show me how to convince Rachel that I love her. Better yet, would You show her that we're supposed to be together? I know You've spoken to me; please speak to her.*

The next day, he rose before sunrise and left camp so that he'd be home in time for breakfast. After four days out in the wild, eating beef jerky and rabbit, Josh was ready for something more substantial. Food was strong on his mind, but thoughts of Rachel were stronger. Would she be happy to see him again? Did she miss him? Eager to see her again, he nudged Sultan into a gallop.

The moment Josh rode into the ranch yard, he knew something was wrong. People scurried around, and six horses loaded with overnight gear and weapons were saddled and tied to the front porch railing. The four Testament boys rode up as he reined Sultan to a stop.

"Josh! Thank God, you're back." Grandma hurried down the porch steps and rushed toward him.

He leaped off his horse and tightened his hold on the gray mare's lead rope. "Whoa, girl," he murmured when he saw the whites of her eyes.

"Hold on, Grandma. Don't come any closer 'til I get this mare in the corral. She's not used to all this commotion." He turned toward the corral. Grandma snagged up the reins of Josh's stallion and led him along. "So what's going on?"

"The girls are missing."

He glanced toward her, and his steps faltered. "What girls?"

"All three of them."

He stopped walking and turned to face her, still not clear who she meant.

"Josh, yesterday morning Lou, Deborah, and Rachel took the buckboard into town, and they're still not back. The men searched for them yesterday evening but came home once the sun set. They're eating breakfast then heading back out."

"Rachel's missing, too?"

Grandma nodded. Josh felt like he'd been shot. He tightened his grip on the lead rope and broke into a jog. Grandma handed Sultan over to one of the hands.

"Shorty," Josh hollered, "get me a fresh mount—a fast one." Shorty nodded and led Sultan into the barn.

Josh hustled over to Grandma, who was heading back toward the house. "Any idea what happened to them?"

"No." The grave expression on her face startled him. Grandma Stafford was the cornerstone of his family, and her feathers rarely got ruffled.

She stopped mid-step and turned to face him. "Josh, what happened between you and Rachel? She's been moping around here like a calf that lost its mother. Poor thing's been miserable. The only time since you've been gone that she perked up was yesterday before the girls headed to town to shop. They were all excited about helping Deborah find some baby clothes and fabric."

Josh wrapped his arm around her shoulders. "Just a big misunderstanding. I'll clear things up when I find her."

She smiled. "I know that a woman can be perplexing. You just have to give her a lot of love and be patient and understanding."

"I know, Grandma. I'm learning. Come on now." He wrapped his arm around her shoulder. "I need to grab some breakfast so I can head out with the rest of the men."

❖

Rachel woke up, chilled and sore. The tiny bedroom they'd been locked in overnight had only a small cot, which she and Lou insisted Deborah use. Rachel stretched then eased to her feet. Sometime during the night, as she had sat praying, an escape plan began to formulate in her mind.

She stooped down and gave Lou a gentle push on her shoulder. "Lou, wake up."

She swatted Rachel's hand. "Let me sleep a bit longer, Trent." Lou turned over onto her side.

Rachel shoved her a bit harder and whispered, "Lou! Come on; wake up. I have a plan."

Lou bolted upright. She rubbed the sleep from her eyes as she yawned. "What sort of plan?"

Rachel nodded. "You know the medical supplies we got at the town store? Didn't we get some sleeping powder?"

Lou looked deep in thought, as if she were checking down her shopping list, and then she nodded. A slow smile tilted her lips; Rachel could see the moment she caught hold of the plan. "We could put it in their food."

Rachel nodded and grinned for the first time since their captivity. "Biscuits and gravy, à la sleeping powder?"

A scuffling sounded on the other side of the door, and then the lock clicked. The door creaked on its rusty hinges, and Cyrus Lawton appeared in the doorway. Both women jumped to their feet. "Well, princess, looks like it's time for you and me to head out."

Fear tugged at Rachel's heart, and she turned to face Lou. Deborah roused in her sleep but didn't awaken.

"What do you want with my friend?" Lou asked, rising to her full height.

Lawton leered at Rachel. She cringed as his eyes ran the length of her body. "I've watched her for months around Dodge. She'd never give me the time of day, then I caught her alone in her pa's barbershop. We'da had a good time if her pa hadn't interrupted and got hisself killed. Looks like I won the prize, though." He grinned with satisfaction, stroked his beard, then reached out and grabbed Rachel's upper arm. "Time to leave, princess."

"B–but what about breakfast?" Rachel asked. "Surely we could eat first. I make real good biscuits, and Deborah can't travel without eating. She'll get sick."

"They ain't comin'. Just you and me." Cyrus flashed her an evil grin then spat on the floor. "But I reckon we could wait and eat first. Didn't have much supper last night."

With a sigh of relief, Rachel nodded. "I'll need to get some supplies out of the wagon."

"Okay, but just you. Them other two can stay here." Cyrus waved his pistol at Lou and Deborah, who had just awakened. He pulled Rachel out of the bedroom into the cabin's main room. As the door closed, she locked gazes with Lou. *Pray*, she mouthed. Cyrus latched the door and locked it.

"Don't try any funny stuff, or you'll be wishin' you hadn't." His long, jagged fingernails bit into Rachel's arm. She clenched her jaw to keep from crying out. "Fix that breakfast, and make it fast. We've got a ways to ride."

Rachel didn't ask where he was taking her. She didn't want to know. Cyrus pulled her outside the small cabin and toward the buckboard loaded with supplies from town. Birds chirped cheerful tunes, blissfully unaware of the danger she and her friends were in. The morning sun warmed her face, even as her prayers warmed her spirit and gave her hope. Cyrus stopped at the back of the wagon, flipped up the canvas flap, and released her. Rachel rubbed her aching arm.

She glanced at the campfire and noticed Cyrus's cronies were just waking up. If they'd still been asleep, she might have been able to get away from Cyrus somehow and ride for help. She peered over the back of the wagon, realizing she had no idea where she was or which way the ranch was. Rachel heaved a sigh and looked heavenward. *Father God, I could sure use Your help right about now.*

"Git busy. We ain't got all day." Scowling at her, Cyrus shoved her toward the wagon. Rachel banged into the corner of a crate loaded with supplies. She cried out at the sharp stab of pain on the back of her hand. The tender area throbbed as a huge welt puffed up. Down the middle of the welt, blood oozed from a two-inch-long scrape.

Cyrus kicked the boots of one of his men. "Git up and find some firewood."

Rachel blinked back her tears. She wouldn't give Cyrus the satisfaction of knowing he'd hurt her.

Chapter 12

The pain of losing something very precious sliced through Josh. Rachel wasn't his, though he believed with all his heart she was supposed to be. An accident might have caused her horses to run off, but deep in his gut he knew Divine Providence had sent him riding in their direction that day.

He glanced at Micah. His tough older brother had said very little since they set out. Josh couldn't imagine the pain he must be feeling over his pregnant wife's disappearance—and regret that he hadn't escorted the women to town, probably. He stood to lose not only his wife but his unborn child, too.

Josh shook his head. That wasn't going to happen. They'd find the women and bring them back home. Then he and Rachel were going to have a talk.

He reached over and squeezed Micah's forearm. His brother looked up, his gray eyes shadowed with pain. "We'll find them."

A muscle twitched in Micah's cheek, and he nodded. He urged his horse into a gallop. Josh did the same, all the time praying for God's guidance and His protection over the women.

"Micah. Over there!" All heads turned toward Slim.

Josh's gaze followed Slim's long arm to where a trail of smoke rose on the morning breeze. "That's the north line shack. Ain't s'posed to be nobody there this time of year."

In unison, the crew spurred their horses to a canter and raced for the shack.

Josh prayed they weren't too late.

⸬

The fresh aroma of skillet biscuits vastly improved the odor of the shack filled with unwashed men. Not sure whether or not cooking would affect the sleeping powder, Rachel opted to wait and add it at the last minute; that way, too, the women could eat. Her stomach swirled from hunger and nerves. Hoping to mask the taste of the sleeping powder, she cut open the biscuits, and using a spoon handle, she lathered them with the store-bought apple butter she'd purchased as a surprise for Grandpa.

She peered over her shoulder. Cy and his two men were hunched over something that looked like a map. With trembling fingers, she reached into her pocket and pulled out a packet of the powder. The packet slipped from her nervous fingers and fell toward the floor. She gasped and snagged it in midair. Relief flooded her, but her knees sagged from the fright.

With another swift peek to ensure the men were still occupied, she dumped a fair amount of the powder onto each biscuit. Would it be enough to put them all to sleep? She hesitated only a moment before retrieving another packet.

"Some'n smells mighty good over there," Cy drawled.

"Mm-hmm," one of his men muttered.

Rachel pressed the tops back on the biscuits and lifted the plate. *Please, Lord, let this work.*

She forced a smile and walked to the men. "I hope you like apple butter. I put an extra portion on each biscuit."

Cy looked at her strangelike. She hoped he didn't suspect anything. The other two men reached for the plate. Cy snarled, reminding her of Josh's dog. "I go first, you fools."

He snatched four of the nine biscuits and walked over to the window. His men gave him a dirty look for not dividing them evenly. Carter split a biscuit and took two whole ones, leaving the rest for the last henchman.

With all three men munching, Rachel returned to the stove. She picked up the other plate with a half-dozen untainted biscuits. "Mind if we women eat, too?"

Cy turned and looked at the plate in her hand. "Open the door," he mumbled as bits of pastry flew from his mouth. Carter muttered under his breath but did his boss's bidding.

Rachel slipped into the room, meeting the anxious gazes of her friends. The door closed behind her, and the lock clicked shut. She collapsed beside Deborah on the cot.

Lou leaned forward, resting her hand on Rachel's knee. "Did you do it?"

The plate shook in her hands. Now that the deed was done, she was even more nervous. She nodded.

"Yahoo," Lou whispered loudly.

Deborah jumped. "Shush, Lou. They'll hear you."

"Come on, you two, let's eat while we have a chance." Rachel held out the plate.

"How much powder did you use?" Deborah asked.

"Two whole packets."

Lou's eyebrows shot up. Rachel's heart took a nosedive.

"You don't think that's too much, do you? I didn't want to kill them—just make them sleep."

Lou shrugged her shoulders while she munched her biscuit.

Rachel looked at Deborah. "I don't know," she murmured.

Rachel pulled a spoon and two forks from her pocket. "These might help us get out of this room somehow."

The women grinned and nodded then ate the rest of their breakfast in silence, listening to the hum of voices from the other room. It was clear the men were packing up, getting ready to leave. Rachel closed her eyes. Would she ever see Grandpa or Josh again?

-:::-

Josh squatted behind a big yucca plant, careful not to get too close. Micah eased in beside him. "There's the wagon. I don't recognize those saddle horses; do you?"

Micah shook his head. Sam and Trent sidled up beside him. "The Testaments are going around to the back. I just hope they don't do anything stupid."

Josh gripped the handle of his pistol. If anyone knew how to skulk around a house, it was the Testament brothers. How else did they steal their women? If he'd had his way, they wouldn't have brought the crazy quartet.

Slowly, the men closed their circle around the shack. For the last half hour, there'd been not a peep from the structure. Uneasiness enveloped Josh. It wasn't normal for things to be so quiet at midday.

"You, in the shack, git yourselves out here. Now!"

Josh tensed. He reached for his pistol.

"Those crazy Testament boys. They're gonna get the women killed," Micah muttered.

"Trent! Micah!"

"That's Louisa." Trent peered over the cactus.

"Yeah?" Micah hollered.

"It's safe to come in. But hurry. We're locked up."

Josh looked at his brothers. The same curiosity and relief flooded their faces. "Let's go."

Together they sprinted toward the shack. Kings One and Two plowed around the corner and burst in the door ahead of them. "They's all asleep in here," one of them yelled.

Josh followed Sam and Micah into the small building while the ranch hands held back. Surprise registered with confusion. Three men slumped against the walls, sound asleep, unaware of the danger they were in.

"Get them out of here," Micah ordered.

Josh saw the Testaments wrestling with a locked door. Reluctantly, he grabbed hold of one of the sleeping men and dragged him outside. He and Sam tied up the slumbering trio. The loud crack of splintering wood told Josh the women were free. Would Rachel be happy to see him?

Micah exited the cabin with his arm around Deborah's shoulders. Hand in hand with Trent, Lou hurried out behind him, grinning and waving at Sam and Josh. Finally, Kings One and Two emerged from the shack, nearly dragging Rachel out between them. Frustration seethed within. The two galoots were going to tear off her arms.

"I found her first. She's mine," King One said—or was it Two?

"Nuh-uh. I did. She's mine." They jerked her back and forth like a rag doll. Poor Rachel looked near tears.

"I'll take charge of the lady," Josh said.

"Nope. We found her first. She's ours."

Rachel's big brown eyes impaled him. He read the unspoken question and hope.

"Actually, I found her first. I just lost her for a bit." He grinned, and Rachel's eyes sparked to life. "Why don't you let the lady decide?"

"So's you want him or us'ns?" King Two asked.

"Oh, uh, well, that's a tough choice. Two of you big strapping men and just one of him." Rachel grinned mischievously but eased toward Josh. Both Testaments puffed out their chests, and their lips lifted in dopey grins. "But since my grandpa's at the Stafford ranch, I'd better go with Josh. Besides, King One, aren't you courting Cynthia now?"

The two Testaments deflated, and King One glanced sheepishly at her. Before they had a chance to respond, Josh stepped forward and grabbed Rachel by the wrist. He pulled her away from the crowd to the other side of his horse then wrapped her tight in his embrace. She collapsed against him.

"I'm so sorry, Josh. I didn't think I'd ever see you again."

"Shhh. I know, honey. It's all over now." He kissed the top of her head, enjoying the feel of holding her close, and sent a prayer heavenward, thanking God.

Mounted on Josh's horse a short while later, they rode back together. Rachel sat in the saddle asleep, wrapped in his arms, as he guided his horse home. Lou, anxious to inform Grandma they were safe, rode ahead with Trent and Sam. Micah and Deborah rode in the wagon, hauling the three tied-up kidnappers. Once the women were safely home, Josh would happily help his brothers escort the men to town for safekeeping in the jail.

The wind tickled his cheeks, and Josh looked skyward. Joy and relief flooded him. Though they hadn't really talked yet, the woman he loved was in his arms. Things would work out. He just knew it.

-:::-

Rachel couldn't hold back the grin on her face as she rode the gray mare Josh had given her. She'd named her Grace because of the way she moved. Josh had scowled and shaken his head, saying that was no name for a mustang. She nudged Grace forward as Sultan pulled alongside. Her mare was swift but no match for Josh's stallion.

Atop the hill overlooking the Stafford homestead, they pulled their horses to a stop. Josh climbed down and dropped his reins. Sultan dipped his head and snatched up a hunk of knee-high grass. Josh helped Rachel down then took her hand and pulled her away from Grace.

"I love this view of the ranch. It's home."

"Yes, it is beautiful. I remember the first time I saw it." Her voice faded to a whisper. "I wished then that it was my home."

Josh turned to face her and lightly clutched her waist. "That's my dream, too. Make this your home, Rachel."

Her golden eyebrows dipped as she struggled to decipher his meaning.

"Marry me, kid."

Rachel jerked her gaze up and stared into his serious sapphire eyes. Her heart turned somersaults of joy, but she had to be sure. "You mean that? You're not just joshin' with me?"

He grinned. "No, honey. I love you. I'd never josh about that. Please, marry me, and make me the happiest cowpoke on this whole spread."

Joy like she'd never known soared through her. "I love you, too. I wanted so badly to tell you when I was locked in that shack."

Josh leaned toward her. Their lips met, and he tugged her against his chest. His kiss was everything she'd hoped it would be. Warm. Filled with love and a promise of tomorrow. For a brief moment she lingered, enjoying it. Hoping it wasn't their last. As much as she wanted to stay there forever, she pulled back.

Something near panic dashed across Josh's face.

"What about Grandpa?"

He sighed a breath of relief. "I talked with Ian. He wants to hang around here for a while. In case you haven't noticed, he and Grandma are getting along better than matching salt and pepper shakers."

He smiled that grin she loved so much. She reached up a finger, tracing a line from his dimple down to the slight cleft in his chin. Josh's eyes closed as he savored the moment.

"I noticed." She didn't want to say what the feel of his rough cheek did to her insides.

Josh opened his eyes. "I talked with Micah and Sam. They've agreed to let me buy some high-quality brood mares. Looks like Sultan's getting his harem. We'll see what happens." He removed a lock of hair that blew across her cheek and tucked it behind her ear. "You were right. I prayed and got my heart straight then talked with my brothers like a man. And they listened."

"I'm so glad."

He ran his hand down her hair and twirled a curl around his finger. "There's only one thing I need to make my dream complete."

Captured by his startling blue gaze, Rachel smiled up at him. "It would seem our two dreams are destined to merge."

Josh's eyebrows dipped in confusion for a moment then lifted with astonishment.

"Yes. I'll marry you, Josh."

He grabbed his hat and tossed it in the air. "Yahoooo!" He twirled her around then pulled her into his arms. His grin was contagious.

Rachel knew she'd finally come home. Like a spiderweb rose, God had taken simple, pliable strands and woven them into a thing of beauty.

THE COAT

by Tracey V. Bateman

Dedication

Special thanks to my mom, Frances Devine.
Not only does she read every word I write,
but she also writes with me when I'm in a crunch.
Thank you for being Supermom and saving the day.
You took my thread of an idea and helped me weave it into
a wonderful story I'm proud to add my name to.
Most of the credit for this project is yours.
I love you so much!

Chapter 1

L eah Halliday clutched her pay envelope tightly and held her head high as she walked down the service street behind Rosemont Industries. Arms linked, she and her two best friends marched side by side, their oxfords in silent step. At least misery had company—the proof being the two dozen women who trudged along behind them down the icy street. *Although,* Leah thought ruefully, *I would have preferred to suffer alone in this case.*

At the corner, the trio turned left and headed down the sidewalk, still not uttering a sound except for an occasional deep sigh. Two blocks away, they walked into Simon's Café. Simon's had been their special coffee klatch hangout for nearly four years now. This was where Susan had sobbed out her misery the day she received the "Dear Jane" letter from her sailor fiancé. It was the place where Janie Brown had shared her doubts about ever being published when the seventeenth rejection letter had arrived in her mailbox. And it was here that Janie and Sue had sat in stunned silence while Leah, trembling and dizzy, told them the news about Bob's death.

Leah hardly noticed the scent of freshly brewed coffee and sweet buns as they walked back to the last booth. She sighed heavily and dropped onto the seat. Sliding over, she made room for Janie.

"They didn't even give us notice! And two weeks before Christmas!" Janie burst into tears and flung her purse onto the table. Grabbing a handkerchief from the open bag, she blew her nose loudly and pressed her lips together.

"I know, sweetie. But ever since the boys came home, we've known it was just a matter of time. At least they gave us two months' severance pay." Leah patted her friend on the shoulder and gave a wobbly smile that wouldn't have fooled anyone.

They ordered Cokes from the waitress and, in silence, listened to the blaring of the jukebox as the Andrews Sisters sang the last roistering chorus of "Boogie Woogie Bugle Boy."

Susan Ryan, the petite blond sitting across from them, blew a strand of hair from her face. "Are they ever going to stop playing that song? Don't they know the war is over?" When none of her friends answered, she frowned, squinting her blue eyes. "Can you believe Mr. Kites—complimenting us on a job well done as we 'held down the fort for the boys in uniform'? Then to say he just knew we would all be happy to give the jobs back to our husbands and fathers. Well, I, for one, don't have a husband or a father, and I need to pay the rent."

Leah bit her lip and stared at the saltshaker that had fallen over on the table. She understood her friend's dilemma; the same war waged inside of her.

"And what about you, Leah? How are you going to take care of Collin?"

"I don't know, Sue. I'll manage somehow. I'm sure another job will turn up." Leah breathed a sigh of relief that she had already bought Collin's Christmas gifts.

"Well, I don't know how you can be so sure." Janie dabbed at her eyes with a clean handkerchief. "After all, everyone's going to be hiring the *returning heroes*. Of course we can always clean houses or wait tables, I guess." She stopped, a look of remorse flashing across her face. "I don't mean to sound like I'm ungrateful for what the boys did. I don't begrudge them their jobs back—" Her voice broke, and she shook her head.

Neither of her friends spoke. There was nothing to be said. Nothing to be done. As many other women in the country were discovering, their usefulness to industrial America had come to a screeching halt the second the first wave of returning GIs stepped off the ships. Leah sipped her Coke, staring glumly at the fizz, and despite her optimistic facade wondered how on earth she and Collin would make it through the winter.

Later, as Leah waited at the corner for her bus, her back turned to the cold December wind, she tried to weigh her options. Since Bob's death, she hadn't had time to think about the future. She fell into bed exhausted most nights, and her days off were spent cleaning and shopping and trying to make up to her ten-year-old son for not having a dad.

But now she had to think about it, and unfortunately, there didn't seem to be any options unless she wanted to sell the house. The thought ripped through her like a jagged piece of glass, but she couldn't rule out the thought that it might eventually come to that if the time came when she had no choice. Their house wasn't fancy, but at least it was a comfortable, roomy place for Collin to grow up. She didn't want to raise him in a three-room flat if she didn't have to.

At the thought, Leah's whole body tensed. Her breathing quickened as the fear she had held at bay for the last four years reached out and wrapped its tentacles around her heart.

Hot grease popped and sputtered as Leah added potato slices to the sizzling iron skillet, then dashed on a bit of salt and pepper. Just as she placed the lid on the skillet, the front door slammed. Her lips curved into a smile while she waited for her reason for living to join her in the kitchen. When too much time passed, she frowned at the silence. Not even Collin's usual "Mom, I'm home" greeted her ears. Grabbing a towel, she wiped her hands on the way to the living room. "Collin?"

Her son stood at the end of the overstuffed sofa, his head down.

"Honey, what's wrong?" Her throat tightened as he raised his head and looked at her with mournful eyes.

Blood trickled from his quivering bottom lip, and dirt smudged his cheeks and forehead. She gasped and hurried to him.

"What happened?"

Looking down at the floor, he shook his head. "Nothin'."

Her heart constricted. "It doesn't look like nothing to me. Come into the bathroom so I can get you cleaned up, and then you can tell me, okay?"

He nodded and went with her without saying anything. Getting cotton and gauze from the medicine cabinet, she cleaned the cuts and scrapes, then leaned back and scrutinized his face.

"Hmm, it doesn't look so bad now that you're all cleaned up. Want to tell me what happened?"

He shook his head.

"Were you fighting?"

His silence answered her question. "All right. Go upstairs, and when you're ready to tell me what happened, you may come back down." He preceded her into the living room, then started to head upstairs, still wearing his coat. For the first time, she noticed he was clutching his arm.

"Honey, is something wrong with your arm? Why are you holding it like that?"

Collin swallowed loudly and blinked his eyes. "Nothin's wrong with my arm, Mom." Avoiding her eyes, he started to climb the stairs.

"Collin, get back down here and let me see your arm."

Sighing loudly, he turned and came back. He looked at her sadly. "Mom, it's my sleeve. It's ripped almost all the way off."

Leah felt her forehead wrinkle up with worry and consciously smoothed it out. "Let me see."

Obediently, he lifted his arm and showed her the sleeve. It was ripped along the seam the length of the sleeve, but Leah sighed with relief when she saw it could be fixed. The thought of having to spend money on a new coat almost made her ill. Worse still was the reality that if the coat had been ripped beyond repair, she couldn't have bought him a new one.

"I think I can mend it, honey. Don't worry. Now, who were you fighting with?"

"Just one of the guys at school."

"Do you want to tell me why?"

"I dunno. Guess he said some mean stuff. Then he grabbed me."

"What did the teacher do?"

Collin widened his eyes in disbelief. "Mom! I'm ten. A fella doesn't squeal."

Leah reached over and brushed back a lock of dark, ash-blond hair from his forehead. When had her baby turned into this boy? When had he begun to think of himself as a fella?

"Okay, Collin. I'll let it go this time. But I don't want you fighting anymore. If you can't avoid it any other way, you'll just have to tell a teacher. If you don't, I'll go to the school and report it myself. Now, put your things away while I stir the potatoes. Supper is almost ready."

Collin stood slowly and started to walk away. Suddenly he spun around and ran back, throwing his arms around Leah's waist. "Mom, can't I just go back to my old school? I hate it here. Those Rosemont kids are nothing but a bunch of stuck-ups."

"Listen to me, Collin. You know Rosemont Academy is a much better school, academically and in every other way. They have up-to-date books and equipment, and it will look so much better on your records. We were blessed that you won that scholarship." She wiped a tear from his cheek. "You'll get used to it. And I'm sure you'll make new friends soon. It's only been a month. Give it time. Won't you do that for me? You know I only want what's best for you."

"Okay, Mom." Collin's expression crashed, and he was obviously trying hard to hold back tears as he headed up the stairs. Leah got up from the sofa with a sigh and walked to the kitchen.

Didn't God even care?

Leah sat in the wooden rocker with her grandmother Collins's sewing basket on the table beside her. Tears of frustration poured down her cheeks and onto Collin's coat. While she'd examined the sleeve earlier, she'd failed to notice the lining inside the coat was ripped to shreds. Beyond repair. What in the world was she going to do? The money from her paycheck added to what little savings she had would have to last them for food and utilities until she could find another job. And there was always the possibility of medical emergencies. She wouldn't dare spend any of their meager funds on a new coat or even fabric for a new lining.

Lord, what am I going to do? It's too cold for Collin to go outside without a warm lining in his coat. The thought was there before she even realized what she was doing. Leah hadn't prayed since Bob died. Why should she? God hadn't seen fit to answer her prayers to keep her husband safe. Apparently He hadn't cared that her son would have to grow up without the love and companionship of his dad. So why bother to pray? Yet, there it was. Leah grew still. Would He answer, or would He ignore her as she'd ignored Him?

Wiping her eyes with both hands, she got up and went to the kitchen to put the kettle on for tea. As she walked back through the dining room with the fragrant brew in her hand, her eye caught a splash of color in the moonlight streaming through the window. She stopped and stared, then inhaled sharply. No, it wouldn't be possible. Or would it?

Leah set the cup on the dining table, and walking over to the window seat, she picked up the patchwork quilt. It was a family heirloom, passed down to her on her wedding day. It was very old and, according to family tradition, had some extremely interesting stories connected with it. She held the quilt close to her and caressed the cool, soft fabric. Did she dare rip it apart? Would her ancestors turn over in their graves at the thought of her pulling out their stitches? Or would they understand that she had no choice?

Still clutching the quilt, she walked back into the living room and sat back down in the rocking chair. Reaching into the loose lining of the sewing basket, she carefully pulled out a slip of paper, now yellowed with age. With a sigh, she read the words she knew by heart.

My dearest son,
  This quilt is the story of your family and the love that binds us together as

truly as the threads that hold together these pieces of cloth.

I began this quilt as a new bride. I didn't know any more about sewing than I did about being a wife, but I knew about love. The pieces of my wedding dress are in here and form the center block. They are the delicate spring-green swatches. It's the same green, by the way, you'll see when the first wildflowers poke their brave stems through the winter-worn earth.

There are a few patches of white in this quilt. They are cut from the shirt your father wore when we got married. Ah, John, what a fine figure he presented that day! I can still see him in my mind, so elegant, so handsome, so sure. . .and so very much in possession of my heart.

The little patches were once your blanket. This was the first earthly fabric that touched your newborn skin. Yellow-spotted flannel looked so warm against your infant skin, like God had poured sun around your tiny body. It was cold the night you were born—so cold the doctor's breath froze midair—but you quickly warmed our hearts.

As our family grew, so did our love—and the quilt. Notice how the stitches get more even and practiced on the outer patches. I was just learning in the center section, but the patches, straggly though they may be, are still holding together after many years of hard use.

Love is like that, John. At first, it's all very new and awkward, but if you're willing to put your heart into it, it'll hold steadfast. There aren't any silk or satin or velvet pieces in this quilt, but to me, its beauty far exceeds the grandest coverlet. Even the littlest, most mundane pieces of life make an extraordinary tapestry when united by love. . .these scraps of love.

Your loving mother,
Brigit Streeter Collins

Leah's heart nearly broke as she read Brigit's letter to her son, John, Leah's own father. She knew what the quilt had meant to her family members. What would they think?

Leah lifted her chin and pressed her lips together. Collin's health and comfort were more important than a quilt, even if it was a family treasure. And inside she had a feeling that if they could see her from heaven, the grand old ladies would agree.

⁂

Max Reilly rubbed frost off the ice-cold, second-story window and peered through at the snow-covered schoolyard below, searching for the taunting voices that had drifted to his office. He located the origin of the noise directly below his window and scowled. A cluster of boys in their early teens stood jeering and occasionally shoving a much smaller boy who stood defiantly in the middle of the circle.

Indignation clutched at Max. He wheeled around and headed for the nearest staircase, taking the steps two at a time until he reached the first floor. Max charged through the double front doors and headed for what had now become a scuffle, as the younger boy had somehow found the gumption to defend himself.

Max pressed through the ring of bullies. Their young victim pulled himself off the ground, his face scrunched up in a valiant effort to keep from crying.

"What's going on here?"

At the sight of the angry headmaster, the boys scattered. Max managed to grab two of the culprits, making a mental note of the ones who were running off.

"No, you don't. Whoa there. Stay right where you are, Mason and Carlisle."

Mason had the grace to look ashamed of himself, while he sputtered, "We were only having some fun. We didn't hurt him any."

"Um-hmm. We'll see about that later. You two get yourselves to my office right now. Sit down, and don't move until I get there."

Shaken by the sternness of their usually good-natured headmaster, both boys obeyed instantly, heading for the building.

Max turned to the younger boy, who was clutching his coat tightly around him and shivering.

"Are you hurt, son?" He knelt down in front of the boy, who tried unsuccessfully to wipe the tears away with his bare hands.

"Here, take my handkerchief. I promise it's clean." He grinned. The kid took the hanky and wiped his face, then blew his nose loudly.

"You're Collin Halliday, the new boy, aren't you?"

Collin nodded. Max picked the boy's hat up from the ground and brushed off the snow. "Here, better put this on. It's mighty cold out here. What was the ruckus about?"

Collin took a ragged breath and bit his bottom lip. "I'm not squealing."

"I understand. But bullies like that don't deserve to be protected. If they get by with treating you like this, they'll do it again to other boys, too. You don't want that, do you?"

A frown furrowed the lad's brow. He shook his head. Looking straight into Max's eyes, Collin said firmly, "No, sir, I wouldn't want that. But I just can't squeal."

Max nodded, wondering how to handle the situation. He had witnessed enough to know that the boys were teasing Collin about something, but unless he knew what it was so he could try to take care of it, the teasing was bound to happen again.

The boy stood shuffling from foot to foot, obviously in a hurry to go.

"All right, Collin. You may go now. But I want to discuss this with you further."

"Yes, sir. Thank you, sir."

Max grinned at the look of relief on the boy's face as he turned to go, but his grin faded as Collin's coat fell open, revealing a multicolored lining. *What in the world?* What kind of mother would line her son's coat with something that looked like a patchwork quilt? Surely she could have found something less conspicuous. Maybe she didn't realize how cruel children could sometimes be to anyone different. This was one reason Max had pushed for uniforms—overcoats included. Unfortunately, the board had overruled him on that.

Max knew what it was like to be the victim of bullies. Being the grandson of Templeton Rosemont, the founder of the academy, hadn't sat too easily upon his own small shoulders when he was a lad in this very school. And the fact that his father, James Reilly, had been the chairman of the board hadn't helped, either. He wasn't sure what he could do to help Collin through this tough time in his life, but at least he could take care of the coat situation. That was the easy part.

Pressing his lips together, he walked with determination back toward the building. First, the boy's tormentors had to be dealt with.

Chapter 2

L eah pursed her lips as she searched through her spice rack for cinnamon, cloves, and ginger. Setting each one on the table, she grinned triumphantly at her son. "Yes, I have everything we need for gingerbread men. Hooray!"

She'd already calculated the cost. Butter and sugar were precious commodities and had cost her more than she should have spent, but after the month they'd just endured, she couldn't say no when he'd asked her to make the treat.

Collin let out a war whoop and jumped off the wooden stool. "Call me when they're done! I'm going to play cowboys with Billy."

Leah shook her head and stared after her son, hands on hips, as Collin grabbed his coat and hat, then headed out the back door. So much for this being a joint effort. Apparently baking cookies with Mom was not Collin's top priority on a Saturday morning.

She walked into the pantry and took out the flour, sugar, and other ingredients she would need. She was just stirring the dry ingredients into the creamed mixture when the doorbell rang.

Leah wiped her hands on her apron and went to open the door.

Max Reilly, headmaster of Collin's school, stood there holding his hat in his hands. He looked down at her with the deepest blue eyes she had ever seen.

"Mr. Reilly?" Her voice almost squeaked, and she cleared her throat. "Is something wrong?"

"Mrs. Halliday, I'm sorry to intrude without sending a note home, but I really need to speak to you if you have a few moments."

Leah frowned. "Collin's not in trouble, is he?"

"No, no, nothing like that." He shuffled his hat from one hand to the other. "But there was an incident in school yesterday that I'd like to discuss if you don't mind."

"Of course. Won't you come in? Here, let me take your coat."

He shrugged out of the wool overcoat and handed it over.

Feeling dwarfed by the size of the headmaster, Leah cleared her throat and angled her head to meet his gaze. "I have fresh coffee on. May I offer you a cup?

"Thank you. Just black, please."

He smiled, and Leah's heart nearly stopped. A dimple winked at her from each cheek, and his black hair and thin mustache reminded her of Rhett Butler.

"Is everything all right, Mrs. Halliday?"

Leah blinked. "Huh?" Then she noticed the amused grin. Heat seared her cheeks. Apparently this man was accustomed to making women lose their ability to speak. "Of course. I'll just hang this up and bring in the coffee. I won't be a minute."

"Take your time."

Oh, that smile again.

Leah walked to the coatrack, caressing the material. The quality was evident, and she carefully hung it up, smoothing imaginary creases. She went into the small kitchen and pulled two cups and saucers from the cabinets. Why did some people have so much while others had nothing? The price of Mr. Reilly's coat alone would have paid for every item of clothing Collin needed and then some.

She pushed back the tears and, squaring her shoulders, returned to the living room with the steaming coffee. Mr. Reilly still stood in the middle of the room, looking ill at ease, his hat between his hands.

"I'm so sorry. You must think me awfully rude. Please sit down." She motioned toward the sagging, worn sofa and pushed back niggles of shame that she had nothing better for the headmaster of the elite boys' school to sit on.

With a wistful sigh, she dropped into the wooden rocker across from him. She crossed her ankles gracefully and sat with her hands clasped in her lap, dreading what must be coming. After the week she'd had, it could only be bad news.

"What brings you all the way over here on a Saturday, Mr. Reilly?"

He leaned forward and placed his cup and saucer on the coffee table. "I don't know quite how to tell you this, but there was a scuffle on the playground yesterday. Some of the older boys were teasing Collin and shoving him around a little bit."

"Again?" Indignation bit a hole in Leah. She sat up straight, leveling her gaze at him. "This is the second time in a month! Isn't it your duty to keep this sort of thing from happening?" She stood, took a deep breath, then stepped back and dropped her arm as she realized she had been shaking her finger almost in the headmaster's face. She sighed and gave him an imploring look. "Why would anyone want to tease a kid like Collin? At his other school, everyone liked him. He had dozens of friends."

Suddenly she noticed that he was looking uncomfortable.

He stood up and then cleared his throat. "Boys can often be cruel. They don't always see things—clothes, for example—as adults do."

Leah's eyes grew wide as understanding dawned. Why hadn't she realized? "His coat?" she whispered. She had been so concerned with keeping her son warm it had never crossed her mind.

"Yes. They were teasing him about the lining. Which is one of the things I wanted to talk to you about." He paused for a moment, then rushed on. "I, uh, took the liberty of purchasing a coat for Collin. Considering—"

A gasp escaped her throat. Her legs felt weak; humiliation burned her cheeks. "I—I appreciate your thoughtfulness, Mr. Reilly, but I am perfectly able to provide for my son. Just because the president of Rosemont Industries believes only the returning soldiers need to provide for their children doesn't mean I am so destitute I would take charity from a stranger."

He blinked in surprise, and a flush washed his handsome face.

Leah's frustration had finally found an outlet, and she planted her hands on her hips. "Perhaps it would be better to teach the boys at your school that just because they come from affluent homes doesn't mean they have the right to bully others who are not so fortunate. Rosemont is a prep school, Mr. Reilly. Prepare them to be good men. That's your job. My job is to teach my son to appreciate what he has. Even if that means wearing an old coat lined with a family heirloom because it was all I had."

Anger fueled her courage, and she walked, straight-backed, to the door. "I am sorry that you had to come all the way over here for nothing. In the future, please confine your attention to Collin's education, and let me take care of matters that are none of your business."

Max's shoes clicked brusquely on the wood floor as he took the bold hint. "Mrs. Halliday, I apologize for offending you. But I do hope you'll reconsider. It's admirable that you want to provide for your son, admirable even that you don't want to accept charity. But sometimes having too much pride is simply foolishness." He gave a curt nod and slipped through the door, which she quickly slammed behind him.

Unable to hang on to composure for another second, Leah threw herself onto the sofa and allowed the tears to flow. Wrenching sobs erupted from a hurting place deep within. When gradually they began to subside, she sat up, wiping furiously at the tears streaming down her face. The audacity of the man. What was he thinking?

She gasped, and her hands flew to her cheeks. Never mind what he was thinking. What had she been thinking talking to him that way? *Let me take care of matters that are none of your business?* Had she really said that? What had she done? Would he expel Collin after her outburst?

The mantel clock chimed noon. Leah had to pull herself together before Collin came home.

Collin! She'd forgotten all about his gingerbread men.

Trembling and heartsick, she got up and forced her legs to carry her to the kitchen. She had to think. She had to find a way to undo what she had just done.

❖

Max drove home in a state of self-condemnation, despite the fact that she'd thrown him out without giving him his coat back. How could he have been so stupid? Why hadn't he at least asked before buying that coat? He just hadn't thought. He simply saw a need and took care of it, just as he had done so many times before. Looking over Collin's records, he had noticed that Mrs. Halliday was a widow and employed at one of his grandfather's factories. What he hadn't known was that she had been let go. Of course she would be angry. He hadn't meant to be insensitive, but the hurt and humiliation on that lovely face were evidence that he had been.

He sat in his living room later that day trying to figure out how to mend the situation, but all he could think of were those soft-brown eyes filled with anguish just before she exploded and let him have it with both barrels. Not that he blamed her.

And he never did get to mention his other idea, which was probably a good thing. He rather doubted she would have wanted him to take her son under his wing. If she had realized his grandfather was the one who signed her compensation check and fired her along with the other women who had held down the fort during the war, she probably would have booted him down the steps rather than simply slamming her door on his back.

All in all, Max, you made a big mess of things.

Still, he couldn't help grinning at her spunk. He'd find a way to make it up to her. Somehow, he'd break through that iron will of hers and convince her to allow Collin to have the coat.

-:¦:-

The heavy wooden doors shut behind Leah, and she stood for a moment, looking down at the gray-painted concrete floor of the long hall. Lifting her chin and taking a deep breath, she stepped to the first door on the right and entered the school office. A middle-aged woman at the front desk looked up from her work and smiled as Leah came through the door. She eyed the man's coat draped over Leah's arm.

"May I help you?"

"Yes, my name is Leah Halliday. Would it be possible for me to see Mr. Reilly?"

"I'll see if he's available."

Leah turned away, looking at the prints on the wall as the secretary spoke into the receiver.

A door at the back of the room opened, and Max Reilly stood, smiling as though he'd been expecting her, which she knew he hadn't. Leah's heart did a strange flip, and she breathed deeply. *I'm just nervous because I don't want him to expel Collin.* Still, those eyes were every bit as deep and intense as she remembered.

"Mrs. Halliday. Please come in."

He ushered her into his office and pulled out a chair in front of his desk. She sat stiffly on the leather-cushioned chair as he went around and sat down behind his desk. "You, um, forgot your coat."

"It was thoughtful of you to bring it down here. You could have just sent it with Collin."

"I didn't want him to get it dirty." Leah felt like an utter fool. All those thoughts about his gorgeous eyes and broad shoulders. Silly girlish thoughts about a man so far out of her reach he might as well be Rhett Butler.

"Mr. Reilly. . ."

"Mrs. Halliday. . ."

They both stopped.

"After you, please," Max said.

Leah swallowed and started again.

"Very well, then. I'm here to apologize for my actions on Saturday. You were only being kind, and I overreacted. It was inexcusable of me, and I hope you won't hold it against my son." She gathered a shaky breath. "It would break my heart if he were expelled from Rosemont due to my outburst and—"

"Whoa, there. Wait a minute." Max stood up and walked around the desk. He sat in the chair next to her, giving her a look of earnest appeal. "You did nothing wrong. I'm the idiot who needs to apologize. In fact, I'd intended to do just that at the end of the school day. I had no idea how the gift would affect you. When the boys told me about the other fight and Collin's coat getting torn, I felt it was the responsibility of the school to replace it. This whole thing was my fault for not consulting you first."

She averted her gaze to her hands. "Oh, Mr. Reilly, now I feel even more foolish. I should have given you a chance to explain." She lifted her chin and looked into his eyes. "To be quite honest, when I made the new lining, I wasn't thinking about anything but my son's warmth and health. Until I find another job, I'm afraid new coats aren't in the budget, so if you still have the one you offered us, I would very much like for Collin to have it."

Max's heart lurched as he stared at the brimming eyes of the young woman beside him. He would have given almost anything to remove the embarrassment she was so obviously feeling. He stood up and leaned against the desk.

Clearing his throat, he said, "There's another matter I'd like to talk to you about."

"Yes?" She looked up at him, a question in her eyes.

His heart jumped again. Making a quick decision, he glanced at his watch. "Look, it's about lunchtime. If you don't have plans, could I take you to lunch and talk about it there?"

"I suppose that would be all right. Or I could just come back."

"No, no," he said quickly. "After all, we both have to eat, so why not take care of this other business at the same time?

Nodding, she permitted him to take her arm and guide her toward the door. Max left a few brief instructions with his secretary, and then he escorted Leah to his car. They drove to a nearby restaurant.

After giving their order to the waiter, Max sat back in his chair and looked across at Leah Halliday. The artificial light in the room brought out gold highlights in the soft brown waves that caressed her shoulders. And her lovely eyes sparkled like stars. He shook his head, wondering where he was getting such poetic notions.

Clearing his throat, he began. "Mrs. Halliday, I hope what I'm about to propose won't offend you or sound strange in any way."

A little frown appeared between her eyes, and he hurried to continue.

"As you may or may not know, Rosemont Industries has begun a program for the sons of soldiers who died in the war."

"What kind of program?"

At the suspicion in her tone, he hurried on.

"It's simply a way to show appreciation for the sacrifices of our soldiers and their families. Of course there is no way we could ever replace a boy's father, but we can try to do things with him that his dad would do if he were here. Fishing trips, baseball games—those sorts of things. And most important, we provide a listening ear. No matter how close a boy is to his mother and how wonderful a mom she is, sometimes he just needs a man to talk to and hang around with."

"I see." She looked down at the plate that the waiter had just put on the table. *She's being too quiet. I've blown it again.*

"I think it sounds like a wonderful idea. And I would love for Collin to have a friend like that." She studied him for a moment. "But I need to think about it. If I do agree to it, I'd be very particular about who my boy went anywhere with."

"Yes, of course you would. A mother can't be too cautious where her child is concerned. Actually, if you allow Collin to take part in the program, I'd be honored if you'd consider me for his companion."

A look of surprise crossed her face, and she looked at him closely as though searching for some ulterior motive.

"That's very kind of you, of course, and I'm sure as the headmaster of Rosemont, your character is above reproach, but I still need to know you better before permitting my son to spend that amount of time alone with you."

"Well, then, how about the three of us doing some things together first?" *Max, you sound like a rambling idiot. She's never going to agree to this.*

"Let me think about it, Mr. Reilly."

"Of course. I'm sure you want to take time to think it over and pray about it."

"I really need to be going, Mr. Reilly. I have an interview this afternoon."

"But you've hardly touched your food."

"I'm not very hungry. Thank you for lunch. I really must go now."

She stood abruptly, nodded her head in his direction, then walked through the busy restaurant and disappeared out the door.

Chapter 3

Max sat hunched over his ancient oak desk, tapping a pencil on the polished surface. His lunchtime conversation with Leah Halliday kept going through his mind—especially her comment about him being a man of good character. He wondered how she'd feel if she knew about Claudia. Pushing his chair back from the desk, he turned sideways and stared unseeing out through the window.

If only he hadn't decided to spend the summer at the family farm that year. If only Jake hadn't chosen that particular summer to spring his new bride on them. Maybe it would have happened anyway, though. Some things were just inevitable, and no matter how many times he replayed that day in his mind, trying to conjure different scenarios, the ending was always the same.

He could sympathize with the H. G. Wells character in his novel *The Time Machine*. No matter how many times the poor, grief-stricken slob went back to try to save the woman he loved, she died in every instance. Some things were simply going to happen. As though they were predestined. Still, nearly four years later, Max failed to see how God could possibly want such a thing to happen to him.

The disruption of his ordered life was unforgivable. The accusation that had rocked him to the core and caused the eye of suspicion to rest upon his up-to-then stellar character caused him to squirm with humiliation and regret. He tried to push it aside and get on with life, but during quiet, reflective moments, he couldn't help but wonder, how did things go so wrong? If only his brother had never brought his young bride home that summer of 1942. His mind drifted back, the images playing through his mind as though it were yesterday. . . .

"Bruiser! Get down!" Max grabbed the Saint Bernard's collar and yanked him back away from the trembling young woman who stood stock still on the circular, stone driveway. His brother, Jake, turned on him with fury.

"Why can't you control that stupid animal? He's going to hurt someone some day!"

Max looked at his brother in surprise.

"Sorry, Jake. He just gets excited when he meets someone new. Don't you, boy?" Max scruffed the dog behind the ears, earning himself a happy half-moan from the Saint Bernard.

He turned to the lovely young woman, who was looking into a tiny mirror she had pulled from her handbag and patting at the platinum-blond locks that had strayed from the roll of hair gracing the top of her head. "Especially when it's someone as pretty as your guest."

The woman glanced away from her reflection and snapped her compact closed. She observed Max as though she'd just noticed his presence. Her arched brow rose with sudden interest that sent a warning signal through Max's midsection.

"I apologize for Bruiser's bad manners. I'm Jake's brother, Max, and you are. . . ?"

"She happens to be my wife." Without another word or look, Jake grabbed one of his wife's mink-draped arms and led her up the path to the house. She followed after him, glancing back over her shoulder at Max. Her full lips curved into a bold smile as her gaze traveled the length of him.

Shock jolted through Max like a lightning strike at her shameless perusal, and as heat crept up his neck and face, he stared after them in embarrassed outrage. What had Jake gotten himself into?

The hiss of the radiator brought Max back to the present. He stood and walked to the window, looking down at the boys on the snow-dusted playground. Most of the students seemed to be occupied in a heated game of dodgeball. Their excited laughter rang out, reaching through the closed window. What innocence. If only life could stay that simple. They say a man controls his own destiny. But Max was proof positive it wasn't always so.

Unbidden, thoughts of the past returned, and he found his unwelcome memories taking him back to that last Sunday in the stable. . . .

"Well, Sadie, how's that little girl doing today?" Max smiled and patted the roan mare on the nose, then reached down and ran his hand over the flanks of the new foal. "Seems to be a fine little filly you have here, Mama."

Without warning, slender arms encircled his waist from behind. Jerking loose, he whirled around to see Claudia grinning.

"Don't be so shocked, Maxie. I've seen you watching me. You've wanted to hold me in your arms all summer, haven't you?"

"I don't know what you think you've been seeing, Claudia, but I'd as soon hold a boa constrictor." He stepped past her and waited 'til she followed him, then closed the door to Sadie's stall.

For a moment, anger clouded her eyes, but then her red-stained lips puckered into a pouting smile.

"Don't be so mean, Max. You know I really like you a lot."

Suddenly she reached up and wrapped her arms around his neck, smiling seductively.

Stunned by her audacity, Max couldn't move. Obviously taking his inaction as an invitation, Claudia stood on her tiptoes and inched closer to him. "You like me a little bit, don't you, Maxie?"

"No!" his mind screamed. And just as he was about to throw her from him, she pressed her lips against his in a very unsisterly kiss.

That's when Jake had walked in, and of course he believed every outrageous lie Claudia had come up with. Finally, he had accused Max, before the whole family, of attacking his wife. His parents had not believed it for a moment. Claudia's character had become fairly obvious to them by that time, but a huge uproar arose among the rest of the family, some of whom were quite eager to believe any piece of gossip they heard. Worst of all, somehow word got around their society set, bringing shame to the entire family.

Earlier in the summer, Max had been offered a position helping with war supplies, so shortly after the scandal arose, he left for Washington, turning down the offer of a teaching position at Rosemont Academy. He hadn't been back to the farm since, and he only visited his parents in their Chicago mansion when he knew Jake and Claudia wouldn't be there. By the time he returned from Washington, the gossip mongers had moved on to other, juicier, more recent scandals, and the incident seemed to have been forgotten by everyone but the family.

His father had helped Max to acquire the position of headmaster at the academy, which had always been his desire, so he had managed to create a stable and happy life, even though his brother Jake still thought the worst. Max avoided him and Claudia as much as possible.

Max shoved back the unwelcome memories. He directed his attention once more to the playground and noticed Collin sitting alone on a bench, staring wistfully at some boys playing dodge ball. Max's heart went out to the lonely looking child. He had to think of a way to convince the nervous mother that he would make a good companion for Collin. Suddenly an idea came to him. He returned to his desk and, pulling out a sheet of school stationery, he wrote a short note inviting Leah and her son to attend church services with him on Sunday morning. He would send the note home with Collin after school.

In the meantime, maybe he could get Collin off that bench for the rest of recess.

·≈·

Leah turned the skeleton key and opened her front door. She had an hour before Collin would be home. Dinner would be a simple meal of leftover meatloaf and vegetables, so all she really had to do was make a salad to go with it.

She put her coat and hat in the closet and made a cup of tea. Sitting at the kitchen table enjoying the steaming, spicy drink, she thought over her afternoon.

After leaving the restaurant, she had gone straight to her appointment at Seville Toy Company. The interview had gone fairly well, but Leah wasn't at all confident. Mr. Monroe had seemed impressed with her shorthand, but her typing wasn't nearly as fast or accurate as it had been four years ago. The factory job at Rosemont had paid so much better than any of the secretarial positions that she hadn't given a second thought to leaving her skills behind. Now she wondered if that had been wise.

Although Mr. Monroe had promised to consider her application, Leah wasn't sure how she would compare to others with more recent experience, especially with so many being let go from the factories. Jobs were scarce. It would be a miracle for her to land this one. Oh, if only she could come up with enough money to start her own bakery! But that would take an even bigger miracle. And Leah just didn't believe in miracles anymore.

"Mom! I'm home!"

Leah jumped up from the table. "I'm in the kitchen, Collin." How in the world had an hour passed by so quickly?

Leah stood and took the meatloaf and vegetables from the ice box, then stopped and stared at Collin as he came in with a big grin on his face.

"Look, Mom. Mr. Reilly said the school owed me this coat because of my other one getting ripped. He said he talked to you about it. Was it okay that I took it?" Leah looked at the navy-blue wool coat that Collin was proudly displaying. Mr. Reilly and Rosemont Academy had obviously spared no expense in replacing the old one.

"Yes, of course. Now, come here and give me a hug."

The boy obliged with a squeeze that almost took Leah's breath away. She laughed and held him away from her.

"Let me get a good look at the new coat. It's very nice, Collin. Much nicer than your old one."

He smiled widely, and then suddenly the grin faded, and he headed back into the living room, coming back a moment later with a bag containing his old coat.

"I really like this one, too, Mom. You did a swell job fixing it. I'll just keep wearing it. I don't need the new one."

Leah looked at her son standing there bravely, willing to sacrifice the new coat to spare her feelings. What could she say to convince him it was all right to keep it?

"You know, Collin, if you don't mind, I'd sort of like to remove that lining and repair Grandma's quilt."

Leah's heart lurched at the look of relief on her boy's face. His expression told her more than any words just how difficult it had been for him to wear the mended coat.

"Sure, I'll just wear the new one then. Isn't it a swell coat? Mr. Reilly's really swell, too. He's an okay guy, not just a headmaster. He came out on the playground at recess and judged us in some races. I almost won the last one." The statement was spoken in such awe-filled tones that Leah struggled to keep from laughing.

"Oh, I almost forgot, Mom—Mr. Reilly sent you something."

"He did, huh?" The thought of "Mr. Reilly" sending her anything raised her defenses. Perhaps she hadn't made it clear that she and Collin weren't charity cases.

Collin reached into his pocket and pulled out a small envelope, which he handed to her.

"Thanks, son. Now run upstairs and change out of your school clothes. I'll just see what Mr. Reilly has to say and get dinner on the table."

The boy headed for the stairs, running.

"Don't forget to wash up," Leah called after him.

She looked curiously at the envelope, hesitating briefly before tearing it open. She nibbled on her bottom lip as she glanced over the note. An invitation to church? They hadn't been to church in years. Not since Bob died. She wandered back into the kitchen, her mind playing scenes of the little wooden church she had attended with her husband before the war had ruined everything.

As she prepared a salad and heated up the leftovers, she thought about her luncheon conversation with the handsome headmaster. Sure, she had wanted to get to know him better before Collin spent time alone with him, but. . .church?

As they ate their supper, Leah glanced over at her son.

"Mr. Reilly has invited us to go to church with him on Sunday. What do you think?"

Collin swallowed a mouthful of milk and grinned at her. "That would be great, Mom. I kind of miss going to Sunday school."

"You do? Why haven't you said anything before?"

"Well, I sort of started to once. But you got a funny kind of look, so I changed my mind."

"Oh, Collin, I'm so sorry." What kind of a mother was so easily read by her ten-year-old son? "Well, I guess we'll go then."

"Really, Mom? Wow, okay by me. Maybe we could go get a hamburger or something after church, too."

"Now, Collin, Mr. Reilly didn't invite us to dinner, and you know we can't afford to be spending our money on hamburgers right now. Don't say anything about dinner to Mr. Reilly. You promise me now."

"Oh, okay, Mom."

The dejected look on her son's face brought a choking sadness to her heart. She knew it wasn't really the hamburger he was yearning for but the male attention.

"Hey, sport, I've got an idea. How about if we invite Mr. Reilly here for dinner?"

"Really?" Collin's shining eyes were evidence that she had been right.

"Sure, but you have to help me decide what to cook. Deal?"

"Deal!" He reached a hand over the table to shake.

"I already know what you can fix for dessert, Mom. How about some of your doughnuts? All the guys around here say yours are better'n the ones at the doughnut shop."

"Better than, Collin, and I don't know about doughnuts for a dinner dessert."

"Okay, then. Chocolate cake. Everybody likes chocolate cake, and yours is the best, Mom."

"I'm afraid I just don't have enough sugar to make it."

Collin's expression crashed. "Aw." He kicked at the ground.

Leah's heart went soft. "Listen, kiddo. I think I have just enough sugar left for about a half batch of molasses cookies. I know it's not chocolate cake, but what do you say I whip some of those up?"

His eyes brightened. "Swell!"

"Good. Now if you're through eating, you can help me with the dishes. Then I'll write a note to Mr. Reilly while you take your bath."

·⁙·

Max couldn't keep the smile off his face as he read Leah Halliday's note for the third time. Not only had she accepted his invitation to church, but she had also extended her own invitation to dinner. That much more time to start building that relationship with Collin. But he had to admit to himself that wasn't the only reason for his elation. The lovely Leah's deep brown eyes and pensive smile had haunted his dreams all night. He'd have to guard his feelings a little better. He certainly didn't need any involvements. Not after what he'd been through. All he needed was a hint of scandal, and even his grandfather's good name wouldn't be enough to keep his job for him. And being headmaster of Rosemont Academy meant everything to him. His heart was here, with the education and upbringing of these boys.

Chapter 4

A soft glow enveloped the sanctuary where Leah sat straight-backed, holding tightly to Collin's hand. The last strains of "Amazing Grace" faded, and the purple-robed choir members seated themselves in the choir loft. The elderly pastor walked to his place behind the pulpit, opened the enormous black Bible that lay there, and smiled out at the congregation.

The pastor greeted the congregation and began to say something about the new addition to the building, but Leah was having trouble hearing him through the loud beating of her heart.

"Mom!" Her son's desperate whisper drew her attention, and she looked down and realized she was gripping his hand too tightly. She gave him a tremulous smile and released it.

"Sorry," she mouthed silently.

"It's okay," he mouthed back, grinning.

She glanced over at Max, who sat at the end of the oak pew on Collin's other side. He smiled, then turned his attention back to the pastor.

Leah closed her eyes and took a deep breath. *Calm yourself down, Leah,* she lectured herself silently. *It's just a church service. You've been to hundreds of them.*

She realized suddenly that everyone was standing, and she quickly rose to her feet and bowed her head as the pastor began to pray.

"Our heavenly Father, first of all we would like to thank You for all the many blessings You have bestowed upon us. Thank You for supplying our daily needs and for guiding us in our walk on this earth. We also thank You, Father, for the boys that You have brought safely home to us. It is such a blessing to see these beloved faces that have been absent from our midst. But, Lord, some of our brave boys didn't come back. We can only accept Your will and ask You to comfort their families and friends. Help us to remember, Lord, they are with You in a better place. . . ."

Is Bob with You, God? Is he really with You? Will we see him again some day? I can hardly remember what he looks like. When I think of him, I see a tall, handsome man in a blue suit standing by me in our wedding picture. But I can't see the twinkle in his eyes or his smile anymore. He loved You. And he taught me to love You, too. But I've strayed away. I can't remember the last time I read my Bible. Does he know about that, God? Does he know I'm not only forgetting him, but that I've just about forgotten You, too?

Leah started as people began to take their seats again. She sat down, wiping tears from her eyes.

⫶

The aroma of roasted chicken filled the kitchen as Leah took the lid off the roasting pan. The potatoes were browned to perfection. The salad was already on the table. She put the chicken on a platter and surrounded it with the potatoes and carrots. After placing it on the dining room table, she stepped back and looked everything over one more time. *Perfect.*

Max and Collin didn't even hear her come into the living room. They were stretched out on the floor putting together a model airplane that Leah had unsuccessfully attempted to help Collin with. From the looks of things, it was pretty much completed.

"Hey, anyone hungry?"

Two heads turned and smiled up at her at the same time. Leah blinked hard in an attempt to stop the tears that were rising unbidden to her eyes. Collin's face was radiant. Leah hadn't realized how much he had missed male companionship.

They both scrambled to their feet.

"I'll say. I'm starving." Collin headed for the dining room, then stopped. "Oops, guess I'd better go wash up."

"Me, too." Max grinned and followed.

Leah shook her head and laughed softly.

The conversation at dinner was light and fun. Leah loved watching the camaraderie between Mr. Reilly and Collin. The boy glowed. It was obvious he had found a new hero.

"Collin, I'd say you are about the luckiest young man in Chicago," quipped Max.

"Why's that, Mr. Reilly?"

"Because, you're mother is the best cook in Chicago, that's why."

Leah blushed and started to speak, but Collin interrupted.

"Yeah, but if you think this stuff's good, wait until you taste the dessert."

Leah shook her head as she watched the two of them clean up a plate of molasses cookies.

Finally, Max gave an exaggerated groan and pushed back from the table.

"You were right, Collin. I've never tasted cookies that good before. Okay, point me to the kitchen sink."

"That's not necessary, Mr. Reilly," Leah said quickly. "I'll just clean up in here while you and Collin finish the model."

"No way, lady. You worked hard preparing this delicious meal, and this fellow pays for his supper. Tell you what—I'll wash, and you dry." His eyes danced as he tossed her a smile that just about took her breath away.

"Well, all right, if you insist." Leah stood up and started to clear the dishes from the table. She stopped suddenly and stared as Max removed his coat. Muscles rippled beneath the white dress shirt as he reached forward to hang the jacket on his chair. Leah felt heat rising to her face as he turned and saw her watching him.

His eyes deepened to near blue-black as he stared at her. She stood mesmerized as his hand reached out toward her hair. Leah jerked around quickly and picked up

410

another plate, almost dropping it. She cleared her throat, hoping she could speak normally. "Kitchen sink is right this way, sir."

After Leah filled the dishpan with hot, sudsy water, she handed Max an apron, which he donned with a flourish.

He turned around, flashing a grin at her over his shoulder. "Afraid you're going to have to tie this. I'm not used to wearing aprons."

Shaking her head firmly, she said, "No way, Mr. Reilly. Your arms can reach behind to those ties quite nicely."

He laughed heartily and tied the apron, then plunged his hands into the suds.

After the dishes were done, they joined Collin, who had disappeared to the living room when he heard the word *dishes*.

Leah watched wistfully as Max helped Collin with the model. It would be wonderful for Collin to have a father. And a husband for Leah wouldn't be bad, either. Especially if that husband was someone like Max Reilly.

He left late in the afternoon, and as Leah followed him onto the wide front porch, he apologized for staying so long.

"Oh no, don't apologize, please. It was so lovely to have you here. I mean for Collin's sake. And, Mr. Reilly, if your kind offer still stands, I see no reason to object to your spending time with my son. He obviously likes you, and you seem to be very comfortable with him."

Max's eyes lit up, and he smiled broadly. "I'm so happy to hear that. Collin is a great kid. I'm going to enjoy this as much as he does."

They stood looking at each other silently for a moment, and then Max smiled again.

"By the way, now that I'm going to be a friend, and not just the headmaster, don't you think you could drop the 'mister' and call me Max?"

"Well, I suppose that would be all right. Then I guess you should call me Leah."

He took her hand. "Thank you for a delicious dinner, Leah, and a wonderful afternoon. I can't remember when I've had such a good time."

Leah watched as Max's car pulled away from the curb. There was no denying the attraction there. Her heart raced every time they were in the same room together.

Leah sighed. She had to think about acquiring a job and taking care of Collin. She didn't have time for distractions. Even if this particular distraction did have the most appealing smile she had ever seen.

She went inside and sat on the worn, overstuffed sofa. Her Bible lay on the side table, where she'd set it after this morning's service. The sermon today had touched her in a way she hadn't felt in years. The words of hope and love that had come forth from the gentle lips of the pastor had pierced her heart as words of condemnation never would have.

Leah reached for the small black book and opened it. Now where was the passage Reverend Hollingsworth had read that morning? *Romans,* she thought.

"Hi, Mom. Hey, are you reading your Bible? I've been reading mine, too. I looked up the part that the preacher was reading today. I wrote it down."

"Oh, Collin. I'm so glad. It was in Romans, wasn't it? Can you tell me the chapter number?

"Sure. Romans, chapter 8. Starting with verse 38."

"Thanks, honey."

Leah leafed through the pages until she found the appropriate verses.

As she read the words of Paul the apostle, hope began to take birth in her heart for the first time since she had received the news about Bob's death: "For I am persuaded, that neither death, nor life, nor angels, nor principalities, nor powers, nor things present, nor things to come, nor height nor depth, nor any other creature, shall be able to separate us from the love of God which is in Christ Jesus our Lord."

·:·

Max whistled a popular tune as he drove away from the Halliday home. He had been telling the truth when he'd told Leah he couldn't remember when he'd had such a good time. Collin was a joy to be with. He wondered what it would be like to have a son like him. And a wife like Leah to come home to every day. His eyes gleamed as he recalled the little dimple that appeared next to her mouth when she smiled. And how he would love to run his fingers through the smooth, silky waves that hugged her shoulders.

Suddenly Max sat up straighter and gripped the steering wheel. What was he thinking? He needed to be careful not to get too close to her. She was bound to start asking questions. He couldn't afford for the scandal to rear its ugly head again.

He pulled into his driveway and sat without making a move to open the door.

Would the shadow of that incident with Claudia haunt him for the rest of his life? Would he have to live with this fear hanging over him forever? Why should he have to continue to suffer for something he hadn't done?

Not only could he not pursue a relationship with Leah, but also if the scandal resurfaced, she wouldn't let him near Collin. He had to do something. He hit his head against the steering wheel in frustrated agony. But what?

Making a sudden decision, he fired up the engine. He had tried, unsuccessfully, to talk to Jake about this before, but Jake wouldn't even speak to him, much less listen to reason. Of course, he was going to believe his wife over his brother. Max couldn't help but wonder, though, how Jake could be so blind to Claudia's lack of morals.

He drove through the gate and parked in front of the huge brick mansion. His father would object to his not pulling into the garage, but he didn't plan to be here that long anyway.

He found his father in the library polishing a rifle from his collection of antiques. Max stood just inside the door, inhaling the familiar smell of leather and old books.

"Well, Max, to what do I owe the honor of this rare appearance?"

"Sorry, Dad. I've been busy lately. Is that a new one?" He walked over and put his hand on his dad's shoulder.

James Reilly held up the rifle by the stock, looking at it proudly.

"I have a certificate of authenticity stating that it belonged to Annie Oakley. It's a rifle she used in Buffalo Bill's Wild West Show."

"Hmm, interesting. Where's Mother?"

"She should be here. So busy running around to her charity functions, she forgets charity begins at home. I could use a little of her tender loving care myself." He ran his hands through his thinning hair in obvious frustration.

Max laughed. Everyone knew that Celia Rosemont Reilly doted on her husband and spoiled him rotten.

"Now, Dad, you just can't stand it if she's away from you for an hour. Admit it."

He laughed as his father threw him an indignant glance and placed the rifle back in the oak cabinet.

"Ring for Helen, son. I could use some strong coffee. How about you?"

Only after they had settled into chairs by the fireplace with hot drinks in their hands did his father turn to him with expectation written across his lined face. "All right, Max. Out with it."

Max buried his head in his hands and moaned.

Taking a deep breath, he looked up.

"It's the thing with Claudia. I have to get out from under this, Dad."

A shadow of pain crossed the older man's face, and he surveyed his son. "I don't think anyone believes that old story anymore."

"Some do. You know they do. And most important, Jake believes it. As long as he believes it of me, believes that I could do such as thing. . .well, his attitude gives credence to it. Not just to those who want to believe the worst. It puts a niggling of doubt even in the minds of people who don't want to think it of me."

A log fell in the fireplace, and Max stared at the sparks as they danced and popped around the blazing wood.

"Dad, I was thinking. Do you suppose it would do any good for me to try to talk to Jake again? Surely after all this time, he has gained some insight into Claudia's character."

"They've gone on vacation. I thought you knew. They left on a riverboat last month for New Orleans and places unknown. Claudia's idea, I'd say. Jake never did like to travel. He wanted to take an airplane, but Claudia is afraid to fly. And besides, riverboats are more interesting." He snorted and curled his lips in derision.

"Well, that's that then."

"What brought this on all of a sudden? I thought you had put it behind you. The board knows all about the situation. You don't need to worry about your job, if that's what's bothering you."

"They know?" A sense of shame invaded Max at the very thought of the board members of the school knowing about the tawdry accusations against him.

"Of course they know. Did you think they had their heads in the sand? They, however, also know me and know that I wouldn't try to cover up for you if it had been true. So stop worrying."

"Well, there are a few other reasons. . . . Oh, never mind. I just want my name cleared."

His father gave him a hard look. "It's a woman, isn't it? Who is she? Why haven't you brought her home to meet us?"

"It's not like that, Dad. She's just a friend." He squirmed in his chair. "The mother of one of the boys at the academy. His father was killed in the war." He smiled as he thought of Collin. "You should see that little fellow. He's great." He ran his hand through his hair. "And she's raised him by herself since he was six."

James Reilly took a sip from his cup, peering at Max over the brim. "I see."

And Max knew that his father did see, way too much.

Chapter 5

I'll miss you, Janie. Are you sure there's not something else you can do?"

"I wish there was. But I'm scared, Leah." Janie's forehead wrinkled, and she bit her lip. "My rent is due in two days, and it would take nearly everything I have left to pay it." Her pink-tipped fingers raked through her hair, and she shrugged her shoulders and smiled sadly. "The last job possibility I had in sight just flew the coop. And believe me, I've pounded the pavement every day."

Leah took a sip of her tea and nodded thoughtfully.

"Yes. Me, too." Leah gave her friend a commiserating smile. "But, Janie, you could live here until something opens up. I have an extra bedroom, you know." Actually, she had been tossing around the idea of renting it out, but Janie didn't have to know that. "So, how about it?"

Janie shook her head. "Thanks, honey. That's sweet of you. But I need to go home while I have money for train fare." She smiled brightly. "Anyway, Dad can always use help in the store."

Leah sighed. "Don't you hate change? Just think how it was a few short months ago. You and Susie and me. The Three Musketeers together forever." She laughed sadly. "Now, Susie is going back to Dallas, and you to Missouri. I'm going to be so lonely."

Janie cut her gaze to Leah, and her lips curved in a teasing smile. "Oh, I don't think you're going to be all that lonely. How are things going with the handsome headmaster? Susie told me you've been spending a lot of time with him."

Leah felt warmth rise to her cheeks. She was going to clobber Susie.

"Really, Janie. Susie is jumping to conclusions. Of course, Max is here quite often because he's spending time with Collin. It's part of the Rosemont program, you know, the one I told you about."

"Um-hmm. And the roses over there? Did *Max* send those to Collin? Are they part of the program also?" She lifted her eyebrows and grinned.

Leah burst out laughing. "Oh, you. All right. I suppose we have been seeing each other some. Actually, he took me to dinner a few nights ago."

"Without Collin?"

"Yes, without Collin. But only because Collin was spending the night with a friend from his Sunday school class."

Suddenly Leah frowned. "Janie, I'm a little bit bothered about something."

Janie, ever the best friend, grew suddenly serious, her eyes alert. "What?"

"It's probably nothing. After all, he has a right to his privacy." Leah paused as anxiety arose as a knot in her stomach. "It's just that every time I ask anything about his family or prior jobs or anything like that, he manages to change the subject." She picked up her spoon and began to tap it against the rim of the saucer. "I'm sure it's okay. After all, a prestigious school like Rosemont surely wouldn't have hired him without a thorough investigation into his personal life. But. . ."

"Hmm. Maybe he's just a private person. Or maybe he's ashamed of his family." Janie slammed her teacup down and snapped her fingers. "Oh, wait, I've got it. His father drinks, and his mother beats him."

Leah exploded into laughter. She was going to miss Janie so much.

After they said tearful good-byes, Leah sat down in her rocker to mend some of Collin's shirts. He'd become so happy and vibrant since Max had taken an interest in him. It was like he had suddenly come to life. There hadn't been a lot of outdoor things they could do because of the cold March winds, but Max had promised fishing trips and baseball games in the spring and summer. In the meantime, he was teaching Collin to play tennis. It never would have occurred to Leah that Collin would be interested in tennis, but under Max's tutelage, the boy was getting quite good at the game.

Still Leah felt she had to be careful where her son was concerned. If only she could be absolutely certain that Max was as upright and responsible as he seemed. It would break Collin's heart if it proved otherwise. And Leah had to be honest with herself. It would just about break hers, too.

···

Max didn't know what he was going to do about Leah. He was falling in love with her. He couldn't get away from that fact. And she seemed to care for him, too. He hadn't been able to resist pursuing a relationship with her that was fast becoming more than friendship. Yet he knew it was hopeless unless he got the situation concerning Claudia settled. Once and for all.

Leah was already asking questions that he couldn't answer without revealing too much. He hadn't even told her yet that his mother was heiress to the entire Rosemont holdings. He knew he had to at least come clean about that. He wished now he had told her from the beginning. It had been foolish to keep it from her.

He had hoped to speak to his brother by now, but Jake and Claudia were back in New Orleans again after traipsing all over the southern states. Apparently Claudia had been enjoying the antebellum mansions of Georgia, Mississippi, Louisiana, and Alabama and had managed to somehow charm her way into southern society. Now, it seemed she was determined to take part in her first Mardi Gras experience.

Max's lips twisted in a wry grin. Poor Jake. That sort of thing was so contrary to his nature. A picture of the young Jake appeared in Max's mind. A picture of Jake shut up in the library with a stack of books on the floor beside him. Max could hardly ever get him outside long enough to go fishing or play a game of catch. His beloved books were always calling him. It was during a rare period of restlessness on Jake's part that he had met Claudia and fallen hard.

Max had no doubt that his brother was smitten soundly. He couldn't help feeling sorry for him. The brothers had been close once. But when Claudia entered the picture, Jake seemed blind to everything but her dubious charms. His eyes were almost certain to be opened one day, and Collin didn't relish the thought of his younger brother getting hurt.

One Sunday in mid-April when he was driving over to pick up Leah and Collin for church, Max made a sudden decision to come clean about his family connections. He hoped Leah wouldn't be too upset. After all, he hadn't actually lied to her; he had just failed to mention a few things. *Yeah, sure, Max,* he thought. *That's going to impress her.*

Leah came to the door looking like she had just stepped off the silver screen. She flashed him a million-dollar smile that nearly made him trip over his feet.

He smiled warmly back and reached for her hand.

"Hi, Max!" Collin scooted past his mother and grabbed the outstretched hand, giving it a hearty shake.

"Hey, sport. Good to see you." Max sent a sideways smile toward Leah, who attempted to hide an amused grin as she headed toward the car.

The service was inspiring, and Max was pleased to notice that Leah seemed every bit as involved in it as he was. In the beginning, he had wondered at the way she seemed to hold herself back from entering in, but lately she seemed to enjoy the services more. They had even spent a few Sunday afternoons discussing the sermon they had just heard.

As Max and Leah stood in the vestibule visiting with a few people after church, Collin and his friend Tommy came hurrying up.

"Mom, is it okay if I go home with Tommy? His mom and dad say it's okay with them."

"And my dad even said he'll take Collin home later if it's okay with you, Mrs. Halliday," Tommy chimed in.

"Well, I think so, but let me go talk to them first." Leah smiled at the boys, and turning to Max, she excused herself, then headed over to where Tommy's parents stood. After a short, reassuring conversation, she headed back to Max.

As Max watched her walking toward him, he decided to take advantage of the opportunity to have his talk with Leah. A few minutes later, as he opened the car door and waited for her to slide into the seat, he said, "If you don't have plans for the afternoon, I'd like to take you out to dinner."

"That would be lovely."

"Oh!" He snapped his fingers. "Would you mind if I ran back inside for a moment? I need to make a fast telephone call."

Leah looked at him in surprise but shook her head.

After making the phone call, he returned to the car and smiled as he slid in behind the steering wheel. "Sorry about that."

As he passed by their usual restaurant without stopping, Leah threw him a surprised look.

He smiled. "I thought we'd go somewhere different today."

417

When Max pulled the car into the drive of a very expensive restaurant, she looked at him in concern but didn't say anything.

He gave his keys to the attendant and offered his arm to Leah.

An elderly doorman opened the door for them, and Max motioned for her to step inside.

She did so, but then turned to him with a decidedly worried look on her face. "Max!" she whispered. "You can't—"

"Good evening, Mr. Reilly. It's nice to see you again. It's been too long." The man who spoke was beaming from ear to ear. "Your table is ready. Please come this way."

-:::-

Leah sat in silence while Max placed their order. The cloth on the table was gleaming white linen, and the settings were silver, crystal, and fine china. Even though it was only noon, a small orchestra played behind palm trees at the end of the room. What was he thinking? She was sure dinner for two here would cost a small fortune. She didn't want to embarrass him by saying anything about it, but. . .

"Max," she said softly, "I wouldn't have minded eating at our usual place. They have excellent food."

"Yes, they do. But I have something to tell you, and I thought this would be the perfect setting. And, Leah, I promise I'm not going to be destitute for the next six months, so enjoy yourself and don't worry about it." He reached over and took her hand for a moment, his eyes warm and affectionate and alive with something else. Uncertainty perhaps?

The food was delicious, and Leah tried to enjoy it, but she was too nervous wondering what he wanted to talk to her about. They both declined dessert, and as they sat with coffee, Leah looked at Max questioningly.

He took a deep breath.

"Leah, I'm not sure how to begin, but I need to tell you who I am."

She sat up stiffly. Uh-oh, here it came. She knew he was too good to be true.

"Do you mean you're not Max Reilly?" she demanded.

A startled look crossed his face.

"Oh no! I am indeed Max Reilly. I suppose I should have said I need to tell you who my family is." He took a nervous breath, then said quickly, "Leah, I'm a Rosemont on my mother's side of the family."

Leah sat waiting for him to go on. When he didn't speak, she realized he was waiting for a response from her. "Do you mean as in Rosemont Industries, Rosemont Academy, Rosemont Gas and Oil?"

He nodded.

"So your mother is. . .what? A cousin or something?"

"Well, no, not exactly. As a matter of fact, my mother is Templeton Rosemont's daughter."

Leah opened her mouth and tried to speak, finally managing to choke the words out. "What? You're Templeton Rosemont's grandson, and you're just now getting around to telling me?"

"Leah, I didn't tell you in the beginning because there wasn't really any reason to at the time, and I don't like to spread it around. Then later. . .well, I wasn't sure how to tell you, especially since my grandfather's factory had let you go."

Suddenly Leah felt a giggle rising up from her chest to her throat, and she coughed to try to cover it up, but to no avail. She chortled with glee while he sat and stared at her as though she had lost her mind.

Finally, she managed to get control of herself.

"Oh, Max, I'm sorry. It's just such a relief. I knew you were holding something back, and I was afraid you had some deep, dark secret. And all the time, you were just afraid I'd be mad at you because your grandfather had fired me."

"Well. . ."

"Don't worry about it, Max. I don't hold you responsible at all."

They left the restaurant shortly afterward, and Max took her hand at the door and said good-bye, promising to see her on Tuesday after school when he and Collin had a tennis date.

Leah felt as though she were walking on clouds the rest of the day, and after Collin had gone to sleep that night, she sat in her grandmother's old overstuffed chair and thought over the day.

Suddenly she closed her eyes.

"Father, I'm so sorry for all my doubts. Please forgive me, and help me not to ever fall into unbelief again. And, Lord, thank You so much for clearing this thing up about Max. Because I guess You know what I've not been admitting even to myself. I've fallen in love with him."

Chapter 6

M r. Reilly, do you wish to dictate those letters about the graduation exercises now?"

Max looked up from the stack of applications on his desk. His secretary stood in the doorway with her steno pad and pencil in hand.

He smiled. "Sorry, Edna. I was supposed to do that this morning, wasn't I?"

She gave him an uncertain smile. "Shall I come back later?"

"No, no, they need to be mailed out right away." He waved her to a chair. "Please sit down, and we'll do that now."

He shoved the applications aside and took his notes for the letters out of the top drawer.

Get ahold of yourself, Maxwell. You're slipping. The thought caused him to exhale loudly, and Edna frowned at him. Max couldn't blame her. She wasn't used to him being absentminded or stressed. He needed to pull himself together.

With an apologetic smile tugging at his lips, he shrugged. "You still have last year's letter on file, don't you?"

"Of course. But—"

"Good! Just use that one, and incorporate these additional notes, please, if you don't mind." He held out his pages of notes to her.

"No, I don't mind, Mr. Reilly." She stood and took the notes, then left the room. But Max couldn't fail to see the confusion in her eyes.

He walked over to the window and looked out. Some of the trees were beginning to bud. A sign of the approaching spring. But he knew that winter could just as easily come rushing back.

His dinner with Leah on Sunday had started out like spring, too. Fresh and joyful. But her words, laughingly spoken, kept ringing through his ears. *I thought you had some deep, dark secret or something.* He hadn't missed the relief in her tone of voice. Apparently she had perceived that everything wasn't as it should be with him. Now he feared he was deeper in the quagmire of deception than before. And he knew Leah didn't deserve to be a part of it.

He had to get this mess straightened out before Leah and Collin got hurt. He supposed he should just back out of their lives. It would probably be the kindest thing to do. But he couldn't. His feelings for both of them were too strong for that now. More than anything, he wanted them for his own. He wanted to be a husband to Leah and a father to Collin. But could that ever happen? Could he ask them to share his life when a shadow hung over his good name? Would God in His mercy show him a way out of this pit?

Max had always believed that God loved him and would take care of the things concerning him. Even when the incident had first happened and the unjust accusations had caused turmoil in his life, he had never doubted God. But now. . . *Why, God? Why?* For the first time in his life, God seemed far away, and no comforting words came to his mind. In sudden grief and frustration, Max doubled up his fist and hit the wall hard, not even feeling the pain.

Leah's high heels clicked against the sidewalk as she almost danced up to her front door. Finally, after all these months of worry, she had a job. Even better, her dream job. The salary was a little lower than she had hoped for, but the owner of the bakery had promised a raise after her initial training. Mrs. Crumply was a widow in her early sixties, and she needed someone who could take over the major part of the pastry making as well as learn the business end. This was just the sort of opportunity Leah had been dreaming of.

God was so good to her. First to clear up her concern about Max and now to provide a real job again. She couldn't wait to tell Collin.

She spent the rest of the day doing laundry and baking cookies. She might as well get all the practice she could. She grinned as she sat at the table sampling one that was warm from the oven.

The door slammed, nearly sending her through the roof.

"Oops! Sorry, Mom!"

Leah grinned at the sound of Collin's voice. Hurrying into the living room, she grabbed him in a tight hug and whirled him around in circles.

"Mom! What are you doing?" Collin stumbled out of her grasp and stared at her with a frown that tried to hide the smile lurking behind it.

Leah laughed and tousled his hair.

"I have a job, Collin. A really good job. Isn't it wonderful?"

"Wow, Mom. That's terrific. Where you going to be working?"

"Crumply's Bakery. Can you believe it?"

Collin leaned his head back and let out a whistle through his teeth.

"Swell, Mom. Peachy keen. When do you start? Do you get to bring home free stuff?"

"I start tomorrow morning. And we didn't talk about free stuff. But there are cookies on the counter. Get changed while I pour you some milk. Then you'd better get your homework done before Mr. Reilly gets here."

She knew Max planned to take Collin out for hamburgers after their tennis practice. This had become a Tuesday ritual. She smiled softly as she poured the milk and put two cookies on a plate.

The doorbell rang just as Collin was closing his notebook, and he jumped up and ran to the door, throwing it open.

"Hi, come on in," Leah called out from the chair where she sat darning socks.

Max walked in with his hand on Collin's shoulder. His eyes twinkled when he saw what she was doing.

"Boys are hard on socks, aren't they?" he queried.

"Well, this one is." They shared a knowing look, and both laughed.

"Guess what, Mr. Reilly? Mom's got a new job. She starts tomorrow. And it's in a bakery." Collin licked his lips and rubbed his stomach, grinning widely.

Leah and Max burst out laughing.

"I can see this is a job after your own heart, Collin. Congratulations, Leah."

"Thank you, sir. I've been walking on cloud nine all day."

"How about joining Collin and me for hamburgers later to celebrate?"

"That sounds very tempting, but I have ironing to do. I need to get it all done up since I'm starting back to work tomorrow."

"Okay, Mom. We'll see you later. We need to go now." Collin's not-so-subtle hint got through to Max, and he laughed.

"You're absolutely right, sport. Let's go. See you later, Leah. We should be back by six. Is that all right with you?"

She nodded, and he flashed her a smile and headed out the door with Collin.

⁘

Leah leaned back in the porch swing and covered a wide yawn with the back of her hand.

Max sent her a crooked smile. "Am I boring you?"

"Oh, sorry. It's not the company. I've just had quite a day."

"I'd probably better be going so you can get some rest."

"Not yet. Let's sit here awhile longer. It's such a beautiful night. I don't know when I've seen the stars so bright."

"Um, you're right." Max leaned back, too, and stretched his arm out behind her. Collin had gone to bed nearly an hour ago, and they had sat here since, talking softly about the tennis game and how well Collin was doing in school.

"Leah. . ."

"Yes?" she answered softly.

A lock of her hair had fallen loose from the velvet ribbon holding it back. Mesmerized, he took it and wrapped it around his finger. She turned toward him, and they gazed into each other's eyes for a moment. He caught his breath as she smiled lazily at him.

"You are so beautiful," he whispered. "Leah, do you realize how much I care for you?"

"I care about you, too, Max. You are so wonderful with Collin, and. . .well, it's not only because of Collin." She took a deep breath and whispered softly, "I care about you for you."

He swallowed and cleared his throat. "There is so much I want to say to you, but. . ."

She reached over and placed her hand on his arm. "It's all right, Max. Let's just get to know each other a little better. I don't want to rush into anything, either."

She smiled warmly, and he thought his heart would melt.

Maybe, just maybe they could make this work. Maybe, when the time was right, he would tell her everything, and she would understand and believe him. But not now. He couldn't, wouldn't spoil this moment.

·:·

Leah swallowed the last bite of her toast, then gulped down her orange juice.

"Collin, you need to hurry, sweetheart. We have to leave in five minutes. I don't want to be late my first day."

Collin stood up silently and took his dishes to the sink. She followed as he turned without looking at her and went into the living room, where he donned his coat, still without speaking.

"Is something bothering you? You haven't said a word since you woke up."

He lifted his eyes and shot her an accusing look.

"I saw you and Mr. Reilly on the porch swing last night!"

Leah felt her face flame.

"Oh. Well, Collin, I. . . What do you mean? We were just talking."

"He's my friend, not yours! Anyway, you're my mom. You're not supposed to have boyfriends!"

Stunned, Leah stared at her son as she felt the blood leaving her face. Her hands trembled as she grasped desperately for the right words to say.

"Collin." She reached for him, but he eluded her grasp and stomped out the door. By the time she followed him out, he was halfway down the sidewalk to the bus stop.

Leah rushed to catch up and reached him just as their bus pulled up. Collin flopped onto a seat and moved over so she could sit next to him.

She turned to him only to see him trying unsuccessfully to hide a tear that had slipped from his eye.

"Collin, I'm sorry you're upset. We'll talk about it this afternoon."

He scowled and turned toward the window.

Leah's heart felt like it would break. It never would have occurred to her that Collin would object to her friendship with Max. What would he do if that friendship did grow into something more, as it appeared to be doing? How in the world would she handle this new development?

Chapter 7

Max whistled as he placed his freshly laundered shirts in the drawer. He had been so busy this week, he had been down to one clean shirt when he finally got time this afternoon to pick up his laundry. He chuckled softly to himself as he started straightening up his bedroom. He hadn't had time to do much cleaning lately, either. Well, to be honest with himself, he probably could have found time before now, but more important things filled his life these days.

Sometimes he felt like pinching himself to see if he was in the middle of a wonderful dream. Leah was the most adorable woman to grace the earth, and he couldn't believe his extraordinary good fortune that she actually loved him, Max Reilly.

Leah had told him about Collin's angry explosion, and Max had been concerned. The boy was refusing to have anything to do with him, but Max had caught him looking at him several times when he thought no one was watching. The expression on his face was proof to Max that the boy missed their times together. It wouldn't be long now. He was coming around. God was answering prayer.

The aroma of lasagna reminded Max it was probably time to take his dinner out of the oven. Ten o'clock was a little late to be eating, and he was starving. He had just settled himself at the kitchen table when the doorbell rang. Max groaned and considered ignoring it, but it continued to ring, getting more insistent with each peal. With another groan, Max pushed his chair back and headed for the living room.

"Okay, okay, keep your shirt on. I'm coming!" He yanked open the door and stared at the disheveled woman who still leaned against the doorbell, causing the repeated ringing.

"Hi, Maxie. Glad to see me?" Claudia's lopsided smile, obviously meant to be seductive, sent a wave of revulsion through Max.

"What are you doing here, Claudia? I thought you were still in Louisiana, ruining lives there."

"Oh, Maxie. You hurt my feelings. Aren't you going to ask me in?" She giggled, then before he realized her intent, she had brushed by him and made her way across the room, falling onto the sofa.

Pursing her lips into a grotesque pout, Claudia beckoned to him with crimson-tipped fingers.

"Come on, Maxie. Sit here and talk to me." She patted the seat next to her.

"You can't stay here, Claudia. You'll have to leave now."

"But, Maxie. I don't want to go anywhere. I want to stay here with you. You know, Max, you're much more handsome than Jake. I've always liked you, and if you'd just get to know me a little, I think you'd like me a lot." She squinted up at him and gave a tipsy smile.

"Claudia, you're drunk. I'm calling a cab to take you home."

Max headed for the phone, and Claudia jumped up and staggered toward him, screaming in protest.

"Don't you dare pick up that phone, Max. I told you I don't want to go anywhere. I'm staying right here with you. I got you in trouble once, Max. And I can do it again!" A calculating look crossed her face. "I hear you have a girlfriend. Does she know about the time you tried to force yourself upon me?"

"Don't start it, Claudia. No one believes your lies anymore."

"Jake does." She threw her head back and laughed, then suddenly bent over as a fit of coughing overtook her.

Max stood looking at the woman his brother had chosen for a bride. Her hair was coming loose, and the bright-red lipstick on her mouth was smeared all over her chin. Maybe a cab wasn't such a good idea. Claudia suddenly put both hands to her head and swayed. Grabbing her arm, Max helped her back to the sofa, where she stretched out with a moan.

"Maybe I'll just take a little nappy, okay, Maxie?" And with that, she was out like a light.

Max stood looking down at her in helpless fury. Would he never be rid of her? Making a sudden decision, he strode firmly to the phone and dialed.

His brother's panicky hello wrenched Max's heart. Apparently Jake had been waiting for the phone to ring. Max hated to cause him pain, but what could he do?

"Jake, you need to come over here and get your wife. She just showed up at my door, and she's not in very good condition."

There was a pause on the other end of the phone, and then Jake answered shakily, "I'll be right there."

Max waited anxiously for his brother, hoping Claudia wouldn't wake up before he got there.

When Jake finally did arrive, he hurried over to his wife, barely looking at Max. He lifted her gently in his arms and carried her out to his waiting car. Max noticed he hadn't availed himself of his chauffeur's services. After he had deposited his wife into the backseat, Jake returned to the front door and confronted his brother. His lips were tight, and Max flinched at the pain and humiliation on his brother's face.

"You won't mention this to Mother and Father, will you?"

"No, of course not." Max reached out to put his hand on Jake's shoulder, but Jake drew back.

"I don't need your pity!"

Max watched sadly as the car squealed away from the curb.

⁘

Leah's days were passing in unbelievable happiness. She loved her job. The baking itself would have been joy enough, but to make things even better, Mrs. Crumply was giving her increasing responsibility for running the business. And as icing on the cake, her relationship with Max was flowering into something precious and wonderful.

His mother had sent an invitation to dinner, and Leah got butterflies in her stomach just thinking about meeting Max's mother. But she also admitted to herself she felt intimidated at the thought of going to one of the largest and grandest mansions in the city.

The only thing that had marred her life these past few weeks was Collin's attitude. After his initial outburst, he had drawn away from Max completely, hardly being civil to him and outright refusing to go anywhere with him. Leah had tried everything she could think of, from reasoning with him to firmly insisting that he straighten up his attitude, but to no avail.

Finally, after she had burst into tears on Max's shoulder one evening, he had cupped her chin in his fingers, turned her face to him, and spoken gently.

"Darling, please don't be so upset. Collin doesn't know how to handle the change in our relationship. Up to now, you have belonged to him alone, and I was his exclusive pal. Give him time to adjust. I really think if we don't make a big issue of it, he'll come around."

They had prayed together that night, and Leah had felt peace wash over her that she hadn't experienced since she and Bob used to pray together. Later, when she was alone, she had cried out her gratitude to God.

Max had continued to come over on every scheduled day to see if Collin wanted to play tennis. In spite of the continuous negative answer, lately she had noticed Collin looking wistfully at Max when Leah and Max were talking or laughing about something. And a couple of times she caught him trying to hide a smile. So maybe things were progressing after all, just as Max had said they would.

Leah hummed softly as she took the mail from her mailbox and went into the house. Another good thing about the bakery was that her day ended at three, and she usually made it home a few minutes before Collin did. Leah had made arrangements with the mother of one of the students to pick him up at their neighbor's house in the morning and bring him home after school. So far it had been working out fine.

She threw her purse on the coffee table, kicked her shoes off, and sat on the sofa. Glancing through the mail, she noticed an envelope addressed in flowing handwriting with no return address and no postage stamp. Puzzled, Leah tore it open. A yellowed clipping fell out, and Leah picked it up and held it while she perused the accompanying note. There was only one line: *I thought you should know the sort of man you are keeping company with.*

Leah's heart pounded as she read the clipping. It was from an old society column, and as Leah read, she felt all her hopes and dreams begin to fade. Her mind grew numb, and her breath came in short, fast gasps.

She started as she heard a car pull up out front, and her heart pounded madly. She had to pull herself together. Collin was home. *Oh no. Collin. What have I done to you? What sort of man have I allowed into our lives?*

How could she have been so wrong? Even in the beginning, when she had doubts, she never would have considered that Max would do the sort of thing this article was accusing him of. Surely this must be a different Max Reilly. But no, it mentioned his father and grandfather by name. How could he have been accepted to his present position if these accusations were true? Leah's mouth twisted, and she gave a short laugh. Of course. The Rosemont name and money could probably buy anything.

She stood up as Collin came bounding into the room.

"Hi, Mom. How was work today?" he asked as he gave her a hug.

She returned his hug, then cleared her throat before speaking. It wouldn't do for Collin to see she was upset. She had no idea what she would say to him if he asked what was wrong.

"Work was fine, Collin. And how was school?" There, that wasn't so hard. It sounded cheerful enough, even to her ears.

"Oh, okay, I guess. Just two more weeks 'til school's out."

"Um-hmm. Looking forward to that, I'll bet."

"Yeah, I guess." He ducked his head and rubbed the toe of his shoe on the worn carpet.

"Is something wrong at school, Collin?"

"No, ma'am."

Suddenly he lifted his face to her, and she could see the pain behind his eyes.

"I'm going to do my homework, Mom. I'll see you later."

"Well, all right, son. Collin, listen. I need to speak to Mr. Reilly privately when he gets here, so would you stay in your room until I call you down, please?"

He tossed her a worried look. "Is something wrong?"

"Nothing for you to concern yourself with, honey."

She watched him tread slowly up the stairs, and anger flared inside her. She could handle the pain of losing her dream, but how dare that cad mess up her son's life? She went outside and sat on the porch swing, clutching the envelope and its contents. The longer she sat there, the angrier she became and the harder she pushed herself back and forth in the swing.

⋅⋗⋅⋉⋅

Max drove slowly to Leah's house. After the episode with Claudia and Jake last night, he knew he couldn't put things off any longer. He was going to tell her everything and just trust in God's mercy and Leah's love for him. Surely she would understand and believe him.

As he pulled up in front of the house, he noticed she was waiting for him on the porch swing. He didn't see Collin anywhere. Good. That would make it easier. And he wouldn't have an excuse to put it off.

"Leah, just the girl I wanted to see." Max smiled as he stepped up onto the porch.

Leah stood up and faced him, and he stopped in shocked surprise at the dark fury in her eyes.

"Leah?"

Her lips were pressed together tightly. She stared at him silently for a moment before she spoke. "Mr. Reilly, please take this little token and leave. I never want to see you again."

Thrusting an envelope into his hands, she turned and walked woodenly into the house, closing the door firmly behind her.

Max stood staring at the closed door for a long moment. When he finally glanced down at the envelope in his hands, he knew he had waited too long.

He didn't have to open it to know that Claudia had kept her word. She had ruined his life once more.

Chapter 8

The days dragged by for Leah. Even her job at the bakery, which should have given her joy, was just busy activity to help her get through another day. Only when confronted with Max's true character had Leah realized how much she truly loved him. The knowledge that he wasn't the man she had thought pierced her heart until she could hardly stand it.

The only ray of light in her life was Collin. Dear sweet Collin. He was going through his own private torment. That was plain from the confusion on his face. He didn't understand why Max wasn't coming around anymore. And he hadn't seen fit to ask her. She knew it must be hard on him seeing Max every day at school and wondering why he had stopped coming over.

One night when Collin was taking his bath, Leah sat in the rocking chair, attempting to concentrate on a new book.

"Mom."

Leah looked up. Collin stood there in his pajamas and slippers, and his wet hair was tousled from a not-so-successful attempt to towel it dry.

"Yes, sweetheart?" Leah reached over and brushed a straying lock of the damp hair out of his eyes.

"I'm sorry."

Puzzled, Leah frowned. "Sorry about what, honey?"

"I'm sorry I was so bad and rude and all about Mr. Reilly." His face seemed to crumple. "It's my fault he stopped coming over, and now you're sad."

"Oh, Collin, no." Leah stood up and pulled her son into her arms. "It's not your fault at all. This is something between Mr. Reilly and me. It has nothing to do with you."

"You sure?" The expression on Collin's face as he looked up indicated he wasn't completely accepting her statement.

"Sure as can be. Now, Collin. . ." She bit her lip and studied her son. "I know it must be difficult for you to be around Mr. Reilly every day under the circumstances, so I'm thinking about letting you switch back to your old school after all. What do you think?"

A totally horrified look crossed Collin's face.

"No, Mom! I mean, do I have to?"

Surprised, Leah stared at her son. "I thought that was what you wanted."

"That was a long time ago. I like Rosemont now, and I've got lots of friends there. Besides, I don't even see Mr. Reilly very much anymore."

Leah peered at her son anxiously, trying to ascertain if he was being truthful or if he was just saying what he thought she wanted to hear.

The tears, threatening to spill over, convinced her he really meant it.

Suddenly his eyes grew wide, and he clapped his hand against his leg. "Oh no!"

He bounded up the stairs and into the bathroom. In just a minute he was back, breathing heavily and holding out a piece of folded paper.

"Wow! I'm glad I remembered this before my trousers went into the laundry. Mr. Reilly asked me to give it to you."

She took the note from him with trembling hands and clutched it tightly.

"Well, all right, Collin. We'll leave the matter of changing schools for now since the term is almost over. Maybe we'll talk about it again before next year."

"Okay, Mom." He reached over and kissed her good night, then went upstairs.

Leah closed her eyes, almost afraid to look inside the folded piece of paper. Finally, with trembling hands, she opened it.

Genesis 39.

Leah stood staring at the words for a moment in stunned surprise.

Genesis 39? What in the world?

Leah picked up her Bible from the side table and leafed through it until she found the passage. She had only read for a few minutes when she inhaled deeply, then continued to read. As she came to the end of the chapter about Joseph and Potiphar's seductive, vindictive wife, her knees grew suddenly weak, and she sat down quickly.

Had she been too hasty in accepting the accusations in the clipping as truth? Could it be that Max was innocent of the charges?

In spite of herself, hope began to rise in her heart and mind. Hope that was quickly replaced with shame. She hadn't given Max a chance to defend himself. On the other hand, this wasn't proof positive that he was innocent. Of course, he would claim innocence if he was guilty. But based on what she'd seen of his character, did she truly believe he was capable of the vile actions the article had accused him of?

When Leah finally went to bed, she tossed and turned in an agony of indecision. Should she give him a chance to explain—and risk her heart again? She was already in so much pain she could hardly function. If she gave him a chance, only to discover that the accusations were true, it would be unbearable. And what would it do to Collin?

Finally, she fell into a restless sleep filled with disturbing dreams. One moment, she would see Max with hurt and pain on his innocent face. In the next, the expression would turn into a gloating sneer. When her alarm clock went off, she felt as though she hadn't slept at all.

Somehow she managed to get through the day at work. They were extra busy due to the Easter weekend coming up, so at least Leah's mind was occupied and unable to wander to the subject that was causing her so much anxiety.

That night when Collin was in his room reading, she went to her room and knelt.

"Lord, I need your wisdom."

1 Corinthians 13.

What? Leah inhaled sharply. Where did that thought come from? She knew that was the chapter on love. Could God be speaking to her? Suddenly a peace washed over her, and she knew it had indeed been God who put the thought in her mind.

She quickly got her Bible and fanned the leaves until she came to the passage. She carefully read each line, each word, not wanting to miss something that God might desire to bring to her attention. As she read all the attributes of love, suddenly she stopped at verse seven and reread the last part. She felt as though a sword had pierced her heart.

"Believeth all things, hopeth all things."

Max had been the epitome of moral excellence from the moment they had met. He had been kind, generous, and godly. Yet when she heard a bad report concerning him, she had immediately believed the worst instead of believing in the qualities she had observed, the qualities that had caused her to fall in love with him.

Lord, tell me what I should do. She was met with silence. Making a sudden decision, she rushed from her room.

"Collin, I'll be right back. I'm going to see if Mrs. Wright can stay with you for a little while. I have something I need to do."

"Okay, Mom."

She quickly changed her dress and smoothed down her hair. As she hurried down the stairs, a knock sounded on the door.

-:::-

Max was having a hard time hiding his misery. He had been so down in the dumps the past weekend when he had gone to his parents' for dinner that his mother had first cried, then grown angry.

"Max, would you like for me to go have a talk with that young lady?" she had asked, her eyes flashing as she patted him on the shoulder.

He had given a little laugh that came out more like a sob.

"Thanks, Mother, but I don't think she would be too convinced by my mother defending me. Mothers tend to do that."

"Well, all I can say is if that woman really loves you, she shouldn't believe a note written by someone she doesn't even know."

"You're right, Mother. But I have to admit, I should have been more forthcoming with her before it was too late."

"Well, be that as it may, we must clear up this misunderstanding." She patted him as only a mother can do, then frowned deeply. "It had to be Claudia who sent the clipping."

"If I thought it would do any good, I would try to reason with Claudia, but she really has it in for me."

Max's father had entered the room about that time, and he emitted what could only be described as a growl. "Good luck if you want to try to talk with Claudia. No one knows where she is. Jake doesn't even know. She's been gone for the past four days."

"Poor Jake." Max couldn't help feeling sorry for his little brother, in spite of his treatment of Max.

"Well, if you ask me, he'll be better off if that woman never comes back," his mother had seethed.

"We may feel that way, Mother, but apparently Jake doesn't."

That had been nearly a week ago. Max wondered if Claudia was still missing. He ate an early supper at the kitchen table and went into the living room. He turned on the radio and searched for something to take his mind off Leah. As if that were possible.

Settling on a music station, he sat on the sofa, leaning his head back against the cushions.

Lord, was I wrong? I was so sure Leah was the woman You intended me to spend my life with.

The doorbell brought him sharply out of his musing. He got up wearily and went to open the door.

"Jake!"

If there had ever been an object of total dejection, it was his brother as he stood in the doorway, hatless, shirt hanging out at the waist. His eyes had the look of a hunted animal, and he ran his hands nervously through his hair.

"Is it all right if I come in and talk to you, Max?" His voice was hoarse as though he had been yelling or, worse, crying.

"Of course." Max stepped back, allowing Jake to come in. "Coffee?"

"Yeah, that'd be good."

"Okay, why don't you just sit down here in the easy chair while I go get it."

Max had never seen his brother so shaken. His face was pale as death, and his hands were trembling when he took the cup from Max. He took a long drink of the hot liquid, then set the cup down on the side table and dropped his head in his hands.

Max sat in silence to give Jake time to pull himself together.

Finally, Jake looked up at Max and took a tortured breath.

The words he spoke were the last thing Max had expected to hear.

"Max, can you ever forgive me?"

Max felt a wave a love for the brother who sat with tears streaming down his face. He knew his own eyes were damp, too. "I forgave you a long time ago, Jake. You're my brother. I love you."

Jake closed his eyes and sighed. "Claudia told me the truth, Max. That she made the whole thing up. She thought it was funny. She played her little games and lied about everything."

Max closed his eyes and breathed a silent prayer of thanksgiving. Finally, after all this time. "Where is she? Did she come back home?"

"Yeah, she came back to try to get some money. A lot of money. Said she needed it to pay off her sister's hospital bill." He emitted a short laugh. "I wasn't buying it. I told her she wanted it to pay off gambling debts and buy booze. That's when she got mad and started screaming and yelling."

Jake's face held an expression of unbelief. "Terrible things. Her language was foul. I couldn't believe some of the things she admitted to. Bragged about, even. Then she laughed and told me she had lied about you."

He dropped his head into his hands for a moment, then looked up at Max.

"I'm so sorry. How could I have believed you would do anything so vile?"

"It's okay, Jake. It's over. She's your wife. She had you fooled. I may have done the same thing in your shoes."

"There's more. She said she had some article from an old newspaper about the supposed attack. Sent it to your friend Leah."

Max was on his feet like lightning and pulling his brother up from the chair.

Jake jerked backward as if he thought Max was about to attack him. "What? What are you doing?"

Max stepped back and looked at his brother.

"Jake, I know you are miserable. I'm going to do everything I can to help you through this. But will you please follow me over to Leah's and tell her about this? She won't talk to me."

"Of course. That's the least I can do for you."

Max drove to Leah's as quickly as he could while making sure Jake was able to follow. When they reached her house, Max knocked on the door with fear and doubt in his heart. Would she believe his brother or just think he was making it up for Max's sake?

The door flew open, and Leah stood there with shock on her face.

"Max!" She was in his arms before he realized what was happening.

"Oh, Max, forgive me for doubting you." She sobbed. "I know you could never do the horrible thing that note accused you of. Will you forgive me?"

⁘

"Sweetheart, it's okay. It's my fault." Max cupped her chin and lifted it so that she was looking into his eyes. The love she saw there left no doubt of its sincerity. "If I had had the courage to tell you about it in the first place, you never would have believed the accusation."

At the sound of a cough, Leah saw for the first time that they weren't alone. She felt her face flame and stepped back out of Max's embrace.

"Leah, this is my brother, Jake. He has something he wants to tell you."

As Leah listened to Jake's story, she felt a conflict of emotions. Anger toward the woman who had caused Max so much pain. Anger toward Jake for believing it, and at the same time pity for his obvious pain and heartbreak. Most of all, she felt shame that she had doubted Max for even a moment.

After Jake left, Max took Leah into his arms once more, and she snuggled closely and wrapped her arms around his waist.

"Leah," he whispered shakily.

She looked up at the expression of love on his face, and as his lips came closer to hers, she closed her eyes and waited in anticipation for this moment she had longed for. She sighed against his mouth as it pressed against hers, finally. All the dreams she'd had of his kisses were nothing compared to the reality. He tightened his hold, and their passion rose, leaving her breathless. "I love you, my girl," he whispered, his forehead resting against hers.

"Oh, Max, I love you, too."

"I'm thinking. . .June."

"June? What are you talking about?" She laughed.

"For the wedding."

Swallowing hard, Leah couldn't resist a grin. "What kind of a proposal is that?"

"The prelude to the real one, which I promise will be everything you've ever dreamed of." He kissed her forehead, her cheeks, her nose, her chin, and finally captured her lips once more. "Or maybe June is too long," he said with a husky growl.

Leah's heart nearly stopped. "I think June will be just fine. We have a lifetime after that."

"So is that a yes?"

Caught by her own words, Leah rose on her tiptoes and initiated a kiss. "Did you have any doubt?"

"Mom! Are you still going somewhere?"

Leah and Max both jumped back as Collin came running down the stairs.

"Mr. Reilly! Hi!"

Max took a deep breath, and, smiling at Leah, he went to meet Collin at the bottom of the stairs.

Leah felt a fleeting moment of disappointment, but at the joy on Collin's face, she caught her breath. There was plenty of time for their love. Plenty of time. Her eyes brimmed with happy tears as she watched Max catch Collin into a tight embrace.

Deep contentment swelled Leah's chest, and her heart soared with the truth that God was good indeed.

About the Authors

TRACEY V. BATEMAN

Tracey V. Bateman is a past president of the American Christian Fiction Writers and has more than 30 stories in print. She believes all things are possible and encourages everyone to dream big. Tracey lives with her husband and four children in the beautiful Missouri Ozarks.

ANDREA BOESHAAR

Andrea Boeshaar was born and raised in Milwaukee, Wisconsin. She and her husband Daniel have been married 40 years. They pride themselves on their wonderful family, including 5 grandchildren.

Andrea's publishing career began in 1994 when her first novel was released by **Heartsong Presents** book club (Barbour Publishing). In 2007, Andrea earned her certification in Christian life coaching, and she'll soon earn her bachelor's degree in Business Management.

Meanwhile, Andrea continues to write. Her latest novels include *Give Me Thine Heart*, *Love's Guiding Light* (Steeple View Publishing), both historical, and a contemporary novel, *Her Hometown Heart* (Pelican Book Group). In 2019, the long-awaited third installment in her **Shenandoah Valley Saga** will release.

For more information and to sign up for her newsletter, visit her website at andreaboeshaar.com. Find Andrea on Facebook: @Andrea.Boeshaar and follow Andrea on Twitter: @AndreaBoeshaar.

CATHY MARIE HAKE

Cathy Marie is a Southern California native. She met her two loves at church: Jesus and her husband, Christopher. An RN, she loved working in oncology as well as teaching Lamaze. Health issues forced her to retire, but God opened new possibilities with writing. Since their children have moved out and are married, Cathy and Chris dote on dogs they rescue from a local shelter. A sentimental pack rat, Cathy enjoys scrapbooking and collecting antiques. "I'm easily distracted during prayer, so I devote certain tasks and chores to specific requests or persons so I can keep faithful in my prayer life." Since her first book in 2000, she's been on multiple bestseller and readers' favorite lists.

SALLY LAITY

Sally Laity considers it a joy to know that the Lord can touch other hearts through her stories. She has written both historical and contemporary novels, including a co-authored series for Tyndale House and another for Barbour Publishing, nine Heartsong Romances, and twelve Barbour novellas. Her favorite pastimes include quilting for her church's Prayer Quilt Ministry and scrapbooking. She makes her home in the beautiful Tehachapi Mountains of southern California with her husband of fifty years and enjoys being a grandma and great-grandma.

VICKIE MCDONOUGH

Vickie McDonough is an award-winning author of nearly 50 published books and novellas, with over 1.5 million copies sold. A bestselling author, Vickie grew up wanting to marry a rancher, but instead, she married a computer geek who is scared of horses. She now lives out her dreams penning romance stories about ranchers, cowboys, lawmen, and others living in the Old West. Her novels include *End of the Trail*, winner of the OWFI 2013 Booksellers Best Fiction Novel Award. *Whispers on the Prairie* was a *Romantic Times* Recommended Inspirational Book for July 2013. *Song of the Prairie* won the 2015 Inspirational Readers' Choice Award. *Gabriel's Atonement*, book 1 in the Land Rush Dreams series, placed second in the 2016 Will Rogers Medallion Award. Vickie has recently stepped into independent publishing.

Vickie has been married over forty years to Robert. They have four grown sons, one daughter-in-law, and a precocious granddaughter. When she's not writing, Vickie enjoys reading, doing stained glass, watching movies, and traveling. To learn more about Vickie's books or to sign up for her newsletter, visit her website at www.vickiemcdonough.com.

JANET SPAETH

In first grade, Janet Spaeth was asked to write a summary of a story about a family making maple syrup. She wrote all during class, through morning recess, lunch, and afternoon recess, and asked to stay after school. When the teacher pointed out that a summary was supposed to be shorter than the original story, Janet explained that she didn't feel the readers knew the characters well enough, so she was expanding on what was in the first-grade reader. Thus a writer was born. She lives in the Midwest and loves to travel, but to her, the happiest word in the English language is *home*.

PAMELA TRACY

Pamela Tracy started writing at a very young age (a series of romances, all with David Cassidy as the hero. Sometimes Bobby Sherman would interfere). Then, while earning a BA in Journalism at Texas Tech University in Lubbock, Texas, she picked up the pen again (only this time, it was an electric typewriter on which she wrote a very bad fiction novel). First published in 1999 by Barbour Publishing, she is a *USA Today* bestselling author who has published more than thirty-five books in multiple sweet, inspiration, and devotional genres. She's a Carol Award winner (from American Christian Fictions Writers) as well as Rita finalist (from Romance Writers of America).